Snowdrops
on
Rosemary Lane

ELLEN BERRY

avon.

Published by AVON
A division of HarperCollins*Publishers* Ltd
1 London Bridge Street
London SE1 9GF

www.harpercollins.co.uk

A Paperback Original 2019

First published in Great Britain by HarperCollins*Publishers* 2019

A catalogue copy of this book is available from the British Library.

ISBN: 978-0-00-815716-6

Typeset in Sabon by Palimpsest Book Production Limited,
Falkirk, Stirlingshire
Printed and bound in UK by CPI Group (UK) Ltd, Croydon CR0 4YY

MIX
Paper from
responsible sources
FSC
www.fsc.org
FSC™ C007454

In memory of Margery Taylor
11.11.35 – 11.11.18

Prologue

30 Years Ago

She scrambled over the high garden wall, scuffing her bare shins. She shouldn't have been there, but that was part of the thrill. Lucy Riddock and her friends were on a fruit-finding mission, and they knew there were redcurrant bushes here. They also knew the old woman whose house it was would go berserk if she saw them.

At least, she seemed old to Lucy, who had just turned ten; at that age, even forty seems ancient. The children certainly knew Kitty Cartwright was prone to outbursts of rage, and that only served to heighten their excitement. It wasn't the first time they had done this. Tellingly, it had never occurred to them to steal berries from anyone else.

Lucy had joined forces with a boy called Hally, which she assumed was a nickname but never thought to ask, as that's what everyone called him. Sometimes, there were others; namely Brenna, Toni and Peter Linton, a trio of siblings with vivid red hair and many guinea pigs. On this occasion, they all jumped down onto the overgrown lawn and darted behind the shed.

Unlike Lucy, who came from a nondescript suburb of Leeds, the others lived here in Burley Bridge. She was just visiting; these were the holiday friends she had met the previous summer, and there had been no contact since then. In those days that was normal. It would be a long time until everyone was easily contactable at all times. Three weeks were all they had together while Lucy stayed with her kind but rather staid and *definitely* ancient Uncle George and Aunt Babs (who were actually her great-aunt and uncle on her father's side).

As both of her parents worked full-time, it helped for Lucy, an only child, to spend time with her aunt and uncle. The Riddocks rarely took holidays beyond the occasional trip away in their caravan, and now Lucy had made friends here, she loved coming to Burley Bridge. Unlike at home, where Lucy's mother kept a tight rein on her, here she was allowed to roam freely.

Stifling laughter, the children crept out from behind the shed and ran to the enormous oak tree that spread its boughs over the entire lower portion of the garden. From here they peeped round, scanning the surroundings. 'The coast's clear,' murmured Hally. They favoured the language of the young adventurers they'd read about in books.

'Go!' Lucy commanded, and they charged as a pack towards the currant bushes around the side of the house. They grabbed at the berries and stuffed them into their pockets and mouths. In truth, the redcurrants were rather tart and not nearly as delicious as raspberries or even the less favoured blackberries that they often found in the wild. It was more about the thrill of the build-up than the actual prize. On a previous occasion, Hally had scoffed so many that he'd been gripped with cramping pains and had had to tell his scary dad that it was a stomach bug. At least, Lucy had gathered that he was scary. She hadn't actually met him. Hally had explained that he was a 'woodsman' and that they had an actual wood, close to their house a little way out of the village – which sounded straight out of a dark fairy tale.

Was chopping logs a real job, she wondered? Hally had mentioned that he sold Christmas trees, but what about the rest of the year? She also knew that Hally's mum had died when he was six, three years before she'd met him. Although the Linton kids had been to Hally's, Lucy understood that it wasn't the kind of home he could just invite his friends to whenever he wanted. Occasionally, on rainy days, they hung out at the Lintons' pink pebble-dashed bungalow in the village. But their most thrilling adventures happened outdoors.

As they grabbed at Kitty's redcurrants, a sharp rap on a side window of the cottage stopped them in their tracks. Moments later, they heard the front door opening. 'What are you lot doing there?' Kitty yelled.

'Nothing!' Hally shouted back.

There was a bang of the front door and they heard her running towards them. They saw her then – skinny and wiry, all furious eyes and flaming cheeks: 'Clear off, the lot of you or I'll phone the police!' Thrilled by the drama, the children charged towards the wrought-iron gate and clattered through it, running as fast as they could until her cries faded away.

'Mission accomplished!' they yelled, once they were safely away down the street. Years later, Lucy would

3

wonder if those childhood holidays would have been half as thrilling without Hally, the Lintons and Kitty's fruit.

It wasn't fair that Kitty lived there, she decided later that night. With its thatched roof and untamed garden filled with flowers, Rosemary Cottage seemed magical – if rather neglected. If Lucy had lived there she'd have given the house a fresh coat of white paint, and cut back the overgrown shrubs to give the roses and lupins room to breathe. She could picture exactly how it would look, under her care. She would paint the dull grey shed a bright sky blue, and the old wooden garage at the side of the house would become an art studio or a den. She would lavish the place with the love it deserved.

When Lucy was thirteen, Uncle George had a heart attack and died suddenly. Shortly afterwards, Babs moved into sheltered housing, where she only lived for a few months longer before passing away in her sleep. As Lucy's family had no other ties with Burley Bridge, her visits there came to an end with no chance to say goodbye to her friends. If she'd had Hally's address she might have written him a letter, but she didn't even know his proper name. So Lucy lost touch with him and the Linton kids, and although she thought of them all occasionally, those memories gradually made way for the all-consuming matter of being a teenager. A few years after that she was going on cheap, rowdy package holidays to Greece and Spain with her college friends, and those summers spent building dens and scrambling over Kitty Cartwright's garden wall seemed a lifetime away.

Gradually, the village that had once shone so brightly

in Lucy's mind began to fade like the image on an over-washed T-shirt. Apart from Rosemary Cottage, that is. It remained as vivid as it had ever been, and she never managed to shake off the fantasy that, one day, it would be hers.

Part One

A New Venture

Chapter One

Now

Whenever someone asked Lucy Scott, 'So, what do you do?' she could truthfully reply, 'I work in lingerie.' Responses varied from, 'Ooh, is that allowed?' to, 'I don't suppose they're hiring?' It was brilliant for getting laughs at parties.

Lucy would then explain that her employer, Claudine, was an online underwear retailer that sounded foxily French, but was actually based on an unlovely industrial estate in Manchester.

Not that Lucy minded. At forty years old, she loved her job as head buyer; it was creative and pretty hectic, and many of her colleagues were also her friends. Throughout the thirteen years she'd worked there – breaking only for two maternity leaves – she had never considered moving anywhere else.

However, recently there had been a sea change. Without warning, the company had been bought out. Her former boss, Ria, who had spearheaded Claudine's image of seductive glamour, had now been booted and a new direction had been announced.

'Hold on to your knickers, guys,' Lucy's right-hand man Andrew had muttered grimly. 'It's going to be a bumpy ride.' And he was right. As the brand veered downmarket, Lucy was involved in numerous heated debates on the subjects of hoistage and underwired support.

'It sounds more like engineering,' her husband Ivan had joked, trying to ease her tension after a particularly trying day.

'It *is* engineering,' she remarked. 'That's exactly what it is – and it's beautiful too. What I'm trying to tell Max is, it can be both. It's next to woman's skin, you know? It's an intimate thing. It should feel lovely to wear—'

'Hey, you don't need to convince me,' Ivan said with a smile. 'I think it's totally gorgeous stuff.'

Lucy sighed. 'Well, unfortunately, our totally gorgeous stuff might not be quite so gorgeous in a few months' time.'

She was right. After she had given an impassioned presentation to the new senior team, it looked as if the future was even bleaker than Lucy had imagined. 'The Claudine customer doesn't give a stuff about heritage,' boomed Max, the flashy new CEO. 'She wants value and fun.'

Lucy glanced at Andrew, who was sitting beside her in the meeting room. They had worked together so long, they could almost read each other's thoughts. 'She also wants beautifully made pieces that last,' Lucy remarked.

'We're not after the granny market here,' retorted Max.

'The average age of our customer is thirty-seven!' spluttered Lucy.

'Hmm, whatever.' The boss drummed his fingers impatiently. 'No one wants to bankrupt themselves over a bra.'

'They're not expensive,' Andrew muttered. 'For the quality and workmanship, they're competitively priced—'

'Never mind that,' Max said, waving a hand dismissively. 'We know what women are looking for. They want *oomph*.'

Lucy inhaled deeply and glanced at the wall clock, wishing she could spirit herself out of here right now. She hated that word. It smacked of uncomfortable, scratchy push-up bras designed to please men – and never mind the poor woman trapped in the darned thing all day. Behind his back, Max was known in the company as MC – Max Cleavage.

The day after her presentation, his secretary phoned through to Lucy at her desk. 'Could you pop in to see Max at three?' she asked.

'Sure,' Lucy said, trying to remain calm. When the allotted time came, she reassured herself that he would simply reiterate his points from yesterday, and she would have to accept that that's how things were going to be. She could handle that, she'd decided. Lucy and her husband Ivan had two young children and she wasn't about to flounce out of her job.

She stepped into Max's office, and he motioned for her to sit down. 'That was quite a heated meeting yesterday.' He flashed a brief smile.

'It was, yes.' Her heart quickened a little.

'I thought we'd have a chat about the restructure, Luce?'

Luce? Only her friends here called her Luce. 'Okay,'

she said warily. Max laced his fingers together and pursed his lips. He was one of those men who seemed to find it impossible to pass a reflective surface without checking out his appearance. Once, she had caught him fixing his hair via his reflection in the microwave door in the kitchen. For a moment now, she wondered if 'restructure' could refer to the controversial redesign of their classic 'Sophia' bra, which was hailed as a miracle in combining beauty and sublime comfort. But no. He was putting together a new senior team, he explained, that would 'fully support our new vision, specifically the novelty undies line'.

'Novelty undies?' Lucy said with a frown. 'What d'you mean?'

'For men,' he said plainly.

'For *men*? But we don't do men's—'

'We do now,' he drawled, 'and it's jungle-themed . . .'

Lucy realised she was gripping the sides of the chair. 'Jungle-themed,' she repeated.

'Yep, starting with elephant pants with an integral trunk section,' Max explained. 'That's for his—'

'Yes, I get you,' she cut in. Lucy wasn't a prude – far from it – but the brand had always taken inspiration from beauties such as Sophia Loren and Lauren Bacall. She couldn't help wondering what these icons would make of elephant pants and, more pressingly, how on earth she would fit in with Claudine's startling new direction.

'But how can a brand called Claudine produce elephant pants?' she started. 'It hardly suggests that kind of product—'

'Ah, but there'll be a separate men's range. We're calling it *Claude* . . .'

She cleared her throat as she took this in. 'So, um . . . what does this mean for me? I mean, will I be expected to work across the men's line too, or—'

'I'll cut to the chase,' Max said firmly. 'Obviously this is a very different kind of market for you. We want people on board who are with us a hundred per cent, who'll *embrace* Claude.'

'Pardon?' she spluttered.

'We can't be po-faced about underwear, Luce.'

'I'm not being po-faced,' she insisted. 'I'm just a little stunned, that's all.'

Max nodded. 'Yes, well, I expected that – and that's why I called you in today.' Her stomach clenched as he regarded her steadily across his vast, entirely bare desk. Lucy suddenly realised what was coming. Her heart rate quickened, and with a wave of despair she pictured their highly praised recent advertising campaign featuring models in oyster silk camisoles shot in the walnut-panelled cabins of an old-style ocean liner. Clearly, those days were gone.

'We appreciate everything you've done here,' Max continued, 'but I think it's best all round if we make you an offer. Take some time to consider it, of course.'

'Elephant pants?' scorned Nadeen over a drink after work. 'I heard a whisper about those. I thought it was a joke.'

'"The Dumbo collection",' Lucy said wryly, still reeling slightly from the admittedly generous payoff Max had just offered her.

'Please don't leave us,' Andrew urged her. 'We need someone around here to talk sense.'

'MC will screw things up, and then he'll be out on

his ear,' Nadeen murmured, and Lucy promised not to do anything rash. However, within a few days, it started to become clear what she should do next.

She had been feeling oddly queasy and flat-out exhausted, and had put it down to the stresses of work. But it turned out that it wasn't that at all. At least, not just that.

Lucy was pregnant. It was unplanned, and quite a shocker at forty years old – when Marnie and Sam were well beyond the baby stage and her boss was trying to force her out. But both she and Ivan were delighted. And maybe, she reflected, this surprise pregnancy would shake up their lives in the loveliest way possible.

There was always the option to fight MC's move to get rid of her. But did Lucy really want to work under him, with his frankly ridiculous ideas? Her maternity leave would be marred by the thought of returning to a company she barely recognised. Alternatively – and the very thought thrilled her – she could accept MC's offer and use it to embark on a new, very different sort of life.

It was obvious now which choice she should make. An adventure lay ahead – Lucy was sure of it – and she couldn't wait.

Chapter Two

If Lucy had known how events would unfold, she wouldn't have come up with her plan. Instead, she and Ivan would have headed straight to her parents' place to pick up their children, and all would have been fine. She might never have set foot in Burley Bridge again for the rest of her life. A few months on, she would wish over and over that she hadn't.

Such a selfish move, she would berate herself. Manipulative, too – and she'd thought she'd been so clever! But none of that had clouded her thoughts on that crisp, blue-skied late October morning when the world had seemed so full of promise.

Lucy and Ivan had spent their tenth wedding anniversary overnight in a country hotel. With two young children it was rare for them to have time alone together. The countryside in this part of West Yorkshire was all green, rolling hills, familiar to Lucy and every bit as lovely as she'd remembered from her holidays. Unbeknown to Ivan, she had planned to make a small detour. She was ready to make a change in their lives, and she was willing him to be positive about it – or, at least, to not think she had lost her mind.

'Where are we going?' he asked as she turned off the dual carriageway.

'Just thought we might have a stop-off,' she replied.

'Oh, whereabouts?' He glanced out of the passenger window.

'Burley Bridge. It's a village a couple of miles away, down in the valley. Remember I told you about my holidays there when I was a kid?'

'Uh-huh . . .' He threw her a bemused glance. 'Feeling nostalgic?'

Lucy smiled. 'I guess so, yeah. I just thought we could have a quick look.'

'Hmm, okay . . . what about your mum and dad, though?' They were both aware that Lucy's mother in particular would be eager to hand back Marnie and Sam at lunchtime as arranged. *No, no, we're fine,* Anna had said in a tight, high voice when Lucy had called last night. *They're quite a handful, but I'm okay – it's your father who's exhausted, you know what he's like, honestly . . . anyway, don't worry about us. You just focus on enjoying your time together. You deserve it, love!*

At that moment, Lucy had almost wished her mother hadn't offered to have the kids, having almost forced her and Ivan to go away overnight. She always made them pay – not in money, of course, but in guilt. It was the currency she used: *Your dad's just a bit upset, that's all. Sam was playing with his models and snapped off a wing . . .* For heaven's sake, couldn't her father have placed his Airfix aeroplanes out of reach on a high shelf?

Hadn't he imagined that his five-year-old grandson might want to play with them? *It was his favourite Spitfire, that's all,* Anna added with a sigh.

'We'll still be there by lunchtime,' Lucy reassured her husband now, as the village came into view. 'Look – see that derelict cottage over there, by the river?' Ivan nodded, and she felt a twist of sadness at the sight of it. It was almost roofless now, the timbers rotted, the stone walls crumbling with weeds sprouting from their crevices. 'That's what's left of George and Babs's place,' she added.

'Wow,' Ivan murmured. 'Was it really habitable back then?'

'Just about. I thought it was wonderful – cosy and crammed with ornaments and artefacts. But according to Mum it was pretty damp and prone to flooding from the river. I don't think there were any more tenants after them.'

'What a waste,' Ivan remarked, adjusting his wire-rimmed spectacles, 'letting it fall into decay like that.' Lucy glanced at him. She could sense his interest waning already, but he perked up again as they drove through the main heart of the village on this perfect autumn morning.

How the place had changed since she was a little girl. There were numerous inviting shops now: a greengrocer with wicker baskets of produce stacked outside, a bijou art gallery, a couple of gift boutiques and a particularly alluring bookshop, which appeared to be wholly devoted to cookbooks. The fading facades Lucy remembered had been painted in cheery colours, and the shops' window boxes and hanging baskets were filled with late-flowering geraniums and winter pansies. Happily, many of the more traditional shops were still there, and appeared to be virtually unchanged – like the general store, and the newsagent's where she had been allowed to spend her pocket money on comics, fishing nets, Sherbet Fountains and whatever else had caught her eye.

Simple pleasures, she reflected, enjoying a rush of nostalgia. 'It's so quaint,' Ivan remarked.

'Lovely, isn't it?'

'Yeah. We should have come here for lunch or something . . .'

Lucy smirked. 'We were kind of busy in the hotel.'

Ivan chuckled. It *had* been wonderful, stealing a little time away from the kids. Life was so hectic with children, it was easy to let intimacy fall away. Her age aside, she couldn't help thinking it was a miracle that they had managed to conceive a third baby at all. These days, they only had to start kissing in bed for either Marnie or Sam to run into their room, desperately 'needing' something: a drink, a cuddle, reassurance after a nightmare. And soon, Lucy and Ivan would be propelled back to stage one all over again, with a newborn. A couple of her friends had recently had their third children. They seemed to have acquired a casualness about parenthood this time around that she hoped she would be able to emulate.

'No pristine babygrows this time,' a chronically sleep-deprived colleague had laughed. 'If there's food on his front, I just pop another T-shirt on over the top. Some days, by bath time, he's wearing six outfits.'

Lucy liked the idea of being more relaxed this time, and being able to fully enjoy their baby, rather than feeling as if they were merely staggering from one day to the next. She slowed down and turned left into a single-track lane.

Ivan looked at her. 'Where are we going now?'

'I just want to show you something,' she replied.

'But what's up here? It doesn't look like it leads anywhere . . .'

'Wait and see,' she said, trying to suppress a smile. There was nothing at first – just trees on either side of the lane, their boughs joining to form a lacy green canopy overhead. There was an old red phone box, a stone trough at the roadside and a huddled cottage with a pale green front door. Someone trotted by on a pony. Surely, Ivan could see how idyllic it was, compared to their neighbourhood of nondescript terraced streets back in Manchester. Whilst perfectly functional, their house had only a tiny paved backyard and a bunch of party-loving students next door. They had been burgled twice, and last November someone had posted a firework through their letterbox. The joys of city life were beginning to wear thin.

'What *is* this?' Ivan asked. 'A mystery trip?'

'You'll see,' she replied, glimpsing the high garden wall now, weathered and patterned with lichen and moss. There was the cottage's whitewashed gable end, the thatched roof, and the wrought-iron garden gate that Lucy, Hally and the Linton kids had charged through in a pack. She could almost hear their plimsoled feet slapping onto the gravel path.

Lucy's heart was quickening now as she stopped the car. She could see the trees they'd climbed and the old wooden shed that they'd hidden behind, like kids in an adventure story. Her strongest childhood memories were here in this semi-wild garden.

And now there was something else too.

A 'For Sale' sign, garish red and white against the cloudless sky. Lucy turned to Ivan.

19

'What's this, honey?' he asked hesitantly.

'Just a cottage.' She was beaming now, unable to stop herself as they climbed out of the car.

They weren't here by chance. Ever since Max had taken over at Claudine, Lucy had been browsing estate agents' websites, fantasising about a cottage in the country. This usually happened late at night, after Ivan had gone to bed, and it had become quite a hobby of hers. She had searched this whole area of West Yorkshire, then found herself homing in on Burley Bridge, just out of curiosity at first. When she had spotted that Rosemary Cottage was up for sale, she had almost fallen off her chair.

This was the reason she had suggested staying in a hotel fairly close by. She'd suspected that Ivan would have resisted coming to view the cottage; Burley Bridge was too remote for them to consider moving here while he was working in Manchester. But she hoped that, when he saw it for himself, he would at least consider taking a look inside.

Ivan met Lucy's gaze, clearly registering her shining green eyes and the flush to her cheeks. 'It's a beautiful house,' he conceded.

She pushed back her thick, long dark hair. 'D'you think we might be able to just – you know . . . have a look around?'

His mouth twitched into a smile. 'What for?'

'Oh, I'm just curious, you know? I remember it really well. Me and a couple of local kids used to sneak into the garden and steal berries . . .'

'You never told me you had a criminal past.' He grinned at her.

'Just a few handfuls,' she chuckled.

20

Ivan turned back to the cottage. 'Looks like it needs quite a bit of work, darling.'

She nodded. 'Yes, but imagine us all being here. Wouldn't it be lovely? You've been saying you've had enough of the crazy hours, the endless meetings, all the pressures—'

'Yes, but—'

'And wouldn't the kids love it? Look at the size of that garden! They could have a Wendy house and a den, and the house would be perfect for bed and breakfast . . .' While she might have lured him here under false pretences, Ivan did know that Lucy had fantasised for years now about running a country B&B.

'Luce . . .' He paused. 'Are you serious about doing bed and breakfast?'

She nodded. 'I know we'd be good at it, you and me together.'

Ivan shook his head and exhaled. 'But how on earth could we do that with the baby coming?'

'We'd manage,' she said firmly. 'We'd only be talking two or three rooms to let out to guests. How hard would that be?'

'Yes, but newborn babies are up all night and demand attention every second of the day. You remember how it was . . .'

'Sam and Marnie were both sleeping through at eight months,' she reminded him.

'But what if this one isn't?'

She exhaled. 'I just thought we could have a look around.'

Ivan slid an arm around her waist. When they'd found out she was pregnant, he had agreed that perhaps now was the time to reduce his working hours in order to spend more time with their young family. With her redundancy payment, they could manage for a while, and he had agreed – tentatively – that it could be an opportunity to live their lives differently. Ivan worked full-pelt at Brookes, a Manchester-based branding agency. Although he loved his job, when deadlines loomed he was often plagued by insomnia and even the odd panic attack. Lucy worried about him. At times, he seemed so stressed and wrapped up in his work, he could barely interact with her or the children at all. 'It's just modern life,' he'd said flippantly, when she'd tried to address the issue. 'No, of course I don't need to see the doctor.'

'But she could sign you off with stress. You could have a break—'

'You know what'd happen then. I'd be edged out of the company, wouldn't I?'

'Like me, you mean,' she'd shot back, knowing he hadn't meant it that way.

He chose to ignore her remark. 'She'd only prescribe happy pills,' he'd muttered – which was Ivan all over: stubborn, dedicated, intent on providing for his young family. And who needed 'happy pills', as he called them – annoyingly – when he could knock back the best part of a bottle of merlot most nights?

Lucy was desperate to make a change. What was the point of Ivan slogging away if the children rarely saw him and the work was making him ill?

'So,' she said now, 'd'you like it?'

He nodded and turned to the cottage again. 'Of course I do, Luce. It's beautiful.'

As she had half-expected a non-committal 'it's okay, I suppose', this was a pleasant surprise. 'I know it's a long way from Manchester,' she conceded, taking his hand in hers.

'Yeah, of course it is.' He nodded thoughtfully and they fell into silence for a few moments. 'But maybe that's not the be-all and end-all anymore,' he added.

She bit her lip as her gaze skimmed the garden. 'You mean—'

'I'm not against it, darling,' he said gently.

She nodded, barely able to believe he was being so positive. 'If we did B&B, I know the baby'd put things on hold for a while . . .'

'Well, yes, obviously . . . but shall we view it anyway?'

It was all Lucy could do not to yelp with delight. 'I'd *love* to.'

'Okay.' His dark brown eyes met hers, and he rested his hand protectively on her stomach, even though she wasn't showing yet. 'Let's phone the agent and just see, shall we? We could come back another time—'

'Well, actually, I phoned already.'

'What?' he exclaimed.

She cleared her throat. 'I told him we'd be in the area today, and he said if you liked the look of it we should give him a call. He's only local. He said he'd pop round with the keys . . .'

Ivan stared at her, feigning outrage. 'You tricked me!'

'I know.' She winced. 'You don't mind, do you?'

'Hmmm.' He slid his gaze back towards the cottage, then turned and beamed at her. 'I *suppose* not. Now you've forced me into this . . .'

They were both laughing now, and Lucy felt as if she could burst with love as she wrapped her arms around his waist. 'Okay, darling,' she said. 'I'll give him a call right now.'

Chapter Three

Three months later, as the village sparkled with late January frost, Rosemary Cottage was theirs and ready to be transformed into the B&B of their dreams. Well, Lucy's dreams really; she was the one driving the project, looking into ways to manage bookings and marketing, as well as overseeing an upgrade of the house. Although it had been spruced up for sale, there was still a substantial amount of work to be done in order to create the kind of B&B she yearned for.

A team of tradesmen set to work upgrading fixtures and fittings. As the days turned milder – there had been no snow so far that winter – they took away the damp-riddled conservatory, and the area where it had stood was transformed into a decked seating space where Lucy planned to serve breakfasts on summer mornings. She was all for dismantling the ancient garden shed, and perhaps building a summerhouse for guests to enjoy – until Ivan and the children made a plea for keeping it. 'But it's falling to bits,' she reasoned. 'It must be as old as the house itself.'

'That's part of its charm,' Ivan reasoned, so she let it go and he set about making it a hobby shed for himself and the children. Although his spare time was still sparse, at least he seemed to be enjoying it now instead of huddling over his laptop, staring at reports, drinking wine. Sam and Marnie were thrilled to have more of his attention, and they were full of ideas for all kinds of construction projects they could get up to together.

'Can we make a birdhouse?' Sam asked.

'Sure!' Ivan replied.

'What about a bird bath and a bird table—' Marnie cut in.

'And bird hotel?' Sam asked, giggling.

'I'd never have guessed you were a shed man,' Lucy teased Ivan.

'I don't think I knew it myself,' he said with a grin. Meanwhile, the cottage's ancient kitchen was refitted in readiness for all the breakfasts – and possibly evening meals – they would be preparing for guests. Gradually, the place started to come together and feel altogether more welcoming.

Lucy had already gathered that the cookbook shop on the village high street had put Burley Bridge firmly on the day-trippers' map. In fact, Della, who had set it up and still ran it, had grown up in Rosemary Cottage alongside her brother and sister. It had been her mother, Kitty, who had shrieked at Lucy, Hally and the Linton children for sneaking into her garden and stealing her redcurrants.

'You were brave,' Della had laughed, when Lucy told her about her childhood antics. 'Mum was pretty scary – especially when she'd had a couple of gins. Even I wouldn't have taken berries without asking.' Lucy and

Della soon became friends, and she made other connections through chatting to neighbours, shop owners and mums at the school gate. Unsurprisingly, Della had only a vague recollection of the Linton family in the pink bungalow, who had apparently moved away many years ago. The name Hally meant nothing to her, and Lucy hadn't really expected it to. Della was a decade older than she was, and would have already left home when Lucy and her companions were running wild through the village.

As Ivan had decided to hang on to his agency job for the time being, Lucy was grateful for these new friendships in the village. His 100-mile round trip was exhausting, but at least it wouldn't be for too long. The plan was for him to go freelance, and work from home once the major bills for the work on the house had been settled. Now and again, he'd call to say he was shattered and couldn't face the drive home, and would be staying over with a colleague in Manchester that night. While Lucy had no problem with that, she looked forward to the day when Ivan resigned from Brookes and was here at her side, being part of village life, being *with* them in every way.

Meanwhile, she took pride in the fact that they had managed the move and Marnie and Sam had settled happily into the village school. It was all going so well, Lucy thought. Too well, perhaps, as one grey March afternoon, she experienced intense cramping whilst out shopping in the village. She made for the bookshop, trying to convince herself that she had just been overdoing things and needed to slow down.

'You don't look well,' Della exclaimed. 'You're kind of clammy.'

'I'm getting these pains,' Lucy said. 'Could I just sit down for a moment?'

'Of course,' Della said, her eyes filled with concern. She turned to her part-time assistant, Rikke, who was manning the till. 'Rikke, I think Lucy should go to hospital—'

'No, I'll be fine,' Lucy protested. 'Maybe if I had a cup of tea . . .' But Della was insistent in her rather motherly way, and drove Lucy to Heathfield Hospital. Lucy tried over and over to contact Ivan, but he was in high-level meetings with clients all afternoon and couldn't be disturbed. Finally, Lucy barked to the receptionist at Brookes that she was in a hospital waiting room and he had to take her call right now.

'Damn his work,' she muttered furiously to Della. But it wasn't his fault – of course it wasn't. Maybe she'd thrown herself into their project with too much gusto? After all, Marnie and Sam were only five and seven. Keeping on top of family life was challenging enough without trying to furnish the guest rooms and their en suites to an impeccable standard, get her head around health and safety rulings and – admittedly, this part was more fun – figure out what she could offer on her breakfast menu to set Rosemary Cottage apart from the rest.

The late miscarriage rocked them, and Lucy couldn't help wondering: should they have stayed in Manchester, where life had just been jogging along? It was likely that the pregnancy had been unviable, a kind young doctor had told them. It was no one's fault. But there was no way of knowing for sure; Lucy had had no tests other than the standard ultrasound, and everything had seemed fine.

At least Ivan had resigned from Brookes now, and was busying himself with putting the final touches to the house as well as starting to establish his own freelance work. Now and again, he'd make slightly disparaging remarks about village life, such as, 'I'm sure they're keeping a dossier on us, Luce. I went into the newsagent's and a woman came over and said, "Oh, I see you've changed the colour of your gate!" They seem terribly interested in what we're up to around here.'

'Who's "they"?' Lucy asked, a tad defensively.

'You know – just, people . . .'

'People who happen to be expressing a friendly interest, you mean?'

Ivan raked a hand through his wavy light brown hair and took off his wire-rimmed spectacles. What was it with middle-aged men and their intolerance of strangers, she wondered? It wasn't just Ivan. Without exception, all of her female friends claimed that their husbands hadn't made any new friends beyond thirty years old, and had no interest in doing so. 'I won't have room for any more mates until some of these old buggers die off,' Ivan once joked. In contrast, Lucy relished making new connections and had actively enjoyed arriving in Burley Bridge, with that 'clean slate' feeling that came with starting afresh. It was the aspect of running a B&B that appealed to her most – the unpredictable nature of welcoming strangers into their home.

'Last week, three people stopped me in the street and asked why we'd got rid of the conservatory,' Ivan went on now, filling two mugs with tea from the pot. 'Someone actually said it was a waste, and that Kitty had loved sitting out there on summer evenings.' Exasperation flickered in his deep brown eyes.

'They're just curious,' she remarked.

'Yes, because there's not enough important stuff for them to think about—'

'That's so patronising,' she retorted, sensing a wave of fatigue now. The children had just gone to bed and she had a list of chores to rattle through before she could kick off her shoes and relax. 'This is what it's like, living in the country,' she added. 'People notice all the little things around them. I know that might seem weird and intrusive to you, but it also means they actually care. Look how Della looked after me, when we lost the baby.'

'Yeah, okay,' he said hotly. 'I s'pose I'm just not used to being so . . . noticed.'

'What've you got to hide?'

'Nothing!' he exclaimed.

'What's this *dossier* you're so afraid of then?'

His face broke into a reluctant smile, as if he had finally realised how curmudgeonly he was being. 'Come on – country life's new to you too,' he added. 'You can't say where you grew up was rural.'

'Well, no,' she conceded.

'So you must know what I mean.'

Of course she did. Naturally, they'd had friends in Manchester – but there had also been that relative anonymity that comes with living in a city. There'd been a pretty transient population in their street; it was the first house they'd bought together, before they'd had kids, and was in a more studenty area than they'd have chosen now. Whilst Ivan seemed to miss their life there, Lucy didn't.

After the miscarriage her new friends in Burley Bridge had showed up with cards, flowers and pot-luck suppers. Women with whom she had only chatted sporadically at the school gate had stopped her in the village and asked if she was okay, suggested a coffee, and given her their numbers in case she ever needed anything. Touchingly, they had also made a point of inviting Marnie and Sam for extra playdates and even days out – as, of course, the children had been looking forward to the new baby coming too.

Burley Bridge was a special place, Lucy felt; even more so since they had lost the baby. Perhaps it had made her put down roots here more quickly than she would have otherwise.

She also knew her husband well enough to realise how stubborn he could be, and that there was no point in trying to *force* him into feeling entirely settled here. Ivan had agreed to move – and that had been nothing short of miraculous. However, Lucy was also convinced that he would come round, and eventually love the village as much as she did. It would just take a little more time.

Chapter Four

As the days had lengthened and Rosemary Cottage's garden had started to awaken, so Lucy began to feel stronger again – more like her old self.

'You're doing too much,' Ivan warned as she launched herself back into the business of readying their home for guests. 'Slow down, darling. We can open when we're ready – there's no rush.' But Lucy didn't want to slow down. She wanted to get things kick-started and found solace in designing a website and setting everything up for online bookings. It was crucial, she felt, to be up and running in good time for the summer season. Being busy certainly helped her to deal with her grief, and by early May they were open.

For those first few weeks, bookings were sparse. But as the mild spring eased into a glorious summer, the guest rooms were generally full at least on Friday and Saturday nights. As well as looking after their visitors, Lucy had thrown herself into decorating the house with flowers and foliage from the garden. She had always loved having fresh blooms around her at home; back in Manchester, she had grown what she could in tubs and window boxes, but been frustrated by the lack of space. Even as a child, she had loved to snip nasturtiums and cornflowers from her parents' neat suburban garden to plonk into jam jars and bring into her bedroom. Now, as something new seemed to burst into life every morning, her imagination began to run riot. This was the first time Lucy had ever had a proper garden of her own, and she adored it.

Her beautiful, cottagey floral arrangements started to be noticed by friends and guests. Through word of mouth she was asked to decorate the local church hall with flowers from her garden, which in turn led to her creating table centrepieces for a coffee morning at the village primary school. Several more occasions were in the diary. It was thrilling to her, how she was building this delightful side hustle, using little more than the natural resources around her.

Meanwhile, Rosemary Cottage was starting to become popular with hillwalkers, and her excellent breakfasts – prepared by Lucy while Ivan looked after the children – were proving quite a hit. As well as the traditional full English, she had introduced home-made creamy yoghurts and berry compotes, made from the currants that still grew in the garden, to be served with toasted brioche from the village bakery. There was also home-made granola, paper-thin crepes drizzled with molten dark chocolate, and fluffy vegan banana pancakes served with maple syrup and coconut cream.

It had all taken an enormous amount of thought and planning – but as the summer went on, Lucy was determined to offer something a little more special than the average B&B. She knew from reading numerous blogs that the days of the greasy fry-up served by a belligerent landlady-type were long gone. Guests were no longer thrown out into the rain straight after breakfast. It seemed that the most loved B&Bs combined the style and comfort of a boutique hotel with the personal welcome of a family home.

'And I thought we'd just be able to throw them some Sugar Puffs,' Ivan joked late one night, as Lucy prepared a batch of pancake mix for the morning.

From time to time, she still suspected her husband was missing his old life with all those client meetings and glittering ceremonies where Brookes had scooped numerous awards. While she chatted happily with guests, Ivan could be rather reserved and prone to hiding away in the tiny study upstairs. He had his freelance work to crack on with, she reminded herself, and perhaps he was still adjusting to rural life.

They grafted all through the summer, with the children spending much of their time playing happily in the garden with their new friends. Just as Lucy had as a child, Marnie and Sam viewed the garden as being full of hiding places, the setting for their imaginative games. 'I used to climb over that wall when I was a little girl,' she told them. 'The lady who lived here used to chase us out!'

'We're allowed to play here any time we like,' Sam remarked with a trace of pride, his lightly freckled face browned from the sun.

'Yeah – we're the luckiest,' Marnie agreed. Her long, flowing light brown hair had turned golden and, like her brother, she glowed from a summer of playing outdoors. Since school had broken up, Lucy couldn't remember seeing them wearing anything other than T-shirts and shorts. They had inherited their father's rangy physique, with slender limbs and skin that turned honey-brown at

33

the merest whisper of sunshine; Lucy was paler and curvier. Both of her children had celebrated their birthdays here in the garden, with vast picnics set out on blankets, bunting strung from the trees and what had felt like the entire village descending for afternoons of games.

It had been a glorious summer so far, and Lucy had grabbed any opportunity to tend to the herbaceous borders and pots of herbs she grew for cooking. Meanwhile, Ivan regarded the lawn as 'his' job – much to the delight of Irene Bagshott, a widow in her sixties who lived further down the lane.

'D'you ever loan him out, Lucy?' she asked with a throaty laugh as she passed by one August afternoon.

'I'm sure we could arrange something,' Lucy chuckled, while Ivan raised a flustered smile. Since she'd met him, he had never seemed aware of his visual appeal, and dressed practically – forever in jeans, a T-shirt or sweater – rather than with any concession to style. In fact, since moving here he was proving himself to be quite the handyman. Whilst Lucy certainly fronted the B&B, Ivan wasn't averse to fixing guttering, replacing a cracked window or sawing a precarious branch off a tree. Whenever he didn't know how to tackle a job, he read up on it or studied YouTube tutorials, then got stuck in. It had felt crucial to Lucy for them to make a real go of their business this summer, and they had, very happily, certainly achieved that. Next summer, she felt, they could take things to another level and start offering evening meals too.

Lucy even allowed herself to believe that Ivan had settled fully into village life, and that he wasn't missing his old workplace – or life in Manchester – at all.

However, it soon became apparent that other plans were afoot, which he hadn't shared with her.

Late one warm September night, they were setting the communal breakfast table for the next morning when he sighed and fiddled with fistfuls of cutlery before finally blurting out, 'I have something to tell you, Luce. A job's come up. A really good one.'

She stared at him and frowned. 'What d'you mean?'

'It's with Si Morley. Remember him?'

'From Brookes, yes, I think so. Didn't you used to go for a drink sometimes?'

Ivan took off his glasses and nodded. 'He has his own agency now – it's small but they're doing incredibly well. A few of the guys from Brookes have already moved over to work with him.'

She nodded, wondering what this was leading to. 'Have you applied for a job with him?' she asked hesitantly.

'God, no, I haven't *applied*,' Ivan said quickly. 'I wouldn't do that without saying anything to you, would I? No, Si approached me.' He repositioned the cups and saucers unnecessarily.

'But why?' Lucy asked. 'Doesn't he know we're living here now, and that you've gone freelance?'

'Yes, of course he does.' Ivan started to polish the glassware with a tea towel even though it was sparkling already. 'He just thought of me when it came up,' he added. 'Apparently I was kinda the obvious choice.' He pushed back his wavy hair that he wore longer now, since he had left his job. He was more stubbly, too, and his more weathered, outdoorsy look suited him.

'Right,' Lucy said. 'Well, you know how valued you were at Brookes.'

He nodded absently, as if the thought hadn't occurred

to him. Lucy crossed the room to one of the two squashy powder blue sofas. As she plumped up the cushions, she tried to ignore the ball of anxiety that seemed to be forming in her gut. Surely he wasn't tempted by this so-called 'approach'? Ivan had agreed that he, too, needed a fresh start, especially after they had lost the baby. He wanted to spend more time with the kids and less on jumping to attention when his clients demanded it. His parents, who lived in the outer reaches of North London, had implied that Lucy had 'forced' him to give up his job – but it hadn't been that way at all.

'What is the job anyway?' she asked lightly.

'Oh, it's a brand manager role. New client. A major repositioning so it'd be all hands on deck for a few months . . .' He repositioned the ketchups, the HP sauce and mustards on the table, as if engaged in a simplified game of chess, with condiments.

When he wandered through to the kitchen, Lucy followed him. 'So, who's the client?'

'A pretty dire hotel chain – you wouldn't know them. They've been hit with a torrent of bad reviews and some of them are pretty disgusting. There's been food poisoning scandals, outbreaks of bedbugs—'

'Nice,' she exclaimed with a shudder. 'Shall I book us in for a treat?'

Ivan smiled. 'Sure. Anyway, they've been bought out with a ton of new investment, and the actual properties are sound, so they're looking to completely refurbish and re-launch as a collection of boutique urban bolt-holes.'

'"Boutique urban bolt-holes."' Lucy gave him a bemused look.

'Ha. Yeah, I know,' Ivan chuckled, his dark eyes glinting. 'Quite a challenge.'

Lucy unloaded the tumble dryer and started to fold Sam's T-shirts. They were emblazoned with planets and robots; outer space and mechanics were his main interests right now. She picked up his polar bear sweatshirt, which he had recently shunned, considering it too babyish at the age of six (although he was still fiercely attached to his panda pillow and refused to sleep on anything else).

'So, are you interested?' Lucy ventured hesitantly, willing Ivan to say no, of course not, but it was flattering to be asked.

He shrugged. 'I might just pop in for a chat. Nothing to lose, is there?'

She stared at him. 'What d'you mean, there's nothing to lose?'

'I just think it might be a bit short-sighted to turn it down flat,' he said quickly.

Lucy stood still, astounded. 'I thought our life was here now? You agreed, Ivan. You said you'd had it with that kind of full-on work. It was doing your head in, you said—'

'Lucy, I'm just saying—'

'So how d'you think it'd work,' she cut in, 'if they did offer it to you? I mean, surely you wouldn't go back to commuting? It was hard enough, those few weeks you did it.'

'Yes, but—'

'Or would it be a home-based job? I suppose that might be okay. You've managed in the study so far, haven't you, with your freelance work? I know it's a bit cramped in there. Could we convert the shed, or build an office in the garden—' Lucy broke off, cursing herself now for not having realised that something was going

37

on. But these days, she felt as if she barely came up for air. It was all she could do to keep on top of day-to-day life here.

'It's not a home-based role,' Ivan murmured. 'They're actually offering a flat with the job.'

'A flat? Where – in Manchester?'

He nodded. 'Yes, love. It's a company flat – just a tiny studio – and it comes with the job. Si's just bought it. They reckon they need *me* to make this work, this rebranding the hotel chain thing. So they've put together this great, um, package.'

Lucy blinked at her husband. At forty-two, his handsome, finely boned face was virtually unlined, his hair showing no sign of thinning. It had amused her, the way some of the women in the village had fussed over him when they had moved in, clearly delighting in the new, eye-pleasing family man who was seen out and about at weekends with his equally attractive children. He had just taught Sam how to ride a bike. He and the children had built a kite in the shed, which had attracted praise from the locals when they'd flown it up on the hill. Whether or not he was prepared to admit it, Ivan really was part of things here, and country life suited him. His wine consumption had reduced dramatically and he looked far healthier and more relaxed.

Lucy turned to him now, trying to remain calm and not over-react when she didn't fully understand what he was telling her. 'So, what are you saying exactly?' she asked. 'I don't quite see how . . .'

'I don't want to upset you, Luce,' he said quickly. 'Honestly, it's the last thing I want.'

Lucy swallowed hard, understanding now what this

meant. 'But we don't need a great package, do we? We've worked so hard to build this. What about school, the kids' new friends, their lives here—'

'No, you'd stay here with them.'

Her heart seemed to falter. 'And . . . *you'd* move back to Manchester? You mean, on your own, without us?'

'Um . . . yeah.' He nodded, and his gaze held hers. So this was it, she realised; finally, he was admitting that she *had* dragged him here, away from the cut and thrust of whizzy city life. It had been her dream – not his – to run a B&B in a picturesque village. He had only gone along with it to please her.

'Are you . . . leaving me?' Her voice cracked.

Ivan looked aghast. 'No! Oh, God, Lucy – no. Of course I'm not. Jesus. Come here, darling.' He wound his arms around her and pulled her close. 'It's just . . . I've really tried, sweetheart. You can't say I haven't.'

'We've only been here ten months, for God's sake. Can't you give it more time?'

'They need someone now,' he said gently. 'I'm so sorry, darling. I promise it's true that they approached me. I didn't go looking.'

'It doesn't matter,' she said sharply, turning away.

'Running a B&B just isn't me, Luce. I've realised that already. I mean, I love the village, and what we've done to this place. But I need more than this.'

'You need more than us?' she exclaimed.

'No, no – not you and the kids. I mean living here, being so cut off from the world, worrying about have we got enough sausages and do we need new pillows, and did we remember lime marmalade, one of the guests asked for it last week, and maybe it's time we started offering evening meals—'

'Sorry your life has become so limited,' she snapped as her tears spilled over.

'It's not limited. It's fantastic!'

'So fantastic that you're moving back to Manchester, away from us?' She was shouting now; she couldn't stop herself. Thank God their children slept soundly at night.

'Listen.' He grabbed at her hand. 'I'll only be away four nights out of seven. I'll set off on Monday mornings and be back on Fridays, and it'll make our weekends all the more special.'

So it was all decided then, she realised. This wasn't a discussion about whether or not he should accept the job. His mind was made up and, whatever her feelings, it looked as if she would be running the B&B virtually alone.

'We can get someone in to help here,' he added, as if reading her thoughts.

'We can't afford that,' Lucy said flatly. 'We're only just managing to stay afloat now.'

'Yes, but we'll have my salary again, won't we? It'll be less pressurised, love. Think what a relief it'll be, having that security again – that regular money coming in. I know it's looking good for the next few weeks, but what about winter? There's hardly anyone booked in past October—'

'I could go all out to get more floristry work,' she said quickly, hating the desperation that had crept into her voice.

'But there won't be any flowers then, will there?'

'I know, but I was thinking of doing Christmas arrangements and selling them locally – even over in Heathfield. There are plenty of shops that sell that kind of thing. Winter foliage, wreaths, there's tons of scope for seasonal decorations with holly, fir cones, berries . . .' Lucy stopped, her cheeks flushing. 'I know it won't make much money,' she added, 'but I have a feeling it could grow and become a bigger part of our lives.'

'I'm sure it could,' Ivan said distractedly. 'I think you're so talented, Luce. It's amazing that you're doing this too, on top of everything else you've got going on here. But it's not about that. It's more about . . .' He paused. 'My future, I guess. *My* working life.'

She rubbed at her eyes and put down the bunch of teaspoons she'd been holding tightly. 'You really want this job, don't you?'

Ivan nodded.

'And it's definitely yours, if you decide to accept it?'

'It is, darling, yes, but please don't worry. I'll still be with you, in every way. You and me will always be a team.'

She inhaled slowly, letting his declaration settle in her mind, and looked around the country kitchen they had planned so carefully. In the past few weeks she had already scrambled hundreds of free-range eggs on that hob. She was immensely proud of what they had achieved, even at this early stage; the glowing online reviews, and a guestbook filling with positive comments. So she *would not* fall to pieces if Ivan had made up his mind to accept the job. She had wanted Rosemary Cottage far too much to let her dreams crumble now.

Lucy smoothed down her long dark hair, which fell in loose waves over her shoulders. 'Okay, then,' she said firmly. 'Go ahead and accept the job, if it feels like the right thing to do.'

Ivan cleared his throat and looked at her. 'I'm sorry, darling. I know I should have talked to you first, but . . . I already have.'

Chapter Five

Two weeks later, Ivan launched into his new routine of heading off to work at six every Monday morning and being gone until Friday evening. Lucy could hardly believe this had been thrown at her, with virtually no warning – but then, that was the way his business worked. It was full on, all-hands-on-deck and, admittedly, Ivan was being well rewarded by his employer. However, it required a big adjustment on Lucy's side. Apart from the wrench of saying goodbye, there were practical aspects to consider; specifically, how could one person simultaneously serve up home-cured Yorkshire bacon to guests whilst chivvying two boisterous children into getting ready and ferrying them to school?

It was impossible, of course, and as Lucy felt uncomfortable relying on her still-new local friends, she decided to enlist some help. In stepped Rikke, the Danish woman in her late twenties who worked part-time at Della's bookshop as well as giving swimming lessons in Heathfield, and harp recitals locally. She quickly proved herself to be quite the godsend.

Marnie and Sam adapted fairly easily to their dad being away during the week. It's not that they didn't miss him; more that children tend to exist in the here and now, and often possess a talent for simply getting on with things. Whereas they used to cause havoc whilst getting ready in the mornings, 'losing' their shoes and suddenly finding themselves splattered with hot chocolate, they would now be eerily helpful and ready in good time for Rikke to pick them up. They would probably have been ready at five a.m. – with shoes polished – if required, so keen were they to impress her.

Within a few weeks, Lucy had managed to adjust too. 'It's amazing what you can get used to,' she told Della when she'd popped into the bookshop one bright and breezy late October afternoon. 'If someone had told me Ivan would be away during the week, I'd have said it'd be a disaster for us. But in some ways . . .' She paused.

'It's made things better?' Della suggested.

Lucy winced. 'I feel terrible for saying it, and of course I miss him. But I must admit, he was getting pretty grumpy with the day-to-day stuff.'

'What kind of stuff?' Della asked with a wry smile.

'Oh, the change-overs, mostly. Cleaning rooms, scrubbing loos.' She paused and smirked. 'Ironing sheets . . .'

'But guests can't have wrinkled sheets,' Della exclaimed in mock horror.

'They absolutely can't.' Lucy grinned. 'And as for the people aspect – well, you know Ivan's sociable enough, when he's in the mood. But with guests, you have to be more—'

'More "on"?' remarked Frank, Della's husband, as he wandered into the shop.

'Yes. That's exactly what Ivan called it.' Lucy laughed.

43

'"I'm not like you," he kept telling me. "I can't be *on* all the time."'

'I guess running a B&B isn't everyone's cup of tea,' Frank added. 'Cutting the toast into perfect triangles—'

'Oh, I'm a stickler for that,' Lucy chuckled, 'with my ruler and set square.'

'You are a natural at it, though,' Della added, handing Lucy a coffee from the percolator. 'Frank, how many times have Lucy's guests told us how much they're loving their stay?'

'Tons,' he said. 'You're obviously doing something right.'

'I'm glad to hear that,' Lucy said, and she caught Della's eye and grinned. She knew her friend was delighted to see her childhood home lavished with care and attention after decades of neglect.

Having chosen a vintage French cookbook, Lucy strolled through the village to pick up Marnie and Sam from school. It was true that she missed Ivan, and by Friday afternoons she was desperate to hear his car pulling up outside the cottage. But they *were* still a team, just as he'd said when he'd dropped the bombshell about the job last month. Ivan wasn't a man to break a promise. Lucy had known that, instinctively, on the day they'd met, on that Euston-to-Manchester-Piccadilly train.

She wasn't normally one for chatting to strangers on journeys. Usually, she preferred to read or simply enjoy watching the landscape sliding by. But that day she'd fallen into conversation with the cute stranger in glasses sitting opposite. When a sudden heavy snowfall caused a two-hour delay, she had been a tiny bit pleased.

Actually, *extremely* pleased. The weekend at an old college friend's in London had been fun, but meeting

Ivan on the journey home had been the icing on the cake. He had made her laugh, fetched them wine from the buffet carriage and they'd got tipsy together. They were at a standstill, not yet halfway home. While other passengers were moaning loudly to each other, and venting their frustrations to the train staff, Lucy had barely noticed time slipping by. *We're sorry about this continued delay,* came yet another announcement. *We're hoping to get moving again very soon . . .*

'I hope we don't,' Ivan had said with a smile that caused her heart to flip. 'I'm enjoying this journey.'

'Me too,' Lucy had said. His eyes were lovely, she'd noticed; dark as espresso with long black lashes. She could hardly tear her gaze away from them.

'So, what d'you do for a living?' he'd asked.

Bingo! 'I work in lingerie,' she'd replied.

'Really?' His eyebrows had shot up. 'And I thought *my* workplace was relaxed.'

She'd smiled. 'It's a lingerie retailer, although sometimes I think it'd be better if we only sold knickers—'

'Then you could say, "I work in pants"?'

'Exactly.' That – or perhaps the wine they'd been sharing – set them off sniggering, and by the time they'd arrived at their home city they had swapped numbers and vowed to meet.

That had been over thirteen years ago. Three years later, she and Ivan were married, and a couple of years after that she was pregnant with Marnie, then Sam followed. Pre-Ivan, Lucy had never lived with a boyfriend or even had anything particularly serious. She'd had wild crushes and the odd, fairly short-lived relationship, but there'd been no one she'd remotely imagined a future with. *Thank God for freak snow,* she'd often thought.

45

And now, as the softly weathered village primary school came into view, Lucy decided Ivan had been right in that their weekends would now feel more special. While there were often guests to look after, they were usually out during the day – and Lucy and Ivan seemed to appreciate each other like never before.

They were so lucky, she reflected as she spotted her new friends clustered by the school gate. She and Ivan had lost a baby, but they had Marnie and Sam and, of course, each other. Now, with Ivan working flat out during the week, it seemed as if they were conscious of making the most of every day they had together.

A few weeks later, when Lucy recalled thinking this, it chilled her to the bones.

Chapter Six

By the time winter took hold, bookings had started to thin out. Lucy had expected this to happen; after all, only the brave-hearted were inclined to hike into the hills with ominous clouds overhead. As the end of term approached, it had rained for what felt like weeks, and she was looking forward to Ivan taking a break over Christmas. Life had been hectic, especially since he had been working in Manchester, and they needed some family time together.

Although Lucy's mother had pushed for them to spend the festive season at theirs, Lucy had put her foot down this time. For years now, they had alternated between going to Ivan's parents', where it would be terribly restrained, with a foot-high tinsel tree sitting primly on a side table, and her own parents' place, which would be decked out in full, extravagant finery.

'But it's our turn this year,' her mother had argued.

'Yes, but we'd love to spend it here for the first time,' Lucy explained. 'Why don't you and Dad come to us?'

'Are you sure, darling? It seems like an awful lot of work . . .'

Lucy smiled, knowing her mother was merely reluctant to relinquish control. 'It's a lot of work for you too, us lot all descending. And we'd love to do it. I don't think Rosemary Cottage will feel properly like our home until we've had Christmas here.'

Reluctantly, Anna had agreed (Lucy's father, Paddy, never had any say in such matters). Ivan's parents had been invited too, but they tended to view visiting Yorkshire as akin to traversing the Arctic tundra, and had politely declined.

And so Lucy propelled herself into preparing for Christmas, scribbling lists and bringing in holly and dark, glossy foliage, plus crispy seedpods and branches with which to create festive arrangements throughout the house.

Although she had enjoyed her run of looking after their guests, it was a relief to block out some time in order to ready the cottage for her parents' arrival on Christmas Eve. In amongst the foliage in the house, she dotted cream tapered candles, red velvet ribbons and silvery fairy lights. Although she had a vague memory that her childhood friend Hally's dad had sold Christmas trees, she gathered from asking around that the nearest source these days was a farm several miles out of the village. So she drove out there with the children and selected a seven-foot Scots Pine, which was delivered later to great excitement. As soon as it was set up in place, scenting the cottage and shimmering beneath an explosion of multi-coloured baubles, it felt as if the festive season had properly begun.

By now, the entire village was strewn with twinkling decorations. A huge tree glinted with jewel-coloured lights, and shop windows were filled with glowing nativity scenes and fuzzed with fake snow. Only an appearance of the genuine stuff could have made Burley Bridge look more festive. Lucy threw herself into every event going, from Della's festive drinks in the bookshop, to a heart-soaring carol concert in the village church. She had never felt such anticipation over Christmas Day itself since she had been a child.

Ivan, too, seemed to be full of festive spirit as the holidays grew closer. He had a buoyancy about him these days, Lucy was relieved to note, and he was certainly doing well in his new post at Si Morley's agency. Thirteen hotels in the once-beleaguered chain had been blitzed of their trouser presses, cheap melamine desks and industrial shower gel dispensers. 'Modern rustic with a hint of hippie' summed up the new look, according to Ivan: 'A little bit of Ibiza in Bradford,' he laughed. They offered green juices, massage and complimentary morning yoga.

Meanwhile, as Rikke had gone home to Copenhagen for the holidays, Lucy's mornings involved getting the children up and ready for school on time and cracking on with some last-minute orders for festive decorations. Happily, her floral displays around the village had led to several requests for handmade Christmas wreaths.

The annual Burley Bridge children's party was also drawing near. Lucy had gathered that the fancy dress element was the highlight, and Marnie and Sam had been talking about it for weeks. Unhelpfully, they had changed their minds about their costumes numerous times, and still hadn't decided when she'd dropped them off at school that morning.

'Can't you just throw something together?' Ivan asked, when he and Lucy caught up on the phone that lunch-time.

'Throw what together exactly?'

'I don't know,' he said distractedly. 'You're the one who's good at that stuff—'

'But it's *tonight*,' she reminded him. 'There isn't enough time. I can't believe we've left it so late.'

'Could you just nip out and buy something?'

Lucy laughed dryly. 'Where are you suggesting I nip out to?'

'Surely there's somewhere. What about that everything-shop on the high street?' The general-store-cum-post-office, he meant.

'Ivan,' Lucy said, shaking her head, 'how many times have you actually been in there?'

'Loads,' he protested, a trace of amusement in his voice.

Lucy smirked. 'What's her name, then? The lady who owns it, I mean?'

'Er . . .'

'You don't know, do you? It's Irene.'

'Irene! Yes, of course.'

'You should remember,' she teased him. 'She has a crush on you.'

'Oh, stop it,' he exclaimed.

'How can you forget Irene? She was all overexcited watching you mowing the lawn.' Lucy was laughing now. 'D'you feel objectified, when that happens?'

'You're being ridiculous.'

'Okay – so who has the hair salon across the road from her?'

'What is this?' he cut in, chuckling now. 'A who's who in Burley Bridge quiz?'

'Yes, and you're doing terribly!'

'Anyway,' he said, quickly changing the subject, 'do they have to dress up? I mean, is it crucial?'

'Of course it is! It's not just the party. There's the parade through the village to the Christmas tree.'

'God, it is quite a number,' he conceded. 'Wish I was there to help.'

'Bet you do.' She laughed hollowly. 'Just hurry home tonight, will you? I can't wait to see you, and neither can the kids. They'll be desperate to show you their outfits – *if* we can cobble something together in time.'

After finishing the call, Lucy headed upstairs, pulled down the ladder from the hatch in the ceiling and climbed up to the attic. Although there was a lamp, it was still dark and shadowy – so dusty she could feel it in her throat – and the abundance of clutter set her on edge. They had shoved any surplus possessions up here when they'd moved in, and never got around to sorting it all out.

Ivan always launched himself into new hobbies and interests, almost to the point of obsession – which would involve buying all the equipment, materials and accessories. Lucy coughed as she picked her way through the evidence of Ivan's long-forgotten passions. There were tennis rackets and a defunct rowing machine. She gashed her shin against the sharp corner of a saxophone case.

'All this *stuff*,' she muttered irritably, relieved to find boxes of fabric remnants now. Once a keen crafter, often making her own clothes during her student days, these days she rarely had the time. She pulled out reams of fabric, hoping for inspiration to strike. Marnie could be an elf, Lucy decided, as she unearthed a length of bright green material. Further delving revealed an ancient light brown onesie, which had belonged to Marnie and could possibly be fashioned into a reindeer outfit for Sam. Lucy transported her finds to the box room where her sewing machine was set up.

By the time she set off to pick up the children from school, she had managed to knock up a basic elf's tunic *and* cut reindeer antlers from sturdy cardboard, which she had covered in felt and stitched to the onesie hood. Pretty impressive, she decided, considering it had all been thrown together at the last minute.

'How come dads never have to involve themselves with this kind of stuff?' Lucy asked with a wry smile at the school gate. There was murmured agreement amongst the mums that men seemed adept at swerving the issue.

'You mean, Ivan wasn't beavering away on the sewing machine last night?' teased Carys, to whom Lucy had grown especially close.

'He wasn't here,' Lucy reminded her. 'He'll just get to admire their costumes later – when it's all over.'

'Is this his last day at work?' Carys asked, and Lucy nodded. 'Bet you can't wait.'

'I'm counting the hours,' she admitted. 'It's been a pretty long haul without him . . .' Lucy caught herself, and felt guilty for even admitting this. There were still five days to go before Christmas and Ivan had agreed to forget about work until after New Year. It meant almost three weeks together as a family. Carys was a single mum to Amber and Noah – Marnie and Sam's new best friends – and rarely got a break. Even when her husband had still been in the picture he had barely lifted a finger, apparently. It had been Glen who had nagged for a dog until Carys had crumbled. Of course, they all loved Bramble, their bouncy springer spaniel. But Glen had never once walked him – Bramble immediately became 'Carys's dog' – and all Glen had done was moan about the hair, the mud brought in on paws, the vet's bills.

More shockingly still, he had never once set foot in

the children's school, figuring that 'We don't need two of us to go to a parents' meeting.' Thank God Ivan wasn't like that. When he was around, he wanted to *do* stuff with his children. Holed up in the shed, he and the kids had already constructed a rather wonky-looking wooden farm, an easel for Marnie and almost completed a birdhouse. The kids loved nothing more than time spent with their dad over spirit levels and pots of paint. Lucy hardly ever ventured into the shed. It was their domain, and she was happy to leave it that way.

The school doors opened and the children surged out. 'See you at the party,' Carys said as her own kids ran towards her. 'Hope they like their costumes!'

'They'll have no choice,' Lucy said with a laugh as Marnie and Sam appeared in the playground. As they set off for home, she described the outfits she'd made. Naturally, the children insisted on pulling them on the minute they were back.

'I love it, Mum!' Marnie enthused, posing for a picture as Lucy whipped out her phone.

'Can we go to the party now?' Sam demanded, clattering about the kitchen in the onesie.

'It doesn't start till half-six,' Lucy said. 'You need dinner first.'

'But I'm not hungry,' he retorted, 'and there'll be cakes and sweets at the party. Noah said—'

'You can't *just* have sweets and cakes, love.'

'Why not?'

''Cause all your teeth'll fall out,' Marnie retorted, slipping into the wise older sister role she so enjoyed.

'Don't care,' Sam huffed.

'Yeah, who needs teeth?' Lucy agreed with a smile. 'We could just *gum* our food—'

'Will Daddy see our costumes?' Sam wanted to know as she put on a pan of pasta.

'Yes, of course,' Lucy replied, 'when you come home. If he's back in time, he might even come out and join us on the parade.'

'Hurrah!' Sam yelled, antlers bobbing.

She looked at her children, aware that it wasn't just the party and parade they were delighted about. It was the fact that Ivan would soon be home. Never mind Lucy's costume-making skills. As far as Marnie and Sam were concerned, nothing could compete with seeing Daddy on a Friday night.

Pesto pasta was shovelled down hastily, and Lucy managed to unearth some queasily coloured lime green face paint to complete Marnie's incarnation as an elf. By the time they set off, the village was already milling with children dressed up and making their way to the party. There were Santas and snow queens and a plum pudding on legs, all hurrying along in the fine rain. As they entered the village hall, Lucy looked around in amazement at a sparkling scene of Christmas trees, model polar bears and stacks of presents. The entire building had been turned into a grotto. Festive music filled the hall as a strident woman wearing tartan trousers and a Christmas jumper – whom Lucy recognised as the school's deputy head – called the excitable children to heel. Clearly in charge of the games, she soon had some kind of dance competition on the go as Lucy found Carys at the trestle table.

'This is pretty impressive,' she said, helping herself to a mince pie. 'Is there always this much food?'

Carys nodded. The table was crammed with plates of cakes and cookies and dishes of foil-wrapped sweets.

'Some people around here have the whole home baking thing wrapped up. It's kind of competitive. No one says so, of course, but there's something shameful about being the one who brought the unwanted ginger cake and brandy snaps.'

Lucy laughed. 'I didn't bring anything. I didn't realise—'

'It'll have been noted,' Carys teased her, 'but you'll be excused, seeing as you're new.'

'Am I still new?'

Carys smiled. '*We're* still new and we've been here for five years. What I mean is, the real villagers are the ones who were born here and you and me will never be one of those.'

Lucy knew what she meant. Ivan had made a similar point: that they would always be 'newcomers', and that villages tended to have their own traditions and rituals that were run by a select few. Well, fine, Lucy thought now, glimpsing Marnie and Sam grabbing cupcakes with their new friends in tow. Occasions like this brought the whole village together. As the party ended, and the children headed outside, she felt lucky to be a part of things here.

Despite the steady rain, the parade was a riotous affair as the children had been handed bells to ring as they made their way through the village. Carys had rushed home to fetch Bramble, who now led the procession in his festive red and white fur-trimmed coat. People waved from their windows above the shops. Several shops had opened late and set out tables laden with yet more mince pies and cups of mulled wine ready for the taking. Lucy took a paper cup of wine with thanks and looked around for Ivan. No sign of him yet – but she hadn't really expected him to come out and join them. He'd be waiting at home, she decided, as she sipped the warm, spicy drink. Hopefully he'd have brought back a decent bottle of red for them to share by the fireside once the children were in bed.

It was almost nine when they finally said their good-byes and started to make their way home. Spirits were still high, despite the rain. Marnie and Sam clutched the bags of sweets they'd been given at the party as they ran ahead down the wet garden path.

Marnie was first to reach their front door. She rattled the handle impatiently. 'Mum, it's locked!'

'Is it?' Lucy frowned, quickening her pace. 'That's funny. I thought Dad'd be home by now.'

'Where is he?' Sam asked, pulling on a wilted antler.

'He's probably just delayed,' she replied as she let them into the house. 'Maybe something happened at work. Don't worry. He'll be back soon.'

'I want Dad,' Sam huffed, ill-tempered now as he stomped into the hallway. He unzipped the onesie, stepped out of it and kicked it aside on the floor.

'So do I,' muttered Marnie, pushing her damp honey-blonde hair from her face. 'Why's he late?'

'I don't know, love. I'll try his phone.' The children plunged their hands into their bags of sweets as Lucy made the call. 'Not too many now, Sam,' she warned as her husband's voicemail message began: *Hey, it's Ivan. Sorry, can't take your call right now. Leave me a message and I'll get right back to you . . .*

She glanced at Sam as he stuffed a handful of jelly snakes into his mouth. No point in trying to limit sweet consumption now, she decided. She wasn't up to a big debate on the matter, and it was a special occasion after all. Instead, she turned her attention to lighting the log fire in the living room in the hope that it would catch quickly, and cosy up the house. Surely Ivan wouldn't be too long now . . . Pushing away a niggle of concern, she herded the children upstairs for their baths, with the promise of hot chocolate once they were tucked up in bed.

Normally, that would have done the trick. Sam adored his bedtime stories, and even at eight, Marnie still regarded them as a treat when she was in the mood for being read to.

'Mum, Marnie took some of my sweets,' Sam complained, swinging on his bedroom door handle.

'No, I didn't,' his sister retorted.

'Yeah, you did! You held my bag for me in the parade. You *stole* some.' He ran at her with a half-hearted kick.

'Ow!' Marnie screamed, unnecessarily.

'Sam, stop that,' Lucy exclaimed.

'I didn't do anything.' His dark eyes radiated annoyance.

'C'mon now, you two. You've just had far too many sweets tonight. *This* is why I try to get you to eat celery.'

'I hate celery!' Sam announced. Lucy's feeble attempt at a joke had clearly misfired.

'Stop shouting, Sam. I'm not going to try and force celery on you now.'

'I hate it more than anything!'

'Yes, we get the message,' Lucy muttered, rubbing at her temples, sensing the start of a headache.

Marnie sighed heavily. '*When* can we get a dog, Mummy?'

Lucy looked at her, figuring that the green face paint would take some shifting in the bath. 'We've been through this hundreds of times before, love—'

'You said we could have one when we moved to the country,' she added with a frown.

'I didn't say definitely. I said we'd consider it.'

'We're in the country now,' Sam announced, perking up instantly. 'Can we get one please, Mummy?'

'Life's a bit busy just now,' Lucy said firmly, although in truth, she would have welcomed a dog into their family. It was Ivan who kept insisting that they had enough on their plate.

'Bath's ready, Sam,' she said now, to swerve them off the subject. 'You're first in tonight.'

'He's always first,' Marnie bleated in the doorway. 'I don't want to go in cold water.'

'It won't be cold. We'll put more hot in—'

'He pees in it,' she moaned, and Lucy wondered yet again where Ivan had got to. She was more than ready for him to take over tonight. The children were much more compliant for him – willing, helpful, eager to please, the way they were with Rikke too; basically anyone who wasn't their mother. Mums always seemed to get the raw deal.

'I *don't* pee in the bath,' Sam muttered.

'You pooed in it once,' Marnie crowed from the landing, which was true – but he'd only been two, and there was no need to bring it up now.

'I didn't,' he growled.

'You did! You pooed!'

'Josh isn't allowed to say poo,' Sam added, referring to a boy in his class.

'What does he say, then?' Lucy asked as she folded towels in the bathroom.

'Chocolate sausage.'

'You're kidding,' she spluttered, at which Marnie guffawed in the doorway. 'Is that true?'

'Yeah.' Lucy handed him a towel as he clambered out of the bath. 'He has to say, "I need a chocolate sausage, Mummy." And he has to put up his hand, even at home!'

The children were giggling now, fuelled by copious quantities of refined sugar, and God knows what kinds of chemical compounds went into those neon-bright jelly snakes. While Lucy was grateful they weren't bickering, she was now clearly visualising the glass of red she would be enjoying soon, whether or not Ivan brought a special bottle home with him. They always had a few in stock, and Friday nights certainly warranted a treat.

Knowing they would be eating later than normal – due to the party and parade – Lucy had planned a quick meal of fresh tuna steaks, seared with olives and peppers. Their weekend evenings were lovely, and she treasured them. They rarely went out, preferring instead to cosy up at home – sometimes sitting out in the garden on warm summer's nights, and in the colder months cuddling up on the sofa by the fire. She checked the time again – it was nine-forty – and willed Ivan to hurry home.

Sam had sloped off to choose a story now, and Marnie was splashing idly in the bath. 'Can you try and wash off that face paint please?' Lucy said.

'It *is* off,' Marnie said, which was clearly untrue. There was some gentle wiping with a flannel – 'Ow!' she screamed, as if she were being attacked with nettles – and finally, bath time was over and the finishing post was in sight.

Lucy usually tried to make their bedtime stories exciting, with her children snuggled on either side of her, tucked up in Sam's bed. However, she might as well have been reading the boiler instruction booklet for all the feeling she was putting into it.

It was her husband Lucy was thinking about on this cold, wet December night. She yearned for him to hurry home and be with her, and to know that everything was all right.

Chapter Seven

James Halsall was relieved to see the Christmas lights of Burley Bridge glinting in the distance. It had rained steadily the whole drive from Liverpool, and now he just wanted to pull up at his dad's and be reassured that everything was okay.

He had pleasant memories of long-ago summers in the village, spent stealing redcurrants from Rosemary Cottage's garden. However, a lot of James's childhood hadn't been fun, and he'd been relieved to leave the place for good the minute he'd found a means of escape. These days, he only came to visit his father who still lived here in a clapped-out farmhouse a mile out of the village. Despite the fact that they were hardly close, James had still seen him regularly – dutifully – over the years.

Until a few months ago there had been a sort of system in place. The unspoken agreement was that he and his older brother, Rod, would alternate visits, passing their father back and forth like a parcel that could potentially blow up in their faces at any moment. Then Rod had moved in with their dad – temporarily, he was keen to stress – and the last time James had visited, everything had seemed fine.

At least, fine-*ish*. Although hardly domesticated, Rod seemed to have things reasonably under control. But the phone call that morning had alerted James to the fact that everything was far from fine after all.

'Sorry to bother you,' Reena had said, 'but I'm really worried about your dad, James. Is Rod meant to be around at the moment?'

'Um, yes, as far as I know. Why, what's happened?' James had asked, immediately alarmed. Reena lived in the village but had a holiday cottage close to his father's place that she rented out. She had never called him before, and he didn't know her too well. James hadn't even known she had his number.

'I went up to the cottage this morning to say goodbye to my guests,' Reena explained, 'and they told me there'd been a bit of an altercation last night. Your dad had been at the door, trying to barge his way in—'

'Into your holiday house?' James exclaimed. 'But why? What did he want?'

'He . . . he was convinced it was his place,' she said apologetically. 'That he lived there, and they shouldn't have been there at all. He was quite, um, insistent. He used some terrible language . . .'

'I'm so sorry . . .' James was aware of a sinking sensation in his chest.

'But finally,' she continued, 'they persuaded him that he'd made a mistake, and he wandered away. I wish they'd let me know last night. They just assumed it was some local eccentric, but by their description – the big beard, the gold earring – it was pretty obvious it was Kenny.'

'Did he seem drunk, do you know?'

'No – just confused, I think.'

'Okay, thanks, Reena,' James said, rubbing at his cropped dark hair. 'I really appreciate you calling.'

'I had to look you up online. You took some finding!'

'Yes, well, I'm glad you have my number now. Please don't worry. I'll try and get hold of Rod and find out what's going on.'

Perhaps it was just as well his father resembled a latter-day pirate, he'd thought bleakly as he called his brother's mobile; it made him distinctive. But Rod's number just rang out. Time after time, James tried it, but no joy.

At forty-four, Rod was three years older than James, and the golden boy as far as their father was concerned. When they were younger, James had wondered if it had simply been an age thing; Rod had done everything first, and had the gift of the gab and a knack of charming everyone. Whilst not wildly academic, he had talked his way into working in 'investments' – James had never quite grasped what this entailed – and made a mint, apparently, which had clearly impressed their father. Weirdly, for someone who had possessed the same pair of slippers since about 1973, Kenny Halsall took a keen interest in money.

Meanwhile, James had been more of a practical type, good at fixing and making things. At seventeen he had gained a joinery apprenticeship in Liverpool through a family friend, and fled.

It wasn't that his childhood had been terrible. Whilst Kenny had hardly been the nurturing type, even as a child James had managed to grasp that raising two boys on his own wasn't easy, especially with his various one-man businesses to attend to. As it was, James and Rod had enjoyed virtually limitless freedom from the ages of six and nine. Even when their mother had still been there, she hadn't been one to establish too many rules.

It was rare to be so unsupervised, even back then in the 1980s. Not for James and Rod the tedious rituals of mealtimes and homework supervision. As Kenny was usually out working, dinner for the boys could mean tinned tomato soup and packets of Monster Munch or whatever else they could plunder from the under-stocked kitchen. James had vivid memories of Rod making some kind of 'pudding' out of jelly, doused liberally in contra-band brandy and set alight. He'd been in awe of his big brother back then.

Although Kenny had various stints of working as a lorry driver, a gardener and a labourer, he always came back to being a woodsman. A couple of acres of forest adjoined their house, and Kenny was often to be found out there, sawing and chopping, then delivering logs all over Burley Bridge and beyond.

Throughout late November and December, Kenny would have virtually decamped permanently to the woods, as he had a seasonal business selling Christmas trees. James and Rod would be enlisted to help with the felling and the dragging of the trees into a makeshift hut, where the young boys were allowed – thrillingly – to use the netting machine. It felt good, the three of them working together when James and his father had little to do with each other the rest of the year. They were a team then. It's why James had a certain fondness for Christmas. It certainly wasn't down to any mince pie-making endeavours on Kenny's part.

Perhaps his father's attachment to wood – and to

forests – had influenced James's own life choices, as once he'd left Burley Bridge and finished his apprenticeship, he had carved out a living as a furniture maker. From building tables and shelves, he graduated towards fitting out boats when his first commission had proven a success. James enjoyed being on the water and seeing a project through from his first visit, when he would start with basic dimensions and often go on to design the whole interior. It was creative, satisfying work. His love life was less successful; he and his ex-wife, Michaela, had split up two years ago, and now they shared the care of their nine-year-old son Spike. But on the whole, life was manageable.

It'll all be a panic over nothing, he tried to convince himself as he turned off the motorway towards Burley Bridge that night.

After Reena's call, James had tried to carry on fitting out the narrowboat he had been working on for the past week. But he'd been unable to concentrate. What the hell was going on with Rod? They weren't close, and never had been really. As for Rod's marriage to Phoebe, a terrifically capable sort, and a national champion swimmer in her youth, all James knew was it had ended messily with Rod somehow acquiring a black eye and his beloved racing bike being smashed up. After that, Rod had moved back in with their father and rarely seemed to see his three children.

Despite still being 'highly successful' in various businesses – which he never seemed keen to divulge any details about – his brother now seemed to have no income at all, as far as James could gather. Still, as Kenny had started to show signs of confusion, it had been a godsend really, to have someone living with him until a long-term solution could be figured out. 'Dad's just a bit ditsy,' was how Rod preferred to describe their father's current state. 'I'm sure it's nothing to worry about.'

As he neared Burley Bridge, James wondered if he had over-reacted wildly by rushing over on this bleak, wet night five days before Christmas. However, there had been no answer on his father's landline either, and there was no one local he felt he could ask to look in on his dad. James's childhood friends had scattered all over the country, and he knew Kenny wouldn't have taken kindly to anyone popping round anyway, checking on his welfare. It had seemed as if there had been no other option than to throw some clothes in a bag, apologise to his client for the delay to the job, and set off. Three and a half hours it took normally, but tonight James had managed it in under three.

As he approached the village, James tried to calm himself in readiness for whatever situation he might walk into tonight. He drove slowly through the quiet streets, noticing how sparkly and festive everything looked. It hadn't been quite as pretty as this when he was a kid. Now all the shop windows glowed with nativity scenes, and lights were strung from the Victorian lamp posts. James thought of Spike, who was currently at his mum's place. He was spending Christmas with her this year so James had planned to visit his father, though not quite this early. The thought of being apart from Spike was never easy at this time of year.

The pitted road rose sharply from the village, cutting between steeply sloping fields, then curving through the woodland that Kenny still owned, although it was only minimally tended these days. The shed his father had built, in which to store Christmas trees ready for purchase, was rotting badly and should probably come down at some point. It was almost impossible to believe how successful they had been, back in the day, when numerous garden centres offered not only a variety of firs but vast selections of Christmas gifts too. The fact was, quite simply, that Kenny Halsall's Christmas trees had been the best around.

As his father's house came into view, standing alone on a muddied stretch of lane, James noted that the living room light was on, which reassured him a little. Illogical, perhaps, but it suggested that Kenny was home, at least. He had always been pretty diligent about switching off all of the lights before he went out. While his heart was still beating he would never waste a single watt of electricity.

James climbed out of his car. He knocked briefly on the front door and pushed it open. 'Dad?' he called out.

'Who's that?' his father boomed from the living room.

'It's me – James.'

'What? *Who* is it?'

'It's me, Dad. Hi!' He stepped into the room where his father was sitting in an armchair with a newspaper spread out over his lap, gawping up at him.

'What are *you* doing here?'

I'm your son, not the bailiff, James wanted to say, but instead he feigned a bright smile and perched on the sofa. 'Just thought I'd come a bit earlier than planned for Christmas,' he said, wondering how best to broach things. He wasn't afraid of his father – not anymore – but he was keen to avoid conflict as far as possible so he could locate his brother and have some kind of discussion of what to do next.

'Why didn't you tell me?' Kenny asked.

'Dad, I've tried to call but you never pick up the landline. And I'm not sure what happened to that mobile Rod bought you.'

'Oh, I lost that,' he muttered.

'Right – okay. So, how are things?' James asked, taking care to maintain a cheery tone.

'Um, all right, I suppose,' Kenny replied.

'So, where's Rod at the moment? Any idea?'

'I'm . . . not sure.' His gruffness had subsided a little.

'Erm, Dad,' James ventured, 'Reena called me today. You know, Reena who owns the yellow house?'

'Uh-huh?'

'Well . . . she sounded a bit worried. She said there'd been some kind of business at the cottage?'

Kenny frowned. 'Oh, she's a nuisance, that woman. Always sticking her bloody oar in.'

'She's always seemed perfectly pleasant to me,' James said quickly. 'She was just concerned that you'd been over to the house, and her guests said you'd, um . . .'

'Is that why you're here? To check up on me?'

'Of course not,' James replied, his jaw tightening.

'What would I be doing at her place?'

'I'm just telling you what Reena said.'

'Well, I don't know what she's on about,' Kenny muttered.

How to proceed from here? They fell into silence, and Kenny scratched at his beard and flicked his gaze down to the newspaper. While he looked reasonably presentable in a navy cable-knit sweater and brown corduroys, the facial hair was always a worry. On previous occasions James had noted all manner of food residue clinging to it. Beards were like dogs, he often thought: if you were going to have one, you had to be responsible for it.

As it was, Kenny owned two obese cats, Horace and Winston, who were currently snoozing on the matted hearthrug. James cast his gaze around the low-ceilinged living room with the faded rose-patterned wallpaper and the dimly flickering open fire. The room reminded him of one of those pubs you'd only ever find yourself in by accident; the kind where there'd be no food on offer apart from some out-of-date pork scratchings, and the barman would look at you with mild disdain as you walked in, as if you had no business being there.

James had grown up in this house, and while his mum had still been there, until he was six, it had seemed forever sunny, filled with her giddy laughter as she tossed her mane of glossy dark hair and cooked up pots of her funny hippie food. When James thought of Evelyn – which he tried not to too often – he remembered glinting green eyes and the sweater dresses she made for herself on her bewildering knitting machine, and often wore with wellies (a look he imagined not many women could have pulled off). It was so long ago, he was sometimes surprised he could remember her at all. But although the images were disjointed – like a handful of random snapshots grabbed from a box – they were still vivid to him. Sometimes, he could almost smell her musky perfume that she kept on the dressing table.

As if he had forgotten that James was there, Kenny snatched the remote control from next to his slippered feet and turned on the TV. Rather than sitting there, trying to communicate, James went through to make two mugs of tea in the kitchen. A quick scan of the fridge revealed that, although the milk was drinkable – just – the only other items in it were two open tins, one partly filled with baked beans and another containing a residue

69

of rice pudding. James had long suspected that Kenny pretty much existed on tins and frozen ready meals. It took him less than one second to weigh up whether to remind his father that opened cans weren't supposed to be refrigerated, before deciding against it. Kenny didn't respond well to household hints.

Hoping his dad wouldn't notice, James binned the tins and made a mental note to do a grocery shop first thing in the morning. At least there was a reasonably fresh loaf on the counter.

Back in the living room, he handed his father a mug of tea. 'So, how long are you thinking of staying?' Kenny asked as he took it without thanks.

'Just thought I'd play it by ear, Dad,' James replied vaguely. 'So, um, when did you last see Rod?'

Kenny shrugged. 'Yesterday, I think it was. He went out.'

'Where to? Did he say?'

'To a meeting or something. That's what he said.'

James frowned. At least they were now communicating civilly, for which he was grateful. But what kind of meeting went on for a whole night and late into the next evening? 'D'you know *who* he was meeting?' James ventured as he sank into the doughy sofa.

'Probably someone important,' Kenny said, adopting a lofty tone now and turning back to the TV, as if that had settled the matter. They drifted into one of those evenings when Kenny would channel-hop randomly, whilst James sat there in bleakness, wondering how long he would have to stay here and feeling tremendously guilty for having such thoughts.

By ten-thirty p.m., his father was showing no signs of wanting to turn off the TV, not when there were life-enhancing documentaries about people-trafficking and migrant workers kept in inhumane conditions in a leaking caravan. To escape the grimness, James went through to the kitchen again, with the intention of washing up the dirty crockery that lay in the chipped Belfast sink.

A mouse scuttled across the kitchen floor. Clearly, the cats were pretty ineffective at keeping them at bay. James checked his phone and tried Rod yet again; he still didn't pick up. It occurred to him that he could call Phoebe, but since Rod's ex had reputedly taken a hammer to his beloved childhood train set, battering the hell out of not only the locomotives but all the tiny buildings and delicate figurines as well, he thought it best not to trouble her with any mention of his brother's name.

James looked around at the scuffed cupboards and reassured himself that it wasn't too bad in here. Perhaps it would have been fine to pop over just for Christmas Day itself.

On numerous occasions he had made an impassioned plea for his father to sell up and move to Liverpool, so he'd be closer – not that James wanted him close especially, but it would have been easier then to keep an eye on him. He had even found the perfect flat, in a new block with a lovely courtyard garden, which his father could have easily afforded – but no, he wasn't having that. 'I'm not moving for nobody,' he'd thundered.

Perhaps, James mused, his brother would come back tomorrow from wherever he'd been, and everything would be fine? Feeling more positive now, he washed up and looked around for a tea towel that didn't look as if a badger had given birth on it. He checked various drawers and cupboards, and finally the tall closet in the hallway where miscellaneous items had always been

71

stored: bicycle parts and broken umbrellas – all those bits and bobs that, apparently, it was against the law to throw out. Only now, such items were no longer visible as every one of the six shelves was entirely crammed with pre-packed supermarket sandwiches.

James stared and felt his stomach shifting. Through their clear plastic packaging it was obvious that many of them had been festering there for some time. His worry about open tins being stored in the fridge seemed suddenly rather pathetic. Clearly, Kenny wasn't 'just a bit ditsy' these days. Of course, James would have to dispose of the stash – but how? Would he tell his father that they had simply 'gone', or that he'd been burgled?

'What are you doing?' Kenny called out from the living room.

'Just looking for a tea towel,' James replied brightly.

'They're not in there.' Now Kenny had appeared in the hallway and was glaring at James, his small gold hoop earring glinting in the dim overhead light.

'No – I can see that.' James moved away from the open cupboard as if he'd been caught prying amongst his father's personal possessions. 'Um, Dad,' he ventured, 'I think you might've forgotten about these sandwiches. Look – there are way more than you need here . . .' *In fact, you actually need none of these, as they are in various stages of decay and would no doubt poison you.*

Kenny frowned. 'They're for the winter. You know I can get cut off up here.'

'Yes, but there's an awful lot, and I think some of them might have been hanging about for a quite a while, like, um, maybe longer than they should have, ideally . . .' James sensed himself growing clammy and wished any kind of confrontation with his dad didn't reduce him to

72

this nervous, sweating state. He was forty-one years old, for goodness' sake, not four.

'I don't believe in all that use-by date stuff,' Kenny retorted.

'But these are sandwiches, Dad. They're bread—'

'I know what sandwiches are made of,' he snapped.

'And they're all egg and cress,' James added as Horace, the larger of the cats – Christ, what did his father feed them? – wandered into the hallway and mewled fretfully around Kenny's ankles. The animal's close proximity seemed to placate his father, and he scooped up the cat, holding him close to his chest. With a sharp kick, Kenny shut the cupboard door on the sandwiches and stalked back into the living room, muttering, 'They're not all egg and cress, are they, Horace? Some are *cheese*.'

73

Chapter Eight

Five bedtime stories, Lucy had read. At a quarter to eleven, she rubbed at her scratchy eyes and shut the last book firmly. 'Okay, that's it for tonight,' she said wearily, kissing Sam and tucking him in, then coaxing Marnie through to her own room.

'I wanted Dad to see my costume,' she announced, radiating disappointment. Marnie wasn't a moany girl usually; she was cheerful and sunny, if a little bossy at times, brimming with energy and ideas.

'You can show him tomorrow,' Lucy reasoned.

'But it's wet. It got rained on.'

'Yes, sweetheart – but if I put it on the radiator it'll be dry for the morning.'

'I'm not tired yet, Mummy.'

'Love, it's so late. You really do need some sleep . . .'

Where's Dad?' Sam yelled from his own room.

'He'll be on his way,' Lucy called back, trying to keep her voice light despite underlying worry that had been niggling her since they'd come home. At least the bedtime routine had been useful in keeping her occupied: bath, pyjamas, drink and biscuit, teeth, stories . . . the whole rigmarole she had been through zillions of times. But now there was nothing left to do but worry – and wait.

She had called Ivan yet again, but his phone still kept going to voicemail. Surely he hadn't decided to go out with colleagues in Manchester tonight, without letting her know? No – that wasn't Ivan at all. He loved his working life, the thrill of being in the midst of a huge project again, but he was also a caring husband and father, keeping in touch with daily calls while he was away. He'd never failed to show up as expected at the end of the week – and this was no ordinary Friday night either. It was the start of his holiday. Lucy was aware of a sharp pang of missing him as she tucked in Marnie and kissed her before padding quietly out to the landing and going to check on Sam.

'I don't want to go to sleep,' Sam muttered from his bed.

'Darling, it's really late now. *I'm* going to bed soon—'

'I feel sick, Mummy.'

'Oh, Sam. It'll be all those sweets. I did say don't eat so many.' She hurried towards him just in time to see him sit up abruptly and throw up all down his front. 'Sam, honey!' Lucy exclaimed. He started crying and scrambled out of bed. Splattered PJs were stripped off, and a naked Sam was ushered through to the bathroom where he was showered, then wrapped up in his favourite dressing gown – the cream one with teddy bear ears, which was far too babyish for him really, but which he needed to wear now, very much.

Back in his bedroom, Lucy bent to cuddle him as he slumped on his bean bag, then stripped his bed and made it up with fresh linen. 'Marnie, please go back to bed,' she muttered as, naturally, his sister had come through to observe the spectacle.

'This room stinks.'

'It'll fade away in a minute,' Lucy fibbed, aware of tiredness pressing down on her now. She was no longer conjuring up images of red wine, but of her own bed, freshly made up as was her custom on Friday nights, with candles ready to be lit on her bedside table. Not that there would be anything terribly thrilling going on in bed tonight, she thought irritably – not after Ivan had worried her so much.

Finally, the children were back in bed. There was a noise at the front door, and she hurried through from the kitchen towards it. But it wasn't Ivan; in fact there was no one there. The wind had got up, and the door was rattling, that was all. Lucy freed her long hair from its ponytail as she strode back to the living room and checked her phone in case she had missed a call.

When she heard a knock, ten minutes later, she wondered if she might ignore it, as who could it be at this time of night? It was near midnight, and no one local would dream of calling. Something clenched inside her as she made her way through to the hallway to see who it was.

Lucy's breath caught in her throat as she opened the door. Two police officers – one man, one woman – were standing there, and that was the moment when Lucy's whole life changed.

Ivan never saw Marnie's elf costume, or Sam in his reindeer onesie. He never saw his wife or children again because, on his drive home from Manchester on that dark, wet night, Ivan had been killed in a head-on collision twelve miles from Burley Bridge. He hadn't been on the motorway but a winding B-road, which was unusual. It wasn't his normal route at all. The other car's driver survived, with serious spinal injuries; Ivan had seemingly skidded on the wet surface and ended up on the wrong side of the road.

It was no one's fault. That was the official conclusion that came out months after the event. It was the fact that water had pooled there on the road surface. But Lucy couldn't stop thinking that perhaps she was to blame for being so insistent about making a new life here in Burley Bridge.

You and me will always be a team, Ivan had said.

As the days and weeks somehow continued without him, Lucy would find herself playing his words over and over as if some terrible loop tape had wedged itself in her brain. And although she knew it was crazy, she couldn't help feeling furious that he had left her this way.

He hadn't kept his promise at all.

Chapter Nine

James had been at his dad's for two weeks now, trying to knock the place into shape and take care of the basics. Christmas had come and gone with Kenny showing little enthusiasm for the roast dinner James had made for the two of them, even though he had cooked his father's preferred beef. 'I don't want some dried-up old turkey,' Kenny had instructed. 'I've never seen the point of that bird.'

He hadn't seen the point of having a Christmas tree, either, but James had insisted on cutting one down from the woods and bringing it into the house. He had even unearthed the box of fragile hand-painted glass baubles his mum had collected, and which he remembered from childhood. Of course, his dad's Christmas tree business was long gone, but the sight of the small, squat pine strewn with tinsel at least cheered the place up. Crucially, James had also managed to dispose of the stash of supermarket sandwiches by flinging them into bin liners and sneaking outside with them while Kenny was watching a young man being apprehended by airport border security on TV.

The man's stash of advent calendars in his suitcase had turned out not to be filled with chocolates, but cocaine. 'How festive,' James had remarked as he came back inside, but his dad had merely cheered on the diligent customs officials (this was rich, considering Kenny had been fond of a gnarly-looking joint well into middle age). Fortunately, Kenny didn't seem to notice that his sandwiches had gone. Perhaps he'd forgotten he'd even bought them.

Meanwhile, James had kept trying to get hold of Rod. He had gone AWOL on several occasions before, during particularly rocky patches in his marriage – otherwise James might have considered reporting him missing to the police. Finally, after a fortnight of his phone just ringing out, Rod finally answered his brother's call. 'D'you realise I've been trying to get hold of you since before Christmas?' James exclaimed. 'Christ – I thought you were dead!'

'Sorry,' Rod said. 'Things have been . . . a bit complicated.'

'You didn't even call Dad on Christmas Day. Even *he* was worried, and you know he's never particularly concerned about us—'

'Yeah. I've just been off-grid for a while.'

'Off-grid?' James spluttered. 'What d'you mean? Where *are* you?'

Rod paused, and James heard a female voice in the background. 'I'm, uh . . . in Switzerland right now.'

'What?'

'I'm skiing,' Rod added curtly, as if it should be obvious. 'Well, not right now – right now I'm talking to you. But I came out for a bit of a break.'

James rubbed at his short dark hair, his breath forming

white puffs as he exhaled. In order to conduct the conversation in private, he was pacing about on the scrubby ground behind his father's house. 'Fine,' he said, keeping his voice steady, 'but couldn't you have let me know? I mean, what about Dad?'

'Hmm, well, maybe you could have a go at trying to live with him for a while?' Rod remarked with more than a trace of bitterness.

James leaned against the dry stone wall, aware of his father's two cats eyeing him keenly from the living room window. 'I know Dad's not easy,' he conceded.

'You can say that again.'

'And of course I don't expect you to stay here indefinitely—'

'Well, thanks for that,' his brother snapped. 'That's hugely generous of you.'

James cleared his throat. 'Okay, I realise you're pissed off. I wish you'd said something, though. Who are you with, anyway?'

'Just a friend . . .'

So, how long d'you plan to be "off-grid"? We really need to get together and talk.'

'No idea,' Rod murmured.

'Right, okay.' James paused. 'But are we talking a few more days, or weeks, or what?'

'It's kind of open-ended at the moment,' Rod replied, infuriatingly.

On that note, the woman – whoever she was – called out for Rod, and they finished the call. Keen to eke out a few more moments alone, James pulled himself up and sat on the wall, gazing out over the valley. It was one of those sharp winter days, blue skied with clear sunshine. Everything seemed incredibly sharp-focused.

It was beautiful here, James reflected. Naturally, he'd never noticed quite how stunning it was when he'd been growing up; to him, the hills that swooped so gracefully were just *there*. He'd taken it for granted that there were rivers to wade in, his dad's very own woodland in which to build dens, and those long, virtually endless days to fill with adventure.

Now James was a dad, and, naturally, he'd never want to be too far away from Spike in Liverpool. But he still had a fondness for this part of Yorkshire – which was just as well, as his father was adamant that he planned to stay here for the rest of his days.

Something had to be done, James decided later as he cleared up after dinner. Although he was no expert, he was aware that if Kenny was showing early signs of dementia, then things were only likely to get worse. James could stay here in the short term, making sure there was food in the house, that the place was reasonably orderly and Kenny didn't harangue Reena's houseguests again – but he couldn't just relocate here permanently. He needed to be close to Spike, and then there was his work, specifically the narrowboat he had started to fit out, and whose owner was being incredibly patient. But he would have to get back to work at some point fairly soon. He had people waiting and a living to earn.

Once again, James looked up sheltered accommodation in the Liverpool area and tried to coax his father into coming around to the idea by showing him the alluring pictures on his laptop. But Kenny wasn't having any of it. It was clear now that getting some kind of help – via his dad's GP, the social work department, or even a private carer if it came to that – was paramount.

There was one thing for it, James decided. He would have to persuade his dad to go to the surgery for something fairly uncontroversial, in the hope that he could sit in on the appointment and somehow communicate telepathically with the GP (*'Do you think my father might be showing the early stages of dementia?'*) while Kenny sat there, oblivious.

'Yes, I think you might be onto something there,' the doctor would transmit back. *'But don't worry, I shall arrange all the help he could possibly need.'*

A few days later, James broached the subject. 'Dad,' he started over breakfast, 'I wondered if it might be a good idea for you to, um, have a few tests sometime?'

'What kind of tests?' Kenny asked with a mouthful of toast.

'Just a few medical things. Blood pressure, cholesterol, the stuff everyone gets checked out from time to time . . .'

'Are you saying I'm falling to bits now?' Kenny asked, frowning.

'Of course not.' James was struggling to keep his tone level.

'Why not shove me over a cliff and be done with it?'

Tempting, James thought – but something must have sunk in as, later that day, his father grudgingly agreed to grace the surgery with his presence. The way things were right now, that seemed like something of a victory.

They went together the following week, finding themselves sitting side by side in the starkly decorated waiting room of the medical centre in Heathfield. There was no surgery in Burley Bridge, and for that, James was thankful; he wouldn't have relished bumping into anyone his father knew.

Kenny's name was called, and James sprang up from

his chair as his father stood up. 'What are you doing?' Kenny asked.

'I thought I'd come in with you, if that's all right?'

'What d'you want to do that for?' His dark eyes narrowed. Across the waiting room, an elderly woman and a thin, pallid teenage boy – the only other people waiting – were clearly pretending not to be paying rapt attention.

'I just thought it might be helpful,' James said.

'Kenny Halsall?' the GP repeated from the doorway. He was wearing tiny round spectacles and had the wiry build of a jockey.

James looked at him, trying to transmit the message: *This is my father; he had fifty-seven egg sandwiches stuffed in his cupboard; could you please diagnose him with something and help?*

Kenny approached the doctor, and both men disappeared around the corner. James inhaled deeply, picked up a ragged copy of *Improve Your Coarse Fishing* magazine that he had no intention of reading, then dumped it back on the table and strode over to the receptionist. 'Erm, my dad's just gone through to the doctor's,' he started.

She nodded curtly as if he really shouldn't be bothering her. 'Yes?'

'I was sort of hoping to go in with him,' he continued, keeping his voice low, 'but he wasn't too keen on that. The thing is, I'd really like to talk to the doctor about my dad, about the concerns I have, about his memory and behaviour and things . . .'

'Are you registered with this practice?' the woman asked. Her mouth was pursed, her lipstick worn off apart from a peachy line around the edges. 'Because, if you are,' she added, 'the best thing to do is make an appointment with your own GP and discuss it with them.'

She turned back to her screen and seemed to be focusing on it intently. 'I used to be registered,' James offered, 'so maybe I'm still on the system . . .' Even as he said it, he knew there was no point in her even checking; there hadn't been a 'system' then, at least no computer as far as he could recall. He was from a pre-systems era when things were written in books and there were drawers of files on everybody. It was the same building, but the last time he was here was probably when he'd chicken pox in something like 1989.

'Date of birth?' the woman asked. As James answered, his father reappeared, looking unusually buoyant and pleased with himself. 'Nothing wrong with me,' he announced.

'Oh, that's good, Dad.' James beamed and turned back to the woman.

'What's your name?' she barked at him.

'James Halsall—'

She shook her head. 'You're not on the system.'

'Right. Okay. Well, could I possibly *get* on it?'

She eyed him with suspicion. 'You'll need to take these forms and bring them back.'

'Great.' He exhaled, aware of his father gazing at him.

'What're you doing?' Kenny asked.

'Nothing, Dad.' He looked at the woman. 'There's no chance I could have a *quick* word with the doctor just now, just for a second—'

She widened her eyes and shook her head, as if he had expressed a desire to set up a burger stall right here in the reception. 'No, sorry. He's very busy today.' He took the forms from her and stuffed them into his back pocket, aware of his father eyeing him curiously as they left the building and climbed into James's car.

'So, did the doctor give you any tests?' James asked.

'Oh yeah, he put that thing on my arm, the blood pressure thing,' his father replied. James sensed him still studying him intently as he pulled out of the car park. 'You think I'm going mad, don't you?' Kenny added.

'Of course not, Dad,' James said.

'Why did you want to talk to my doctor, then?'

'Just, you know, to see how things are.'

His dad regarded him steadily as they waited at a red light. 'You think I don't know you threw all that food away.'

'What food?'

'My sandwiches!'

James let out a gasp of exasperation. 'Oh, Dad. I was just trying to clear out the—'

'Well, don't *try* anything,' Kenny said firmly. 'You know I hate waste.'

As they fell into a rather surly silence on the drive back to Burley Bridge, James wondered what to do next. The thought of suggesting to his father than he might be suffering from anything more than perpetual ill humour filled him with horror. But then, James was an adult man of forty-one, and sometimes, being an adult required one to face up to bloody awful situations and figure out a way of dealing with them.

No matter how maddening he was, and how fervently he railed against the idea of any kind of 'help', James was determined that he would not let his father down.

Chapter Ten

Sometimes it was hard for Lucy to remember what she was like before the accident. But, somehow, the weeks had gone on and she was still here, alive. Christmas had happened, apparently, although naturally it had been a write-off. Lucy's parents had arrived at Rosemary Cottage, and Lucy had a vague recollection of a few presents and a cobbled-together dinner, and her mother cooking and cooking as the days went on – mostly pies, as it happened, as if copious quantities of pastry might save them all. But Lucy was still a mother herself, which required her to be stoic and strong – all those motherly things – so she did her best and tried not to fall to pieces in front of Marnie and Sam.

You were supposed to hold it together, just because you'd given birth. You had to comfort your children when they were inconsolable and stand there, clutching their hands because you'd decided it was best for them to go to Daddy's cremation, to say goodbye properly with the other people who loved him. As if you were capable of making any kind of rational decision. Should they have gone? Was it too traumatising for them, even though Lucy had somehow got it together to find a young, female celebrant who had followed her request to make the ceremony a celebration of Ivan's life?

It was beautiful – everyone had said so. Well, nearly everyone. Lucy became convinced that Ivan's mother, Penny, had glanced at her with fury – as if she thought she were somehow to blame for the accident. Perhaps she was being hypersensitive, and of course, his parents were devastated too. Ivan had been their only child, and although they were hardly demonstrative, she knew they adored him. Back in their North London semi, his child-hood bedroom had remained just as he'd left it when he'd departed for university at eighteen years old.

In contrast, Lucy had always suspected that they had never fully approved of her. Penny was a retired ward sister, while Nigel had worked as a quantity surveyor. She'd sensed that they had viewed her job in lingerie as faintly ridiculous: 'Underwear? Really?' Penny had remarked, paling slightly as if Lucy had explained that she was a pole dancer, and would they like to come watch her next show? Their move to Burley Bridge, and the opening of their B&B, had clearly baffled them too.

'What d'you do all day, Lucy?' Penny had asked one day last summer.

'I do most of the stuff connected with the guests,' she'd explained, her jaw set tight with the effort of remaining pleasant. She'd wanted to add, *as well as looking after the children and the house and doing my floral commissions*. Of course she hadn't said that – but Christ, it was hard to be civil sometimes. It had been her in-laws' first visit to Burley Bridge; they were obviously uncomfortable with venturing beyond the North Circular, and had apparently been appalled that Ivan had chosen to stay on in Manchester after university.

Penny dropped the phrase 'The North' regularly into conversation: 'Are you sure there's enough of a holiday market in The North, Lucy?' And, 'Do you think people in The North really want this kind of sophisticated breakfast menu?' As if bread and dripping, shovelled in before they clomped off in clogs to plough the fields, was more the normal kind of fare.

'Oh, our guests come from all over the place,' Lucy replied cheerfully. *D'you know, some of them have even encountered granola!*

'Well, I never imagined we'd see Ivan living in a place like this,' Nigel had announced, the implication being that Lucy had bound his beloved son tightly with rope and dragged him away from the city to play at country living with her.

Of course, all of that was in the past now. Penny hadn't looked angry, Lucy's friends had reassured her; no one thought anything bad of her. How *could* they?

Because she'd been the one to come up with the scheme of buying Rosemary Cottage and running a B&B. It had been her stupid dream, and if they'd stayed in Manchester, she would still have her husband and Marnie and Sam would have their dad.

Although Penny and Nigel headed straight back to London after the service, Lucy's mother had announced that she would stay on in Burley Bridge 'for the time being', to help out. Lucy's father was sent home in the meantime to look after Tilly, their flatulent miniature schnauzer, and would return to pick up Anna when summoned.

'I think you should all come back and stay with us,' her mother remarked one evening, after the children had gone to bed. 'I know you're not up to moving, love, but we could find you somewhere eventually. And in the meantime, you could stay with us.'

'Mum, I can't make any decisions like that right now,' Lucy replied.

Her mother scanned the living room. There were no flowers now, not so much as a wisp of fresh greenery, and the numerous sympathy cards had been stashed away. They had been lovely to receive, and occasionally Lucy browsed through them, but she didn't want them all lined up on show, like Christmas cards. 'But this house is full of memories,' Anna remarked.

'We've only been here for a year,' Lucy reminded her, although her mother was right; Ivan's things were everywhere, as was the evidence of his hard work in finishing off the house.

'We just wish you were closer to us.'

'You're only an hour away, Mum.'

Anna pursed her lips. 'You're not going to do B&B anymore, are you, darling?'

'Not at the moment,' Lucy said firmly. 'Of course not.'

'I mean, *ever*. You can't, can you, on your own—'

'Mum,' she cut in, then paused. 'Please, can we not discuss this right now? I'm not being evasive. I just don't know what I'm going to do.'

It was true; Lucy hadn't even started to consider what her future might hold. It was only late January – a month since she'd lost Ivan. It seemed incomprehensible that a few weeks ago, she had been tossing crepes, whipping up berry compotes and arranging vases of lush, glossy foliage snipped from the garden. Surely it can't have been her who'd been chatting so easily with guests as she'd brought out fresh coffee to the breakfast table?

Back then, a glowing comment in the visitors' book would make her heart soar:

A lovely cottage, and Lucy was so welcoming!

The best breakfast we can ever remember having at a B&B.

Rosemary Cottage is our new fave in the area. We can't wait to come back!

Well, sorry, Lucy thought bitterly whenever she reread those words – but they would have to find somewhere else to stay for the time being. These days, Lucy was barely capable of boiling an egg, and more often than not, the kitchen smelt of burnt toast and stress.

As the weeks went on, she barely ventured into the garden she'd loved so much last year. She just marched through it, head bent down, barely able to glance at the shed where Ivan and the children had whiled away so many hours together, or the wrought-iron gate he'd painted cornflower blue as a surprise, knowing it was her favourite colour. Rikke still popped in to see Lucy and the children, and brushed off Lucy's apologies over being unable to offer her regular working hours at the moment. 'That doesn't matter,' she'd said kindly. 'I just like to see you all as friends. Please let me know if I can help.'

Meanwhile, Lucy had put a blunt message on the B&B website explaining that they would be closed until further notice. Incredibly to her, Ivan had no life insurance – she felt guilty even thinking of such things – as he'd been notoriously disorganised when it came to admin and finance, those tedious matters that had never seemed important until now. Anna had expressed surprise too, but Lucy had dismissed the matter. She certainly wasn't prepared to have a conversation that might have shown Ivan as even slightly thoughtless or irresponsible. After all, they had arranged the mortgage together, so it had been her responsibility too. Anyway, money wasn't an issue, Anna kept insisting; she mustn't worry about a thing.

Gradually, Marnie and Sam started back at school – a couple of hours at first, then half-days, to ease them in gently. They seemed stunned and bewildered by what had happened, but would then amaze Lucy by playing happily together with Sam's farm for an entire afternoon – the one they had built with Ivan in the shed, with the wooden enclosures, a farmhouse and a milking shed. It was almost as if, for the duration of a game, they were capable of forgetting what had happened. Then it would all come crashing down upon them and there'd be a squabble, and tears, and hails of tiny plastic animals flung at each other.

At night, Sam started wetting the bed again (previously, there hadn't been any mishaps since he was three) and Marnie would wake up crying about a robber in her room, some kind of animal's paw at her bedroom window, all kinds of nightmarish stuff. They went through phases of being shouty and demanding, then barely speaking at all; of shunning the meals she'd cooked then nagging for sweets, crisps and copious amounts of junk food. Lucy found herself doing her utmost to accommodate their whims – because how could she possibly enforce petty rules when their dad had died?

Once upon a time, she had gone to great lengths to conceal vegetables in their food. Now, if they begged for chips from the village chippie – well, they got chips. 'It won't do them any harm,' Anna agreed. Lucy was grateful to her mother for just being there, happy to tackle the laundry or read bedtime stories when Lucy simply didn't have the energy.

But having her around had its downside too.

It was now early February, and Lucy had turned forty-two, having allowed her mother to put on a small tea party to mark the occasion, even though the last thing she felt like doing was celebrating it ('Please, love,' Anna had cajoled her, 'even if it's only for the kids'). Now that was over, Lucy was starting to crave her own space. Any suggestions that Anna might like to think about going home soon were brushed off. 'Oh, I'm quite happy here!' she trilled, dusting and hoovering as if her life depended on it. An unstoppable force, Anna set about deep-cleaning and reorganising the kitchen without being asked, exclaiming, 'There – that's *much* better now.' As if they had been living in squat-like conditions until Anna had arrived as a one-woman taskforce to sort things out.

There's an awful lot of guilt around death, Lucy noticed. Guilt about sometimes not answering the door when friends came around, because she just wasn't in the mood for coffee and chat – and guilt about *really* wanting her mother to go home now.

And guilt about Ivan, of course. Lucy wondered if that would ever go away.

'There! *Now* you'll be able to find things,' Anna announced proudly one Friday evening when – once again, without prior consultation – she had pulled out everything from the linen cupboard and put it all back, according to her own, supposedly superior system.

'Thanks, Mum,' Lucy said flatly, blinking at the neatly ordered shelves.

'See, I organised it in colours rather than—'

'Yes, I can see that – it's totally brilliant.' Lucy felt a twinge in her jaw as her mother frowned at her.

'I just thought it'd be easier if—'

'Mum, it's fine!' Lucy snapped.

Anna stared at her, her cheeks flushing pink. 'Don't you think it looks better this way?'

'I, I don't know. I mean, yes. It looks great. I'm sorry, I just . . .' *I don't give a stuff how our duvet covers and pillowcases are stored,* she thought, sensing the tears welling up.

Anna blinked at her. 'I could put everything back the way it was, if you like?'

Oh, for heaven's sake! From then on, they stepped carefully around each other, with Anna asking permission before she did virtually anything: 'I was going to peel some potatoes for dinner; is that okay, love?' And: 'Is it all right if I throw out this banana? I think it's past its best . . .'

It felt to Lucy as if the cottage's walls were closing in on her, and late that Sunday night, she sat with her mother at the fireside and explained, 'I think we just need a bit of time alone now, Mum. Me and the kids, I mean. We're so grateful to you for spending all this time with us, but—'

'You mean, you want me to go home?' Anna's finely plucked brows shot up.

'I don't mean it like that,' Lucy said quickly. 'It's just – we'll have to get used to managing on our own at some point, won't we? And Dad must be really missing you . . .'

'He's fine! He's probably enjoying the peace.'

'I just feel sorry for him, though, being alone. It's been over a month, Mum.'

93

'He's not alone, is he? He has Tilly . . .' Anna picked at her dark red nail polish. 'Is this because of the linen cupboard?'

'No – of course it's not,' Lucy exclaimed. 'No, Mum. You've been an amazing help to us . . .'

'I just think I should be with you at the moment.'

Lucy inhaled. 'We'll all be coming to you really soon, in the Easter holidays.'

'Oh, I hope so,' Anna said. 'But that does seem like a terribly long time away . . .'

'It's only a few weeks.' Lucy leaned over and squeezed her hand.

'I'll go tomorrow, then. I'll call your dad and ask him to come.'

'Okay, Mum.' Lucy knew she had hurt her feelings, and she was being punished with a crashing wave of guilt.

Anna looked up at her, her grey eyes moist. 'I'm sorry if I've got on your nerves, love. I was only trying to help.'

Chapter Eleven

James had made a decision. Pretty soon, he would have to return to Liverpool to pick up his own life again. However, during the past few weeks it had become clear that Kenny needed some kind of help around the house – someone to keep an eye on him in between James's visits, and report back if anything untoward was going on. The challenge now was to persuade his dad to accept any kind of assistance at all.

James had already contacted social services to see if a carer could be provided. Well, of course they couldn't. Even if Kenny had been diagnosed, it wasn't as simple as a kindly person turning up and taking care of everything. He had also filled in those GP registration forms and returned to the doctor's in Heathfield, where his buddy, the hostile receptionist, informed him that he still couldn't register if he already had a GP in Liverpool (as if he was a two-timing rat, but with doctors). It was all he could do not to rip out his hair in frustration and shout, 'Why are you being so obstructive? I am only trying to help my dad!' But of course, she was just doing her job, and at least she hinted that a GP's home visit might be possible, if his father were to consent to it.

'How should I put that to him?' James wanted to ask. '"Dad, would you be okay with the doctor coming to your house and performing various mind tests on you?"' He had looked up the standard tests online and could imagine his father's response when quizzed about who the Prime Minister was, or asked to draw a cube. He feared for any medical professional who expected any kind of compliance on that score. Meanwhile, since Christmas, James had been dashing back on the odd quick visit to Liverpool, to see Spike and squeeze in a bit of work whenever he could. But it was far from ideal and certainly wasn't sustainable.

Then a breakthrough happened, and Kenny finally agreed to James advertising for what they were loosely terming a 'home help'. It felt like a small miracle. James had outlined his plan to try an old-school-style advert – more like a plea for help, if truth be known – in the general store's window in the village, and Kenny was reasonably okay about this, 'as long as it's no more than a couple of hours a day. I s'pose the place has been getting a bit out of hand,' he conceded. 'But I don't want someone constantly flitting about and bothering me. I'm not an invalid, okay?'

As his father had also demanded to check the ad's wording, James was approaching it with extreme care. On a small white card, he wrote: *Daily home help/ companion required for a local man in his 70s.*

Was that enough detail, he wondered? Deliberately, he had shied away from using the word 'carer', aware that it might suggest duties of a personal nature when really, he just needed someone to keep an eye on his dad, and to contact him immediately if he had been repeat-purchasing perishable food items or exhibiting any other worrying behaviours.

Of course, what he really meant was: *Spy wanted for confused and often ill-tempered old man.* But obviously, that would have attracted zero applicants, and Kenny would have vetoed it anyway. *Around 2 hours per day,* James added, *but can be flexible for the right person.* In other words: *please, for crying out loud, somebody help.*

The ad was duly placed in the shop window, and a handful of respondents got in touch. However, James had underestimated his father's notoriety in the area. In a village like Burley Bridge, everyone seemed to know everyone, albeit vaguely – and once Kenny's identity had been confirmed, the interested parties suddenly became rather less keen.

'You're Kenny Halsall's son?' remarked one woman with a deep, gravelly voice. 'Moved away a long time ago, didn't you?'

'Erm, yes, but I'm back and forth a lot these days.' He kept his tone bright to try and convey that this was an entirely convivial situation.

'Um. Well, look – I was just curious about your ad, but I don't think it's the job for me.'

'Oh, yes, I know your dad,' another, extremely well-spoken woman remarked. 'We used to buy our Christmas trees from him. Still living up there by the woods, is he? Wow. Well, um, thanks for clarifying. I might get back in touch.' James soon realised that this meant, 'You will never hear from me again.'

A couple of weeks came and went, and James suggested to his father that they should increase the proposed hourly rate to a level that would make it irresistible.

Although Kenny had agreed to pay for the help, James was more than willing to chip in, if that would clinch it. Hell, he'd do whatever it took, he reasoned to himself. However, his father's thriftiness was legendary, and he was adamant that the rate they were offering was fair. James should have known. Kenny hadn't reacted well when he had inadvertently dumped a returnable lemonade bottle into the recycling bin instead of taking it back to the shop and reclaiming his father's 10p. James hadn't even realised that returning bottles was a thing people did anymore. He'd assumed it had gone the way of children reading *The Beano*, playing with catapults and stealing berries from Kitty Cartwright's garden.

Those were the days, he mused occasionally when he happened to glimpse the gable end of her cottage from the main road (as it was tucked away down a lane, he had no reason to actually pass it). When James looked back, his childhood had been mainly happy, despite what had happened to his family.

He thought of it often, now he was back in the village so frequently, and could hardly believe he had once been so carefree.

On a bitingly cold February afternoon, he found himself sitting across a table in the village pub discussing his father's situation with an impressively confident Danish woman who happened to have been working for the family who now lived in Rosemary Cottage.

'I started helping out with the children,' Rikke said, 'when the dad was working away during the week. They were running it as a B&B.'

'Oh, yes,' James said. 'I noticed the sign by the garden wall.'

Rikke nodded. 'Only . . .' She winced. 'The dad was killed in a road accident just before Christmas. Maybe you heard about that?'

'No.' James shook his head and frowned. 'No, I didn't. I've been pretty much wrapped up with Dad, really. But, God – that's terrible.'

'Lately, I've just been visiting and keeping in touch.' She paused and sipped her tomato juice. 'I do a few shifts a week in Della's bookshop,' she added. 'Do you know Della?'

'Um, yes, a little . . .' James only knew *of* her, really, but he didn't want to seem totally oblivious to village life. He was aware that she was one of the three Cartwright kids – Kitty's children – but she was older than him, and their paths hadn't really crossed.

'And I teach swimming at the pool in Heathfield,' Rikke went on, 'and do the occasional wedding too.' She beamed a bright, white smile. 'I play the harp,' she added. 'Do you know Lorna and Rory Macklin – she works at the hair salon, and he helps Len at the garage . . .'

'Er, I think so,' he fibbed.

'Well, I played at their wedding.'

'This is all very impressive,' James said, wondering how on earth this young woman had become so entrenched in village life when these days, he felt quite out of touch with the place. Naturally, people recognised him from time to time, and said hello when he was out and about in the village. However, the place had changed dramatically and there were lots of new faces too.

'I suppose none of that's terribly relevant,' Rikke went on, 'to the kind of job you're looking to fill. But I'm hard-working, I drive and I'm good with people.'

'I'm sure you are,' James said.

'If you need references, I could ask Della at the shop. It might not be the right time to talk to Lucy at Rosemary Cottage but—'

'I'm sure it's not,' James said quickly. In fact, Rikke seemed so infinitely capable that he really wanted to say, 'The job's yours,' without further questioning. However, sensing that he should at least find out a little more about her, he went to fetch more drinks from the bar – he was sticking to Coke – and then pressed on.

'Are you sure you have time to take on another regular job?' he asked. 'I'm looking for a visit every weekday, and on occasional weekends too, if I can't manage to get over and see Dad.'

'I prefer my life to be busy,' she said, 'and I like a lot of variety rather than being tied to one thing.'

'D'you live locally?' he asked.

'Couple of miles outside the village. I was married,' she added, which astounded him – although why shouldn't she have been? He already knew she was twenty-nine, although with her fresh, pink-cheeked complexion, she looked even younger. 'It didn't work out,' she continued, 'but I liked it so much here I decided to stay. It's so friendly, so warm.'

'It is, yes,' he said. 'So, um, how about meeting my dad and seeing how you get along?'

'I'd love to,' she said.

Happily, she was still as keen after he had admitted that his father could be 'challenging', and had told her about the sandwich hoard. It seemed that nothing fazed her as he drove them up to his father's house.

He marvelled at how Rikke greeted him in such a cheery manner that Kenny couldn't help but be charmed by her. He was astounded at how friendly she was to his dad's cats, even though they had never struck James as particularly amenable to humans or even to each other. Yet there she sat in his father's overstuffed living room, happily chit-chatting with Kenny, with Horace plonked on her lap like a hairy ginger cushion, and seemingly not minding when James's father asked, 'So is it true your Danish sandwiches never have tops on? Isn't that a bit of a rip-off?'

James felt his back teeth jamming together. 'It's not compulsory,' she said with a smile, 'but, you know, they are more about the filling than the bread. I could make some for you, if you'd like to try them?'

'Is it all cold pickled fish?' Kenny asked, eyes narrowed suspiciously, although James could tell he was enjoying himself now.

'Again, it's not compulsory, Mr Halsall,' Rikke replied.

'Oh, call me Kenny—'

Rikke smiled warmly. 'Yes, herring is pretty popular. That and rye bread.'

'Actually, I do enjoy a herring,' Kenny conceded, and so the conversation turned to favoured Danish fare. Soon Rikke was promising to bring Kenny some of her own salt-cured salmon, and by the time they said goodbye, it had been agreed that she would start the following week when James returned to Liverpool.

As he drove her home, she chatted happily about the children at Rosemary Cottage. 'They're such a joy,' she said, 'even after everything they've been through. It's incredible how much children can cope with – but then, their mum's amazing too.'

'It must've been dreadful for all of them,' James murmured, wondering why on earth he'd been feeling as if the weight of the world had been pressing down on his shoulders when others had it so much worse. Yes, he still had to somehow persuade his father to see his GP or a specialist, and deal with his denial – or even wrath – if he was diagnosed with something like dementia. And God knows what else they would face, further down the line. But for now, at least, his dad would be looked after.

James glanced at Rikke as the narrow lane snaked down towards the village. 'So, are you absolutely sure about taking this on?' he asked. 'Working for my father, I mean?'

'Yes, of course,' she replied. 'He's a lovely man.'

James couldn't help chuckling at that. 'I'm glad you two got along. He can be, you know, a little tricky.'

'It'll be fine – honestly,' she said firmly, 'and, like you said, you're only a text or a phone call away.'

He nodded, realising that he was no longer annoyed that his brother had swished off to some Alpine resort with a mysterious woman. Perhaps it was for the best, in that it had highlighted how urgent the situation here had become. Anyway, Rikke Svendsen would be a match for his father, he was sure of it. Kenny had actually seemed keen to impress her, and James had barely been able to keep a straight face as the two of them had rattled on about the delights of the Danish *smorgasbord*. His father was terribly set in his dietary ways, and James knew for a fact that he detested pickled fish.

Chapter Twelve

During those few months last year, Lucy had become used to managing family life by herself while Ivan worked in Manchester. However, being entirely alone was a different matter. These days the house could feel stifling, and she was immensely grateful whenever Marnie and Sam were whisked off for an outing or playdate for a few hours. It wasn't that she was trying to palm them off. However, her energies were severely diminished and she hated to think of them missing out. Three months on from the accident, Lucy was still overwhelmed by the kindness of her friends in the village.

There had been a monumental 'rallying round' with a slew of provisions brought to her door: curries and casseroles, soups and risottos and towering Victoria sponges that even the children had struggled to plough through. There were foil-covered pies and a tsunami of Tupperware. Lucy didn't like to admit that, most days, all she could manage were a few slices of toast. She was aware of the difference between good and bad weight loss, and her new, angular frame was a result of the latter. She was pale and gaunt, her long dark hair drab, her eyes dull and haunted. However, after weeks of insomnia at least she was finally managing to fall into a deep, exhausted sleep each night, and wake when the new day came rather than at something like four a.m.

Homework was now being done and school-related events attended once more. Lucy had emerged from what had felt like madness, when she could barely get it together to dress herself, and was now beginning to at least function on a basic, day-to-day level. After all, everyone needed fresh milk and clean clothes, and she started to think: of course, Ivan would want her to be on top of things, to be clean and appropriately dressed and not slumped in a puddle of wine.

As daffodils sprang into life in her garden, she started to venture out and cut some to bring a splash of brightness inside. When Della happened to mention that her bookshop's window could do with a refresh, Lucy offered to create a display for her. The resulting confection of cherry blossom, narcissi and delicate greenery lifted Lucy's spirits a little every time she walked past the shop.

As the days warmed and lengthened, Sam and Marnie seemed to have become a little more settled too. Of course, they still had their moments; on several occasions Lucy had had to rush to school to pick up one – or both – of them when they had become inconsolable or, more likely, developed a sudden and apparently symptomless illness, requiring cuddles and buttered crumpets at home. Mealtimes could still be difficult, as that was when they tended to bicker, and every nuance of their moods was clearly on display.

One particularly fraught tea time, some insignificant

spat saw Sam grabbing the glass bottle of ketchup and flinging it across the kitchen where it smashed into the fridge door before shattering all over the floor. The resulting mess seemed to shock him as much as it did Lucy and his sister. He sobbed fervently and demanded to be allowed to clear it all up himself, becoming even more distraught when Lucy wouldn't let him handle the broken glass. So, yes, there were occasional dramas – but, for the most part, the three of them seemed to be coping. The kitchen calendar was once again smattered with reminders for after-school gymnastics in the village hall, plus football, Brownies and the occasional party and school trip.

Ivan had gone, but birthdays still happened and, now and again, Lucy found herself having to choose a present for a seven-year-old who wasn't hers. Clearly, her instincts on such matters were somewhat impaired these days, and she would stare at the racks of games and gizmos in her favoured toyshop in Heathfield, like someone who was entirely unfamiliar with children and the stuff they enjoyed. In fear of making a terrible gaffe, she took to upscaling her level of gift-giving and, on more than one occasion, was aware of the recipient's look of startled delight when they unwrapped the kind of Lego kit that might normally be given by grandparents at Christmas.

'Lucy, that's way too generous!' was uttered by a shocked parent on more than one occasion.

Some days she even managed to force herself to social events in the village. There was the odd barbecue and party, a PTA fundraiser and a gathering of the primary school mums in the pub. Occasionally, when Lucy couldn't face going out, one of her friends would send a thoughtful text, asking if she'd like them to pop round for coffee and a chat.

Carys worked part-time at an estate agent's in Heathfield, and on the days she was at home she and Lucy fell into a pattern of spending time together. They had become friends almost instantly when they'd first met at the school gates; it had always amused Ivan how easily Lucy chatted to strangers. However, since his death they had become even closer. They would walk Bramble, Carys's spaniel, up in the hills, or hang out in her kitchen together. She lived in an old stone cottage on the edge of the village that reminded Lucy a little of her great-aunt and uncle's place – except, whereas George and Babs's house had been crammed with a lifetime's worth of porcelain ornaments, Carys's was pleasingly clutter-free.

'It's the only way I can function,' she'd told Lucy, the first time she'd gone round there, when Ivan was still alive. 'Can you imagine how it'd be, with just me and the kids if I let things get out of control?' It had occurred to Lucy that Noah and Amber were incredibly grown up and helpful for their ages. Even at five and seven they had been making their own beds, putting toys away and – mind-bogglingly – washing up without flooding the kitchen. Lucy had always adopted an 'easier to do it myself' approach, which she was starting to regret. It was just the three of them now, and they would need to pull together somehow. She found herself trying to almost *inhale* the serenity of Carys's surroundings and take it back home with her.

In contrast, Rosemary Cottage now seemed oppressive, and the thought of sorting through Ivan's possessions was still too awful for Lucy to contemplate. An entire wardrobe and chest of drawers were still full of his clothes. If she couldn't bring herself to send so much as his raggedy old paperback thrillers to charity, how would she deal with the grey cable-knit sweater that hung over the back of a chair in their bedroom, and still smelt of his skin? What about his wellies that sat at the back door, his waxed jacket that hung from a hook alongside the children's coats, and his toiletries in the bathroom?

Everything was there, just as he'd left it. His car had been written off, so that was no longer around, but the lawnmower felt as if it had been 'his', and to her shame, Lucy had never attempted to get the thing started. It was unwieldy and ancient, and had been here when they'd bought the house, strewn with cobwebs and smattered with rust. Ivan had conceded that it was 'bloody temperamental, but once it's going it's fantastic. It'll probably outlive us all.'

One bright, sunny Sunday at the end of March, Lucy ventured out to the ramshackle wooden garage, which they used only to store tools, camping furniture and the mower. As spring had been particularly warm and showery so far, the lawn was already crying out for its first cut. Lucy knew it didn't matter really, and that no one would judge her if the garden looked a little unruly this year. It wasn't even visible from the main road. However, the lawn issue had started to build in her mind as something she must attend to without delay, in order to prove *something* – she wasn't entirely sure what that was – to herself.

As Rikke had taken the children out on a walk, it was the ideal opportunity to do it. She dragged the contraption out onto the lawn and swore as she yanked its starter cable. Of course nothing happened. She tugged on it several more times, then stood back and glared at the mower as if it were deliberately refusing to cooperate with her.

'Bloody useless thing,' she muttered, pushing a lank strand of dark hair from her face. She pulled the cable again and gave the mower a sharp kick when it failed to respond, then realised she was being watched.

Her neighbour Irene had stopped at the garden gate. Lucy leapt away from the mower as if it were a small animal she'd been caught abusing. 'Hi, Irene!' she chirped with a quick wave. These days, Lucy was no longer adept at making casual chit-chat, especially when caught unawares. She preferred at least twenty-four hours' notice before being expected to have a proper adult conversation with anyone.

'Hi, love,' Irene said with a kind smile. 'Need some help with that?'

'Oh, no, it's fine, thanks . . .'

Irene stood there at the gate, watching her. Lucy sensed her own smile setting as she willed her neighbour to leave her alone and move on, even though she often gave Sam and Marnie free sweets in her shop and had been one of the prime movers in the bring-hot-food-to-Lucy movement, supplying weekly shepherd's pies throughout January. Irene was also one of those sturdy rural women who could probably push-start a tractor if required – but still, Lucy would *not* ask for help.

'Those old mowers are a real bugger to get going,' she remarked.

'Yes, they are,' Lucy said with a bemused eye-roll, as if they were discussing an endearingly headstrong toddler.

'You can borrow mine if you like,' she added, and now Lucy was reminded of Ivan's remark: *I'm sure they're keeping a dossier about us, Luce. They seem terribly interested in what we're up to . . .*

'I'll be fine with this one, thanks,' Lucy said, more firmly now.

'Mine's very lightweight. It's as easy as dragging a carpet sweeper around.'

'A carpet sweeper?' Lucy repeated, thinking for a moment that she meant a person – like a road sweeper, but for indoors.

Irene jerked an arm back and forth like a piston, to mime hoovering. 'You know – those manual vacuum things. Don't think I've seen one for years, mind you. I wonder why they went out of favour when they're so easy and you don't have to plug them in?'

What on *earth* was she blathering on about?

'Anyway,' Irene concluded, crossing her arms across her grey polo-necked sweater, 'my little mower's no more bother than that.'

'I'll bear it in mind,' Lucy said, adding, ''S'cuse me, Irene – but I've got to dash in. I've left something bubbling away on the hob.'

'Oh, don't let me keep you.' Lucy flashed another quick grin as she strode purposefully back into the house, finding herself in the ridiculous position of having to skulk about indoors now, until she could safely assume that Irene had moved on.

A few minutes later, back at the lawnmower, she told herself sternly that Ivan wasn't going to materialise magically; she would just have to man up and deal with this ruddy thing by herself.

She pulled the cord again, then remembered him once mentioning the throttle and wondered where the hell that was. Could there be an instruction book kicking about in the garage? She had a quick look, but of course there wasn't; this wasn't a newly bought Argos sandwich toaster but a hulking contraption built in something like 1952. Back in the garden she wondered if in fact there was any petrol in it – or maybe it was horse powered? She screwed off a grubby plastic cap and put her eye up against it, but there was no way of telling what was in there, if anything at all. She replaced the cap and rubbed at her face, the task of mowing the lawn feeling insurmountable now to the point where she wondered if, actually, she would be better hacking at it with shears.

Why had she allowed Ivan to take charge of so many of the 'man jobs' about the place? As well as mowing the lawn he'd maintained both of their cars and cut the hedge with his big, manly trimmer. He'd been the one to hang pictures, put up shelves, fix bicycle punctures and assemble flat-pack furniture with minimal fuss: basically, anything that required a tool rather than a utensil. Since she'd met him, Lucy couldn't remember one occasion when she had used a screwdriver, apart from to get the back off the controller for Sam's toy helicopter when the batteries needed to be changed. Even then, a tiny screw had pinged off to be lost forever.

It was appalling, really, how she had allowed this to happen, even though she had been perfectly capable of tackling the odd home maintenance job when she'd been single. She had unblocked several U-bends and fixed a washing machine by accessing its inner workings and fishing out a tangle of bra underwires. But then she'd met Ivan, and unwittingly turned into a feeble lady who couldn't contemplate so much as changing the head on her electric toothbrush without bleating for assistance from her strong and capable male. Until she'd lost him, it had never occurred to Lucy how traditional their roles had become. What kind of example was she setting for her own daughter? Now, as she stood there helplessly in her garden, Lucy felt at once abandoned by her husband – and furious with herself.

She was furious with Ivan, too, because surely, the accident would never have happened if he'd been driving with due care and attention that wet December night? Driving was one area where she *had* retained control in their relationship. She preferred being behind the wheel rather than sitting there as a passenger, partly due to Ivan's tendency to speed, which had always made her nervous. And she was pretty certain he'd have been driving too fast that Friday evening, having just finished work for the festive period. He'd have been eager to get home to her and the kids, to kick off his shoes, crack open the wine and start his holidays. Or *would* he? Perhaps he'd had something else on his mind, some kind of distraction that had caused him to take that bend in the road too fast?

The fact that Ivan hadn't been taking his normal route home was something that still niggled Lucy. For those first few weeks, it been on her mind pretty much constantly, and once the almighty shock and devastation had flattened out into a plateau of grief, she had been determined to find out why he'd been going that way. It didn't seem as if there had been any road closures or detours that night. She had spent hours online, studying local news reports, and had even phoned the police and the council's highways department to check. Still no explanation. So where had Ivan been going when, only that lunchtime, he had called from his Manchester office to say how desperate he'd been to finish work and hurry home?

111

Lucy had been through every possibility she could think of: he'd been tired and taken a wrong turning. Yet that was unlikely, as Ivan had driven that journey hundreds of times and often remarked, 'Christ, Luce – the car could do that trip by itself.'

Maybe he'd intended to stop off along the way – but where, and what for? She had studied the map of the area until it ceased to represent anything at all, and even driven the route herself. There were a couple of rather nondescript villages; neither seemed to have any amenities, like a shop or petrol station, that he might have planned to stop at in order to buy something. He wouldn't have anyway. If he'd planned to bring treats home, he'd have bought them in one of the chi-chi independent food stores that had popped up close to Si Morley's offices in Manchester.

After the accident, the police had brought her the contents of Ivan's car. There had been some work documents, his zip-up bag containing his laundry, his gym kit and a couple of novels, and a beautiful Christmassy bouquet, wrapped in cellophane with a plain white card attached.

Thank you so much! the message read – in Ivan's handwriting. What had he been thanking Lucy for, and why was he bringing her flowers that night? Although Ivan was far from mean, it wasn't his usual sort of gift. Maybe he'd just grabbed them in a hurry?

Of course, there was an alternative version of events, but that would have forced Lucy to accept that things hadn't been as they seemed, and that perhaps her loving, loyal husband wasn't quite the man she'd thought he was. In this version, the flowers hadn't been intended for her at all.

This thought tore at her mind now as she hauled the wretched lawnmower back across the straggly grass. *He'd been seeing someone else.* She could think of no other explanation for his movements that night. Maybe it had started after they'd moved here, when he'd admitted that he'd felt under-stimulated and 'spied upon', living in the country. After all, she had tricked him into viewing Rosemary Cottage in the first place – and he had never truly wanted to run a B&B. Or perhaps the miscarriage last year had been the trigger, when she'd been so down and distraught and hadn't felt like having sex for months on end? Was *that* why he'd done it? It was classic, wasn't it – husband feels neglected and unloved so he jumps into bed with someone else.

And who could blame him, really?

Lucy's eyes were brimming with tears as she dragged the mower up the small ramp into the garage. When Ivan had still been here, she had never considered that he might have lied to her. She had trusted him absolutely, right up until the day he died. But now, as she gave the mower one final kick for humiliating her in front of Irene Bagshott, she no longer knew what to think.

Tears were falling freely now; thank God the kids were out with Rikke. They'd gone up into the hills to collect bits and pieces for a nature project they were doing at school. That's what Lucy should have been doing right now – enjoying the spring day, collecting fluffy pink blossom instead of imagining Ivan being with someone else.

That was why she lost concentration as she reached up to close the up-and-over garage door. She grabbed at the plastic handle on the end of the rope and tugged it hard – but her mind was so filled with anguish about

Ivan cheating on her that she forgot to step out of the way. There was a metallic clang as the door slammed down onto her head, and Lucy reeled backwards, falling to the ground.

Chapter Thirteen

Her first thought as she came to was: *Someone attacked me. They hit me over the head but I'm okay, I'm alive.* Then: *Christ, I'd never have imagined something like that happening here* . . . Lucy's eyes were open now, and although her vision was blurry she managed to assess her surroundings as she gathered herself up to a seated position.

She was on the gravel next to her house, and that appeared to be her old wooden garage in front of her. How bizarre this was. Its door was hanging half open. Had someone burgled it? If so, what had they been after in here – some half-used cans of emulsion and foldable camping chairs? She exhaled slowly and looked upwards. The sky was clear blue and streaked with transparent clouds, and the sun was shining brightly. There was a light breeze and the distant sound of cars. Slowly, Lucy moved one hand until it was resting lightly on the top of her head. She prodded about, fingers spread, assessing the tenderness of her scalp.

That had been some whack. As her hair didn't seem

to be sticky or wet, she decided it was probably only her skull and/or brain that had been damaged so at least she wouldn't look a fright around the village. There'd be no rush of concern or fussing over her at the school gate.

Lucy lived in fear of people deciding she 'wasn't coping', and the onslaught of casseroles starting up again.

For a few moments she just sat there, aware of a swill of nausea and a dull pounding in her head as she remembered now what had happened. She hadn't been attacked after all. She had slammed the garage door down on top of herself. She let out a gasp of exasperation, for being incapable of mowing the lawn – it was all coming back to her now – and, worse still, being unable to shut the garage without knocking herself out.

She stood up unsteadily, the nausea intensifying and causing her to grab at the side of the garage for support, like a drunk person. *Oh,* she didn't feel well at all. She needed to get into the house and sit down and drink something sweet. But for now, all she could do was stand there, a hand placed across her eyes, waiting for the swell of sickness to subside.

'Mum!' Sam's voice rang out from down the lane.

She pulled her hand away from her face. 'Hi, love,' she said, trying her best to look normal. She smiled wanly.

He was approaching with Marnie and Rikke, and Lucy could see that all three were giving her curious looks as they grew closer. 'What are you doing, Mum?' Marnie asked with a frown.

'I, uh, just bumped my head, love.' Now she felt as if she might actually throw up. She touched her forehead; it was clammy with sweat.

'What happened?' Rikke asked, hurrying towards her. 'Oh, you look terrible, Lucy. You're so pale.'

'I pulled the garage door down on my head,' she admitted. 'It was so stupid of me.'

'Poor Mum!' Marnie exclaimed, clutching at her arm. 'Are you okay?'

'I'll be fine in a few minutes,' she said.

'Does it really hurt?' Sam asked, peering up at her.

'Just a bit,' she fibbed.

Rikke stepped forward and examined Lucy's head, parting her hair gently. 'Looks like there'll be some bump here.'

Lucy flinched. 'There isn't a cut or anything, is there?'

'No, I don't think so . . .' How reassuring Rikke seemed; this strong, capable young woman with her no-nonsense blonde crop and pink cheeks. 'You need to be checked out, though, just to make sure.'

'No, I don't,' Lucy said quickly, moving away from her now. 'It was just a bit of a shock, that's all. What an idiot I am! I'll be fine.' She started to make for the house with the children scampering along at her side, staring up at her.

'But you might have concussion,' Rikke said firmly. 'It can be dangerous, you know.'

'What's going to happen to you, Mum?' Sam cried out, grabbing her hand.

'Nothing,' Lucy replied. 'I just banged my head and I need to rest and then I'll be—'

'No, you *must* see a doctor,' Rikke said firmly. 'The Heathfield surgery is closed on Sundays so it'll have to be hospital, I'm afraid.'

'I'm not going to hospital,' Lucy exclaimed. 'They'll just look at me and send me straight home.'

'I hope they do,' Rikke said, pulling out her phone from her pocket, her nostrils flaring now as she exhibited a fierce determination that Lucy hadn't witnessed before.

And now she found herself complying – albeit rather huffily – as Rikke made a brisk call to Della, then outlined the plan: she would drop off the children at the bookshop ('Hurrah!' whooped Marnie, who loved the place, mainly because there was always a jar of home-made cookies on the counter for customers). Then she would return with her car to pick up Lucy and take her to Heathfield Hospital – so could she please go and get ready?

Lucy nodded and hugged the children, and as they were whisked away she hurried into the house to grab her bag.

'There's nothing wrong with me,' she reminded Rikke several times on the journey to hospital.

'Lucy,' Rikke said with a trace of exasperation, 'what would you do if one of the children had banged their head so badly they'd lost consciousness?'

'Well, I'd take them to hospital of course.'

'So there you go then.'

'Yes, but I'm not a child. I'm forty-two and I—'

'I don't think there's an age when concussions stop being dangerous,' she retorted, and despite her thumping head, Lucy couldn't help smiling at that. Oh to have a Rikke type on hand constantly to take care of her. Someone to make the numerous decisions that were required of her throughout the day: what to cook for dinner, whether to battle with Marnie over her maths homework or just let it go, whether to agree to spend the whole two weeks' school holiday at her parents' over Easter, as her mother was urging her to do, or stick to her guns and make it a shorter visit . . . None of these were major issues really, but they all piled up and sometimes Lucy felt frozen in indecision.

She glanced at Rikke as she slowed her speed. They were coming into Heathfield now, a pleasant historical market town with a medieval castle and a wide selection of artisan shops. Rikke drove smoothly through town and towards the hospital. Occasionally, Lucy yearned to tell her about Ivan being on the 'wrong' road home the night he died – because Rikke would probably come up with some kind of sensible explanation. For the flowers, too. Maybe the bouquet of poinsettias and red Christmas roses had been intended for someone they knew in the village? Lucy tried to imagine Ivan explaining that he'd bought them for Della or Irene – but she knew in her heart that it wasn't the kind of thing he'd do. He was kind, yes, but not in a random, bestowing-presents-upon-neighbours kind of way.

He must have bought them for me, she tried to reassure herself – but that didn't feel right either, and she knew she couldn't risk mentioning it to Rikke without it sounding weird.

The only person she had told was Andrew, her closest friend back at Claudine. They had worked together for over a decade and often had lunch and after-work drinks; she had met his partner, Roger, many times, and Andrew had met Ivan – but they had never really socialised as couples (Ivan had often referred to Lucy's workplace friends as 'your fashiony mates').

Andrew had come to the crematorium for Ivan's service, and visited again when Lucy's mother had gone home. 'I think maybe Ivan was having an affair,' she'd blurted out, going on to explain about the wrong road and the flowers.

'That's crazy talk,' Andrew exclaimed. 'Oh, Luce. You know he'd never have done that to you. It was probably just a nice, spontaneous gesture to mark the start of the Christmas holidays.'

'But it wasn't his kind of thing,' she'd protested. 'He was more likely to buy me a book, or a necklace or perfume – never flowers.'

'Look.' Andrew put an arm around her as they sat up late by the fire. 'If Ivan was up to something, d'you really think he'd put "Thank you very much!" with an exclamation mark on the card?'

It was typical of Andrew to home in on punctuation. He'd almost had a seizure when their new boss had sent out a group email at work, announcing: *Meeting in board room at 3 to discuss social media push. Come brimming with idea's!*

'Maybe you're right,' she'd conceded, 'but what would he have been thanking *me* for?'

'For being all-round bloody brilliant?' Andrew had said with a smile.

Now Rikke turned to Lucy as they parked up in the hospital car park. 'How are you feeling?' she asked.

'Much better,' Lucy replied. 'In fact, I'm really not sure about going in and bothering them. They're only going to say I'm wasting their time.'

'Well, look,' Rikke said, already unbuckling her seat-belt and clambering out of her car, 'we might as well have you looked at anyway, seeing as we're here.'

Now Lucy understood why Marnie and Sam behaved so impeccably for Rikke. Although not yet thirty, she had that air of authority that made people do as she asked, just as Lucy was doing now.

Into the hospital they went, to sit and wait amongst the genuinely sick and injured, the limping and bleeding, to finally be examined and told that Lucy's responses seemed fine. Rikke had even insisted on accompanying her, as if she thought Lucy might underplay the seriousness of the incident.

'You're okay to go home now,' said a young doctor with a milk-pale face, 'but remember that the effects of concussion can sometimes be delayed. Make sure you have someone responsible with you for the next few hours.' As if Lucy were seven years old, when this supposed medical professional looked as if he might be just about of age to join the high school chess club.

'Thanks for bringing me,' she said to Rikke, as they left the building.

'That's no problem,' Rikke said. 'It's best to be safe.'

'Yes, of course.' Now Lucy just wanted to get back to the village, pick up the children from Della's and pour herself a large wine. She glanced at Rikke, noticing that she seemed a little distracted as they made their way across the car park.

'You really don't need to stay with me when we get back,' Lucy added. 'I don't need looking after. If I feel dizzy or sick, I can call someone.'

'It's okay, we can watch a film or something.'

'Rikke, you're welcome to come around,' Lucy added, amusement in her voice now, 'but it wouldn't feel like we were just watching a film together, would it? It'd seem like you were babysitting me . . .' She broke off as Rikke raised a hand. At first, Lucy thought she was just dismissing her protestations. But as she followed her gaze she saw that she was waving to two men who looked as if they, too, had just left the hospital.

'Hi!' Rikke called out, and both men acknowledged her with a wave back. Rikke glanced at Lucy. 'That's the guy I work for, with his son. Remember I told you about Kenny?'

'Yes, of course,' Lucy said. Rikke had mentioned that she was helping out an elderly man who lived just outside the village – although she hadn't gone into much detail about his circumstances. Not for the first time, Lucy had marvelled at how she managed to keep her numerous plates spinning.

Both men were tall and slim, wearing jeans and sweaters, and were making their way between the parked cars towards them. *Please don't come over,* Lucy thought, her heart sinking. On good days she was just about capable of socialising with people she knew well. She certainly wasn't keen on chit-chat with strangers.

But now here they were and there was nothing she could do about it. 'Lucy, this is Kenny and James,' Rikke said with a bright smile.

'Hi,' Lucy said, as cheerily as she could manage. Despite the older man's full beard, she surmised immediately that there was a strong father–son resemblance. Both had intensely dark eyes and were strong-looking, handsome men; Kenny was the older, hairier version. There was something familiar about James, she decided. Perhaps she'd seen him out and about around the village.

'What're you doing here?' James asked Rikke.

'Lucy had a bit of an accident,' she explained.

'Oh, really?' He turned to her with a look of concern.

'But I'm fine,' Lucy said quickly. 'Just a bump on the head.'

'How about you two?' Rikke asked. 'Is everything okay?'

'Seems like it is,' James replied. 'I just wanted to make sure—'

'He *made* me come,' Kenny cut in with a disgruntled shrug. 'I said I thought I'd swallowed a bone, a fishbone.'

'We had cod and chips at the chippie for lunch,' James explained.

'And I got this scratchy feeling,' Kenny added, indicating his throat. 'Wish I'd never mentioned it now, wasting the NHS's resources when they have proper emergencies to deal with.'

'Okay,' James said, laughing now as he held up his hands in mock surrender. 'But you said you could feel it in your throat, Dad. You said it was annoying you, that it wouldn't go away and you thought it was *lodged*.' He shook his head and exhaled. 'I made the mistake of looking it up online.'

'That's what we all do when we're ill,' Rikke conceded.

'They gave me an X-ray,' Kenny added, 'and there was nothing there. They said it's probably just scratched. A *phantom* bone, they called it.'

'Well, that's good, isn't it?' Rikke said brightly. 'Better than a real bone, anyway?'

'I guess so,' James said, turning to his father. 'Wouldn't you say so, Dad?'

As Kenny mumbled disgruntedly, Lucy found herself observing the scene as if she wasn't a part of it. She was convinced now that she had definitely met James before – and gradually, it came to her where their paths had crossed.

He was chatting away now about a job he'd been doing on his dad's house. Something about a rotten

123

windowpane, and now Rikke was telling James about an outing to the cinema that she and Kenny were planning next week. But Lucy wasn't listening properly. Her mind was racing. All she wanted was to hurry away to Rikke's car and go home.

She'd had this urge to hide herself away ever since Ivan died. It was why she still didn't answer the door sometimes when friends and neighbours came around to see how she was doing. Lucy still wasn't functioning properly – she was only too aware of the fact. It was probably why she still fixated on those wretched Christmas flowers that were found in Ivan's car, and the 'other woman' she had conjured up in her mind who would of course be incredibly gorgeous and sexy and successful.

It was probably also why she had pulled the garage door down on top of her head today.

Lucy had tried to gather her faculties together – and, on the surface, she seemed to be coping reasonably well. *You're so strong and brave and a wonderful mum. Ivan would be so proud of you* . . . All of those things had been said to her many times. But Lucy knew she wasn't brave really. She lived in a state of near-perpetual anxiety, and the last thing she wanted right now was to pretend she was delighted to run into an old friend.

She glanced at James, a little furtively, knowing exactly who he was now. That wide smile, those dark brown eyes, the lilting voice: it was Hally from all those years ago.

Hally with whom she'd spent so many blissful days when she was just a child. Hally whom she'd loved, in her own giddy, immature way, before she'd really known what love was. And now he was a fully grown adult, chatting away to Rikke about a rotting window and the thing with his dad and the fishbone, as if everything was normal.

Lucy gazed over at Rikke's red car in the distance, trying to dredge up an excuse as to why she must run to it right now. She felt ill and needed to sit down immediately! She'd left something incredibly valuable in it and really should check if it was still there! Everyone knew there were *tons* of thieves in the hospital car parks of small market towns . . .

'Erm, Rikke—' she started.

'*Lucy* . . .' James had turned to her with an incredulous look on his face. Oh, God, he'd realised. There'd be no rushing to Rikke's car now.

She blinked at him, her cheeks flushing hot, feeling idiotic now for pretending she hadn't known.

'You're . . . you're Lucy, aren't you?' he exclaimed. 'I mean – Lucy who used to come to the village, for your summer holidays when you were a kid—'

'Uh . . . yes.' She mustered a smile. 'Yes, that's me.'

'I'm James! I, I mean . . . I'm Hally. D'you remember me?'

Kenny prodded his son's arm. 'We should get back home now, shouldn't we?'

'Yes, Dad, in a minute,' James said distractedly. He beamed at Lucy. 'Remember, we used to hang out together, get up to all sorts?'

She nodded. 'Yes, of course I remember.'

Now Rikke was looking first at James, then at Lucy. 'You two were friends as children?'

'Yeah,' James said. 'This is amazing!'

'*What's* amazing?' Kenny asked, looking puzzled.

James looked at his father. 'Lucy used to come to

125

Burley Bridge every summer. Well, for a few years at least. We had such great times ...' He grinned at her. 'We stole berries—'

'—From Kitty Cartwright's garden,' Lucy finished for him. 'That's where I live now.'

'Really? You're the one living at Rosemary Cottage?'

'Yes!' She smiled stiffly and glanced at Rikke, trying to transmit that they really should go now. However, James was chattering on, seemingly oblivious to her reticence and the fact that his dad clearly wasn't too happy about hanging around on this chilly March afternoon.

'I had no idea you two knew each other,' Rikke marvelled.

James chuckled, his eyes crinkling, and he pushed back his short dark hair. 'How *are* you?'

'Oh, I'm good,' Lucy said in a strained voice.

'You look great. You've hardly changed!'

'Ha. I doubt that really but, um, thank you . . .' She shuffled and cleared her throat. 'I really should get back, though . . .'

'Oh, of course,' Rikke said, and James nodded.

'Well, it's lovely to see you again,' he said. 'We should catch up properly sometime. Would you like to take my number?' Before she could answer he had pulled his phone from his pocket.

'Er, yes, hang on.' She sensed a tic on her left eyelid as she pulled her own phone from her bag. Numbers were exchanged, because what else could she do when they were all standing there, looking at her expectantly? There was a rather stilted hug goodbye, as if James had finally picked up on her awkwardness, before they parted company.

'Well, that was amazing,' Rikke said as they climbed into her car, and Lucy agreed that it was. As she drove them home, Rikke shared what she knew about James's life these days; that he lived in Liverpool, worked pretty flat out as a joiner and boat fitter, and was a single dad to a young son called Spike. Lucy gathered that, until he'd employed Rikke, James had been darting back and forth to keep an eye on his dad. Apparently, there was an older brother – whom Lucy remembered vaguely – who'd been staying with their dad, but had up and left in pursuit of a woman and was now seemingly living in Switzerland. 'James seemed pretty keen to find someone to help out,' Rikke added. 'He's brilliant with his dad, though – incredibly patient. Kenny can be a little, uh . . ,' she grinned '. . . challenging.'

Encouraged by Rikke, Lucy told her more about the adventures she'd had on her visits to the village. 'That sounds such fun,' Rikke said with a smile, adding, 'D'you think you'll get in touch with James?'

'Erm, maybe,' she said vaguely. She sensed Rikke glancing at her.

'You should,' she added. 'He's a lovely person.'

'Yes, he was always fun.' Lucy smiled tightly, aware of an awkward silence settling over them. To fill it, she pulled out her phone again and called Della at the bookshop to check if Marnie and Sam were okay, and to say they'd be back soon. There was no need to phone because of course, the children were having a lovely time hanging out in the bookshop. But Lucy didn't want to talk about James, or speculate on whether they might pick up on their friendship.

She didn't want to rekindle it. The thought of telling him what had happened to Ivan appalled her, and she hoped she wouldn't run into him again and have to explain her situation. James seemed like a good, decent man, but he belonged to her past, when she'd been young and carefree.

He'd been wrong, too, when he'd said she'd hardly changed. She had – more than he could ever imagine.

Chapter Fourteen

Rather than battling with the mower again, Lucy took note of an advert stuck up in Irene's shop window for regular garden maintenance. A couple of days later a cheerful gardener with a shock of red hair came round and had the lawn cut in less than half an hour. Like the doctor at the hospital, he looked incredibly young – but then, a lot of people did to Lucy these days. He had brought his own (twenty-first-century) machine and seemed taken aback when Lucy rounded up his fee with a generous tip. 'Could you come round every couple of weeks throughout the summer?' she asked.

'Sure, of course,' he replied. It was as simple as that; sod the expense, she decided. Len from the garage – whom she knew enjoyed tinkering with ancient machinery – was more than happy to take the antique machine off her hands. Getting rid of the darn thing, despite Ivan's fondness for it, seemed like a major step forward, and it propelled Lucy to bag up all the detritus that was lying about in the garage, and give it a thorough sweep-out.

This might have seemed hardly life-changing to some,

but Lucy allowed herself a glint of pride on having completed the job. While she wasn't ready to tackle the attic – packed as it was with Ivan's things – she did feel able to attack the utility room, which had amassed a colossal amount of clutter during the past few months. It felt good to tick jobs off the list, even though she was aware that she was probably going to great lengths to 'keep busy' – also known as 'flailing madly with no coherent plan', like when she gave up smoking a few months after meeting Ivan. As he was a non-smoker, she had become suddenly self-conscious about her habit and vowed to quit. He'd laughed at the way she had thrown herself into baking multiple loaves – more than they could possibly eat – and painted her kitchen bright yellow and installed window boxes on the previously bare ledges of her flat. She was a whirl of activity, trying to stem nicotine cravings by ensuring that there was no opportunity for them to invade her brain.

'Just popping out to the shop,' Ivan had told her. 'By the time I come back I'll expect you to have built a helipad.' For years afterwards, the term 'helipad madness' continued to be used to describe any kind of fervent activity undertaken to fill some sort of void.

Only, with cigarettes, the cravings gradually subsided and normal service was resumed, and Lucy wasn't sure that that would ever happen to her now.

Still, being busy was good, she decided. And when the local hairdresser, Nicola, stopped her to compliment her floral display in the bookshop, and asked if she could decorate her windows too, Lucy said yes without thinking. She really needed to spend more time in the garden, to immerse herself in something practical. Just as it had helped to heal her after the miscarriage last year, tidying the borders and filling terracotta pots were easy, soothing tasks. She threw herself into filling the salon's window with irises and narcissi, shrugging off Nicola's offer of a complimentary haircut on top of payment for the flowers.

'It'd be no trouble,' the hairdresser said. 'We could even try a restyle . . .'

'Maybe sometime,' Lucy replied vaguely, wondering if Nicola was hinting that she really should sort herself out.

Word of Lucy's floristry talents seemed to be spreading. The manager of a local hotel a little way out of the village had called to ask if she would decorate their foyer. It was early April now, and she agreed to do the job as soon as she was back from her trip to her parents'; already, she knew she would cut freesias, peonies and anemones in cheering yellows, lilacs and pinks. It seemed that this side of Lucy's life was beginning to take flight without her having to do very much in the way of trying to attract jobs. Compared to doing B&B on her own, which felt utterly daunting now, here was something she *could* do, with minimal stress.

Lucy was aware that, if she wasn't planning to ever take in guests again, perhaps she should consider downscaling. After all, that had been the whole reasoning behind buying Rosemary Cottage – to run it as a small business. She and the children could easily manage in a much smaller place; plus, it would be easier and cheaper to run.

Overwhelmed by the thought of making such a momentous decision, she preferred to push such thoughts from her mind. And when a text came from James a week after their car park encounter – *Lovely to see you, fancy a coffee this weekend?* – she took what felt like the easiest option. She simply didn't reply. If she felt slightly guilty, she soon shrugged it off as there was a more pressing matter on her mind.

The Easter holidays were upon her. After much cajoling on her mother's part, Lucy had agreed to spend a week at her parents'. In panic, she had examined the thatch that was supposed to pass as a hairstyle and decided it wouldn't do; if she turned up looking like that, her mother would surmise that she wasn't coping at all, and would muscle in and start trying to take over her life. An avid believer in the importance of keeping up appearances, Anna had even had a manicure for Ivan's cremation service, opting for polish in a discreet shell pink.

On the day they were due to set off, Lucy examined her reflection in her bedroom mirror some more, wondering how her hair had managed to grow so long and out of control. Once, she'd regarded it as her best feature. It was a rich dark brown, with the occasional grey hair now which Lucy yanked out, and it used to attract all kinds of compliments. Ivan had told her that her mane of waves – 'So long and full, like a French film star's' – plus her deep green eyes had been what had first attracted him to her. 'As well as all the other bits,' he'd added, teasing her.

These days it was self-cut with any old scissors that were kicking about, and her eyebrows were fuzzy and lacking in definition. For goodness' sake, even Tilly, her parents' schnauzer, went for a thorough grooming every eight weeks.

As she hadn't planned to set off for her parents' until after lunch, Lucy called Nicola at the salon on the off-chance that she might be able to fit her in.

'No problem,' she said cheerfully. 'I've just had a cancellation this morning – and remember, it's my treat. Could you come over right away?'

'Sure,' Lucy said. Marnie and Sam were still flopping about in pyjamas, but the unashamed bribe of sweets from the newsagent's propelled them speedily into T-shirts and jeans, and they were off.

'So, what are we looking at doing today?' Nicola asked, meeting Lucy's gaze in the mirror while the children lounged on the leather sofa. She had popped in recently to refresh the flowers in the salon window. That's what *she* needed, she decided; a perk-up in order to face her mother.

'I just need . . . reviving,' Lucy said with a smile.

'Right,' Nicola said brightly. 'I think we can lose quite a bit of length, don't you? And we'll bring in some layers, create some lightness. Let me get you shampooed.' Apart from a part-time assistant who wasn't here today, Nicola's salon was really a one-woman operation. A decade or so older than Lucy, she had run this place for twenty years and knew pretty much everything that happened in the village.

'I've had so many comments about your flowers,' she said as she rinsed Lucy's hair. 'I've been passing on your number.'

'That's great,' Lucy said, distracted now by the children. Generally, they could be trusted to behave reasonably well, but today she could sense that Sam was intent on high jinks. Sweets had been guzzled, and now he'd got up to investigate the various tubs all set out on a wheeled trolley. 'Sam, please sit down,' Lucy said.

Ignoring her, he picked up a spongy hair doughnut and mimed biting into it, at which Marnie laughed.

Nicola gave him a quick glance. A tub of long-handled combs was knocked over and Nicola sprang across the room to gather them up.

'Sam!' Lucy exclaimed. 'Just sit down. We'll only be a few more minutes . . .' Without apologising he perched beside his sister and whispered conspiratorially in her ear. *This isn't fair,* Lucy wanted to snap. *It's my first proper haircut since, well, God knows how long* – but of course, a six-year-old didn't care what she looked like, he didn't care about things being 'fair'.

'I've got something for you two,' Nicola said, breaking off from attending to Lucy to fetch a small stack of rather ancient-looking comics from a cupboard. She also handed them glasses of orange juice.

While they accepted these with thanks, Lucy knew their patience was limited and she willed Nicola to do a speedy job. Sam was now loudly telling Marnie a story about Daniel from school pooing in his greenhouse and having to wipe his bottom on leaves.

'What kind of leaves?' Marnie asked.

'Dunno. Big, soft, papery ones.'

'Why didn't he use the toilet in the house?'

'His dad was on it. And then he had all these pooey leaves to get rid of, so he put 'em in the watering can, and then his mum found—'

'*Thank you,* Sam,' Lucy cut in sharply, wondering when he might grow out of this fascination-with-poo phase and hoped it would be soon (surely he should have already? Was this normal?). Then the bickering started, the comics having been tossed aside in favour of half-hearted poking and prodding. An orange juice was spilled. Lucy apologised profusely as Nicola mopped it up.

'Honestly, it's no problem,' she insisted, but Lucy still

sensed a wave of relief from her as, having barely even acknowledged her finished hairstyle, she grabbed the kids' hands firmly and they all tumbled out of the salon door.

So that's what happened when she had the audacity to try to look like a normal, sane person instead of a crazy woman with a thatch.

And so to Leeds, where Lucy could at least cast off the shackles of responsibility and be looked after for a week.

'You look lovely, darling!' exclaimed her mother. She had shot out of the house the instant Lucy had pulled up outside.

'Thanks, Mum. Just had a quick cut and blow-dry this morning.' *Hardly the most relaxing one of my life, but never mind.*

'It really suits you. Oh, it's so good to see you all!' Anna swept back her highlighted hair and bobbed down to embrace her grandchildren. Lucy's dad, Paddy, had stepped out from their smart white 1950s semi to greet them too. As Tilly scampered out, panting and yapping at nothing in particular, the children fell upon her, all thoughts of grandparents momentarily forgotten.

'Hello, Dad,' Lucy said, kissing her father. 'Good to see you.' He grinned and ruffled Lucy's hair as if she were nine years old.

As soon as they entered the house it was clear that Anna had thrown herself into preparations for their visit. Whilst Christmas was always a big deal at the Riddocks', this year Anna had clearly treated Easter with similar gusto. In the hallway a gigantic silver birch branch lurched precariously from a ceramic planter, laden with dangling foil-wrapped chocolate rabbits.

'Can we have some, Grandma?' Marnie asked, wide-eyed.

'Of course, take as many as you like.'

'But not too many,' started Lucy, knowing there was no point. She had certainly relaxed on the confectionery front lately. Ivan had been pretty laissez-faire about such matters, but she suspected even he would be calling a halt now as they grabbed at the treats. There were further delights in the living room – bowls of sweet speckled eggs set out on the coffee table – and every windowsill bore arrangements of miniature straw nests containing fluffy yellow chicks.

There were Easter-themed balloons at the fireplace, and paper chains in yellow and pink had been draped across the gilt-edged mirror. 'Wow, this is amazing!' Lucy enthused.

'I thought we'd make it fun,' Anna said. 'We're having a big lunch tomorrow, and then drinks on Monday. Everyone's coming – including your aunts.' Anna meant her two sisters.

'Great,' Lucy said, sensing her back teeth clamping together.

'Okay,' Anna went on, addressing the children, 'as soon as you've taken your bags upstairs, Grandpa has another surprise for you.' The children hared up to the room the four of them – three of them now – always shared when they stayed here, and reappeared demanding to know what the surprise was. It turned out to be an egg hunt and yet more chocolate. Her father had apparently been briefed to throw himself into the proceedings – despite clearly suffering from a cold – as eggs were hidden all over the garden.

Lucy took a glass of wine gratefully from her mother

and sipped it, then inhaled deeply. So, this was Easter with her parents. The aunts were coming, and many others besides; there would be a huge fuss, with everyone giving her the big-eyed look – the *poor Lucy* face. But it would be okay; she would get through it somehow.

Lucy's aunts arrived before lunch next morning. Elspeth, the eldest of the three sisters, never married and child-free, was brandishing a terribly complicated-seeming board game for them all to play ('Please pretend to like it,' Lucy willed her children). Flora, the youngest, a widow and apparently terribly spoiled, so Lucy's mother always claimed, immediately bagged the best seat in the living room. While Elspeth set out the board game, Flora sat regally in the corner like an Egyptian queen.

'I might sit this one out,' Paddy said apologetically, frowning down at the game's indecipherable rules that had been thrust at him. 'My cold's coming on really strong now.'

'What cold? You look absolutely fine to me, Paddy,' scoffed Anna, ever the expert on ailments despite possessing no medical training (before her retirement she had reigned over the homewares floor of a now defunct department store).

'Well, he says he wants to sit this one out,' Elspeth added, as if Paddy were no longer capable of speech.

'Sit what out?' asked Flora, who was slightly deaf.

'The game,' Elspeth announced. 'In fact, Easter. Paddy wants to sit Easter out,' at which the sisters laughed.

It was usual for sympathy to be lacking whenever Paddy was under the weather. A couple of Christmases ago, Anna had complained of him 'malingering' and 'wanting attention' – and shortly afterwards he had been diagnosed with acute shingles. 'Anything to have me running around after him,' she'd complained.

However, despite all the jibing and mild bullying, Lucy couldn't help admiring her mother's levels of commitment on the entertainment front. There was a vast, sprawling lunch, involving a saddle of lamb that the children picked at reluctantly, then coffees and a gigantic Easter cake, swathed in yellow buttercream and covered in tiny eggs. There were presents for the children – more chocolate, naturally – all wrapped outlandishly with cellophane and enormous sheeny bows. However it was the presence of Tilly that won Marnie and Sam's attention throughout the day.

'They adore her, don't they?' Anna remarked, spotting them curled up by her basket in the living room later on in the day, petting and talking to her.

'They do, Mum,' Lucy agreed. 'It's lovely to see.'

'Dogs are very comforting,' Flora offered, giving her a meaningful glance. 'Nick and I loved our Honey.'

'I know you did.' Lucy smiled tightly at the sight of her aunt's watering eyes.

'Oh, Lucy. You know what you should do, love?' Now Elspeth had joined in.

Drink more? Lucy wondered, draining her glass. 'Um, not really, Aunt Elspeth.' *Please don't say it. Don't suggest I should try to fill the void left by Ivan by getting a dog.*

Elspeth frowned. Although her hair was a fine silvery shade now, her brows had remained dark and dense, with the texture of Brillo pads. 'It might be a comfort for them,' she offered.

'Oh, I don't think—' Lucy started.

'Pets are very good for children,' continued Elspeth, clearly being an expert in such matters despite never having produced a child of her own. 'They teach empathy, and that it's not all about them.'

Bloody charming! Lucy thought, bringing her glass to her mouth then remembering it was empty.

Marnie looked up hopefully. 'Can we, Mum? Can we get a dog please?'

'I'm not even thinking about that right now,' Lucy said quickly.

'Why not?' Sam asked, his face drooping. *Well done, Aunt Elspeth, for bringing this up . . .*

'Because it's not the right time to make a big decision like that,' Lucy said.

'You always say it's not the right time,' Marnie announced.

'Yeah,' Sam muttered. 'Everyone else has a dog. Why can't we?'

'Honey helped us so much when the children moved to Australia,' Flora added.

But Ivan isn't in Australia, Lucy wanted to remind her. *He is ash, in a little pot on the shelf in my bedroom.* She spent the rest of the evening busying herself with handing out cups of tea and steering Sam away from his grandpa's Airfix model collection, which still sat, defiantly and within easy reach of small hands, on the sideboard in the dining room.

Later that night, when the day was finally over, Lucy lay in the narrow single bed in the room she was sharing with Marnie and Sam. While they slept soundly on blow-up mattresses, Lucy was starkly awake with one thought burning in her mind:

If there was a single thing one should never say to the recently bereaved, it would be: 'So, have you thought about getting a dog?'

*

139

The next day another cluster of relatives arrived late in the afternoon, for drinks and nibbles: Paddy's brother and sister-in-law, their son and his wife, plus their three children. Lucy suspected her mother had pulled out all the stops in order to blast away the slightest hint that something terrible had happened just four months before.

Paddy, who was still sneezing intermittently ('Really milking that cold now,' Anna observed) was given the role of cocktail maker, and Marnie and Sam were festooned with yet more Easter eggs. Lucy was relieved, at least, to see that they were still capable of having fun. However, as the afternoon went on, she started to wonder if Rosemary Cottage was okay, as if it were a person she had left all alone. There was no need to fret, as Della had promised to keep an eye on the place. But even so, Lucy had started to count the days when she and the children could return home, to normality – or, at least, as normal as it was possible to be these days.

Her parents' house always felt too hot, with the central heating on even though the days were warm, the sky incessantly blue. By day three, as they cleared up after yet another huge meal, Anna had managed to corner Lucy alone in the kitchen.

'You can't go back to that village,' she announced, giving her daughter a concerned look.

'Of course we're going back, Mum.' Lucy stared at her, astounded by the implication that she might not.

'Well, yes, I know you'll have to go *back*,' Anna conceded, 'but just to pick up your things.'

'Pick up our things?' Lucy spluttered. 'It's not a holiday house, Mum. It's our home!'

'Yes, I know that,' she said impatiently. 'But promise me you'll put that house on the market as soon as you can, love. If you need to do anything to it, I can come over and help.'

'I'm not promising that,' Lucy said firmly, grateful that the children were out of earshot, playing with Tilly in the garden.

Anna frowned. 'It might seem daunting now, darling – the upheaval of a move and everything. But it's the best thing to do, isn't it? There are good schools here. I've talked to some people . . .'

'Who?' Lucy asked, aghast.

'Um, the school secretary. The lady in the office. She said you just have to contact the council, and as long as you're in the catchment area—'

'Marnie and Sam aren't moving schools! They love their school. It's fantastic, Mum. They've been so supportive.'

'But children are adaptable, aren't they?' Anna clutched at her arm. Lucy managed to resist the urge to shake her off. 'They'd soon settle in,' she added, 'and your dad and I would take care of everything – the house sale, the move . . .' Lucy stared at her, mutely. Children were adaptable; they should have pets. Was everyone a ruddy child-rearing guru now?

'We're *not* moving,' Lucy snapped, aware of a twinge of guilt now. In some ways, her mother was right, in that she and the children would have the support they needed, plus a home; at seventy-one, Paddy still kept a finger in his property-letting business. She knew he'd find her the perfect place.

'We just care about you, Lucy,' her mother murmured. 'Why stay in that village?'

141

'Mum, our life's there now,' Lucy reminded her, struggling to assume a patient tone. 'The children have their friends, and we love our house.'

'Don't tell me you're still going to try to run a B&B?'

'I . . . I still don't know about that, Mum.' Lucy faltered and her voice cracked.

'Oh, darling.' Her mother took her in her arms. 'Please, just accept you gave it your best shot – but you can't carry on alone. You're thin as a rake. Your dad and I are so worried, aren't we, Paddy?' She raised her voice to a shrill pitch.

'What's that, love?' he called from the living room.

'We're worried about Lucy! *Aren't* we, Paddy? Could you show an interest, please?'

'Of course I'm interested,' he blustered, scuttling through the door as if shamed into participating in the worrying. Anna glared at him.

'Mum, I'm okay, honestly,' Lucy said quickly. 'Well, I'm not *exactly* okay. But I will be at some point. I have to be, don't I?'

Anna pursed her lips. 'But how can you possibly look after the children, and yourself, *and* run a business?'

'Mum,' Lucy said firmly, plonking a dish towel on the worktop, 'please don't do this. We're very happy to be here, but we're going home on Friday, as we planned to, and I'm absolutely not deciding to do anything – anything at all, I mean – right now.'

Although she didn't quite know what she meant by that, it seemed to put a lid on the matter, and for the next few days, Anna managed not to bring up the subject again. However, it hung over them like a cloud, and as the week went on, Lucy was overcome by an urge to escape back to Burley Bridge.

It was their home, just as she'd said. It was where they belonged. In the end, she cracked a day early, making an excuse that a floristry job had come in and she needed to go home to prepare for it.

She felt bad about lying (more guilt!). However, as they said their goodbyes, Lucy sensed that Marnie and Sam were as relieved as she was to be escaping from the steady stream of well-meaning relatives who insisted on hugging and kissing them constantly.

The children had had their hair ruffled so many times it was a wonder they had any left. They had been festooned with sweets and chocolate, and their complexions had taken on peaky hues. Anna had launched into one final, impassioned plea for Lucy to sell up and move closer. 'I'm not making any decisions right now,' she said firmly as she stashed their belongings into the boot of her car.

Her mother was wet-eyed as they said goodbye on the drive. 'Mum, you're coming over to see us in a couple of weeks, remember?' Lucy said, her patience waning now.

'Yes, I know, love.' She nodded stoically.

'I'll miss Tilly.' Sam gazed after her morosely as she pottered back indoors, presumably sick of all the hugging.

'Will you miss me too, Sam?' Anna asked, needily.

'Yes, Grandma.'

'Of course they will,' Lucy said, catching her dad's eye with a smile as she ushered her children into the car.

'We'll miss Tilly the most, though,' Marnie whispered conspiratorially to her brother as soon as the doors were shut.

And now, as they sped homewards under a clear April sky, Lucy knew she would somehow make their own place feel like home once again – for Marnie and Sam, and for Ivan. Lucy had stood her ground, and she felt oddly proud of the fact – and now she realised she would go on to make a life for the three of them on her own. What other choice was there? Falling apart simply wasn't an option.

She glanced back at her children as they waited at a junction. They were talking about Tilly, and how sweet she was, how cuddly and soft with those cute little ears, and now they were debating what they would call *their* dog, if they were ever allowed to have one, which they probably wouldn't as Mum didn't like them (that was patently untrue). And why *wouldn't* she let them when they'd promised to do all the walking and putting out her dinner and everything, all the work?

'Mum,' Marnie started, 'can we please have a—'

'We've talked about this, love, and you know the answer.'

'But Grandma and Grandpa have Tilly.'

'Yes, and that's different. They have time for her; they're retired.'

'Grandpa's not, is he?' Marnie remarked. 'He's always on the phone. He's always talking about *houses*.'

Hmm, well, that was true. She doubted if her father would ever give up his business entirely. 'Yes, but he doesn't go to work every day. He's mostly at home.'

'So are you!' Marnie announced. 'You're always at home.'

Well, thanks very much! Lucy thought wryly, although of course it was true. *I didn't used to be,* she wanted to remind them. *I was at the epicentre of bra engineering and my life was swishy and dynamic.* Then she remembered how she'd have to rush like a mad thing to the childminder's, and then to nursery and school, cursing every red traffic light and panicking that she'd be late. *I don't miss that,* she decided. *I don't miss it one bit . . .*

'When will *you* retire?' Sam asked.

'Oh, not for a very long time, love. I'm still young.' *Although I feel about ninety-seven.*

'But you don't have a job,' Sam pointed out.

'My life's pretty full, though,' she replied.

'Full of what?' he asked.

Hmm. Lucy decided not to answer that honestly. 'Full of looking after you two!'

He sighed loudly, and whispered to his sister, loud enough for Lucy to hear: 'Maybe when she's really old, she'll let us have one.'

Lucy turned up the car radio, reflecting that when Ivan was here, even when he worked away during the week, it had felt as if the kids' constant barrage of demands and questions was at least partly divided between them. *Is God real? Does Father Christmas exist? How are babies made?* And the perennial: *Why can't we have a dog?* And now it was just her, and maybe she would have to figure out a different way of being with them; a new way of living really, terrifying though that was. Being on her own with two children was something she had never considered, not for one moment – but this was how her life was now.

Thankfully, the dog issue seemed to have been forgotten as they started chatting about chocolate-sausage-Josh. And soon they were giggling as if everything was completely normal in their world.

They didn't notice that, as they neared home, Lucy had turned onto a minor road that would wend through open countryside, passing through a couple of hamlets until it led to Burley Bridge. It would probably add a good fifteen minutes to the journey. If the kids had looked out, they would have seen little more than a nondescript road with nothing to distinguish it from the more direct route. But it wasn't just any other road to Lucy.

It was where the accident had happened. Pretty soon, they would pass the bend where Ivan had skidded and smashed headlong into an oncoming car. She had driven this route several times before, on high alert for clues – about what, she didn't quite know. In a horrible, self-torturing way Lucy had been almost drawn to it.

If Ivan had been seeing another woman in Manchester – perhaps someone he'd met through work – that still wouldn't have explained why he'd come home this way. But the fact is, he had, which would have lengthened his journey on the night when, surely, he'd have been desperate to get home.

It had been five days before Christmas. Like a kid, he'd always loved the whole festive season. Back in their Manchester house he'd always insisted on a tree that was slightly too big for their living room, its top branch poking at the ceiling, then he'd rally the kids around to festoon it with baubles and tinsel. The latter was contentious; Lucy wasn't a tinsel lover but she was happy to let them run amok with it if it made them happy.

'If it was left to Mum we'd have coordinated baubles – all in silver,' he'd joked. As it was, Ivan and the kids' approach to tree decorating was crazily beautiful, and she hadn't actually minded the tinsel after all.

Lucy inhaled now as she passed the spot where the accident happened, and cursed herself silently for coming this way – especially with the children. What if one of them had asked her why they were here? What would she have said? As the church spire of Burley Bridge came into view, Lucy made a silent promise to herself that she would never come this way again. It was time to move on; to stop raking over the details and keep her memories intact.

She had loved Rosemary Cottage since she was a little girl. A terrible thing had happened, and now she no longer knew how she felt about the house, the village – or indeed about anything in her life. But she was still a capable person; she had survived almost a week at her parents'; she had listened to Elspeth and Flora implying that she might consider 'replacing' her husband with a pet. She had even coped with her mother's insistence that she should give up on Rosemary Cottage altogether.

Lucy decided now that she would never do that. It seemed childish and ridiculous but she wanted to prove her mum wrong – and, crucially, she knew she had to carve out a new life for herself and her children. A wave of determination filled her heart as she fixed her gaze firmly on the road ahead. While she wasn't sure whether she believed Ivan was watching over them – or was merely a billion dust particles now – she knew with absolute certainty that she would survive alone, and do her utmost to make her husband proud.

147

Part Two

A Year Later

Chapter Fifteen

Bacon, tomatoes, sausages, mushrooms. Eggs any way. If poached, they were perfectly done in silicone pouches, and if scrambled, they were buttery and soft. With a simplified breakfast menu, Lucy had been up and running again for several months, and business was looking good.

Fortunately, one of her earliest guests had been a reviewer for a travel website, and through his glowing report a flurry of bookings had kept her going throughout the winter and well into spring. *A characterful thatched cottage in a quaint and thriving West Yorkshire village,* he had written. *It's one of those places where you find yourself pretending you live there. You want this to be your local high street with its quirky shops including, amazingly, a shop selling nothing but cookbooks. No wonder people come from far and wide – Rosemary Cottage is a perfect home-from-home.*

He had even sent someone along to take photos of Lucy, beaming brightly in the garden at the cottage's front door. If she hadn't known the truth, she might have looked at the picture on the website and thought, 'Well, *she* has it all with her picture-perfect life.'

Affecting a cheery smile, she had formulated a way of minimising the risk of any awkward questions from guests about her personal situation. Lucy was aware that no one wanted to arrive at their B&B to learn that the host's husband had died in a road accident a little more than a year before. No – it had to be all perky chit-chat, attentive service and reams of recommendations for local delights. Part of Lucy's job was to convey the impression that, at Rosemary Cottage, all was right with the world.

'Such a beautiful day,' she remarked one bright and sun-filled April morning as she brought out a pot of fresh coffee to her guests in the dining room. Graeme and Amanda were a couple in their early thirties who had seemed notably affectionate with each other – touchy-feely and cuddly – when they had arrived last night.

'It's lovely,' Graeme agreed. 'We're so lucky.'

'It's our first time away without our little boy,' his wife Amanda added. 'So it's kind of a big deal to us.'

'Oh, that's pretty special,' Lucy said. 'How old is he?'

'He's just had his first birthday.' Amanda's eyes met hers, and Lucy detected the flicker of curiosity that she had started to recognise recently. The couple had already met Marnie and Sam first thing that morning as Rikke had breezed in to take them to school. It was always the women who picked up on what was perhaps a slightly odd situation; Lucy apparently running things alone, with no mention of a partner.

'It's lovely to get some time together, just the two of you,' Lucy added.

'It is.' Graeme nodded and grinned. 'We so appreciate it.'

'How old are your two?' Amanda asked.

'Sam's seven, Marnie's nine,' Lucy replied, and there it hung – that pause again, holding a silent question: *so, are you running things here by yourself?* When they'd first moved here Ivan had been working away during the week, and there'd been no such flicker of curiosity then. But then, Lucy would have dropped him casually into conversation: 'My husband works in Manchester'; 'Ivan's back this evening. Hopefully you'll meet him later.'

And these days – at least where her guests were concerned – her husband had become unmentionable.

When Amanda and Graeme had headed out for the day, Lucy spruced up the downstairs rooms, threw in a load of laundry, peeked in at Marnie's devastated bedroom, felt instantly depressed, and decided to take advantage of the beautiful weather by getting stuck into weeding the garden instead. Although she still missed Ivan on so many levels, sometimes it was the practical issues that hit her hardest; someone to *do* stuff, to reach up to high places and lift heavy things, even to twist off a jam jar lid. But it was the parenting side mostly – having someone to share all the worries, the joys and basic hard graft; to whisk the kids off for a few hours at the weekend to give her the peace to tackle a few jobs or, occasionally, sink into a bath with a magazine. Although she was hugely thankful to friends like Carys, who certainly helped out – and she hoped she reciprocated sufficiently – it wasn't quite the same.

After a couple of hours' gardening she stood up, brushing the soil from her gardening gloves as she cast her gaze along the blaze of colour that stretched all the way from the house down to the shed at the bottom of the garden. There were swathes of pale pink sweetpeas

153

and deep red peonies. A climbing rose that clung to the gnarly garden wall – the one Lucy, James and the Linton kids had scrambled over as children – was such a glorious deep yellow that she couldn't help feeling uplifted whenever she glimpsed it in bloom. She cut some flowers and took them inside, placing the vase of blooms on the windowsill next to the framed photo of Sam and Marnie as a baby and toddler. Until recently, there had been a wedding photo there too. But one morning, a lone, robust hillwalker type – who wore her bobble hat to breakfast, and smelt of Deep Heat – had spied it and asked, 'So, is your husband involved much with the B&B, Lucy? Or is it really your thing?'

'Oh, um, we lost him, unfortunately,' Lucy said quickly, unprepared for such a direct question (it was fair enough though, particularly as she still wore her wedding ring; there hadn't seemed any reason for her to take it off). 'There was a road accident,' she added.

'I'm so sorry,' the woman said, looking alarmed. 'I didn't realise. I mean, I shouldn't have—'

'No, really, it's okay.' Lucy's cheeks blazed, mostly from embarrassment at making her feel uncomfortable. Her guest also blushed, as if it were catching, and there had been an excruciating few moments during which Lucy had babbled. 'We're managing all right, you know. We're just getting on with things. You have to, don't you? So, um, would you like some more toast? Or maybe another pot of tea?'

'Oh, no, I think I'm all done, thank you,' she said, clearly wanting to scuttle out of the house and run for the hills. As soon as she'd left, Lucy had snatched the photograph and taken it upstairs to her room. When the children asked where it had gone, she had explained, 'It's

154

on my bedside table now. I like seeing it before I go to sleep.' Feeling oddly disloyal, she had gone on to remove all traces of Ivan's existence from the 'public' parts of the house.

If the children noticed, they didn't say anything and life went on, hectic and full, leaving Lucy little chance to brood. She barely had time to dwell on the attic that still needed clearing out – or even Ivan's wardrobe, for that matter. Everything was still as he'd left it. One day she'd deal with it all.

Lucy was aware that, on the outside at least, she probably seemed like any other normal mother. Perhaps she appeared to be even more capable and gung-ho than most with her open-door policy when it came to welcoming the village children into her home. For the most part, she was buoyant and brimming with energy: 'Hero Mum,' as Carys had called her recently, when she had hosted a sleepover for seven children during the Easter holidays. However, she would still wake up some mornings to experience a fresh wave of devastation on realising that Ivan wasn't beside her.

It infuriated her that this still happened. When would she be able to trust herself to just wake up and *know*? But she refused to allow herself to be pulled down by her grief. Ensuring that life was as full as she could possibly make it had become her way of scrambling through the days.

These days, Lucy rarely mentioned Ivan to anyone, apart from when the children wanted to talk about their dad. She had no desire to go over the details with anyone – which was why, when she spotted James Halsall in the village one bright and sunny afternoon, she was tempted to dart into the greengrocer's to avoid him.

Too late. He'd already seen her, and waved, and she waved back as if she'd only just spotted him. As he strode towards her, she arranged her expression into what she hoped looked like a genuine smile.

Chapter Sixteen

As soon as he spoke, she felt foolish for even considering hiding from him. Because James already knew about Ivan; of course he did. Burley Bridge was the kind of place where everyone knew pretty much everything – and anyway, they had Rikke in common. 'Sorry I never got in touch,' she said as they strolled through the village together. 'Last year, when I ran into you at the hospital . . . well, I wasn't in a good state, you know. I wasn't really thinking straight. It had only been a few months.'

'Of course, I understand,' he said quickly. 'So . . . how are things now?'

She hesitated, wondering how best to explain it. 'We're getting there, I suppose. Me and the kids, I mean. Starting up the B&B again has helped, in a weird way. Some people – well, my mother, mainly – thought it was completely mad, but it's been good for me. There are people around and always tons to do. And time helps, of course.'

'I'm glad to hear that.' James glanced at her. He had barely changed since childhood, Lucy decided. Yes, life was etched on his face; there were fine lines around his brown eyes and his short dark hair was flecked with grey around the temples. But those eyes were still bright, his build still rangy and slim. 'I'm so sorry, Lucy,' he added. 'I can't imagine how you got through it, with the children being so young too.'

'You just have to,' she murmured, gripping her basket, which was filled with loaves and the children's favourite chocolate and almond pastries from the artisan bakery. They fell into silence for a few moments. 'You texted me, remember?' she added. 'And I didn't reply.'

'Oh, I just assumed you had a lot on your plate,' he said quickly. 'Don't worry about it.'

She glanced at him. 'How are things with your dad these days?'

'Not too bad at the moment – thanks to Rikke, mainly. Things are ticking along.'

'She's amazing,' Lucy remarked, and James nodded. 'She started helping out when Ivan was still here and took a job back in Manchester, so it was just me running the B&B during the week. I don't know how I'd have managed without her.'

'It must've been a lot to take on with a young family,' James said.

'Yes, but in some ways it was easier than the grind of working nine-to-five. I used to work for a fashion retailer in Manchester – an underwear brand. That used to be my joke: "I work in lingerie".'

James laughed. 'And you gave up *that* line to move here? You must have fallen hard for that house.'

'Yes, I did.' Lucy paused and smiled. How easy he was to chat to, she decided, wondering again what had possessed her to consider avoiding him. 'Are you busy right now? Would you like a coffee? I'd love you to see the cottage.'

'That'd be lovely,' James said, 'if *you're* not too busy . . .'

Lucy shook her head. 'I have an hour or so before I have to pick up the kids from school. C'mon – you can see what we did to the place.'

Sometimes, it took an enthusiastic visitor to remind Lucy how much they – and, latterly, she – had done to Rosemary Cottage. The garden was enchanting now, the herbaceous borders abundant with colour, the oak tree's boughs spread wide over the expanse of lush green lawn. 'This takes me back,' James said with a smile as they made their way to the front door. 'It really is picture-perfect.'

'As long as you don't look too closely,' she joked.

'No, it really is lovely.' She led him in and made coffee, indicating for him to take a seat at the worn old kitchen table.

Although she hadn't planned to talk about the night Ivan died, it all came out as they sat together. He listened as she talked, commenting occasionally but never interrupting. Lucy wasn't sure how much he'd known already, and it didn't seem important to ask. She felt the sun on her face through the kitchen window as she sipped her coffee and described how life had been since that night.

It was so easy to tell him, and she didn't cry. She just talked and talked, encouraged by his gentle, considered responses. She wondered if this was what therapy was like; in fact, several friends, including Carys and Andrew, had suggested she might consider 'talking to someone'.

I don't need that, Lucy had said firmly, meaning:

159

Obviously, I'm going to take the far more sensible approach of bottling it all up and pretending to be fine. But now, she wasn't pretending anything at all. She described the searing grief in the aftermath of the accident, and how she had wondered, sometimes, if she was going quite mad. Although she didn't mention Ivan's mysterious route home, or the flowers in the car, she somehow knew she would probably tell him about that too, one day. It felt as if, now she had started to talk properly about Ivan, she couldn't stop.

'That's a hell of a thing to have gone through,' James said finally, when she paused for breath.

Lucy nodded and pushed her dark hair from her face. 'Before it happened, Ivan had been working away during the week. He was only here at weekends.'

'But it's entirely different, not having someone at all,' he said gently, 'and I guess you really looked forward to the weekends.'

'Yes, I did.' She inhaled slowly at the recollection. 'There were all the rituals, you know – planning a special supper, making sure there was wine in the fridge. It was a kind of date night thing.' She hesitated. 'That sounds terribly corny, doesn't it?'

'It sounds great,' he said.

'It's the kind of thing they always tell you to do in the magazines.'

'Maybe my ex and I should've tried that,' James said with a wry smile.

'I'm sorry, I haven't even asked about your life,' she said quickly. 'I'm really going on about Ivan today. I don't normally—'

'Please don't apologise,' he said.

'It's just . . .' She broke off, remembering now how

160

she would put fresh sheets on the bed for those Friday nights, and have her lingerie ready to slip into – usually one of her favourite fripperies, in black or cream silk, from Claudine. Ivan loved that stuff – well, he was a heterosexual man, wasn't he? – and so did Lucy. It made her feel womanly, alluring and, well, *gorgeous*, actually, cut as it was to flatter and enhance. She'd pile up her hair messily and apply a little of her favourite body oil, the stuff that made her skin so glowy and soft, and she'd light a scented candle on the bedside table and – oh God, now she was remembering being in Ivan's arms, and it was so vivid and real she could actually feel the warmth of his skin against hers . . .

Startlingly, her eyes had flooded with tears. 'I'm sorry,' she muttered, rubbing at them with the sleeve of her cotton shirt.

'No, *I'm* sorry,' James said, looking alarmed. 'I shouldn't have mentioned that thing, about the weekends.'

'It's not your fault,' she blurted out as, mortifyingly, hot tears began to fall and, worse still, her nose began to run. 'Most of the time I'm fine,' she said quickly, furious at herself now as she rubbed at her face, 'but occasionally it takes me by surprise. It just *hits* me. I miss him so much and I can't help it.'

She looked at James across the table: this kind, patient man who had been such a good friend to her all those years ago. She hadn't seen him since she was thirteen years old and now she was a mess of tears and snot, using her sleeve as a hankie. She hadn't even asked about his son, his work or anything, and no doubt he thought she was completely self-obsessed. Lucy could sense him staring at her – perhaps in horror – as she leapt up from her chair and grabbed a tea towel patterned with the

161

top ten British garden birds, and blotted her wet face with it. A choking sob came out.

James leapt up too. 'Lucy,' he started, touching her arm as he hovered beside her now, 'is there anything I can do, anything at all? I'm so sorry if I said something . . .'

'No, it wasn't you.' She shook her head and turned her back to him, willing the tears to stop and for James to get the message that he should go now and just leave her alone.

Chapter Seventeen

But he didn't go. He waited, seemingly not appalled by
the sight of a woman weeping and snotting all over the
blue tits and chaffinches on the tea towel. And when
Lucy finally stopped – thank God the children hadn't
witnessed her display – he beckoned her to sit back down
at the table as he took the seat beside her.

'Are you okay?' he asked gently.

Lucy exhaled and nodded. 'Yeah. God, I'm mortified,
James. I didn't expect that to happen.'

He looked at her, and she decided there was something
incredibly kind about his dark brown eyes. She rubbed
at her own, aware that they were puffy and probably
bright pink. 'I'm not sure you can plan these things,' he
added.

'Yeah.' He got up and filled a glass of water and
handed it to her, and she sipped it gratefully. 'It just seems
so unfair sometimes,' she murmured. 'For Marnie and
Sam especially . . .' She broke off. 'You know what that's
like, don't you?'

'Sorry, I don't . . .' He sat back down next to her, looking puzzled now.

'Losing your mum, I mean,' she said. 'I remember you telling me.'

James cleared his throat and reddened slightly, and she regretted mentioning it. 'Erm, yeah . . .'

She drank some more water and mustered a smile. 'Anyway, enough about all this sad stuff. It's a beautiful day. Would you like to see the garden properly? The one you trespassed in all those times?'

'Sure,' he said brightly. 'I'd love to.' So they headed outside, and as they walked she quizzed him about Spike, his work as a boat fitter and life in Liverpool.

'Spike's with me half of the week,' he explained. 'It's worked out okay since his mum and I split – not too many dramas.'

She looked at him, intrigued now about what had gone on in his life in the interim years. 'How old's Spike?' she asked.

'He's ten. A great kid – bit quiet, bookish, does his own thing. Likes coming on jobs with me when he's not at school.' James smiled fondly. 'He's pretty handy, actually. Knows one end of a hammer from the other.'

Lucy grinned. 'Sounds like you're really close.'

'Yeah, we are, although of course I drive him mad sometimes, and he's just reached the stage where I embarrass the hell out of him.'

Lucy chuckled. 'Hormones kicking in?'

James nodded as they strolled down towards the shed. 'That looks interesting. Spike would love that.'

'The shed? Come and see it . . .' Partly hidden by overhanging willows, and in the shade of the oak, it was looking rather shabby with its wonky timbers and peeling

164

pistachio paint. She opened the creaky door and James peered in at the clutter. 'Wow. Looks like there's been a lot of creativity happening in here.'

Lucy nodded. 'Ivan and the kids used it as a sort of den. They made things together – probably not a patch on your standards, but they made that . . .' She pointed at the birdhouse attached to the trunk of the oak.

'That's impressive!'

'But I should really deal with what's in here sometime,' she continued, 'and the attic too. It's absolutely stuffed.'

'What with?' James asked.

'Oh God – all sorts. But mainly Ivan's things. It's where I put all his stuff that I couldn't make a decision about. So, basically, pretty much everything.'

He nodded, clearly understanding. 'I imagine the last thing you needed was to sort through everything, and have to make all those decisions.'

'Yep. I just shoved it all away out of sight. All his paperwork, his work-related books, his hobby stuff – and Ivan had a *lot* of hobbies.'

'What kind?' James asked.

'He went through quite a few,' she said, smiling now. 'Ivan was the kind of person to throw himself into something, and that would involve buying all the equipment, the materials, the accessories. There was the fitness phase, the gym equipment, the weights and treadmill and cycling gear, then the artistic period when he got into screen printing. Then he bought a saxophone.'

James nodded. 'So he was an enthusiast.'

'Yes, I guess you could say that,' she said as they made their way back towards the house.

Back in the kitchen, Lucy poured more coffee from the pot, hoping James really hadn't minded her having a good cry in front of him today. She hadn't done that for months now; in fact, she couldn't remember the last time. When someone died, it felt as if there was a specific period when you could talk all the time, and cry and be crazy and nothing sensible was expected of you. It was fine to not wash your hair – or even your face – and to look terribly shabby and forget that the children were supposed to take in old family photographs for a class project.

It was okay to be the disorganised mum who accidentally wandered out of the greengrocer's with a bunch of bananas without paying for them.

It was even okay to snap at the children for some tiny misdemeanour and then apologise and hug them as if your lives depended on it. *All* of that was okay.

But then time moved along, and the bereavement cards and kindly texts gradually petered out. People stopped bringing shepherd's pies and cakes – of course they did. They couldn't nurture you forever; they had their own lives to get on with, and worries of their own. And it felt as though your allotted grieving period had run out, as if it were time on a parking meter, and so you decided that from now on you'd better keep your feelings to yourself.

Nearly a year and a half had passed since Ivan had died. Lucy was still a little shellshocked by her outpouring of tears today.

She glanced at James as he drained his mug. 'Well, I guess I'd better get up to Dad's,' he said. 'Thanks for the coffee. It's been lovely seeing you.'

'I really am sorry for getting upset,' she said quickly.

James stood up and touched her arm fleetingly. 'Please don't say that. I'm glad you've told me all that stuff, you know? It's important. And I was thinking just then. You know all the stuff in your shed, and in your attic that you can't bring yourself to sort out?'

'Yes?'

'Erm . . .' He rubbed at his sun-browned neck. 'Would you like me to help you with it sometime?'

Lucy pulled a face. 'Oh, it'll be a horrible job. It'll be filthy and messy and I'll probably get quite emotional.' She paused, wondering how best to put it. *I'm still not sure I can bear to throw anything way*, is what she meant.

'All I mean is,' James continued, 'it might be useful to have a friend with you, helping you to work your way through it. You know – a bit of moral support. What d'you think?'

Lucy put down her mug on the worktop and looked at him. Instinctively, she knew she could trust him to be sensitive, and not try to make decisions for her; but still, the thought appalled her. 'It's lovely of you to offer,' she said as she saw him to the front door. 'I'll think about it, okay?'

'Well, you know where I am. You can call anytime.'

She nodded and smiled. 'Thank you. I don't mean just for that offer, although that really is kind of you. I mean, thank you for letting me—' She broke off, sensing her cheeks flushing now, and pushed her hair back awkwardly. 'It's just been good to talk,' she added quickly. 'Next time it won't be all about Ivan, I promise.'

He fixed her with a curious look. 'It would've been strange for us *not* to talk about it, wouldn't it?'

She thrust her hands into her jeans pockets. 'I guess so, yes.'

He made his way to the front door. 'Just drop me a

text anytime you fancy a coffee. I'm still here for a day or two once a week.'

'I'll do that,' Lucy said.

'It's been great seeing you again.' He smiled warmly and kissed her briefly on the cheek, and then he was gone.

Lucy stood for a moment, wondering whether he was being truthful with her. She hoped he was; it would be a shame if she'd scared him off forever. Well, it was done now, she decided as she headed off to school to pick up the children. Later, once they were home, she decided it was too lovely an afternoon to cajole them into doing their homework right away. Her time with James had lifted her spirits, and she felt inspired to make the most of the glorious spring afternoon by bringing a blanket and makeshift picnic tea outside. Once they'd finished, and the children were pottering around in the early evening sun, Lucy strolled around the garden, gathering ideas for her next floral decorations. Despite everything, she still loved it here.

She'd had grand ideas for the place when they'd moved in. The garden had been the main reason she'd yearned to live here; after all, she had never been inside the cottage before that first viewing with the estate agent. Once it was theirs, she had planned to create a new border down by the shed. She'd envisaged a vegetable plot to supply salads and potatoes for the simple bistro-style evening meals she had hoped to offer to guests eventually.

Some hope of that now, she thought wryly, but she did have a seemingly unstoppable supply of fresh flowers, which she picked and carried back indoors. They hardly needed arranging at all. She just plunged them into glass jugs and vases, fluffing them out with her fingers and placing them in all the downstairs rooms. Instantly, it was as if spring had breathed new life into the cottage.

'Mum!' Sam yelled from the front door. 'Can we take Bramble for a walk? *Please*?'

'Oh . . .' She paused, her default response being to say, 'Not today.' But why not, she reasoned? She called Carys, who was busy with visitors but said they were welcome to borrow their dog. So the three of them picked him up and headed off on a stroll into the hills.

Going for walks was something Lucy and the children had started doing together in recent months, even when they didn't have a canine companion. She suspected it was unusual for children to enjoy it quite as much as Sam and Marnie did; but then, at home she was often busy with B&B guests, and this way they had her all to themselves.

Curiously, they had never got around to exploring the countryside quite as much when Ivan had still been here. He had never really embraced the idea of heading up into the hills – although he'd implied that it was the kids who were reluctant. 'Moving to the country doesn't mean they'll suddenly love hoofing for miles,' he'd teased Lucy, shortly after they'd moved in. 'They're city kids, remember. They're used to having stuff all around them, loads to look at, all kinds of life going on.'

'There's loads going on here too,' she had argued, but he'd been right: back then, the delights of spotting cows, sheep and even ponies had worn off after some twenty minutes, and many of their early meanderings involved a barrage of moaning and complaints of sore feet. But earlier this year Sam's love of space exploration had made way for a keenness on nature, and he'd decided to set up a natural history museum in his bedroom, which

169

would require exhibits (as well as an admission fee of 20p). Was this unusual for a seven-year-old boy, Lucy wondered? In some ways, he seemed young for his age – or perhaps just a little old-fashioned, not that this was a bad thing at all. She loved to see Sam collecting interesting pebbles, feathers, scraps of sheep's wool and even the occasional tiny animal skull on their walks.

Before long he was *asking* to go out. Whilst the museum was very much 'his' project, Marnie enjoyed helping him, crying out, 'Sam – how about this?' when she spotted a tiny blue egg or an unusual pine cone lying on a path. It had sharpened their perception and turned their walks into treasure hunts. They were now hugely pleasurable for all three of them, and Lucy suspected the walks were doing them all good, in all kinds of ways.

As they walked, they chatted. She discovered that the children were far more likely to share their feelings as they plodded along – sometimes holding her hands, sometimes running ahead – than if she tried to sit them down for A Proper Talk at home. Today, Bramble was the focus as they strode up through the hills and the woods, returning with armfuls of foliage to add to the jugs of flowers in the house.

'It looks lovely in here,' Carys enthused later, when she turned up with Amber and Noah to collect their now exhausted spaniel. Much later still, when her own children were in bed, Lucy picked up her phone and noticed a text.

Great to see you today, it read. *Look forward to next time and please remember my offer, James.* He'd only just sent it. There was no mention of him being appalled at her tearful outburst, or the fact that she had mopped up a gallon of snot with the tea towel that now lay in the bin.

Thank you, great to see you too, Lx, she replied. While she wasn't sure whether their friendship would rekindle properly, she couldn't help being impressed with how he'd been with her today. Some people ran away from grief. They treated it like an unpredictable dog; it scared them, and they didn't know how to handle it. But James had known, and a sense of warmth filled her heart now as she thought of him. And something else happened too. Somehow, as Lucy headed upstairs to bed that night, she felt a little less alone.

Chapter Eighteen

James couldn't quite believe what he was doing. He never talked about personal stuff, not even with friends, really – because the men he knew didn't really act like that. They tended to be practical types he'd met through his boat-fitting work and emotions were generally kept under wraps.

Yet here he was, two weeks after Lucy had invited him over for coffee, back here again. She had spotted him in the bakery and darted in to say hi. It had surprised him how happy he'd been to see her. She looked lovely with her dark, glossy hair worn loose, and a flush to her face.

Now they were sitting at her garden table, and he was telling her that the mother of his child – the woman he'd been with for eleven years – had had an affair. Lucy pushed back her hair and encouraged him to go on. 'So, you really had no idea?'

He shook his head. 'I suppose I should have. I felt like an idiot for not spotting the signs. But Michaela was a brilliant mum, and in the early years I'd assumed she was happy to not be going out to work, and spending as much time as possible with Spike.'

It was true. She'd always seemed to have endless energy and patience, and Spike adored her. But as he grew older and started school, she started to suffer from anxiety and insomnia. She had returned to work as a legal secretary and said that her job was stressing her out. 'I'd tried to convince her that we could manage on my earnings,' he continued, 'but she was adamant that she wanted to be working too – and of course that was fine. I understood that. A couple of years went by, and when Spike was seven, she started to act all weird and jumpy and not like herself at all.'

Lucy nodded as if she understood, and again, James wondered why he was telling her all this. He hadn't planned to tell her anything really; it had just tumbled out.

'Was she stressed?' she asked. 'I mean, it's hard going out to work when you have young children. You want to work, and be part of the outside world again – but then there's guilt about not being there constantly . . .'

He sipped from his mug. 'Yeah, she said that was it – that she was stressed and anxious. I suggested she see her GP, but Michaela was always a bit anti-doctors and started seeing an acupuncturist instead – first for the anxiety and then for other stuff, like migraines, back pain, toothache, stuff I had no idea she had . . .' He broke off and paused. He knew he should head off to his dad's place soon – he'd stopped off at Lucy's as soon as he arrived – even though he could happily sit here all day.

'Toothaches?' she prompted him.

'Yep. I suggested she saw a dentist for that, and she said, "Why are you so closed-minded?"'

173

They both smiled, and he noticed how very green Lucy's eyes were in the sunshine. 'Because you'd suggested that a dentist might be the best person for seeing to teeth?'

He nodded. 'She said the acupuncture was really helping her, and she did seem more content generally, since she'd been seeing her. It was all Ally-this, Ally-that. She said it was therapeutic.'

As they got up and went inside for more coffee, James decided he'd babbled on enough. It had been a painful time in his life, but he was over it now and, again, he wasn't quite sure why or how he'd ended up sharing all of this with Lucy. She seemed genuinely interested – and, yes, she'd been the one to start on the subject, by gently asking about Spike, and Spike's mum and what had happened between them. But he didn't want Lucy to think he was badmouthing his ex, and he hoped it wasn't coming across that way. It surprised him, the way it seemed to matter what Lucy thought of him. He was a little in awe of her, he realised. Despite everything that had happened to her she seemed so capable and strong.

Today, he'd learned more about her impressive floristry sideline: parties, christenings, all kinds of special occasions. There were plenty of grand country weddings around here, and as word spread he was sure she would soon be in high demand. James had a wedding to attend to himself in a few weeks' time. Phyllida Somerville was a local dignitary whose daughter was getting married. His father was invited; he had supplied firewood to the family for many years, and they were still fond of him. When the invitation had arrived, James had realised he'd have to brace himself, dig out a suit and accompany his dad.

In Lucy's kitchen now, she refilled their mugs from the

percolator and motioned for him to take a seat at the table. He spotted her glancing at her phone on the table. 'I need to pick up the kids from school in half an hour,' she started.

'Oh, God – I'm sorry,' James exclaimed. 'I've taken up way too much of your time yet again.'

'No, I didn't mean that,' she said, smiling now. 'But you were telling me . . .'

'I've really gone on. I'm sorry.' He raked at his hair and cleared his throat.

She laughed, and just then it was as if she hadn't changed at all from the girl who'd been up for all kinds of adventures. '*I* went on last time, didn't I? I told you all about Ivan, and I cried, and—'

'Yes, but that was different.'

'Anyway, you're not going on,' she said firmly. 'What I meant was, I'm really curious to know what happened next, about the acupuncturist, I mean.'

Ah, so she'd guessed. Of course she had.

'I don't mean that in an idle gossip kind of way,' she added quickly, 'but, well, there's this thing with Ivan – this thing that doesn't quite add up. You know.' She flushed and looked down momentarily at her mug. 'But never mind that. What I meant was, I'm genuinely interested. And you were saying?'

'You don't have much time—'

'So, what happened?' she cut in. 'I mean, how did you find out?'

And so he told her, and by the time they left the house – with her heading to school and him to his car – James had shared more about his personal life with Lucy than he had ever told anyone else.

He parked at his dad's house, but he didn't go in

175

immediately. Instead, he sat there in his car, feeling a little overwhelmed by how much he'd shared with Lucy today. And now he was replaying that scene, three years ago, when he'd stupidly said to Michaela, 'Aren't these acupuncture sessions costing quite a lot? I don't mean it's a problem. Of course, you can see whoever you like.'

'Oh, so you're saying I should ask your permission?' Michaela had shot back.

'Of course not,' he'd exclaimed.

'Why are you bringing up the cost issue, then?' She'd glared at him, her hazel eyes narrowed in disdain.

James had been stuck for words for a moment. What had started with a casual enquiry had been turned around to look as if he begrudged her spending money on looking after herself, which of course he didn't.

'What about all the money you've spent on those tents and sleeping bags, the camping stove and chairs and all that?'

'But . . . that was for camping,' he'd pointed out.

'Obviously,' she remarked, 'and that's fine, isn't it – because it's something *you* wanted to do.'

James had stared at her, unsure of how to proceed, or what the real issue was here. This whole exchange was being conducted in muttered, angry tones, so that Spike – who was watching something on his laptop upstairs – wouldn't hear them. 'I thought you liked camping?' James said.

'No, actually, I hate it!' Michaela snapped. 'It's you who loves being outdoors, sleeping on a bloody blow-up bed and heating up beans on that crappy little stove.'

'Spike loved it!'

She glared at him. 'Of course he did. He's a child. But what about me, and what I might enjoy?'

'Why didn't you say,' he started, 'if you hated it?'

'After you'd spent all that money? What would've been the point?'

He'd felt as if he'd been punched. The previous summer they had driven from Liverpool to Plymouth and taken the ferry to Brittany, where they had booked a pitch at a beautiful campsite right on the coast, and had had two glorious weeks there. They'd swum and fished and built campfires, and come back to the tent happy – at least, he'd thought they were happy – and reeking of woodsmoke from the driftwood they'd burnt. He could hardly bear to think of it now. 'I thought you loved it too,' he'd said.

'I'd have loved it a lot more,' Michaela retorted, 'if we'd had a hotel room with a bed in it.' The implication that he not only begrudged Michaela spending money on acupuncture, but had also forced her to spend a fortnight in a tent, wholly against her will, made him feel terribly uneasy, and a few nights later he found her sitting bolt upright at the kitchen table as if she were about to make an announcement.

'Could you sit down please, James?' she asked him.

Obediently, he lowered himself onto a kitchen chair. 'Kels . . .' That had been his nickname for her. 'What is it?'

He saw her mouth twitch as she picked at the varnish on a fingernail. 'I'm sorry, James . . .' She looked down. 'I've been seeing somebody else.'

He blinked at her across the table. Her expression seemed oddly neutral, as if she had mooted the possibility of upgrading their kitchen worktops.

'What d'you mean, *seeing* someone? You mean sleeping with them?'

She nodded, her cheeks flushing pink.

'Who is it?' he asked hollowly.

Michaela cast her gaze downwards. 'It's, um . . . my acupuncturist.'

At first he thought it was a joke, perhaps to get him back for 'dragging' her camping. But now her eyes had filled with tears and he realised it wasn't a joke at all.

'You're having an affair?'

Michaela had nodded mutely. So many questions had rushed through James's mind then, such as: 'You're leaving me for a woman?' Not that that would have been any worse, or better; just even more startling, if that were possible. But no, it turned out that Ally was actually *Ali*, a man called Alistair Jenkins, who lived a couple of miles away in an area of Liverpool far more salubrious than their own. James had just assumed the acupuncturist was female. He had also assumed that he and Michaela were still happy – or at least, content enough in that long-term-couple kind of way.

How wrong he had been. That evening he learned that Ali hadn't even been Michaela's acupuncturist beyond that first appointment; they'd taken to meeting for pots of chamomile tea instead. 'It was all very cerebral,' she explained, which had made him want to punch a hole in the wall. 'For ages, we just chatted about stuff.'

Oh, how sodding cosy! How bloody *therapeutic* that must have been.

'Right – so you held off jumping into bed,' he snapped. 'That makes me feel so much better!'

The next day Michaela had moved in with a friend from work, which turned out to be a temporary measure as, within a couple of months, she and Ali had rented a place together (it had turned out that he was married too). And soon, a rather bewildered but accepting Spike was spending half the week there. Ali was 'all right', he said, when James quizzed him. His mum's new flat was 'nice', his bedroom 'pretty good really'. He was seven at the time. Michaela had bought him the Xbox he'd been asking for (i.e. bribed him) and all seemed right with his world.

It wasn't that James had been utterly passive in all of this. He had tried to reason with her, and on one sorry occasion, after downing two-thirds of a bottle of scotch – he wasn't a whisky drinker normally – he had phoned her and cried and begged her to come back. He had even told Lucy that part today, about the whisky (what the hell *had* he been thinking?). But Michaela had said no, and told him that he should have 'known' she wasn't happy. James had ranted some more and kicked the kitchen bin, making a huge dent in it, which he would later have to explain away to Spike by saying, somewhat unfeasibly, that he 'knocked it with some shopping'. Cerebral Ali grabbed the phone and barked, 'Accept it's over, James. It's time to move on.'

'Oh, is it?' James had fumed. He must have hurled his phone at a vase Michaela's mother had given them, because hours later James had woken on the sofa wondering why his broken phone was lying in a puddle of water and flowers and broken glass.

He'd told Lucy that bit too – about the phone and the broken vase. What must she think after hearing about him being a phone-smashing, bin-kicking maniac who'd necked almost an entire bottle of whisky in one go? And he wondered again: why did it matter to him what she thought? After all, they hardly knew each other really.

But it did matter, he realised, as he climbed out of his

car and made his way across the scrubby ground to his father's house. It mattered very much and actually, he felt okay that he'd shared it all with her. At least, he thought he did. Anyway, he'd done it now.

Chapter Nineteen

As spring edged its way into a glorious summer, the steady stream of guests brought benefits – and not just in providing Lucy with an income. It meant there was little time for her to stop and wonder where her life was going, and what her future held. Looking after these strangers, as well as her children, was pulling her along, and the long summer's days often saw Rosemary Cottage's garden filled with children as Marnie and Sam had friends over to play.

Whereas once Lucy had crept in to steal redcurrants, now her own kids' friends would arrive en masse for lengthy games and sprawling picnics that Lucy would somehow manage to throw together with zero notice. She made real lemonade, syrupy flapjacks and mounds of chocolate chip cookies, which she would dole out whilst still warm from the oven. She had become known amongst the other mums for 'going the extra mile', as Carys put it, fondly – and perhaps she was trying to compensate for something she *couldn't* give Marnie and Sam.

She probably didn't need to go to such lengths. Her garden seemed irresistible to children anyway – perhaps because everything grew abundantly and was wild and cottagey, rather than neat. Lucy was happy for the children to play freely here, and so tents were pitched, dens constructed, blankets and cushions dragged outside, and Bramble the spaniel was a near-permanent fixture as he scampered around on the lawn.

James had taken to dropping round too, and she welcomed his company. She had learned more about his home life and about Spike, whom he clearly adored, and even more about the break-up with his son's mother.

'Things settled down,' he told her, when she'd gently quizzed him about where things stood one Sunday in June as they drank tea in her garden. Chocolate-sausage-Josh was here, and the three children were busily building a den, involving a wooden clothes horse and blankets and no small degree of bossing by Marnie.

'After the phone smashing and whisky slugging,' Lucy remarked with a smile.

James nodded and smiled too, and told her that he'd managed to behave rationally even when, that first summer after she'd left, Facebook had buckled under the sheer quantity of Michaela's holiday photos – just like *their* photos, but with James replaced by Ali, and the Brittany coast swapped for Ali's holiday home in Gran Canaria, complete with hot tub on the decking, in which the three of them were pictured, grinning in the bubbles, as if life was just one big long jacuzzi now. But at least Spike seemed fine, which was all that mattered really.

She learned that James had met Ali, the acupuncturist, numerous times, when he'd picked up or dropped off

Spike from his ex's new place – and managed to remain civil, partly because Ali was something like six foot five with a barrel chest and oddly dense, vertically sitting hair, 'like a sandy-coloured shag-pile carpet,' as James put it. They chuckled over his description.

The two men's encounters tended to be mercifully brief, he explained: the first involving an awkward handshake on Michaela and Ali's doorstep, when it had felt as if Ali had wanted to crush his bones, and James had certainly wanted to punch him extremely hard. However, over the months and years, James – and, crucially, Spike – had become used to the new shape of things.

'Are things still working out with Rikke?' Lucy asked as they headed indoors; the day was growing cooler and she needed to cook dinner for the kids. Sam and Marnie had accepted her friendship with James without question, and why not? She enjoyed him being around. It made a pleasant change to have a man about the place from time to time.

'She's brilliant,' James replied. 'I don't know what I'd do without her, to be honest.'

'No sign of your brother coming back?'

'Doesn't look like it at the moment. Seems like Switzerland's his home now – at least, for as long as this liaison lasts.'

Lucy smiled and gave James a quick glance as she extracted pizzas from the freezer. Occasionally, she wondered whether he had had many 'liaisons' since he and Spike's mum had split up. He hadn't mentioned anyone, and she got the impression that with his son, his work and weekly dashes to Burley Bridge to see his father, James's life was pretty full.

'I forgot,' he said as he was about to leave. 'I have

something in the car for you. It came from a boat I was working on—'

'What is it?' Lucy asked.

They headed outside where he lifted an enormous cork pinboard from the boot of his car. 'Please say if you don't want it,' James said quickly. 'I just thought, with Sam having that museum in his room, maybe it'd be handy—'

'Oh, I'm sure it would,' she started.

'I don't want to dump it on you.' He smiled apologetically.

'No,' she said, beaming, 'it's fantastic. That's so thoughtful of you . . . but doesn't Spike want it?'

James shook his head. 'He's always rescuing bits and bobs from the boats I work on. There's not a spare inch of space on his bedroom wall.'

'Well, thank you for thinking of us.' Lucy called Sam over as James carried the board towards the house. 'Look what James brought for your room, love. You could pin exhibits to it – feathers, leaves and all sorts . . .'

'That's great,' he enthused. 'Thanks!' The sight of her son grinning up at James made Lucy's heart turn over. How lucky they were in so many ways, she reflected, with friends who cared about them. And how lucky *she* was that she had run into James in the hospital car park last year.

As he left that day, she hugged him warmly without a second's thought, and it felt just right.

Chapter Twenty

How good it felt to be back in Manchester for the day, in a buzzy bistro with bare wooden tables and bright Sixties graphic prints on the walls. Andrew and Nadeen, Lucy's best friends from her old workplace, had finally persuaded her to drive over for a long lunch. Although they had always kept in touch, it had shocked Lucy to realise that it had been months since she'd ventured further than Heathfield. The trip had required lipstick, plus a thought-about outfit including her low-heeled patent shoes that hadn't seen the light of day since she'd left the city. In Burley Bridge she was welded to her walking boots, Birkenstocks and wellies and, admittedly, sprucing herself up again had felt pretty refreshing.

She had bought Marnie's birthday presents in town – Sam's eighth birthday had passed the previous week – and now she and her friends were catching up, talking over each other, repeatedly having to apologise to the waiter for not even having looked at the menu yet. 'You kept this talent quiet,' Nadeen exclaimed as Lucy showed them pictures of her latest floral displays on her phone.

'I always dabbled,' she said with a grin, 'but I kept it under the radar at work.'

'Like a dirty secret,' Andrew sniggered.

Lucy nodded. 'I didn't think flower arranging would rank that coolly as a hobby.'

Nadeen laughed. 'You thought it sounded a bit nana-ish, didn't you?'

'Yeah.' She chuckled. 'And I knew MC had me down as being a bit traditional anyway. Anyway, how are things there—'

'We'll come to that later,' Andrew said impatiently, peering at her screen. 'Look at that gorgeous shop display, Nads. God, Lucy – it's so professional!'

'I *am* professional,' she teased him. 'At least, I try my best to appear so.'

'Talk about multi-tasking,' Nadeen murmured approvingly. 'Any more jobs coming up?'

'Funnily enough, my hairdresser called to say someone wants me to do some wedding flowers. Phyllida-someone. It's her daughter's wedding next month and apparently the florist has let them down so they're pretty stuck.'

Nadeen's dark eyes widened. When she'd arrived, Lucy had noticed how pulled-together her friends looked: Andrew in his box-fresh pale blue T-shirt and black skinny jeans, his dark hair immaculately cropped, and Nadeen in a snug-fitting pink sweater and denim skirt, her glossy, jet-black bob looking perfect as ever. Both child-free, her friends had always exuded glamour at work, as had most of Lucy's other colleagues; it was just the way things were at Claudine, and back then, she had probably stopped registering it. Although she knew Nadeen and Andrew would never judge her, Lucy was thankful now that she had made a special effort with her appearance today.

186

'Are you going to do it?' Andrew asked after their orders had finally been taken. 'This wedding, I mean?'

'I haven't heard anything yet,' Lucy said. 'My hairdresser just wanted to check it was okay to pass on my number.' She paused. 'So, come on. What's the latest at work?'

Andrew glanced at Nadeen and rolled his eyes. 'It's a car-crash, Luce. You know Claude was supposed to be a separate brand, so it didn't affect the main lingerie lines?'

She nodded. 'So MC's still going ahead with that? I thought it might be just a whim.'

'A flash in the pants?' Andrew quipped, and they all sniggered before he turned serious. 'Unfortunately not. Those elephant briefs are already out there in loads of stores. Have you seen the press coverage?'

Lucy shook her head. 'Not really, no.' She felt lamentably out of touch with the fashion retail world these days.

'Well, we've pretty much lurched down the stag party route now,' Nadeen said with a grimace. 'It's awful, Luce. You wouldn't recognise the place.'

'What made him do this?' Lucy asked, baffled. 'It seems mad. It's not what Claudine's known for at all. It'd be no weirder if he suggested launching a range of, I don't know – air fresheners or biscuits. It just doesn't fit.'

Nadeen shrugged. 'I guess he assumed the party thing's a massive market, and we all know that kind of tat costs pennies to produce. It's his background, apparently – stag and hen novelties. He made a huge success of it in his last job.'

'But so far, not with us,' Andrew added. 'It's completely bombed, as far as we can tell. We'll probably all be out on our ear soon. Don't suppose you need a gardener at Rosemary Cottage?'

187

Lucy gave him a pained smile. 'You can't even keep a cactus alive,' she reminded him, 'and the countryside makes you feel weird.'

'No, I like it – to visit.' He grinned.

'Anyway, you're lucky to be out of it all,' Nadeen added, then caught herself: 'Sorry, I didn't mean—'

'No, I know I'm lucky in a lot of ways,' Lucy said quickly.

'You're amazing,' Nadeen added. 'You seem so . . . together these days. So positive again.'

'You really do,' Andrew said, squeezing her hand.

Lucy chuckled. 'Don't make me cry, you two. Let's not get emotional—'

'Check out this then.' Andrew whipped out his phone and brought up a picture to show her. '*This* is what you're missing at work.'

'What is it?' Lucy leaned forward.

'More creatures have been released into the wild,' he sniggered.

'Tiger pants!' Lucy gasped, peering at the screen.

'Yep, they're the newest,' Andrew explained. 'And look – there are bears, hippos, a cuddly koala . . .' The three became hysterical as Andrew scrolled through the new additions.

'Just in case you ever find yourself missing the place,' Nadeen said with a smirk.

Lucy smiled. 'I miss you two but I don't miss, you know – the job.'

'Well, you have a job anyway,' Andrew reminded her. 'Two, in fact. You run a thriving B&B *and* you're a top florist now.'

'I don't know about that,' she said, 'but, you know, I am thinking, maybe I could step things up a level.'

'What d'you mean?' he asked.

They broke off as a selection of small plates were brought to their table: delicious tapas-style dishes of the kind that Lucy hadn't encountered since she left the city. Lucy considered Andrew's question for a moment. She would always love and miss Ivan, of course she would; her life had changed forever on that Euston-to-Manchester-Piccadilly train. Likewise, she would forever be Mum to Marnie and Sam, and remember the baby that might have been. Those aspects were all vital parts of her, but they weren't *all* that she was. She was only forty-three years old – since when did forty start being preceded by 'only', she wondered? – and, hopefully, there were decades ahead of her.

'I'm thinking,' she said, 'there are a few old-fashioned florists in Heathfield, the kind that do bog-standard bouquets and centrepieces, that kind of thing. If I was more proactive in actually attracting work, then I'm sure I could be a lot busier.' She paused as they all started to tuck in. Lucy had already decided she would avoid offering funeral flowers; she couldn't face being involved in anyone's loss, even from a distance. For Ivan's cremation service – operating on autopilot, really – she had ordered a casket spray, and along had come a stiff arrangement of lemon and cream roses, which hadn't seemed right at all.

'D'you think you'd manage,' Andrew asked, spearing a marinated pepper, 'on top of the B&B and the family . . .?'

'Rikke helps out,' she said. 'I'm sure I could handle it if I was organised. I've been thinking about dropping off cards at local businesses,' she went on, 'and setting up a website and social media accounts. What d'you think of

189

"Sweetpea Special Occasion Flowers" for my business name?'

'I love it,' Andrew enthused.

'It's perfect,' Nadeen added. 'Honestly – I know you can do it.' By the end of their lunch, Lucy did too, and as they hugged goodbye she had already made up her mind that she was ready to take things to the next level. The day had done her so much good, she decided as they parted company.

Lucy was climbing into her car when her phone rang in her bag. The children were at Carys's for the day – school had broken up for the summer – and instinctively, she snatched it in alarm. But it wasn't Carys. It was a number she didn't recognise.

'Lucy? It's Phyllida Somerville,' the woman said. 'Nicola was kind enough to give me your number. Is this a good time?'

'Yes, it's fine,' Lucy said brightly as she buckled her seatbelt.

'Great. So, I gather you do flowers for all kinds of occasions?' Her accent was clipped upper class; she said 'flarze' rather than 'flowers'.

'Yes, that's right,' Lucy said.

'I've phoned a couple of times,' Phyllida added, in a tone that suggested to Lucy that she was being told off. She realised now that the missed calls she'd noticed yesterday must have been from her too. Lucy really would have to become more organised. She was terrible at remembering to check her voicemail messages.

'I'm sorry,' she said.

'Not to worry. I have you now. It's just, my daughter's getting married in three weeks' time and our florist has pulled out.'

'Oh, that's terrible.'

Phyllida sighed loudly. 'She says she's taken on far too much and sounds like she's having a bit of a breakdown – but honestly, she's really let Emma and Dylan down. I'd have thought we'd be a priority, seeing as we booked months ago. So, anyway – I'm really hoping you can help.'

Lucy wondered if Phyllida was always this unsympathetic when it came to other people's mental health.

'What kind of thing are you looking for?' she asked.

'Something natural and fresh,' Phyllida explained. 'We don't want imported flowers and we certainly don't want any of those nasty, artificially dyed monstrosities. I'm thinking a casual, country look at the church. Just garden flowers, a few sweetpeas and whatnot . . .'

Lucy smiled at her brusqueness. 'Well, I only use natural materials I've gathered locally,' she explained. 'I don't buy in any flowers at all. In fact, at the moment, most come from my own garden.'

'Oh, that sounds perfect,' Phyllida announced, sounding relieved, as if Lucy had agreed to take on the job already. 'I'm thinking a casual, country look. You're highly recommended around the village – but have you done any weddings before?'

'No, not exactly . . .'

'What *have* you done?'

Lucy frowned. Was this a phone interview? 'Various shops in the village,' she started. 'The bookshop, hair salon, bakery, gallery – that kind of thing. And the foyer at Lupin's Hotel.'

'Hmm.' Phyllida paused. 'I'm sorry – I don't mean to be pushy or rude. My daughter is adamant that it doesn't matter, but of course it does. She's young, you know. She thinks it's cool to not care, to be ever-so-casual – but I know she'll regret it later if we don't pull something spectacular together.' Her voice had softened. 'Would you mind terribly if I asked you to come over for a chat?'

'Phyllida—' Lucy hesitated. 'I'd love to help out but a whole wedding, by myself—'

'We're only talking flowers at the church, then the reception here at my home,' she said firmly, which didn't sound *quite* like a few sweetpeas and whatnot. But now Lucy remembered how full of enthusiasm she'd felt in the restaurant with Andrew and Nadeen. Hadn't she just said she wanted to step things up? 'Do you know Fordell House?' Phyllida went on. 'That's where I live.'

'Oh, yes, of course.' Sam and Marnie had been fascinated by the grand, turreted house when they had passed by on one of their walks recently. Who lived there, they'd asked? Would they have servants?

'Emma always planned to make the bouquets for her bridesmaid and herself,' Phyllida went on. 'So you wouldn't need to worry about those.' *Oh, that's okay then!* Lucy smiled, warming to Phyllida now the curtness was starting to fade away.

'Okay,' she said. 'I could pop over tomorrow, if that suits you, and bring a list of suggestions—'

'That's wonderful, thank you,' Phyllida cut in, sounding immediately relieved. 'I'm very much looking forward to meeting you, Lucy. It's been a terrible worry and you really are helping us out.'

As if everything was agreed already, Lucy thought with a smile as she pulled out of the parking space. Clearly, Phyllida Somerville was a woman used to getting her own way.

Chapter Twenty-One

'I'm just dashing out, Mum,' Lucy said when Anna called the following afternoon. 'Can I ring you a bit later?' Her mother had a habit of calling at inopportune moments. She had already made it clear that she thought Lucy was crazy to start doing B&B again, and she knew how she'd react if she mentioned the possibility of doing wedding flowers on top of everything else.

'Oh, are you going somewhere with the children?' she asked.

'No, they're at holiday club today,' Lucy replied, checking the kitchen clock. She had agreed to be at Phyllida's in twenty minutes.

'Really? Are you . . . working?' What on earth did she mean by that? She knew how Lucy filled her days.

'Mum, I'm just . . .' She paused, reminding herself that her mother probably didn't mean it in a critical way. Lucy was aware that she was still prone to bouts of hypersensitivity. 'They enjoy it,' she said. 'Lots of their friends go too. But, look, I really have to go. I have an appointment . . .' There was a pause, during which she was probably supposed to furnish her mum with more details, but she just left it hanging there.

'Right. Well, I just wanted to say, your dad and I have been talking.'

'What about?' Lucy asked, her heart sinking a little as she picked up her bag and slung it over her shoulder, then made her way to the front door.

'I know what you'll say but please bear with me.' Lucy inhaled deeply. She knew what was coming next. 'A house has come up,' Anna continued. 'I know you want to see the year out—' *See the year out?* When had she ever said that? '—but it's so lovely – just right for you and the kids. The best part is – it's in our road!'

Lucy opened her mouth to speak but no words came. She stepped outside, locked the door and marched to her car. 'Dad's holding it for you,' Anna continued. 'Will you at least come over and look at it? You could be all moved in and settled by—'

'Mum, we're not moving,' she exclaimed. 'You know I'm running a business again here. Well, two businesses really.'

'But don't you think—'

'Could you put Dad on please?' Lucy said tersely.

'He's having a lie-down right now,' she muttered.

'What's wrong? Is he okay?'

'Oh, he's just going on about some dizziness thing now, *another* ailment, as if I have time for that.'

'What kind of ailment?' Lucy asked, frowning as she climbed into her car.

'Nothing really. He's fine when his friends call and they ask him out for a drink, but at home – no, he's dying—'

'Mum!'

'You know what I mean,' she said briskly.

'*What* does Dad have?'

'Oh, something with a ridiculous name,' her mother remarked. 'Labyrinth-something. Sounds like a board game to me.'

'D'you mean labyrinthitis?' Lucy asked. 'That's a real thing, Mum. It can affect the balance and be pretty nasty. Has he seen a doctor?'

'He's never away from the doctor's,' she crowed.

'Well, maybe he's actually ill!'

'What about me? I never catch any of these peculiar viruses. I don't have *time* to be ill.'

Knowing the conversation would continue in this vein, Lucy turned on the ignition. 'Mum, I'm really sorry but I can't talk now—'

'You're going to your appointment?'

'Yes.'

A beat's silence. '*You're* not ill, are you, darling?'

'No, Mum,' Lucy said, trying to keep her voice level. 'I'm not ill. I'm great, actually, but sorry – I really do have to go.'

Lucy's exasperation soon dissipated as she pulled into the expansive grounds of Fordell House. There was a huge, peeling Victorian greenhouse, and what she could see of the garden looked rather formal and uninspiring, as if someone certainly kept it tidy but didn't possess much in the way of creativity or love for the place. The house itself looked a little faded too, although the vast, pale pink landmark was still impressive, nestling amongst the hills with nothing else around. Lucy trotted up the wide stone stairs, and before she had even reached the door, it opened.

195

'Lucy, hello, thank you so much for coming.' Phyllida greeted her warmly and shook her hand. She was a tall, statuesque woman with neatly coiffed silvery hair and piercing blue eyes, and was wearing casual checked trousers and a peachy-hued sweater. Although in her seventies at a guess, she had a vibrancy about her and looked as if she led an active life, and Lucy decided she was the kind of woman who took no nonsense from anyone.

She was led into a panelled hallway and along a corridor lined with numerous paintings of the kind of rural landscapes that could have depicted almost anywhere: hills, lakes, forests, in ornate gilt frames and dulled with age. Phyllida showed Lucy into a sun-dappled drawing room with yellow drapes and richly patterned rugs scattered about. The atmosphere was of faded opulence, and Lucy had a fleeting sense of wondering why she was here and how on earth she would manage to pull off this job by herself.

'Do sit down,' Phyllida said. They no sooner perched on stiffly upholstered chairs than a young man in a crisp white shirt and smart black trousers swept in. He was carrying a cake stand laden with scones and pots of cream and jam, plus a tray bearing a teapot, cups and saucers.

'Lucy, this is Davide,' Phyllida said.

'Hi,' she said, and he greeted her with a warm smile and handshake before pouring their teas.

'Thank you so much,' Lucy said, at which he just nodded and murmured something in French. Once he'd melted away into another room, Lucy outlined her ideas for seasonal flowers, with Phyllida making grand, rather confusing statements such as, 'I'd like a sense

196

of *abundance* – you know? We're looking to decorate the church pews, and have some fabulous display by the altar, and perhaps by the entrance too?' She paused. 'Do have a scone. Davide bakes them – they're very good . . .'

Obediently, Lucy helped herself, and it was indeed delicious, even though she barely felt like eating in her rather nervous state. 'Then we'll need flowers here at the house, of course,' Phyllida went on. 'I'd love to see something spectacular going up our main staircase, let me show you . . .' She leapt up and marched across the room with Lucy in pursuit.

'Okay, yep,' Lucy was now scribbling in her notepad as she gazed up at the impressive stairwell. The house was furnished with antiques, seemingly from a mishmash of eras, and cluttered with china ornaments of horses and dogs. There was a velvet-upholstered chaise longue in the hallway, which was shabbily beautiful, if a little moth-eaten. Dust particles danced in the air.

'We'll need table centrepieces,' Phyllida continued, waving an arm around as she led Lucy into a panelled dining room, 'and perhaps something dramatic for the porch. I'm thinking tall structures, bursting from pots.' She frowned suddenly. 'You don't go around tearing up plants from the countryside, do you?'

'Oh, no,' Lucy said quickly. 'As I said on the phone, most of it comes from my own garden, and a neighbour says it's fine to cut foliage from the land behind her house. D'you know Irene, from the post office in the village?'

'Yes, of course, I know everyone around here.'

'Well, she's been very generous.' Even as she said it, Lucy had figured that she would have to be especially inventive in order to source such a vast quantity of

197

materials without having to plunder the countryside too much. It was fine to take a little – but she was careful about never damaging wild plants or leaving them looking depleted. She would certainly need to find new places to forage if this second business of hers continued to grow at this pace.

Lucy wound up the meeting by showing Phyllida some sketches she'd done, showing various arrangements she could pull together, plus photographs of her recent creations on her iPad. However, it seemed as if Phyllida was sold on her already.

'I have every confidence in you, Lucy,' she said as she saw her out. 'I've walked past your place and I have to say I'm impressed with what you've done to the house and garden.' She paused. 'I am right, aren't I, that you're the family in Rosemary Cottage?'

'Yes, that's right,' Lucy replied, wondering if she, too, had heard about Ivan.

'How lovely! Kitty was a great friend of mine. I miss her terribly. You always do, don't you, when you lose someone who was dear to you?'

'Uh, yes, I guess so,' Lucy said, sensing a twist in her heart.

Phyllida smiled wistfully. 'I still find it hard sometimes to accept that she's gone. We spent so many happy afternoons together in her garden.' Lucy nodded, momentarily stuck for words. 'But she'd be delighted that those redcurrant bushes of hers are in such capable hands,' she added, patting Lucy's hand.

As she pulled out of the wide, sweeping drive, she wondered how on earth she would make a start on all of this, and pictured Ivan, gently teasing her. Before the accident, she had never thought she believed that the dead had any connection with the living. Once you were gone, you were gone, she thought: into the earth, to nourish the soil and fertilise new growth, or to be scattered and carried away on a breeze. It was the natural way of things and she supposed she was okay with that. But now, her views had shifted. It wasn't so much that she believed in heaven in an angels-on-clouds sense, or indeed in any kind of afterlife; more a feeling that the man she loved was still with her, somehow. She could feel him close, and picture him smiling at what she had agreed to take on.

'I do hope I've been clear,' had been Phyllida's parting shot today, 'and it's not too much for you, Lucy. Please do say now, if you're not sure.'

'No, I'm sure it'll be fine,' Lucy had said firmly, trying to exude confidence and smiling now at the thought of the task ahead of her. An entire lavish wedding, all by herself? It was helipad madness all right.

Chapter Twenty-Two

'Well, I do hope you're going to call her and say you've changed your mind,' Lucy's mother announced when she arrived the following week. A mercifully *short* stay was how Lucy regarded it; guilt-making, naturally, but she was still feeling rather prickly about Anna's insistence that she must sell up and move to Leeds.

When it was just Lucy and the children, they muddled along. The three of them were a tight little unit now. They had found their new rhythm, and as Lucy launched herself back into day-to-day life, starting to plan and gather materials for Phyllida's daughter's wedding flowers, she had reflected again that they had a great deal to be thankful for.

'Of course I'm not going to change my mind,' she said. 'I'm delighted to be asked. It's about time I moved the business up a gear, Mum.'

She sensed her mother glancing at her as they strolled across the garden. Lucy had brought out coffee and cakes, thinking it would be lovely to enjoy them outdoors on this mild July afternoon. But Anna had been fidgety and

200

kept rubbing at her arms, even though she was wearing a sweater, and had finally asked if they could head back indoors.

'Would you ever consider going back?' she asked as they stepped into the house.

'Back where, Mum?' Lucy frowned.

'Back to Claudine – to that job of yours. You seemed happy there.'

'Of course not,' she said firmly. 'We're not moving back to Manchester. The thought has never even occurred to me. Anyway, they got rid of me, remember? A new boss came in and decided my face didn't fit. They wouldn't just have me back.'

'Well, if not there, how about looking for something in Leeds?' Anna suggested, affecting a casual tone. Lucy glanced at her, wondering where this was leading to. She had never intimated that she would consider going back to a full-time job. 'There must be plenty of fashion retailers based there,' Anna added.

'I'm sure there are,' Lucy said, 'but why would I—'

'I'm just worried you're not thinking things through,' her mother cut in.

'What d'you mean?'

Anna pursed her lips. 'Doing all these flowers – these occasions – as well as running things here.'

'Well, Rikke still helps out when I need her to, and there's the holiday club for the odd day when I'm really hectic and need to catch up on stuff—'

'Is the B&B really doing okay?' Anna asked, wincing.

Lucy frowned. 'We're doing great, Mum. Why d'you ask?'

'Well, there aren't any guests now . . .'

Lucy exhaled. There was no pleasing her mother;

according to her, Lucy was either too busy, taking on far too much, or not busy enough. 'I deliberately didn't accept any bookings for these few days you're here,' she explained, as patiently as she could manage. 'And there's Marnie's birthday coming up too. We have enough going on.'

Anna nodded, seemingly taking this in. 'But this wedding . . . it's a bit of a step-up from decorating a shop window, isn't it?'

Lucy looked at her. 'Yes, it is – and isn't that a good thing?'

She sensed her mother trying to figure out how best to put it. 'It just seems . . . a lot to take on, love. And using only local, natural plants, not even buying anything in – for a *wedding* . . .' She pulled a concerned face, as if Lucy had declared that she would be using only road-kill and decaying fish. Anna was a fan of bright, zingy, artificially dyed chrysanthemums and Lucy's more natural approach seemed to baffle her. 'It doesn't sound as if you'll be able to pull it all together from your garden,' she added.

'No, I realise that, Mum.' Lucy glanced at the kitchen wall clock and quickly calculated how long it would be until the children were back from a gymnastics session in the village hall. Carys had offered to walk them home, but now Lucy wished she and her mother had gone to meet them instead. Things were easier with Anna when the children were around to dilute things; plus, her mother would never badger her in this way in front of the kids.

'And I'm sure you're not allowed to wander all over other people's land willy-nilly,' Anna continued. 'That's the thing with the countryside, isn't it? You look at it, and you think, "Oh, isn't it stunning? I'm looking forward to exploring all of this!" Then you find out that pretty

202

much all of it belongs to someone and you're not allowed on it.'

Lucy exhaled slowly as she trimmed some green beans on the worktop. Anna had already rifled through a drawer and located a duster, and was now flicking it across the crockery on the dresser. It was going to be trying, this visit – but Lucy must remain calm. 'You're right – but there are footpaths, you know,' she remarked.

Anna fell silent for a few minutes. 'I wish you'd think about selling up,' she murmured eventually. 'You know it's the sensible option to move closer to home.'

'But this *is* our home, Mum,' Lucy said, as patiently as she could manage. 'We've been through this, haven't we? And we're doing okay – honestly. Can't you see that?' She watched her mother stretching up to dust the row of hand-painted coffee cups on the top shelf. Couldn't she ever relax and just *be*?

'Yes, but what about winter?' Anna asked.

'What d'you mean? It's only July, Mum. I'm not even thinking that far ahead.'

'*You* know,' Anna said, sounding impatient now. 'Spring and summer are fine here, I can see that. Even autumn's quite pleasant. But, God, the winter, darling – it's so long here. So bitter and dark.' As if it were northern Finland, and not rural West Yorkshire.

'You don't need to do that, Mum,' Lucy said, immediately regretting the sharpness in her voice.

'You mean worry about you? Of course I do.'

'No, I mean dust. I did it yesterday.'

'Well, it looked like it needed doing. I only want to help.'

Those five little words. Each time she'd visited since the accident, Anna must have uttered them dozens of times. On each occasion Lucy would feel her blood pressure rising.

I only want to help . . . Having left Lucy's father at home with Tilly for company, Anna seemed to have made it her mission to up the domestic standards at Rosemary Cottage.

Lucy detected lingering tension as she made a pot of tea, having virtually had to force her mother to sit down and drink it. 'So, would you like me to help with any jobs while I'm here?' Anna asked.

'No thanks,' Lucy replied. 'Just spend time with the kids when they get home. They'll love that. They should be home by five.'

'Yes, but I'd like to be useful,' Anna added.

'Spending time with Marnie and Sam *is* useful, Mum. Remember, I'm on my own here and I do virtually everything with them. I'm sure they'd love to play a game with you when they get home. There are loads in the cupboard . . .'

'Okay,' Anna said, clearly less than enamoured with the thought. Lucy could virtually hear her brain whirring as she tried to think of a more appealing alternative. 'Or,' she added, 'I could make a start on that shed.'

'What?'

'Well, I had a quick peep in earlier,' Anna remarked. 'It's a terrible tip.'

When had she managed to do that? *Fast work, Mum,* she thought dryly, reminding herself to remain as pleasant as possible and not lose her rag. It was difficult, though. Somehow, Anna's presence seemed to propel her back into being an irritable teenager. She was seized by an urge to stomp out of the room and hurtle upstairs to her bedroom.

'The shed's fine,' Lucy said firmly. 'It was a special place for Ivan and the kids and I don't really want to do anything with it right now.'

'Oh . . . okay, love.' Anna nodded, and a pause settled over them. 'What about the attic then?' she asked eventually. 'You said you'd just dumped stuff up there when you moved in. I was thinking, while I'm here, I could have a real go at it.'

'Please, Mum,' she exclaimed, 'I really don't want you taking on any of these jobs.'

Her mother looked at her. 'Darling . . . maybe it's time to tackle them. It's been, what . . .'

Lucy stared at her, aghast at what she knew her mother was going to say.

'It's been a year and a half,' Anna murmured, flushing a little.

Lucy cleared her throat and pushed away a strand of dark hair from her eyes. 'I know how long it's been, and I'll do those jobs when I'm ready.' The effort of sounding calm and reasonable was causing her heart to thump.

'Yes, love,' her mum said softly.

'Anyway, a friend's offered to help me with all that.'

'Which friend?'

'Um – d'you remember me mentioning a boy called Hally, when I used to come here when I was little?'

'I think so,' Anna said vaguely.

'Well, we've been in contact again. He lives in Liverpool but his dad's place is nearby so he's here most weeks. He usually drops by and we have a coffee.'

'Oh!' Anna looked a little shocked, and Lucy realised with a stab of alarm how that might have sounded. For the first time it occurred to her that others might think that too: that there was something other than friendship developing between her and James, when the idea was ridiculous. 'Are you spending much time with him, then?' her mother asked.

Lucy looked at her, trying to read her face. 'Like I said, he just pops by every so often when he's visiting his dad.'

A small silence hung over them and, for some ridiculous reason, Lucy was aware of her cheeks burning. Not because she had anything to hide or to feel guilty about – but because the actual possibility was out there now, floating around like a peculiar fragrance they couldn't ignore. Her mother actually thought she might be interested in another man, romantically. Lucy gathered up the green beans and dropped them into a pan. 'He just said he'd help,' she said briskly.

'*I* could help, if you'd let me get up in that attic,' Anna remarked.

'I'll deal with it when the time's right, when I have a moment to *think*—' Lucy broke off, sensing her heartbeat quickening to an alarming rate. Anna had been here less than three hours and already Lucy could sense a vein thudding urgently at her temples. How were they going to get through three days together?

A fresh wave of guilt whooshed over Lucy for even having such thoughts. 'I don't want to upset you,' Anna murmured, making Lucy's heart twist even more.

'You're not.' She squeezed her mum's hand. 'I'm glad you're here. You're a big support, you know.'

Anna smiled wanly, and Lucy could sense her edging towards martyr mode. 'Shall I just tidy up the children's rooms,' she suggested meekly, 'before they come home? I mean, just make their beds, pick up their toys, make the place *nice* for them?' As if it were a rancid hovel.

'Yes, okay, Mum,' Lucy said, slumping into submission now. But at least it would keep her occupied, she reasoned. At the risk of treating her like a child, perhaps this was the best way of handling her mum; by coming up with a list of jobs she could do, to keep her happy and make her feel useful, in the way that Lucy had let the children help by 'sweeping' (i.e. riding the floor brush broomstick-style) and 'weeding' (playing in the soil).

While Anna was upstairs, Lucy caught up with her messages on her phone. There was a rush of alerts from Andrew, her old friend from work:

Big news!

MC has quit. Or maybe been pushed? Went for a meeting and came back ashen, cleared desk and left.

MORE NEWS apparently big backer appalled by decisions he's made. And that concludes your newsflash today! Call me. Axx

Intrigued, she yearned to find out more, but she couldn't call him now, not when she was aware of her mother clonking about upstairs, no doubt moving things around even though Marnie didn't especially like her things being rearranged.

There was also a text from James: *Hope all goes well with Marnie's birthday. Good luck! Loved the pic you sent of Sam's pinboard in all its glory. Looked great. Glad he could put it to good use. Jx.* She blinked at it, wondering why on earth her mother's reaction had rattled her so much.

Because of what other people might think of their friendship? That was crazy. No one thought anything, she was sure of that. Trying to shake off her unease, she sat at the table, grateful for a few moments' peace. She vaguely registered her mother coming downstairs, striding along the hallway and out to the garden, then coming back in and clomping back upstairs again.

Eventually, guilt niggled at her and she headed upstairs to see how her mother was doing. The whiff of furniture polish engulfed her as she reached the landing. 'Mum?' she called out.

'In Sam's room, love!' Anna sing-songed.

Lucy stepped in and gazed around at the immaculate surroundings. 'Wow,' she marvelled. 'This is fantastic, Mum. I'd forgotten what colour the carpet is.' Admittedly, these days the kids' rooms tended to escalate out of control quickly. She'd had to learn to prioritise, directing most of her energies into the public parts of the house whenever she had guests. They were unaware of the scattering of pants, socks and Lego garnished with pencil shavings and broken biscuit in the kids' rooms.

However, Sam's lair was now neatly ordered. His books were perfectly aligned on the shelf, grouped according to spine colour. His bed had been changed and made up immaculately, shoes paired up neatly, and . . . Lucy stopped and stared at the wall where the pinboard had been, covered in leaves and feathers, all the flatter exhibits that Sam had been able to display that way.

It wasn't there anymore. There was just a space, and a grubby smear on the pale blue wall.

'Mum . . . where's Sam's pinboard gone?' Lucy asked, frowning.

'It's over there, love.' Anna indicated to where it was propped up against his wardrobe.

Lucy exhaled with relief. 'Oh, thank goodness. I thought you might've thrown it away . . .'

'No, of course not. But I've—' she started.

'Why did you take it down?' Lucy asked, wandering

over and checking that it was just as Sam had left it. Everything appeared to still be in place.

'I was going to clear it up,' Anna said quickly.

'You were going to *clear up* the pinboard? What d'you mean?'

She smiled tightly. 'All that old, grubby stuff on it. I thought it'd look so much nicer with pictures on, postcards and stickers like he used to have on his wall . . .'

'Sam reckons he's too old for stickers,' Lucy murmured.

'Oh, does he? Anyway, I've already done the shelf, look—' Lucy turned and looked at the shelf that, since early spring, Sam had designated as his museum. Last time she'd looked, it had been covered by the small objects he'd collected on their walks. And now it was bare.

'Where are Sam's things?' Lucy asked.

Anna beamed at her. 'His Lego's all in that box over there. Gosh, that took some gathering up!' She chuckled. 'His other toys are in the basket – I've put that under the bed. And his cuddly toys—'

'No, Mum,' Lucy cut in, 'I mean the things from the *shelf*.' She pointed at it.

'Oh, that?' She shrugged. 'I thought they were just odd bits.'

Lucy could sense her heart rate quickening as she looked at her mother. 'They're not just *bits*. They're important to him.'

'Sorry, I didn't realise.'

'Well, can we put them back, please?' Lucy asked, trying to remain calm. 'The kids'll be home from Carys's soon – she's dropping them off. Sam'll be upset if everything isn't how he left it.'

Anna winced. 'They were awfully dirty, love. Bits of

209

bone and a nasty little skull, and I don't think feathers are hygienic. God knows what was living on that lot.' She paused, seemingly oblivious to the appalled expression that was forming on her daughter's face. 'I thought the room would look fresher without them,' she added.

'Fresher?' Lucy exclaimed. 'When did an eight-year-old boy ever care about things being fresh?' They stared at each other for a moment. 'Can we put them back?' Lucy implored her.

'I got rid of them,' Anna said quickly, 'so I could give the shelf a thorough wipe-down.'

Lucy gawped at her, then scanned the room and snatched at a knotted bin bag that was lying by the door.

'They're not in there,' Anna muttered. 'I took them outside.'

'Outside? D'you mean to the garden?'

'Yes, but . . .' She stopped as her daughter turned and hurtled towards the bedroom door. 'Lucy! Where are you going?'

'That was Sam's museum,' she yelled back. 'What were you *thinking*, Mum? I have to get it before he finds out.'

Chapter Twenty-Three

She raced downstairs and through the house, aware of her mother calling out after her. 'Which one did you put them in?' she snapped. They were both down at the bottom of the garden now, having stopped at the row of wheelie bins. Anna stared, open-mouthed as Lucy flipped up one of the lids.

'They're not in there,' she said, trying to grab at her daughter's arm. Lucy shook her off and flung the next lid open.

'They're not in that one either.'

Lucy swung round to face her, close to tears now. She hated the way this still happened to her occasionally: the sudden loss of control, as if someone had stamped on her accelerator pedal when she'd always thought of herself as a calm and level-headed person. In her old job, when the pressure had been on, Lucy had been the one to soothe her colleagues, to help them prioritise and hang on to the belief that everything would work out okay. 'Panicking won't help,' she'd often say during meetings. 'There's nothing that can't be fixed here. No one's died.'

But now the smallest thing could set her off. She had cried in frustration the other day when she'd tried to buy bread in the village and discovered that she'd left her purse at home. A few days earlier, she had kicked the garage door violently when she couldn't get it to shut properly – which was perhaps unwise of her, considering it had smashed down on her head last year.

But this wasn't a small thing, like a forgotten purse or temperamental garage door. To Sam, it would be enormous.

'Mum,' Lucy said steadily, 'please try and remember which one you put them in.' Someone on the road caught her eye. It was Lucy's neighbour, Irene, strolling by. She waved over the gate and, distractedly, Lucy waved back.

'They're not in a bin,' Anna murmured. 'Come with me.' They walked around to the side of the shed where Anna pointed towards the pile of shrub clippings. 'I brought them out in a bag and then tipped them over there,' Anna explained.

'What? You just *scattered* them?'

'I know what you're like with recycling,' her mother mumbled. 'You don't like things going to landfill, do you? You're always saying that.'

Lucy scanned the pile of foliage. None of Sam's exhibits were immediately visible; perhaps they'd slipped down through the gaps, or her mother had scattered them more widely than she'd realised. *For crying out loud,* she wanted to yell, *what kind of idiot would throw out a child's precious things from his bedroom?*

She started to delve through the pile, scattering twigs, barely noticing that her hands were becoming scratched as she raked through the greenery.

'I'm sorry, love.' Her mother looked quite distraught now.

212

'Are you sure this is where you threw them?'

'I think so. Now I'm not sure. Is it really important?'

'Of course it's important!'

Anna touched her arm. 'Please don't shout. Let's not make a huge thing of it. It was just a mistake.'

'I'm sorry, Mum. I'm just upset.'

'I was only trying to help.'

'Yes, I realise that.' Could anyone crank up the guilt more effectively than a mother, she wondered? She would rather die than make Marnie and Sam feel that way.

'I'll make it up to him,' Anna added. 'I'll buy him a . . .' She paused. 'What's he into these days?'

Making museums! Lucy wanted to snap, but managed to stop herself. Anna had never been terribly in touch with the children's latest whims and obsessions. For years, she had insisted on buying dolls for Marnie even though she had never shown the slightest interest in them. Diplomatically, Lucy had tried to suggest other possible gifts, like art materials, accessories for her bike or even a gift token if she was struggling for ideas. But the dolls had kept coming – bought out of love, of course, Lucy realised that – dressed in their gauzy outfits with their pouty mouths, and Lucy hadn't had the heart to ask her to stop. For this coming birthday, Lucy had suggested she contributed to the keyboard Marnie had asked for.

'Don't worry about it,' Lucy muttered now.

'No, really. I can get him a present,' Anna insisted.

'It's fine,' Lucy said, wishing they could rewind to the moment when her mother had arrived earlier that afternoon, and start over again. Anna was a fusspot – but Lucy knew she loved her, and she *did* only want to help. Maybe cleaning and tidying were the only ways Anna could think of to lend a hand.

If she had been able to think straight, Lucy would have reminded herself that, as a bereaved daughter, she probably wasn't easy to be around these days. Her mother wasn't to know how important those tiny finds were to Sam; she hadn't been there when he'd found that delicate skull lying on the path in the woods. Was it from a shrew, they'd wondered? Or a vole? Sam had wrapped it in tissue and slipped it carefully into his jacket pocket.

How would she tell him it had been thrown away, and what did it matter if feathers weren't especially hygienic when this little boy had lost his dad?

Tears blurred Lucy's vision now as she spotted a smooth white pebble next to the clippings pile. But was it a museum exhibit or just an ordinary pebble, and would Sam even be able to tell the difference? She spied a feather, too, and tried to figure out whether it had just been lying there, or was it one that Sam had picked up on a walk? There was no sign of the skull, though, or the tiny bird bones.

'Hi!' Carys's voice cut through the air.

Lucy straightened up quickly at the sight of her friend and the children – Marnie, Sam, and Carys's children, Noah and Amber – who had wandered in through the gate.

'Hi!' She beamed as Bramble charged into the garden, ears flapping, and proceeded to tear around excitedly.

'Hi, Grandma!' Sam called out, and hurried towards her, closely followed by Marnie. It twisted Lucy's heart to see how happy they were to see her. Carys greeted Anna – they had met several times before – and turned to Lucy.

'They did so well at gymnastics,' she said, 'but the

teacher said there's going to be a lot of rehearsals before the show . . .'

'What show?' she asked distractedly.

'Mum, I told you,' Marnie groaned. 'There's a gymnastic display at the end of the holidays.'

'Oh, yes!' Lucy feigned recollection. 'Yes, of course. Well, that's great.'

Catching her eye, Carys frowned. 'Sorry we're a bit late. They wanted to stop off for an ice cream.'

'Oh, that's nice. Thanks so much for having them. We were thinking we'd like to do another sleepover soon?'

'That'd be great.' Carys's gaze met Lucy's and a look of concern crossed her face. 'Everything okay?'

'Er, yes . . .' Lucy's chest tightened as she tried to work out what to do. She wasn't about to tell tales – 'My mother threw Sam's museum away!' – and had no desire to establish blame. But what other explanation could she give? Perhaps she could delay Sam from going upstairs, just for long enough to give her the chance to have another hunt for his exhibits. Things would be a whole lot better if she could sneak at least some of them back onto the shelf.

Miraculously, both Marnie and Sam took their grandma's hands and started to lead her around the garden, showing her the purple and yellow pansies they had planted themselves, and the haphazard rockery they had built in the patch of border Lucy said they could have as their own. Noah and Amber tailed after their friends, all of them chatting in a happy group with Bramble moseying along beside them. Sam was now pointing out the bird box that he and Marnie had partially constructed with their dad, and Lucy had helped them to finish without knowing how he had intended it to be, or able to find any kind of plan

215

or diagram. It was a little wonky, but it had held together and they had painted it pea green, fixed it to the oak tree and were immensely proud of it. 'I wish Dad could see it,' Marnie had said.

'You seemed a bit stressed there, when we arrived,' Carys murmured.

Lucy grimaced and waited until Anna and the children had disappeared around the corner to where the redcurrants grew. 'Mum's been a bit overenthusiastic with her tidying up,' she explained. 'You know Sam's museum in his room?'

Carys nodded. 'The V&A of Burley Bridge?'

'Yeah, well, it's no more, I'm afraid. She decided it was a health hazard and threw it all out.'

'Oh no!' Carys looked aghast. 'Where did she put it all?'

'Down there, she *thinks*,' she said, motioning towards the pile of clippings. 'C'mon, I'll have another quick look.'

They both strode towards the pile of clippings. However, before they had even reached it Sam had reappeared and shouted, 'I need to pee!' and hurtled into the house.

Lucy stared at her friend. 'Oh, Christ.'

'It'll be okay,' Carys whispered. 'Tell him it was a mistake, and you can go out and find new things – even better things – and he'll have an even more amazing museum.'

Lucy wanted to believe it was possible, and that she'd lost perspective and was over-reacting wildly, as often seemed to be the case these days. After all, some of the exhibits had only been bits of bark and tufts of lichen. Even with the egg and the animal skull, they were hardly talking a crisis of international proportions.

216

As Anna and Marnie strolled back into view, Lucy made her way towards the house. 'I'm just going to check if Sam's okay,' she said quickly.

'He's gone to the loo,' Marnie announced.

'Yes, I know, love.'

Marnie frowned at her, clearly confused as they only ever used the downstairs loo when they were playing outside, and of course Sam was capable of negotiating it without help. Perhaps he'd come straight back out, Lucy tried to reassure herself as she strode towards the front door, aware of her mother, Carys and all three children staring after her.

But no, 'Mum!' Sam's voice rang out from upstairs. '*Muuum*!'

'What's the matter, Sam?' she called back, her heart thudding.

'My museum's gone!' There was a scramble of footsteps on the landing, then he scampered downstairs and ran towards her, juddering to a halt on the front step.

'Sam . . .' She bobbed down and pulled him towards her. 'It's okay, love. There's just been a slight . . . mistake, okay?'

'What mistake?' He pulled back and looked at her, his wavy brown hair mussed, his dark eyes wide and indignant.

'Well . . . Grandma was tidying up your room and she didn't realise, she didn't mean to—'

'What did she do?' he barked at her.

Lucy reddened, aware how unpleasant it was to be referred to as 'she', but now wasn't the time to pick him up on his manners. She straightened up and looked around at her mother for help.

'I, um . . . I threw your things away, love,' Anna

murmured, quickly striding towards them. 'I'm sorry, Sam.'

'Why did you do that?' He gawped at her, tears forming instantly and rolling down his lightly freckled cheeks.

'I didn't know they were important. I just thought they were – I don't know – just bits you'd picked up from outside.'

'Why did you *let* her?' Sam seemed to be redirecting his anger towards his mother now. Amber and Noah gawped at her, all agog.

'Yeah, why did you, Mum?' Marnie growled.

'It's no one's fault,' Carys said quickly. 'These things happen.'

'Grandma was only trying to help,' Lucy tried to explain. 'She was making your room nicer for you.'

She reached for Sam's hand but he whirled away, yelling, 'I don't want it nicer. I want Dad!'

'So do I,' Marnie cried, her face crumpling.

'Oh, Lucy, I'm so sorry,' Anna started.

'It's okay, Mum,' Lucy muttered.

'No, it's not!' Sam raged. 'I want Dad and I want my things back. I want Grandma to go.'

'Sam!' Anna exclaimed. 'I was only trying to help.'

'Well, you weren't helping,' he yelled.

'Sam, please stop this now,' Lucy implored him, trying to pull him in for a hug, but he pushed her off and ran away from her, towards the bottom of the garden.

'Come back, darling,' Anna called out weakly.

He stopped suddenly and swung round to face her. 'Go away, Grandma,' he cried, wiping his wet face with his hands. 'I don't want you here anymore. Just go home.'

Chapter Twenty-Four

Lucy apologised for Sam, and hated herself for apologising. Shouldn't she be on her son's side? Years ago, she'd jumped to his defence when she found out that he'd been put in 'the naughty corner' for refusing to join in a game at his old nursery. The naughty corner! It had astounded her that such a thing still existed. But Anna wasn't a nursery employee. She was his grandma, who loved him and regularly drove over to spend time with them all – and, yes, she had only wanted to do a kind thing by decluttering his room.

They struggled through the early evening, and once the children were in bed, Lucy found her mother leafing pointedly through a gardening magazine at the kitchen table. 'Mum, I'm sure Sam didn't mean it,' she ventured, offering her a cup of weak tea, two sugars, the way she liked it.

'I think he's a little too old for that sort of thing,' she murmured.

Too old for what? Lucy wanted to ask. Having a museum, or shouting at his grandma? He'd only just

219

turned eight, for goodness' sake! She prickled with shame at even entertaining such thoughts, and when her mobile trilled on the worktop she just gave it a cursory glance.

An unknown number. Bound to be someone wanting to book, she decided. She dithered over whether to accept the call, wondering whether it would annoy her mother further and if she should just ignore it and give her her full attention – oh, sod it, she decided. Her mum had already turned back to the magazine and didn't seem to *want* her attention right now.

'Hello?' she said sharply. Not the usual, *Hello, Rosemary Cottage, Lucy here. Can I help you?*

'Hi, is that Lucy?' It was a male voice.

'Yes?'

'Erm, you might not remember me. It's Connell. Connell Davies—'

She paused for a moment. 'Connell from college?' she asked, taking the phone out into the hallway away from her mum.

'Yeah, that's me!' He sounded all buoyant, and she could tell he was smiling as if he expected her to be delighted to hear from him. She rubbed at her face distractedly and hoped that, whatever the reason for his call, he wasn't expecting a lengthy reminiscing session right now. 'I know it's been a heck of a long time,' he added.

'Yes, it really has . . .' He was coming into focus now, gradually sharpening in her mind: tall and lanky, in skinny jeans before they were properly fashionable. A mop of straight, floppy light brown hair that forever hung in his eyes, and a wide, eye-crinkling smile. They hadn't been close friends, although they'd known plenty of people in common. Connell had run with a cooler

220

crowd than hers – or she'd always had the impression that he liked to think he did.

'So, how *are* you?' he asked.

'I'm good, thanks. All's fine. How about you?' Why on earth was he calling? It occurred to her that there might be some kind of college reunion in the offing, and her heart lurched with panic. While she could hang out happily with James, Carys and her other friends in the village, she'd rather hack off her own leg than be thrust together with a pile of people she hadn't seen for twenty years.

'All's great,' Connell said breezily. 'Anyway, I'd better explain why I'm calling. I got your number from your B&B website.' A brief pause. 'Hope you don't mind me calling so late . . .'

It had just gone nine-thirty. At least his call had rescued her from the stony vibes that were still emanating from her mother in the kitchen. 'It's not late at all,' Lucy said.

'Great. Well, look, I'm back down in Nottingham these days—' she remembered now that that was where he was from '—but I need to come up to your area for work. It's not for ages yet. I'm thinking October, probably. But I heard through the grapevine that you and your husband set up a B&B, and from what Jennie said, it sounded like it might be in the right area . . .'

'Jennie?' Lucy asked, partly in order to shrug off his mention of her husband. Mostly, whenever that happened, it was easiest to just let it fly over her.

'Yeah, I'm still in touch with a few of the old faces sporadically,' he said. Jennie had been Lucy's flatmate in the first two years of college, but they had lost touch during the interim years. 'So I was intrigued and thought I'd try to look you up,' Connell continued. 'That's how I found you.'

'Wow,' Lucy murmured, stepping out into the cool evening. 'Well, of course I can put you up in October. I don't have any bookings that far ahead.'

'I'd love that,' Connell said. 'I thought, rather than staying at some miserable chain hotel on my own, it'd be a much nicer trip if I could find a cosy-looking B&B – and yours looks lovely. I found it on a travel blog. Something about the best B&Bs in the north? Was that it?'

'Yes, we were lucky to be picked for that.'

'I couldn't believe it when I saw you on the website! That picture of you, standing in front of your beautiful house . . .' Ivan had taken that photograph when they'd first opened up for guests. 'You looked so happy,' he added.

'I was. *Am*, I mean,' she added quickly. 'But I'm still amazed you knew it was me.'

'Yeah, 'course I did. Obviously, you have your married name now, and your hair's quite a lot longer. But I recognised you right away. You haven't changed a bit.'

She smiled, sensing the stress of the day ebbing away a little. She should probably be in the kitchen now, trying to placate her mother rather than chattering on her phone, but never mind. She would try to make it up to her tomorrow. Instead, she found herself wandering down to the shed, where she started to poke around in the hope of spotting some of Sam's exhibits, but also knowing there was no point. 'That's very kind of you,' she said, 'but the photo was taken from quite a distance.'

'Well, you looked great,' he said firmly. '*Really* happy. I was actually a little bit envious. I mean, I'm not sure it'd be for me, running a B&B, living way out in the wilds—'

'It's not quite the wilds,' she cut in, 'but yes, it is pretty rural. So, what's bringing you up here, anyway?'

'I've been asked to do a project with the village school,' Connell replied. 'Burley Bridge Primary, I mean. I assume that's pretty near you.'

'My two children go there,' Lucy exclaimed. 'It's a ten-minute walk from my house. What kind of project is it?'

'A sort of art project involving the kids,' he explained. 'I need to come over and meet with the head teacher and look at the building – the space we'll be working with. We're doing a stained-glass installation.'

'That sounds brilliant!'

'Yeah, it should be. Like I said, I don't have a date yet but we're looking at late October. I'll let you know as soon as it's definite. I was hoping I could book in for a couple of nights—'

'Great,' Lucy said, figuring now that she would tell him about Ivan when he came, but not now; it wasn't the kind of news she wanted to land on him out of the blue. 'But it wouldn't be on a B&B basis,' she added. 'I mean, I wouldn't dream of charging you.'

'Nope, I'd only stay as a proper paying guest,' Connell said firmly. 'It's your business, isn't it?'

'Well, yes . . .'

'Please – it's only fair. I'll get in touch nearer the time when I know the exact dates, okay?'

'Great,' she said, feeling happier now as they finished the call. It would be fun to see him, she decided as she made her way back inside to face her mother, and get through the rest of the evening trying to make chit-chat and being rebuffed. In fact, it would be easier than having a regular guest, with all the small talk *that* involved.

223

Although she had been adept at chatting with strangers when Ivan had still been alive, since the accident it was the one aspect she still found tricky. No one would guess – at least she hoped they wouldn't – but sometimes, the effort of being constantly cheery could sometimes feel a little like wearing another woman's lipstick: slightly wrong, as if it didn't quite suit her. But with Connell, they had shared history.

Like her, he had grown up in a bleary suburb and yearned to escape and find out what the wider world had to offer. He'd studied product design, while she had been on a fashion-buying course. Lucy remembered now that he'd gone from a ramshackle flat-share, its red kitchen walls covered in pages ripped from art magazines and something terrible festering in a forgotten saucepan, to relative domesticity with Zelda, a fabulously glamorous Italian girl.

Connell and Zelda had hosted a dinner party once – the first Lucy had ever been invited to. It seemed terribly ambitious with around a dozen guests, numerous courses and proper cloth napkins, which Lucy had never encountered outside of special occasions at her parents' house (her mother kept them neatly ironed in a drawer). Zelda had whisked a seemingly endless succession of sensational dishes from their tiny Baby Belling oven.

'Is that what being a grown-up is like?' Lucy's flatmate Jennie had laughed as the two of them had tottered home tipsily together. 'We don't even have an oven glove!'

Soon after that, their paths had diverged. Lucy heard that Connell had sailed straight into some brilliant design job down south, while she had floundered for some years in mundane admin roles around Manchester before landing a job as a junior buyer at Claudine. She had no idea whether Connell and Zelda had stayed together. Perhaps they had produced a host of gorgeous children by now?

Intrigued, she was keen to find out more when they had the chance to catch up properly. But all thoughts of his October visit disappeared as she found her mother pacing the kitchen, her own mobile clamped to her ear. 'Get her to the vet, Paddy,' she commanded without making eye contact with Lucy. There was more pacing, then: 'Yes, I know she doesn't like him. She'll have to be muzzled. What d'you expect? Last time you took her, he squeezed her anal gland.'

Lucy winced, hovering in the doorway, waiting for her mother to finish the call. 'What is it?' she asked finally when she'd rung off. Anna snatched her cardigan from the back of the chair and trotted upstairs with Lucy in pursuit. It turned out that, although she had expressed zero concern over Paddy's labyrinthitis, her mother was alarmed by the news her beloved Tilly – a fervent snaffler of pavement food – had experienced 'digestive issues' all day.

'I'm sorry to miss Marnie's birthday,' she murmured as they reached the landing, 'but I think it's best if I go home first thing tomorrow. Say bye to the children from me if they're still in bed when I leave.'

Chapter Twenty-Five

Lucy and the children stood in a clump in the fine rain, waving Anna off as she drove away. 'Sorry, Mum,' Sam murmured as they all sloped back inside.

'Oh, Sam, it's okay. It's not your fault. I told you, it's about Tilly being ill really.'

He threw her a quick *don't-give-me-that* look as they all ambled back inside. 'I don't want that stuff anymore anyway,' he mumbled, flopping onto the sofa in the living room and kicking off his shoes. 'It's stupid having a museum. That kind of stuff's for little kids.'

'No, it's not,' Lucy exclaimed. 'It was brilliant, what you put together. Really inventive and clever.'

'Josh thought it was stupid.' Ah, the so-called friend who had also laughed at Sam's panda pillow the first time he'd been over to play. Chocolate-sausage Josh. No wonder the kid had issues.

'But he didn't even go up to your room last time he was here,' Lucy remarked. 'He never saw it, did he?'

Sam tugged at a falling-off sock. 'I told him about it.

I asked if he wanted to see it and he said no, he hates museums, and then everyone laughed.'

'Oh, never mind him,' Lucy said quickly. 'Listen – shall we do something nice today instead of moping around?' He shrugged sulkily. 'C'mon, darling. How about we go swimming or something?'

'Nah.' He shook his head. Marnie, who was sprawled on the rug with a notebook and pens, didn't even deign to answer.

Lucy glanced towards the window. The bleary morning was turning even greyer, and faint rain was still speckling the glass. She was aware that she had to pull *something* out of the bag today. Anna had left a cloud of despondency in her wake, and although Marnie was idly drawing now, Lucy suspected it wouldn't keep her occupied for long.

'How about Let's Bounce?' she asked, bracing herself before they had even answered. The gigantic soft play centre was forty minutes' drive away and today – a wet Saturday – it would be particularly hectic. Lucy and Carys had braved it a couple of times. They were realistic enough to know that, while they loved to think they were providing all the benefits of a country childhood – all rosy cheeks and splashing in rivers – what their kids *really* wanted was to thrash around in an artificially lit barn amidst hordes of other screaming children, depressed-looking parents and the stench of fried food.

Of course, Marnie leapt at her suggestion, and even Sam perked up, especially when she said they could take a couple of friends too. So, on the day her mother had flounced off home, Lucy found herself picking up Noah and Amber from Carys's, and sipping a terrible coffee by herself whilst the four children in her care threw themselves round a cavernous barn in a state of high giddiness. Whilst they were certainly having fun, the banging music and the fact that a toddler had just vomited on the floor a few feet away served only to plummet Lucy even further into a pit of gloom.

It was still raining steadily as she drove them, exhausted but at least happy again, back home. Her sense of flatness was lingering on like the burger smell that had clung to her hair, and now she wondered if she could have handled things differently with her mother. It wasn't that Lucy didn't appreciate everything she did for her. Anna kept in touch constantly and often sent little notes in the post to her and the children. In contrast, Ivan's parents had virtually melted away, so consumed were they by their own grief. They had come to the service at the crematorium but rushed off straight afterwards with barely a goodbye. After driving all the way up from London, they hadn't even come to Rosemary Cottage for the small gathering afterwards, or exchanged more than a few choked words with Lucy.

Like her, Ivan had been an only child. She knew it had been devastating for them, but then Marnie and Sam would ask about them occasionally – 'Why don't we ever see Grandma Penny and Grandpa Nigel?' – and what was she supposed to say? 'They live so far away, and it's such a long drive for them.' How feeble that sounded.

'Can't we visit them, then?' Marnie had asked. 'I love London!' Lucy didn't know how to explain that, if they did visit, it probably wouldn't be like last time, which had been all about the thrill of Hamleys, where remote controlled airships were flying across the store, or a vast dinner in Chinatown and the theatre in Covent Garden. Lucy phoned Penny and Nigel occasionally, but there was either a stilted exchange or it was just the answerphone, and they didn't always call back.

'I don't think we got your message,' Nigel said once, and apparently their answerphone was so old and decrepit – possibly steam-powered – that that might have been the case.

'We have quite a lot on at the moment,' explained Penny last time Lucy asked if they'd like to come up to stay, which meant *no thank you*. Lucy had known from Ivan that they rarely socialised and seemed to have few interests apart from watching TV. At least her own mother wanted to be involved. The situation frustrated Lucy, more for Marnie and Sam's sake than her own. To her, they were in-laws with whom she had never been close. But Marnie and Sam were their only grandchildren, and Lucy had hoped that they would continue to play a part in her children's lives.

Next day was Marnie's birthday. She knew it was touch and go whether a card and present would arrive from them, as nothing had turned up yet (at least Sam had received a card and book token; it had hardly thrilled him, but it was better than it not being acknowledged). Last year there'd been nothing for either of them, but Lucy had forgiven her in-laws for – presumably – forgetting. After all, it had only been six months since Ivan had died. But now here they were, a whole year further on without him. A wave of loneliness consumed her that evening, and no amount of 'keeping busy' with chores could help her to shake it off.

When she'd still been at Claudine, Lucy had noticed the phrase 'reach out' creeping into common parlance, specifically in MC's emails: *Hey all, can I reach out and ask for your opinions on our new packaging options?*

Or, worse still, directed to her personally: *I'm reaching out to you, Lucy, asking you to get on board with the men's fun range.*

And I'm reaching out to you, she'd wanted to fire off back, *to remind you that we are a much-loved quality lingerie brand but if you want to wreck all of that with your trunk pants, go ahead.*

However, later that night, following her mother's abrupt departure and an afternoon at Let's Bounce, Lucy lay in bed thinking that she would very much like to reach out to someone right now. Not in a physical sense; she had no desire to touch or be touched, and probably never would again, at least not in any intimate way. The idea of sleeping with someone was as alien a concept to her now as Morris dancing. No, what Lucy craved now was just to feel *close* to another person, just to talk, just to *be* together. Someone she could be utterly honest with and know she wouldn't be judged.

At just gone eleven it was too late to call anyone, and she decided her feelings were too muddled to be compressed into a short, neat text – so she decided she had better not contact anyone at all. But still it surprised her when she realised who she really wanted to be with right now.

She didn't quite know why this was, and this acknowledgement made her feel a little unsettled, as if something was changing in her as she lay there in the dark. Yet it was definitely James Halsall who filled her mind as she drifted off to sleep that night.

Chapter Twenty-Six

Something weird had happened to James. His jeans were fine – jeans were jeans, after all – but his T-shirt looked terrible, faded and sad, and now he was rummaging through the few bits of clothing he kept at his dad's, which wasn't much.

He wasn't one to think about clothes normally. He just grabbed the nearest thing and that was that – if it was clean, comfy and fairy plain, then it did its job. But not now on this hazy Saturday afternoon, the last day of July. Right now, he was giving his attire serious thought, and he seemed to be incapable of making a simple decision.

'James?' Kenny called through from the living room. 'Something's up with my heating again.'

'What's wrong with it?' James was in his room, with the door ajar. He could hear his dad clonking about in the kitchen, muttering and swearing occasionally. Although certainly forgetful and prone to bouts of confusion, he was still managing okay with Rikke's daily visits and James making his weekly trips over. These days,

James enjoyed his trips – looked forward to them, even, if Lucy was going to be around. They hung out in her garden mostly, drinking coffee and chatting, doing a few jobs together if something needed attention. He found it incredibly soothing and enjoyable – but he wasn't soothed now.

'It's gone off!' Kenny announced accusingly, as if James might have been tampering with it.

James had whipped off the substandard T-shirt. Now he was pulling on a cotton shirt he'd found in a drawer and must have left here ages ago. It was burgundy with a tiny black check – was that too much, he wondered, for the occasion? Christ, he'd have to iron it. Did his dad still possess a working iron?

'James!'

'You don't need the heating on now,' he called back. 'It's summer. It's a lovely day out there.'

He looked down at the shirt, wondering now if he'd be too hot in this, or look overdressed – but then it was only a shirt and jeans, he was hardly talking a dinner jacket, and actually it didn't look *too* creased, not when it was on . . .

'There's no hot water,' his father yelled. 'That's what I'm trying to tell you . . .' With the shirt unbuttoned James strode through to the kitchen where his father was holding a hand under the running tap. 'It's stone cold,' he announced. 'Something's broken. We're going to have to get a man.' He turned and stared at his son. 'Where are *you* going?'

'Um, just a little gathering,' James replied. 'I told you about it, remember? I'll only be out for a couple of hours.'

His father narrowed his eyes. 'With your shirt open?'

James exhaled loudly and tested the water with his hand; as his father had reported, it was freezing. He checked the main switch. 'Dad, you've turned off the main heating control again. Please just leave it alone . . .'

'I never touched it!'

James flicked the switch on and waited a few moments until the low rumble of the boiler could be heard. 'That's it back on now.' He started to button up his shirt and sensed his father's bemused gaze upon him.

'So . . . where did you say you're going?'

How old did his dad think he was? Nine? 'Just to a thing in the village, Dad.'

'Can I come?'

He pushed back his hair and studied his father's eager face, the small, intense brown eyes that still glinted with mischief, the pink mouth only just visible through the greying beard. 'It's a children's birthday party,' James said, smiling now. 'It'll be games and cakes and tons of kids charging around . . .'

His father smirked. 'You're going to a kids' party?'

'Yes, Dad.'

He chuckled and, with the hot water issue miraculously rectified, sauntered back to the living room. 'Right, I see. The way you've been acting, I thought you were going on a date.'

Every children's party they'd hosted at Rosemary Cottage had been blessed with brilliant weather, and today, Marnie's tenth birthday, was no exception. The sky was a wash of turquoise, the freshly cut lawn bathed in sunshine. Lucy was grateful for that. Having a pile of children running about, playing games and enjoying a sprawling picnic was so much easier outside than everyone being in the house. It wasn't that she was madly house-proud by nature, but she had B&B guests due later (having checked her bank account, she had decided she couldn't really afford to turn down a booking just because it was her daughter's birthday).

Lucy's friends had turned up to help: Carys and Jodie – known as the most glamorous mum at the school gates, and never un-manicured – plus several others whom she had got to know through their children. Other mothers were great, she reflected, at running indoors to fetch a fresh jug of juice without being asked. They gathered up discarded paper plates, handed out cake, administered plasters to cut knees, found someone's lost bangle and rallied children around for a game – women were *brilliant*. But it wasn't just the mums who had made the party such a success. James had proved invaluable too, noticing that Bramble had disappeared through the bars of the gate and run off in pursuit, as well as fetching and carrying to and from the kitchen virtually all afternoon.

Towards the end of the party, Sam found a dead mouse by the shed. The younger ones gathered around him in fascination and disgust as he held it in his hand. 'Will your mum let you keep it?' came Noah's voice.

'Probably not,' Sam said.

'It's perfect,' Josh marvelled. 'Looks like it could be alive!'

'Yeah,' Sam said, ignoring Lucy as she called over for him to throw it back into the undergrowth. The children continued to study the mouse. Next thing she knew, James had gone over and spoken to the boys. A small hole was dug by the fence, and the mouse placed in it, and everyone seemed satisfied with that.

He looked so smart today, Lucy reflected. The fact

that he had opted for a shirt rather than a T-shirt struck her as particularly endearing. He'd had a haircut, too, in the week since she'd last seen him. He hadn't seemed to mind that, by the end of the party, his shirt had been daubed with ice cream (an overexcited Josh had collided with him whilst clutching a cone).

She had told him about her mother flouncing off home a couple of days previously, and that Ivan's parents hadn't sent Marnie anything in time for her birthday. 'I think she still had a pretty good time,' he remarked as they cleared up together. Once he'd gone, she did a final spruce-up of the downstairs rooms, in preparation for her guests' arrival. And here they came now: a retired head teacher called Moira with a wiry yoga body, who enthused madly over the house and garden, and her rather shy-seeming, bald and bespectacled husband, Jeremy.

'We've had my daughter's birthday party today,' Lucy told them, as she spotted a deflated balloon lying on the stairs on the way to show them to their room.

'You must be a powerhouse of energy,' Moira remarked.

'I don't know about that.' She smiled. 'But my children are having a friend each to sleep over tonight. I've asked them to be especially quiet, but if you're disturbed at all, please let me know. I mean, don't think twice about it.'

'I'm sure we won't be,' Jeremy said warmly. 'It's a family home. We expected there to be people around.'

'And we've just driven up from Kent,' Moira added, 'so we'll be out like lights tonight.'

The party crowd had long gone now, apart from Amber and Noah, the designated sleepover friends, so Lucy spruced up the flowers throughout the house and set the breakfast table for her guests. Her mother called, ostensibly to ask how the party had gone, but really, Lucy suspected, to smooth the waters between them. 'They had a lovely time,' she said. 'Thanks for the money towards the keyboard. Marnie really loves it.'

'Oh, that's good,' her mother said. 'I'm sorry I wasn't there to help today.'

'There were plenty of adults,' Lucy said. 'Most of the mums stayed, actually. And James came too—'

'James?' her mother repeated.

'Yes, Mum.' Now Lucy regretted mentioning his name.

'Does he have children, then?'

Lucy set a tiny vase of honeysuckle flowers on the breakfast table. 'Yes, he has a son called Spike.'

'That's a funny name!'

Lucy cleared her throat. 'I think it's sweet actually. It's unusual. It has character . . .'

'You could say that.'

'Mum!'

A small pause. 'So, how does Spike get along with Marnie and Sam?'

'Erm, they haven't met yet.' Lucy frowned, wondering why her mother was probing her in this way. She never quizzed her about her women friends in the village. Should she feel *guilty* for some reason?

'*Will* they?' her mum asked.

'Will they what, Mum?' Exasperation was beginning to rise in Lucy's chest. She wanted to end this conversation and go to bed. She didn't remember their relationship being anything like as prickly as this when Ivan was still alive; these days, they seemed to be permanently about to teeter over into some kind of row.

'Meet. Will your children meet Spike?'

'I don't know!' Lucy exclaimed. 'I expect so, yes, when he comes over to visit sometime—'

'Well, anyway,' her mother cut in, 'I'm glad all went well today.' She coughed dryly. 'And Tilly's fine now, in case you were wondering.'

'I meant to ask,' Lucy said quickly. 'So, was it just a stomach bug?'

'Something like that. We had to buy this special bland tinned food – it's ten pounds a can – and of course your father made a big fuss about the expense, wanted to keep her on plain boiled rice for a few more days, but you know how that bungs her up . . .'

'I do indeed,' Lucy said gravely. 'Anyway, Mum, thanks again for the money towards the present and all the little gifts you left for Marnie. She loved them all. She'll be sending you a note . . .'

'Oh, that's okay, love.'

Her stomach twisted with guilt now. 'And, um . . . I'm sorry for what happened when you were here. With Sam, I mean.'

'Don't worry about that. He was just upset.' There was still a briskness to her tone, but at least they were communicating more normally.

They said goodnight, and Lucy watched TV for an hour or so but couldn't settle to anything. She hardly watched it at all these days. She and Ivan had had their shows they loved, the off-beat comedies and Scandi dramas, but she would never have dreamed of continuing to watch them on her own. She would never know how these lengthy dramas would end and she no longer cared. There were so many activities she associated with Ivan; even watching TV came under that category. Not walking, though, or collecting all those natural things, the bits of bark and dried berries and feathers. That was something she and the children had learned to love without him. Damn her mother, throwing away Sam's museum . . .

Guilt needled at her again, and she quickly pushed it away.

At eleven-thirty Lucy made a mug of tea and took it upstairs, the Spike issue turning over in her mind. She would love to meet him, and in fact she was intrigued as to how he and her children would get along. She knew James brought him over occasionally to see his granddad, but she'd either been busy, or away at her parents', on his last couple of visits. But James had mooted that he'd like her to meet him, and she hoped it would happen soon.

All was quiet as Lucy made her way along the landing to the main bathroom. As she passed Sam's room, she heard Noah's voice: 'What d'you think'll happen to that dead mouse?'

'It'll rot away, I 'spose,' Sam replied.

Lucy looked down. A chink of light shone from beneath the bedroom door; torches were on, even though the boys had been asked to go to sleep an hour ago. But they were having a sleepover, and only talking in murmurs – her guests were at the other end of the house – so she wasn't going to nag at them now.

'Yeah,' Noah said. 'The flesh'll decay – the fur and insides and all that. Bugs'll eat it. That's what happened to Benjy before we got Bramble. He got buried in the garden and rotted away.'

'Aw,' Sam murmured.

'It's natural,' Noah went on. 'They go back into the ground and that helps other things grow, like fertiliser. When we'd buried Benjy I wanted to see what he was like after, I dunno, a year or something. But Mum said no, he'd just be a skeleton and it'd be horrible.' The boys fell silent. Lucy was standing there with a hand on the bathroom door handle, knowing she shouldn't be listening in.

Then: 'Did your dad get buried?'

Oh, Christ . . .

'No, he wasn't buried,' Sam replied carefully. 'He was cremated.'

'What's that?'

Her back teeth were jammed together now, and she felt oddly weightless.

'It means the person gets burned,' Sam said matter-of-factly.

'Oh.' A pause while Noah digested this. 'D'you think that's better?'

'Better than what?'

'Being buried.'

'Um . . .' Another lull. 'I think cremation's better,' Sam said finally, ''cause if you're buried you need space for the coffin, and if you're cremated you turn into dust that goes in a little pot.'

Lucy braced herself for the next question, which she was certain would be: *Is your dad in a little pot?* Yes, he was – on a shelf in her bedroom. But it wasn't.

'Has your mum got a boyfriend?' Noah asked.

She inhaled sharply and touched her face. Her cheek felt warm and tight from the sun; she'd been so busy ensuring that the kids applied sunscreen, she'd forgotten to put any on herself.

'Uh?' Sam sounded surprised.

'The man who helped us bury the mouse. Is that her boyfriend?'

Lucy placed a hand on the cold porcelain bathroom

door handle. It was clearly an innocent line of questioning, with no other intent than mild curiosity. She knew what kids were like. But was that what people thought of her – that she and James were more than platonic friends? When her mother had hinted at the idea, she'd convinced herself that no one else would see it that way. But perhaps they did. Maybe gossip was flying around: *Her husband's only been gone for eighteen months and she's seeing someone already . . .*

Was she being talked about like this – not by Carys, or the other mums she knew well, but by peripheral people? This was a village, after all, and she was a single woman now, and James was a single man. People liked to talk, and it was likely that they had put two and two together . . .

'I'm sure they're keeping a dossier on us, Luce,' Ivan had said once. 'They seem terribly interested in what we're up to around here.' An hour ago she'd felt happy that Marnie's party had gone so well, and lucky to have so many lovely supportive friends, and now she felt . . . well, Lucy didn't know what she felt as she shut the bathroom door and perched on the edge of the bath.

Putting her head in her hands, she groaned audibly as she exhaled. She didn't hear Sam say, 'Don't be stupid, Noah. That really is stupid. James isn't her boyfriend – he's just her friend.'

Chapter Twenty-Seven

'Could we meet up to go over your thoughts please, Lucy?' It was just before dinner on a rain-lashed Monday, and Phyllida was on the phone. Lucy had been trying to catch up with her accounts and updates to the B&B website. Josh, the boy who had mocked Sam's museum, now seemed to be firmly in favour as he was here again, hammering away on an old xylophone the boys had found in a box of forgotten toys that hadn't seen the light of day since they'd moved here.

'Of course, Phyllida,' Lucy replied, clicking into what she hoped was a professional tone.

'It would be helpful to know your colour scheme so we can tie in the table settings and canapés, you know?'

Bang-bang went the wooden hammer on the battered old instrument. At eight years old, Sam had mostly passed the stage of wanting to make a god-awful racket just for the hell of it. Shouldn't Josh be past that too? 'Josh, please,' she said with a quick smile. 'D'you mind . . .'

As he carried on bashing, Lucy marched out with the phone to the hall. 'Sorry. Summer holidays,' she said wryly.

'Ha, yes . . .'

'Erm, I can come over to talk things through,' Lucy added, 'no problem.'

'Great,' Phyllida said briskly. 'I wanted to mention, the wedding is being featured in *Country Style* magazine so they'll be sending a photographer along.'

Holy cow. 'Oh, that's lovely.'

'Not that I want you to feel pressurised,' Phyllida chuckled. 'We're a family who doesn't like fuss.' Lucy grimaced. She had already gathered that 'doesn't like fuss' meant 'we expect a tremendous palaver'. 'Could you pop over in the morning?' Phyllida asked. 'My daughter and her fiancé are visiting to go through the last-minute arrangements and I know they'd *love* to talk things over with you.'

'Yes, that's fine . . .'

'Great. So, we'll see you tomorrow, bright and early. We're so looking forward to seeing your ideas!' With that, Phyllida rang off.

That evening, with panic mounting now, Lucy combed her own garden, taking photographs, making notes and pulling together a doable plan in her mind. She had already assessed the land behind Irene's house, and while there were abundant shrubs there, she realised now that she would have to venture further afield in order to amass enough fresh greenery that was in peak condition to combine with her own garden flowers.

She thought about calling James to ask if it would be okay to venture onto his father's land and see what she could find in the woods. He'd fallen into a habit of texting to let her know when he would next be visiting his father, and she loved that. She found him so easy to be with. However, now she looked down at the phone

242

in her hand, and instead of texting him, she called Rikke to ask if she could look after the children for an hour or so next morning. Arrangements made, she pushed her phone back into her bag and decided to leave it for now.

Perhaps she *had* been seeing too much of James lately. If a visiting eight-year-old boy had imagined that there might be something between them, then it was probably better to give each other some space. After all, the last thing she wanted was for Marnie and Sam to worry, even for an instant, that she would ever consider replacing their dad.

Next morning Phyllida was at the front door of Fordell House before Lucy had even knocked. She beckoned her in, calling out, 'Emma, our florist is here!'

'Oh, hello there,' beamed the reed-slim blonde woman in a pink sweater and jeans as she trotted downstairs. She was closely followed by a young man – presumably her fiancé – in a pale denim shirt, black jeans and sunglasses.

'Lucy, this is Emma and Dylan,' Phyllida announced, then cried out: 'Davide!' In rushed the short, slim man with a neat beard whom Lucy had met on her last visit. 'Davide, I think we're ready for our coffees now,' Phyllida added with a quick smile.

Lucy watched the butler scuttling off in his russet corduroys and a moss-coloured sweater, his polished shoes clacking against the wooden floor. Phyllida led them all to the drawing room where they had discussed wedding plans on her first visit. He returned within minutes with a tray laden with tiny pastries and coffee for the four of them. 'Do tuck in,' Phyllida said as a hovering Davide poured the coffees. 'Don't we have any of those *pains au chocolat*?' she asked with a small frown. 'You know Emma loves them.'

'Mum, it's fine,' Emma said, with the kind of impatience Lucy recognised from her recent exchanges with her own mother. She smiled apologetically at Lucy. 'Thanks so much for coming out here today. I'm sure you're terribly busy. We could have discussed it by phone.'

'It's no trouble at all,' Lucy said quickly, and they all tucked into the pastries as Lucy started to outline her plans. When they'd finished, and everything had been whisked away by Davide – Lucy was the only one to thank him, which she did profusely – she brought out her sketchbook and showed Emma and Dylan her copious ideas.

'So, what I like to do at this time of year is a mixture of fresh garden flowers,' she explained. 'I'm thinking of freesias, hollyhocks, sweetpeas, that kind of thing. Fresh, pretty colours with lots of greenery to offset them. It'll all look quite loose and cottagey, nothing too structured.'

Emma nodded politely, but her hand had wound around Dylan's – he was jammed up close at her side – and Lucy suspected that perhaps this couple, whom she guessed were in their early thirties, weren't terribly interested in the specifics of what she planned to do.

'It all sounds great,' she said in a whisper when her mother had disappeared from the room, 'and we're happy for you to do whatever you think best.' Emma glanced at Dylan and smiled. 'But to be honest, this wedding is actually Mum's project and we decided to just let her run with it. Left to us, we'd have had it in a pie and mash shop in Hackney.'

The couple laughed, and Lucy sensed herself relaxing finally. 'But don't tell Phyllida,' Dylan offered, finally removing his shades and pulling a mock-horrified face. He was classically handsome with sculpted cheekbones and clear blue eyes edged by long dark lashes.

'I wouldn't dream of it,' Lucy said with a grin.

'Also, you must come to the wedding,' Emma added, touching her hand.

'Oh, um – you really don't need to ask me,' she said hastily. 'I'm very happy to put everything in place and then leave . . .'

'No, we'd really love you to come,' Emma insisted. 'Lots of people from the village are invited. We just want to make it a fun event for everyone.'

'Well, if you're sure?' Lucy asked hesitantly. Christ – she wasn't sure if she was up to attending a wedding yet. Managing run-of-the-mill social occasions had been enough of a challenge over the past eighteen months.

'Absolutely,' Emma said. 'D'you have children?'

'Yes, er – two.'

'Bring them along too. There'll be lots of kids there. Bring your partner too—'

'Um, it's just me actually,' she said quickly.

'Bring a friend, then.' Emma beamed at her. 'Please, it's just a buffet, very informal, and lots of people from the village are coming. You'll know them, I'm sure.' She looked at Dylan. 'We can't believe that magazine photographer's coming.'

Dylan shuddered dramatically. 'Nothing to do with me!'

'Oh, you know what Mum's like—' Emma broke off as Phyllida reappeared.

'I told Davide that next time we must have those *pains au chocolat.*'

'Please stop going on about them,' Emma said quickly. 'Poor Davide.'

'Poor Davide?' Phyllida laughed hollowly, then turned to the kitchen and called out: 'Davide, darling! Come here please.'

Lucy's mouth fell open as he hurried back into the room. 'Yes, darling?'

'Please tell Emma where we're going for your birthday next weekend.'

He beamed at her – this dapper, much younger Frenchman who, Lucy could see it now, clearly adored her. 'We are going to Vienna for coffee and cakes.'

Phyllida smiled and reached out to squeeze his hand – but still he didn't sit down and join the gathering. Perhaps he wasn't allowed, Lucy mused.

'We're very much looking forward to it, aren't we?' she asked, as if he were a child.

'Yes, darling,' he said, and in a gesture that seemed so sweet and affectionate, he reached out and smoothed down a stray strand of Phyllida's fine silvery hair. The older woman smiled too, despite his faux pas with the pastries, and it occurred to Lucy that before Ivan died, she might not have even registered such a tiny thing. But it occurred to her now that Ivan used to do things like that all the time: touching her hair and face, picking a hair off her sweater or wandering over and rubbing her shoulders gently while she read.

She pushed the memories away quickly, thanking Emma and Dylan again for the wedding invitation – hoping it sounded as if she was *thrilled* to be asked – and wondered what the heck she was thinking, agreeing to take this on when her focus should be on getting through the days, one at a time, keeping family life intact.

But still, she'd done it now.

Chapter Twenty-Eight

So much for creating a little distance between her and James. Pressure was mounting to start assembling her wedding displays, and when he dropped by next day, en route to his dad's, it would have felt ridiculous not to invite him in for a coffee.

'Did you get my text yesterday?' he asked as she filled his mug. 'I didn't want to pester you but I was worried you weren't okay.'

'Yes, I'm sorry, I forgot to reply,' she said vaguely.

She filled his mug and he perched on the edge of the kitchen table. 'So, how're you getting on with those wedding flowers?' Of course, as he and Kenny were attending as guests, James was well aware of her pressing deadline.

Lucy pulled a face. 'I have to admit, it feels like a heck of a lot to pull together.'

'Can I help at all?' he asked.

'Oh, I don't think so . . .'

James laughed, his dark eyes sparkling. 'I didn't mean

with the actual arranging, though I guess I could follow instructions—'

'Actually, you *could* help,' Lucy cut in, aware of a sense of relief now. 'Would you mind asking your dad if it'd be okay to take some bits and pieces from the woods? I wouldn't decimate it, just a few sprigs . . .'

James was beaming now. 'Lucy, you could fill your car ten times over with what you plundered from there and no one would notice. Just let me know when's a good time and I'll meet you, okay?'

So, next morning, after dropping off the children at holiday club, Lucy drove towards James's father's forest. The narrow lane climbed steeply away from the village, cutting through a dense wood before emerging again into open fields. She pulled up at the tumbledown hut at the roadside where James was waiting for her. 'Hi,' he said, greeting her with a brief hug.

'Hi.' She smiled. 'Thanks for doing this. I hope it's not terribly dull for you.'

'What else d'you think I'd be doing?' he asked. 'No, actually I've always loved it around here. The woods, I mean. This was the centre of Dad's Christmas tree empire, believe it or not.'

'Really?' She looked around at the tall pines that bordered both sides of the road, and the badly rotting shed. 'So, this was your shop?'

He nodded. 'It didn't look much better then than it does now, but no one seemed to care about that. C'mon – if we head through the forest there's a clearing. I think you'll find what you need there.'

Lucy looked at James. He was all rangy and tanned in a roomy grey T-shirt, faded jeans and battered old walking boots. As he marched on it became clear that he knew these woods as if they were part of him. 'Was your dad's business really successful?' she asked as they followed a shady path through the trees.

'Yes, amazingly,' he replied. 'It was the only thing he did that ever made decent money and he took it pretty seriously – by his standards, anyway. Of course, at thirteen years old I thought I knew much better than he did. One time, I persuaded him to drive me and my brother to a couple of garden centres so we could assess the competition.' He chuckled. 'I thought it might persuade him that we could up our game a bit.'

Lucy smiled. She had already decided she had overreacted to Noah questioning Sam about her relationship to James, and to her mother's quizzings too. It had just been a little too much, too close together, and it had touched a nerve. But since when had she based her life choices on what other people thought of her?

'So, what did you have in mind?' she asked. 'For your dad's business, I mean?'

'Oh, you know – I thought we could build a shop, sell all kinds of Christmas paraphernalia seeing as people were coming from all over to buy our trees anyway.' He grinned at her. 'I had an idea that we might be a sort of festive superstore.'

'Nothing wrong with ambition. So what happened?' They had emerged from the woods into a wide clearing, filled with clear sunshine on this cool, bright morning. It was the kind of secret glade she'd have delighted in finding as a child.

'He was furious,' James replied. 'Stomped around the place, going, "Who the hell wants scented candles and potpourri?"'

Lucy laughed. 'Potpourri angered him?'

'Made him livid. I remember him shouting, "Why have you brought me to a bloody grotto?"'

'With Christmas music playing, no doubt.'

'Oh, don't get him started on Christmas music.'

Armed with laundry-style bags and secateurs, they started to gather lush ferns and eucalyptus; the kind of greens that were often regarded as 'fillers' but which Lucy found as beautiful as the flowers they would be arranged to set off. There was a wild bay tree, from which she clipped sprigs, having paused to ask, 'Are you sure it's okay, taking all of this?'

'Of course it is.'

'Does your dad know I'm doing this?'

'I told him I was meeting you,' James said, as they carried on filling the bags.

'Honestly, this is fantastic,' Lucy said. 'How did you know all this was here? I mean, it's perfect.'

He turned and looked at her. 'I grew up here, remember. This is where I spent pretty much all of my childhood.'

Onwards they went, filling all of the bags Lucy had brought, before heading back into the woodland and making their way towards the road. Lucy breathed in the scent of the firs as they followed the pine-needle-carpeted path. Chinks of sunshine eked in through the branches. It was so soothing in here, dark and shady and blissfully silent apart from their footsteps on the soft ground. Every so often, Lucy stopped to pick up small objects – a speckled feather, a particularly exotic fir cone – in the hope that they might inspire Sam to start a new museum in his bedroom. He would probably reject them, as the whole point had been that he'd found the items himself. Maybe he'd outgrown the whole idea anyway. But it was worth a try, she decided.

Back at her car, they loaded the bags into the boot. 'D'you think you have enough here?' James asked.

'Oh, yes, more than enough.' She closed the boot and smiled at him. 'Thank you so much. This has really helped me.'

'Hey!' a voice rang out, and they both swung around to the direction of its source. There didn't seem to be anyone in sight.

Lucy frowned. 'This *is* your dad's land, isn't it?'

'Yes, of course.' James sighed, and a look of resignation settled on his face as someone – it was Kenny, she saw now – appeared from the woods and stomped towards them.

'What're you doing here, Dad?' he asked pleasantly.

'I'm not on house arrest, am I?' he retorted. 'I mean, I am allowed out into my own woods from time to time?'

'Of course you are,' James said, exasperated. 'It's just, I wasn't expecting—'

'What *you* two are doing is more the point,' Kenny cut in, smirking now and turning to stare at the bags sitting there in Lucy's open boot, greenery bursting from them.

'James was just helping me out,' Lucy started. 'We were just—'

'Helping you out in the woods? Bet he was!' Kenny guffawed loudly.

She looked away, her face burning hot. Christ, what *was* he inferring? Did everyone assume she and James were have some kind of fling—

'Dad, I told you I was meeting Lucy,' James said, clearly mortified by his father's remark too. 'I said she was doing some wedding flowers. Emma Somerville's wedding, remember? The one you're invited to?'

'I didn't realise you meant *this* Lucy,' his father muttered.

James laughed hollowly and shook his head. 'How many Lucys d'you think I know, Dad?'

Now Kenny was scratching at his beard, fixing his gaze on Lucy. 'Well, I don't know. He never tells me anything about his private life.'

James groaned and shook his head, like a teenager in the presence of his embarrassing dad. Lucy edged towards her car, keen to escape before Kenny announced that he was considering taking out a full-page ad in the *Heathfield Gazette*, saying something like: *James and Lucy. What's really going on between those two?* Silly her, for thinking it was so normal and unremarkable for a woman to be platonic friends with a man! 'I've met you before,' Kenny added, studying her intently now.

'Yes – it was at the hospital. You'd had an incident with a fishbone . . .'

'You were with Rikke. *Our* Rikke.'

'That's right,' she said. 'I hope you don't mind me gathering up a few bits and pieces from the woods,' she added, indicating the pile of bulging bags.

'A few bits and pieces? Is that what you call it?' He raised an extravagantly sprouting eyebrow and strode over to her car to peer into the boot. She really couldn't tell if he was teasing or not.

'Remember I told you Lucy's decorating the church and the house for the wedding?' James said.

'Right,' his father said, his dark eyes gleaming with amusement now. 'Well, you just come and take whatever you like anytime, Lucy. I'm sure James will be very happy if you do . . .'

'Kenny, I—' she started.

'. . . Something like nine hundred Scots Pines and Douglas Firs out here,' he went on, sweeping an arm as if to indicate his kingdom, 'so I'm hardly going to miss a few bits.' He paused and looked at them both. 'Sorry to disturb you two today.'

'Dad,' James said quickly, 'you weren't disturbing anyone.'

'So you keep saying.' Kenny chuckled as Lucy climbed into her car, and James threw her an apologetic, *what-can-you-do?* kind of look as she drove away.

Had Kenny really thought they'd been 'up to' something, other than gathering plants? The idea was so ridiculous it was actually funny. Amused now – in a mortified way, as if she'd come out of the ladies with a trail of loo roll stuck to her shoe – she fixed her gaze on the narrow road that led back to the village. At least she had virtually an entire garden centre stuffed in her boot – which meant she would never need to venture into Kenny Halsall's woods again.

And thank heavens for that.

Chapter Twenty-Nine

Although she suspected it wasn't entirely good for her, Lucy would occasionally wake up and just lie there for a few minutes, playing a game with herself. These games often involved making a list in her head, and today it was entitled:

If I Still Had Ivan

I wouldn't try to cajole him into being more sociable. She was going to a wedding today – Emma and Dylan's wedding – and if her husband were here he'd be huffing and puffing, saying they didn't even know them – so did they really have to go? Like a grumpy teenager he'd be sulking and poking about in his wardrobe – the one that was still stuffed with his clothes, as if he might appear miraculously and need something to wear. And he'd be grumbling about having to put on a suit (in a sort of protest he had only ever owned one at a time, to be brought out for special occasions).

Although he had always been perfectly lovely with her

friends, Lucy had wished sometimes that Ivan would make a little more effort – with the B&B guests too, for that matter. As it was, he was only truly sociable where his own friends and colleagues were concerned. Now, of course, she berated herself for having nurtured any criticisms of him at all. That's what happened when someone died; you couldn't bring yourself to acknowledge that they had any faults at all. Instead, you decided you'd been an overcritical harridan and not appreciated them enough.

. . . Or mind if he didn't want to come on a walk. When Ivan started working back in Manchester, Lucy's expectations of their weekends had shot off the scale. While she was eager to get out in the countryside, once he'd put in a couple of hours in the garden here, Ivan had often just wanted to flop on the sofa and bury himself in a book. 'What a waste of our precious time together!' she'd fume. Had she been awful to live with back then, she wondered now? It had been perfectly reasonable, she reflected, for Ivan to prefer to stay home – 'Those clouds look ominous, Luce' – rather than hiking up a hill with Sam, Marnie and a bunch of their friends to pick raspberries that they could have easily bought from a shop. 'Without bugs in them,' he'd pointed out on more than one occasion. Shop-bought raspberries were one of about eight million things that made her think of him.

. . . Or get cross if he started mansplaining. When she had been trying to shift a little weight after being pregnant with Sam, Lucy had taken up running. 'I'll tell you the right way to train,' Ivan had said – proceeding to jog around the park with her, rattling off a list of must-dos including 'never slap your feet down like that, all right? Unless you want to damage a tendon.'

'Of course, that's my goal for today,' she'd shot back, 'to wreck my body.' She'd glared at him. 'Anyway, before today, when was the last time you did any purposeful running?' He'd just laughed her off and continued, irritatingly, to dispense tips – and if that happened today, she would not mind a bit. Nope – today, he could stand there, instructing her on the best way to pack her delicate wedding decorations into her car (he had always been an extremely precise car-packer) and she would bow to his superior knowledge, and bestow thanks.

. . . I'd also let him 'help' with the cooking. While Ivan had cooked occasionally – on special occasions, when praise was in the offing – Lucy had tended to take care of meals day-to-day. But Ivan couldn't resist 'helping', giving a curry an idle stir as he ambled past, or squirting in some lime juice or tasting it and saying, 'Mmm, I think it needs salt.' It didn't count as *helping*, as it had no impact on her workload; in fact it served only to rile her. However, now she would embrace his lime-squeezing, salt-adding tendencies, which led her to the next point . . .

. . . Crisps! 'God, I fancy some crisps,' her husband would often exclaim, such was his rabid desire for salt when she could barely tolerate any at all. 'Why do we never have any in the house?' If Ivan were here now, the cupboards would be so crammed with his favourite variety (good old salt and vinegar) that, whenever he opened a cupboard, an avalanche of family packets would tumble out.

But the truth was, she didn't have Ivan, so these games were pointless – and anyway, what was she doing, lying in bed, remembering Ivan nagging about her tendons and claiming all the cooking glory when the wedding was happening in a few hours' time? She jumped out of bed, conscious of unfamiliar twinges from the hours she had spent piecing the final floral arrangements together last night. For seven hours straight she'd been bent over mounds of greenery, her eyes scratchy with tiredness and her fingers sore from all the twisting and bending of branches and stems.

Having served up nothing more elaborate than beans on toast, followed by Angel Delight – luckily, the children regarded such offerings as treats – she had zoomed through the bath time and story time routines with brisk efficiency, letting them get away with a perfunctory teeth clean, before settling down to toil away at the kitchen table until two-thirty a.m. Prior to that – for most of the day, with Rikke helping out – Lucy had put the indoor decorations in place in the church (the outdoor ones would have to wait until morning). Then they'd driven out to Fordell House to drop off the table centrepieces and decorate the banisters of the sweeping stairwell, twisting them with eucalyptus and ivy and inserting fresh flowers, with cunningly disguised spongy pouches at the bases of their stems to keep them fresh until the next day. Phyllida had been delighted, thank goodness.

Now it had just gone six-thirty a.m. and dawn was creeping through the white linen blinds in Lucy's bedroom. She hadn't had nearly enough sleep, and she registered the tiredness in her eyes, the dark shadows lurking beneath and the prominent crease between her brows – the 'mum line', as it was known – as she checked

257

her reflection in the dressing table mirror. She would need to perform some kind of rescue job with make-up, and do her nails, too. They were grubby and ragged after her endeavours with the foliage last night. She hadn't even thought about her hands until this moment.

At least her hair was in better shape, she decided after her shower. She'd been back to Nicola, who'd done a brilliant job, and as Lucy blow-dried it she realised she was starting to look more like old-Lucy – i.e. *younger* Lucy – from the days when she'd still made an effort each morning for work. When she had been at Claudine – in the pre-Max Cleavage days – they used to say lingerie was 'a woman's best friend'. It was on all their packaging and advertising material in elegant script. Granted, it was hardly a genius tagline, but it summed up the fact that, like a dear friend, the perfect bra and knicker ensemble could lift the spirits like nothing else.

Only now, with her interest in lingerie long gone, Lucy decided that an excellent haircut had an even more marked effect. It fell in loose waves around her face, glossy and healthy-looking, by some kind of miracle. To think, back in her Claudine days she would have given a tiny rural salon like Nicola's a wide berth, assuming they still used the rubber-cap method for highlights, and recommended poodle perms.

She applied light make-up quickly, and when she'd finished she was pleased to see that she looked like a fully fledged member of the human race again. Pleasingly, Lucy had also managed to unearth one jar of nail polish that hadn't entirely glooped up.

Sam and Marnie were up and dressed now, and Carys had stopped by to whisk them off for the day. Lucy had decided not to take them along to the wedding, in spite of Emma's generous invitation. She knew they'd have a far better time with their friends. 'Look at *you*!' Carys exclaimed. 'God, Lucy. You look fantastic!'

'Thanks,' she said, unused to such an enthusiastic response to her appearance.

Carys beamed at her. 'Good luck for today.'

'Thanks,' Lucy said again, seemingly incapable of more meaningful speech.

Her friend grabbed her hand. 'You should feel really proud of yourself, doing all of this, and going to the wedding . . .' She paused. 'Are you nervous?'

'Just a bit,' she admitted.

'It'll be great. Lucky you – I hear it's the wedding of the year, around here.'

Agh, please don't say that, Lucy thought. Then Carys hugged her and called for the children; Amber and Noah had hared straight up to Sam and Marnie's rooms.

In the now empty house, she caught herself pacing from room to room, straightening cushions, picking up the odd lidless felt tip and, disconcertingly, a whole toasted crumpet that was poking out from beneath the sofa. Hopefully it hadn't been there for long enough for any of her guests to spot it. Taking a deep breath, she tried not to dwell on the last conversation she had had with her mother, during which Anna had enquired about how things were going with the B&B, and the wedding flowers – implying yet again that it was far too much for Lucy to manage. At least she hadn't started on how Lucy must sell Rosemary Cottage and move to Leeds or Manchester or anywhere else. And she hadn't asked her about James either.

Lucy made herself a strong coffee and sipped it, re-assuring herself that the flowers looked great, and that she'd know plenty of people at the wedding. Della and her husband Frank would be there, and James and his father, of course – although she might have to keep a distance if Kenny was still on that, 'Ooh, what were you two up to in the woods?' trip like a sniggering thirteen-year-old rather than a seventy-something man.

It was finally time to set off. Lucy mentally added one more point to her 'If I Still Had Ivan' list: *I'd be perfectly satisfied if he told me I looked 'okay'.*

It used to frustrate her, the way he'd say, 'Yeah, it's nice,' whenever she put on a new outfit for him to express an opinion on. She'd craved a more enthusiastic response – perhaps to reassure her that he still found her attractive, or 'ravishing', as he used to say, back in the old days.

One last check in the mirror: 'You're *fine*, Luce,' her husband would say whenever she dithered like this, kissing her cheek and giving her a teasing smile. She smoothed down her long dark hair and tried for a smile. He was right; she *was* fine. That was good enough for her.

Chapter Thirty

She arrived early at the church to meet Davide, as arranged, and a couple of his brothers who had come over from Narbonne, their hometown in France. While Lucy checked the bouquets she had already fixed to the ends of each pew, Davide and one of the brothers hopped up and down on a flimsy stepladder in order to set up the wire frame that would support Lucy's cascade of flowers and foliage at the entrance. Rikke was on hand to help, although at the reception she would be focusing on her harp recital. It still surprised and delighted Lucy to notice how lives intertwined here in this small, close community. Her path would never have crossed with Emma and Dylan's if Phyllida hadn't mentioned to her hairdresser that she had been let down by her florist.

Soon, everyone began to congregate outside the church. 'The flowers look gorgeous,' Della said, scuttling over to her, with Frank at her side, adding, 'You can sit with us if you like.'

'Thanks,' she said gratefully. Lucy had been aware of this before: the feeling that she was being taken care of at a social event so she wasn't left hanging about on her own. She had already glanced around for James, but there was no sign of him yet. The guests were all filtering into the church now, and Lucy sensed a swell of pride as she looked around. Although she had put everything in place last night, it was a different matter seeing her work on display on the actual day. It was a crisp, bright morning, and sunshine beamed in through the stained-glass windows, scattering patches of jewel-coloured light onto the tiled floor and polished woodwork. The effect of the copious greenery, plus sprays of hollyhocks and freesias was beautifully fresh and cheery, and as they took their seats Della whispered, 'So many people are talking about your flowers. You should be so proud of what you've managed to do.'

Lucy beamed with delight, and the beautiful couple glided in, Emma a slip of a thing in cream chiffon, her long blonde hair scooped up, her equally stunning brides-maid in dusky pink. The ceremony began.

Although Lucy had only met Emma and Dylan on that one occasion, she couldn't help feeling moved as hymns were sung and they said their vows. Lucy and Ivan's marriage had been a ramshackle affair in a registry office. In a fit of rebellion, she had worn a black leather jacket over a plain white shift. Her mother had pushed for a traditional, lavish do, but she and Ivan hadn't wanted that.

'You had to be unconventional,' her mother had said, mustering a stoical smile, but with disappointment clouding her grey eyes. They had all reconvened at Lucy and Ivan's flat where their friends had brought various dishes to form a mishmash of a buffet. They drank cava, not champagne. Much later, after copious quantities had been downed, she heard her mother whispering to her Aunt Elspeth, 'My only daughter – and we're sitting here eating garlic bread and pizza! Still, I suppose young people like to do things their own way.'

Emma and Dylan's ceremony came to an end. Lucy caught Della's glance; clearly, her friend had picked up on her wave of emotion, and squeezed her hand. 'Better not cry,' she whispered with a smile. 'See that photographer over there? She's from *Country Style* magazine.'

'Oh, God, I'd forgotten about that,' Lucy exclaimed as they all started to file out of the church. There was a real mixture here, she realised now: Emma and Dylan's friends, most of them so ridiculously good-looking that Lucy couldn't help staring, fascinated. It wasn't as if the inhabitants of Burley Bridge wore sackcloth and had never encountered mascara. However, such high-octane glamour was distinctly lacking in regular village life, and these beautiful young things were attracting plenty of attention from passers-by as they boarded the waiting coach.

Then there were the locals. Phyllida had certainly had an inclusive approach as Lucy spotted numerous familiar faces: Len, who owned the garage, plus many of the shopkeepers, and even the head teacher from Marnie and Sam's school.

They were greeted at Fordell House by a cluster of waiting staff bearing trays of champagne. In the rather faded but still opulent lounge, Davide fluttered from group to group, topping up glasses as if he were staff himself, and Lucy gratefully took a sip of champagne.

'What a job you've done,' exclaimed Len's wife, Pauline. 'It looks stunning. Honestly, I don't know how you do all this.'

'Oh, I enjoyed it,' Lucy said, thankful that no one had

seen her in the early hours of the morning, hand-tying the final decorations and picking out thorns from her fingers. Yesterday, when she and Rikke had come here to wrap swathes of greenery around the polished mahogany banisters, she had wondered if it was opulent enough. She had created centrepieces of birch twigs and sweetpeas, with tiny white fairy lights nestled within. Now, as the waiters started to do the rounds with trays of canapés, she allowed herself a swell of pride on seeing that it *had* worked.

But where was James? Lucy caught herself looking out for him, and when he and his father appeared, smartly suited but with James looking rather harassed, she waved to attract their attention.

James arrived at her side as his father wandered off. 'We had a bit of a wrangle this morning,' he murmured. 'It was kind of tricky. I wasn't sure we'd make it at all.'

'What happened?' Lucy asked, surprised to note how pleased – and, actually, relieved – she was to see him.

He grimaced. 'Dad couldn't see why it might not be the thing to turn up in ancient cords and a holey Snoopy T-shirt.'

Lucy chuckled. 'Mmm, yes, they're relaxed – but possibly not *that* relaxed.'

'I had to virtually force him into that suit,' James added, shaking his head. 'He's like a teenager sometimes.'

'The suit thing can be quite an issue,' she murmured, 'for someone who doesn't like to conform.'

'Yeah.' James chuckled. 'It's only clothes, though, isn't it? No big deal really.' Across the room, Kenny was chatting animatedly with Phyllida, making her laugh.

'You look very smart,' she added truthfully. 'Both of you, I mean.'

He shrugged and smiled and said, '*You* look wonderful—' He seemed to catch himself then, and quickly reached for a glass from a passing tray.

'Oh, thank you.' Lucy smiled, a little taken aback by the compliment. It felt lovely, though, to have someone say that to her. She glanced around and wondered if anyone might be making assumptions about them standing together and chatting, then decided she was being ridiculous – and that she didn't care anyway.

She was, quite simply, happy. She had friends all around her, a glass of champagne in her hand, and everyone loved her flowers. The realisation lifted her heart.

'Erm, I just wanted to say,' James added, 'I'm sorry about the other day, in the woods. I think Dad thought he was being funny.'

'Oh, that's fine,' she said quickly.

'He can just be a bit, you know . . . he doesn't think before he speaks these days.' Their eyes met, and she could see how important it was to him to straighten this out with her.

'It really is okay,' Lucy said, more firmly now as Phyllida tapped a teaspoon against a glass and called out, 'Can everyone head outside to the front lawn for the group photograph, please!'

Out they all shuffled, to be arranged in rows around Emma, Dylan, his parents and Phyllida, who was presiding over the occasion like the figurehead of a ship, dressed in elegant mauve silk with a matching hat with a tuft of netting sprouting from the front. Davide had been relegated to standing at one end, with Kenny and James. Lucy, who was standing next to Della and Frank, caught James's eye. She smiled, glad that he was here, his 'You look wonderful!' declaration still ringing in her

265

ears, probably because she was unused to such an enthusiastic response ('You're *fine*, Luce!'). And it was true that he looked good in his dark grey classic suit; he scrubbed up extremely well.

'Okay, everyone – bright smiles please.' The photographer – who looked barely old enough to be in charge of the expensive equipment – commanded everyone's attention from behind her tripod. 'Ready . . .' The gaggle of young children in attendance were called to heel. 'That's it . . . but I can't quite see everyone at the back.' There was some last-minute reshuffling, and then a collective gasp as Kenny burst from the group to assume a dramatic pose – arms outstretched – at the front.

'Dad!' James exclaimed, to a ripple of amusement from the guests. 'Dad – please, come back here.'

Lucy glanced with amusement at Della. 'So where *should* I stand?' Kenny asked, possibly feigning confusion.

'Perhaps not right at the front, Sir?' the photographer offered diplomatically, as James lurched over and tried to take his father's arm.

'Stop manhandling me!' he snapped. 'What're you doing?'

'C'mon, Dad, you need to come back a bit . . .'

'Why?' Kenny blustered.

'Because you're not actually getting married and you're standing in front of the bride . . .' James glanced over at Lucy, and she caught him suppressing a smile, surprised by the surge of warmth she felt for him. Was she too harsh on her own mother? She couldn't imagine ever being as patient as James clearly was as he managed to coax Kenny, gently but firmly, back to his allocated position. As if fearful that he might break rank again, the photographer rattled off the shots at remarkable speed.

266

The incident seemed to have only added to the occasion, as the level of chatter and laughter had risen by several notches by the time the buffet was set out, and Rikke's harp music rippled beautifully across the room.

So much praise was heaped upon Lucy that, by now, she was unsure of what to do with it. As the afternoon tipped into a convivial evening, she was pencilled in for three future events. The photographer was doing the rounds of the room now, taking reportage shots as the guests mingled.

'Could I get one of you two, please?' she said, at which Lucy and Della obligingly beamed at the lens.

'And me!' It was Kenny again, lurching over with champagne sloshing out of his glass.

'Dad – stop photobombing!' And now James had appeared, smiling wearily.

'You did all of this?' Kenny barked at Lucy, indicating the floral arrangements on the tables.

'Er, yes . . .'

'Amazing what you can do with a few bits of old twigs, Lucy,' Kenny chuckled, swaying slightly and resting a bony hand on the table for support. James rolled his eyes good-naturedly. 'Where's the champagne?' Kenny added, looking around. 'My glass is empty, James. Where's that girl with the tray?'

'Dad, maybe have a water or an orange juice this time around?'

'Stop trying to police my drinking,' he retorted, catching Lucy's eye as though she might be an ally. 'He's always like this,' he added.

'That's right, Dad,' James said resignedly. 'Put on this earth to ruin your fun.'

And so the evening went on, and now the pressure

267

was off, Lucy realised that she was enjoying herself very much. A couple of champagnes had given her a warm, fuzzy feeling. While she would have loved Ivan to have seen her flowers, she didn't feel completely at sea without him at her side. 'Look how patient James is with his dad,' she murmured to Della later, as they watched Emma and Dylan leave in a vintage Bentley.

'He's so good with him,' she agreed. 'You and James know each other from way back, don't you?'

'Yes, we met when we were nine and I used to come on holidays here.' She wasn't rattled this time by the mention of her and James having some kind of connection. Perhaps it was the champagne, or the general conviviality of the occasion, but today she was just happy to be here. Anyway, she had nothing to be embarrassed about and nothing to hide.

'I hadn't realised he was your partner in crime when you were nicking Mum's fruit,' Della teased her.

Lucy laughed. 'Did he say it was his idea?'

'No, he blamed you!' They both chuckled. 'So, whose idea was it?'

'I couldn't possibly say,' Lucy said as they drifted back inside. The two women settled on a chaise longue. The party was starting to thin out now, but Lucy was in no rush to leave. The children were sleeping over at Carys's tonight. She was lucky, she decided, despite everything that had happened. Last Christmas she was still barely managing to struggle through the days – and now here she was, on this beautiful August day, at a wedding.

'You know James and his brother didn't have the easiest time, don't you?' Della's voice cut into her thoughts. 'After their mum died I mean.'

'Yes, I do.'

Lucy remembered the day James had told her he'd lost his mum, when they had sat by the river, eating prawn cocktail crisps that dissolved on their tongues, and drinking tepid Coke. The Linton kids had been there too. Being local, they had known about James's history already. Unlike Lucy, they had visited Hally at home, and had known his mum as well as his crazy-sounding dad. 'His mum was so sweet,' Toni Linton had told her later, when Hally had gone home. 'She made us a picnic and we took it to the woods. There was a clearing and we lit a fire and all sat around it. It was so fun.'

Now, in the faded grandeur of Fordell House, Lucy sipped her champagne, wondering if Toni had been talking about the clearing where she and James had gathered eucalyptus a few days ago.

Lucy's heart had ached for Hally back then. To lose a parent when you were only a child seemed like the most brutal thing imaginable. How could you possibly fill that gap, she wondered? 'You should come here in winter,' Toni had added. 'We're all allowed up to Hally's then 'cause his dad needs help selling Christmas trees.' What fun that sounded: helping the customers to choose their trees, taking the money and – best of all – bagging up trees with the netting machine Hally had told her about.

More guests were leaving the wedding now, and Lucy told Della she'd like to say goodbye to James and Kenny before Frank drove them home. The front door was open, and she spotted James outside, tie loosened now, seemingly having been cornered on the steps by a middle-aged woman in a powder blue silk suit. Lucy stood and waited.

'I worry for your dad, James,' she was saying, hand plonked on her ample hip. 'I really think you should have him diagnosed as soon as possible.'

'Reena, look,' he started, 'I know there's an issue but it's not as easy as you might think.'

'But he thought my holiday house was his place! He tried to barge his way in, James.' The woman was tipsy, Lucy realised, her voice strident.

'Yes, but that was just the once – it hasn't happened since.'

'But surely, if he saw a psychiatrist . . . There's someone who comes to the GP's surgery in Heathfield twice a month. I hear he's very good with elderly people.'

'He's really not keen.'

'I realise you have help,' she went on, 'but is it enough? I worry about him . . .'

'Well, I do too.' Just as she was about to head back to Della, Lucy saw James registering her presence, perhaps with a trace of relief. He made his excuses with a tight, distracted smile and beckoned her outside. They strode to a low stone wall and perched on it.

'Sorry,' she said. 'I didn't want to interrupt you there, but we're about to leave.'

'No, it's fine,' he said quickly. 'Reena's a decent person and she does want to help. But with Dad . . .' He paused. 'It's kind of tricky.'

Lucy nodded, wary of saying anything insensitive, and reluctant to show that she had heard the details of the conversation. 'I'm sure you do whatever you can.' She paused. 'Where is he now?'

He nodded towards the cars on the drive. 'He's having a doze in the passenger seat. I'd better take him home in a sec.'

Lucy nodded again. 'Well, it's been lovely seeing you today. I'm so glad you were here, James.'

'I'm glad you were too.' He looked around the huge

but rather neglected garden, and when he turned back to her, their eyes met for a moment. Maybe it was the champagne, or the headiness of the occasion, but it startled her as she sensed a flicker of something between them; then, suddenly, it was as if they were thirteen again, hatching plans as they sat together with their feet dangling in the shallow river. She had nurtured a crush on him then – secret and powerful, before she'd properly known what one was. But it had been a crush all the same.

'D'you fancy Hally?' Brenna Linton had asked once, when it had just been the two of them lying on the warm, clipped grass in the Lintons' back garden.

'Of course not!' Lucy had retorted, sensing her cheeks reddening. 'Why do you ask that?'

'A lot of girls do,' she said, giving her a sideways look.

'Well, I don't.'

'My sister does,' Brenna had added, meaning Toni. 'She's *mad* about him.'

'Really?' Lucy had tried to act casual but had been aware of a flicker of envy catching fire now in her belly. After all, the Lintons were here all year round. Hally was bound to be closer to them than he was to her; they spent way more time together.

Now Lucy cleared her throat, and James fished his car keys out of his jacket pocket. 'Is your dad okay,' she asked quickly, 'after all those champagnes?'

'He thinks he had champagne,' James replied with a conspiratorial smile, 'but between you and me, I made sure the ones he was offered were alcohol free.'

'That must have taken some doing!'

'It did,' he chuckled, 'but the girl serving us took care of it. The way Dad is, he can't handle alcohol, although he used to love a drink.'

'But didn't he notice? And I thought he seemed tipsy . . .'

James chuckled. 'He thought it was booze, so it affected him that way.'

'Placebo effect,' Lucy suggested, and James nodded.

'Very clever.' She touched his arm without thinking. 'You're brilliant with him.'

'Oh, God, not at all,' he blustered. They parted ways with the briefest of hugs, and she went back inside to find Della and Frank, who were ready to head home.

Later that night, as she wiped away her make-up, she wondered if she had imagined that moment between her and James, out in the garden. Although she had been drinking, he hadn't, and she hoped she hadn't hung around him too much, or been too gushy, or . . .

Lucy caught herself fretting momentarily as she undressed, but by the time she had climbed into bed, her worries had faded and she lay there, not lonely tonight but . . . she wondered quite *what* she was feeling, and realised it was contentment. That's what it was.

She was truly content, and not just because of the champagne – perhaps for the first time since Ivan died. In fact, she had felt happy for most of the day. To any normal person that might have sounded unremarkable: after all, weddings were generally joyous occasions. But to Lucy, it felt nothing short of miraculous. She lay there in her cool white bed, thrilled and amazed that she could still feel that way after all.

Some day that had been, James mused, sitting up in bed in his old childhood bedroom in a T-shirt and PJ bottoms, with an unread book on his lap. The wedding – Christ, the effort it had taken to persuade his father to go. James hadn't been crazy about going either but the Somervilles had always been so good to Kenny, sending over a huge ham or a boulder-like fruitcake at Christmas, paying him generously for his logs and giving him the odd handyman job when he'd been out of work. In the summer months he'd come home with a box of lettuce, accepted out of politeness (his father would rather have eaten his own eyeball than consume salad), and in autumn there were apples and blackberries from the orchard. To not attend the wedding would have been rude, James had reasoned – and now he was delighted that they'd gone.

To think – Lucy was living here now. He'd loved those days when they were just kids, getting up to all sorts. He'd always thought of Burley Bridge as a pretty drab place, where nothing ever happened – then she'd show up at her aunt and uncle's without warning. From one year to the next, he'd never know if she was coming, but when she arrived, it would immediately feel as if she had never been away.

It felt, he thought rather wildly, like the sun had come out when she'd returned. And now she lived in that beautiful house and had her floristry business, and of course she'd been through hell, with her husband's death. He didn't want to come across as pushy, keeping in touch when her life was obviously full, but all the same, he was aware of a sense of lightness about him, and some other emotion that he hadn't experienced for quite a long time. Of course he felt happy when he and Spike were hanging out together, or when he'd finished a particularly challenging job and the boat owner was pleased. There were lots of great things in his life – but this was different.

He'd had a couple of large glasses of rather fierce red wine since he'd come home from the wedding. He knew his father hated it, said it made his joints sore and that it was 'a posh people's drink' (champagne – even the alcohol-free version – clearly didn't fall under that banner) so James had decided it was okay to have a bottle in the house. And now, as he sat in his bleak, dimly lit childhood bedroom, the happiness he was experiencing was as bright and vivid as a summer's day spent by the river. It didn't seem to matter that, long term, he hadn't a clue about what to do about his dad, or that he could hear him muttering to himself through the mottled partition wall.

At that moment, James Halsall was definitely, one hundred per cent happy. And also, quite possibly, a little drunk.

Part Three

October

Chapter Thirty-One

Autumn had arrived, turning the West Yorkshire valley burnished orange and gold. With it had come a new business to the village, the brainchild of Della's younger sister Roxanne: a vintage shop, selling not only exquisite clothes but also carefully chosen pottery, picture frames, jewellery and the like. Lucy was delighted to be asked to create an autumnal window display for the opening. Although her herbaceous borders didn't offer the abundance of fresh flowers as they had during the summer months, she was learning to work with the seasons, bringing home foliage from her walks with the children.

The utility room at Rosemary Cottage quickly filled up with branches encrusted with pine cones. Galvanised buckets held acorns, dried berries, silver birch twigs and velvety leaves. Lucy found herself becoming as keen-eyed as Sam had been when hunting for museum exhibits, and she soon devised ways to incorporate these autumnal treasures into her arrangements. She only wished she could rouse his enthusiasm to start collecting again.

One crisp October morning, she had just seen her

overnight guests on their way when James called. 'I'm at Dad's,' he said. 'Spike's here for a couple of days. D'you fancy coming up and meeting him later? With the kids, I mean? I thought we could have a campfire . . .'

'We'd love to,' she said, delighted, but also wondering what Marnie and Sam would make of Kenny. He wasn't the normal kind of grandpa, she reflected, as they drove up through the woods towards his cottage later that afternoon. No, clearly he was far better than normal with his mad beard and hoop earring as he welcomed them in, with the announcement that they could do whatever they liked here. James caught Lucy's eye and smiled.

'What, anything?' Sam asked, wide-eyed as he gazed around the cluttered living room.

'That's a dangerous thing to say to kids, Dad,' James chuckled, which his father chose to ignore.

'Sure,' Kenny said to Sam. 'What d'you want to do? Tell you what. Have a think about it while I get you a drink – orange juice okay?'

'If it's no trouble,' Lucy said quickly, answering for them.

'It's no trouble,' Kenny called back, already in the kitchen. 'I'd offer you a sandwich as well if some smart-arse hadn't thrown them away.'

With closed-lipped smiles at Kenny's choice of words, Marnie and Sam perched on the old worn-out sofa. 'That was, what – nearly two years ago,' James murmured to Lucy. 'Christ, sometimes I wonder if there's anything wrong with his memory at all.'

She smiled, squeezing in next to the children and looking around the room as James went to fetch his son from one of the bedrooms. From James's previous descriptions of the place, she could see that a major tidy-up had been undertaken, although the shelves were still crammed with what looked like old magazines, newspapers and assorted paperwork. 'I'm off to sort through Dad's boxes of receipts, used jiffy bags and concert tickets stretching back to the Seventies,' he'd told her with a stoic smile one evening, as he was setting off. 'Thank God the scented candle craze passed him by or the whole place would have been up in flames by now.'

A few moments later, orange juice was handed out in mugs, and James had reappeared with Spike: a tall, angular and rather timid-looking boy clutching a paperback, with a shock of sandy hair brushing into his dark eyes.

'I was just finishing a chapter,' he remarked apologetically as a large ginger cat wound its way around his legs, quickly disappearing again on glimpsing the visitors.

'Okay, well, this is my friend Lucy,' James said, 'and this is Marnie, and Sam.' There were mumbled hellos from the children, then James rubbed his hands together and said, 'So I thought we could build a campfire out the back, if you'd like that?'

Spike's face brightened instantly. 'Yeah!'

James put an arm around his son's shoulders. 'There's work to do first. We'll need you all to help collect some wood.'

They headed outside, leaving Kenny, who brushed off their invitation to come out and join them. Outside now under the slowly darkening sky, they started to gather whatever wood they could find littering the scrubby ground. Lucy turned to James. 'How's your dad doing these days?' she asked.

'He's still managing,' he replied, 'but things are changing, you know? It's so gradual it's barely noticeable, but I can see it happening.'

She nodded and touched his arm. 'It must be so hard.'

James nodded. 'He remembered the sandwiches, which is amazing. But then he won't remember little things like where the cutlery's kept, or where he's put his keys, his glasses – we lose a lot of glasses and keys.'

'What d'you think you'll do?' she asked, glancing over to the children, her heart lifting to see Spike patiently explaining that only dry wood would do; the thinner pieces, not the moss-covered log that Sam was attempting to drag over.

'I'm still trying to persuade him to move,' he replied, 'but no joy with that so far. He's the most stubborn man on earth, but I understand it. This is his home.'

'That sounds familiar,' she said. James gave her a quizzical look. 'Every so often,' she added, 'Mum has a go at convincing me that we should move closer.'

'Closer to Leeds, you mean?' He frowned.

'But we're not,' Lucy added quickly as they started to build the fire. 'At least, I don't think we are. Our lives are here.' She glanced at him, wondering why his demeanour had changed, and told herself he was just concentrating on lighting the fire.

It caught quickly and the children gathered around it, entranced by the flames. 'Can't we persuade your granddad to come out and join us?' Lucy asked Spike.

He smiled at her and shook his head. 'He says it's too damp out here, bad for his bones.'

'Like it's not damp inside the house,' James said ruefully.

'Granddad used to sell Christmas trees,' Spike was telling Marnie and Sam. 'That was his job, before he got too old for it.' James caught Lucy's eye and smiled.

'That's a good job,' Sam observed, holding the palms

280

of his hands out to the fire as James went inside for blankets.

'What's *your* job?' Marnie asked him when he reappeared, handing them one each – including Lucy – which they all draped around their shoulders.

'I'm a carpenter,' he replied. 'I make things with wood.'

'Everyone knows what a carpenter is, Dad,' Spike said with an eye-roll.

James smirked. 'Yeah, well, mainly I'm a boat fitter. I build the cabinets, I fit them out – I work out the best way to use all the space inside.' He paused. 'I think we need more wood if we're going to keep this fire going. Could you find some?'

Off the three of them went, still within sight but far enough away that their conversation was only audible as murmurs now. There was a sharp bite to the October night, and Lucy pulled her blanket tighter around her shoulders.

'Want to go inside?' James asked.

'No, it's lovely out here and the kids are enjoying it.' They fell into an easy silence, and Lucy looked at James. It happened sometimes, when she least expected it; she could be having a lovely time – and what could be nicer than sitting here at the fire with James, finally getting to meet his son – then those thoughts would sneak in, darkening her mood and however hard she tried, she couldn't push them away. It was happening now. Lucy was aware of the children pottering about and chatting at the far end of Kenny's land, but she felt oddly dislocated.

'Everything okay?' James asked gently.

She nodded, wondering how to broach what she wanted to say. 'You must know it really well around here,' she started.

'Yeah, well – of course. I lived here until I was seventeen.'

'I mean, the other villages around here,' she added.

He gave her a curious look. 'Um, yeah – most of them. Why, is there something—'

'This might sound a bit mad,' she murmured, willing the children not to come back to the fire just yet, because she had to tell him; it was threatening to burst out of her.

He looked at her encouragingly. 'I'm sure it won't. Try me.'

She inhaled deeply. 'That night, when Ivan was killed in the accident – he wasn't driving his normal route home. He was close to those villages, Little Morton and Denby Cross – that's where he crashed. But he didn't usually come that way.'

James nodded thoughtfully. She could hardly believe she was telling him this. 'So why do you think—' he began.

'I don't know! There's nothing there really – just a few houses and a pretty dismal children's playground. I've driven the route myself, just to check in case I'd missed something, and I keep thinking maybe *that* was the real reason for the crash.' He gave her a baffled look. 'I mean, maybe Ivan drove that way because he was distracted,' she went on. 'He'd been thinking about someone else, or maybe he was actually on his way to see her . . .'

'To see *who*? What d'you mean?'

She shrugged dismissively. 'I don't know. Some woman, I suppose—'

'You don't really think that, do you?' The flames flickered in his dark eyes as he looked at her.

282

'I've no idea, James. I don't know what was going on that night. Can you think of any reason why someone would go there?' It was a ridiculous question; she knew it.

He shook his head. 'As far as I can picture it, the only reason you'd drive that way is if you were stopping at one of the villages, or maybe heading out to a farm. There's a couple down that road. I don't know who has them, though. They've probably changed hands since I was a kid.' He paused. 'Was he the kind of person who just enjoyed driving?'

'Not really. And certainly not on a Friday night after a week at work. He was always eager to get home. At least, he *seemed* like he was.' She squinted as the wind turned and smoke gusted into her eyes. 'There was a bouquet of flowers on the back seat of his car,' she continued.

'That was kind of him,' James murmured, but Lucy shook her head.

'They weren't for me. I'm pretty certain about that. I don't think he'd even got me a Christmas present.' Her voice cracked, and he squeezed her hand briefly.

'Oh, Lucy. Don't put yourself through this—'

'But I don't know what else to think,' she cut in. 'After he died, I thought maybe he'd kept my Christmas gift hidden at the Manchester flat where he stayed during the week. Perhaps he'd just forgotten to bring it home with him that night. But I went there myself eventually to collect his things. His boss had gathered everything together for me and packed it all up. He'd offered to drive over with it all, but I sort of wanted to see the place for myself. Where he'd been living during the week, I mean.' She paused, looked at James, and continued:

'There were some clothes, books, toiletries and stationery – that was about it.' She pushed her hair from her face, feeling foolish now. 'I don't mean I care about a present, of course I don't. But I wanted to know that he'd at least thought about me that Christmas.'

'I'm sure he had,' James said softly. 'The thing is, there's no point in raking over this now. You'll never actually know, and you're just torturing yourself by imagining scenarios—' He broke off as the children approached with armfuls of wood. It was piled onto the fire, and Lucy tried to join in with the chatter, but it was impossible when all she could think was: had Ivan rearranged his life to be away from her during the week, in a flat where he could get up to anything? And had he planned one last visit to this mysterious person before the Christmas holidays, when they'd be forced apart?

As the fire started to die down, they carried their blankets inside. Lucy forced a bright smile as she said goodbye to Kenny and Spike, murmuring to James before she climbed into her car: 'And now you must think I'm completely crazy.'

'Of course I don't,' he said. 'But I think there must be some innocent explanation.' Although she hoped he was right, she couldn't imagine what that could possibly be. But at least the hug he gave her told her that he didn't think she was crazy at all.

Chapter Thirty-Two

Halloween had arrived, and Burley Bridge was decked out in festive finery: shop windows displayed black cats and cauldrons filled with foil-wrapped sweets, and glowing lanterns and fairy lights were strewn everywhere. If anything, things had ramped up several notches from last year. Lucy couldn't remember giant glowing pumpkins in clusters in the Red Lion's garden, or a flock of ghosts (did ghosts *flock*?) dangling on fine threads in the window of the village hall.

At the request of Marnie and Sam, Lucy was hosting a party this year for the village children. She had ensured that there would be no B&B guests that night; her old college friend Connell had texted a couple of weeks ago to say he would be arriving the day after Halloween so Lucy figured she could let the kids invite twenty or so friends and she would lay on a fabulous feast. She had already made bat biscuits, spider cakes and blood-red jelly, and had a batch of skinny sausage rolls ('wizened fingers') and black spaghetti ('witches' hair') to attend to, as well as pinning up strings of doughnuts for the kids to nibble. Another case of helipad madness, definitely.

While the children were busy dressing up, she set about carving an enormous pumpkin for the Halloween table. As she started to hack at it, she turned to see Sam in the kitchen doorway in the Dracula outfit she had resorted to buying online. 'It's scratchy,' he announced.

'I'm sure it's fine,' she said, poking her knife into the pumpkin's tough flesh. And now another list formed in her mind: *Things I took for granted when Ivan was here.* Zipping up her party dress. All those little things like changing lightbulbs and fuses, checking her car's tyre pressure, removing a particularly stubborn cork from a bottle – and carving pumpkins which, she decided now, was a stupid tradition.

'Ow!' she yelped.

'What's wrong?' Sam asked.

'I just cut my hand.'

She stared down at where the knife had slipped and sliced into her flesh, halfway up her index finger.

'Is it bleeding?' he asked, clearly more concerned with his costume than her minor injury.

'Yep. It'll be okay, though.' She grabbed at the kitchen roll and wrapped it around as a makeshift bandage.

'I can't wear this,' he added, her wound apparently forgotten now. 'It's itchy.'

She frowned at him. 'It's just a cape and trousers, Sam. The cape isn't even touching your skin – you have your own T-shirt on. So how can it be itchy?'

'It is! I can't wear it.'

'Well, what else are you going to wear?'

'Don't shout!' he barked.

'I'm *not* shouting. I'm just trying to get the party

286

ready—' She broke off. 'Oh, God.' She ran to the oven, grabbed the oven gloves and yanked open the door to see three neat rows of entirely blackened sausage rolls. 'Oh, shit.'

'You swore,' Sam announced, bristling with self-righteousness as Marnie swished in in her Scooby-Doo costume. Carys's children were being Velma and Shaggy, but Sam had refused to follow the theme. *Bet you wish you had now,* Lucy thought darkly as she plonked the burnt offerings on the draining board and wrapped a fresh strip of kitchen roll around her finger.

'At least it's seasonal,' she muttered to herself. 'A bleeding wound to scare everyone.'

'Did you hurt yourself, Mum?' Marnie asked with vague concern.

'Just a little bit but never mind,' she said in a clipped voice, wondering now what had possessed her to take on the hosting of a party tonight. But at least the table was laid, with all the food put out and streamers thrown haphazardly around the kitchen. She had to admit, it looked pretty inviting.

With half an hour before everyone was due to arrive, Lucy boiled a vat of spaghetti and managed to transfer it, portion by portion, into a ziplock bag with a little water and black food colouring, only mildly scalding herself in the process. Party food attended to, she figured that she, too, should make an effort to dress the part. Leaving the children watching spooky cartoons in the living room – with Sam still grumbling about his scratchy cape *and* the fact that Josh would be bound to win the fancy dress prize – she hurried upstairs, stripped off her jeans and sweater and pulled on an ancient, shapeless back maternity dress that had somehow avoided being taken to the charity shop. She had also sourced a scraggy black wig from the newsagent's meagre selection of Halloween accessories, and pulled it on. Poised at her dressing table mirror now, she started to sponge on the greyish face paint she'd bought for Marnie the previous year.

'Mum!' Marnie yelled from downstairs.

'Just a minute, honey.' Lucy wedged white plastic fangs over her own teeth (another newsagent purchase) and studied her reflection in her mirror. She looked hideous – just as the occasion required.

'Mum!' Marnie yelled again. 'It's your phone. It's ringing *again*.'

Lucy pulled on a witch's hat, which Carys had unearthed for her, and hurried downstairs. She took her ringing mobile from Marnie's outstretched hand. 'Hello?' she said briskly.

'Lucy, hi – it's Connell.'

'Oh, hi, Connell.' She strode through to the kitchen where it was quieter.

'I'm sorry,' he started, his voice echoing, 'but I think there's something wrong with my sat nav.'

She frowned. Much as she was looking forward to seeing Connell after all these years, she wasn't entirely sure why he was telling her this.

'And I'm not getting GPS on my phone,' he added. 'Maybe I'm out of data.'

She pulled out her fangs and slipped them into the pocket of the dress. It was impossible to concentrate with them in. 'I'm sorry to hear that,' she started, 'but I'm actually just about to—' She broke off at the sound of a sharp rap on the front door.

'Pretty sure I'm only three or four miles away,' Connell

went on. 'I've turned off the main dual carriageway and the road was signposted to Burley Bridge, but then it forked and I think maybe I took the wrong—'

'But, Connell—'

'Mum! Someone's at the door!' Marnie shouted from the living room.

'Could someone answer it please?' Lucy yelled back. Her request was ignored. She gripped her phone and strode through to the hall. 'You mean you're on your way here *now*?' she exclaimed.

'Yes! I've just pulled over to call you.'

Panic rose in her chest as she opened the front door, pulling an apologetic face as she beckoned in Roseanne, one of the school-gate mums, and her three little boys who were dressed as a trio of wizards. Marnie and Sam ran through to greet them, leaving the TV blaring. 'Come in, come in,' she said distractedly. 'I won't be a minute. There's food in the kitchen.' She waved a hand towards it and raked her wig back from her already clammy forehead.

'Sorry, Connell – some friends have just arrived. Um, look, I don't know what's happened but it's actually tomorrow night you're booked in for. You've made a mistake.' As she said it, doubt started to creep into her consciousness. *Had* it been tomorrow, or had she been the one to mess up? Certainly, she'd been prone to forgetfulness since Ivan died. Too many demands on her time, too many plates to keep spinning, coupled with broken sleep and general mental woolliness. She wasn't proud of the fact that she had sent Marnie and Sam on a school archaeology trip to Ilkley Moor without packed lunches and they'd had to settle for 'a dry cracker and some grapes' (as reported by Marnie) donated by a friend. She

289

had missed her own doctor's and dentist's appointments – but so far, she had never messed up a guest's booking.

'I really don't think so,' Connell said.

'Okay. Just hang on a sec.' She tried to exude calm as she marched through to the living room and flipped open her laptop to check her spreadsheet of bookings. *There* he was. 'No, it was definitely November the first and second,' she said firmly. There was another knock at the door, and Lucy hurried through and waved in the new arrivals, still making apologetic gestures for being on the phone.

'Everything okay?' Carys mouthed.

Lucy grimaced and nodded. As everyone surged into the kitchen, and the noise levels rose, she stepped into the downstairs bathroom and shut the door.

'Connell,' she said, 'I've checked my bookings diary. You're definitely in there for tomorrow night.'

'Oh, Christ,' he groaned. 'I'm so sorry. I don't know how I messed up.'

She held the phone to her ear, remembering again how scatty and chaotic he'd been at college. 'Could I possibly stay tonight?' he asked. 'The head teacher's expecting me first thing tomorrow. I reckon I'm literally five, six miles away.'

'But . . . my whole house is full of people right now.' Another mum had arrived with her offspring (why was it *always* the women out trooping the streets in the wind and the rain with gangs of hyped-up children?).

'Look, I won't really need anything from you,' Connell went on. 'Just a bed to sleep in, basically. I won't even need breakfast. I'm sure I can get something in the village.'

'Tomorrow morning's not the problem,' she said. 'It's tonight. It's Halloween.'

'Christ, is it?'

'Yes! And I'm having a party and then I'm going to be out with the children till God knows when. I really can't have any guests tonight.'

'Well, look – I could help.'

'What with?'

'Um, anything really. Anything you need me to do. I could, er . . . clear up after the party?'

Despite the fact that this situation was far from ideal, she couldn't help smiling at that. 'I don't expect my guests to wipe jelly off the floor.'

Connell chuckled. 'I don't mind, honestly. If you just could tell me how to get to you?'

Wearily, Lucy lowered herself onto the toilet lid. 'You mentioned a fork in the road, once you'd taken the Burley Bridge turn-off?'

'Yep. I turned right.'

'Well, go back to the junction and take the other fork and carry on for a couple of miles . . .' She broke off. 'But please take that road carefully. It's been raining, there are sharp bends and it's quite skiddy.'

'Hey, I'll be fine,' he said jovially.

She cleared her throat. 'And when you get to the village, go right along the high street until the end of the shops, then turn left up the lane and that's our cottage on the left. You should be here in ten minutes. Oh, and there's one other thing . . .'

'Yes?'

She stepped out of the tiny bathroom and made her way down the hall and into the melee of the kitchen. 'I don't suppose you're any good at carving pumpkins?'

Chapter Thirty-Three

It didn't matter that he lacked a cape. Connell had barely put down his bags and given Lucy a hug before he was being hailed as a Halloween hero by the assorted women clustered around him in her kitchen.

'So good to see you,' he said warmly. 'You're *just* the same!'

'I don't think so,' she said, laughing, 'but thank you.'

There was no time for more pleasantries as Roseanne – who was dressed as a particularly slinky Morticia Addams – strode over to him and announced, 'We need your help.' Roseanne won the mums' race at every sports day and her smart, modern home was crammed with her sons' sporting trophies. Used to getting others to do as she asked, she thrust the handle of a serrated knife towards Connell, plus the enormous, unyielding vegetable, which Lucy had started to hack at.

'Oh! Right, okay.' He looked bemused as he glanced at Lucy, then registered the makeshift bandage on her finger. 'Have you cut yourself?'

'Just a tiny bit,' she said quickly, 'but it's okay now.'

Even the children had quietened down when this new face had arrived, but before long everyone had revved up again as they strained to bite at the doughnuts that were strung across the kitchen.

'Please don't feel obliged to do this,' Lucy said quickly, aware of the women watching with rapt attention as Connell, stationed at the kitchen table now, deftly sliced the top off the pumpkin.

'Ooh,' breathed Roseanne admiringly.

'It's no problem,' Connell said, face set in intense concentration as he continued to carve. Roseanne handed him a spoon, which he accepted with a charming smile, then proceeded to scoop out the inner flesh.

'Gosh, you do know what you're doing,' breathed Carys – who knew she had the flirting gene? – as he set about carving an impressively sinister-looking eye.

'I'm not so sure about that.' Connell glanced around and smiled at Lucy. 'So sorry about the mix-up tonight.'

'That's no problem,' she said.

'Well, I'm just glad you could fit me in.'

Lucy caught Roseanne trying to quell a smirk as she looked at Carys, who raised a brow suggestively. Christ, Lucy thought, struggling to keep a straight face herself: they were acting like teenagers recently released from a girls-only boarding school, where the only male they'd seen with any regularity had been the ageing janitor. And Connell *was* attractive, she conceded; his eyes were a striking pale blue, like those old-fashioned air mail envelopes, and he wore his light brown hair cropped short. Although he'd been clearly a little taken aback to walk into a kitchen full of women and children, he had gathered himself together with admirable speed. Lucy was intrigued to find out what had happened in his life since she'd last seen him eighteen years ago.

'That's very good,' Roseanne observed as Connell completed the second eye.

He chuckled. 'I'm just winging it here. I really don't have a clue.'

'False modesty,' Carys chuckled.

'Don't let us put you off,' Roseanne added, having bagged the chair next to him now. If she edged any closer, Lucy thought, she'd be on his lap.

'Well, you look like you've done this before,' remarked Carys.

'Not since I was a student,' he replied.

'So, you two know each other from college?' asked Jodie, another of the school mums who'd just arrived, having perhaps been alerted that a handsome stranger had shown up at Lucy's tonight.

'Yeah, that's right.' Unlike everyone else's costumes, there was nothing scary about Jodie's white leotard, frothy pink tutu and lilac wings; on the contrary, it showed off her enviably lithe body. However, Lucy feared that it wasn't suitable for the cold, wet night – the ballet slippers especially – and hoped she had brought a warm jacket.

'So, where are you from, Connell?' she wanted to know.

'Nottingham,' Connell replied, 'but I studied in Leeds. That's where Lucy and I met . . .'

'And what brings you up here?'

'I'm an artist,' he replied. 'These days, I work mainly in stained glass—'

'Ooh,' Roseanne exclaimed. 'That's . . . *amazing*.' If Connell's pumpkin-carving skills were impressing the assembled audience, with this new factlet they were agog.

'So it's a working trip, really,' he continued, getting up to wash his hands at the sink, and gratefully accepting a mug of tea from Lucy. 'I'm here to do a project with the primary school.'

'We're getting stained glass at the school?' Roseanne beamed at him, seemingly oblivious to her own children's altercation over who got to bite the chocolate-covered doughnut off the string.

'Yes – there's been funding awarded,' Connell explained. 'The idea is that we involve the kids right from the start. So they'll come up with ideas in art sessions, and then we'll work together to translate these into glass.'

'How will you do that?' Lucy asked, handing out mugs of tea – although she could be offering absinthe for all the attention her guests were paying her.

'Some pieces will be made from simple leaded glass,' he explained, 'just like you'd see in a typical church window.'

Jodie was gazing at him, nodding, as if she was about to slither off the chair and dissolve into a pool of joy.

'And with others we'll actually fuse the colours,' he continued, putting the finishing touches to the pumpkin now – carving out *eyebrows*, for goodness' sake, 'so they merge together. The effect's like melted jelly sweets.'

Roseanne looked orgasmic now, and Lucy considered dampening a tea towel with which to dab at her brow. Connell stopped. 'I don't want to bore you all with this. You look like you have a busy night ahead.'

'Oh no, not at all. It's fascinating!' Jodie exclaimed. With all this talk of fusion and things melting, Jodie, too, was looking quite flushed. And now Roseanne was praising the finished pumpkin – 'It's a show-stopper!' – as if Connell had carved St Paul's Cathedral out of ice.

'Look, everyone!' Jodie called out to the children. 'Isn't this the *best* pumpkin you've ever seen?' But they were too thrilled by the doughnuts to care about a frankly inedible vegetable, and soon they all started demanding to set off into the cold, damp night.

'Let me show you to your room,' Lucy said to Connell, surprised that none of the other women had offered to do it for her.

'Oh, you're too busy for that,' he said. 'Just point me in the right direction and I can sort myself out.'

She frowned. 'Are you sure? I'm sorry you've arrived to such chaos.'

'Of course I'm sure,' he said firmly. 'And, look – please, don't worry about entertaining me.' Cue another quick look between Lucy's friends. 'It's just lovely to see you,' Connell added warmly, 'and I'm really looking forward to catching up.'

Despite the wind and the rain, Connell's arrival seemed to have sprinkled no small amount of joyfulness on the proceedings as the women herded their children outside, and they made their way towards the village hall.

'I wouldn't mind helping him with his project,' Jodie said with a grin.

'What d'you know about stained glass?' Lucy teased her.

'Nothing, but I could learn,' she chuckled. 'There are courses, night classes. Sounds like you just fuse a few things together. How difficult can it be?' There were gales of laughter and several suggestions of how Connell might be 'entertained' during his brief stay. So buoyant was the mood that no one really cared when, naturally, Josh's dragon costume scooped first prize, while his mother fluttered about, saying, 'I don't know how he won. It was all thrown together at the last minute.' Because naturally, it was uncool to admit that one had been hand-stitching individual dragon's scales over the preceding weeks.

By the time trick or treating was finished, and the children were laden with goodie bags, Lucy had to concede that Halloween had been pretty successful. Her finger had finally stopped bleeding and, as she and her children approached Rosemary Cottage, she saw that Connell must have found tea lights somewhere as the pumpkin was flickering in the porch window now, as if to welcome them home. And when she stepped inside, she saw that the party devastation had all been cleared away in the kitchen, with order almost restored. Connell was beaming at her from the sink, wearing a slightly crumpled wizard hat that someone must have left behind.

'Wow!' She looked around in wonder. 'You shouldn't have. You're supposed to be a guest here. I could have done it.'

'After schlepping around out there all night?' He laughed and dropped a stray paper plate into the bin bag, then knotted it up.

'Look,' she said to Marnie and Sam, 'Connell's cleared up all the mess!'

'Oh, yeah,' Marnie said, more concerned with delving into her goodie bag. Although Lucy had already introduced them, the children were accustomed to new people around the place, and so what, if a guest happened to have cleared up?

Lucy smiled. 'Well, I'm very grateful. That was so thoughtful of you. I'll just get these two ready for bed and scrub off this face paint.'

'I was going to say it suits you,' he teased, and she laughed.

'And while I'm doing that,' she added, 'maybe you could do *one* more thing and pour us a glass of wine?'

Chapter Thirty-Four

It was one of those nights that just seemed to unfold with no concern over the time. As they worked their way through the bottle of wine, Lucy told Connell what had happened to her husband, and he'd expressed concern and shock, of course, but mainly, he had listened.

In turn, Connell had sped through the significant events of his life since he had last seen her. No, it hadn't worked out with Zelda. She had ditched him for a wealthy record company executive and, the last he'd heard, she had a chi-chi homewares shop in the Cotswolds. 'You know the kind of place,' he said, grinning. 'Fifty quid for a set of coasters.'

Lucy smiled. He was easy to be with after all this time. In fact, it was the first time they'd ever spent an evening together, just the two of them, and he seemed far more considered than she remembered. He'd been pretty boisterous back then, concocting ridiculous cocktails in the blender his mum had bought him, involving vodka, coconut milk and cherries, she remembered now. 'Not quite what Mum had in mind,' he said, laughing as they reminisced. 'I assume she'd been thinking more banana smoothies, to get some nutrients into me.'

Lucy opened a second bottle of wine and topped up their glasses as they relocated from the kitchen to the squashy sofa in the living room. 'So, after Zelda, what happened then?' she asked.

'Um, well, the rest of my twenties were dedicated to prolonging my adolescence as long as possible,' he said with a self-deprecating shrug. 'I lived with another girl for a few years. We worked together at the same design studio, before I decided to go freelance. But it wasn't right. My thirtieth birthday was thundering towards me and I had to make a decision. I knew she wanted kids and it wasn't fair to keep things going.' He broke off and sipped his wine. 'They're a bit of a milestone, aren't they, those decade birthdays?'

'I guess so,' she replied. Her last one – her fortieth – had been marked by a wonderful party in a Manchester bar, masterminded by Ivan, and she could hardly bear to think of it now. 'So, you broke up?' she prompted Connell.

He nodded. 'Yeah, it was kind of sad, but she moved on quickly and married someone much better, someone who really had their act together. She's mum to twin girls.'

'And you've never been married yourself?'

'Nope – never came close. These past ten years or so – well, I was seeing someone on and off, but that's petered out now.' He chuckled. 'Not sounding terribly good at this, am I?'

She almost felt sorry for him, hearing all of this. One relationship after another, which ended up going nowhere. Like her, Connell was forty-three. While she wasn't of the belief that everyone should be settled down into coupledom and domesticity, she sensed a hint of phoney bravado in the way he'd described his life so far.

'It's just the way things have worked out for you,' she said. 'Better to not be in a relationship than one that's not right.' She paused as her phone bleeped on the coffee table, and she checked the text. It was James to say he'd be here tomorrow, and did she have time for coffee? ''Scuse me a sec,' she said, quickly tapping out a reply: *Old college friend Connell's here, we'll prob. spend time together catching up.* She pressed send, wondering now if that had sounded a little abrupt, and if she should add, *You're welcome to come over of course.*

'Everything okay?' Connell asked.

'Oh, yeah. It's just, a friend's coming to the village tomorrow, and I'm wondering whether to say to come over, but maybe it'll sound like I don't really want him to now.'

He smiled. She realised they were both pretty tipsy now. 'It's hard for an afterthought not to sound like one when that's what it is,' he remarked, immediately understanding her conundrum.

Lucy grimaced. 'It would've been okay if I'd said it in the first text.'

'Yeah.' Connell nodded. 'And things can easily be misinterpreted in texts. Like how you got the date wrong about me coming . . .'

'*I* got the date wrong?' she exclaimed in mock outrage. 'I think you'll find it was you . . .' She placed her phone back on the coffee table, having decided it was better to leave it than risk offence. 'So, anyway,' she added, 'I was hearing all about your life.'

Now he was the one grimacing. 'I hope I'm not going on.'

301

'Not at all! So, you don't have any kids of your own?'

'Sadly not,' Connell said, adding, 'Yours are so like you, you know. Both of them, but especially Marnie.'

'They're like Ivan too,' she said with a smile.

'Hmm, maybe. But they have your bone structure. Your smile, too. They're both really striking. All of you are.'

'Oh, thank you.' She beamed at him, touched by the compliment.

'I have to say, you seem so together, Luce,' he went on. 'With this amazing house, I mean. Running a B&B on your own and being a single mum . . . it's incredible really. I feel like a total underachiever compared to you.'

'Don't be crazy.' She laughed kindly and looked at Connell, realising now why it was often said that there was nothing quite like being with an old friend, someone who knew you way back, when you could feasibly sleep on a staircase or feel chuffed that you had 'invented' a particularly thrifty dish, involving penne and baked beans.

'No, I mean it,' he said, turning serious now.

'It's lovely of you to say,' she said. 'Things are going okay but, you know, sometimes it's been incredibly difficult.' Her gaze met his. How funny, she thought, that the college party boy was sitting here with her now, in her cottage in the country. 'My mum's adamant that I should sell up and move closer to her and Dad,' she added.

'You don't want to do that?'

She shook her head. 'What I *really* don't want is for someone to make decisions for me.'

'Yeah, I can understand that,' he said.

Lucy stood up, overcome by a wave of tiredness now

after the party and schlepping around the village, and now all that wine. 'You seemed to be quite a hit with my friends,' she added with a smile as they made their way through to the kitchen.

Connell grinned self-deprecatingly. 'Only due to my pumpkin-carving skills.'

'I don't think it was just that,' she teased him. 'Looks like you've still got it.'

He coloured a little, his blue eyes crinkling with amusement. 'Well, they all seemed very friendly.'

Lucy laughed, feeling extremely glad now that he had persuaded her to let him stay tonight. She could tell he was going to be fun to have around. 'That's what it's like here in the country,' she said. 'The locals *are* friendly. But if you run into them around the village and they get too much for you, don't worry. You have a safe haven here.'

Over the past few months James had started to look forward to his visits to Burley Bridge. He'd never imagined that would be possible, but that's how it was now, despite his dad's perpetual cantankerousness and the fact that even the cats seemed pretty pissed off whenever he turned up. 'He's not normally like that,' his father had remarked recently when Horace had hissed at him. 'He's like a docile little kitten when you're not here.' Of course, the fact that James now felt his heart lifting – rather than crashing to his feet – on his drives over from Liverpool wasn't really anything to do with his father at all.

He loved the time he spent with Lucy and valued their friendship immensely. There was something special about being with a friend who knew you from way back –

303

before you were a dad and a working man, with an ageing father to take care of, and all of the other responsibilities everyone accumulated as they grew older. He supposed he didn't really have that with anyone else.

He'd been a little nervous of introducing Spike to her and her kids. In fact, he'd been conscious of putting it off, as his son was prone to shyness, just as James had been as a child, and seemed happiest when the two of them were pottering about on a boat together. Spike was one of those kids who had a couple of good mates and that was enough. It usually took him some time to relax around new people. But not so that evening with Lucy, Marnie and Sam in his granddad's garden. Building a fire came under the banner of those camping-type activities that Spike had always loved, and he'd known what kind of wood they needed, and how to arrange it so it would catch and burn steadily, and had clearly enjoyed his role of chief fire-maker that night.

That night had felt pretty significant in other ways too. James had been flattered that Lucy had shared her concerns about Ivan's route home the night he died (even though he'd been pretty certain there must have been a perfectly innocent explanation). But then, James had shared things with her too over the past few months. She was the only person he'd ever told about slugging all that whisky on his own and smashing that glass vase.

He'd wanted to tell her something else too that night. It was something that had been brewing in him for a long time now. But the children had come back to sit around the fire and the opportunity had slipped away. He'd hoped to grab the chance on this visit. But this time, Lucy had another old friend over, and had made no indication that it would be okay for him to pop in tomorrow. In fact, she'd made it clear that she didn't want him to as she was spending time with Connell.

That was fine, of course. Lucy had mentioned that he was coming to stay – this old college mate who'd been so popular, clever and fun, a bit of a rebel when it came to attending lectures and handing in assignments on time, but massively talented (of course). Apparently, he was going to be working on a stained-glass project at the village school. As James washed up his dinner things in his small, cramped kitchen, he figured that Connell sounded pretty impressive, travelling the country to undertake projects like that. He caught himself feeling a little put out, and silently chastised himself for it.

Don't be so bloody ridiculous, he told himself as he went to bed that night. *So, she doesn't want to see you this time. She's busy. She's spending time with this Connell person. So just get over yourself.*

Chapter Thirty-Five

Connell was full of praise for Lucy's breakfast. 'That's the best fry-up I can ever remember,' he enthused. 'But I feel bad, sitting here when you're rushing about.'

'This is my job,' Lucy reminded him. 'Anyway, remember how much clearing up you did for me last night. Just enjoy your coffee.'

'Yes, you're the guest here,' Rikke added as she chivvied Marnie and Sam into their coats.

'Did you know Connell's coming to your school today?' Lucy asked.

'Why?' Marnie asked.

'There's going to be an art project,' she explained.

'We're going to turn the big window in the main hall into a work of art,' Connell explained. 'It'll be made up of loads of pieces of stained glass, all designed by you guys . . .'

'By *us*?' Sam said, brightening.

'Yeah.' Connell nodded. 'By all the pupils, I hope. I'd love as many kids as possible to take part.'

Yesterday, the children had been too full of excitement

over Halloween to pay much attention to their guest. But now they were regarding him with interest. 'Have you been to our school before?' Marnie asked.

'Nope, I've only seen pictures,' Connell replied. 'This'll be my first time. Will you look after me?'

Marnie chuckled. 'Yeah. Are you moving here?'

'No, I'm just here for one more night. But I'll be coming back before Christmas and there'll be more visits until the project's all done.' He looked at Lucy. 'And I'd love to stay here, if that's okay with you.'

'Of course it is,' she said. 'You're always welcome.'

'We're heading off to school in a few minutes,' Rikke added. 'Would you like to walk over with us?'

'Sure.' Connell beamed at her. 'I'll just get my stuff together.' Minutes later, they were all heading out, leaving the house suddenly quiet and Lucy alone and feeling somewhat fuzzy with her mild hangover.

As she hadn't had one for so long, the sensation felt almost novel. In the early days, after losing Ivan, there had been several evenings when she had knocked back too much wine alone and woke up hours later, having napped on the sofa, feeling bleary and a little ashamed of herself. It had been all too tempting to lurch for a bottle the minute the children were tucked up in bed. So gradually, she had cut back on wine until she was hardly drinking at all, and only on social occasions. Last night had been fun, though – and as she headed out to the shops, she reflected upon how funny it was that James had popped up from her childhood, and now Connell from her student years too.

It was a cloudy morning with a heaviness in the air. Lucy did the rounds of the village shops, slightly regretting that text she'd sent to James last night, saying she was busy today – but it was too late to do anything about that now. She wasn't about to mess him around by suddenly being available after all. Instead, she focused on selecting fresh vegetables with a plan to make soup, grateful for the easy chatter of the girls who worked in the greengrocer's.

When they had first moved here, Ivan had remarked, in his bemused way, that buying something as simple as an apple generally involved a chat about the weather and children, and what did he think about the pub's new lunchtime menu – had he tried it yet? 'Everything takes a hundred years,' he'd said, clearly still operating on city time. But Lucy had loved it then, and she was starting to love it again now. There was a feeling of generosity here – that people actually cared. And when Connell returned from his meeting just before lunch, she was keen to show him why she had fallen in love with Burley Bridge way back when she'd been a child.

As she often did when requested by guests, Lucy had made packed lunches in brown paper bags. 'So Famous Five-ish,' Connell said with a grin. 'Are we off to find some smugglers?'

'You never know what we'll find,' Lucy replied, catching the scent from the rosemary bush at the front door as they left the house.

The sky had darkened a little as they climbed away from the village and up into the hills. 'The kids were so enthusiastic about the project,' Connell was telling her. 'The idea is, they'll come up with ideas for the glass panels from nature around them. We talked about using the landscape as a starting point for ideas.'

'There's plenty of inspiration around here,' Lucy said.

'It's stunning,' he agreed. 'I can see why you decided

to settle here.' He pulled out his phone and took pano-ramic photos of the valley. There were still patches of copper and gold in the distant forests, dulled now as the sky turned darker still. 'What's winter like here?' he asked, which struck her as a naive question as they perched on a rock and delved into their brown paper bags. It was rural, yes – but hardly remote.

'Last year was pretty mild,' she replied, although in truth she had still barely been aware of much going on around her then. At least she wasn't like that now. It was important to recognise that she was making progress, and to recognise how far she'd come. She caught Connell giving her a curious look.

'Are you okay? Want to head back now?'

'Oh, no,' he said quickly. 'I was just thinking, we never spent much time together back in the old days, did we?'

'No, I guess not.'

'You always seemed very focused and driven,' he added, 'and I assumed I was probably a bit flippant and stupid for you.'

'Of course you weren't! We just moved in different circles, that's all. I suppose I was a bit of a swot. Maybe I should have kicked back more, not taken myself so seriously.'

'And maybe I should have knuckled down and done some proper work.' Connell chuckled and then bit into a sandwich.

'You did really well, though,' she added. 'You sailed straight into a proper, grown-up job, as far as I heard.'

'Yeah – the corporate world,' he said dryly.

'A design studio, wasn't it? Hardly a bank or an insurance company.'

'But a bit of a factory,' he explained, 'churning out

work without having enough time to think things through properly. There was always way too much work and not enough people. I'm a lot happier now, doing this.'

'And d'you have enough commissions to keep you going?' She paused. 'It seems very niche, doing stained glass.'

'Oh, there's plenty of work,' he said. 'There's what you'd expect – church restorations, community projects and the odd commission for a house or a garden piece. And then a job like this one – at the school – comes along, and it's a dream, really.'

'You're very lucky.' She caught him glancing at her again.

Connell nodded, and she was aware of a stillness in the air now. 'I suppose what I was *trying* to say,' he added, 'is that I was pretty in awe of you in college.'

'You're kidding,' she said, genuinely amazed.

He smiled, looking almost bashful now. 'No, I really was. And I, um . . . actually thought you were very cute.'

'Did you?' she exclaimed.

'Well, yes. You were. You are, I mean . . .' Her heart quickened as she studied his face. Was he flirting, or just teasing her, or what?

'No one's said anything like that to me in a long time,' she said with an awkward laugh.

'I'm sorry, I didn't mean to embarrass you . . .' He pushed back his light brown hair.

'You're not. You're not at all.' Her heart was racing now, and his hand brushed against hers. She was keenly aware of something happening between them, something intensely disconcerting but somehow thrilling too. She held Connell's gaze, feeling emboldened now and convinced that they were about to kiss.

Oh my God, she thought. *I am going to kiss someone who's not Ivan.* She couldn't even remember kissing anyone else, not really; it had been so long ago and seemed insignificant. They were the kisses from her distant youth, from way back in her twenties, and even her teens – on sofas, at parties and in beds, from the odd boyfriend here and there and even a one-night stand, once in a blue moon when she had been far wilder than she was now.

Her heart was still thumping as she realised that the thought of kissing Connell Davies, on whom her flatmate Jennie had nurtured a year-long crush, didn't appal her at all. In fact, quite the opposite. She wanted his lips upon hers, his hands all over her body. She craved someone to touch her lovingly, to kiss her deeply and make her cry out in the throes of passion. And she feared that, if no one ever made her feel that way again, she might wither and die.

Chapter Thirty-Six

A fat raindrop splashed onto her cheek. Lucy leapt up from the rock as if it had burned her. Of course she wasn't going to kiss him! Christ, what on earth was she thinking? 'What's wrong?' Connell blurted out, scrambling up too.

'I think we'd better get back,' she said quickly, her cheeks flaming. 'Look at those clouds.'

He glanced up, and then back at her. 'We won't dissolve, will we?' he asked in a bemused tone, hurrying after her as she started to stride down the path.

'You might. You're not used to our Yorkshire rain.' As they made their way down towards the village, it was as if that moment had never happened.

'I did study in Leeds, remember,' he murmured. 'I'm not completely allergic to the north.'

She forced a smile. 'I'd better get back anyway. Tons to do.'

They walked in silence for a few minutes, until Connell remarked, 'The good thing about this job is, it means a few trips up here to work with the kids.' He had already told her this. Perhaps he'd forgotten. 'I hope I can stay again?'

'Of course,' she said, glancing at him now. *Why* had she wanted to kiss him just then? Because she was genuinely attracted to him – which meant that she still had that in her, the ability to experience desire – or maybe it had just been a moment of madness? She did feel pretty crazy sometimes, her emotions still intense and unpredictable, knocking her off balance when she least expected it. Perhaps she'd just been flattered, or carried away in a whirl of nostalgia after their chats last night. Thank God she'd come to her senses there.

'I was hoping you'd say that,' he said lightly. 'I should be here again before Christmas.'

'Braving winter in Burley Bridge?' she said with a quick smile.

'I'd love to see it actually.'

'It's lovely,' she said, 'although I haven't really been in the frame of mind to fully appreciate it yet. But there are snowdrops everywhere – on all the verges. You'd never know they were there, and they spring up wherever you look. It's stunning—' She broke off as the rain started to pelt down full force, and they hurried back towards the village. Within minutes, they were drenched in their lightweight jackets – and she was supposed to be a proper country person now! As for the way he'd looked at her there just a few minutes ago? It was nothing, she told herself as she let them, hair dripping, back into the house. Guilt still burned in her, but at least nothing had actually happened.

Although she was tempted to sit up chatting over another bottle of wine that night, Lucy had garlands of dried branches, interwoven with fresh bay leaves and

313

rosemary, to make for an herbalist's shop in Heathfield. She made soup for dinner, and as they ate Marnie and Sam fired questions at Connell about stained glass. When he fetched his portfolio of work, and the children sat with him on the sofa, eyes wide as they leafed through it, she felt a rush of warmth for him.

Perhaps she had misread everything today, she considered now. He had made her feel good about herself again, and she had got carried away and imagined that there might be the possibility of something developing between them.

Of course, it was ludicrous. Even if she wanted to, there was no way she could cope with a proper, romantic relationship with anyone. She had no need for one, and no time for one either. However, she had enjoyed Connell being around, and was sorry he would be leaving tomorrow.

Once the children were in bed, and Connell had headed upstairs to his room, having explained that he would be making an early start, she set to work at the kitchen table. In her pyjamas with a baggy sweater thrown on top, she inhaled the scents from the herbs and expertly twisted them into the garlands. It was soothing work, and she felt lulled by the steady patter of rain on the kitchen window. So engrossed was she that a distant rumble of thunder barely registered. A sharp crack followed, and a flash of white filled the kitchen as lightning struck.

Lucy stood up, made her way to the front door and opened it. Rain was still pelting down, and there was a heaviness in the atmosphere that made her shudder. Normally, she loved the garden at night, and would stroll around it, just for a breath of air before going to bed.

She was clutching a mug of tea, her eyes scratchy with tiredness. Another crack sounded. 'Mum!' Sam yelled from his room. 'Mum – a thunderstorm!'

'It's okay, love,' she called back, tripping quickly upstairs and finding him, pale and scared-looking, on the landing. Sam had never enjoyed storms, and even at eight he was still afraid of them.

'Hey, darling,' she said gently, pulling him close. 'Come on, let's get you tucked up in bed. We don't want to disturb Connell.'

'Could lightning strike our house?'

'I very much doubt it,' she replied.

'If it did, would it catch fire?'

'Darling, no.' She kissed the top of his head. 'Come on – shall we watch it together from your window? Sometimes that's better, being able to see for yourself what's happening out there, rather than lying in bed and worrying.'

Sam nodded. 'Okay.'

Kneeling side by side on the window seat now, they peered out over the garden as wind tore through the trees, whipping up twigs and leaves from the lawn and sending plant pots flying with a clatter. Marnie appeared too, ghostly pale in her lilac nightie. The three of them huddled close, transfixed as the garden lit up blue-white with each flash of lightning, following by the rumble of thunder.

'It's so loud, Mum,' Marnie murmured, snuggling closer to her mother.

'Yes, I can't remember a storm quite like this,' Lucy said, kissing the top of her head. Another violent thunderclap made the three of them start, and Lucy pulled her children close, having lost track now of how long

315

they had been there in the cosy warmth of Sam's room. The wind was howling, the trees in the garden bending and swaying, as if dancing, and there was another sharp crack as something hit the ground.

'Was that our bird box?' Marnie exclaimed.

'I don't know, sweetheart. I can't see from here.'

'I'm scared,' Sam whimpered, biting the edge of his pyjama top sleeve, in the way that he used to gnaw on the pale blue satin-edged blanket he'd been virtually welded to as a toddler.

'It's okay, love,' she said, aware of footsteps on the landing, 'but maybe we should all get some sleep now. I'm sure it'll finish soon.'

'How d'you know?' Sam asked. Lucy was trying to formulate an answer that would reassure him that it really was okay, she was the grown-up and she knew about storms, when a violent crash seemed to rock the house.

'Our tree!' Marnie screamed.

'Is everything all right?' Connell called out from the landing.

'I don't know.' Lucy jumped up from the seat and hurried past him as she ran downstairs and along the hallway to the front door. In her PJ bottoms and thin sweater, without stopping to consider that she was barefoot, she ran out into the garden where the wind still raged, branches cracking, plant debris whipping up into the air.

'Lucy! Come back in, you'll get soaked out there.' Connell was standing on the front step.

'I'm okay!' she called back.

'C'mon, you can't do anything out here tonight. We'll check the damage in the morning.'

But Lucy wasn't listening anymore. She didn't want

to be told to go back inside; she was breathing deeply, trying to steady herself as her eyes became accustomed to the dark. The street lamps were out – not that there were any in their lane, but normally light would carry from the high street. Here in her garden, the only light source came from the feebly glowing lamp above their front door, which she had meant to upgrade, but never got around to.

There was no moon visible that night. But once her eyes had adjusted, she could see that, while the oak still stood defiantly, one of its heftiest branches had come down and smashed onto the roof of the shed, which was no longer a shed at all, but a tumble of broken timbers as if it had been made from balsa wood.

She walked slowly towards it, aware of the cold, wet grass between her toes as she surveyed the debris that, until a few minutes ago, had been the shed that Ivan insisted on keeping just as it was ('What do we need a summerhouse for when we have this?'). Countless hours he'd spent in there with the kids, building and making things together. Lucy had hardly put a foot in it since he'd died. On one occasion she had stood at the open door, surveying the shelves crammed with boxes and tins of tools and screws and all the materials he had worked with, and it had torn at her heart.

She had never wanted to go in there again. When James had suggested helping her to clear it out, she had known deep down that she wouldn't ever do that. The attic, perhaps, with all of Ivan's hobby accoutrements – but not the shed. She crouched down and touched the soaking timbers. It was still raining, although less heavily now, and she was aware of soft footsteps behind her, a hand placed gently on her shoulder.

317

'Lucy?'

Tears were pouring down her face, merging with the rain, as she stood up and turned to look at Connell.

'Are you okay?' he asked. He, too, was soaking, wearing just a white T-shirt and black tracksuit bottoms. He was barefoot like her, and his hair was plastered to his head.

'Yeah,' she replied, although she wasn't really; and now, as he took her hand and they crossed the garden, back to the warmth of the house, she wondered if she would ever be.

She pretended she was. Lucy had become adept at pinning on a bright smile for guests, serving up bacon and eggs and recommending local walks, always busy, busy, busy. Her friends thought she was fine; 'I don't know how you do all of this,' Carys had said on more than one occasion.

Now Lucy didn't either.

Connell hugged her in the hallway, but she just wanted to go to bed now and be alone. She thanked him for coming outside – for being there – and headed upstairs ahead of him, where she tucked in the children and kissed them goodnight. Then she padded quietly into her own room and lay on top of her bed, not caring that her wet sweater and pyjamas were soaking the bed linen.

That was it, she decided. She had tried, and done her damnedest to persuade everyone that she was coping fine – but in fact, her mother had been right.

It was over.

Chapter Thirty-Seven

It was Rikke who had persuaded Lucy not to do anything rash. 'Look how happy and settled the children are here,' she'd said next morning when she'd showed up to take the children to school, and Connell had headed back to Nottingham.

In the bright, cool sunshine after the storm, Lucy agreed that she wouldn't make any major decisions right now. However, after she had battled on alone for nearly two years, last night had taken something out of her. Her fight, perhaps, or her grit. She had surveyed the damage again, and tried to console the children, who were devastated by the sight of the smashed shed and ravaged oak. And she decided: she really had had enough. In early spring, when the garden was starting to bloom, she would put Rosemary Cottage up for sale. Which left Christmas to consider . . .

'You will be coming to us this year, won't you?' Anna had asked a couple of days before.

'Maybe,' Lucy had replied, 'but d'you mind if I talk it over with the kids first? I'd just like to make sure that's what we all want to do.'

'Oh. Don't they want to come to us?' She'd sounded hurt.

'I'm sure they do,' Lucy had said quickly. 'It's just, I don't want to assume anything. I still have to be careful with them, you know.'

'Of course I know that, love. But we'd love you to come.'

Lucy had exhaled slowly. Lately, she had started to feel that she wanted to regain some control over what they did as a family. She no longer had that dinghy-in-a-storm feeling; she was stronger now, and surer of what was right for her and the children. And if they were to move, Lucy felt that it was only right to have Christmas here, just the three of them. She couldn't leave this house without celebrating it here for the last time. And now, she wondered, would Kenny perhaps let her buy one of his trees? The shed was just a pile of smashed timbers, but she could go all out to make the house as sparkly and beautiful as possible.

If they were to have Christmas at Rosemary Cottage, it would be the Christmas to end all Christmases.

Fuelled by sheer determination, she had ploughed through the last few weeks, being attentive to the few guests who came to stay during the colder months. While James still popped in from time to time, and she was always happy to see him, she sensed a slight distance emanating from him and wondered if she had offended him somehow. When the children told him about the ongoing stained-glass project at school, masterminded by Connell, she detected a catch in his voice as he expressed enthusiasm. What on earth was going on with him? His dad seemed pretty stable, as far as she could gather, and she assumed – and hoped – nothing was going on with Spike, or his ex. James just seemed rather troubled and she couldn't fathom why. Had he been offended when she'd turned down his offer of helping to rebuild her shed?

'There's no point,' she'd said, perhaps a little sharply. Couldn't he understand that it would never be the same, and that she had no need for it anyway?

'I can help out more, if you need me to,' Rikke said as they sat having coffee at Lucy's kitchen table one icy December morning, while the children were at school.

'You have so much else going on, though,' Lucy remarked. 'I know how busy you are. Are you still visiting Kenny?'

She smiled. 'Oh, yes. Need to keep *him* on his toes. But if it would make a difference to you, and persuade you to stay in the village . . .'

'You're an enormous help already,' Lucy murmured.

Rikke sipped from the white china mug. 'I'm really fond of Marnie and Sam. I'd really miss you all if you moved away.'

Lucy reached across the table and squeezed her hand. 'Let's just focus on Christmas at the moment.'

'You know I'm going home for a couple of weeks?'

Lucy nodded; Rikke had mentioned her forthcoming trip to Copenhagen. 'Don't worry,' she said firmly. 'We'll still be here when you get back.' She paused and picked up her phone. 'I got this email this morning. It's from the new CEO from my old company. Max, the one who wanted me out, has been ousted and this new woman wants me to pop in for a chat.'

'You'd seriously give up all of this, to go back to your old company?' Rikke looked aghast.

'I'm not making any decisions right now,' Lucy said. 'A short-term contract's coming up, but it doesn't start until April. It's a maternity cover and it's at a much higher level than I was working at before.' She caught Rikke's concerned gaze. 'And then, if it worked out, there might be a permanent position at that grade.'

'Oh.' Rikke placed her mug on the table and smoothed back her short blonde hair. 'It's a fashion company, isn't it?'

'Yes, that's right. Well, lingerie actually, but my friend Andrew told me they're looking to branch out into other areas. Nina, the new boss, wants to expand into luxury nightwear, yoga wear, that kind of thing. It's kind of appealing.'

Lucy passed her her phone, and Rikke frowned as she read the email. 'She seems very keen.'

'Nothing's definite,' Lucy added, 'and please don't mention anything to the children right now.'

'No, of course not.' She handed Lucy's phone back to her. 'Is this all because of the storm that night? Is that it?'

'Oh, no,' Lucy said firmly, 'it's more than that. It's . . . well, it's the whole thing really. It's everything.'

She was oddly touched by how deflated Rikke seemed when she left, and she didn't even want to consider how the children would feel about leaving Burley Bridge. However, they were resilient kids, as they had proved in the way they had settled here, made friends and even coped with losing their dad. Lucy was immensely proud of them, and she was convinced that they'd manage this next step together, if it happened. Max's brash approach had failed dramatically and Nina Kerridge had been brought in to sort things out.

Alone now, she reread the email:

Hi Lucy,

I hope you're well. I've been meaning to get in touch with you since I started here at Claudine. I wanted to give you the heads up as early as possible. I know you have your thing going on in the country, and you've had an awful lot to cope with in the past couple of years. I was so sorry to hear about your husband and I do hope it's okay to get in touch now.

I have considered this carefully and I keep coming back to the fact that you're the obvious person to step in when Dana goes on maternity leave this spring. You know the company so well and have a rounded, considered approach as well as a respect for the brand heritage. You work so well with people and would be a real asset here. It's not your old head buyer position I'm thinking of. I'm looking for someone to work closely with me, as my second-in-charge.

Lucy sipped the dregs of her tepid coffee. She knew Nina a little, from way back; in fact, Connell knew her too. They had moved in similar circles at college, and Lucy had kept tabs on Nina's career as she had cut her teeth with a middle-of-the-road high street brand, before moving to a more senior position at a cutting edge chain. She was rather chilly, Lucy remembered – hugely driven, undoubtedly gifted and razor-sharp. She would be inspiring to work for. Maybe a new challenge like this was just what she needed.

As you probably know, the email concluded, *it's been a bit of a rescue mission here, but once things*

*are steady again we have lots of new developments
that I'd love you to be part of. Do give me a ring
if you'd like to meet up to discuss this further. I do
hope it's a yes.*

With all best wishes,
Nina

Lucy would contact her, certainly, but first she had a
more urgent call to make. She picked up her phone and
took a deep breath before calling her mother to tell her
that she and the children would be staying at Rosemary
Cottage for Christmas.

Chapter Thirty-Eight

James was washing up after lunch at his father's house when the police arrived. 'Is there a Mr Halsall here?' asked the younger of the two officers at the front door.

James frowned. 'I assume you mean my dad – Kenny Halsall?'

'That's right. He made the call.'

'Dad called the police?' he exclaimed. 'What about?'

'Can we come in?' the same officer asked.

'Yes, yes, of course.' He beckoned them in, wondering whether to wake his father from his nap. He had been even more cantankerous than usual today, irritated to hear that Rikke would be going to Copenhagen for Christmas – 'She needs a holiday, Dad,' he had pointed out – and hadn't taken well to James's suggestion that perhaps they should try to find someone else to drop in daily to help out.

The two officers glanced around the room, and James saw his father's home through their eyes: superficially tidied but still cluttered, the cats prowling between books and newspapers piled against the walls, the semi-drawn curtains adding to the general feeling of gloom. 'There's been a theft reported,' the older man replied.

James rubbed at his forehead, trying to make sense of this. 'Dad's having a nap and I don't want to disturb him. Can I deal with this?'

'We really need to speak with your father,' the younger man said, so James tapped on Kenny's bedroom door and he emerged a few moments later, slightly dishevelled, in a voluminous checked flannel shirt and jeans, scratching at his beard.

'Dad – the police are here,' James started. 'Can you come through?'

'The police?' Kenny looked startled. 'What do they want?'

'I think you called them,' James said, as patiently as he could manage. 'They want to discuss something about a theft?'

Shaking his head and shrugging, Kenny followed James through to the living room and peered at the officers, clearly having no idea why they might be there. 'Mr Halsall,' the older one started, having immediately adopted a gentler tone, 'you called to say there's been a theft of power tools?'

'Oh!' Kenny nodded self-righteously and folded his arms across his chest. 'Yeah. You can't leave anything around these days, can you?' He looked at James. 'Have *you* seen them?'

'Erm . . . not exactly. I mean, not recently, no.' James glanced at the police officers, then turned to Kenny. Maddening though he was, he was still his father and he wished to avoid – or at least minimise – any humiliation for him. 'Dad . . .' He raked his hair at the back of his neck. 'If you've been looking for your power saws and stuff well, um . . . Rod took them.'

326

Kenny glared at him, dark eyes blazing now. 'You can't blame our Rod!'

'I'm not blaming him,' he said quickly. 'I'm just stating a fact.' He exhaled loudly, the enormous ginger cat catching his eye as he slunk out from behind an ancient curtain. James turned to the officers. 'My brother was living here with Dad for a while and he decided, um . . . he made the decision that it was probably best to look after his tools, so . . . he locked them in the boot of his car.'

'They're in his car?' Kenny's face paled.

'Yes, Dad.' He nodded.

'Where's his car now?' Kenny thundered.

'I haven't the faintest idea. He went to Switzerland, remember? I hardly ever hear from him but I assume he's still there.' James paused and cleared his throat. 'So there hasn't actually been a theft—'

'So what am I meant to use for cutting down Christmas trees?' Kenny snapped. 'A butter knife?'

The younger officer's mouth quivered, and he covered it with a hand. Being country police officers they were incredibly understanding, brushing off James's apology for their time being wasted; so no harm done really. In fact, James suspected they had rather enjoyed their visit. After they'd left, and he had managed to convince his father that Rod had merely been 'looking after' the tools – 'in case of burglars' – the older man sat heavily in the armchair, grabbed the remote huffily and turned on the TV.

Great – a cheery documentary about the dreadful conditions in a garment factory in Cambodia.

'Can't I even get a nap around here?' Kenny complained to the TV.

327

He had no recollection of calling the police, James realised. Nearly two years ago now, he had hoarded sandwiches and harassed Reena's holiday guests, thinking her house was his own. Less worryingly – but hardly ideal – he had photobombed a society wedding. It all added up to the fact that, really, all James was doing was patching over the problem – doing his best, which clearly wasn't enough, with fingers firmly crossed. And at some point, something would have to change.

He didn't know quite what that meant, and before Connell's visit to Lucy's, he might have called her to talk it through. But he sensed a bit of distance between them now, and he knew there was another visit pending, which she seemed pretty excited about, with this art project and everything. The whole thing made him feel out of kilter, which he knew was ridiculous, so it now seemed easier to step back a little and not contact her quite so often. Perhaps, he reasoned, she needed a little space.

Meanwhile, James had one radical suggestion to put to his father. While it might not solve things long-term, it would certainly provide an immediate solution, and ensure no further calls to the police over the festive season.

'Dad,' James said levelly. His father swung round and peered at him. 'Dad, how would you feel about coming – you and the cats, I mean – to my place for Christmas?'

A mile away in Rosemary Cottage, Lucy clutched her phone to her ear, knowing that whatever she said, there would no changing her mother's mind. It would be as hopeless as trying to halt the tide.

'So, what your father and I have decided,' Anna had announced, 'is we can't have you and the children spending Christmas alone in that house. We just can't bear it.'

'But Mum—' she'd started.

'Now, before you say no, it's too much work and all that – we've thought it all through, Lucy, and it's the best solution all round. We're coming to yours this year, and there'll be nothing for you to worry about. *We're* bringing Christmas to you.'

Chapter Thirty-Nine

Although Lucy wouldn't say she was a crier normally, certain triggers sent her from respectably dry-faced to awash with tears and snot, virtually dissolving, within seconds.

Watching *The Railway Children* with Marnie and Sam generally did the trick, specifically the end scene where the steam cleared on the railway station platform, and 'Daddy' appeared. *Daddy, oh my Daddy!* Cue copious weeping into tissues. When one of her children was deeply upset, that too could turn on the taps – like when Sam had been devastated about his museum exhibits being thrown away. Even their scruffy old shed – Lucy had cried over that. But nothing guaranteed instantaneous eye flooding like the school Christmas carol concert.

Lucy's family had arrived en masse: her parents, Aunt Elspeth and Aunt Flora, plus Tilly, the flatulent schnauzer who had apparently stunk out the car. They dragged in sack loads of presents like eager elves, plus mountains of food, which they had dumped in the kitchen before exclaiming how lovely and cosy Lucy's home was (the aunts), and that 'it's quite a small tree, Lucy' (her mother). 'I thought you'd have had a bigger one,' she added.

'I decided this size would be easier to handle,' Lucy had explained, glancing at what she'd thought was a perfectly respectable five-footer. 'I thought I might be able to get one from James's dad, but there was no one at the house when I called round, and I didn't think I should just hack one out of the ground.' In truth, she had half hoped James would be around to help her, and perhaps assist with setting it up in the house. But she hadn't heard from him for a couple of weeks, and she didn't want to bother him if he was busy. Now she assumed he and his father had gone away for Christmas.

Still, Lucy's mother's decorations more than made up for the seemingly disappointing pine. The life-sized reindeer had migrated from her parents' house and were now bracketing her front door.

'Ooh, someone's feeling festive,' Irene had chuckled as she'd marched by.

The living room was strewn with tinsel – despite Lucy's protestations – and no horizontal surface was without a glittery Santa, a herd of reindeer or a cluster of twinkling lights. It was as if the John Lewis Christmas department had relocated to Rosemary Cottage.

'This is quite . . . eye-popping,' Connell had said with an amused glint when he'd arrived that morning. It was a flying visit; he was only staying for one night. 'I could always stay at the pub,' he'd said, 'if you have a houseful.' Lucy thought she'd detected slight disappointment when she'd mentioned that her family were planning to descend on her. But no, she'd insisted; her parents would share one guest room, her aunts the other; they could make it work, if he could bear them – plus her parents' excitable schnauzer – all fussing around, and didn't mind the tiny study with its single bed. Connell's plan was to visit the school on the last day of term, having brought the made-up glass panels featuring the children's designs. They were currently displayed on a table in the foyer for the parents to see.

'They look wonderful,' Lucy said now, mopping at her face.

Connell smiled. 'I'm glad the kids are happy with them.'

'How sweet of the artist to come to the concert,' her Aunt Elspeth had whispered into her ear on her other side. She had been thrilled to discover that Connell was an old friend of Lucy's. 'And what a lovely man, Lucy,' she added approvingly. 'He's a very handsome chap, isn't he?'

'Yes, I guess he is,' Lucy murmured. During the small gap between carols, Elspeth's voice seemed to be carrying clearly across the hall.

'I'm just *saying*, love.'

Mercifully, the children launched into the next carol. Lucy focused ahead, wondering if her puffy eyes would ever recover from the sight of thirty-five children singing 'Silent Night'.

As the evening progressed, a rogue thought kept flashing into her mind – *I wish Ivan was here* – but she pushed it away, and when it was time for everyone to join in with a rousing rendition of 'Ding Dong Merrily on High', her voice rang out clearly, and she felt happy to be here, to be part of this, despite the fact that her mascara had undoubtedly run, and her face was still entirely wet.

The concert had been lovely, and she had planned

drinks back at her place, having decided to knock back some fizz to get into the spirit of things. While Lucy walked with her mother, the children and the aunts, Connell and her father lagged a few feet behind. The odd snowdrop had appeared on the verges, each as delicate as a tear, but it was after Christmas when they tended to appear in full force.

Snow had started to fall now – flat, soft flakes, drifting slowly, catching in their hair and delighting the children who were grabbing at handfuls and throwing them, it was settling that quickly.

Lucy glanced back to see Connell and her father still chatting happily, and she smiled.

Handsome chap indeed. Was Aunt Elspeth trying to set her up, or what? Luckily, there had been no awkwardness when Connell had showed up, and no hint of flirtation either, for which she was relieved. But Lucy would need to keep her wits about her if she were to get through tonight and tomorrow – before Connell headed back home to Nottingham – without humiliation.

There was no snow in Liverpool, although James had heard on the radio that it was falling incredibly quickly in the area of Yorkshire around Heathfield and Burley Bridge, and he almost wished he was there. Still, it was festive enough here. As he turned into Michaela and Ali's modern estate, it seemed to him that the houses were competing as to which was the gaudiest.

Illuminated Santas were clamped to the roofs, and gardens were populated by elves and reindeer with fairy lights strung on every available structure. At one time, he might have thought it over the top, but tonight, after a rather sullen drive over from Burley Bridge with his father – the cats mewling in their baskets on the back seat – he had to concede that it was cheering. He would have to do a speedy job of raising the festive standards at his own place as soon as they arrived home.

'I'll wait here with the cats,' Kenny announced as James pulled up in front of the spangliest house of them all. Icicle fairy lights dangled from the roof, and the clipped hedges had been sprinkled with what appeared to be some kind of outdoor glitter. Michaela had always loved a bit of glitz at Christmas, and the glossy black door bore a ritzy garland constructed from baubles, golden bows and red velvety leaves.

'Come in, Dad,' James insisted. 'They'll be fine. I'm not leaving you sitting out here all alone.'

'I'm not speaking to that man,' he said gruffly, which baffled James; his father had never met Ali, and probably wouldn't remember Michaela either now. The thought triggered a rush of sadness in him, and he hung on to the hope that he would still be interested in Spike, and what was going on his life. Only a few weeks had passed since the bonfire, when Lucy and her children had come over for the evening, but since then James had noticed a deterioration in his dad's ability to grasp what was going on around him. And there'd been that call to the police.

'Please come on in,' James said firmly. 'We'll only be a few minutes.' Grudgingly Kenny climbed out of the car and followed his son to the front door.

'Hi, James,' said Ali as he opened it.

'Hi,' James said. 'This is Kenny, my father.'

'Kenny, hi!' Ali beamed at him and shook his hand vigorously. 'Come in. They should be on their way back. Spike's been at some party or other. Incredible social life, he has.'

334

'He's been out a lot, then?' James asked.

'God, yeah. Social whirl for the kids around here,' Ali said, leading them into the kitchen with its vast island unit and row of dangling copper-shaded lights. 'I think they were expecting you at eight.'

'I did say seven,' James said, not wanting to make a big thing of it but silently urging them to appear as quickly as possible.

'Ah, well. Can I make you coffee?' Ali asked, in a tone that suggested he hoped James would say no.

'Yeah, that'd be great. How about you, Dad?' But Kenny was already wandering out of the kitchen, and when James looked around the corner he saw that he had sunk heavily into the concrete-coloured sofa in the living room. 'Excuse Dad,' he said to Ali, back in the kitchen. 'He's just not feeling terribly sociable at the moment.'

'Don't worry. Spike's told me all about his granddad.' As he set about fiddling with the seemingly complex coffee machine like some jumped-up barista, James perched on one of the high chrome stools at the island, and stole a glance at Ali's hair. It was the thickest, densest hair James had ever seen on a man – not that he registered blokes' hair normally – and the precise shade of a digestive biscuit. James had an urge to press a flattened hand on the top of it, to see if it would 'give', or even put a match to it to check whether it was flammable. As Ali bobbed about, fiddling with cups and levers and making steam hiss out – not from his hair but the coffee machine – James checked his watch, willing Michaela and Spike to hurry home.

Ali turned to face him. 'So, we'll miss Spike this Christmas. Unusual, isn't it, for Kenny to come to your place?'

'He usually refuses,' James said, distinctly unkeen on

discussing his family arrangements with this man. 'But I sort of insisted,' he added. 'I'm, uh, trying to keep an eye on Dad at the moment.'

'I gather he's not too well these days?'

'Um . . . he's okay.'

Ali winced. 'Michaela mentioned he's pretty confused.'

James baulked at this. However difficult his father may be, he was also unkeen on Michaela discussing Kenny's mental health with her boyfriend. How much longer were she and Spike going to be anyway? *Hurry up,* he willed them. *Hurry up home and then I can get the hell out of here.*

'I hope you don't mind me asking, but have you had him diagnosed?' Ali met James's gaze directly.

'Um, no – not yet.' The question caught him off guard.

Ali pulled a sympathetic face. 'You know, it might be helpful.'

James exhaled, reluctant to discuss any of this – but, equally, he had no desire to cause friction that might affect Spike by being surly with Ali. So he tried to pretend that Ali was just somebody's husband whom he had met in the kitchen at a party, and not the so-called medical practitioner his partner had been sleeping with on the sly.

'I realise that,' he said lightly, 'but he actually refuses to see a GP at all, so it's tricky.'

'Ah, yes – but that's a *conventional* doctor.'

James frowned. 'What d'you mean?'

'Well, we all know what happens when you go to see a GP, don't we? You're in for ten minutes max, quick diagnosis – treating the symptom, not the person – and then you're pinged out into the street.'

He prodded some more at the coffee machine. The

making of a simple hot drink seemed to be on par with preparing a lobster bisque in terms of complexity. Coffee machines were the new sports cars, James decided: the bigger and shinier and whizzier the better. Ali slammed down a lever, patted the machine on its top as if praising it for a job well done, and handed James a tiny cup of tepid tar-like liquid.

'I think we have everything under control,' James fibbed, 'where Dad's concerned.'

'Right. So, would you consider taking him to see an alternative practitioner?'

'Are you kidding?' James spluttered, unable to stop himself. 'It's hard enough persuading him to go to the GP. So I doubt he'd agree to see someone with a bunch of herbal pills or some foul-tasting tea or whatever.'

Ali looked aghast. 'Alternative therapies can be highly successful in the treatment of cognitive impairment.'

And that meat tenderiser hanging on the hook over there looks like it'd be highly successful for whacking you over the head with, mused James, clenching his back teeth together. 'Well, we'll see what happens,' he said firmly, sipping the acrid dark liquid. After all the palaver, he made far better coffee at home with a simple cafetière.

At the sound of voices and footsteps in the hall, he experienced a surge of relief.

'Oh, hi, James.' Michaela smiled tightly as Spike beamed and hugged his dad.

'Hey, buddy.' James's spirits rose at his son's heartfelt greeting. 'I think there was a mix-up with times,' he started, addressing Michaela now.

'Was there? No, I don't think so.' She frowned. 'Anyway, are you all ready, Spike? You haven't forgotten anything?'

'I'm all ready.' Spike beamed at his dad. 'I packed last night.'

'Good for you, being so organised. Granddad's sitting in the living room if you want to say hi.'

Spike hurried through. Kenny might never have been a conventional cuddly grandfather, but he was of endless fascination to Spike. Michaela greeted Kenny briefly, and then they were off, clambering into James's car, which he tried to start up and drive normally, instead of shooting off with a gleeful screech.

On the back seat, Spike was already bestowing all his attention on the cats. His light brown hair was roughly cut, and he was wearing his customary oversized jeans and a khaki sweatshirt. The flush of happiness and anticipation on his face gladdened James's heart. 'Can we camp out in your garden, Dad?' he asked. Unlike Michaela, Spike regarded sleeping in a tent as the ultimate treat.

'Sorry, not at this time of year,' James said.

'But we do winter camps with the Scouts.'

'Yes, but my place isn't right for it. People walk right by the garden and, anyway, you know it's shared. You'd probably get someone chucking a bottle at your tent.'

Spike sniggered.

'You can do it at Granddad's in the springtime, okay? We can take all the kit over.'

'Great,' Spike enthused. 'Is that all right, Granddad?'

'Sure it is,' Kenny said from the passenger seat, and James sensed him relaxing now, his prickliness ebbing away. 'I like your house,' Spike added. 'But I'm learning about living outdoors and surviving in the wilderness so I'd rather sleep outside.'

'The wilderness?' Kenny exclaimed with a chuckle. 'Is that what you call my garden, after all the work I've put in?' In truth, Kenny's ancient lawnmower hadn't been liberated from the rotting shed since something like 1987.

Spike laughed. 'It *is* pretty wild out there.'

'Spike's been watching a series about outdoor survival,' James explained.

'Well, you need to come over and see me again,' Kenny growled, 'and I'll show you how it's done properly.' He glanced sideways at James. 'Although I reckon your dad thinks I'm just an old fool who doesn't know anything.'

'No, he doesn't,' Spike exclaimed.

'Of course I don't, Dad,' James said, focusing on the road ahead now, and sensing that Christmas with Kenny wasn't looking to be too awful after all.

Spike embraced the task of plundering James's box of decorations and putting up the artificial silver tree. When he'd finally gone to bed, at the same time as Kenny, with whom he was sharing a room – plus the cats – James called his brother.

'How are things with you?' he asked, surprised when Rod picked up.

'Oh, pretty good,' he said blithely. 'Been doing some skiing, helping out with Livia's accounts.'

'So her name's Livia?' It was the first time Rod had mentioned anyone by that name.

'Uh-huh. She has a chain of opticians. I'm kind of helping her run things out here.'

James let this new information settle for a moment. 'So, any plans to come back at some point?'

'Well, uh, not at the moment,' Rod replied.

'D'you think we could make some time for a proper chat, then? Not now, but sometime soon. Could I Skype you?'

'What for?' Rod sounded genuinely baffled.

'You know,' James murmured, 'to talk about Dad's future. What we're going to do long-term.'

'Sounds like you've got it all sorted,' he said, 'with that Swedish girl?'

'Her name's Rikke, and she's actually Danish, but—'

'Well, she sounds great!'

'Yes, but she's only there for a couple of hours a day,' James reasoned. 'And what if she leaves?'

'Oh, I'm sure there's plenty of others,' Rod retorted, but he was wrong, James was certain of that. There was only one Rikke. 'Gotta go,' Rod said briskly. 'Wish Dad a happy Christmas from me, would you? And you too. And Spike.'

James sat for a moment in the glow of the tree lights, making the firm decision to not get annoyed with his brother tonight. He'd soon find a solution, he was sure of it. With Rod clearly out of the picture, it was up to him to take care of his father now.

He got up to go to bed, still clutching his phone. One of the cats prowled in and hopped up onto the sofa where he stretched out luxuriantly. James went to pat him but he recoiled and hissed. 'Make yourself comfortable, mate,' he murmured, turning his attention back to his phone.

Should he message Lucy? She'd been flickering into his thoughts since he'd seen her last, and now, he couldn't think of a reason not to. He knew she'd been devastated about the shed being destroyed, and he had an idea that he might be able to help somehow. He didn't mean that in a patronising way. In fact, Lucy gave the impression that she was managing admirably without anyone's help.

Hi Lucy, he texted, *sorry I haven't been in touch for*

*a while. Things a bit hectic with Dad, life – you know.
I'm in Liverpool now with Dad. Remember I'm happy
to help with* . . . He paused. No – that wouldn't do. He
erased the 'Remember I'm happy to help with' part and
wondered why the sending of a simple text to an old
friend suddenly felt so difficult.

Have a lovely Christmas, he typed quickly, before he
could change his mind, *and hope to see you soon. Love
James. x*

Chapter Forty

Snow had started to fall on the night of the carol concert, and by Christmas Eve morning the cottage was covered in it. Though Connell had said goodbye, it turned out that he wouldn't be leaving after all. 'Can you believe this?' he announced, pulling off his snow-speckled black jacket as he re-entered the cottage. 'The village is snowed in. We're cut off!'

'Really?' Lucy was astounded. 'I don't think that's happened here for years. Are you sure all the roads are closed?'

'At the moment, yes, but hopefully they'll clear them pretty soon. I've had to leave my car outside the pub. Couldn't manage to turn back.' She handed him a coffee which he sipped distractedly, then plonked the mug on the windowsill.

'Well, there's not much you can do at the moment,' she added.

He exhaled loudly. 'But I have to get back today. It's really important. They'll grit the roads, won't they?'

'At some point, yes,' she said, trying to convey optimism.

She sympathised; of course Connell wanted to get home to Nottingham for Christmas Day rather than being trapped with her and her family. But right now, there was nothing anyone could do. 'I'm sorry you're stuck here,' Lucy said, 'but why not enjoy it for now? The kids have sledges, and I'm sure we can get hold of a couple of spares.'

'Uh . . . no thanks,' Connell said quickly, as if she had suggested abseiling. 'I just need to focus on getting out of here.' As if he was planning to *stare* the snow into submission. So Lucy, the children and her parents set off without him – the aunts had also decided to stay at home – and they met up with a whole bunch of villagers who were already whizzing down the slopes, whooping and screaming, hats and gloves flashing brightly against the white. The sky was a clear unblemished blue, the sun shining brightly. It seemed as if the whole village had come out to play. With a twinge, Lucy realised she was missing James and wished he was here too, with Spike. They would love this. At least he'd texted, and she had replied immediately. She wondered if, after her 'moment' with Connell last month, she'd been unwittingly creating a little distance from James, even though it made no sense to do so. Whatever had happened, they'd been seeing less of each other recently and she felt a little hurt that he hadn't told her he'd be taking Kenny to Liverpool for Christmas.

Lucy's boots crunched into the snow as she dragged a sledge up the hill. Marnie and Sam were already scooting downwards at top speed, her parents cheering from the bottom of the slope, Tilly running in excited circles.

This was what Christmas was about, Lucy decided,

sitting gingerly on her own sledge, unprepared for Jodie rushing over and giving her a firm shove. What a pity Connell was missing this, she thought fleetingly – then she wasn't thinking about anything at all because she had gathered speed and was whizzing so fast that she felt as though she might take off. Lucy yelped with joy, feeling like a child herself as the cold air rushed past her face. She swooped over bumps and dips, coming to a juddering halt as she rammed the heels of her flat boots into the snow as a primitive brake.

Two hours went by, before Lucy finally decided that her stoic parents looked freezing, and they all headed back home, with the addition of Amber and Noah, who had begged to come over when they'd heard that pancakes were promised. As they all warmed themselves in the kitchen, Lucy whipped up a batch of batter and fried numerous pancakes, two pans on the go simultaneously to minimise waiting time for the hungry kids.

The mood dipped a little when Aunt Elspeth produced the mountainous panettone she'd brought, and none of the children seemed particularly interested in eating it. 'Try a bit,' she urged Sam, rather sharply.

'I've had it before,' he announced. 'It's just bread.'

'No, it's a cake, Sam.'

Keen to avoid an endless it's-bread-no-it's-cake loop, Lucy called out, 'Who'd like hot chocolate?'

'We've got marshmallows!' Marnie reminded her, delving into a cupboard. 'Pink and white ones.'

'And Flakes,' Lucy added, 'to sprinkle on top.'

'And squirty cream!' Sam yelled, diving for the fridge, while Aunt Elspeth looked on with mild disapproval, as if the shunning of her panettone came under the banner of bad manners, which must surely be Lucy's fault for not raising him properly. Lucy's slight fear of her eldest aunt had clearly never quite gone away.

'This year it's the panettone,' Aunt Elspeth said dryly. 'Last year it was the glazed camembert.'

Lucy was tempted to hand her a pen and paper and say, 'Would you like to list more foods my children won't eat?' But instead, she busied herself by topping up the adults' mugs as the children tucked into the hot chocolates before charging out to the garden to play in the snow.

When Connell reappeared, accepting a steaming mug from Lucy, he sank wearily onto a kitchen chair. 'So it looks like I definitely won't be going home for Christmas.'

'Oh, I am sorry,' Lucy said. 'Who were you planning to have it with?'

'Just . . . just friends,' he said vaguely. 'It's more . . .' He sighed. 'That feeling of being cut off from civilisation, you know?'

It's hardly the Arctic Circle, she wanted to say. *It's a village that has pretty much everything.* 'I know it's frustrating,' she said, 'but we'll have a lovely time here. You're welcome to spend it with us, of course.'

'Christ, that's going to go down well!'

He seemed to catch himself then, and at the moment she knew there was someone waiting at home, someone who would be terribly disappointed by his absence. 'You said you were planning to spend it with friends?' she prompted him gently.

He sighed and nodded. 'Well . . . *a* friend, actually. It's all pretty new. She's only just moved into my place.'

She studied his face, which had barely changed at all since the time when she'd first known him. He still had the air of a hapless student, trying to figure out a tricky

345

situation with a girl. 'Your first Christmas together, then,' she remarked, and he nodded.

'It was supposed to be, yes.'

She smiled, trying to lift him out of his gloom. 'I'm sure she'll forgive you. I mean, you can't help the snow. And, as I said, you're very welcome to spend the day with us – *if* you can stand us.'

He glanced dolefully out of the window, then back at her. 'Of course I can. That's very kind of you.'

'Honestly, we'd love to have you here with us.' But before she turned away to clear the plates and scraps of pancake the kids had left in their wake, she caught Connell's bleak expression. And she guessed it would take more than a hot chocolate to put a smile back on his face.

Christmas Day dawned, and Lucy saw that yet more snow had fallen when she got up at six. The children were already up and highly charged, tearing open their stockings, and a couple of hours later everyone had drifted into the kitchen, looking expectant as if waiting for the magic to begin.

Lucy had never been good at asking for help. But today she'd decided that, as everyone had bowled up here, they could all take part – including the children, who were tasked with setting the table and prepping smoked salmon starters, and her father, who willingly grabbed a peeler and set to work on a mound of potatoes.

Lucy's mother, who never caught 'any of these peculiar viruses' – who didn't have *time* to be ill – was in bed, stricken down with flu.

'We could have done this last night,' her dad said cheerfully, 'after those cocktails we had. It would have been quite fun, attacking 200 sprouts and putting little crosses on their bottoms.'

'No need for that, Paddy,' muttered Aunt Elspeth, who was prepping the turkey in some mysterious way, tying it up tightly with string as if preparing to send it overseas, while Aunt Flora, the precious one, was making terribly hard work of chopping carrots.

'So much food,' Aunt Elspeth exclaimed. 'I hope none of it's wasted. I don't know what Anna was thinking, bringing that huge Stilton wheel.'

'I'm sure we'll get through it,' Lucy said cheerfully.

'There'll be loads of leftovers,' she lamented, as Lucy thrust a glass of Prosecco into her hand.

'We haven't even had Christmas dinner,' she remarked. 'Let's not worry about the leftovers yet.'

'Couldn't this have all been done last night, like Paddy said?' Christ, would Aunt Elspeth ever stop moaning?

'Mum doesn't believe in it,' Lucy informed her, as if prepping ahead were a kind of religion. 'She thinks the vegetables lose their taste. "If they were meant to lie about soaking," she always says, "they'd have grown in water, like seaweed."'

Her father spluttered with laughter. Despite the hectic scene, the mood was high, and Lucy swung around happily at the sound of Connell arriving.

'Hey, Connell,' she said. 'Are you any good at gravy? We might need you to help out.'

'Have you looked outside this morning?' he said, frowning.

'Yes – there's even more snow.' She shrugged. She loved it and refused to apologise for it.

He inhaled deeply, as if trying to bolster himself. 'So, what would you like me to do?'

'The gravy? I'm sorry to thrust a job at you right away. It's just, there's an awful lot to do.'

'Gravy's not quite my forte,' he said apologetically.

'Okay. Could you peel the parsnips?'

'Um . . .' He looked rather reticent about this too. Surely a man who could create intricate stained glass was capable of cutting up small root vegetables? She handed him a knife, feeling quite the project manager now as she hurried upstairs with a cup of tea and toast for her mother who was sitting up amidst a sea of crumpled tissues.

'Oh, Mum. Poor you. Today of all days.'

'Never mind, love. You all have fun.' She blew her nose noisily. 'Was that Connell I heard?'

Lucy laughed. 'It was, Mum. Your hearing's as keen as ever.'

'He's stuck here then, because of the snow?'

'That's right.'

'Hmm.' Lucy could sense her mother mulling over this state of affairs. 'He might be around for quite a long time, then.'

'I very much doubt it,' Lucy said briskly, making for the door now. 'He's not at all happy to be here, you know. If he could dig himself out with a teaspoon, he would.'

Occasionally, when Lucy still worked at Claudine, they would have away-days. These would usually involve some kind of team-building enterprises like building go-karts or making a short documentary about the history of the bra. But nothing she had ever done demonstrated the brilliance of the teamwork today, in her own kitchen, in which everyone had played a part – even Aunt Flora, with her feeble carrot chopping, and *even* Connell who had grudgingly sliced up a grand total of three parsnips before hitting the wine.

They all ate until they could barely move, but somehow they still managed Christmas pudding with brandy sauce, which was also shunned by Sam (take note, Aunt Elspeth!). As dictated by both aunts, everyone – even a reluctant Connell – was rounded up to watch the Queen's speech, and once that was done there were shouty board games of a less serious nature than those usually favoured by Elspeth.

They all flopped out in front of *It's a Wonderful Life*, with Lucy's father snoring softly in his Christmas jumper, and Aunt Flora guarding the wooden box of Turkish delight, even though no one else wanted any. Even Anna had managed to rouse herself and join the party downstairs.

And as the day drew to an end, with Tilly making off with a mince pie before anyone could grab it off her, Lucy poured herself a large glass of wine and stood at the open back door, looking out on her snow-covered garden. The broken shed was still thickly covered, the snow on the lawn kicked up by the children, but softening now as flakes still fell, light and gentle, slowly covering their tracks.

It had been a wonderful Christmas. Everyone said so as they got ready to leave three days later, by which point pretty much all of the leftovers had been eaten, and Aunt Elspeth had reminded Lucy about seventeen times that the Stilton wheel would make excellent soup.

'Cheese soup?' Marnie cried out in horror. Aunt Elspeth glanced over, no doubt adding yet another item to the list of *Things Lucy's Children Won't Eat*. But nothing – not even a sour-faced relative – could spoil this Christmas, possibly Lucy's last Christmas in Rosemary Lane.

Chapter Forty-One

James had spent almost a week with Spike, Kenny and the cats in his house. It had been surprisingly cordial, considering that his place was tiny and the cats had commandeered the sofa ninety per cent of the time. Trying to coax them off had annoyed his father so James had decided to let them be. However, five days after Christmas, he was faintly relieved this morning to hear that the thaw had finally come, and that today he stood a pretty good chance of being able to drive back to Burley Bridge.

He planned to stay with his father while he investigated all kinds of care in the area. He was prepared to stay a couple of weeks, maybe more – as long as it took, really. He was fine with that. Saying goodbye to Spike was harder, as he dropped him off at his mother's place. James suspected that the real wrench for Spike was number one: saying bye to the cats, followed by number two: his granddad. James was wryly aware of where he stood in the pecking order, according to his son.

They were halfway home, and Kenny was dozing in the passenger seat when James's mobile rang. He quickly checked the screen, saw that it was his brother, and pulled over at the next services so he could call back.

Rod rarely called him. It was usually James who was left to attempt to keep some line of communication going. 'Rod?' he said. 'You just rang.'

'Look, yeah – I wanted to apologise actually.'

'Apologise? What for?' *What for exactly?* was what he really meant.

'Um, the thing with Dad. Leaving you in the lurch like that.'

For a moment, James was lost for words. More than two years had passed; his annoyance had faded away long ago. He had accepted that taking care of their father had become his sole responsibility. 'Let's talk about this some other time, Rod. I'm at a service station right now. I'm taking Dad home.'

'Yeah, well, I'm coming back,' Rod muttered. 'I can't stand it here,' he added, in case James might have assumed he was only coming back to help.

'Why? What's happened?'

'Oh, man – the rules out here,' he drawled. He seemed to have affected some kind of accent. Perhaps he'd had a skiing accident and bumped his head?

'What kind of rules?' James asked.

'Rules about everything,' Rod declared. 'This building we're in – it's no washing machine on after seven p.m., no running a bath after nine. God help you if you use a coffee grinder before ten in the morning or flush the loo in the night, and as for smoking – you're not even allowed to do it on the bloody balcony, as if there's a

352

shortage of fresh air here. The place is like one gigantic blue-skied, breezy Alpen box! It's like there's too much oxygen. You *need* to smoke to dampen it down.'

James laughed, and not for the first time it struck him how similar to their father Rod was, and that perhaps he was more like his mother, a fact that, actually, he preferred not to dwell on too much. 'But you've never stuck to a rule in your life,' he remarked.

'That's not true,' his brother said, aghast.

'It is,' James insisted. 'And, look – they're not the actual building's rules, are they? It's not Switzerland that won't let you smoke on the balcony. It's your girlfriend, isn't it?'

'Well, um, yeah. She's a bit picky about certain things.'

'So, it's not the building you're splitting up with, is it?' James added. 'It's – what's her name again?'

'Livia.'

'Right. So, when you are you thinking of coming home, then?'

Some kind of announcement blotted out Rod's voice. '. . . I'm at the airport now.'

James frowned, and it dawned on him that he couldn't have Rod turning up at their father's place, simply because he had nowhere else to go. He glanced at his dad, who was still dozing.

'Well, look – we can get together sometime soon, okay? But not right now. Don't come straight to Dad's.'

'But I thought—'

'No, Rod,' James said firmly. 'If you're stuck, call Phoebe. I'm sure she'll be delighted to have you back.'

After they'd finished the call he sat for a moment, wondering if he'd been a little harsh there – but sod it. He really couldn't face his brother today. He sat for a few moments, twisting his phone about in his hands and finally he called Lucy's number.

'James, hi!' There were street noises around her; perhaps she was in a hurry to be somewhere. He sensed that it wasn't the best time.

'Hey, Lucy. Just calling to catch up really. I wondered how your Christmas went.'

'It was eventful,' she chuckled. 'I'll tell you all about it when we meet up.' She sounded happy to hear from him, at least. 'Are you coming back anytime soon?'

'Right now, actually. We're on our way. I don't suppose you'd like to grab a coffee or something later on?' He realised now how very much he wanted to see her, and to tell her the secret he'd been carrying. He *had* to share it with her. He just hoped she'd understand why he'd kept it from her all this time.

'I'd love to but I'm in Manchester right now. I'm just about to go into an interview.' She paused. 'Well, she says it's not an interview – more of a chat. But they're sort of the same thing really.'

It surprised him, how crushing this news was. 'So . . . are you definitely moving back to Manchester?'

She hesitated again. 'I . . . I'm not sure. I really don't know what I'm doing right now, but I'm due in ten minutes. I'd better go.'

'Well, good luck,' he said.

'Thanks, James. Bye!' And she was gone.

He glanced at his father, figuring that they should be back in under an hour as long as no more snow came. James loved snow, he always had – but he wanted a clear run now as there was something he needed to do. But before he pulled out of the services, he played the voice-mail message that had been left while he was driving.

354

Hello, James? It's Phyllida here. Phyllida Somerville. As if his world was littered with Phyllidas. *I wondered if you could give me a call please? As soon as you can. There's something I think you might be very interested in. So do call me. Thank you. Bye.*

Chapter Forty-Two

Both James and Connell had told Lucy she hadn't changed, which she knew wasn't entirely true. She was an older, softer version of the girl they'd known – still recognisable, though. The basic components were pretty much the same. But Nina Kerridge looked so startlingly different that Lucy wouldn't have recognised her at all.

'So good to see you,' she said, hugging Lucy in her expansive corner office – the one MC had commandeered – and standing back and beaming at her.

'You too,' Lucy said, fascinated by the smoothness of her forehead, the plumpness of her lips; once brunette, now ash blonde, she appeared to be a different creature entirely. Even her teeth had been done, Lucy noticed. They beamed brightly, Tipp-ex white. 'It looked as if I might not make it,' she added. 'With the snow, I mean. But the roads are just about cleared . . .'

'That's good,' Nina said, obviously disinterested in the weather conditions. 'Would you like a coffee? Tea? Please, have a seat.'

Lucy sat down. 'Coffee please.'

Nina's manner had changed too. While she had always exuded confidence, now her assuredness had ramped up several levels. Nina was clearly a woman who liked to get things done. With a nod and wave, she communicated with someone through the glass wall in the main office. As they were still in that no man's land between Christmas and New Year, few staff were around. Lucy was slightly relieved that none of her friends appeared to be here today. The last thing she wanted was to catch Andrew or Nadeen's eye while she was here in Nina's office. She hadn't even told them she was coming today; she had wanted to keep it low-key, and would fill them in later.

'So, I'll get straight to the point,' Nina said, leaning back in her chair as a young woman brought in a tray of coffees, 'about the new direction we're taking.'

Lucy nodded. She was interested in the yoga and sleepwear collections that Andrew had mentioned, and was keen to hear it from the boss.

'Bottoms are the new boobs,' Nina announced, pausing as if to gauge her reaction.

'I'm sorry?' Lucy frowned.

Nina grinned, baring those big white teeth at her. 'You know how in beauty, eyes are the new lips? You *must* have read that.'

'Oh yes. To be honest, I always find that idea of something-being-the-new-something really confusing.'

'Well, it's all about emphasis and priorities.'

Lucy nodded. 'So our customers – I mean, Claudine's customers – are prioritising their bottoms now?'

'Not exactly,' Nina said, 'but, you know, the last few years have been about the new bra – the bralette – and the trend's been about softness, hasn't it? Less structure, a friendlier wear.'

'Yes, of course.' Lucy knew all about that.

'Well, now we're looking at the same kind of idea, but for knickers.'

'The knickerlette?'

Nina laughed. 'More of a soft, hugging pant.'

'But isn't that what all pants are like? Good pants, I mean. The pants most women prefer to wear.' She heard herself saying 'pants' repeatedly and felt faintly ridiculous.

'Exactly. Forget thongs, boy shorts – even briefs. We're going all out to focus on the comfy pant, the pant that *loves* your bottom.'

'D'you mean *big* pants?' Lucy asked hesitantly.

Nina beamed. 'Yes! We want to give women permission to wear big pants.'

'I've never needed permission,' Lucy said with a smile. 'I've worn them for years.'

'Oh, me too – but always with slight embarrassment, you know? The what-if-I'm-knocked-down-by-a-bus kind of thing and I'm found wearing giant monstrosities.' Lucy nodded, although she had never had such concerns herself. 'So what we're doing,' Nina continued, 'is making the big pant a gorgeous, sexy item. It'll be a new brand – still under the Claudine umbrella of course, but with its own unique identity.' She fixed her with a blue-eyed stare. 'And we'd love you to head that up.'

Lucy hesitated. 'Head up the big pant?'

She laughed. 'You could put it that way.'

'What would the role be exactly? You know I was head buyer, and you mentioned it would be more of a second-in-charge to you . . .'

'You'd take full control of the brand, really,' Nina said,

as if it was obvious. 'It would be your baby for the duration of the contract, then we could see how the pants are performing.'

Without warning, Lucy was seized by a desire to laugh. As Nina went on, enthusing wildly about the *scope* and *potential* of the big pant, Lucy tried to focus hard on non-funny things – like Aunt Elspeth's dry panettone, and the time the children had nits. In an attempt to rein in her mirth, she choked.

'Are you okay?' Nina lurched forward.

'Yes, sorry. Just, um – something in my throat.' She inhaled deeply, trying to steady herself.

Nina's gaze flicked to her phone on the desk. 'Right – well, I have a two o'clock meeting so I'm sorry – we'd better wind this up for now. Could you think it over and get back to me, and we can talk again in more depth?'

'Of course,' Lucy said, slightly shocked that it was all over so quickly. She'd arranged for Marnie and Sam to play at Jodie's and schlepped all the way to Manchester – and Nina had given her all of eleven minutes. Lucy had forgotten that this was how things were in the business world. She hadn't even finished her coffee.

'Thanks for coming in,' Nina said, jumping up and hugging her again. 'I have to say, you look amazing, Lucy. Country life is obviously suiting you very well.'

By the time she arrived back in Burley Bridge, it was already starting to get dark, and Marnie and Sam were happily worn out from an afternoon's trampolining in Jodie's garden. Yet they still wanted to play out, so she wandered into her garden with them, scanning the borders now that the snow had somewhat melted away, and figuring that she would need to do some cutting back and tidying.

She noticed then that something was different. Her eyes lighted upon the place where the shed had been crushed by the falling branch.

Lucy stared. The pile of wooden pieces was no longer lying there. She strode towards the spot, seeing that the base of the shed was still where it had always been, but all of the pieces – the broken walls and the roof, had been stacked neatly against one wall. Beside them, something lumpy was shrouded in black polythene.

She lifted it gingerly. There were several plant pots underneath, filled with what looked like the shed's contents: small tools, screws, spools of wire – the things Ivan and the children had used when they had been tinkering about in there.

Someone had sorted it all in an organised fashion. One pot was filled with tiny tins of enamel paint, another with brushes, another with offcuts of wood. The children hadn't noticed yet. They were too busy playing – Marnie was charging about with Sam on her back – and they never noticed when things had been tidied anyway. Only when their possessions had been thrown away.

Then Lucy's gaze lighted upon a smaller pot at the end of the row. Its contents weren't tools or art materials, but a mixture of odd things. She dipped in a hand and touched a round white pebble, a speckled feather, a gnarly pine cone and a tiny animal skull. There was a pale blue bird's egg, miraculously undamaged, and a thin white bone, smooth as porcelain.

She picked carefully through the objects, only faintly aware of her children's voices as she found a small note. She picked it up and examined it. It looked as if it had been ripped from a lined notebook. *Found these lying all together,* the loopy but neat handwriting read, *as if they'd been tipped out onto the ground. Wondered if it was some sort of collection? James.*

She stood up now, unable to stop smiling as she called out, 'Sam? Come here a minute, love. I think this might be your museum.'

Chapter Forty-Three

James had felt fine when he'd pulled up at Lucy's on the morning of New Year's Eve. He was going to tell her, he decided. He'd just splurge it all out and that would be that. But now, as she welcomed him in and poured him a coffee, his mouth was dry and his heart was hammering against his ribs. He took a seat and Lucy sat opposite him.

'So, are you looking forward to tonight?' she asked. There was a New Year's Eve gathering in the village hall and she knew he planned to drop by with his father.

'Yeah, I guess so, are you?'

Lucy nodded. 'I've promised the kids they can stay until the bells. It's their first time. They're pretty thrilled about that.' A pause settled over them. James could sense Lucy studying his face, as if she knew something was coming, and that he hadn't just dropped by for a casual chat. 'So, your Christmas went pretty well?'

'Yeah.' He nodded. 'Better than I could have hoped for, really.' He looked at her and smiled. 'I've missed you lately.'

Well, he hadn't planned to say *that*. Lucy smiled, cupping her coffee mug with both hands.

'I've missed you too. Thanks so much for what you did – with the shed and Sam's museum exhibits . . . it was so kind of you.'

'That's okay,' he murmured. He inhaled and sipped his coffee, trying to muster the courage to say what he'd come to say. He looked at her. 'Lucy,' he started, 'I want to say . . . I'm sorry.'

She frowned. 'What on earth for?'

'Um . . . look, I lied about something pretty major a long time ago. Not just to you,' he added quickly. 'I lied to everyone. Even the Linton kids – *all* my friends. It wasn't just you.'

She met his gaze, as if waiting for him to go on. 'What did you lie about?'

He cleared his throat, aware of Marnie and Sam chatting upstairs. He willed them to stay up there just a few minutes longer. 'D'you remember,' he started, 'how I said my mum had died when I was six?'

'Yes, of course.'

'Well, she didn't. She left us because she'd fallen in love with someone else. But Dad was so distraught and humiliated, he said that was what we had to tell everyone, and we did. Rod and I stuck to the lie. It seemed so important to him.'

For a moment, Lucy just looked at him. There had been another flurry of snow overnight and everything was still and white and perfect. 'So . . .' Lucy hesitated. 'She never tried to contact you or your brother?'

'Not that I know of,' he replied. 'Even if she did, she obviously didn't try very hard.'

'And you've never thought of trying to contact her?'

James shrugged. 'I'm starting to think I might do that. You know when we were talking about you sorting through Ivan's things – and you said maybe you would, when the time was right?'

Lucy nodded. James could feel the thud of his heart. 'Well, maybe it's that time now for me.'

'Maybe it is,' she murmured. Then they were no longer sitting opposite each other across her kitchen table. She was up on her feet, and so was he, and she was hugging him. 'Oh, James. I wish you'd told me. Why didn't you say?'

He stood back and looked at her, stuck for words for a moment. Why hadn't he said? 'I didn't know how,' he replied, knowing how ridiculous that sounded.

'You just had to say it,' she said, squeezing his hand.

James nodded. *And I needed to find the right person to tell,* he reflected, turning to the doorway as Sam wandered in, saying a bleary hello to James and asking if pancakes might be possible.

It was the following Saturday when James arrived to pick up Lucy, Marnie and Sam. Lucy had been puzzled when he'd called the previous day, suggesting 'a drive', if they were free. 'But where to?' she'd asked.

'It's a kind of surprise,' James had replied.

'Can't you give me a hint?' She'd laughed.

'Nope. No hints! You'll just have to wait and see . . .'

Now he was drinking coffee in her kitchen while the children got ready upstairs.

Of course, Marnie and Sam wouldn't settle for that, and now, in the back seat of James's rather battered old car, they asked repeatedly where they were heading to – until Lucy had to ask them, firmly, to be patient.

'We're just going for a drive,' James said, which made her smile. It sounded like something her mother would do or, more likely, demand to be taken on. But gradually, as they left the village behind, her curiosity started to niggle.

'You can give *me* a clue, if you like,' she said, throwing James a quick glance.

'Sorry. No clues.' James looked back at Lucy, and something stirred in her. She remembered clearly the first day she'd seen him, when they were nine years old. Suddenly, Burley Bridge had seemed full of promise.

They all fell silent now as he drove out into open countryside. 'I was thinking,' she murmured a few minutes later, 'I *would* like you to help me to clear out the attic sometime, if it's not too much trouble?'

'Of course it's not,' he said. 'I'd love to help. Just say when it suits you and we can get started.' He indicated and made a turn off the main road.

Lucy frowned. 'James . . . why are we going this way?'

'I just want to show you something,' he replied.

'But . . .' A small chill ran through her. There was nothing to see, and nowhere to visit on this road – just two hamlets, with no reason to go this way unless you lived here.

It was the road where Ivan had crashed. The one there was no reason for her husband to be on at all, unless . . .

James had slowed down now and switched on the radio, which did nothing to soothe Lucy's growing anxiety. 'James—'

'Here we are,' he said quickly. He indicated and turned into a gravelled area in front of a large, fairly modern detached house.

'What are we doing here?' Sam demanded as they all climbed out of the car.

'Wait and see.' James smiled, and now Lucy registered the sound of dogs barking. *Lots* of dogs.

'What *is* this place?' she asked.

James pointed at a sign next to the front door: *Candy Bank Dogs Rescue Centre.*

'A dog rescue centre?' She stared at him and grinned.

'Are you getting a dog, James?' Marnie exclaimed.

'Not exactly, Marnie.'

'James . . .' Lucy started. 'Please tell me what's going on . . .'

He cleared his throat and indicated the neat side garden with its swing and rabbit hutch. 'Marnie, Sam,' he said, 'could you guys play there, just for a couple of minutes while I talk to your mum?'

'Okay,' Marnie said, somehow managing to rein in her curiosity. 'C'mon, Sam.'

As the two of them strolled over to investigate the hutch, James turned back to Lucy. 'I'm sorry,' he started. 'Maybe I should have said. It's just – Phyllida called me yesterday. She seems to know everything that goes on around here, and she told me about a new development that's just been finished along the road here. It's retirement flats. Well, sheltered housing, really – lovely apartments, with a resident warden and a garden. Just four of them, and one's still vacant. I'm thinking about showing it to Dad.'

'Oh . . . that's fantastic,' she said. 'So, d'you think he might agree to sell up?'

'We'll need to figure it out,' he said. 'I hope he'll be persuadable. He'd be a lot safer somewhere like this. Spike might be a bit disappointed that he won't get to camp in his granddad's garden, but—'

'He could camp in ours,' she said quickly. 'He's always welcome to do that, and my kids would love it.'

'I'll tell him that.' He smiled.

'I still don't understand why we're here,' she added, feeling confused now.

James grinned and laughed. 'This is going to sound crazy. I called the manager yesterday – I hope you don't mind. It's just, when I drove past on the way to those new flats, I saw this place and something just registered with me. About you, I mean. You and Ivan.'

She was about to ask why when the door opened and an older woman with long silvery hair, fringeless with a Seventies-style ponytail, stepped outside. 'James?' she said. 'Come on in.' She smiled broadly.

'This is Lucy,' he added.

'Ah, Lucy Scott. I'm Melanie.' A hint of something flickered in her eyes. Lucy was good at picking up signs like that, like when her guests wondered why she was running a B&B alone, but didn't like to ask. She had become very perceptive.

'How d'you know my surname?' she asked as Melanie led them inside, through a neat waiting room and into a small office. The walls were adorned with posters of dogs; all the different breeds, and a map of the world to denote where they originated from. There were glass jars of dog treats on shelves, and a bunch of leads hanging from a hook on the door.

'Lucy,' Melanie said, indicating for them to sit down at the desk, 'your husband came here, just over two years ago.' She opened a red leather-bound diary on the desk and flipped through the pages. '*Here* we are. Ivan Scott, 8pm, 20th December.'

Lucy felt as if her heart had stopped. 'What d'you mean? Why was he here?'

She looked around the room, then back at Melanie who was smiling now.

'Well, he'd been here before he made this appointment,' she said tapping the page, 'and he'd chosen a dog he thought you'd all love. A little cocker spaniel called Bob. He was planning to come that evening to pick him up and take him to his new home.'

They went to get the children then, and Melanie led them all round to the back of the house where a low-rise building housed kennels, and dogs of all different breeds were lounging in baskets and on sofas or pottering around. 'Are we getting a dog?' Marnie exclaimed, tears springing instantly to her eyes. Lucy's eyes were moist too as she looked at James.

'I'm afraid Bob has been adopted,' Melanie explained. 'When Ivan didn't turn up that night, I assumed he'd just changed his mind. People do that. They have second thoughts, a change of heart.'

'Yes of course,' Lucy said quickly. She gazed around. There were dogs of every imaginable colour and breed and she didn't even know where to begin.

'I'll give you some time to get to know them,' Melanie said. 'All the dogs here are fine with children and very friendly. Ivan filled in all the questionnaires and forms, so unless your circumstances have changed—'

'No, they haven't changed at all,' Lucy said quickly.

'Then you're already an approved adopter,' Melanie said. Lucy grinned, lost for words. 'I'll be in the office if you need me, but do take your time.'

'Thank you,' Lucy said, turning to James when Melanie

had disappeared through the back door. 'And thank *you*. I can't believe you thought of this, and made that connection!'

'Hey, that's okay.' He smiled, looking around now as Marnie and Sam just stood and stared in wonderment, as if they couldn't believe they were here. His hand brushed against Lucy's, and she turned and looked at him.

James Halsall, the boy she had been in love with before she had known what love was, and who had lifted her heart again. She would never stop missing Ivan, but maybe she had found a different kind of love.

Maybe. Time would tell, and they had all the time in the world.

'Mum?' Marnie's voice cut into her thoughts.

She turned and looked at her children. Even on Christmas morning, they hadn't looked as happy as this.

'Are we really getting a dog?' Sam asked, staring up at her in delight.

Lucy smiled, catching James's gaze again briefly as she answered, 'Yes, darling, it looks as if we are.'

Chapter Forty-Four

It had been Hally first, before the Linton children. He was the one who had caught up with Lucy that first day and said hi. Her mother had just dropped her off at her Uncle George and Aunt Babs's place. Lucy was ten years old and she didn't really want to be there. She didn't know anyone here, and she had no idea how she would fill three whole weeks when there was nothing to do. It felt like forever.

She was mooching through the village, fed up and alone, when she happened to turn down a narrow lane which, she soon discovered, led to a cottage. It was white with a thatched roof and a garden bursting with flowers. She stood and stared. It was the cottage she had imagined from hundreds of stories, and the one she had visited in her dreams. Lucy wanted to sneak into the garden, but what if someone saw her? She wished she had a friend here, someone at her side to bolster her courage, but she didn't, so – stuff it – she was going in alone.

Walking in through the gate was too obvious, so she clambered up the rough stone wall, grazing her knees

370

on the way. Once at the top she could see that there were redcurrant bushes round at the side of the house. She jumped down, ran to the bushes and started to help herself to the fruit.

A boy was watching her, although she hadn't known that then. She hadn't spotted Hally yet. Apparently, he saw her stuffing berries into her pockets and scrambling back over the wall, and he caught up with her in the lane.

'Hello?' he said.

She whirled around. A boy had spoken – a tall, skinny boy with a shock of dark hair and deep brown eyes with tiny flecks in them. 'Hi,' she said, sensing herself flushing a little.

'I'm Hally,' he said.

'I'm Lucy.'

'You're brave,' he remarked with a grin. 'D'you know who lives there?'

'No?' Lucy shrugged.

'Kitty Cartwright.'

She shrugged again in a 'so?' kind of way.

'Did you steal her redcurrants?' She could tell he was impressed.

'Only a few,' she said, smiling now. 'Want some?'

'Yes please.' Hally told her later that he'd never heard of anyone daring to sneak into that garden before. That woman in there was *crazy*.

'C'mon then,' she said. 'We can go to my auntie and uncle's garden and eat them there.'

They started chatting easily as they walked together, filling each other in on their ages and lives, all the important stuff.

Lucy stopped suddenly. 'Hey, Hally!' She nudged him.

He looked at her quizzically. 'What is it?'

She nodded back towards the cottage. 'See that house?'

'Yeah?'

She smiled and started walking again, her face warmed by the afternoon sun, her heart soaring as he caught up with her, already knowing they would be friends.

'I'm going to live there one day,' she said.

Acknowledgements

Huge thanks to Rachel Faulkner-Willcocks, Sabah Khan and the brilliant Avon team. Hugs and mince pies to my fabulous agent, Caroline Sheldon, and to everyone who sponsored me in the Virgin Money London Marathon 2019 (special thanks to Caitlin at Home-Start Glasgow South and Iain and Dexter at Virgin Money Lounge, Glasgow). Thanks to Wendy for excellent hospitality at Hotel du Rigg, and to Jimmy, Jen, Kath and Susan for cheering at the finish. Festive love to the staff at McClymont House, Lanark, who looked after my mum, Margery, so wonderfully, to Keith and Beatrice for their support, and for Tania's kind visit during Mum's last days. Finally, thank you to Elise Honeyman's coaching group: Annie, Anne, Christobel and Mif. You're an inspiration x

Loved *Snowdrops on Rosemary Lane*? Go back to where it all began in the first of the Rosemary Lane series.

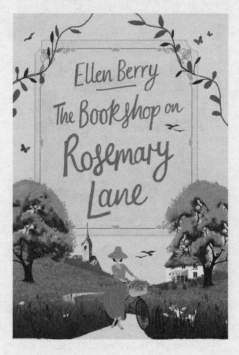

Take a trip to the Yorkshire village of Burley Bridge, where a special little cookbook shop is about to open its doors . . .

And don't miss the second book in the series . . .

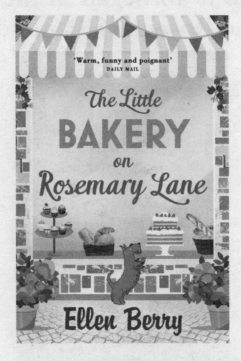

'Warm, funny and poignant'
DAILY MAIL

The Little
BAKERY
on
Rosemary Lane

Ellen Berry

Prepare to fall in love with the beautiful village of Burley Bridge all over again in this gorgeous, heart-warming read.

More from Ellen Berry, writing as Fiona Gibson.

The laugh-out-loud *Sunday Times* bestseller is back and funnier than ever in this hilarious romantic comedy!

More from Ellen Berry, writing as Fiona Gibson.

A laugh-out-loud romantic comedy perfect for fans of Milly Johnson and Carole Matthews.

FRENCH
GRAMMAR

Jean-Claude Arragon, M.A., L es L, MIL

TEACH YOURSELF BOOKS
Hodder and Stoughton

First published 1986
Fourth impression 1989

Copyright © 1986
Jean-Claude Arragon

British Library Cataloguing in Publication Data

Arragon, Jean-Claude
  French grammer.—(Teach yourself books)
  1. French language—Grammar—1950–
  I. Title
  448.2′421   PC2112
  ISBN 0 340 39148 0

Printed and bound in Great Britain for
Hodder and Stoughton Educational,
a division of Hodder and Stoughton Ltd,
Mill Road, Dunton Green, Sevenoaks, Kent,
by Richard Clay Ltd, Bungay, Suffolk.
Typeset by Macmillan India Ltd., Bangalore 25.

Contents

Introduction

When we speak or write our own language, we make up sentences, which are, in general, understandable by all those who are familiar with the language. Such sentences are not built haphazardly. The words appear in a certain order and, like the pieces of a jigsaw puzzle, occupy a specific place in the overall pattern. This means that our minds have discovered the acceptable (and unacceptable) ways of speaking and writing. In other words, we have worked out the grammar rules of the language, and if we hear a child or a foreigner say *I has done that or *I very like it, we know instinctively that those phrases are not acceptable (although they may still be understandable), because they break the rules which our brain has worked out, even though we may not always be able to state why this is so or exactly what the rule is. Similarly, when learning another language, we have to acquire the vocabulary and the grammar of that language in order to build up a store of knowledge which will enable us to understand and to communicate. This can be done in different ways with varying degrees of success. One way, perhaps the more effective, is to spend long periods of time in the foreign country, but this is not always possible. Another way is to learn every word and every grammar rule you need mechanically, but this is very tiresome and, unless you are blessed with a superb memory, very frustrating. Yet another, and perhaps more practicable method, is to build up our knowledge of words and structures by becoming *actively involved* in the learning process and in the discovery of the rules, as we did when we learnt to speak our own language.

Looking back over our formative years, it may seem that doing so was quick and easy but this is not so! Long before we even began to talk, our brain was doing an amazing amount of 'detective work' using the language information which was coming to our ears, 'examining' it, piecing things together, mastering sounds, phrases, sentences, making up its own rules and later inflicting the results of all those thoughts on other people. That is precisely what you must learn to do once again. However, instead of having to work out all the rules by yourself, you will have this book at your elbow. The book is, in

*Here and throughout the book an asterisk (*) is used to denote an unacceptable utterance.

essence, not very different from a recipe book. It will give you a list of the 'ingredients' you need (grammatical words) and the order in which to use them to turn your efforts into acceptable and palatable recipes (sentences). But it is essential that you experiment on your own: you must prepare your own sentences from the 'ingredients' used in the examples given, using the latter as models. Teach yourself to listen or look for similarities or differences in any new material you come across. Compare words, phrases, sentences. In that way, you will develop positive attitudes which are the key to linguistic success. And whenever you *discover* a rule, however small, you will have made excellent progress because that is a rule you will not forget!

The aim of this book, therefore, is to help you improve your skills in French through active participation. It would be unfair to claim that you will find all the answers in it. However, an honest attempt has been made to present the main rules of French grammar in a clear and precise way. The vocabulary used in the examples is largely based on *le Français fondamental*, a list of the 3000 most commonly used words in the language. In this way, useful memory space will not be taken up with seldom-used items. It is hoped that by so doing, the author will have provided a useful tool for the beginner and at the same time encouraged more advanced learners to develop and refine the knowledge already acquired.

NB: Whenever a very important or problematic point is encountered in the course of the explanations it will appear in a boxed section which will be immediately recognisable. Particular care should be taken to remember the context of such sections.

The book is designed to be read through once to get 'the feel of the language' and then returned to as often as necessary, to learn a specific point, to refresh your memory, or to check on one of your own 'theories'. Let us take an example of this 'theory-building' which is so crucial to the learning process. If you come across phrases like the following:

Voici la voiture rouge. *Here is the red car.*
Voici le chat noir. *Here is the black cat.*
Voici les pommes vertes. *Here are the green apples.*

you should examine them carefully. This examination should enable you to formulate the following theories:

Theory I: The word **voici** can be used with a masculine noun (**le chat**), with a feminine one (**la voiture**) or with a plural one (**les pommes**). Therefore it could mean either *here is* or *here are*.

Theory II: Words expressing colour (**rouge**, **noir**, **vertes**) all appear after the name of the thing or being they refer to. Therefore, this seems to indicate that, in French, adjectives of colour follow the noun they refer to, whereas in English they are placed before it.

Theory III: The adjective **vertes** and the noun **pommes** both have an s in the plural. Therefore it could mean that
(*a*)   French nouns take an s in the plural (which is similar to English);
(*b*)   French adjectives take an s in the plural (which is totally different from English).

If you check in the relevant sections of this book, you will find that theories I and II are absolutely correct, but that III is incomplete and needs to be refined further.

The more you become accustomed to looking at the language in this way, the more rewarding your learning will be and the quicker your progress.

Finally you should remember two crucial points:
1   A language is a living thing; grammar rules are there to capture its individuality and its vitality, not to destroy them.
2   Every language has its own identity and you must not try to 'bend' the rules of French to fit those of your own language.

If this book helps you to gain greater confidence in the use of French and a clearer view of the way the language operates, it will have more than met its goal.

1 The Development of the French Language

The present state of the French language is the result of a long and complex evolution and of numerous external influences. At various stages in its history, France was invaded by different ethnic and linguistic groups: Greeks, Romans, Celts, Franks, Arabs . . . and each of those groups left its mark on the country and its language. There is little doubt, however, that the most profound influence of all was exerted by the Romans and by their language, Latin, both in its classical and popular forms. However, the words and grammatical structures borrowed from Latin were modified to fit the needs and the patterns of the developing French language, thereby contributing to its originality. Some of the original features of French are given below.

The gender of nouns

French nouns are divided into two gender categories: masculine and feminine. To the learner, the division may sometimes seem arbitrary or even amusing, but there are reasons, obscure though they may be, for the classification. At this stage, it would not be helpful to go into those reasons. For those who have studied Latin, however, it may be helpful to know that borrowed masculine and neuter Latin nouns are masculine in French whilst borrowed feminine Latin nouns have retained their original gender.

Although there are useful rules which can help you recognise the gender of certain nouns, the best method is to learn any new noun with a word which will give an indication of its gender. That is why every new noun should be associated with the singular form of its definite (*the*) or indefinite (*a*) article. Unlike their English counterparts those words carry information about the gender of the noun that follows.

Thus you should learn:

not: voiture	*but*: **la voiture**	*or* **une voiture**
car	*the* (fem.) *car*	*a* (fem.) *car*

not: sac   *but*: **le sac**   *or* **un sac**

bag   *the* (masc.) *bag*   *a* (masc.) *bag*

This is very important and may save you a great deal of trouble at a later stage.

Gender and number agreements

Since French nouns are divided into two gender categories, masculine and feminine, it is logical that words related to those nouns should also bear the mark of the noun's gender; that is why it is vitally important to know what the gender of a given noun is; failure to do so would result in a cascade of mistakes.

Compare: le grand homme brun   *the tall dark-haired man*

and: la grande dame brune   *the tall dark-haired woman*

The above examples clearly show that, whereas in English the definite article *the* and the adjectives *tall, dark-haired* are the same in the masculine and in the feminine, it is definitely not so in French.

French nouns can, whenever necessary, bear the mark of the plural. This also occurs in English. However, there is a striking difference between the two languages in this respect: the plural form of an English noun nearly always sounds *different* from the singular one:

a wall ⟶ *walls*

a home ⟶ *homes*

The plural form of a French noun nearly always sounds *exactly the same* as the singular one:

un mur ⟶ **des murs** } the **s** is not

une maison ⟶ **des maisons** } sounded

It is therefore vital that some other signal or 'advance warning system' be present to indicate whether the noun is in the singular or the plural. This is done with the help of a category of words called determiners; the definite article **le**, **la**, **les** (*the*) and the indefinite article **un**, **une**, **des** (*a, some*) belong to that category.

Compare: **la** grande dame brune   *the tall dark-haired woman*

and: **les** grandes dames brunes   *the tall dark-haired women*

The *only* difference in sound between the two comes from the definite article **la/les**.

This explains why, in French, determiners cannot usually be omitted.

Vowel removal (or elision); liaison

In certain circumstances, some vowels (**a**, **e**, **i**) are removed at the end of a given word and are replaced by an apostrophe (') which is a marker used to signal the elision. The reason is that French does not usually permit a 'clash' of vowels between two adjoining words. So, if such a clash is likely to occur because a word beginning with a vowel or a 'silent' (mute) **h** follows another word ending with a vowel, the last vowel of the first word disappears and is replaced by '. Therefore:

    *le enfant becomes l'enfant   *the child*
    *le hôtel becomes l'hôtel   *the hotel*

NB Vowels cannot be removed from the end of nouns, adjectives, verbs, adverbs (important grammatical words); they can only be removed from *specific words* like the definite article, pronouns or the preposition **de** (*in*, *at*, *from*) for instance. In the case of the definite article, the result of this process is that the reduced form **l'** no longer carries any gender information. That is why, when learning new nouns, you should replace **l'** by the appropriate indefinite article **un**, **une** (*a*).

Thus you must learn:

    not: l'orange *the orange*   *but*: **une** orange *an orange* (fem.)
    not: l'acteur *the actor*   *but*: **un** acteur *an actor* (masc.)

The need to eliminate the 'vowel-vowel clash' across word boundaries, has also led the French to make use of liaison (or word-linking). As we have already seen, certain letters at the end of a word are not sounded; this may result in the occurrence of a 'clash'. To avoid this clash the French *either* sound the last letter of the preceding word:

Compare: un peti**t** homme *a small man* – the **t** is sounded
and: un peti**t** garçon *a small boy* – the **t** is not sounded

or they modify the preceding word whenever possible:

Compare: **ce** garçon *this boy*
and: **cet** enfant *this child* – **ce** has become **cet** to avoid the
             clash

    For a fuller treatment of this point, you should refer to Appendix I, where you will also find a list of words beginning with 'non-silent' (aspirated) **h**, before which vowel removal or elision does *not* occur.

The 'tu' and 'vous' forms

In French, there are two ways of addressing a person: you can either use the **tu** (*thou*) form or the **vous** (*you*) form. Most English people seem to have great difficulty in deciding which to use. The rule is in fact quite simple:

tu is used between relatives or close friends but not normally with strangers or passing acquaintances. There are, however, some exceptions:

(*a*)   members of a close-knit group, students for instance, use the **tu** form, even though they may not know each other; in this case the **tu** form creates a bond between members of the group;

(*b*)   the **tu** form can be used with a complete stranger as a mark of contempt. Parisian taxi-drivers use this quite often!

vous is used in all other cases. It should not be seen as a sign of stand-offishness, but as a *mark of respect*. The best thing to do is take your cue from the French: if they use **tu** with you, you may use it with them, if not use **vous**.

Sentences and their components: the jigsaw puzzle

Sentences in French, as in other languages, are made up of sections called clauses or phrases, which in turn are made up of words.

To the beginner it may be useful to consider the French sentence as a linear jigsaw puzzle, each word representing a piece of the whole pattern, for which the right place must be selected. In English, you know instinctively how the pieces fit together. It is crucial for you to realise that they may not fit the same way in French:

| Compare: | (Le | — | beaujolais | nouveau | est | arrivé. |
| and: | (The | new | Beaujolais | — | has | arrived. |

| or: | (Voici | le | — | chat | noir. |
| and: | (Here is | the | black | cat. | — |

| or: | (Je | le | vois | — |
| and: | (I | — | see | him. |

You must therefore beware not to impose upon French the rules of your own language.

The pieces of the jigsaw puzzle (words) are not all alike in shape or status, but they all have a specific role to play. Because of this, they have been grouped in grammatical categories; it would be extremely awkward and wasteful to try and explain grammatical rules without using grammatical words. Grammatical categories are recognised the world over and used in the teaching and description of all languages. Therefore, if you wish to consult a dictionary, or other reference books, you will have to become familiar with a few 'technical' words. After all, when you go to an ironmonger's, it is easier to ask for 'a screw' than for 'a tapering cylindrical piece of metal with a spiral ridge running on its outside and a slotted head, for fastening pieces of wood or metal together'!

Below is a list of the grammatical categories which will be examined in subsequent chapters. Rather than presenting the categories by order of importance it has been decided to introduce them to reflect, as far as possible, the order in which they would occur in a sentence.

Determiners

A determiner is an element which occurs before the name of a thing or being, and gives some useful additional information as well as (in French) giving advance warning of the *gender* (masculine or feminine) and/or the *number* (singular or plural) of that name. In English, determiners do not have exactly the same role.

Compare: **le** sac *the* bag – masculine

la carte *the* map/card – feminine

les visiteurs *the* visitors – plural

The main categories of determiners are:
- (*a*) the definite article: **le, la; les** (*the*);
- (*b*) the indefinite article: **un, une; des** (*a; several*);
- (*c*) the partitive article: **du, de la, des** (*a certain amount of*);
- (*d*) the possessive adjective: **mon, ma, mes** (*my*);
- (*e*) the demonstrative adjective: **ce, cette; ces** (*this/that; these/those*);
- (*f*) the exclamative adjective: **quel, quelle, quels!** (*what(a)!*);
- (*g*) the interrogative adjective: **quel, quelle, quels?** (*what/which?*)
- (*h*) the indefinite adjective: **quelques, plusieurs, certain(s)** (*a few, several, certain/some*);
- (*i*) the numeral: **un, six, dix, cent** . . . (*one, six, ten, a hundred* . . .)

Adjectives

Adjectives are words which are added to the names of things or beings, to give details about (some of) their characteristics.

le **vieux** monsieur **barbu**   the *old bearded* man.

la **petite** maison **blanche**   the *small white* house

Some adjectives can be found before the noun, some after. This is not a matter of choice; there are definite rules governing the position of adjectives: adjectives expressing colour are placed *after* the noun and not before it as in English. Adjectives are also found after a small number of verbs such as: **être** *to be*, **devenir** *to become*, **sembler** *to seem*, **paraître** *to appear*, **rester** *to remain*:

Il est **riche.**   *He is rich.*

Elle devient **belle.**   *She is becoming beautiful.*

> In French, as already mentioned, adjectives agree in *gender* (masculine/feminine) and *number* (singular/plural) with the name of the thing(s) or being(s) they qualify. This is *not* the case in English.

le **grand** garçon   *the big boy* – masc. sing.
la **grande** fille   *the big girl* – fem. sing.
les **grands** garçons   *the big boys* – masc. plur.
les **grandes** filles   *the big girls* – fem. plur.

Nouns

Nouns are the words that name things, or beings, for example le **bois** *wood*, la **table** *table*, un **docteur** *a doctor*, des **touristes** *some tourists*. Nouns are usually divided into two categories:

(*a*)   *common* nouns, like those above;
(*b*)   *proper* nouns, i.e. those naming countries, rivers, mountains, seas, etc., or giving the surname or name(s) of people. They begin with a capital letter:
La **Tamise**   *the Thames*,   les **Alpes**   *the Alps*,
Léonard de Vinci   *Leonardo da Vinci*

Pronouns

A pronoun is a word which can replace a noun or a noun-phrase (determiner + adjective + noun). It is very useful because it allows us to avoid tiresome repetitions.

Le pauvre homme n'est pas malade, **il** est mort!   *The poor man is not ill, he is dead!*
Tu vas au cinéma ce soir? J'**y** suis allé hier!   *Are you going to the pictures tonight? I went there yesterday!*

In the above sentences, **il** represents and replaces **le pauvre homme** and **y** represents and replaces **au cinéma**.

Verbs

Verbs are words which express an action or a state:

les enfants **chantent**   *the children sing/are singing* (action)
le professeur **est** malade   *the teacher is ill* (state)

Adverbs

Adverbs are words or expressions which indicate where, in what manner, when, how often, etc., an action is (was, will be . . .)

performed. They are used to modify the sense of a verb, or of another adverb; they can also modify the sense of an adjective.

L'autobus **roule** vite.   *The bus is going fast.*
L'autobus roule **très** *vite*.   *The bus is going very fast.*
L'autobus est **très** *rapide*.   *The bus is very fast/quick.*

The use of bold italic indicates which word the adverb modifies. Adverbs, unlike adjectives, do not normally vary in gender (masculine, feminine) or number (singular, plural). There are only very few exceptions to this rule.

Linking words

They connect together words or phrases in the speech chain. Among those, we find:

(*a*)   *Prepositions* like **à** *at/in*, **de** *of/from*, **dans** *in*, **sur** *on*, **devant** *in front of*, **pour** *for*, **contre** *against*, etc. They are used to link two words or phrases, and they clarify the relationship (generally of purpose, space or time) existing between the two:
Ils attendent **sur** le quai.   *They are waiting on the platform.*
Êtes-vous **pour** ou **contre** cette idée?   *Are you for or against this idea?*
Ils se préparent **à** partir.   *They are getting ready to go.*

(*b*)   *Conjunctions* like: **ou** *or*, **mais** *but*, **et** *and* which are used to link two phrases of equal status:
Ils ont accepté **mais** nous avons refusé.   *They accepted but we refused.*
or like: **bien que** *although*, **parce que** *because*, **pour que/afin que** *so that*, etc. which serve to introduce a phrase (sometimes called subordinate clause) which will 'complete the picture' as far as meaning is concerned. Those words establish a relationship between two sections of a sentence.
L'accident s'est produit **parce qu'**il allait trop vite.   *The accident occurred because he was going too fast.*
Je te le dis **pour que** tu ne sois pas surpris.   *I tell you so that you won't be surprised.*

Note: Words in this category do not vary in gender or number.

Interjections

These are small words, which are used to convey a feeling, a command, or a noise.

Ouf! nous l'avons échappé belle.   *Phew! we had a narrow escape.*
Clac! la porte se ferme.   *The door closes, bang!*

Registers and styles

When we speak (or write) our own language, we use a wide range of words and expressions (register) arranged in a certain way (style). Register and style are strongly influenced by the circumstances in which we speak or write. We do not express ourselves in the same way when addressing a close friend or a relative, a stranger, a superior or a subordinate. Our expressions can be colloquial, familiar, normal, formal, etc. Using the wrong type of language in a given situation could amount to committing a serious social gaffe.

Let us take as an example the following questions:
1   What can I do for you, sir?
2   What do you want, mister?
3   What can I do you for, squire?
It will be immediately obvious to a native English speaker that although all three expressions are aiming to elicit the same information, they contain important overtones and cannot be used at random.

If it is normally easy to 'gauge' the appropriateness of a given register or style for a particular occasion in one's native tongue, it is extremely difficult to do so in the case of a foreign language. In any case, you will normally be forgiven for using a type of language which is too formal, whereas careless use of slang or colloquial expressions may offend, particularly in view of the fact that such utterances always sound worse than when used by a native speaker.

The problem is very complex and goes beyond the scope of a book such as this. The following suggestions, however, should prove useful in this matter:

1   You should acquire a good, recently-published dictionary, in which differences in register and style are clearly indicated.
2   You should pay close attention to the *social context* in which a given word (or turn of phrase) occurs, so that you may use it in similar circumstances in the future. As your knowledge increases, you will be able to refine your sense of appropriateness.

The following devices, however, are very often used in familiar French by native speakers and would therefore not raise many eyebrows if you were to adopt them.

(*a*)   Omission of the **ne** element of the **ne . . . pas** (*not*) negation.

Compare: Il mange **pas.**

and: Il **ne** mange **pas.** } *He does not eat.*

or: Elle est **pas** partie.

and: Elle **n'**est **pas** partie. } *She has not gone.*

(*b*) Systematic use of **on** (*one*) as a replacement for **nous** (*we*).

Compare: **On** est arrivés à midi. } *We arrived*

and: **Nous** sommes arrivés à midi. } *at midday.*

or: **On** ira voir le film. } *We shall go and*

and: **Nous** irons voir le film. } *see the film.*

(*c*) Use of **c'est** (*it is*, singular) instead of **ce sont** (*it is*, plural) with a third person plural.

Compare: **C'est** les voisins
qui reviennent. } *It is the neigh-*

and: **Ce sont** les voisins
qui reviennent. } *bours coming back.*

or: **C'est** eux les coupables. } *It is they*

and: **Ce sont** eux les coupables. } *who are guilty*

(*d*) Formulation of questions without using an inversion or a question marker.

Compare: Vous êtes sûr?

and: Êtes-vous sûr? *or* Est-ce
que vous êtes sûr? } *Are you sure?*

or: Tu écoutes?

and: Écoutes-tu? *or* Est-ce
que tu écoutes? } *Are you listening?*

Note: In such cases, the 'question quality' is given by the intonation (voice pitch) which rises instead of going down as it would in a normal statement.

Whenever you come across a new familiar expression, make a mental note of the context in which it occurred so that you may, in turn, use it in the right way.

Pronunciation

Refinement of one's oral performance can be achieved in several ways, and in particular with the help of phonetics. Phonetics is the study of speech sounds. In modern dictionaries, each word entry is followed by its phonetic transcription composed of symbols from the International Phonetic Alphabet (IPA). This means that if you know the value of the relevant IPA symbols, you will be able to pronounce a given word accurately, even though you may never have seen or heard it before. This is why a section containing the description of the relevant IPA symbols, along with information on stress patterns and syllable structure, has been included as an appendix. Learning those symbols and their values will be a great help in your future language studies.

In addition, your oral performance may be dramatically improved by listening regularly to authentic French language material such as songs, stories or news broadcasts. All you need to do is to record such items and listen repeatedly to their contents to absorb the meaning and the sound of French words, thereby increasing your linguistic competence.

Accents and diacritic signs

Accents have a very important role to play in written French. They can be used to modify the sound of a vowel or to serve as markers to differentiate between certain words which would otherwise look exactly alike:

Compare: **la** *the* and: **là** *there*
or: **ou** *or*   and: **où** *where*
or: **a** *has*   and: **à** *at, to*

In the above cases, a grave accent is used to distinguish the two forms.

Similarly, diacritics like the apostrophe ('), the diaresis (¨) or the cedilla (˛), signal a change in the syllable or sound structure of a word. An explanation of the role and position of such signs has also been included in the Appendix.

Remember: Accents (and diacritics) cannot be used at random; they must *always* be carefully and properly placed.

Explanations concerning French pronunciation, syllable structure, stress and the role of accents and other signs have been included in the appendices. It is hoped that some readers may find them informative and profitable.

Key points

1 French nouns fall into two categories: masculine and feminine.

2 When learning a new noun, it is advisable to learn it with the relevant definite or indefinite singular article to avoid agreement mistakes later.

3 In French 'vowel-vowel clashes' at word boundaries are avoided by a variety of means: (elision, liaison and even alteration of the form of some words).

4 Certain types of words (determiners and adjectives) carry gender or number information about the noun(s) they are related to; certain other types (prepositions, adverbs) do not.

5 In French there are precise rules concerning the relative position of words in a sentence. These rules may be quite different from those which apply in English.

SECTION I

Some of the Jigsaw Pieces:
The Noun and its Associates

2 The Definite Article

The French definite article is broadly equivalent to the English *the*. It varies in gender (masc/fem) and in number (sing/plur) with the noun which follows.

Form

	Singular	*Plural*
Masculine	le/l'	les
Feminine	la/l'	les

Le mari   *The husband* (masc. sing.)
La femme   *The wife* (fem. sing.)
Les garçons   *The boys* (masc. plur.)
Les filles   *The girls* (fem. plur.)

Remember: The **e** of **le** and the **a** of **la** disappear if the next word begins with a vowel or 'mute h', to avoid the vowel-vowel clash (see appendix I).

L'ami   *The friend* (masc. sing.)
L'amie   *The friend* (fem. sing.)

NB   Because of its importance as an 'advance warning system', the non-reduced singular form of the article **le**, **la**, should not be separated from the noun when learning new vocabulary. Consider the two words as a whole **article + noun** and not as separate entities.

Special forms

When linking words (prepositions) like **à** (*at*, *to*, *in*) or **de** (*of*, *from*) are used before the article, they combine with it in the following way:

(*a*)   In the case of **à**:

	Singular	*Plural*
Masculine	au/à l'	aux
Feminine	à la/à l'	aux

Il va **au** travail. (and not *Il va à le travail.)   *He is going to work.*

Nous allons **aux** Etats-Unis (and not *Nous allons à les Etats-Unis.)   *We are going to the United States.*

Note: **à l'** is used when the next word begins with a vowel or a mute 'h' to avoid the vowel-vowel clash.

(*b*)   In the case of **de**:

	Singular	*Plural*
Masculine	du/de l'	des
Feminine	de la/de l'	des

Il vient **du** travail. (and not *Il vient de le travail.)   *He is coming from work.*

Nous arrivons **des** Etats-Unis. (and not *Nous arrivons de les Etats-Unis.)   *We have just arrived from the United States.*

Note: **de l'** is used when the next word begins with a vowel or mute 'h' to avoid the vowel-vowel clash.

Important remarks concerning the use of definite articles

The definite article is used far more frequently in French than in English. Consequently, its meaning may not be exactly the same in the two languages.

Compare: **Les gens** = 'people' as a category, as opposed to animals or plants, *but also* 'a specific group of people'

and: **The people** = people belonging to a specific group: a nation, an estate, a gathering . . .

Because of this, it is safe to assume as a general rule that, if the definite article is used in a given context in English, it will be used in the corresponding French context. (There are very few exceptions.)

the boy   le garçon
the queen   la reine
the guests   les invités
The Alps   Les Alpes

In addition to the above the definite article is used before the noun in the following cases:

1   With the names of continents, countries, regions, states, lakes, rivers, mountains.

L'Afrique   *Africa*
La Hollande   *Holland*
Le Yorkshire   *Yorkshire*
La Bretagne   *Brittany*
La Tamise   *The Thames*
Les Pyrénées   *The Pyrenees*

Note: In the case of feminine-singular names of countries and regions **à la** will be replaced by **en** if the meaning is *going to* or *staying in*.

> Il va **en** Espagne (and not *Il va à l'Espagne.)   *He is going to Spain*. (fem. sing.)
> Ils sont **en** Bretagne (and not *Ils sont à la Bretagne.)   *They are in Brittany*. (fem. sing.)

With the same category of names, if the meaning is *coming from*, **de la** or **de l'** will be replaced by **de** or **d'**.

> Il arrive **d'**Allemagne (and not *Il arrive de l'Allemagne.)   *He's just arrived from Germany*. (fem. sing.)
> Vous venez **de** France. (and not *Vous venez de la France.)   *You are coming from France*. (fem. sing.)

2   With names of substances, materials and processes.

> J'utilise **le** bois, **le** sable, **le** ciment et **la** pierre.   *I use wood, sand, cement and stone*.
> **Le** charbon et **le** pétrole sont rares.   *Coal and oil are rare*.
> **L'** or, **l'**argent et **les** diamants sont chers.   *Gold, silver and diamonds are expensive*.

3   With nouns representing a broad category, group or profession.

> **Les** jeunes protestent.   *Young people are protesting*.
> **Les** riches ont tout.   *Rich people have everything*.
> **Les** politiciens sont ambitieux.   *Politicians are ambitious*.

4   With nouns expressing a general quality, trait or fault.

> **La** paresse est un défaut.   *Laziness is a fault*.
> **La** gourmandise est un péché.   *Greed is a sin*.
> **Le** courage est une qualité assez rare.   *Courage is a fairly rare quality*.

5   With nouns representing an abstract concept.

> **Le** beau, **le** bien, **le** vrai sont là pour nous guider.   *Beauty, goodness, truth are here to guide us*.
> **La** mort me fait peur, **la** vie aussi.   *Death frightens me, so does life*.

6   With names of languages and nationalities

> Il apprend l'espagnol.   *He is learning Spanish*.
> **Les** Français sont individualistes.   *French people are individualistic*.

7   With names of seasons, days, parts of days (if speaking in general terms)

   Il fait froid l'hiver, mais **les** étés sont doux.   *It is cold in winter, but summers are mild.*

   En automne, **les** soirées sont courtes.   *In autumn, evenings are short.*

   Le samedi et **le** dimanche nous sortons.   *We go out on Saturdays and Sundays.*

But: If you refer to *last* or *next* Monday, Tuesday, etc. you do *not* use the definite article:

   Samedi soir, je passerai le voir.   *(Next) Saturday evening I shall drop by and see him.*

   Ils sont partis lundi.   *They left on Monday.*

The phrase *in the morning* meaning *tomorrow morning* is translated in French by **demain matin**.

In **le lundi**, **le jeudi**, etc., the singular form of the article is sufficient to give the idea of a regular occurrence; the plural is not normally acceptable.

---

8   With nouns indicating title, rank, whether or not they are followed by the name of the bearer.

   le président Kennedy   *President Kennedy*

   la reine Elizabeth   *Queen Elizabeth*

   le comte Dracula   *Count Dracula*

   le général de Gaulle   *General de Gaulle*

   le général et **le** premier ministre arrivent.   *The General and the Prime Minister are arriving.*

Note: If you are talking *directly* to the bearer of the title, you should use Monsieur, Madame, Messieurs—before the title, unless a special form of address is available like **(Votre) Excellence** *your Excellency* etc.

   Madame **la** Comtesse   *Countess/Your ladyship*

   Messieurs **les** Députés   *Honourable Gentlemen* (to MPs)

   Monsieur **le** Président   *Mr President*

9   With names of academic subjects, crafts, hobbies, sports:

   Je déteste **la** chimie.   *I hate chemistry.*

   Il adore **les** langues.   *He adores languages.*

   Elle apprend **la** poterie.   *She is learning pottery.*

   Vous aimez **le** football?   *Do you like football?*

   Elle préfère **la** lecture.   *She prefers reading.*

10   With nouns indicating parts of the body, where in English you would use *a* or a possessive.

Ce chien a **le** nez froid.   *This dog has a cold nose.*

Il met **les** mains dans **les** poches.   *He puts his hands in his pockets.*

Il a **le** crâne fracturé.   *He has a fractured skull.*

Je me brosse **les** dents.   *I am brushing my teeth.*

Vous vous lavez **les** mains.   *You are washing your hands.*

Elle a mal à **la** tête.   *Her head is hurting.*

But: If the noun indicating a part of the body is qualified by an adjective, **le** is replaced either by the appropriate indefinite article **un**, **une**, **des** (*a*; *some*):

Le chien a **un** petit nez froid.   *The dog has a small cold nose.*

or by the appropriate possessive adjective: **son**, **sa**, **ses** (*his/her*):

Il met **ses** grosses mains dans **ses** poches.   *He puts/is putting his big hands in his pockets.*

11   In expressions where a price per item or speed per unit of time is given.

Ce vin coûte *70F* **la** bouteille!   *This wine costs 70F a bottle!*

Il roulait à 140 km à l'heure.   *He was driving at 140 km an hour.*

12   With the preposition **à**, to describe a peculiarity or a distinguishing feature characterising a person, animal or thing.

L'homme **à la** jambe de bois   *The man with a wooden leg*

La femme **à la** robe rouge   *The woman in the red dress*

La maison **aux** volets verts (aux = *à les- masc. plur.)   *The house with the green shutters*

Omission of the definite article

In certain circumstances, the definite article can be omitted:

(*a*)   in proverbs:

Pauvreté n'est pas vice.   *Poverty is no vice.*

Pierre qui roule n'amasse pas mousse.   *A rolling stone gathers no moss.*

(*b*)   in set expressions/phrases:

Travail – Famille – Patrie   *Work – Family – Country*   (the motto of the Vichy Regime)

Liberté – Egalité – Fraternité   *Freedom – Equality – Fraternity* (the motto of the French Republic)

(c)   in lists of items or people:

Tables, chaises, vaisselle, tout était cassé.   *Tables, chairs, crockery, everything was broken.*

Hommes, femmes et enfants ont péri dans les flammes.   *Men, women and children perished in the flames.*

(d)   if, in a sentence, two nouns follow each other and the second is in apposition to the first (that is to say if it gives extra information about the first), the article of the second noun is omitted:

Paris, capitale de la France, est une belle ville.   *Paris, the capital of France, is a lovely city.*

(e)   in expressions of the type: *the more . . . the more, the less . . . the less* (or a combination of the two):

Plus il travaille, plus il devient riche.   *The more he works, the richer he becomes.*

Plus je regarde, moins je comprends.   *The more I look, the less I understand.*

Note: (d) and (e) above are two of the rare occasions when the English definite article is not translated by its French equivalent.

(f)   in expressions where two nouns are present and the second noun is used as an adjective:

La Banque d'Angleterre   *The Bank of England*

Le vin de Bourgogne   *Burgundy wine*

Les fromages de France   *French cheeses*

Un tapis de Perse   *A Persian carpet*

Key points

1 The French definite article can be used to indicate either a broad category or concept, or (as the English *the*), a specific and well defined sub-category.

2 The definite article is used far more frequently in French than in English. If it is used in English, it is very likely that it will also appear in French.

3 The definite article (except in its reduced form l') carries advance information about the gender and/or number of the noun that follows.

4 When learning a new noun, you should always try to remember it with its article (singular form).

5 The definite article is required before names of countries, regions, rivers, mountains, seas and lakes, languages or nationalities.

6 The definite article *must* also be used when the noun refers to a broad category or concept, a representative group or profession, a given type of activity (artistic, scientific, scholarly, etc.).

7 With nouns expressing abstract concepts (Good, Evil, Life, etc.) or general qualities or faults (Beauty, Laziness, etc.), the definite article *must* also be used.

8 With nouns referring to parts of the body two possibilities may occur:

(*a*) If 'ownership' is unambiguous, particularly through the use of **avoir** (*to have*) or of a reflexive construction, the definite article will suffice.

(*b*) If 'ownership' may be open to ambiguity or misinterpretation, or if the noun is qualified by an adjective, the definite article must be replaced by a possessive adjective.

9 In expressions where a quantity (distance, money, weight) per unit is stated, the definite article will be used to translate the English *a* or *per*.

10 The definite article may be omitted in proverbs and set expressions as well as in (long) lists of things or beings.

11 The definite article is *not normally* used before a noun placed in apposition to another (i.e. following *and* giving extra information about it), unless an expression individualizing the second noun is also included.

3 The Indefinite and Partitive Articles

The indefinite article

The French indefinite article is, in the singular, the equivalent of the English *a* or *an*. In the plural it has the meaning of *some/several, a certain number of* or, in interrogative sentences (questions), the meaning of *any*.

Note: **un** and **une** can also have the meaning of *one*.

Form

	Singular	Plural
Masculine	un	des
Feminine	une	des

Note: The indefinite article, like the definite one, varies according to the gender (masculine/feminine) and number (singular/plural) of the noun which follows. Like the definite article, it serves as an 'advance warning system':

Un chien	⟶ **Des** chiens
A dog	*(Some) dogs*
Voici **une** lettre	⟶ Voici **des** lettres
Here is a letter	*Here are (some) letters*
J'ai **un** visiteur	⟶ J'ai **des** visiteurs
I have a visitor	*I have (some) visitors*
Vous avez **une** allumette?	⟶ Vous avez **des** allumettes?
Do you have a match?	*Do you have (any) matches?*

Important remarks concerning the use of indefinite articles

In English, the use of a plural noun without the article (e.g. dogs), could convey two different meanings:

1 the noun could refer to a *general category*:
   Dogs are faithful.

In this case, the French equivalent would be preceded by the definite article (see p. 16 above):

Les chiens sont fidèles.

2   the noun could refer to an *unspecified number of individual things or beings*:

There are dogs in the garden.

In this case, the meaning would be *some, a certain number of* and the French equivalent would be preceded by the indefinite article **des**:

Il y a **des** chiens dans le jardin.

So, it is essential to choose the right type of article if you wish to convey the correct meaning!

Normally, the French indefinite article is used in the same way as its English equivalent (*a, an*). There are, however, certain differences in its usage between the two languages, as illustrated below.

Characteristic differences in usage

The indefinite article is *not* used in French in the following cases:

1   Before the words **cent** (*a hundred*) and **mille** (*a thousand*)

Voilà cent francs.   *There's a hundred francs.*

J'ai mille et une choses à faire.   *I have a thousand and one things to do.*

It should be noted that in the above examples *a* really means *one*.

2   After the word **sans** (*without*), *except* if the meaning is *without a single* or *without so much as a . . .*

Il sort sans chapeau.   *He's going out without a hat.*

Le voyageur sans bagages.   *The traveller without luggage.*

But: Il part **sans un** mot, **sans un** regard. *He's leaving without a single word, without a single glance.*

3   Before nouns indicating nationality, occupation, religion, creed, etc:

Je suis Français.   *I am a Frenchman.*

Il est chauffeur de taxi.   *He is a taxi driver.*

Elle est catholique.   *She is a Catholic.*

But not when **c'est** (*it is/he is/she is*) is used:

C'est **un** ingénieur.   *He is an engineer.*

C'est **une** Anglaise.   *She is an Englishwoman.*

4   In exclamative phrases or sentences expressing a strong feeling: surprise, admiration, distaste, loathing, etc. beginning with **quel**, **quelle** (*what a . . . !*)

Quel désastre!   *What a disaster!* (masc. sing.)

Quelle vie!   *What a life!* (fem. sing.)

Quels imbéciles!   *What fools!* (masc. plur.)

24 *The Indefinite and Partitive Articles*

5 After **comme** when the meaning is *as* (occupying the post of . . .)
Il travaille ici comme jardinier. *He works here as a gardener.*
But: if the meaning is *like* (in the same way as), the indefinite article is used:
Compare: Il travaille comme apprenti. *He's working as an apprentice.*
and: Il travaille comme **un** apprenti. *He's working like an apprentice.* (i.e. badly)

6 After **ni** in the expression **ni . . . ni** (*neither . . . nor*)
Compare: J'ai **une** écharpe et **des** gants. *I have a scarf and gloves.*
and: Je n'ai **ni** écharpe **ni** gants. *I have neither scarf nor gloves.*

Special forms of the indefinite article

1 *All* forms of the indefinite articles (**un, une, des**), become **de** (or **d'** to avoid the vowel-vowel clash), in the following circumstances:

(*a*) In negative sentences, with such expressions as **ne . . . pas** (*not any*), **ne . . . plus** (*no longer*), **ne . . . jamais** (*not . . . ever*), **ne . . . guère** (*hardly*).

Compare: Elle a **un** enfant.
She has a child
and: Elle **n'a pas d'**enfant.
She doesn't have a child.

or: Il y a **une** plage.
There is a beach.
and: Il **n'**y a **pas de** plage.
There isn't any beach.

or: Je fume **des** cigares.
I smoke cigars.
and: Je **ne** fume **jamais de** cigares.
I never smoke cigars.

or: Vous avez **des** problèmes.
You have problems.
and: Vous **n'**avez **guère de** problèmes.
You have hardly any problems.

But remember: Elle n'a pas **un** ami means *She doesn't have one single friend* (see 2 above).

(*b*) After words and expressions denoting a collection (small or large) of things or beings, such as: **beaucoup** (*many*), **un petit nombre** (*a small number*), **un grand nombre** (*a large number*), **un certain nombre** (*a certain number*), **une foule** (*a crowd*), **une poignée** (*a handful*), etc.

Compare: J'achète **des** cadeaux.
I'm buying gifts.
and: J'achète **beaucoup de** cadeaux.
I'm buying a great many gifts.

or:	Voici **des** pièces.	and: Voici **une poignée de** pièces.
	Here are (some) coins.	*Here is a handful of coins.*
or:	Il y a **des** gens.	and: Il y a **une foule de** gens.
	There are people.	*There is a crowd of people.*

2   In addition, the plural form **des** of the indefinite article becomes **de** (or **d'** to avoid the vowel-vowel clash), when the noun in its plural form is preceded by an adjective:

Compare:	**Des** enfants	and: **De** petits enfants
	(Some) children	*(Some) small children*
or:	**Des** amis	and: **De** bons amis
	(Some) friends	*(Some) good friends*
or:	**Des** pommes	and: **D'**énormes pommes
	(Some) apples	*(Some) enormous apples*

But: if the elements **adjective + noun** are 'welded together' to form a set expression, **des** remains intact.

Compare:	**De** jeunes filles	and: **Des** jeunes filles
	Girls who happen to be young	*Girls*
or:	**De** petits pois	and: **Des** petits pois
	Peas which happen to be small	*Garden peas*

Note: The above remarks concerning special forms of the Indefinite article also apply to the partitive article, which is studied below.

The partitive article

The French partitive article is, in its singular form, the equivalent of *some* or *a certain amount of* when referring to a noun which cannot easily be divided into countable units, (e.g. some water, some bread). The plural form of the partitive article is the same as that of the indefinite: **des**.

Form

	Singular	*Plural*
Masculine	du/de l'	des
Feminine	de la/de l'	des

The partitive article varies according to the gender and number of the noun that follows.

In the singular (masc. and fem.), it changes to **de l'** before a vowel or a mute 'h', to avoid the vowel-vowel clash (see appendix I).

Du pain! *I want some bread!*
Il boit **de la** bière. *He's drinking beer.*
Voulez-vous **de l'**eau? *Do you want some water?* (fem. sing.)
Je mange **des** confitures. *I'm eating jam.* (fem. plur.)
Voilà **de l'**argent. *There's some money.* (masc. sing.)

Important remarks concerning the use of partitive articles

Normally, the partitive article is used in French when in English *some* or *a certain amount of* (or *any* in a question), followed by a noun in the singular, would be required:

De l'eau minérale   *Some mineral water*
De la viande   *Some meat*
Du café   *Some coffee*

Compare:	**De la** bière	and:	**Une** bière
	Some beer		*A beer*
or:	**De l'**ordre	and:	**Un** ordre
	A certain amount of order		*An order*
or:	**Du** travail	and:	**Un** travail
	Some work		*A job*

In certain circumstances, however, the partitive article has to be modified as indicated below.

Special forms of the partitive article

1   As was the case for the indefinite article, all forms of the partitive article become **de** (or **d'** to avoid the vowel-vowel clash) in the following constructions:

(a)   In negative sentences (see 1(a) on page 24).
Il n'a **jamais d'**argent. *He never has any money.*
Pas de chance! *No luck!*
Vous n'avez **plus de** travail. *You have no more work.*

(b)   After words and expressions denoting a collection of things or beings (see 1(b) on page 24).
Ils ont **beaucoup d'**argent. *They have a great deal of money.*
J'ai **peu de** patience. *I have little patience.*
Une pincée de sel   *A pinch of salt*

2   In the plural, **des** becomes **de** or **d'** in the circumstances outlined in 2 on page 25.

Des confitures	⟶	**De** bonnes confitures
Jam (fem. plur.)		*Good jam*
Des épinards	⟶	**D'**excellents épinards
Spinach (masc. plur)		*Excellent spinach*

Key points

1   The indefinite article is, in its singular forms **un**, **une**, the equivalent of *a* or *an*; in the plural, it can be translated by *some, a certain number of* or simply by the noun without any article.

2   The partitive article is, in its singular form **du**, **de la** (or **de l'** to avoid a vowel-vowel clash), the equivalent of *a certain amount of*. The plural form **des** is *not normally* translated in English.

3   The indefinite and the partitive articles can act as 'advance warning systems' for the noun which follows; because of this, they cannot normally be omitted, except in very precise circumstances.

4   In negative sentences and after phrases referring to a collection of things or beings, *all* forms of the indefinite and partitive articles become **de** (or **d'** to avoid the vowel-vowel clash).

5   The indefinite article is *not* used in French in the following circumstances:

(*a*)   before **cent** (*a hundred*) and **mille** (*a thousand*);

(*b*)   before nouns expressing creed, nationality, occupation, religion, *except* when those nouns are introduced by **c'est/ce sont** (*it is*);

(*c*)   in exclamative sentences, after the appropriate form of **quel . . . !** (*what (a) . . . !*);

(*d*)   to translate *as* (*in one's capacity as*). *But* if the meaning of *as* is *like*, the article will be required;

(*e*)   in the negative expression **ni . . . ni** (*neither . . . nor*).

6   If, in the plural form, the indefinite (or partitive) article is followed by an adjective preceding a plural noun, **des** will be reduced to **de** (or **d'** to avoid the vowel-vowel clash), *except* if the group **adjective + noun** forms a recognised set phrase.

7   After expressions indicating a quantity, large or small, the plural form **des** (indefinite or partitive) will be reduced to **de** (or **d'** to avoid the vowel-vowel clash).

8   Negative expressions meaning **not any** are normally translated as **ne . . . pas de/ne . . . pas d'** as applicable. If, however, the meaning is: *not a single . . ./not so much as a . . .* , the expression **ne . . . pas un(e)** should be used.

4 The Demonstrative Adjective

The demonstrative adjective is used in French as in English to 'attract attention' to the noun which follows, to make the thing(s) or being(s) it refers to 'stand out' from others in the same category.

Form

	Singular	*Plural*
Masculine	ce/cet	ces
Feminine	cette	ces

(a) In its above forms, the demonstrative adjective is the equivalent of *both* this/these *and* that/those.
(b) The alternative masc. sing. form **cet** is used when the following word begins with a vowel or mute 'h', to prevent the vowel-vowel clash.
(c) The demonstrative adjective varies according to the gender and/or number of the noun which follows. So, like most other determiners (definite, indefinite and partitive articles) it serves as 'an advance warning system' for that noun.
    Ce travail est difficile. *This work is difficult.*
    Regardez **cette** chambre. *Look at this room.*
    Ces fleurs sont superbes. *Those flowers are superb.* (fem. plur.)
    J'adore **ces** enfants. *I adore those children.* (masc. plur.)
But: **Cet** animal est féroce. *This animal is ferocious.*
or: **Cet** hôtel est complet. *This hotel is fully booked.*

Important remarks concerning the use of demonstrative adjectives

In most cases, the French demonstrative adjective is used in the same circumstances as its English equivalents (*this/these* or *that/those*). If, for any reason, it becomes necessary to distinguish between the two meanings, in order to indicate an opposition (either clearly stated or implied) in space or time, all that is needed is to place **-ci** (*here*) or **-là** (*there*) after the noun. The words in brackets may be stated or implied.

Cette bière-**ci** est bonne (mais **cette** bière-**là** est mauvaise). *This beer is good (but that beer is bad).*

J'aime **ce** costume-**là** (mais pas **ce** costume-**ci**). *I like that suit (but not this suit).*

Cette remarque-**ci** est plus logique (que **cette** remarque-**là**). *This remark is more logical (than that remark).*

In French, the demonstrative adjective, usually followed by **-là**, can be used to express a strong feeling (distaste or affection).

Ne parlons pas de **ces** choses (**-là**). *Let's not talk about those things.*

Je déteste **ces** gens (**-là**). *I hate those people.*

Ah **ces** enfants! *Oh, those children!*

Note: In French, the demonstrative adjective is normally repeated after each noun in a series:

Compare: **Ces** hommes, **ces** femmes et **ces** enfants sont perdus!

and: *These/those men, women and children are lost!*

or: Achetez **ces** livres et **ces** magazines.

and: *Buy these/those books and magazines.*

Special uses

Apart from its ordinary usage, the demonstrative adjective can be present in the following circumstances:

(a) In certain exclamations with the meaning of *what (a)...!* or *such (a)...!*

Mon Dieu, **ce** travail! *My goodness, what a (=an awful) job!*

Cette idée! *What an (= a preposterous) idea!*

(b) In commercial correspondence, **ce jour** (lit: *this day*) can be used for *today* and **à ce jour** for *to date*.

Nous avons reçu **ce jour** votre lettre du ... *We have received today your letter of ...*

A **ce jour**, nous n'avons pas reçu votre chèque. *To date, we have not received your cheque.*

(c) When the English definite article *the* is used with a strong demonstrative meaning, it is better to translate it with the French demonstrative adjective:

Cette femme est malade. *The (= this) woman is sick.*

Cet homme est un fou! *The (= this) man is a lunatic!*

Key points

1   The demonstrative adjective agrees in gender and/or number with the noun which follows.

2   In the masculine singular, **ce** is replaced by **cet** whenever the next word begins with a vowel or a mute 'h' (to avoid the vowel-vowel clash).

3   The French demonstrative adjective can have the meaning *this/these* or *that/those*. If a distinction needs to be drawn, you simply need to add **-ci** (*-here*) or **-là** (*-there*) after the noun.

4   In general, the French demonstrative adjective is used in the same way as its English equivalent. There are, however, a few cases where usage differs.

5   When a list of nouns is involved, the demonstrative adjective (if required) must appear before *each* item.

6   The demonstrative adjective may be used in exclamative sentences with the meaning of *what (a) . . . !/such (a) . . . !*.

7   In commercial correspondence, the expressions *today* and *to date* may be translated in French by **ce jour** and **à ce jour** respectively.

8   The strong demonstrative value of the English definite article *the* makes it necessary, in certain circumstances, to translate it with the appropriate form of the French demonstrative adjective.

5 The Possessive Adjective

Possessive adjectives in French, as in English, are used to indicate ownership or close relationship. There are, however, very important differences in their use between the two languages. In French, the possessive adjective does not agree in gender with the possessor (owner) but gives information on the gender and number of the being(s) or thing(s) owned.

Compare: Voilà **sa** chaise.

and: *Here is his chair.*

In French, the possessive tells us that only one chair is involved (**sa** as opposed to **ses**) and that the word **chaise** is feminine. It also tells us, as does its English equivalent, that one owner is involved.

In English, the possessive tells us that the owner is male (*his* as opposed to *her* or *its*) but gives no information about the thing owned: the clear difference in sound between the singular (*chair*) and the plural (*chairs*) makes it unnecessary for the possessive to carry information about number.

So *remember*:

in French = **possessive** agrees with '**owned**'

in English = **possessive** agrees with **owner**

Form

	Person	OWNED			Engl. equivalent
		One		More than one	
OWNER		masc.	fem.	masc./fem.	
	1st	mon	ma	mes	*my*
	2nd	ton	ta	tes	*your* (familiar)
One	2nd	votre	votre	vos	*your* (polite)
	3rd	son	sa	ses	*his/her* *its/one's*
More than one	1st	notre	notre	nos	*our*
	2nd	votre	votre	vos	*your*
	3rd	leur	leur	leurs	*their*

Notes: As previously mentioned, the form **vous** (*you*) and its corresponding possessives **votre/vos**, can be used to address *either* one person (it is then a mark of politeness and respect) *or* several people.

> Monsieur Legrand, **votre** femme et **vos** enfants sont ici!   *Mr Legrand, your wife and (your) children are here!*

The familiar form **tu** and its corresponding possessives **ton/ta/tes**, are used when talking to relatives, close friends, fellow-members of a close-knit group *or* to express contempt towards a stranger (see Unit 1, pp. 3–4).

Since in French certain nouns are masculine and others feminine and since the singular and plural forms generally sound the same, it is *logical* for the possessive adjective to have separate forms to denote masculine singular, feminine singular and plural.

Compare: **Mon frère** est parti.   *My brother has gone.*
and: **Mes frères** sont partis.   *My brothers have gone.*
or: **Ta soeur** est malade.   *Your sister is ill.*
and: **Tes soeurs** sont malades.   *Your sisters are ill.*
    The words in bold indicate the agreement relationship.

NB   When the word following the possessive adjective is feminine singular and begins with a vowel or a mute 'h', **ma, ta, sa** are replaced by **mon, ton, son** to avoid the vowel-vowel clash (see appendix I).

> **ma hôtesse** becomes: **mon** hôtesse   *my hostess*
> **ta énorme gaffe** becomes: **ton** énorme gaffe   *your enormous blunder*.
> **sa idée** fixe becomes: **son** idée fixe   *his/her fixed idea*

The use of bold indicates the agreement relationship.

Important remarks concerning the use of possessive adjectives

Although in most cases possessive adjectives are used in a similar way in both languages, there are divergences due to different sentence patterns or grammatical categories. One such case occurs when reflexive verbs are used. A reflexive verb indicates that the action performed by the subject 'falls back' upon the subject, e.g. **je me coupe** *I cut myself*. In such a case, ownership being determined by the verb, there is no need to use a possessive as well. So ***je me coupe ma main** becomes **je me coupe *la* main** *I cut my hand*, or ***il se lave sa figure** becomes **il se lave *la* figure** *he is washing his face*.

Similarly, when ownership is clearly determined by the general meaning of the sentence, the possessive is not used. So *il marche avec ses mains dans ses poches* *he is walking with his hands in his pockets* becomes il marche avec *les* mains dans *les* poches; *il met son chapeau sur sa tête* *he is putting his hat on his head* becomes il met son chapeau sur *la* tête; *ouvrez vos yeux et vos oreilles! open your eyes and your ears!* becomes ouvrez *les* yeux et *les* oreilles!

If, however, the noun 'owned' is qualified by an adjective or adjectival phrase, the possessive will be used:

ouvrez **vos** jolis yeux et **vos** belles oreilles! *open your pretty eyes and your beautiful ears!*

Normally, a possessive adjective will be used in the singular with *each* being or thing 'owned', because of the gender problem.

Compare: il est venu avec **son** père et **sa** mère

and: *he has come with his father and mother*

but in the plural, one possessive can be used before a list if no special emphasis is required.

Où sont **vos** frères et soeurs? *Where are your brothers and sisters?*

In some cases, when addressing a superior, particularly in a military context, the possessive is used.

Pardon, **mon** capitaine! *I beg your pardon Captain!*

Bonjour, **mon** lieutenant! *Good morning Lieutenant!*

Key points

1 In French, the possessive adjective agrees with the thing(s) or being(s) 'owned' and *not* with the owner(s).

2 Since there are 2 genders in French and since the plural form of most nouns sounds identical to their singular form, there are 3 sets of possessive adjectives: masculine singular, feminine singular and plural.

3 The forms **votre** (sing.) and **vos** (plur.) can be used to refer either to *one* owner (polite use) or *several* owners (normal use).

4 When ownership is clearly indicated by the context (use of reflexive verb or general meaning), the possessive adjective is normally replaced by the appropriate definite article.

5 When the noun of the thing(s) or being(s) owned is qualified by an adjective or adjectival phrase the possessive adjective is used *even* if the context clearly indicates ownership.

6 Indefinite, Exclamative and Interrogative Adjectives

Indefinite adjectives

Indefinite adjectives are used in French, as in English, to indicate reference to an undefined quantity or number of things or beings. They cover the whole spectrum of sense from 'none' to all. They agree in gender (masc./fem.) and/or number (sing./plur.) with the noun they refer to; they, too, serve as an 'advance warning system' for that noun, and are therefore generally placed before it.

Note: Because of their sense, it is not normally possible to use adjectives expressing 'none' or 'one' quantities in the plural; nor is it possible to use adjectives meaning 'more than one' or 'all' in the singular. There are, however, some indefinite adjectives which can vary in number as well as in gender. Such adjectives are listed in each of the relevant sense categories of the chart on pp. 36–7.

Important remarks concerning the use of indefinite adjectives

Indefinite adjectives are used when the exact number or quantity of beings or things referred to is not specified (if it were, a numeral would be used). This means that normally, the two categories, indefinite adjective and numeral, are mutually exclusive in a sentence.

However, the following points should be carefully noted:

1 In phrases of the type '**quelque** trente personnes' (*some thirty people*), **quelque** is not an indefinite adjective but an adverb meaning 'approximately' and, as such, does not agree with the noun-phrase 'trente personnes'.

2 If **même** is used with the meaning of *even*, it is not an indefinite adjective but an adverb. As such, it will not be subject to number agreement.

Compare: L'argent, les chèques, les bijoux **même** ont disparu!
The money, the cheques and even the jewels are gone!

and: Les **mêmes** clients reviennent cette année. *The same customers are coming back this year.*

3 Such expressions as **tout le monde** (*everybody*), **toute la famille** (*the whole family*), **tout le village** (*the whole village*) etc., although

obviously referring to a *group* of things or beings, will be considered as singular for the purpose of agreement.

Tout le monde **est** là.   *Everybody is there.*

Toute la famille **est** en vacances.   *The whole family is on holiday.*

Tout le stock **est** vendu.   *The whole of the stock is sold.*

4 Indefinite adjectives expressing 'zero quantity' are used with the negative **ne** (or **n'** if the next word begins with a vowel — see Appendix I), and the noun they relate to is in the singular:

Aucun voyageur **n'**a été blessé.   *Not a single traveller has been wounded.*

Pas une lettre **n'**arrive.   *Not a single letter is arriving.*

NB   **Aucun/aucune** and **nul/nulle** (*not any/not a single*) are, on very rare occasions, used in the plural (in spite of their meaning), if the noun they refer to does not have a singular form.

Ne payez **aucunes** arrhes, **aucuns** frais.   *Do not pay any deposit, any charges.*

Arrhes (f. pl.) *non returnable deposit* and **frais** (m. pl.) *charges/costs* have no singular form with the same meaning.

Exclamative adjectives

They are used in French (as in English) to express a strong feeling — surprise, admiration, indignation, despair, loathing, etc. — about the thing(s) or being(s) to which they refer. The utterance in which they appear always ends with an exclamation mark. They are equivalent to the English *What (a) . . . !*

Form

	Sing.	*Plur.*
Masc.	quel	quels
Fem.	quelle	quelles

The exclamative adjective carries advance information about the gender and number of the noun which follows:

Quel idiot! (m. sing)   *What a fool!*

Quelle agréable surprise! (f. sing)   *What a pleasant surprise!*

Quels beaux yeux! (m. pl.)   *What beautiful eyes!*

Quelles robes magnifiques! (f. pl.)   *What magnificent dresses!*

	VARIATIONS				MEANING	
	singular		plural		sing.	plur.
	masc.	*fem.*	*masc.*	*fem.*		
GROUP I	aucun	aucune	—	—	*not any*	—
	nul	nulle	—	—	*not any*	—
number referred to = none	pas un	pas une	—	—	*(not a single)*	—
	autre	autre	autres	autres	*other*	*others*
	certain	certaine	certains	certaines	*some*	*some*
	chaque	chaque	—	—	*each/every*	—

GROUP II	number referred to = one		number referred to = more			
	—	—	différents	différentes	—	different
	—	—	divers	diverses	—	various
	maint	mainte	maints	maintes	many a	many
	même	même	mêmes	mêmes	same	same
	pareil	pareille	pareils	pareilles	such (a)	such
	—	—	plusieurs	plusieurs	—	several
	quel	quelle	quels	quelles	what/which	what/which
	quelconque	quelconque	quelconques	quelconques	any	any
	quelque	quelque	quelques	quelques	some	several
	tel	telle	tels	telles	such (a)	such
	tout	toute	tous	toutes	every	all

NB The dashes signal that certain forms of a given adjective are not available. The correct form of the adjective *must* be chosen to correspond with the gender and number of the noun it qualifies. For example:

Il n'y a **pas une** (seule) place libre. (**place** = fem. sing) *There isn't a (single) seat free.*

Leur retard doit avoir **quelque autre** cause. (**cause** = fem. sing.) *Their lateness must have some other cause.*

Certains jours, il est bizarre. (**jours** = masc. plur.) *Some days, he is peculiar.*

The French exclamative adjective is used in the same circumstances as its English equivalent. The following points should however be noted:

1   In the singular, it cannot be followed by the indefinite article **un** or **une** (*a*).

> **Quelle** superbe bague!   *What a superb ring!*
> **Quel** scandale!   *What a scandal!*

2   The exclamative adjective can sometimes be replaced by the corresponding definite article (**le**, **la**, **l'** or **les**) provided the same exclamative intonation is preserved.

> **Quels** imbéciles! = **Les** imbéciles!   *What fools!*
> Oh! **quelle** belle robe! = Oh! **la** belle robe!   *Oh what a beautiful dress!*

Interrogative adjectives

Interrogative adjectives are used to express a query about the character or identity of the thing(s) or being(s) referred to. The utterance in which they appear often ends with a question mark. They are translated in English by *which . . . ?* or *what . . . ?* They give advance warning of the gender and number of the noun that follows.

Form

They have the same form as exclamative adjectives:

	Sing.	*Plur.*
Masc.	quel	quels
Fem.	quelle	quelles

Use

Interrogative adjectives are used in a similar way in both languages. The following points should, however, be borne in mind:

1   Sometimes, an exclamative phrase and an interrogative one may have exactly the same components. It is therefore important to be particularly attentive to the intonation (voice-pitch movement) of each of them to differentiate meaning, as you would in English.

Compare: **Quel** courage!   *What courage!*
and: **Quel** courage?   *What courage?*

2   In certain types of sentences, the interrogative adjective is followed by a change in the normal word order (inversion), particularly in 'careful' French. But in 'casual' speech, the inversion is often not made:

Compare: Quelle heure **est-il**? (careful French)
and: Quelle heure **il est**? ('casual' speech)   *What time is it?*
or: Dans quelle chambre **sont-ils**? (careful French)
and: **Ils sont** dans quelle chambre? ('casual' French)   *Which room are they in?*

Key points

1   Indefinite adjectives are used to refer to an undefined quantity or number of things or beings. They cover the whole range of meaning from 'none' to 'all'.

2   Many indefinite adjectives, because of their meaning, cannot vary in number, i.e. they are *either* singular *or* plural. Some, however, can be used in the singular and (with the appropriate agreement) in the plural. Indefinite adjectives vary in gender as required.

3   **Même** and **quelque** can either be indefinite adjectives or adverbs. As indefinite adjectives, they mean *same* and *some* (= *a few*) respectively and agree as appropriate. As adverbs they mean *even* and *approximately* respectively and they are invariable.

4   Indefinite adjectives expressing 'zero quantities' — **aucun, pas un, nul** — are used with the negative adverb **ne** (or **n'** to avoid a vowel-vowel clash). They are normally used with a noun in the singular; if the noun they refer to has no singular form, **aucun** and **nul** can be put in the plural (masculine or feminine).

5   Exclamative adjectives are used in French, as in English, to express a strong feeling — surprise, admiration, indignation, despair, etc. — about the noun they refer to. They carry advance information about the gender and number of that noun.

6   Exclamative adjectives used with a masculine or feminine noun *cannot* be followed, as they can in English by the indefinite article (**un** or **une**).

7   The exclamative adjective is sometimes replaced by the corresponding definite article. The meaning is equivalent so long as the exclamative intonation is retained.

8   Interrogative adjectives are used in French, as in English, to express a query about the character or identity of the thing(s) or being(s) referred to. They have the same form as exclamative adjectives and they, too, carry advance information about the noun's gender and number.

9   In certain types of interrogative sentences, the interrogative adjective is normally followed by an inversion (change in word-order). In 'casual' *spoken French* however, the inversion is often not made.

7 Numerals

In French, as in English, numerals are used with nouns to indicate an exact number of things or beings (cardinal numbers) *or* the rank or position occupied by the thing(s) or being(s) the noun refers to (ordinal numbers).

In each category, there are numerals made up of one word only and numerals made up of several words (usually linked together by a hyphen- or **et** (*and*).

1   Cardinal numerals do not agree in gender or number with the noun they refer to except for the following:

(*a*)   **un** (*one*) which becomes **une** in the feminine:

  un homme et **une** femme   *one man and one woman*

(*b*)   **vingt** (*20*) and **cent** (*100*) which take an **s** *if* they appear in numbers which are multiples of 20 and 100 *and if*, at the same time, they end the numeral adjective:

  quatre-vingts personnes   *80 people*

but: **quatre-vingt-trois** ans   *83 years*

  deux cents kilomètres   *200 kilometres*

but: **deux cent dix** kilomètres   *210 kilometres*

  However, if the last element of the number is either **millier** (*approximately   a   thousand*), **million** (*million*), **milliard** (*thousand million*) or **billion** (*million million*), **vingt** and **cent** will take an **s** because those elements *are not adjectives* but nouns which are followed by **de** (or **d'** to avoid the vowel-vowel clash).

  quatre-vingts millions de centimes   *80 million centimes*

  neuf **cents** milliards de déficit   *900,000 million deficit*

2   In compounds using numbers between 21 and 71 inclusive, the first unit (= one) of a new decimal set, i.e. 21, 31, 41, 51, 61, 71, will be preceded by the word **et** (*and*); in all other such cases, **et** will *not* be present:

  vingt **et** une cartes postales   *21 postcards*

  soixante **et** onze invités   *71 guests*

but: cent un jours   *101 days*

  six cent un litres   *601 litres*

Form

Cardinal numbers	Corresponding ordinal numbers	Cardinal numbers	Corresponding ordinal numbers
0 zéro			
1 un/une	premier/première		
2 deux	deuxième (second/seconde)		
3 trois	troisième		
4 quatre	quatrième		
5 cinq	cinquième		
6 six	sixième		
7 sept	septième		
8 huit	huitième		
9 neuf	neuvième		
10 dix	dixième		
11 onze	onzième		
12 douze	douzième		
13 treize	treizième		
14 quatorze	quatorzième		
15 quinze	quinzième		
16 seize	seizième		
17 dix-sept	dix-septième		
18 dix-huit	dix-huitième		
19 dix-neuf	dix-neuvième		
20 vingt	vingtième		
21 vingt et un(e)	vingt et unième		
22 vingt-deux	vingt-deuxième		
		30 trente	trentième
		40 quarante	quarantième
		50 cinquante	cinquantième
		60 soixante	soixantième
		70 soixante-dix	soixante-dixième
		71 soixante et onze	soixante et onzième
		72 soixante-douze	soixante-douzième
		80 quatre-vingts	quatre-vingtième
		81 quatre-vingt-un(e)	quatre-vingt-unième
		90 quatre-vingt-dix	quatre-vingt-dixième
		91 quatre-vingt-onze	quatre-vingt-onzième
		92 quatre-vingt-douze	quatre-vingt-douzième
		100 cent	centième
		101 cent un(e)	cent unième
		200 deux cents	deux centième
		201 deux cent un(e)	deux cent unième
		1000 mille (mil for dates)	millième
		1001 mille un(e)	mille unième
		2000 deux mille	deux millième
		1,000,000 un million	millionnième
		1,000,000,000 un milliard	milliardième
		1,000,000,000,000 un billion	billionnième

3   In compound numbers, the components indicating less than a full hundred are hyphenated *except* when **et** is present (see 2 above):

    quatre-vingt-dix-huit ans *98 years*

    cent dix-sept mètres *117 metres*

but: vingt **et** une bougies *21 candles*

Fractions

Except for $\frac{1}{2}$ (**un demi**), $\frac{1}{3}$ (**un tiers**), $\frac{1}{4}$ (**un quart**), fractions are composed, as in English, of a cardinal over an ordinal:

    trois huitièmes *three-eighths*

    un sixième *one-sixth*

    les neuf dixièmes de la population *nine-tenths of the population*

Important remarks concerning the use of numerals

Broadly speaking, numerals are used in a similar way in French and English. However, the following points should be remembered.

1   When referring to Kings, Queens, Emperors, Popes or other eminent people sharing their name with others, the cardinal number is used, except for the first bearer of the name. In this case *only*, the ordinal is used. In both cases, the number is placed after the name.

    Louis II (Deux) *Louis the Second*

    Henri IV (Quatre) *Henry the Fourth*

but: Elizabeth Iere (Première) *Elizabeth Ist*

    Napoléon Ier (Premier) *Napoleon I*

2   For the days of the month, cardinal numbers are used *except* for the first day which is indicated by the ordinal number

    le 14 (**quatorze**) juillet et le 15 (**quinze**) août *the 14th July and the 15th August*

but: le 1er (**premier**) mai *May 1st*

du 1er (premier) janvier au 31 (trente et un) décembre *all the year round* (lit: *from January 1st to December 31st*)

3   **Un millier** (*approximately a thousand*), **un million** (*a million*), **un milliard** (*a thousand million*), **un billion** (*a million million*), etc. are *nouns*, not adjectives; they will therefore take an **s** in the plural, and the noun which follows will be preceded by **de** (or **d'** to avoid the vowel-vowel clash):

    un million de francs *1 million francs*

    quatre milliards d'individus *4 thousand million individuals*

> With French numbers, a dot is used where a comma would
> appear in English and vice versa:
> 3.250.000 kilomètres *3,250,000 kilometres*
> 3,265 mètres *3.265 metres*

4 When a cardinal number is qualified by another adjective like
premier (*first*), **dernier** (*last*), **suivant/prochain** (*next*), **autre**
(*other*), etc. the cardinal number appears *before* the qualifying
adjective, and not after as in English:
les **trois** premiers mois *the first three months*
les **deux** dernières années *the last two years*
les **dix** autres jours *the other ten days*

5 Some one-word cardinal adjectives up to and including **cent**
(*100*), can be turned into feminine nouns by the addition of the
suffix **-aine**. Such nouns generally indicate an approximate number.
They are followed by **de** (or **d'** to avoid the vowel-vowel clash).
une **vingtaine** d'années *about 20 years*
une **douzaine** de jeunes gens *a dozen (or so) young people*
but: in commercial transactions, **une douzaine** has the meaning of
exactly twelve.
une **douzaine** d'oeufs s'il vous plaît *a dozen eggs please*

(*a*) In the case of **dix**, the noun indicating the approximate number
becomes **une dizaine** (with a **z** not an **x**).
(*b*) Such nouns, when used with the definite article **la**, tend to
indicate an (approximate) age bracket:
Elle approche de **la trentaine**. *She is nearing 30 (years of age).*
Il avait atteint **la cinquantaine**. *He was in his fifties.*

6 For numbers between 1100 and 1999 you can *either* say **mille cent**,
mille deuxcent(s) etc. (**mil cent, mil deux cent(s)** for a *date*), *or* **onze**
cent(s), douze cent(s), etc.

Nous avons dépensé $\begin{cases} \textbf{mille cinq cents} \text{ francs.} \\ \textbf{quinze cents} \text{ francs.} \end{cases}$ *We have spent 1500 francs.*

Kennedy est mort en $\begin{cases} \textbf{mil neuf cent soixante-trois.} \textit{ Kennedy died in 1963.} \\ \textbf{dix-neuf cent soixante-trois.} \end{cases}$

Note: In everyday French, it is more common to write dates with
figures than with letters.

7 **Mille un(e)** is used for a precise number (*1001*); **mille et un(e)**
indicates *a great many*:
J'ai **mille et une** choses à faire. *I have a thousand and one (= a*
lot of) things to do.

8 In conversation, it is normally accepted when talking about dates
of the 20th century, to omit **mil neuf cent** or **dix-neuf cent**:

la guerre de 14–18 (quatorze-dix-huit)   *the 1914–18 war*
le débarquement de juin 44 (quarante-quatre)   *the June 1944
landings*

9   When referring to a specific decade of the 20th century, the
relevant number must be preceded by the expression **les années**
les années trente   *the thirties*
les années soixante   *the sixties*

10   For official time-tables and on radio and television, the 24-hour
system is used:
Voici les informations de **20 heures**.   *Here is the 8 o'clock
(p.m.) news*
départ: **18 heures 12**, quai numéro 6   *departure: 18.12, platform 6*

Cardinal numbers used to indicate particular pages or chapters
of a book, acts or scenes of a play, are placed after the noun.
When **vingt** and **cent** are used in this way, they do not take an s
even if the conditions of Note 1 (p. 40) are met
Ouvrez le livre à la page **deux cent**.   *Open the book page
200.*
Lisez *l' Avare* de Molière, Acte **II [Deux]** Scène **II [Deux]**
Read 'l' Avare' by Molière, Act II Scene II.

Key points

1   Numerals are divided into 2 categories: *cardinals* which indicate a number
and *ordinals* which denote a rank or relative position.

2   Cardinal numeral adjectives are invariable except for **un** (*one*; fem.: **une**)
and for **vingt** (*20*) and **cent** (*100*) which, in very specific circumstances, take
an s in the plural.

3   Numerals are made up of either one word only or several words which
are, in certain circumstances, linked by **et** (*and*) or a hyphen.

4   The words **millier** (*approximately a thousand*), **million** (*million*), **milliard**
(*thousand million*), **billion** (*U.K. billion*) and others denoting still larger
numbers, are *nouns* not adjectives; they take an s in the plural.

5   Although there is great similarity in the use of numerals in French and
English, usage sometimes differs. For Kings, Queens, Popes and for the days
of the month, only *the first* is translated by an ordinal number; for all the
others the cardinal number is used. When a cardinal number is qualified by
another adjective the cardinal number generally comes first.

6   Some cardinal numerals can be transformed into nouns expressing the
corresponding approximate number by deletion of the final **e**, if applicable,
and addition of the suffix **-aine**.

8 Adjectives

Note: Determiners (possessives, demonstratives, exclamatives) are dealt with in separate chapters.

Adjectives are single or compound words which are used to give certain indications about some of the characteristics, traits, qualities, etc. of the thing(s) or being(s) they refer to. For example:
> la **petite** valise **noire**   *the small black case*
>
> ses **grands** yeux **étonnés**   *his/her large wondering eyes*

Although adjectives have the same role in French and English, their position and agreement patterns are totally different in the two languages:

1 In the great majority of cases, adjectives in English are placed before the noun. In French the situation is far more complex and can be influenced by such factors as meaning or length.

Compare:	Il entre dans sa **propre** maison.	
	He goes into his own house.	change in meaning
and:	Il entre dans sa maison **propre**.	according to position
	He goes into his clean house.	

or:	une idée **courageuse**	of the 2 words (adjective
	a courageous idea	and noun), the shorter
and:	une **courageuse** intervention	comes first
	a courageous intervention	

2 In French most adjectives vary in gender and number with the noun(s) they qualify, whereas in English they do not.

Compare:	un **bon petit** restaurant pas **cher** (m. sing.) *a good, small, inexpensive restaurant*
and:	une **bonne petite** auberge pas **chère** (f. sing.) *a good, small, inexpensive inn*

Position of adjectives

The following important points must be remembered about the position of adjectives in French:

1   The majority of adjectives are placed after the noun; if in doubt, it is fairly safe to place the adjective in that position (but see the specific rules stated below).

2   Adjectives denoting colour or shape are placed *after* the noun (except for special stylistic effects).

>   Je vois les collines **vertes** et les toits **rouges** du village.   *I see the green hills and the red roofs of the village.*

but: allons dans la *verte* prairie (*poetic effect*)   *let us go into the green meadow*

3   Certain adjectives have different meanings according to their position. They must therefore be placed correctly to convey the right meaning. A list of the most common adjectives belonging to that category is given below.

ancien = *former/ancient*
>   un **ancien** cinéma   *a cinema no longer used as such*
>   un cinéma **ancien**   *an ancient cinema*

brave = *good/brave*
>   une **brave** femme   *a good-hearted woman*
>   une femme **brave**   *a brave woman*

certain = *undefined/definite*
>   un **certain** changement   *a certain change*
>   un changement **certain**   *a definite change*

cher = *close to one's heart/expensive*
>   mon très **cher** bijou   *my dearly loved jewel*
>   mon bijou très **cher**   *my very expensive jewel*

dernier = *the last of a series/the one before this*
>   la **dernière** semaine   *the last week*
>   la semaine **dernière**   *last week*

grand = *illustrious (great)/tall*
>   un **grand** homme   *a great man*
>   un homme **grand**   *a tall man*

mauvais }
méchant }   = *of poor quality/vicious (hurtful)*
>   un **mauvais/méchant** livre   *a book of no literary value*
>   un livre **mauvais/méchant**   *a hurtful book*

pauvre = *wretched/penniless, destitute*
>   une **pauvre** femme   *a wretched woman*
>   une femme **pauvre**   *a penniless woman*

propre = *own/clean*
>   sa **propre** voiture   *his/her own car*
>   sa voiture **propre**   *his/her clean car*

4   If the noun is qualified by several adjectives, these can *either* retain their normal position, for example:
>   une **petite** femme **pauvre**   *a small, destitute woman*

or go after the noun and be 'linked' by a comma or **et** (*and*):
>   une femme **petite** et **pauvre**   *a small and destitute woman*

5   Adjectives denoting duration, size or magnitude are generally placed *before* the noun:
>   une **énorme** vague   *an enormous wave*
>   une **longue** attente   *a long wait*

6   Adjectives indicating permanent or semi-permanent characteristics are generally placed *after* the noun (but see also no. 5 above):
>   un homme **chauve**   *a bald man*
>   une femme **édentée**   *a toothless woman*
>   des enfants **intelligents**   *intelligent children*

7   Adjectives derived from verbs are placed *after* the noun:
>   Voici une maison **abandonnée**. (verb = **abandonner**)   *Here is a deserted house.*
>   Quelle blancheur **éclatante**! (verb = **éclater**)   *What dazzling white(ness)!*

8   Adjectives which are themselves qualified by another expression are placed *after* the noun even if on their own they normally go before it

compare: une **belle** fille   *a beautiful girl*
and: une fille **belle** comme le jour   *a stunningly beautiful girl* (lit: beautiful as the day)
or: un **grand** jardin   *a big garden*
and: un jardin **grand** comme un mouchoir   *a garden the size of a handkerchief* (= *tiny*)

9   Adjectives denoting origin (geographical, geological, historical, social, religious, ethnic, spatial, etc.), are placed *after* the noun they qualify:
>   une chanteuse **américaine**   *an american singer*
>   la période **élizabéthaine**   *the Elizabethan period*
>   l'église **catholique**   *the Catholic church*
>   la classe **ouvrière**   *the working class*

10   Certain adjectives have *no fixed position* and could theoretically be placed either before or after the noun they refer to. In such cases, the *shorter word*, i.e. the one with the smaller number of syllables (on this point see appendix I), will normally come *first*:

Compare: une idée **importante**   *an important idea*
           (2 syl)   (3 syl)
and: une **importante** manifestation   *an important demonstration*
           (3 syl)   (4 syl)

Most of the above rules are often broken to produce special stylistic effects.

Agreement of adjectives

Preliminary remarks

As previously mentioned, most French adjectives agree in gender and number with the noun(s) they refer to. If an adjective is used with several nouns, agreement is made according to sense:

Compare: un homme et un enfant **fatigués**   *a tired man and a tired child*

and: un homme et un enfant **fatigué**   *a man and a tired child*

If there are one or more feminine nouns and one masculine one, the adjective(s) qualifying them will be in the masculine plural.

Des femmes, des fillettes et un petit garçon **fatigués** dormaient.   *Several tired women, girls and a little boy were asleep.*

The basic form of the adjective to which agreement endings will be added, is the masculine singular. That is the form in which the adjective appears in a dictionary.

Most adjectives agree in the normal way indicated below. Some, however, have slightly or markedly modified forms in the feminine singular and/or the masculine plural. Note, though, that however 'irregularly' an adjective may behave, its feminine singular form will only need an **s** to become a feminine plural.

Deux **vieilles** personnes (f. pl.), une **vieille** dame (f. sing.)   et un **vieux** monsieur (m. sing.), attendaient l'autobus.   *Two old people, an old lady and an old gentleman, were waiting for the bus.*

Elle est **heureuse** (f. sing.) et ses filles sont **heureuses** (f. pl.) elles aussi.   *She is happy and her daughters are happy too.*

Adjectives ending in **x** or **s** in the masculine singular do not change in the masculine plural:

un enfant **malheureux**   des enfants **malheureux**
an unhappy child   *unhappy children*
le **gros** colis (m. sing.)   les **gros** colis (m. pl.)
the big parcel   *the big parcels*

Normal agreement of adjectives

In the case of a 'normal' adjective, the following endings are added, as required, to make it agree in gender and number with the noun(s) it qualifies:

	Sing.	Plur.
Masc.	—	s
Fem.	e	es

le **petit** hôtel (m. sing.) ⟶ les **petits** hôtels (m. pl.)
the small hotel   *the small hotels*
la **petite** chambre (f. sing.) ⟶ les **petites** chambres (f. pl.)
the small bedroom   *the small bedrooms*

Note: Adjectives ending in **e** (without an accent) in the masculine singular will have the following agreement pattern:

	Sing.	Plur.
Masc.	—	*s*
Fem.	—	*s*

le feu est **rouge** (m. sing.) ⟶ les feux sont **rouges** (m. pl.)
the light is red   *the lights are red*
la robe est **rouge** (f. sing.) ⟶ les robes sont **rouges** (f. pl.)
the dress is red   *the dresses are red*

Adjectives undergoing slight modifications in the feminine

Certain adjectives undergo a slight change of spelling in their feminine (singular and plural) forms. The most common of those (and, if applicable, the exceptions) are given below.

(*a*) Adjectives ending in **eil**, **el**, **et**, **ien**, **ol**, **on**, in the masculine singular, double their last consonant in the feminine singular (and plural).
    Compare: un fauteuil **ancien**   *an antique armchair*
    and: une chaise **ancienne**   *an antique chair*
    or: le destin est **cruel**   *fate is cruel*
    and: la vie est **cruelle**   *life is cruel*
    Exceptions: The following adjectives, instead of doubling their last consonant, take a grave accent over the **e** preceding that

consonant in the feminine singular (and plural): **complet**
complete, **concret** *concrete*, **discret** *discreet*, **inquiet** *worried*,
replet *plump*, **secret** *secret*. For example:

il est **inquiet** (m. sing.) ⟶ elle est **inquiète** (f. sing.)
he is worried   *she is worried*
un voisin **discret** (m. sing.) ⟶ une voisine **discrète** (f. sing.)
a discreet neighbour (man)   *a discreet neighbour (woman)*

The following adjectives have an alternative masculine singular
form used to avoid a vowel-vowel clash (see Appendix I) with
the next word.

m. sing. *normal form*	*alternative form*	*m. pl.*	*meaning*
beau	bel	beaux	*beautiful*
nouveau	nouvel	nouveaux	*new*
fou	fol	fous	*mad*
mou	mol	mous	*soft*
vieux	vieil	vieux	*old*

Their feminine singular is formed by doubling the last consonant of that alternative form before adding the usual **e**:

un **beau** jour (m. sing.) ⟶ une **belle** soirée (f. sing.)
a beautiful day   *a beautiful evening*
un désir **fou** (m. sing.) ⟶ une course **folle** (f. sing.)
a mad desire   *a mad race*

(b) Adjectives ending in **ieux** or **eux** in the masculine singular will
normally end in **ieuse** or **euse** in the feminine singular.

un **curieux** incident   ⟶ une **curieuse** lettre
a curious incident   *a curious letter*
un **heureux** événement   ⟶ une **heureuse** union
a happy event   *a happy union*

Remember: Since those adjectives end in **x** in the masculine
singular, they will retain the same form for their masculine
plural (see page 48).

(c) Adjectives ending in **ot** in the masculine singular will follow the
normal pattern of agreement. However there are exceptions to
this rule. The following adjectives will double their last conson-
ant before doing so: **boulot** *dumpy*. **palot** *palish*, **sot** *silly*, **vieillot**
old fashioned.

un garcon **palot**   ⟶ une fillette **palotte**
a rather pale boy   *a rather pale girl*
cet homme est **sot**   ⟶ cette femme est **sotte**
this man is silly   *this woman is silly*

(*d*) Adjectives ending in **in** in the masculine singular follow the normal pattern of agreement, although there are two exceptions: **bénin** *slight = not serious* and **malin** *sly/crafty*.

un rhume **bénin**   ⟶ une maladie **bénigne**
a slight cold   *a minor illness*
Il est **malin** mais sa femme est encore plus **maligne**.
He is crafty but his wife is craftier still.

(*e*) Adjectives ending in **al** in the masculine singular follow the normal pattern of agreement except in the masculine plural, where the ending changes to **aux**. Nine adjectives ending in **al**, however, follow the normal agreement exactly; **banal** *banal*, **bancal** *lame*, **fatal** *fatal*, **final** *final*, **glacial** *freezing*, **idéal** *ideal*, **jovial** *jovial*, **natal** *natal*, **naval** *naval*.

un entretien **cordial**   ⟶ des entretiens **cordiaux**
a cordial discussion   *cordial talks*
But: un accident **fatal** ⟶ des accidents **fatals**
a fatal accident   *fatal accidents*

(*f*) Adjectives ending in **ais**, **as** or **os** in the masculine singular follow the normal pattern of agreement for the feminine (both singular and plural). Again, though, there are a few exceptions: **bas** *low*, **épais** *thick*, **gras** *fat*, **gros** *big*, **las** *tired*, which double the **s** in the feminine (sing. and plural).
Compare:

le temps est **mauvais**   ⟶ la mer est **mauvaise**
the weather is bad   *the sea is rough*
and:
le brouillard est **épais** ⟶ le fumée est **épaisse**
the fog is thick   *the smoke is thick*

The above adjectives do not change in the masculine plural because they already have an **s** in their masculine singular form.

(*g*) Adjectives ending in **gu** in the masculine singular follow the normal agreement pattern except for the fact that in the feminine (singular and plural) the **e** will take a diaresis (¨):

un son **aigu**   ⟶ une plainte **aiguë**
a shrill sound   ⟶ *a shrill cry*

(*h*) Adjectives ending in **if**, **ef** or **euf** in the masculine singular follow the normal pattern of agreement but change their **f** into a **v** in the feminine (singular and plural):

J'achète un pantalon **neuf** et une chemise **neuve**.
I am buying new trousers and a new shirt.

(*i*) The stem of the following adjectives undergoes a marked change in the feminine (singular and plural), but they nevertheless follow the normal agreement pattern (see, however, page 48).

m. sing. form	*f. sing. form*	*meaning*
blanc	blanche	*white*
franc	franche	*frank*
favori	favorite	*favourite*
frais	fraîche	*fresh/cool*
sec	sèche	*dry*
doux	douce	*soft*
roux	rousse	*reddish*
faux	fausse	*false*
public	publique	*public*

For example:

du pain **blanc** ⟶ de la poudre **blanche**
white bread   *white powder*

(j) Most adjectives ending in **eur** or **teur** form their feminine singular in **euse** or **teuse** (for the plural, an **s** is added to the relevant form):

un avenir **prometteur** ⟶ une attitude **prometteuse**
a promising future   *a promising attitude*

However, certain more *unusual* or *learned* adjectives, change **teur** into **trice** in the feminine (for the plural, an **s** is added to the relevant form):

l'argent est **corrupteur** ⟶ la puissance est **corruptrice**
money is corrupting   *power is corrupting*

(k) Adjectives ending in **g** in the masculine singular add a **u** in the feminine:

un **long** voyage ⟶ une **longue** marche
a long journey   *a long walk*

Adjectives which break the normal agreement rules

Although some of the adjectives studied hitherto deviate from the normal pattern of agreement, they still vary in gender and number with the noun they refer to. The adjectives listed/indicated below however, are either partially or totally outside the agreement rules as outlined above.

(a) Nouns used as adjectives of colour *do not* vary in gender or number. The most common are: **cerise** *cherry*, **chocolat** *chocolate*, **marron** *chestnut*, **mastic** *putty = grey/beige*, **noisette** *hazel*, **olive** *olive*, **orange** *orange*

la fille aux yeux **noisette**   *the girl with hazel eyes*

Il achète des chaussures **mastic**. *He is buying putty-coloured shoes.*

(b) Adjectives of colour made up of more than one word do not vary in gender *or* number:

Compare: Il porte une chemise **bleue**, une veste **verte** et des chaussures **grises**. *He is wearing a blue shirt, a green jacket and grey shoes.*

and: Il porte une chemise **bleu clair**, une veste **vert pomme** et des chaussures **gris foncé**. *He is wearing a light-blue shirt, an apple-green jacket and dark-grey shoes.*

(c) Certain adjectives are sometimes used as adverbs to modify the sense of verbs. In such cases the adjective will *not* vary in gender *or* number. The most frequently encountered adjectives of that type are: **bas** *low*, **bon** *good*, **cher** *dear*, **clair** *clear*, **doux** *soft*, **dur** *hard*, **faux** *false*, **ferme** *firm*, **haut** *high*.

Ces fleurs sentent **bon**. *These flowers smell good.*

Elles parlent **bas**. *They speak in a low voice.*

Nous travaillons **dur**. *We are working hard.*

Note: Adjectives used with the verbs **être** (*to be*), **devenir** (*to become*), **sembler** (*to seem*), **paraître** (*to appear*), **rester/demeurer** (*to stay/remain*), agree in gender and number with the thing(s) or being(s) they refer to:

Compare: La visite est **chère**. *The visit is dear*

and: La visite coûte **cher**. *The visit cost a lot of money.*

or: La rivière est **basse**. *The river is low.*

and: La rivière descend **bas**. *The river goes down a long way.*

(d) The words **demi** *half*, **nu** *bare*, **excepté** *except*, **ci-joint/ci-inclus** *herewith*, **compris** *included*, **supposé** *supposed*, **vu** considering, when placed *before* the noun, do not agree in gender or number. If placed *after* the noun, they agree as required.

Compare: Il marche **nu**-pieds. *He is walking barefoot.*

and: Il marche pieds **nus**. *He is walking barefoot.*

or: attendez une **demi**-heure *wait for half an hour*

and: attendez une heure et **demie** *wait for an hour and a half*

(e) Adjectives following the expression **avoir l'air** (*to seem/have the appearance of being*) can *either* agree normally if a subjective opinion is expressed (**avoir l'air** = *to seem to be*) *or* agree with **l'air** (m. sing.), if an objective assessment is given (**avoir l'air** = *to have the outward appearance of*).

Compare: Cette maison a l'air **vieille** (agreement with **maison**) *This house seems (to be) old.* (Subjective opinion)

and: Cette maison a l'air **vieux** (agreement with **l'air**)
This house looks old. (objective assessment)
Note: The difference in meaning is sufficiently slight for you not to worry unduly about it at this stage.

(*f*) The following adjectives do not vary in gender *or* number: **chic** *chic*, **kaki** *khaki*, **rococo** *rococo*, **snob** *snob*, **sterling** *sterling*.

un uniforme **kaki** ⟶ des uniformes **kaki**
a khaki uniform   *khaki uniforms*
une livre *sterling* ⟶ dix livres **sterling**
a pound sterling   *ten pounds sterling*
Note: Usage is not totally consistent and some of the above are sometimes written with **s** in the plural.

(*g*) The adjective **grand** when used as part of a compound feminine noun singular or plural, does not vary in gender or number. In such cases its meaning is *great/grand/main*.
Compare: ma **grande** tante *my tall aunt*
and: ma **grand**-tante *my great-aunt*
or: nos **grandes** mères *our tall mothers*
and: nos **grand**-mères *our grandmothers*
Note: In such constructions, **grand** is followed by an apostrophe or a hyphen.

(*h*) The adjective **possible** (*possible*) follows the normal pattern of agreement *except* if preceded by such expressions as **le plus** *the most*, **le moins** *the least*, **le mieux** *the best*.
Compare: Il y a deux solutions **possibles**. *There are two possible solutions.*
and: Elles font le moins de fautes **possible**. *They make as few mistakes as possible.*

NB This lesson will seem complex because the behaviour of adjectives in French is dramatically different from that of English adjectives. Return to it as often as needed.

Key points

1 Adjectives are single or compound words used to give certain indications about (some of) the characteristics of the thing(s) or being(s) they refer to.

2 Most adjectives in French agree in gender and number with the thing(s) or being(s) they qualify.

3 Most adjectives have a clearly defined position in the sentence. Some of them change their meaning if their position changes. Since the majority of adjectives are normally placed after the noun, it will be fairly safe to use that position when in doubt.

4 Most adjectives add an **e** to the masculine singular to form the feminine-singular, and an **s** to form the plural for both genders. Certain adjectives, however, do not follow this normal pattern of agreement.

5 Adjectives ending in **x** or **s** in the masculine singular remain the same in the masculine plural.

6 A limited number of adjectives have an alternative masculine singular form used to avoid a vowel-vowel clash with the next word.

7 Nouns used as adjectives of colour do not vary in gender or number with the thing(s) or being(s) they qualify.

8 Compound adjectives of colour do not vary in gender or number.

9 Adjectives used as adverbs do not vary in gender or number.

10 A small number of adjectives remain invariable if placed before the noun they refer to, but agree as required if placed after that noun.

11 The adjective **grand** (*great/grand/main*) when used as part of a compound feminine noun remains invariable and is linked to the following word by an apostrophe or a hyphen. In masculine plural compounds **grand** takes an **s.**

12 The adjective **possible** (*possible*) does not agree in gender or number when used after **le plus** (*the most*), **le moins** (*the least*), **le mieux** (*the best*).

9   The Gender of Nouns

General remarks

Nouns are words (single or compound) used to name beings (human and non-human) and things (substances, processes, feelings, etc.). There are two types of nouns:
- *common nouns* which indicate things or beings belonging to a given class, e.g. **la porte** *the door*, **le travail** *work*, **les enfants** *children*;
- *proper nouns* which identify a specific thing or being, or a specific set of things or beings, e.g. **L'Angleterre** *England*, **Londres** *London*, **le Maroc** *Morocco*, **Churchill** *Churchill*, **les Alpes** *the Alps*. Note that all proper nouns begin with a capital letter.

In French, nouns fall into two gender categories — masculine and feminine. This classification was originally influenced by the Latin system: nouns derived from masculine or neuter Latin names are normally masculine; nouns derived from feminine Latin names are normally feminine. Whether you have studied Latin or not, you may find the following suggestions useful to memorise the gender of French nouns:

1   Always learn the noun *with* its definite *or* indefinite singular article (which give advance warning of the gender). For example, you should learn **le** gouvernement (*government*) and not just gouvernement or **la** chance (*luck*) and not chance.

Remember: Using the wrong gender would, as previously pointed out, result in a cascade of mistakes, since not only most determiners, but also most adjectives, have to agree in *gender* as well as *number* with the noun they refer to.

Compare: un petit village accueillant et reposant   *a small welcoming and restful village*

and: une petite ville accueillante et reposante   *a small welcoming and restful town*

There is no such agreement problem in English.

2   Pay attention to the sense of the noun. Generally, nouns referring to male beings are masculine and nouns indicating female beings are feminine (but see 6 below). For example:

un homme *a man*, **une** fillette *a young girl*, **une** poule *a hen*, **un** étalon *a stallion*

Note: There are exceptions to this rule, which shall be examined later in this chapter.

3 Look carefully at the endings of nouns. They often give useful guidance about gender.

le développe**ment** (**-ment** = masculine)

la propor**tion** (**-tion** = feminine)

NB: the formulation of 'theories', as outlined in the introduction, will be of particular use in the discovery of 'rules' concerning gender classification by ending or by meaning.

Since the plural form of most French nouns sounds exactly the same as their singular form, it is vitally important for the speaker to indicate clearly the right gender by using the appropriate form of the determiner and/or adjective.

wrong = *Le vieux dame est mort.

right = **La** vie**ille** dame est morte. *The old lady is dead.*

Before proceeding to a detailed study of the gender of nouns, the following categories should be distinguished:

1 Nouns which refer to things or beings of one gender only; they will vary in number only:

la maison (*the house*)	⟶	les maisons (*houses*)
le mur (*wall*)	⟶	les murs (*walls*)
un arbre (*a tree*)	⟶	des arbres (*trees*)

2 Nouns which, without any alteration in spelling, can refer to a male being in the masculine and to a female being in the feminine. The following are the most commonly encountered.

Masculine	*Feminine*	*Meaning*
un adversaire	une adversaire	*opponent*
un artiste	une artiste	*artist*
le camarade	la camarade	*friend*
le collègue	la collègue	*colleague*
un élève	une élève	*pupil*
un enfant	une enfant	*child*
un esclave	une esclave	*slave*
le locataire	la locataire	*tenant*
le partenaire	la partenaire	*partner*
le secrétaire	la secrétaire	*secretary*
le touriste	la touriste	*tourist*

NB: In this category, there is no change in the meaning of the word (apart from the gender).

3   Nouns which, with some alteration of their masculine form (ending), can be made to refer to a female being of the same species.

Masculine	*Feminine*	*Meaning*
le travailleur	la travailleuse ⎱	*worker*
un ouvrier	une ouvrière ⎰	
le cousin	la cousine	*cousin*
le chien	la chienne	*dog*
le fou	la folle	*mad person*
le Parisien	la Parisienne	*Parisian*
le nouveau	la nouvelle	*newcomer*

4   Nouns which remain exactly the same in spelling when changing from masculine to feminine, but which take on a different meaning in the process. The following are the most common nouns of that type:

Masculine	*Feminine*
un aide (*male assistant*)	une aide (*help*)
le critique (*critic*)	la critique (*criticism*)
le garde (*guard = person*)	la garde (*guard = action*)
un guide (*guide*)	une guide (*rein*)
le livre (*book*)	la livre (*pound*)
le manche (*handle*)	⎰ la manche (*sleeve*)
	⎱ la Manche (*the Channel*)
le moule (*mould*)	la moule (*mussel*)
le manoeuvre (*unskilled worker*)	la manoeuvre (*manoeuvre*)
le page (*page-boy*)	la page (*page = sheet*)
le pendule (*pendulum*)	la pendule (*wall clock*)
le poste (*post*)	la poste (*Post Office*)
le physique (*physique*)	la physique (*physics*)
le radio (*radio operator*)	la radio (*radio*)
le tour (*turn/tour*)	la tour (*tower*)
le vase (*vase*)	la vase (*silt*)
le voile (*veil*)	la voile (*sail*)

5   Nouns which are masculine in the singular and feminine in the plural (sometimes with altered meaning):

Masculine	Feminine
un amour malheureux *(an unfortunate love)*	des amours malheureus*es* *(unfortunate loves: poetic)*
un aigle *(an eagle: actual bird)*	des aigles *(eagles: emblems on flags/shields)*
le délice *(delight)*	les délices *(ecstasies)*
un orgue *(an organ: music)*	des orgues *(an organ: music-poetic or pompous)*

6 Nouns of living creatures (singular or plural), which can refer *either* to beings of one sex (as indicated by the noun's gender), *or* to any member of the species *regardless* of sex:

les vaches (fem.)   *cows/cows, oxen and bulls*
les souris (fem.)   *female mice/mice of either sex*
les moutons (masc.)   *rams/sheep of either sex*
les poissons (masc.)   *male fish/fish of either sex*
les mouches (fem.)   *female flies/flies of either sex*
les éléphants (masc.)   *bull elephants/elephants of either sex*
les hommes (masc.)   *men/men and women*

For example:

Les **vaches** sont dans le pré.   *The cows are in the meadow.*
Les **hommes** sont mortels.   *Men are mortal.*

Note: If the ambiguity needs to be removed, this can be done in one of two ways: *either* by using the specific male or female term, if it exists:

Les **vaches** et les **taureaux** sont dans le pré.   *The cows and bulls are in the meadow.*

or by adding the words **mâle** (*male*) or **femelle** (*female*) after the noun as required:

une souris **mâle**   *a male mouse*
un éléphant **femelle**   *a female elephant*

7 Certain nouns referring to human beings which, although of one gender only, can apply to individuals of either sex:

la connaissance   *acquaintance — man or woman*
la personne   *person — man or woman*
la recrue   *recruit — man or woman*
la sentinelle   *sentry — man or woman*
le témoin   *witness — man or woman*
la victime   *victim — man or woman*

8 Certain nouns indicating a profession or status traditionally held

by men have no feminine equivalent. The following are the most frequently-encountered examples:

l'auteur	*author*	le journaliste	*journalist*
le bourreau	*executioner*	le magistrat	*magistrate*
le chef	*chief*	le ministre	*minister*
le diplomate	*diplomat*	le peintre	*painter*
le docteur	*doctor*	le possesseur	*owner*
l'écrivain	*writer*	le professeur	*lecturer*
le guide	*guide*	le successeur	*successor*
l'ingénieur	*engineer*	le tyran	*tyrant*

NB   If needed, it is possible to indicate in one of two ways that the noun refers to a woman:

(*a*)   By using the words **femme** (*woman*) or **dame** (*lady*) in connection with that noun, which then takes on the value of an adjective. For example:

J'ai parlé à une **femme docteur**.   *I spoke to a lady doctor.*
Cette **dame** est peintre.   *This lady is a painter.*

(*b*)   By referring to the person as **Madame le . . .** if addressing her directly:

Excusez-moi, **Madame le Ministre**   *Excuse me, Minister*

Hints for the determination of the gender of nouns

The information given below is designed to help you learn and remember the gender of French nouns. For each gender, the information has been subdivided into two sections:

(*a*)   determination of gender by *meaning*; and
(*b*)   determination of gender by *ending*.

Masculine nouns

Determination of the masculine gender by meaning

(*a*)   Nouns referring to beings of the male sex, for example **le fils** *son*, **le cheval** *horse*, **le chien** *dog*.

(*b*)   Nouns identifying the following:

– *chemical substances and gases*, for example **le carbone** *carbon*, **le sulfate de cuivre** *copper sulphate*, **l'azote** *nitrogen*, **le cyanure** *cyanide*;

– *colours*, for example **le blanc** *white*, **le jaune** *yellow*, **le rose** *pink*, **le violet** *purple*;

– *holidays*, such as **le quatorze juillet** *14th July — Bastille Day*,

le quinze août *15th August* — *Assumption*, but **la Toussaint** *All Saints Day* and **la Noël** *Christmas*. Note, however, that in greetings, or if accompanied by an adjective, **Noël** is masculine. For example:

(Je vous souhaite **un**) joyeux Noël! *(I wish you a) happy Christmas!*

Nous avons passé **un** excellent Noël. *We have had an excellent Christmas.*

— *languages*, for example **le chinois** *Chinese*, **le grec** *Greek*, **le russe** *Russian*;

— *metals*, for example **le cuivre** *copper*, **le fer** *iron*, **le plomb** *lead*, **le zinc** *zinc*, but: **la fonte** *cast iron*, **la tôle** *sheet iron*;

— *seasons, months, days of the week*, for example **le printemps** *Spring*, **en décembre dernier** *last December*, **un dimanche** *one Sunday*;

— *trees, shrubs and bushes*, for example **le chêne** *oak tree*, **le peuplier** *poplar*, **le rhododendron** *rhododendron*, **le rosier** *rose-bush*, but: **une aubépine** *a hawthorn*, **la vigne** *vine*, **la ronce** *bramble*;

— *countries not ending in 'e'*, for example **le Portugal** *Portugal*, **le Guatémala** *Guatemala*;

— *flowers not ending in 'e'*, for example **le géranium** *geranium*, **le lilas** *lilac*, **le mimosa** *mimosa*, **l'oeillet** *carnation*;

— *fruit and vegetables not ending in 'e'*, for example **le citron** *lemon*, **le melon** *melon*, **un artichaut** *an artichoke*, **le navet** *turnip*;

— *items of clothing not ending in 'e'*, for example **le blouson** *lumber jacket*, **le pantalon** *trousers*, **le soulier** *shoe*, **le veston** *jacket*;

— *illnesses not ending in 'e'*, for example **le choléra** *cholera*, **les oreillons** *mumps*, **le typhus** *typhus*, but: **la malaria** *malaria*;

— *rivers not ending in 'e'*, for example **le Mississippi** *Mississippi*, **le Nil** *Nile*, but: **la Volga** *Volga*;

— *sciences and scholarly disciplines not ending in 'e'*, for example **le dessin** *drawing*, **le droit** *law*;

— *letters of the alphabet*, for example **un 'a'** *an 'a'*, **un 'c'** *a 'c'*. *Note:* Usage sometimes differs, but the masculine is generally seen as being acceptable in all cases;

— *lorries, ships and aircraft*, for example **le Ford** *Ford Truck*, **le Boeing** *Boeing*, **le Concorde** *Concord*, **le France** *the France* (liner), but: **la Caravelle** (aircraft), **la Marie-Céleste** (ship). *Note*: Usage sometimes differs in the case of ships, but the masculine gender is by far the most widely used;

62 *The Gender of Nouns*

- *wines, spirits and cheeses named after their region/country of origin*, for example **le bourgogne** *Burgundy wine*, **le cognac** *brandy*, **le roquefort** *Roquefort cheese*, **le hollande** *Dutch cheese*. *Note*: In such cases, the gender is obviously influenced by the fact that the words **vin** (*wine*) and **fromage** (*cheese*) are masculine;
- *nouns borrowed from English*, for example **le parking** *car park*, **le snack-bar** *snack bar*, **le week-end** *week end*, but: **un/une interview** *an interview*, **la star** *top artist*. *Note*: If the borrowed noun refers to a person of the female sex, it will be feminine in French, for example **la Cover-girl** *covergirl*, **la Script-girl** *script girl*.

Determination of masculine gender by ending
Nouns with the following endings are (normally) masculine:

age, for example **le passage** *passage*, **le lavage** *washing*, **le ménage** *housework*, but: **la cage** *cage*, **une image** *an image*, **la nage** *swimming*, **la page** *page*, **la plage** *beach*, **la rage** *rage/rabies*;

ail, for example **l'émail** *enamel*, **le travail** *work*, **le vitrail** *stained glass window*;

al, for example **le carnaval** *carnival*, **le métal** *metal*, **un oral** *an oral examination*;

as, for example **le bas** *lower part/stocking*, **le gras** *fat*, **le tas** *heap*;

eau, for example **le chapeau** *hat*, **le drapeau** *flag*, **le taureau** *bull*, but: **l'eau** *water*, **la peau** *skin*;

eu, for example **le feu** *fire*, **le jeu** *game*, **le pneu** *tyre*;

eur if indicating a person or machine performing a job or task, for example **un aviateur** *an airman*, **le chauffeur** *stoker/driver*, **le mélangeur** *mixer*, **le compresseur** *compressor*;

eux, for example **le creux** *hollow*, **le sérieux** *seriousness*, **le vieux** *old man*;

er/ier if referring to a person performing a job/task, for example **le boucher** *butcher*, **le plâtrier** *plasterer*, **le portier** *doorman*;

in/ain/ein, for example **le lin** *linen*, **le matin** *morning*, **le pain** *bread*, **le sein** *breast*, but: **la fin** *end*, **la main** *hand*;

is, for example **le colis** *parcel*, **le commis** *apprentice*, **le tapis** *carpet*, but: **la vis** *screw*;

ment, for example **le changement** *change*, **le développement** *development*, **un élément** *an element*, but: **la jument** *mare*,

oir, for example **le devoir** *duty*, **le dortoir** *dormitory*, **le pouvoir** *power*, **le savoir** *knowledge*;

ou, for example **le chou** *cabbage*, **le cou** *neck*, **le fou** *madman*, **le trou** *hole*, **le voyou** *thug*, but: **la nounou** *nanny*.

Note: It is possible for you to create many more such categories of nouns, but there may be numerous exceptions to your 'rules'. Nevertheless, it is a worthwhile exercise which will accustom you to look at the language in the right way.

Feminine nouns

Determination of the feminine gender by meaning
(*a*) Nouns referring to beings of the female sex (but see also notes 6, 7 and 8 on pp. 59–60), for example **la fille** *daughter*, **la jument** *mare*, **la chienne** *bitch*.
(*b*) Nouns identifying the following:
   – *countries ending in 'e'*, for example **l'Autriche** *Austria*, **la Belgique** *Belgium*, **la Tunisie** *Tunisia*, but: **le Cambodge** *Cambodia* (now Kampuchea), **le Mexique** *Mexico*, **le Zaïre** *Zaire*;
   – *flowers ending in 'e'*, for example **la rose** *rose*, **la tulipe** *tulip*, **la violette** *violet*, but: **le chèvrefeuille** *honeysuckle*;
   – *fruit and vegetables ending in 'e'*, for example **l'amande** *almond*, **la carotte** *carrot*, **la fraise** *strawberry*, **la pomme de terre** *potato*, **la prune** *plum*, **la tomate** *tomato*, but: **le pamplemousse** *grapefruit*;
   – *garments ending in 'e'*, for example **la chemise** *shirt*, **la cravate** *tie*, **la veste** *jacket*, but: **un imperméable** *a raincoat*, **le passe-montagne** *balaclava*;
   – *illnesses ending in 'e'*, for example **la fièvre** *fever*, **la peste** *plague*, **la rougeole** *measles*, **la tuberculose** *tuberculosis*, but: **le malaise** *feeling of sickness*;
   – *rivers ending in 'e'*, for example **la Loire** *Loire*, **la Seine** *Seine*, **la Tamise** *Thames*, but: **le Danube** *Danube*, **le Rhône** *Rhone*, **le Zambèze** *Zambezi*;
   – *sciences and scholarly disciplines ending in 'e'*, for example **la biologie** *biology*, **la chimie** *chemistry*, **la politique** *politics*;

- *sports, games and leisure pursuits ending in 'e'* (but *not* in **isme**), for example **la marche** *walking*, **la course** *running*, **la danse** *dancing*, **la peinture** *painting*, **la poterie** *pottery*. *Note*: **le culturisme** *body building*, **le cyclisme** *cycling*, etc.

- *vehicles other than lorries, aircraft, boats*, for example **une Austin** *Austin car*, **la Citroën** *Citroen car*, **la Suzuki** *Suzuki motorbike*, **la bicyclette** *push-bike*, **la motocyclette** *motorbike*, but: **le tricycle** *tricycle*.

Determination of feminine gender by ending
Nouns with the following endings are (normally) feminine:

ance/anse/ence/ense, for example **une avance** *advance*, **la chance** *luck*, **la danse** *dance*, **la défense** *defence*, **la prudence** *care = prudence*, **la violence** *violence*, but: **le rance** *rancid taste*, **le silence** *silence*;

ée, for example **l'arrivée** *arrival*, **l'épée** *sword*, **la gelée** *frost/jelly*, **la montée** *climb*, but: **un athée** *atheist*, **le lycée** *Grammar school*, **le mausolée** *mausoleum*, **le musée** *museum*;

esse, for example **la caresse** *caress*, **la finesse** *finesse*, **la messe** *mass*, **la paresse** *laziness*, **la tresse** *plait*;

ette/otte, for example **la chambrette** *small bedroom*, **la botte** *boot*, **la buvette** *refreshment bar*, **la chemisette** *short-sleeved shirt*, **la flotte** *fleet*, **la fourchette** *fork*, **la roulotte** *gipsy caravan*;

eur if expressing an abstract notion, for example **l'ardeur** *passion = fire*, **la chaleur** *heat*, **la hauteur** *height*, **la peur** *fear*, **la valeur** *valour/value*, but: **le bonheur** *happiness*, **le malheur** *unhappiness*. Note that if the noun ending in **eur** refers to a *machine* or *person* doing a specific type of activity, it will be masculine, for example **le brûleur** *burner*, **le contrôleur** *inspector*, **le coureur** *runner/racing driver*. **le mélangeur** *mixer*, **le voleur** *thief*;

rie, for example **la boucherie** *butcher's shop*, **la cavalerie** *cavalry*, **la galerie** *gallery*, **la patrie** *fatherland*;

sie/tie, for example **la bourgeoisie** *middle class*, **la courtoisie** *courtesy*, **la démocratie** *democracy*, **la fantaisie** *whim*, **la partie** *party*, **la sortie** *exit*, but: **le messie** *messiah*, **le sosie** *look-alike*;

sion/tion, for example **la confusion** *confusion*, **la contraction** *contraction*, **l'érosion** *erosion*, **la perfection** *perfection*, **la question** *question*, **la version** *version*, **la vision** *vision*, but: **le bastion** *bastion/stronghold*;

té if expressing an abstract notion, for example **la beauté** *beauty*, l'égalité *equality*, **la fraternité** *fraternity*, **la liberté** *freedom*, but: **le doigté** *touch = knowhow*. *Note*: If the noun ending in **té** refers to a *non-abstract* thing or being, it will be masculine, for example **le comité** *committee*, **le pâté** *pâté*, **le velouté** *velouté = soup/sauce*;

ture, for example **la confiture** *jam*, **la couverture** *blanket*, **la facture** *bill*, **la fracture** *fracture*, **l'ouverture** *opening*, **la structure** *structure*, **la voiture** *car*.

Note: As mentioned above, it is possible for you to create more categories by examining noun endings and formulating your own theories. Doing this will accustom you to look for the underlying 'logic' of the language.

Key points

1 French nouns fall into two distinct gender categories: masculine and feminine.
2 In spite of the apparent arbitrariness of the division, it is possible to organise categories based on meaning which, with some exceptions, will help learners to find out which gender a given noun belongs to.
3 In addition to categories based on meaning, it is also possible to assign many nouns to one or the other of the two gender categories according to ending. *Note*: With practice, learners will develop a 'feel' for the gender of the new nouns they encounter.
4 It must be remembered that the gender of a noun affects the adjectives and other determiners associated with it. All the necessary agreements *must* be made where appropriate.
5 *Generally*, nouns referring to beings of the male sex are masculine and nouns referring to beings of the female sex are feminine.
6 There are, however, cases when a noun of one gender may refer to:

(a) beings of the other sex;
(b) beings of both sexes.

7 There are a number of cases when, for a given noun, a change in gender will determine a change in meaning. Special care should be taken to try and remember such nouns.
8 It is possible for learners to experiment with 'theories' concerning the gender of nouns according to meaning and, to a larger extent, according to endings. It is a worthwhile exercise, which will encourage them to look for the 'underlying unity' of the language.

10   The Plural of Nouns

Simple (one-word) nouns

The majority of French simple nouns form their plural by adding an **s** to their masculine or feminine singular form.

Remember: Most adjectives connected with a plural noun will follow the agreement pattern as appropriate. For example:

La grande porte	⟶ Les grandes portes
The big door	*The big doors*
Le petit garçon	⟶ Les petits garçons
The small boy	*The small boys*

Some categories of nouns, however, do not follow the general rule outlined above. They are examined below:

1   Nouns ending in **s**, **x** or **z** in the singular do not change in the plural. For example:

Un **bas** nylon	⟶ Des **bas** nylon
A nylon stocking	*Nylon stockings*
Le petit **vieux**	⟶ Les petits **vieux**
The little old man	*The little old men*
Un joli **nez**	⟶ De jolis **nez**
A pretty nose	*Pretty noses*

2   Nouns ending in **au**, **eau** or **eu** in the singular, add an **x** in the plural. For example:

Le **noyau**	⟶ Les **noyaux**
The kernel/core	*The kernels/cores*
Le **bateau**	⟶ Les **bateaux**
The boat	*The boats*
Le **feu** rouge	⟶ Les **feux** rouges
The traffic light	*The traffic lights*

Exceptions: The following take an **s** in the plural: **le bleu** *bruise/boiler suit*, **le landau** *pram*, **le pneu** *tyre*. For example

   Mes quatre **pneus** sont à plat.   *My four tyres are flat.*

3   Nouns ending in **al** in the singular form their plural in **aux**:

Le **cheval** sauvage	⟶ Les **chevaux** sauvages
The wild horse	*The wild horses*
Un **métal** précieux	⟶ Des **métaux** précieux
A precious metal	*Precious metals*

Exceptions: The following six nouns take an s in the plural: **le bal** *dance*, **le carnaval** *carnival*, **le chacal** *jackal*, **le festival** *festival*, **le récital** *recital/concert*, **le régal** *delight/feast*.

Note: **Un idéal** (*ideal*) has two plural forms: **des idéals** *or* **des idéaux**

4   The following six nouns ending in **ail** in the singular, form their plural in **aux**: **le bail** *lease*, **le corail** *coral*, **l'émail** *enamel*, **le soupirail** *air vent*, **le travail** *work*, **le vitrail** *stained glass window*. For example
>   Les **vitraux** de la cathédrale sont magnifiques.   *The stained glass windows of the cathedral are magnificent.*

5   The following *seven* nouns ending in **ou** in the singular, form their plural in **oux**: **le bijou** *jewel*, **le caillou** *stone*, **le chou** *cabbage*, **le genou** *knee*, **le hibou** *owl*, **le joujou** *toy* (child's word), **le pou** *louse*. For example:
>   Ciel, on m'a volé mes **bijoux**!   *Good Heavens, someone has stolen my jewels!*
>   L'enfant adorait ses **joujoux**.   *The child adored his toys.*

6   Four nouns have two plural forms (regular and irregular), which may have quite different meanings, as shown in the table below:

Singular	Regular plural	Irregular plural
un aïeul	des aïeuls	des aïeux
a grandfather	*grandfathers*	*forefathers*
l'ail	les ails	les aulx
garlic	*garlic: modern form*	*garlic: obsolete form*
le ciel	les ciels	les cieux
the sky	*skies: in paintings*	*skies/heavens*
un oeil	des oeils	des yeux
an eye	*round windows*	*eyes*

7   Nouns created from invariable words (adverbs, prepositions, conjunctions), remain invariable in the plural, for example:
>   Les **si** et les **mais**   *The ifs and buts*
>   Les **pourquoi** et les **comment**   *The whys and wherefores*

Compound nouns

Compound nouns can be made up of a combination of the following elements:

(*a*)   variable words (adjectives, nouns, past participles), which may take the mark of the plural according to the rules stated below.

(*b*)   invariable words (adverbs, conjunctions, prepositions, verbs), which will remain invariable at all times.

Both these elements are illustrated in the examples below:

Le petit-fils   ⟶ **Les petits-fils** (adj. + noun)
The grandson   *The grandsons*
Un ouvre-boîte   ⟶ Des ouvre-boîtes (verb + noun)
A tin-opener   *Tin-openers*
Le haut-parleur   ⟶ Les haut-parleurs (adv + noun)
The loudspeaker   *The loudspeakers*

The following cases must be distinguished:

1   Some compound nouns are so closely 'welded' together that the identity of the components has been forgotten and they are now treated as one word.

Un portefeuille   ⟶   Des portefeuilles
A wallet (lit: *leaf-carrier*) *Wallets*
Le contrevent   ⟶   Les contrevents
The shutter (lit: *wind-shield*) *The shutters*

Exceptions: Le bonhomme   ⟶ Les bónshommes
              The (old) fellow   *The (old) fellows*
              Un gentilhomme   ⟶ Des gentilshommes
              A gentleman   *Gentlemen*

Note the plural of the following forms of *direct* address:

              Madame   ⟶ **Mes**dames
              Madam   *Ladies*
              Mademoiselle   ⟶ **Mes**demoiselles
              Miss   *Young ladies*
              Monsieur   ⟶ **Messieurs**
              Sir   *Gentlemen*

2   *Noun + noun compounds*   Normally, both components can be put into the plural when required:

Un chou-fleur   ⟶ Des choux-fleurs
A cauliflower   *Cauliflowers*
Une chauve-souris   ⟶ Des chauves-souris
A bat   *Bats*

There are, however, some exceptions to this rule.

(*a*)   If the nouns are linked by a preposition: **à** *to*/*for*, **de** *of*/*from*, **en** *in*, **pour** *for*, etc., *stated or implied*, the second noun will remain singular. For example:

Un arc-en-**ciel** ⟶ Des arcş-en-**ciel**
A rainbow *Rainbows*
Le timbre-**poste** ⟶ Les timbres-**poste**
   (= pour la poste)
The postage stamp *The postage stamps*

(*b*) If the second noun represents a 'generic' name (i.e. the name of a whole species, class or group of beings or things), it does not take the plural form.

Le ver à **soie** ⟶ Les vers à **soie**
The silkworm *The silkworms*
Un soutien-**gorge** ⟶ Des soutiens-**gorge**
A bra (lit: *Support-bosom*) *Bras*
Le moulin à **vent** ⟶ Les moulins à **vent**
The windmill *The windmills*

(*c*) A small number of such compounds do not change in the plural.

Un (des) coq-à-l'âne   *Abrupt change(s) of subject*
Un (des) pied-à-terre   *Small occasional lodgings (−)*
Un (des) pot-au-feu   *Stew(s)*
Un (des) tête-à-tête   *Tête-à-tête(s)*

3 *Noun + adjective compounds*   Normally, both elements take the plural form when required.

Un coffre-fort ⟶ Des coffres-forts
A safe *Safes*
Un franc-maçon ⟶ Des francs-maçons
A freemason *Freemasons*

Note: In *feminine plural compounds*, **grand** (*grand/great*) can either remain invariable or take an **s**. For example:

Une **grand**-mère ⟶ Des **grand(s)**-mères
A grandmother *Grandmothers*
La **grand**-tante ⟶ Les **grand(s)**-tantes
The great-aunt *The great-aunts*

4 *Adjective + adjective compounds*   Normally, both elements take the plural form when appropriate:

Le dernier-né ⟶ Les derniers-nés
The last-born child *The last-born children*
Le sourd-muet ⟶ Les sourds-muets
The deaf-and-dumb man *The deaf-and-dumb men*

Note: If one of the adjectives is used in an adverbial sense, it will remain invariable

Un **nouveau**-né   Des **nouveau**-nés
A newly born child *Newly born children*

5   *Verb + noun compounds*   The verb element remains invariable in the plural. The noun normally agrees in number, *except* if it represents a 'generic' name (i.e. the name of a whole species, group or category).

Le couvre-feu	⟶ Les couvre-feux
The curfew	*The curfews*
Un garde-fou	⟶ Des garde-fous
A hand-rail	*Hand-rails*
But: Un abat-**jour**	⟶ Des abat-**jour**
A lamp-shade	*Lamp-shades*
Le gratte-**ciel**	⟶ Les gratte-**ciel**
The sky-scraper	*The sky-scrapers*
Un coupe-**papier**	⟶ Des coupe-**papier**
A paper-knife	*Paper-knives*
Un brise-**glace**	⟶ Des brise-**glace**
An ice-breaker	*Ice-breakers*

Note: If the word **garde** used as the first element of the compound refers to a *person*, it will take an s in the plural. If it refers to an *object*, it will remain invariable:

Compare:	Un **garde**-malade	⟶ Des **gardes**-malades
	A male nurse	*Male nurses*
and:	Une **garde**-robe	⟶ Des **garde**-robes
	A wardrobe	*Wardrobes*

6   *Invariable word + noun compounds*   In such compounds, the noun alone may take the plural form when required.

Un à-coup	⟶ Des à-coups
A jolt/jerk	*Jolts/jerks*
Un non-sens	⟶ Des non-sens
A meaningless phrase	*Meaningless phrases*

Note: If a compound noun is made of two (or more) invariable words, it will of course remain invariable in the plural.

Un (des) on-dit   *Rumour(s)* (lit: *one says*)
Un (des) passe-partout   *Master-key(s)*
Un (des) va-et-vient   *Two way switch(es)*

Foreign nouns

For this category, the rules of plural formation are fairly unstable, but the following guidelines may be helpful:

If the word comes from a language in which plural formation is the same as in French, it will easily be integrated and follow the normal rule. For example:

Un pullover	⟶ Des pullovers
A jumper	*Jumpers*
Le parking	⟶ Les parkings
The car-park	*The car-parks*

2 If the word comes from Latin or Italian and is commonly used, it may follow the normal rule.

Un maximum	⟶ Des maximums (*also* maxima)
A maximum	*Maxima*
Un référendum	⟶ Des référendums (*also* référenda)
A referendum	*Referendums*

3 If the word *is not* fully assimilated, its plural form may be the one used in the language of origin.

Un graffito	⟶ Des graffiti
A graffito	*Graffiti*
Un barman	⟶ Des barmen
A barman	*Barmen*
Un lied	⟶ Des lieder
A ballad	*Ballads*

Note: There is, as yet, great confusion about the word **media** (= *mass media*):

	Un medium	
or	Un media	Des media (*or* des média *or* des médias)

Proper nouns

In this category, several cases must be distinguished:

1 Proper nouns referring to famous royal families take the plural when required:

Les Bourbons *The Bourbon family*
Les Stuarts *The Stuarts*

2 Proper nouns referring to families other than those mentioned above, remain invariable:

Les **Dupont** sont invités par les **Lebrun.** *The Duponts are invited by the Lebruns.*

3 Proper nouns referring to works of art produced by a given artist, take the plural form when required:

Trois **Picassos** ont été volés. *Three Picasso paintings have been stolen.*

4 Proper nouns used to refer to people of the same artistic or intellectual calibre as the original bearer of the name take the plural form when necessary:

Les **Einsteins** et les **Flemings** sont rares. *People like Einstein and Fleming are rare.*

Note: Usage often differs in this latter category.

Nouns which can only be used in the plural or in the singular

1   The following are some of the nouns which *cannot* be used in the singular:

les archives   *archives* (fem.), **les arrhes**   *non-returnable deposit* (fem.),
les confins   *confines (*masc.), **les entrailles**   *entrails* (fem.),
les frais   *expenses* (masc.), **les mathématiques**   *mathematics* (fem.),
les menottes   *handcuffs* (fem.), **les pourparlers**   *discussions* (masc.),
les ténèbres   *darkness* (fem.), **les vivres**   *food supplies* (masc.), etc.

2   The following categories of nouns are *not normally* used in the plural:

(*a*)   adjectives used as nouns and expressing broad concepts and 'eternal' values; for example **Le beau** *Beauty*, **le bien** *Good*, **le mal** *Evil*, **le vrai** *Truth*;

(*b*)   Infinitives used as nouns; for example **L'avoir** *financial possessions*, **le devenir** *evolution*, **le savoir** *knowledge*, etc.

(*c*)   generic names of products, materials, substances; for example **le bois** *wood*, **le fer** *iron*, **la laine** *wool*, **le pétrole** *crude oil*, etc.

(*d*)   names of intellectual or artistic disciplines; for example **la biologie** *biology*, **la chimie** *chemistry*, **la musique** *music*, **la sculpture** *sculpture*, etc., but: **les mathématiques** *mathematics*.

Nouns which change their meaning in the plural

A small number of nouns change their meaning when put in the plural:

Singular		Plural	
la bonté	*goodness*	⟶ les bontés	*favours*
la chance	*luck*	⟶ les chances	*opportunities*
la douceur	*softness*	⟶ les douceurs	*sweets*
la volonté	*willpower*	⟶ les volontés	*whims/fancies*
le ciseau	*chisel*	⟶ les ciseaux	*scissors*
la lunette	*spy-glass*	⟶ les lunettes	*glasses = spectacles*

Nouns which change their pronunciation in the plural

Three nouns, although they follow the normal rule of plural formation, change their pronunciation in the plural (for an explanation of phonetic symbols see Appendix I):

Un boeuf	[bœf]	⟶ Des boeufs	[bø]
An ox		*Oxen*	
Un oeuf	[œf]	⟶ Des oeufs	[ø]
An egg		*Eggs*	
Un os	[ɔs]	⟶ Des os	[o]
A bone		*Bones*	

Key points

1 *The majority* of French nouns form their plural by adding an s to their masculine or feminine singular form. Some, however, do not follow this rule.

2 Nouns ending in s, x and z remain the same in the plural.

3 *Most* nouns ending in **au**, **eau** and **eu** in the singular, take an x in the plural.

4 *Most* nouns ending in **al** in the singular, change **al** to **aux** in the plural.

5 *Most* nouns ending in **ail** and **ou** follow the normal rule of plural formation. There are, however, exceptions in both cases.

6 *Four* nouns have two plural forms (regular *and* irregular). The meaning of those two forms is *not* automatically identical.

7 Nouns created from invariable words (adverbs, conjunctions, prepositions, verbs) remain invariable in the plural.

8 Compound nouns may be composed of two types of elements: *invariable ones* (mentioned in 7 above); and *variable ones* (adjectives, nouns, past participles). The first category will *not* take the plural form *in any circumstances*. The second will take the plural as appropriate, unless the general sense of the word makes the agreement illogical (reference to generic categories, broad concepts, etc.).

9 The rules of plural agreement for foreign nouns are not absolute: if the noun is 'well integrated' (i.e. very frequently used) the normal rule will apply (add an s). If not, the foreign noun may retain its original plural form.

10 The rules governing the plural of proper names in French are complex and flexible. If the proper name refers to the members of an illustrious family or to the intellectual or artistic production of the rightful bearer of the name, the plural agreement will be made when appropriate. In most other cases the proper name will remain invariable in the plural.

11 Some French nouns have no singular form and *must*, therefore, *always* be used in the plural.

12 A certain number of nouns representing broad concepts, intellectual disciplines or 'generic categories' are not normally used in the plural. If they are, the meaning of the plural form may be quite different from that of the singular form.

11　The Pronoun

Note: for the purpose of exemplification, some pronoun categories are, at times, mentioned out of turn. Please refer to the sections clarifying those categories if in doubt.

Pronouns are words which can replace nouns or nominal expressions. Some pronouns can even replace whole sentences:

> La neige est épaisse. **Cela** m'inquiète. *The snow is deep. That worries me (that = the fact that the snow is deep)*.

Pronouns enable us to speak and write in a more concise and elegant way, and to avoid tiresome repetitions.

Compare:　La dame regarde ses deux enfants. Ses deux enfants jouent. Ses deux enfants sont heureux. Cet enfant-ci court; cet enfant-là chante. La dame est fière de ses deux enfants.

and:　La dame regarde ses deux enfants. **Ils** jouent. **Ils** sont heureux. **Celui-ci** court; **celui-là** chante. **Elle** est fière d'**eux**. *The lady is looking at her two children. They are playing. They are happy. This one is running; that one is singing. She is proud of them.* (In the second version most of the nouns have been replaced by the appropriate pronouns.)

French nouns, as stated on many previous occasions, are not all of the same gender and can generally vary in number. The pronouns which are to replace them must therefore carry as much information as possible about gender and number. Consequently, there will be marked differences between the French and English pronoun systems. For example *I need them* could be translated in French either as: J'ai besoin d'**eux** (if *them* represents a masculine plural) or as: J'ai besoin d'**elles** (if *them* represents a feminine plural). It is therefore wise to assume that not all pronouns will function in the same way in the two languages.

There are six distinct categories of pronouns. Each category has a special role to play and it is crucial, whenever the forms are different, to distinguish clearly between them. The categories are as follows: personal, demonstrative, possessive, relative, interrogative, indefinite. They will be examined in turn.

Personal pronouns

As their name suggests, they 'point out' who is the 'performer' (subject) or the recipient (object) of the action.

Subject pronouns

They indicate the performer(s) of an action.

Number	*Person*	*Pronoun*	*Meaning*
Singular	1st 2nd 2nd 3rd 3rd 3rd	je/j'† tu vous il elle on	*I* *you* (familiar form) *you* (polite form) *he* (also used to replace non-human masculine nouns) *she* (also used to replace non-human feminine nouns) *one* (neutral pronoun to avoid specific reference to persons of one or other gender)
Plural	1st 2nd 3rd 3rd	nous vous ils elles	*we* *you* (normal plural) *they* (masculine only or masculine + feminine) *they* (feminine only)

† When **je** is followed by a vowel or a mute 'h' it loses its **e**.

There are a number of points to bear in mind with the use of subject pronouns:
1 On their own, **je** (*I*) **tu** (*you*—familiar) **on** (*one*) **nous** (*we*) and **vous** (*you*—plural or polite singular) do not carry any gender information. That information will often appear in the ending(s) of the accompanying adjective(s) (if any).

Compare: **Je** suis content. *I am pleased.* (The ending of the adjective **content** reveals that the subject **je** is masculine.)

and: **Je** suis contente. *I am pleased.* (In this case, the ending of the adjective reveals that the subject is feminine.)

or: **Vous** êtes fatigué. *You are tired.* (The ending of the adjective indicates that **vous** refers to a male person — polite singular.)

and: **Vous** êtes fatiguées. *You are tired.* (The ending shows that the remark is addressed to several female persons — normal plural.)

NB Using the polite form **vous** to address one person in French is *not* a sign of stand-offishness but of respect.

2 **Il**, which normally refers to a masculine being or thing, can also be used in French as an impersonal pronoun. In such cases, it does not refer to any specific thing or being and is then the equivalent of the English impersonal form *it*. For example:

Il pleut? Non, **il** neige. *Is it raining? No, it is snowing.*

Il faut partir! *It is necessary to go.*

Il importe d'être calme. *It is important to be calm.*

3 In good French, **on** (*one*) is always followed by the 3rd person singular of the verb (even though it may have the meaning of *people*):

Le soir venu, **on** rentrait fatigué mais ravi. *When the evening came one* (i.e. *people) went home tired but delighted.*

NB For the purpose of agreement, **on** is considered as a masculine singular pronoun. The endings of the adjectives in the preceding example make the fact clear.

4 In familiar French, **on** is often used instead of **nous**. In this case any agreement is made as if **on** was really **nous**:

On est sorti**s** tous les quatre hier soir. *The four of us went out last night.*

5 Sometimes, for the purpose of emphasis, another set of pronouns is used to 'reinforce' the subject pronouns; in this case such pronouns, called *disjunctives*, usually appear before the subject ones. They are listed on pages 81–2.

Compare: J'abandonne. *I give up.*

and: **Moi**, j'abandonne. *As for me, I give up.*

6 To translate English constructions where two subject pronouns are linked by *and* or *or*, two disjunctives will be used in French. For example:

Lui et **moi** (and not *il et je) viendrons vous chercher. *He and I will come and fetch you.*

Qui va répondre, **toi** ou **moi**? (and not, *tu ou je). *Who is going to answer, you or I?*

7 When translating expressions of the type *It is (not) I . . .* the subject pronoun will be replaced by the corresponding disjunctive:

C'est **moi** (and not *c'est je) qui ai appelé la police. *It is I who called the police.*

C'est **lui** (and not *c'est il) que je veux voir. *It is he I want to see.*

Ce n'est pas **toi** (and not *ce n'est pas **tu**) le coupable. *You are not the culprit.* (lit: *it is not you the culprit*)

8   More generally, the subject pronoun cannot be used without a verb or solely with the auxiliary **être** (*to be*) or **avoir** (*to have*) as it can in English.

Compare: *Who has broken the vase? I have!*

and: Qui a cassé le vase? Moi! (and not *j'ai)

To all intents and purposes, it is as if the expression *It is . . . who . . .* had simply been omitted and rule 8 above does therefore apply.

9   In comparisons, after expressions such as **plus . . . que** (*more than*) **moins . . . que** (*less than*), **aussi . . . que** (*as . . . as*) **comme** (*as*), the subject pronoun is replaced by the corresponding disjunctive pronoun (see pages 81–2):

Elle est plus jeune que **toi**.   *She is younger than you (are).*

Ils gagnent moins que **moi**.   *They earn less than I (do)*

Object pronouns

They are used to refer to the thing(s) or being(s) affected by the action performed by the subject(s). They are sub-divided into two groups: *direct object* (accusative) and *indirect object* (dative). Since the distinction between these two groups seems to create confusion in the mind of some learners, here is a simple (if not foolproof) way of finding out which is which. After the subject and the verb have been stated, ask the question **qui?** (*who?*) or **quoi?** (*what?*). If this question has an answer, you will have to substitute the appropriate direct object pronoun when required:

Tu vois la rivière?   *Do you see the river?*

Oui, je **la** vois. (je vois quoi? = la rivière, fem. sing.) *Yes, I see it.*

Et votre repas?   *What about your meal?*

Nous **le** mangeons! (nous mangeons quoi? = le repas; masc. sing.)   *We are eating it!*

Note: Be sure that the answer you obtained was to the question **qui?** or **quoi?** *and not* **à qui?** (*to whom?*) or **à quoi?** (*to what?*), otherwise the pronouns you need are the indirect object ones!

Compare: Il regardait le tableau; il **l'**admirait. (il admirait quoi? = le tableau; masc. sing.)   *He looked at the painting; he admired it.*

and: Il regardait le chien; il **lui** parlait. (Il parlait à qui? = au chien; masc. sing.)   *He looked at the dog; he spoke to it.*

Direct object (*accusative*) pronouns

Number	Person	Pronoun	Meaning

Singular	1st
	2nd
	2nd
	3rd
	
	3rd
		me/m' (moi)
		te/t'
		vous
		le/l'
		
		la/l'
			me
			you (familiar form)
			you (polite form)
			him (also used to replace
			    non-human masc. nouns)
			her (also used to replace
			    non-human fem. nouns)

Plural	1st
	2nd
	3rd
		nous
		vous
		les
			us
			you (normal plural form)
			them (to replace masculine
			    or feminine human or non-
			    human nouns)

For example:

Il a perdu sa fille de vue. Est-ce que vous **la** voyez? (vous voyez qui? = sa fille; fem. sing.) *He has lost sight of his daughter. Do you see her?*

Tes parents sont là; je **les** ai appelés. (j'ai appelé qui? = tes parents; masc. plur.) *Your parents are here; I called them.*

Note: When the next word begins with a vowel or mute 'h', **me**, **te**, **le** and **la** lose their e or a to avoid the vowel-vowel clash. For example:

Cette affiche, nous **l'**avions vue. *We had seen this poster.* (lit: *this poster, we had seen it.*)

There are a number of points to observe regarding the use of this pronoun:

1   Throughout the system **vous** could refer to a masculine singular, a feminine singular, a masculine plural or a feminine plural. Information about the gender and number of the noun referred to, will be carried by the past participle (if any).

Compare: Je **vous** ai **vu**. *I have seen you.* (masc. sing.: no e and no s at the end of **vu**)

and: Je **vous** ai **vue**. *I have seen you.* (fem. sing.:e at the end of **vu**)

and: Je **vous** ai **vus**. *I have seen you.* (masc. plural: s at the end of **vu**)

and: Je **vous** ai **vues**. *I have seen you.* (fem. plural: es at the end of **vu**)

2   The rules concerning gender and number agreement should be respected *every time* the pronoun is used, not only in the case of the past participle, but with any adjective or determiner relating to the pronoun.

Compare: Ils l'ont conn**u** tout petit.   *They have known him since he was very small.*

and: Ils l'ont conn**ue** tou**te** peti**te**.   *They have known her since she was very small.*

Here again, the endings give the clue to the gender and number of the being(s) or thing(s) referred to.

3   A number of English verbs give the impression that they take a direct object complement (accusative) when the recipient is a person. Beware of them: in French they are used with **à** and take an indirect object pronoun. The most frequent of those are:

to allow = permettre (à)	to order = commander (à)/
to ask = demander (à)	ordonner (à)
to forbid = interdire (à)	to permit = permettre (à)
to forgive = pardonner (à)	to sell = vendre (à)
to give = donner (à)	to telephone = téléphoner (à)
to grant = accorder (à)	to write = écrire (à)

With those verbs, the appropriate question to ask would not be **qui/quoi?** (*who/what?*), but **à qui/à quoi?** (*to whom/to what?*), as previously mentioned.

Compare: Tu as vendu la voiture? Oui, je l'ai vendue. (j'ai vendu quoi? = la voiture)
Have you sold the car? Yes, I have sold it.

and: Tu as vendu la voiture à Robert? Oui, je la **lui** ai vendue. (je l'ai vendue **à qui** = à Robert)
Have you sold Robert the car?   Yes I have sold it to him.

DO NOT write or say:
   *Je **le** vends la voiture *for*: Je **lui** vends la voiture.   *I sell him the car.* (= *to him*)
or   *Elle **le** permet de sortir *for*: Elle **lui** permet de sortir. *She allows him to go out.* (= *to him*).

---

4   There are some verbs in French which admit a direct object (accusative) but which are used in English with a preposition (*for, to, at*). Among those are the following: **attendre** *to wait for*, **demander** *to ask for*, **écouter** *to listen to*, **espérer** *to hope for*, **regarder** *to look at*. For example:

Nous **les** attendons depuis hier.   *We have been waiting for them since yesterday.*

Voulez-vous **les** écouter?   *Do you want to listen to them?*

5   In the positive imperative tense, the pronoun **me** (*me*) is replaced by **moi**, which is then placed after the verb. For example:

Suivez-**moi**!   *Follow me!*

Ecoutez-**moi**!   *Listen to me!*

but: Ne **me** suivez pas!   *Do not follow me!*

Ne **m**'écoutez pas!   *Do not listen to me*

Indirect object (dative) pronouns

These pronouns are used to replace the noun of the recipient(s) when the latter is separated from the verb by the preposition **à**.

Number	Person	Pronoun	Meaning
Singular	1st 2nd 2nd 3rd	me/m' (moi) te/t' vous lui	*(to) me* *(to) you* (familiar) *(to) you* (polite form) *(to) him or her* (also used to replace masc. or fem. non-human nouns)
Plural	1st 2nd 3rd	nous vous leur	*(to) us* *(to) you* *(to) them* (used to replace *all* masc. or fem. nouns)

Il faudrait **lui** téléphoner. (téléphoner à qui?)   *We should telephone him/her.*

J'espère que vous **leur** donnerez le bonjour de ma part. (donner à qui?)   *I hope that you will give them my regards.* (lit: *that you will give to them 'good day' from me*)

There are a number of points to observe regarding the use of these pronouns.

1   Some verbs, although constructed with the preposition **à** (*to*), do not take the indirect object pronouns but the disjunctive ones when referring to a *person*. The most common of those verbs are:

aller à	= to go to	
courir à	= to run to	
penser à	quelqu'un	= to think of	somebody
rêver à	= to dream of	
venir à	= to come to	

For example:

Je pense **à toi**. (and not *je te pense)   *I think of you.*

Elle courut **à moi**. (and not *elle me courut)   *She ran towards me.*

2   In the positive imperative, **me** (*to me*) is replaced by **moi**. This, however, *does not* occur in the negative.

Compare: Donnez-**moi** du pain (and not *me donnez du pain) *Give me some bread.*

and: Ne **me** donnez pas de pain.   *Do not give me any bread.*

3   Since **lui** can refer to a masculine or to a feminine (human or non-human), this may give rise to some ambiguity. The context should normally clarify the meaning. If, however, you wish to make absolutely clear who or what you are referring to, you may do so by using the appropriate disjunctive pronoun (see below) together with the indirect object pronoun.

Je les ai vus tous les deux; je ne **lui** ai rien dit **à lui**, mais je **lui** ai tout raconté **à elle**.   *I saw them both; I said nothing to him, but I told her everything.*

The pronoun **leur** must not be confused with the possessive adjective **leur/leurs** (*their*). For example:

Je **leur** ai donné leur argent de poche et leurs bonbons.   *I have given them their pocket money and their sweets.*

Disjunctive (or prepositional) pronouns

These pronouns, apart from the specific uses outlined in the above sections — reinforcement of the subject pronoun, replacement of subject pronouns in structures with **et** (*and*) or **ou** (*or*) and in expressions of the type **C'est moi qui . . .** (*it is I who . . .*) or after the positive imperative — *must also be used* whenever the verb and the 'recipient' of the action are linked by a preposition such as **avec** (*with*), **de** (*to/of/about*), **contre** (*against*), **derrière** (*behind*), **devant** (*in front of*), **pour** (*for*), **sous** (*under*), **sur** (*on*), **vers** (*towards*) etc., and in some cases **à** (*of/to*), as previously mentioned.

For example:

Elle a fait une petite promenade à pied avec **eux**.   *She went for a little walk with them.*

Nous ne pouvons rien faire pour **elle**.   *We can do nothing for her.*

Restez derrière **moi**!   *Stay behind me!*

Number	Person	Pronoun	Meaning
Singular	1st	moi	*me/myself*
	2nd	toi	*you/yourself* (familiar form)
	2nd	vous	*you/yourself* (polite form)
	3rd	lui	*him/himself* (also used to replace masc. non-human nouns)
	3rd	elle	*her/herself* (also used to replace fem. non-human nouns)
	3rd	soi	preposition + *one/oneself* (used for human nouns when no specification of the gender is possible or required)
Plural	1st	nous	*us/ourselves*
	2nd	vous	*you/yourselves* (normal plural)
	3rd	eux	*them* (masc. plural)
	3rd	elles	*them* (fem. plural)

There are a number of points to observe regarding the use of these pronouns:

1   It should be remembered that **vous** (*you/yourself/yourselves*) could refer to any of the following:
  (i) a male person;
 (ii) a female person;
(iii) a group of people (male or male + female);
(iv) a group of people (female).

Therefore great care should be exercised about possible agreement.

2   **Soi** (*one/oneself*) is, in modern French, only used in connection with the indefinite personal pronoun **on** (*one/somebody*) followed by the 3rd person singular of the appropriate verb. It may, however, refer to an unspecified number of persons. For example:

On doit toujours porter ses papiers sur **soi**. *One* (= *people*) *must always carry one's* (= *their*) *papers with oneself* (= *them*).

Those two pronouns are used when the speaker or writer does not know (or does not want to specify) the gender of the person or persons concerned.

Very often, French people avoid the use of **on** and **soi** and replace them with **vous** with the appropriate person of the verb. So, the above example often becomes:

> **Vous** devez toujours porter vos papiers sur **vous**. *You must always carry your papers with you.*

3 For the purpose of emphasis or clarification, the word **même(s)** (*self/selves*) is sometimes used after the disjunctive pronoun, particularly to translate the emphatic forms *myself, yourself*, etc.

> Elles ont fait tout le travail **elles-mêmes**. *They did all the work themselves.* (fem. plur.)
>
> Je vais vérifier cela **moi-même**. *I am going to check that myself.* (masc./fem. sing.)
>
> On n'est jamais mieux servi que par **soi-même**. (proverb) *Don't count on others* (lit: *one is never better served than by oneself*)

Reflexive pronouns

Such pronouns are used with certain verbs or in certain constructions to indicate that the action stated by the verb 'falls back' on the performer(s). In a reflexive construction, therefore, the reflexive and subject pronouns refer to the same person(s). For example:

> Je **me** prépare à partir. *I am getting ready to go.* (lit: *I am preparing myself to go*)
>
> Nous **nous** arrêtons. *We are stopping.* (lit: *we are stopping ourselves*)

Number	Person	Pronoun	Meaning
Singular	1st	me/m'	*(to) myself*
	2nd	te/t'	*(to) yourself* (familiar form)
	2nd	vous	*(to) yourself* (polite form)
	3rd	se/s'	used for all 3rd persons singular including the impersonal **on**
Plural	1st	nous	*(to) ourselves*
	2nd	vous	*(to) yourselves*
	3rd	se/s'	used for all 3rd persons plural (masc./fem.; sing./plur.; human/non-human)

Note: Although there are in French some verbs which are exclusively reflexive, such as: **s'enfuir** *to flee*, **s'évanouir** *to faint*, etc., there are a great many others which can be used reflexively *or* non-reflexively. It is therefore essential to use the reflexive pronoun wherever the action 'falls back' on to the performer(s), even if in English the reflexive construction (myself, yourself, etc.) is not considered essential or acceptable.

Compare: Il a lavé.   *He has washed (something/someone).*
and: Il s'est lavé.   *He has washed (himself).*
or: Nous regardons les enfants.   *We are looking at the children.*
Nous **nous** regardons.   *We are looking at ourselves.*

For example:
Ce soir, nous **nous** coucherons de bonne heure.   *Tonight we shall go to bed early.* (verb = **se coucher**)
Je **me** suis coupée avec le couteau à pain.   *I cut myself with the bread knife.* (verb = **se couper**)

Notes:
1   The ending of coupée in the previous example indicates that the performer (who is also the recipient) is feminine.
2   **me**, **te** and **se** lose their **e** when the word which follows them begins with a vowel or mute 'h' (to avoid the vowel-vowel clash).

Points to bear in mind regarding the use of these pronouns:
1   From the above examples, it is obvious that the compound tenses of reflexive verbs are always constructed with the auxiliary **être** (and not with **avoir**):
Nous **nous sommes** réveillés à six heures. (and not *nous nous avons réveillés à six heures) *We woke up at six o'clock.* (verb = **se réveiller**)
Je **me suis** trompé (ad not* je m'ai trompé) *I made a mistake* (verb = **se tromper**)
2   It is important, in order to make the past participle agree correctly, to know whether the reflexive verb is constructed with the accusative (direct object) or with the dative (indirect object). The following suggestion may prove useful to distinguish between the two.

(*a*)   reconstruct the sentence *mentally* with the auxiliary **avoir** (*to have*);
(*b*)   then, ask the question **qui?** or **quoi?** after the past participle, as in the case of object pronouns. If the question **qui?** or **quoi?** admits the subject pronoun as an answer, the construction is an

accusative one and the accompanying past participle will agree in gender and number with the subject (i.e. performer). For example:

Elle s'est lav**ée**. (Elle a lavé qui? = elle-même, fem. sing.) *She washed*. (Whom did she wash? = herself)

Ils se sont **vus**. (Ils ont vu qui? = eux-même, masc. plur.) *They saw themselves*. (Whom did they see? = themselves)

But if it is the question **à qui?/à quoi?** which admits the subject pronoun as an answer, this will indicate an indirect object construction and no agreement will be needed. For example:

Elle **s'** est d**it** que c'était fini. (Elle a dit **à qui** = à elle-même) *She said to herself that it was all over*. (To whom? = to herself)

Ils **se** sont donné deux jours. (Ils ont donné deux jours **à qui?** = à eux-mêmes) *They gave themselves two days*. (They gave to whom? = to themselves)

Compare: Elle s'est donn**ée** à lui. (Elle a donné **qui?** = elle-même) *She gave herself to him*.

and: Elle s'est donn**é** du mal. (Elle a donné du mal **à qui?** = à elle-même) *She went to a lot of trouble*. (lit: *She gave trouble to herself*)

3 Under the heading 'reflexives' are sometimes included verbs which are really 'reciprocal', i.e. denoting that the action of the performer(s) affects the recipient(s) who in turn reciprocate(s). For example:

Robert et Paul **se** sont battus. *Robert and Paul fought (each other)*, i.e. *Robert fought Paul and Paul fought Robert*.

Note: It is therefore possible to come across sentences which may be ambiguous. For example **Ils se sont blessés** could mean either *They wounded themselves* (reflexive), or *They wounded each other* (reciprocal).

Usually, the context will clarify the meaning; if the ambiguity needs to be removed, this can be done by selecting the appropriate form from the following: **l'un l'autre, l'une l'autre, les uns les autres, les unes les autres** (*each other/one another*) and placing it after the verb to indicate reciprocity.

Compare: Aidez-**vous**, le ciel vous aidera. (reflexive; proverb) *God helps them that help themselves*. (lit: *help yourself and Heaven will help you*)

and: Aidez-vous **les uns les autres**. *Help one another*. (reciprocal)

4 There is another small group of verbs which also use the reflexive pronouns in their construction. Unlike the previous categories, they

cannot be used without those pronouns. The most common are: **s'écrouler** *to collapse*, **s'emparer de** *to seize*, **s'enfuir** *to flee*, **s'évanouir** *to faint*, **se repentir** *to repent*. Here the pronouns have no reflexive value. For example:

> La jeune femme s'est évanouie. *The young woman fainted.*
> Les soldats **se** sont emparés des armes. *The soldiers seized the weapons.*

NB The agreement is made as in the case of direct object reflexives.

Notes:

1 The reason why the above three categories are often treated as one is obviously because they all use the same pronouns (**me, te, se, nous, vous, se**).

2 Normally 'reciprocal' verbs should not be used in the singular (since they need two performers). In practice, however, it is possible with the help of a preposition such as **avec** (*with*), to retain the reciprocal meaning with a singular.

> Il **se** bat avec son frère. *He and his brother fight.* (= with each other)
> Elle s'est disputée avec son mari. *She and her husband had a row.* (= with each other)

5 A reflexive construction is sometimes used idiomatically in French to replace a passive one. For example:

> Les oeufs **se vendent** à la douzaine. *Eggs are sold* (lit: *sell themselves*) *by the dozen.*
> Un grand bruit s'est fait entendre. *A loud noise was* (lit: *made itself*) *heard.*
> *Cette maison* **se** construit vite. *This house is being built* (lit: *building itself*) *quickly.*

The pronouns *en* and *y*

They are often called pronominal adverbs because they can be used both as adverbs and as pronouns.

1 *As adverbs* they are used to indicate the place where (for **y**) and whence (for **en**) the action takes the performer(s). For example:

> Il y a le feu à l'usine. J'**y** vais. *There is a fire at the mill. I am going (there).*
> Ne parlez pas de la guerre, il **en** vient. *Do not talk about the war, he has just come back (from it).*

2 *As pronouns* they are normally used to replace nouns (or equivalents) referring to things or non-human beings, in sentences where the verb is constructed with the following prepositions:

> **de** *of/with* in the case of **en**
> **à** *to/about* in the case of **y**

before a noun or nominal expression. For example:

Tu penses à l'accident? Oui j'**y** pense. *Are you thinking about the accident? Yes I'm thinking about it.*

Tu parles du film? Oui j'**en** parle. *Are you talking about the film? Yes I'm talking about it.*

Notes:

1 It is possible to find **en** and **y** used in constructions referring to humans:

Vous avez parlé de lui? Oui j'**en** ai parlé. *Did you talk about him? Yes I talked about him.*

Pensez-vous à moi? Oui j'**y** pense. *Do you think of me? Yes I do.*

2 **En** can have a partitive meaning (= *some of it/them*):

Vous avez de la viande? J'**en** veux! *Do you have any meat? I want some!*

3 **Y** is omitted before the future and conditional forms of aller:

Vous irez la voir? Oui j'irai. (and not *j'y irai) *Will you go and see her? Yes I will (go).*

The position of object pronouns

A close look at the examples given so far in this chapter, reveals that the position of direct object pronouns follows a certain pattern in relation to the verb.

Two cases must be distinguished:

(*a*) constructions where the imperative affirmative is used;
(*b*) all other constructions (including the imperative negative).

We shall examine each case in turn.

Constructions with the verb in the imperative affirmative
The pattern is as follows:

	Number	*Persons*	*1*		*2*	*3*	*4*
			A	B			
		1st	moi (me)		moi/m'		
	Singular	2nd	toi (te)		toi/t'		
		2nd	vous		vous		
Verb +		3rd		le, la/l'	lui	Y	en
		1st	nous		nous		
	Plural	2nd	vous		vous		
		3rd		les	leur		

Notes:
1   The combination of pronouns, when permissible, will occur in the order shown (1 to 4).
2   The pronouns of column 1 A and B are direct object pronouns (answers to **qui?/quoi?**).
3   In column 1 A the direct object pronouns **me** and **te**, unacceptable in this context, are replaced by **moi** and **toi** respectively.
4   The pronouns of column 2 are indirect object pronouns (answers to **à qui?/à quoi?**).
5   Some of the pronouns of columns 1 B and 2 lose their vowel when the next word itself begins with a vowel or mute 'h'.

Main combinations and restrictions
1   Only one of the two groups (A *or* B) of column 1 can be used with a given verb.
2   Group B of column 1 can be used before the pronouns of column 2:

> Vendez-**le-moi**.   *Sell it (masc. sing.) to me.*
> Rends-**la-leur**.   *Give it (fem. sing.) back to them.*

3   The pronouns of column 2 should *not* be used with the pronoun of column 3.
4   The pronouns of column 2 can be used with the pronoun of column 4:

> Prêtez-**m'en** deux.   *Lend me (= to me) two of them.*
> Donne-**nous-en** un morceau.   *Give us (= to us) a piece of it.*

The verb in any other tense (including the imperative negative)
In this case the object pronouns are placed, in the order shown, before the verb (in a simple tense construction) or before the auxiliary (in a compound tense construction).

Number	Person	1 A	1 B	2	3	4	5	
Singular	1st 2nd 2nd 3rd	se/s'	me/m' te/t' vous	le, la/l'	lui	y	en	+ Verb aux
Plural	1st 2nd 3rd	se/s'	nous vous	les	leur			

Notes:
1   The combination of these pronouns, when permissible, will occur in the order shown (1 to 5).

2   Some of the pronouns of columns 1 and 2 lose their vowel when the next word itself begins with a vowel or mute 'h'.

3   The pronouns of column 1 B represent the following three categories: *direct object* (accusative), *indirect object* (dative) and *reflexive*; since they have the same form and are mutually exclusive, little harm is done by having one column instead of three.

4   The pronouns of column 2 are direct object pronouns (answers to **qui?/quoi?**).

5   The pronouns of column 3 are indirect object pronouns (answers to **à qui?/à quoi?**).

Main combinations and restrictions

1   Only one of the two groups (A *or* B) of column 1 can be used in 'good' French with a given verb.

2   The pronouns of column 1 B can *only* be used in connection with those of column 2 *if* they are indirect object (dative), or reflexive

> Je **vous le** donne.   *I am giving it* (masc. sing.) *to you.*
>
> Est-ce que vous **nous les** avez rendus?   *Have you given them back to us?*

Note: The ending of **rendus** indicates that **les** refers to a masculine plural noun.

3   The direct object pronouns of column 2 can be used with the indirect pronouns of column 3:

> Vous allez **la lui** présenter.   *You are going to introduce her to him* (or *her*).
>
> Nous regrettons de ne pas **la leur** avoir donnée.   *We regret not having given it* (fem. sing.) *to them.*

Note: The object pronouns are placed before the verb which they relate to *even* if it is in the infinitive mood.

4   The direct object pronouns of column 2 can be used with either that of column 4 *or* 5:

> Elle **l'y** a poussé.   *She pushed him to it.*
>
> Je **l'en** avais averti.   *I had warned him of it.*

5   The pronouns of column 1 can be used before the one in column 4:

> Vous **m'y** faites penser.   *You make me think of it.*

6   The pronouns of column 4 and 5 can usually be used together:

> Nous **y en** avons discuté.   *We discussed about it there.*

Demonstrative pronouns

Demonstrative pronouns are used to 'single out' the noun they replace. They can be divided into two groups with unequal demonstrative power. Except in the case of neutral pronouns (see below) they vary according to the gender and number of the noun they represent. For example:

> Je vais prendre **celui-ci** et **celle-là**.   *I shall take this one* (masc. sing.) *and that one.* (fem. sing.).

The two groups are as follows:

Simple (one-word) demonstrative pronouns

As their demonstrative power is weak, extra information is needed to clarify the identity of the noun they represent. That is why they have to be accompanied by a relative clause (giving additional information about the noun they refer to, with or without a preposition (**à** *to*, **de** *of*/*from*, **avec** *with*, **contre** *against*, **pour** *for*, **sans** *without*, etc.

		Singular	Plural
Masc.	celui	neutral form =	ceux
		ce	
Fem.	celle		celles

Points to bear in mind regarding the use of these pronouns:

1   The neutral form **ce**, which is still considered as a masculine singular for agreement purposes, is used when the speaker is unable (or unwilling) to ascribe a specific gender or number to the noun which the pronoun replaces.

Compare: Voici des fruits; prenez **celui** que vous voulez.   *Here is some fruit; take the one you wish.* (**fruit** = masc.)

and: Voici des fruits; prenez **ce** que vous voulez.   *Here is some fruit; take what (whatever) you wish.*

or: Il y a trois menus. Choisissez **celui** qui vous plaît.   *There are three menus. Choose the one you like.* (**menu** = masc.)

and: Voilà la carte. Choisissez **ce** qui vous plaît.   *Here is the list of dishes. Choose what you like.*

In the first instance the pronoun refers to a specific noun, so a gender can easily be ascribed to it, whereas in the second, the thing referred to is vague, unspecified.

2   Be sure not to forget to make the necessary gender and number agreements if there are adjectives or past participles involved:

Cette cliente est **celle** qui est venue ce matin. (**cliente** = fem. sing.)   *This customer is the one who came this morning.*

Ces clefs sont **celles** que j'avais laissées sur la table. (**clés** = fem. plur.)   *These keys are the ones I had left on the table.*

3   There are a few cases when the neutral form **ce** can be used without an accompanying clause. It can be explained by the fact that, in such constructions, **ce** is really a modification of **cela**, which belongs to the second category of demonstrative pronouns. For example:

Ce disant, (= en disant cela) il ouvrit le coffre-fort. *As he was saying that, he opened the safe.*

4 **Celui** and **ceux** can often be used to refer to a person or persons of either sex.

Celui qui sortira le dernier fermera la porte. *The person who comes out last will close the door.*

Que **ceux** qui ne sont pas contents le disent. *Let those who are not happy say so.* (*those = the people*)

Compound (two-word) demonstrative pronouns

They are formed by combining the above pronouns with **-ci** (*here*) or **-là** (*there*) to distinguish between things or beings relatively closer or further away, in space or time, from the speaker. They have a very strong demonstrative value and are used to replace a noun preceded by a demonstrative adjective. Unlike the first category, they can function on their own (i.e. without additional information). Their form varies according to the gender and number of the noun they replace.

Note: **ceci**, **cela** and **ça** can be seen as contractions of **ce . . . ici** and **ce . . . là** and therefore deserve the denomination 'compound demonstrative pronouns'.

	Singular		*Plural*
Masc.	celui-ci celui-là	*neutral sense*: ceci cela/ça	ceux-ci ceux-là
Fem.	celle-ci celle-là		celles-ci celles-là

Points to bear in mind regarding the use of these pronouns:

1 Although in theory **-ci** is supposed to refer to someone or something relatively closer in space or time, and **-là** to someone or something relatively further away, pronouns formed with **là** are preferred in everyday French, except in cases where some misunderstanding is likely to occur. For example:

Quel costume prenez-vous, **celui-ci** ou **celui-là**? (costume = masc. sing.) *Which suit are you taking, this one or that one?*

Ouvrez cette fenêtre-ci; **celle-là** est bloquée (fenêtre = fem. sing.) *Open this window; that one won't open.* (lit: *is blocked*)

But: J'ai besoin d'un cendrier; passez-moi **celui-là**. *I need an ash-*
tray; pass me this (or that) one.

2 The neutral forms **ceci** and **cela/ça** (without an accent!), whilst
being considered masculine-singular for the purpose of agreement,
are used when the subject is unable (or unwilling) to ascribe a specific
gender or number to the noun they replace. For example:

Il est toujours en retard; **cela** est irritant. *He is always late; that*
is irritating. (that = the fact that he is always late)

Faites ce que vous voulez, **ça** m'est égal. *Do what you want, it's*
all the same to me. (it = whatever you want to do)

3 **Ça** is used in familiar French to replace **cela** which seems to be
considered as elevated in style. In this case, the pronoun often retains
its vowel *even* when the next word begins with a vowel:

Ça a marché! (fam.) *It worked!*

4 A distinction between what has been said and what is going to be
said can be made by using a pronoun with **-là** (in the first case) and **-ci**
(in the second).

Compare: Ecoutez-bien **ceci**: Je veux que vous partiez à
l'instant. *Listen carefully to this: I want you to go this*
minute.

and: J'exige la vérité, rappelez-vous **cela**. *I demand the truth,*
remember that.

Possessive pronouns

Possessive pronouns are used to replace a 'noun phrase' containing a
possessive adjective or, more generally, whenever ownership needs to
be indicated.

They are equivalent to **mine**, **yours**, **his/hers**, etc. in English:

C'est le sac de ta soeur? Oui c'est **le sien**. *Is it your sister's bag?*
Yes it's hers.

It is crucial to remember that, in French, the possessive pronoun
agrees with the being or thing owned and not with the owner.

Since possessive pronouns replace nouns which can vary in gender
and number, they have different forms to indicate those variations.

Compare: J'ai trouvé un sac. C'est **le mien**! (**sac** = masc. sing.) *I*
have found a bag. It is mine!

and: J'ai trouvé une montre. C'est **la mienne**! (**montre** = fem.
sing.) *I have found a watch. It is mine!*

Owner	person	Owned				
		one		*more than one*		
		masculine	feminine	masculine	feminine	*Meaning*
one	1st	le mien	la mienne	les miens	les miennes	*mine*
	2nd	le tien	la tienne	les tiens	les tiennes	*yours* (familiar)
	2nd	le vôtre	la vôtre	les vôtres	les vôtres	*yours* (polite form)
	3rd	le sien	la sienne	les siens	les siennes	*his/hers/its*
more than one	1st	le nôtre	la nôtre	les nôtres	les nôtres	*ours*
	2nd	le vôtre	la vôtre	les vôtres	les vôtres	*yours* (normal plur.)
	3rd	le leur	la leur	les leurs	les leurs	*theirs*

For example:

Pouvez-vous me prêter une carte? J'ai perdu **la mienne**. *Can you lend me a map? I have lost mine.* (**carte** = fem. sing.)

Ne touchez pas à ces livres; ce sont **les miens**. (**livres** = masc. plur.) *Do not touch those books; they are mine.*

There are a number of points to bear in mind regarding the use of these pronouns:

1 Since those pronouns include a definite article, **le**, **la**, **les**, that article will combine in the normal way with **à** (*at/to*) and **de** (*of/from*) when those prepositions precede the pronoun. For example:

Quand je parle de problèmes, je ne pense pas **aux vôtres** mais **aux miens**. (**problèmes** = masc. plur.) *When I am talking about problems, I am not thinking of yours but of mine.*

2 In some idiomatic expressions it has become difficult, if not impossible, to find out what noun the possessive pronoun stands for. Such expressions have to be remembered and used *as they are*:

A **la vôtre**! *or* A **la** bonne **vôtre**! *Your health!* or *Your very good health!*

Il y met **du sien**. *He is pulling his weight.*

Elle a encore fait **des siennes**. *She has been up to her old tricks again.*

3 Unlike the possessive adjectives, which they resemble, **nôtre** and **vôtre** as pronouns take a circumflex accent in all cases:

Ce n'est pas votre tour, c'est **le nôtre**. *It is not your* (adj.) *turn it's ours.* (pron.)

4 The masculine plural possessives -**les miens**, **les tiens**, etc. — can be used to refer to parents or relatives. For example:

Je vous déteste, vous et **les vôtres**! *I hate you and your family!*

5 The 3rd person singular possessive pronouns -**le sien**, **la sienne**, etc. — can be used with the indefinite subject pronoun **on** (*one/*

somebody) or any other singular indefinite adjective or pronoun with the meaning of *one's own*:

> J'ai apporté les cadeaux: chacun aura **le sien**.   *I have brought the presents: everyone will have his own.*
>
> Voulez-vous ma voiture? Non, tout le monde a **la sienne**.   *Do you want my car? No, they all have their own.*

Relative pronouns

Relative pronouns are words used to connect a noun or phrase they represent (called the antecedent), with a sense-group which follows (called a relative clause) and which contains useful additional information about the antecedent. They correspond to the English pronouns *what, which, who, whom, that*. For example:

> Voici l'*homme* **qui** vous a insulté.   *Here is the man who insulted you.*
>
> Voilà l'*endroit* **où** j'ai vu l'animal.   *There is the spot where I saw the animal.*

(The word in bold is the pronoun; the one in bold italic the antecedent.)

Relative pronouns can be divided into the following two categories:

Simple (one-word) relative pronouns

They do not vary according to the gender or number of the antecedent.

For example:

> C'est lui **qui** est parti le premier.   *It is he who went first.*
>
> Le travail **que** vous faites est excellent.   *The work you are doing is excellent.*
>
> Connaissez-vous la ville **où** je suis né?   *Do you know the town where I was born?*
>
> C'est un film **dont** on parle beaucoup.   *It is a film which people talk a great deal about.*

Note: **que** will lose its **e** when the next word begins with a vowel or a mute 'h' to avoid the vowel-vowel clash:

> J'aime le disque **qu'**il a acheté.   *I like the record he bought:*

Form	Usage	Meaning
qui	It is used to refer to the subject (performer) of the action, whether thing or being. It can be used on its own or with prepositions.	*who/which/whom* (subject)
que	It is used to refer to the object (recipient) of the action, whether thing or being. It *cannot* be used with a preposition.	*that/which/whom* (direct object)
quoi	It is used to refer to things only and is *always* preceded by a preposition.	(*with, on, above*, etc.) *which*
dont	It is used to replace constructions in which the noun was preceded by the preposition **de** (*of/from*). It can refer to things *or* beings.	*of which/of whom/where*
où	It is used to indicate position or destination in space or time. It can be used with certain prepositions: **de**, **par**, **vers**, etc.	*where (when)*

Points to bear in mind when using these pronouns:
1 All the above pronouns, with the exception of **quoi**, can refer to things or beings:

Regardez les rochers **qui** sont tombés. *Look at the rocks which have fallen.*

2 **Quoi**, which refers to things only and must be preceded by a preposition, is very often used in neutral constructions with **ce**, when the gender or number of the thing(s) referred to is not known, or not clearly defined:

Vous savez **ce** à **quoi** je fais allusion. *You know what I am alluding to.* (lit: *that to which I am alluding*)

3 In sentences where the antecedent of the relative pronoun **que** is not clearly stated, the neutral demonstrative **ce** will automatically be used as antecedent. This is *not* the case in English:

Compare: Je ne comprends pas **ce qu'**il veut.
and: *I don't understand what* (lit: *that which*) *he wants.*
or: Faites **ce que** vous pouvez.
and: *Do what* (lit: *that which*) *you can.*

4 Whereas in English it is sometimes acceptable to omit certain relative pronouns, it is not possible to do so in French:

Compare: C'est cette plage **que** je préfère.
and: *It is this beach (that) I prefer.*
or: Le vendeur à **qui** j'ai parlé est malade.
and: *The salesman (whom) I talked to is ill.*

5   Although **qui** and **quoi** can be used immediately after the preposition **de** (*of/from*) to introduce a relative clause, a construction with **dont** will normally be preferred:

Possible: La victime **de qui** j'ai entendu les cris . . .
Preferred: La victime **dont** j'ai entendu les cris . . .
             The victim whose screams I heard . . .
Possible: La chose **de quoi** vous parlez est scandaleuse.
Preferred: La chose **dont** vous parlez est scandaleuse.
             The thing you are talking about is scandalous.

6   Relative pronouns are regularly used after the simple demonstrative pronouns **celui, celle, ceux, celles** (*the one(s)*). For example:

Prenez **celui que** vous préferez.   *Take the one* (masc. sing.) *you prefer.*

Note: **Ce** will be used in such a construction when the speaker does not know, or does not wish to state, what the gender or number of the antecedent is:

Dites-moi **ce qui** vous inquiète.   *Tell me what (the thing which) worries you.*

7   Compound demonstrative pronouns — **celui-ci, celle-là**, etc. — can also be used before single relative pronouns when a very strong demonstrative meaning is required:

Je vais prendre **celui-ci, qui** a l'air plus tendre.   *I shall take this one* (masc. sing.), *which seems more tender.*

Note: In such cases, the demonstrative and the relative pronouns are normally separated by a comma.

8   **Qui** is sometimes used in idiomatic phrases to refer to any individual, male *or* female, with the meaning of *whoever* or *he/she who*:

Qui va à la chasse perd sa place. (*saying*)   *He who leaves the queue loses his place.* (lit: *He who goes hunting . . .*)
Qui dort dîne. (*saying*)   *He who goes to sleep will not feel hunger pangs.* (lit: *He who sleeps dines*)

9   **Que** is sometimes used in proverbs and sayings as a subject pronoun instead of **qui**:

Advienne **que** pourra. (**que** = **ce qui**)   *Come what may.*

10   Certain relative clauses introduced by **qui** can be replaced by a present participle, providing the verb they contain describes an action in progress at the time.

Compare: Je vis mon père **qui** lisait son journal.

and: Je vis mon père **lisant** son journal. *I saw my father (who was) reading his paper.*

In such cases the present participle remains **invariable**.

11 Although the pronoun **où** is generally used to give spatial information, it can also be used in French with expressions of time. Its English equivalent is then *when*:

Compare: C'était l'époque **où** j'étais heureux.

and: *It was the time when I was happy.*

or: Le jour **où** tout ira bien . . . *The day when everything will be fine . . .*

Compound (two-word) relative pronouns

These pronouns are formed by the relevant combination of the definite article *and* the pronoun **quel** (*which*) 'welded' together. They vary according to the gender and number of their antecedent. They are normally used in constructions involving a preposition — **à** (*at/to*), **pour** (*for*), **sans** (*without*), etc. — as are their English equivalents *which/whom*.

	Sing.	*Plur.*
Masc.	lequel	lesquels
Fem.	laquelle	lesquelles

For example:

L' idéal pour **lequel** nous luttons. (**idéal** = masc. sing.) *The ideal which we are fighting for.*

C'est l'homme avec **lequel** je travaille. (**homme** = masc. sing.) *It is the man whom I work with.*

Note: Since those pronouns include the definite article **le, la, les**, it is logical to expect that, when they occur immediately after the prepositions **à** and **de**, they will combine with them in the following way:

with **à**: auquel, à laquelle, auxquels, auxquelles

with **de**: duquel, de laquelle, desquels, desquelles

Ces vacances **auxquelles** je pense sans arrêt. (**vacances** = fem. plur.) *Those holidays which I think about all the time.*

Je ne connais pas l'incident **auquel** vous faites allusion. (**incident** = masc. sing.) *I do not know the incident you are alluding to.*

Points to bear in mind regarding the use of these pronouns:

1   In French, the preposition which is used with the pronoun *must* be placed immediately before it. In English, it is normal to place the preposition at the end of the clause.

Compare: Le stylo **avec lequel** il écrivait.   *The pen (which) he was writing with.*

> The French relative pronoun *cannot* be omitted in any circumstances.

2   In constructions where the compound relative is to appear immediately after the preposition **de**, the use of **dont** is normally preferred. This makes for a shorter, more elegant sentence.

Compare: C'est la vie **de laquelle** il rêve.

and: C'est la vie **dont** il rêve.   *That is the life he is dreaming of.*

or: Les monuments **desquels** vous parlez.

and: Les monuments **dont** vous parlez.   *The monuments you are talking about.*

But: If the antecedent is separated from the relative by a prepositional phrase, **dont** cannot be used:

Ced La dame **dans l'auto** de laquelle j'ai laissé mon sac.   *The lady in whose car I left my bag.*

Le bâtiment **à l'entrée** duquel il se tenait.   *The building at the entrance of which he stood.*

3   **Lequel, laquelle, lesquels, lesquelles** are sometimes used to replace the subject pronoun **qui** to give a feeling of emphasis or to avoid ambiguity.

Il téléphona à sa soeur, **laquelle** lui annonça la nouvelle.   *He telephoned his sister, (and it was she) who told him the news.*

Le fils du boulanger, **lequel** était fort riche, acheta la ferme. *The son of the baker who* (the son) *was very rich, bought the farm.*

Note concerning relative clauses introduced by single or compound pronouns: The learner must bear in mind that agreement rules, whenever applicable, must be respected across clause boundaries.

Les photos **que** nous avons pris**es** et **qui** sont prêt**es**, sont excellent**es**.   *The photos that we took and which are ready are excellent.*

The participle and adjectives agree with **photos** = fem. plur.

Interrogative pronouns

Interrogative pronouns are used to formulate direct or indirect questions (see below) about the thing(s) or being(s) they relate to.

With the exception of **dont**, they are identical with the relative pronouns presented in the preceding section. They are the equivalents of the English interrogatives *who, whom, what, where,* etc. They can, with the exception of **que** (*what*), be used with a preposition which will be placed immediately before them. For example:

Pour qui travaillez-vous? *Who do you work for?*

Avec quoi écrivez-vous? *What are you writing with?*

As in the case of the relatives, we shall divide them into two categories:

Simple (one-word) interrogative pronouns

Form	Usage	Meaning
Qui . . . ?	It is used to refer to persons only. It can be used alone or with a preposition.	*Who? Whom?*
Que . . . ?	It is used to refer to things or non-human beings only. It cannot be used with a preposition.	*What?*
Quoi . . . ?	It is used to formulate a question about things when a preposition is present. (it can also be used on its own in a small number of cases.)	*(With, For, on . . .) What?*
Où . . . ?	It is used to ask information about the position or destination of a thing or being. It can be used with *or* without a preposition	*Where?*

For example:

Qui est là? *Who is there?*

Que décidons-nous? *What are we deciding?*

Par quoi allez-vous commencer? *What are you going to begin with?*

Où veux-tu aller? *Where do you want to go?*

Note: When followed by a word beginning with a vowel, or a mute 'h', **que** becomes **qu'** to avoid the vowel-vowel clash:

Qu' avez-vous dit? *What did you say?*

Qu' est-ce qu'il y a? *What is the matter?*

Compound (two-word) interrogative pronouns

Their two constitutive elements (matching definite article and pronoun) are 'welded' together. They vary according to the gender and number of the thing(s) or being(s) they refer to and their use suggests the formulation of a choice. They correspond to the English pronoun *Which one(s)?*

	Sing.	*Plur.*
Masc.	lequel	lesquels
Fem.	laquelle	lesquelles

Notes:
1   The above pronouns combine with the prepositions **à** and **de** in precisely the same way as the similar relative pronouns:

> **Auquel** de ces deux livres tenez-vous le plus? (**livre** = masc.)
> *Which one of those books do you value most?*
> J'ai deux frères. **Duquel** parlez-vous? (**frère** = masc.)   *I have two brothers. Which one are you talking about?*

2   Compound interrogative pronouns can be used on their own or with a preposition:

> J'ai vu un des dossier. Ah oui? **Lequel?**   *I saw one of the files. Oh yes? Which one?*
> Ils ont deux filles. **Avec laquelle** sortez-vous?   *They have two daughters. Which one are you going out with?*

Points to bear in mind regarding the use of simple and compound interrogative pronouns:
1   Simple (one-word) pronouns do *not* carry any gender or number information. They can therefore refer to any number of things or beings of either gender:

> **Qui** est venu à la réunion?   *Who came to the meeting?*
> **Où** irez-vous? En France, en Espagne et au Portugal!   *Where will you go? To France, Spain and Portugal!*
> **Que** plantez-vous? Des légumes!   *What are you planting? Vegetables!*

2   **Qui, quoi** and **où** can be used on their own or with a preposition:

> **Qui** viendra me chercher?   *Who will come and fetch me?*
> **Avec qui** partez-vous?   *Who are you going with?*
> **Où** se cachent-ils?   *Where are they hiding?*
> **Par où** sont-ils descendus?   *Which way did they go down?*

3   All interrogative pronouns can be used in elliptical (i.e. shortened) constructions with an infinitive. In such cases, the performer of the action is not stated but the context should make

things clear. In the following examples *one* is arbitrarily used as the subject.

Qui croire? *Who is one to believe?*
Que faire? *What should one do?*
Où aller? *Where should one go?*
or: **Lequel** choisir? *Which (one) should one choose?*

4 Questions are classified into two distinct categories:

(*a*) Those asked *directly* to someone, as in a face to face dialogue. In this case, the question stands on its own as an independent clause (this is the case in all the above examples), and ends with a question mark.

(*b*) Those asked *indirectly*. In this case, it is as if the speaker were asking the question to himself. Indirect questions normally follow a main clause in which verbs like **se demander** (*to wonder*), **ne pas savoir** (*not to know*), **n'être pas sûr** (*not to be sure*) etc. are used.

Compare: **Avec qui** déjeunez-vous? (direct)
Who are you having lunch with?
and: Je ne sais pas **avec qui** vous déjeunez. (indirect)
I do not know who you are having lunch with.

The distinction between direct and indirect questions is important because the word order used in the formulation of the question may differ:

In direct questions there is (normally) an inversion: the verb is followed by the pronoun. For example:

Où sont-ils? *Where are they?*
Avec quoi écrirez-vous? *What will you write with?*

In indirect questions there is no inversion: the normal word order is preserved. For example:

Je ne sais pas **où** ils sont. *I do not know where they are.*
Je me demande **avec quoi** vous écrirez. *I wonder what you will write with.*

Note: Question marks are *not* used at the end of indirect questions.

5 In ordinary French (written and spoken) it is possible to formulate questions about people in the following ways. Instead of just beginning a question with **qui** we can say **Qui est-ce qui** . . . (subject) or **Qui est-ce que** . . . (object). For example:

Qui est-ce qui parle? = **Qui** parle? *Who is speaking?*
Qui est-ce que vous invitez? = **Qui** invitez-vous? *Who are you inviting?*

6   It is also possible to formulate questions about things or non-human beings in a similar way. Instead of beginning a question with **que** we can say **Qu'est-ce qui** . . . (subject-with impersonal verbs) or **Qu'est-ce que** . . . (object). For example:

> **Qu'est-ce qui** se passe? = **Que** se passe t-il?   *What is happening?*
> **Qu'est-ce que** tu fais? = **Que** fais-tu?   *What are you doing?*

7   It is possible to use similar structures with **où** (or **quoi** if preceded by a preposition). For example:

> **Où est-ce qu'**ils habitent? = **Où** habitent ils?   *Where do they live?*

Note: The above alternative structures can be used with a preposition, *except* when they replace que, as in 6 above:

> **Avec qui est-ce que** tu sors?   *Who are you going out with?*
> **D'où est-ce que** tu viens?   *Where are you coming from?*

The less elevated but nevertheless correct ways of formulating a question outlined in 5, 6 and 7 above, eliminate the need for a change in word order, often perceived as highbrow by ordinary speakers. This perception explains why, in 'spoken' French, the inversion is often not made, *even* in the absence of the alternatives mentioned above.

Compare: **Où** vas-tu?   ('good' French)
> **Où est-ce que** tu vas?   ('ordinary' French)
> **Où** tu vas?   ('spoken' French)   *Where are you going?*

or: **A qui** téléphonez-vous?   ('good' French)
> **A qui est-ce que** vous téléphonez?   ('ordinary' French)
> **A qui** vous téléphonez?   ('spoken' French)
> *Who are you telephoning?*

> **De quoi** parliez-vous?   ('good' French)
> **De quoi est-ce que** vous parliez?   ('ordinary' French)
> **De quoi** vous parliez?   ('spoken' French)
> *What were you talking about?*

Indefinite pronouns

Indefinite pronouns are used when no precise indications are given about the identity — or number — of things or beings referred to. They correspond to the English pronouns *everybody*, *nobody*, *people*, *someone/somebody* etc.

Note: If an indefinite pronoun does not have a plural form, it cannot be used in a plural construction; conversely, if a pronoun has no singular form, it cannot be used in a singular construction.

So, you must say or write:	**Quelqu'un a** frappé. *Someone knocked.*
and not:	*__Quelqu'un ont__ frappé.
or:	**Plusieurs ont** péri. *Several perished.*
and not:	* **Plusieurs a** péri.
or:	**Tout le monde est** malade. *Everyone is ill.*
and not:	* **Tout le monde sont** malades.

It is very important to remember those constraints to avoid making strings of agreement mistakes. For example:

Chacun est content. *Everyone* (masc. sing.) *is happy.*
Chacune est contente. *Everyone* (fem. sing.) *is happy.*
Certains sont descendus. *Some* (masc. plur.) *went down.*
Certaines sont descendues. *Some* (fem. plur.) *went down.*
On s'était perdu dans le noir. *One* (masc. sing. i.e. *people*) *had got lost in the dark.*

Points to bear in mind regarding the use of these pronouns:

1 The pronouns of Group I (meaning = 'none') are normally used with the negative particle **ne**. For example:

Personne n'a voulu attendre. *Nobody wanted to wait.*
Rien n'a changé. *Nothing has changed.*
Aucun ne bougea. *No-one* (masc. sing.) *moved.*

In such sentences, the **verb** is in the **singular** and the negative particle **pas** must *not* be used.

2 Very rarely, the expression **d'aucuns** (*some people*) can be encountered in sentences of the type:

D'aucuns disent que . . . *Some people say that . . .*

3 **Autrui** is used as a masculine singular, usually with a preposition:

Soyez bon **envers autrui**. *Be kind to your fellow-beings.*

4 **Certains, certaines** (*some*), are only used in the plural:

Certains disent qu'il a quitté sa femme. *Some say he has left his wife.*

5 The pronouns **l'un, l'autre**, etc. are often used in the same sentence to distinguish between two individual things or beings or two groups:

La vieille avait deux fils; **l'un** était médecin, **l'autre** journaliste. *The old woman had two sons; one was a doctor, the other (was) a journalist.*

6 There is often hesitation as to whether agreement with **plus d'un** should be in the singular or the plural. Both are usually accepted and you could say or write

either: **Plus d'un a** refusé.
or: **Plus d'un ont** refusé.
More than one refused.

| | VARIATIONS | | | | MEANING | |
| | Singular | | Plural | | | |
	masc.	fem.	masc.	fem.	sing.	plur.
GROUP I number referred	aucun	aucune (nulle)	—	—	no-one	—
	nul		—	—	none	—
	pas un	pas une	—	—	{ not a single one	—
to = none	personne	—	—	—	nobody	—
	rien	—	—	—	nothing	—
GROUP II	—	—	d'aucuns	d'aucunes	—	some (people)
	autrui	—	—	—	{ every fellow human	—
	—	—	certains	certaines	—	some
number	chacun	chacune	—	—	each one	—
	le même	la même	les mêmes	les mêmes	the same one	the same ones
referred to =	{l'un	l'une	les uns	les unes	one	some
one or more	{l'autre	l'autre	les autres	les autres	the other	(the) others

n'importe qui	—	—	—	anyone / whatever	—
n'importe quoi	—	—	—	anything / whatever	—
plus d'un	plus d'une	plus d'un	plus d'une	more than one	more than one
quelqu'un	quelqu'une	quelques-uns	quelques-unes	someone	some (people)
qui que	—	—	—	whoever	—
quiconque	—	—	—	whosoever	—
quoi que	—	—	—	whatever	—
tel	telle	tels	telles	such (a)	such
tout	toute	tous	toutes	everything / everyone	all
tout le monde	—	—	—	everybody	—

NB   The dashes signal that certain forms of a given pronoun are not available; any necessary agreement (of verbs, adjectives, past participles) should be made accordingly.

7   **Qui que** (*whoever*) and **quoi que** (*whatever*) are both used as masculine singulars and *must* be followed by a verb in the subjunctive mood:

  Quoi que vous fassiez, vous ne gagnerez pas.   *Whatever you do you shall not win.*

8   **On** (*one*) is used in singular constructions as a subject pronoun

  On mange pour vivre.   *One eats (in order) to survive.*

In addition, **on** may sometimes be used to replace any one of the subject pronouns in familiar French:

  On sort ce soir?   *Are we going out tonight?*

  Ah je vois, **on** se repose!   *Oh I see, you are having a rest!*

  On travaille dur au Japon.   *They work hard in Japan.*

9   **Quiconque** (*whoever*) is always used as a masculine singular and any agreement should be made accordingly:

  Quiconque a accepté ne le regrettera pas!   *Whoever agreed shall not regret it!*

10   Although **tout** is generally used with the meaning of *everything*, it can also mean *everyone*. In both cases, agreement is made in the singular.

Compare: **Tout** est en ordre.   *Everything is in order.*

and: **Tout** dormait dans la ville.   *Everyone was asleep in the town.*

Key points

1   Pronouns are grammatical words used to replace noun-phrases, thereby avoiding tiresome repetitions. They can, in certain circumstances, even replace whole sentences.

2   There are six distinct categories of pronouns: personal, demonstrative, possessive, relative, interrogative and indefinite. Each of these has a specific grammatical role.

3   Personal pronouns serve to indicate the performer(s) or recipient(s) of an action. *Note*: It should be remembered that the French system makes it *imperative* that *all* suitable agreements (masculine/feminine, singular/plural) of adjectives, past participles, etc. be made as appropriate.

4   The indefinite pronoun **on** can only be used as a subject pronoun and *must*, in 'good' French, be followed by the 3rd person singular of the relevant verb.

5   Direct object (accusative) pronouns must *not* be confused with indirect object (dative) pronouns. The former replace the direct object complement (answer to **qui?/quoi?**). The latter replace the indirect object complement (answer to **à qui?/à quoi?**).

6   There are very clear rules for the agreement of the past participle in transitive and intransitive constructions. Those rules should be followed faithfully.

7   Certain verbs function differently in the two languages; their construction (accusative, dative, etc.) should be carefully checked, since the choice of the suitable pronoun is dictated by the type of construction involved.

8   Disjunctive pronouns must be used after prepositions (**à, de, pour, sans,** etc.). In addition, they may appear in certain circumstances to replace *or* reinforce subject pronouns.

9   Reflexive pronouns serve to indicate constructions in which the action performed by the subject 'falls back' upon him/her (reflexive) or affects someone else, who in turn reciprocates (reciprocal).

10   Although a small number of verbs *cannot* be used in non-reflexive (or more accurately non-pronominal) constructions, e.g. **s'enfuir** (*to escape*), **s'évanouir** (*to faint*), etc., many others can be constructed non-reflexively as well as reflexively.

11   The prescribed rules of gender and number agreement apply in reflexive constructions whenever appropriate.

12   The relative position of the above pronouns in a sentence is fixed and the rules governing it must be adhered to. It should be noted, however, that a special set of rules applies if the verb is in the Imperative *positive* Tense.

13   Demonstrative pronouns are used to 'single out' the noun they replace. If, for any reason, special emphasis is required, simple (one word) pronouns may be reinforced with the use of the appropriate particle **-ci** (*here*) or **-là** (*there*).

14   The neutral form **ce** (*this/that*) is used whenever it is not possible — or desirable — to ascribe a definite gender or number to the thing(s) referred to.

15   Possessive pronouns agree in gender *and* number with the noun of the thing(s) or being(s) 'owned' and not, as in English, with that of the 'owner'.

16   Relative pronouns are used to introduce subordinate (relative) clauses. Those pronouns *represent* the noun-phrase expressed in the (preceding) main clause.

17   In French, it is *not possible* to omit relative pronouns.

18   Relative pronouns preceded by **de** are normally replaced by **dont** (*whose/of which*).

19   Interrogative pronouns are used to formulate direct or indirect questions. With the exceptions of **dont**, they are identical with the relative pronouns. It must be remembered that the word order in *direct* questions is often not the same as in *indirect* ones.

20   Indefinite pronouns are used when no precise indications are available about the gender or number of things or beings referred to.

21   Indefinite pronouns can be divided into two groups:

(*a*)   those referring to 'zero things or beings'. They are used in *negative* constructions with **ne** (but *not* with **pas**) and the verb of the sentence *must* be in the singular;

(*b*)   those referring to 'one or more things or beings'. With those, the correct gender *and* number agreements *must* be made as appropriate.

22   Some indefinite pronouns have no singular form. Others have no plural. Any necessary agreement (of verb, adjective(s), etc.) must be made accordingly.

SECTION II

*Some More Jigsaw Pieces:
The Verb and Its Associates*

12 Tenses, Moods, Voices; Types of Verbs

Note: This is an important chapter which you are advised to read carefully before proceeding to the study of verbs.

General introduction to Tenses

Language learners are sometimes disconcerted by the large number of tenses which are used in French, as in other languages, to situate events in time. Yet those tenses are necessary to give our speech the shades of meaning needed for efficient and unambiguous communication.

Different languages have different ways of indicating whether something happens regularly, is happening now, happened in the past, will happen in the future, would happen (or have happened) if . . . , etc. Such information is usually conveyed by one of several tenses.

In French, tenses can be divided into 2 categories:

1 Tenses where the verbal group is made up of one word only; they are called *simple tenses*. The verb is made up of two distinct sections 'welded' together: a stem and an ending. Whereas the stem will remain reasonably stable, the ending will vary according *to the person performing* the action and also *according to the tense required*: In the following examples the stem is marked in bold, the ending is italic:

Nous **regard**_ons_   *We are looking* (Present)

Je **parl**_ais_   *I was talking* (Imperfect)

Elle **arriver**_a_   *She will arrive* (Future)

2 Tenses where the verbal group is made up of several words (usually two): the auxiliary and the main verb; such tenses are called *compound tenses*. In this category, the main verb will remain reasonably stable; it is the auxiliary which has the task of indicating the performer(s) of the action *and* the tense used. A closer look at the auxiliary will reveal that it is itself made up of a stem and an ending. In the following examples the stem of the auxiliary is marked in bold, the ending in bold italic, and the main verb in italic:

Nous **avons** regardé   *We have looked* (Perfect)
J'**avais** parlé   *I had talked* (Pluperfect)
Elle **sera** arrivée   *She will have arrived* (Future Perfect)
Note: There are sometimes slight variations in the way a verb is divided into a stem and ending. This will be clarified at a later stage.
3   Two auxiliaries are used in French for the formation of compound tenses: **avoir** (*to have*) and **être** (*to be*). They cannot be used at random: certain categories of verbs take **avoir**, others take **être**. This will also be clarified in the next chapter.

The Six Moods and their Tenses

Tenses are grouped into broader categories called Moods. Each Mood is used to convey specific shades of meaning and includes both simple and compound tenses. There are six distinct Moods in French: four Personal Moods (so called because they make it possible, through the person of the verb used, to determine the 'identity' of the performer(s) of the action), and two Impersonal Moods, (so labelled because they give no indication at all about the performer(s) of the action).

Each of those Moods, along with the currently used tenses within it, is presented below.

The Indicative Mood

It is used to indicate the straightforward occurrence of an action along the time-axis. Its tenses are as follows:

The Present
Formation: Stem + endings of the relevant group.
Usage: The present is used to indicate:
1   That an action is occurring at this precise moment:
   Il **mange.**   *He is eating.*
2   That an action has been occurring for a while and is likely to continue for some time to come:
   Il **mange** trop.   *He eats too much.*
Note: If a distinction between the two is required, it is possible to use an expression which will indicate the fact that the action is in progress: that expression is **être en train de** (*to be in the process of*). For example:
   Il **est en train de manger.**   *He is eating (at this very moment).*
3   an 'eternal' truth valid for all times:
   Le crime ne **paie** pas.   *Crime does not pay.*

4 eagerness or anticipation:
Nous **partons** en vacances demain. *We are going on holiday tomorrow.*
5 a veiled order:
Tu **prends** le train de huit heures! *You are taking the eight o'clock train!*
6 the dramatic importance of an action which would normally be expressed in the Perfect Tense:
Il s'est arrêté au coin de la rue. Soudain il **se retourne**. . . *He stopped at the street-corner. Suddenly he turned* (lit: *turns*) *round* . . .

The Immediate Future
Formation: Present of **aller** (*to go*) + Infinitive of main verb.
Usage: This tense is used to state that an action is going to happen soon:
Nous **allons acheter** une voiture. *We are going to buy a car.*
Note: In spoken French, this tense is often used instead of a Future.

The Immediate Past
Formation: Present of **venir** (*to come*) + **de** + Infinitive of main verb.
Usage: This tense is used to indicate that an action has just taken place:
Ils **viennent de sortir**. *They have just gone out.*

The Past Historic
Formation: Stem + endings of the relevant group.
Usage: It is used to indicate that an isolated, finite event took place at a given time in the past:
Elle le **vit** et **courut** vers lui. *She saw him and ran towards him.*
It is crucial to remember that the Past Historic can be used to indicate actions which may have lasted a long time, but that the duration (or even repetition) of those actions is seen as *non-important*. The occurrence of the action is the key-point. That is why the Past Historic is the ideal tense for biographies and reports of past events.

    A   B
Il **naquit** à Paris en 1923. Il **fit** ses études au Lycée Montaigne,
       C   D
puis il **alla** à la Sorbonne où il **passa** trois ans . . .
He was born in Paris in 1923. He studied at the Lycée Montaigne, then went to the Sorbonne where he spent three years . . .

In the above example, the periods of study obviously lasted several years and the person attended regularly; but the tense *merely* records the events as having happened separately along the time-axis:

Past   Present   Future

A   B   C   D

Note: Nowadays, the Past Historic is often avoided, particularly in spoken French, because it is seen as 'affected', and replaced by the Perfect (see below). But in good written style, its use is still recommended.

The Perfect

Formation: Present of **avoir/être** + Past Participle of main verb.

Usage: The Perfect is now used in *everyday speech* to replace the Past Historic:

> Il **est descendu** à huit heures et **a commandé** son petit-déjeuner. *He came down at eight o'clock and ordered his breakfast.*

Note: The above example could be formulated in the Past Historic with the same meaning:

> Il **descendit** à huit heures et **commanda** son petit-déjeuner.

The Perfect (as the Past Historic which it often replaces), is used to indicate the *occurrence* in the past of isolated, finite actions along the time-axis, *without placing any emphasis* on their duration.

Note: The combination Perfect + Present is sometimes used in spoken French as an alternative to the more formal Future Perfect + Future.

So you may say: Quand tu **as fini**, tu **viens** me voir.

                     Perfect   Present

as well as: Quand tu **auras fini**, tu **viendras** me voir.

                     Fut. Perfect   Future

                     When you have finished you will come and see me.

The Imperfect

Formation: Stem + Imperfect endings (identical for all groups).

Usage: This tense is used to emphasise the duration, repetition or habitual occurrence of an action in the past. In English, the Imperfect is marked by structures like *was . . . ing, used to . . . , was in the habit of . . .* or sometimes *would* (i.e. *used to*). A list of the most common shades of meaning this tense conveys is given below:

1   It is used to indicate that an action *was in progress* when another isolated action occurred:

Les enfants **dormaient** quand nous sommes rentrés. *The children were asleep* (i.e. *sleeping*) *when we came home.*

2 It serves to indicate that an action *used to happen* regularly in the past. Here again, it is the *duration or repetitive aspect* which is emphasised, as opposed to the mere 'recording' of the event.

Compare: Il **allait** au restaurant tous les jours. (Imperfect)
He used to go to the restaurant every day.

and: Il **alla** au restaurant tous les jours. (Past Historic)
He went to the restaurant every day.

In the second example, all the visits to the restaurant are seen as *one global event.*

3 It is used to indicate that an action, through its lasting or recurring quality, used to be *characteristic of a given period* in the past:

Quand j'**étais** jcune, je **sortais** souvent.
Imperf. Imperf.
When I was young, I used to go out often.

4 It is sometimes used instead of the Perfect (or Past Historic) to dramatise an event, to give it special prominence.

Les Alliés **ont débarqué** le six juin. Quelques semaines plus
Perf.
tard, ils **libéraient** Paris.
Imperf.
The Allies landed on 6th June. A few weeks later, they liberated Paris.

In this latter sense, the Imperfect should be used seldom and with great care by learners.

---

5 It is used *in conjunction with the Present Conditional* in sentences with **si** (*if*) expressing a condition:

Si j'**avais** le temps je leur **écrirais**
Imperf. Pres. Cond.
If I had time I would write to them.

Note: Structures similar to those of the Immediate Future and Immediate Past presented earlier, but using the Imperfect of **aller** (*to go*), or **venir** (*to come*), make it possible to express such shades of meaning as *was/were about to . . .* or *had just . . .* respectively:

J'allais partir quand il a appelé. *I was about to leave when he rang.*

Vous **veniez de partir** quand il est arrivé. *You had just left when he arrived.*

Both constructions are normally used in conjunction with a Perfect (or Past Historic).

The Pluperfect

Formation: Imperfect of **avoir/être** + Past Participle of main verb.
Usage: The Pluperfect is used:
1   To indicate that a past action was totally completed at the time another action occurred. The importance placed on the completed aspect of the action rather than on its simple occurrence, makes it an ideal partner for the Imperfect when it is necessary to highlight the repetition of certain events in the past. For example:

    Quand il **avait bu** il nous **racontait** sa vie.
           Pluperf.   Imperf.
    When he was drunk (had been drinking) he used to tell us his life-story.

    Lorsqu'elle **avait fini** le ménage, elle **lisait** un roman.
           Pluperf.   Imperf.
    When(ever) she had finished the housework she used to read a novel.

2   To present a request in a very polite almost apologetic way:

    J'avais pensé que vous **apprécieriez** . . .
      Pluperf.   Prest. Cond.
    I had thought you would appreciate . . .

3   In conjunction with the Conditional Perfect, in sentences with **si** (*if*) expressing a condition:

    Si **j'avais su**, je ne **serais pas venu**
        Pluperf.   Cond. Perf.
    Had I known (lit. *if I had known*), *I would not have come.*

Note: In such a sentence, the condition is purely academic because it is too late to alter the course of events.

4   In indirect speech, to indicate that the action it describes came before another action expressed in the Perfect (or Past Historic).

    Il **a dit** qu'il **avait oublié**. (indirect speech)
    Perf.   Pluperf.
    He said that he had forgotten.

which corresponds to: Il a dit: "J'ai oublié". (direct speech)
                        He said: "I have forgotten".

The Past Anterior

Formation: Past Historic of **avoir/être** + Past Participle of main verb.
Usage: This tense is used to indicate the occurrence of an isolated event in the past, *before* another isolated event took place. This makes

it the ideal partner of the Past Historic (or Perfect) to indicate a close correlation between two actions, *without any reference* to duration or repetition. For example:

Dès qu'il **eut terminé**, tout le monde **applaudit**.
Past Ant.   Past Hist.
As soon as he had finished, everybody clapped.

Quand elle **fut partie** il **se leva**.
Past. Ant.   Past. Hist.
When she had gone, he got up.

Note: The use of such expressions as: **après que** (*after*), **aussitôt que/dès que** (*as soon as*), **lorsque/quand** (*when*), emphasises the logical link which exists between the two actions expressed in that type of sentence.

NB: In short, the Past Anterior is to the Past Historic what the Pluperfect is to the Imperfect (or what the Future Perfect is to the Future).

Double Compound Tense (Passé surcomposé)

Because of the loss of popularity of the Past Historic in spoken French, an alternative tense had to be introduced to replace the Past Anterior which was also perceived as 'affected'. That alternative tense is constructed as follows:

Present of **avoir** + Past Participle of the relevant Auxiliary + Past Participle of main verb.

Thus: Quand elle **fut partie,** il **se leva**.
Past. Ant.   Past. Hist.

becomes: Quand elle **a éte partie**, il **s'est levé**.
Passé surcomp.   Perfect

and: Dès qu'il **eut terminé**, tout le monde **applaudit**.
Past Ant.   Past. Hist.

becomes: Dès qu'il **a eu terminé**, tout le monde **a applaudi**.
Passé surcomp.   Perfect

Note: Other **Temps surcomposés** may be constructed on the same pattern, as spoken alternatives to less frequent compound tenses.

Future

Formation: Stem + endings (identical for all verbs).

Usage: The Future is used:

1   To indicate *objectively* that an event will take place at some time in the future:

Nous **reviendrons** demain. *We shall come back tomorrow.*

Vous **finirez** cette lettre tout à l'heure. *You will finish this letter in a while.*

Note: A subjective overtone may be introduced if the future is replaced by an Immediate Future or a Present.

Compare: Nous **partirons** ce soir. (Future = objective statement)
We shall leave this evening.

and: Nous **allons partir** ce soir. (Immed. Fut. = eagerness)
We are going to leave this evening.

or: Nous **partons** ce soir. (Present = eagerness/veiled order)
We are leaving this evening.

2   A moral obligation, an order, a request:

Tu ne **tueras** point.   *Thou shalt not kill.*

Je vous **demanderai** de garder cela pour vous.   *I would like you to keep that to yourself.*

Future Perfect

Formation: Future of **avoir/être** + Past Participle of main verb.

Usage: This tense is normally used in conjunction with the Future, to indicate that the completion of an action will precede, and to some extent determine, the occurrence of another action:

Quand tu **auras fini** le travail je te **paierai**.
    Fut. Perf.   Fut.
When you have finished the work I shall pay you.

Note the difference in timing between:

Vous sortirez quand la cloche **sonnera**.

You will go out when the bell rings.

and: Vous sortirez quand la cloche **aura sonné**.

You will go out when the bell has rung (has stopped ringing).

The Future Perfect is also used to indicate:

1   That an action will soon be over:

J'**aurai fini** la réparation à midi.   *I will have finished the repairs by lunchtime.*

2   That an action is very likely to have happened:

Ils **se seront perdus** dans les bois.   *They will have got lost in the woods* (they most probably have).

Tu **auras** mal **compris**.   *You must have misunderstood.*

The Conditional Mood

This Mood is normally used to indicate the possible occurrence of an action if certain conditions were (or had been) met. In addition, it can convey other shades of meaning (polite request, guarded statement etc.) which will be examined in turn.

The two most commonly used tenses in this mood are the Present and the Perfect.

The Present

Formation: Stem + endings (identical for all groups).

Important: The *stem* used to form this tense is *exactly the same* as the one used for the Future. In addition, the *endings are the same* as those of the Imperfect.

Usage: The Present Conditional is used:

1 To express the idea that an action would occur, *in the present or the future*, if certain conditions were met:

    Si j'**avais** de l'argent j'**achèterais** un bateau.
       Imperf.   Pres. Cond.
    If I had money I would buy a boat.

Note: In this type of structure, the Conditional can *only* be used in conjunction with an Imperfect. So you must say:

    Si nous **étions** riches, nous **serions** heureux.
          Imperf.   Pres. Cond
    If we were rich we would be happy.

(and not *Si nous **serions** riches nous **serions** heureux).

2 To soften a command into a polite request:

    Nous **voudrions** une chambre pour deux personnes.   *We would like a double room.*

3 To express longings, vague desires or wishes

    J'**aimerais** voyager.   *I would like to travel.*

4 To announce the occurrence of a present or future event which has not yet been *officially* confirmed:

    Le Président **arriverait** demain à Paris.   (*According to rumours*) *the President will arrive in Paris tomorrow.*

    Selon la radio française, la Reine **serait** souffrante.   *According to French radio, the Queen is unwell.*

Note: This use of the Conditional is very frequent in Radio and Television broadcasts.

5 To express a strong feeling about a present or future action (disbelief, anger, scorn):

    Il me **donnerait** des conseils!   *He has the audacity to give me advice!*

The Perfect

Formation: Present Conditional of **avoir**/**être** + Past Participle of main verb.

Usage: This tense is used:

1   To express the idea that an action *might have occurred* if certain conditions had been met:

   Si j'**avais su**, je ne **serais pas venu**.
   Pluperf.   Cond. Perf.
   If I had known, I would not have come.

Note: In this type of structure, it can *only* be used in conjunction with the Pluperfect.

You must say: Si nous **avions** été riches, nous **aurions** été heureux.
   If we had been rich, we would have been happy.

and not: *si nous **aurions** été riches nous **aurions** été heureux.

2   To express regrets for lost opportunities:

   J'aurais aimé la revoir.   *I would have liked to have seen her again.*

3   To announce the *unconfirmed* occurrence of a recent event:

   Selon lui, trois personnes **auraient été** blessées.   *According to him three people have been wounded.*

The Imperative Mood

This Mood is used for the formulation of commands, request, directives or advice.

   Note that the tenses which compose it have only three persons each — 2nd person singular, 1st person plural, 2nd person plural — and that no subject pronoun is used. The Tenses are as follows:

The Present

Formation: Stem + endings of the relevant group.
Usage: The Present Imperative is used:

1   To formulate a command or a warning:

   Mange ta soupe! (2nd pers. sing.)   *Eat your soup!*
   Ne **regardez** pas! (2nd pers. plur.)   *Don't look!*

2   To express a request, suggestion, or advice:

   Essayons encore! (1st pers. plur.)   *Let's try again!*
   Prenez votre temps. (2nd pers. plur.)   *Take your time.*

3   To give instructions:

   Prenez la deuxième route à gauche, et **continuez** tout droit. *Take the second road on your left and carry straight on.*

Notes:

1   In order to soften the strong command value of this tense, it is possible, in the second person plural, to use **veuillez** (*would you please*) followed by an Infinitive:

Veuillez me suivre. *Would you please follow me.*

Veuillez accepter l'assurance de mes meilleurs sentiments. (polite formula to end a letter) *Yours faithfully* (lit: *please accept the assurance of my best feelings*)

2 The Present Imperative can be used as an alternative to the **si** clause of a sentence expressing a condition, *provided* the verb of the main clause is in the Present or the Future Indicative.

Compare: **Ayez** bon coeur, on vous exploite.

and: Si vous avez bon coeur, on vous exploite.

If you are kind-hearted, people exploit you.

or: **Soyez** sévère, on vous craindra.

and: Si vous êtes sévère, on vous craindra.

If you are strict, people will fear you.

The Perfect

Formation: Present Imperative of **avoir/être** + Past Participle of main verb.

Usage: This tense is used to indicate that an order, a request, a directive, etc. will have to have been carried out by a certain time given as a deadline.

Soyez parti à mon retour. *I want you gone when I return.*

Ayez fait vos valises quand je monterai. *Have your cases packed when I come up.*

Note: Since the Imperative has only 3 persons, it often borrows from the subjunctive the 3rd persons singular and plural to complement its range.

Qu'il **entre**. *Let him come in.*

Qu'ils **mangent** de la brioche! *Let them eat cake!*

The Subjunctive Mood

This Mood is generally used to indicate that an action is envisaged as a vague possibility, a thought, a hypothetical event *and not* as a reality or a certainty.

That is why the Subjunctive is found, in subordinate clauses, after a verb or phrase expressing command, desire, doubt, fear, urgent request, etc. In addition (see Unit 16, pages 203–4 on conjunctions), certain expressions used to introduce a subordinate clause *must be* followed by a Subjunctive. Although this Mood is essentially the Mood of subordinate clauses, it may also be found in main or independent clauses (an independent clause is a clause which is not followed by a subordinate one), to express a strong feeling (enthusiasm, anger), a desire or a wish:

Vive la République!   *Long live the Republic!*
Que dieu vous **garde**!   *May God be with you!*

Important: Using the subjunctive is *not* a matter of choice. Because of its overtones, that Mood must only be used in the appropriate context.

The Tenses which are relevant to our study are presented below.

The Present
Formation: Stem + endings (identical for nearly all verbs).

The two auxiliaries **avoir** (*to have*) and **être** (*to be*) do not follow the pattern exactly (see detailed conjugation charts in the next chapter).

Usage: the Present Subjunctive is used to express the hypothetical or possible occurrence of an action *in the present or the future*:

Je ne crois pas qu'il **parle**.   *I do not believe he will talk (now or later)*.

The present Subjunctive must be used after main clauses containing the following:

1   (*a*) Verbs expressing an order, a request (positive = do or negative = do not), a wish:
   commander (*to command*), **demander** (*to ask*), **exiger** (*to demand*), **ordonner** (*to order*), **préférer** (*to prefer*), **souhaiter** (*to wish*), **vouloir**, (*to want*), etc.

   (*b*) Expressions also indicating those shades of meaning:
   il faut (or **il faudrait**) **que/il est nécessaire que** (*it is necessary that*), **il est recommandé que** (*it is recommended that*), **il est souhaitable que** (*it is desirable that*), **il serait bon que** (*it would be advisable that*), etc.

   Nous voulons que vous **restiez**.   *We want you to stay.*

   Il faut que vous **achetiez** le disque.   *You must buy the record.*

Note: The impersonal structure: **il est** + adjective + **que** *must be* followed by the subjunctive, *except* if the adjective expresses an obvious, inescapable fact (in which case the Indicative will be used):

Compare: Il est important que vous **répondiez**. (Subj.)
            It is important that you answer.
and: Il est clair que vous **répondrez**. (Indic.)
            It is clear that you will answer.
or: Il est souhaitable qu'il **réussisse**. (Subj.)
            It is desirable that he should succeed.
and: Il est certain qu'il **réussira**. (Indic.)
            It is certain that he will succeed.

2 (*a*) Verbs expressing doubt, fear, longing, regret: **avoir peur que** (*to be afraid that*), **craindre que** (*to fear that*), **douter que** (*to doubt that*), **regretter que** (*to regret that*), etc.

(*b*) Expressions also indicating those shades of meaning: **il est douteux que** (*it is doubtful that*), **il est peu probable** que (*it is improbable that*), **il est regrettable que** (*it is regrettable that*), **il est triste que** (*it is sad that*), **il n'est pas sûr que** (*it is not sure that*), **il ne semble pas que** (*it does not seem that*), etc.

Il craint que vous ne **disiez** non. *He fears that you may say no.*

Il n'est pas sûr que je vous **croie**. *It is not sure that I will believe you.*

3 Interrogative and negative phrases introducing such overtones as doubt, disbelief, reluctance, etc.

Compare:	Je suis certain qu'elle **est** malade. (Indic.)
	I am certain she is ill.
and:	Je ne suis pas certain qu'elle **soit** malade. (Subj.)
	I am not certain she is ill.
or:	Elle est sûre que nous **sommes** contents. (Indic.)
	She is sure we are pleased.
and:	Est-elle sûre que nous **soyons** contents? (Subj.)
	Is she sure we are pleased?

4 A Superlative:

le mieux (*the best*), **le moins** (*the least*), **le pire** (*the worst*), **le plus** (*the most*);

C'est le garçon le plus doué que je **connaisse**. *He is the most gifted boy I know.*

C'est le meilleur repas que j'**aie** jamais mangé. *It is the best meal I have ever eaten.*

In addition to the above-mentioned cases, the subjunctive *must* be used in a subordinate clause if the latter is introduced by certain 'prescribed' conjunctions, some of which are presented below (for a fuller list, please consult the chapter on conjunctions): **A condition que** (*provided that*), **à moins que** (*unless*), **afin que** (*so that*), **avant que** (*before*), **de crainte que/de peur que** (*for fear that*), **jusqu'à ce que** (*until*), **sans que** (*without*), etc.

The Perfect

Formation: Present Subjunctive of **avoir/être** + Past Participle of main verb.

Usage: This tense is used in the same environment as the Present Subjunctive (i.e. after expressions of command, desire, doubt, regret; after certain 'prescribed' conjunctions, etc.), but it expresses the possibility of the hypothetical action *having already taken place* at the time of the utterance:

Je crains qu'il n'**ait abandonné**.   *I fear he may have given up.*
Croyez-vous qu'il **ait eu** peur?   *Do you think he was frightened?*

Compare: Je ne pense pas qu'ils nous **voient**. (Pres. Subj.)
I do not think they will see us (now or later).

and: Je ne pense pas qu'ils nous **aient vus**. (Subj. Perfect)
I do not think they have seen us (already).

Note: It is possible to use the Subjunctive Perfect to indicate the completed aspect of a projected action by a certain deadline. For example:

Je veux que vous **soyez parti** demain.   *I want you gone by tomorrow.*

Points to bear in mind regarding the use of the subjunctive:

1   Many learners are unduly worried by this seemingly daunting Mood. Just remember that it must be used in very precise and clearly prescribed circumstances. Whenever those circumstances arise, you will know that the Subjunctive is needed.

2   Although the conjunction **que** is almost always present before a subjunctive, it does *not* follow that every time **que** is used, it must have a subjunctive after it!

3   The Subjunctive is generally considered as stylistically 'heavy' (some of its tenses are already fading into oblivion). For that reason, it is often avoided, if at all possible, in spoken French. The main methods used are:

(*a*)   replacement of *the whole* subordinate clause by an Infinitive, whenever the main and subordinate clauses share the same subject.

thus: *Je* ne crois pas que *je* **puisse** rester.

becomes: Je ne crois pas pouvoir rester.
I do not think I can stay.

(*b*)   replacement of *the whole* subordinate clause after certain impersonal constructions (so long as no ambiguities in meaning are created by the substitution).

thus: Il faut que nous **partions**.

becomes: Il nous faut partir.
We must go.

(*c*)   replacement of *the whole* subordinate clause by a noun.

thus: Je doute qu'il **soit** honnête.
I doubt whether he is honest.

becomes: Je doute de son honnêteté.
I doubt his honesty.

All the Moods examined so far were Personal Moods, with the subject(s) performing the action clearly indicated. The following Moods are called Impersonal Moods. They offer no information about the identity of the performer(s) of the action (the context will normally supply that information).

The Infinitive Mood

This Mood merely expresses the abstract idea of the action stated by the verb, without any indication about the performer or of any further shade of meaning. It is considered as the *nominal* (noun-like) form of the verb.

The Tenses it contains are as follows:

The Present

Formation: Stem + **er/ir/re** (according to the group).
Usage: This form is used to situate the action referred to in the present or the future. For example:

Il veut **partir**. *He wants to go (now or later).*

This is the form in which the verb is found in the dictionary. The ending will tell you which group (1st, 2nd or 3rd) the verb belongs to (see next chapter). This information is useful because, within a given group, verbs tend to behave fairly consistently as far as tense-formation is concerned. Thus, knowing one verb will normally help you to recognise (and form the tenses of) *most* of the other verbs in the same group.

Specific uses of the Present Infinitive

1 It can sometimes be used to replace a whole subordinate clause (s.c.):

Je l'ai vu **partir** = Je l'ai vu **qui partait**.
                                          s.c.
I saw him go.

Il me faut **refaire** le travail = il faut **que je refasse le travail**.
                                                          s.c.
I must redo the work.

Note: This is particularly useful to eliminate a 'ponderous' subjunctive.

2 It can be used to shorten an interrogative clause:

Que **faire**? = Qu'est-ce qu'il faut faire?
What is one to do?
Où **aller**? = Où doit-on aller?
Where is one to go?

3   It can replace a noun (and its article):
Mieux vaut **mourir** = Mieux vaut la mort.
It is better to die.
J'adore **marcher** = J'adore la marche.   *I love walking.*
4   It is used with the meaning of an Imperative in *written* notices,
instructions for use, recipes, etc.
Ouvrir avec soin = Ouvrez avec soin.
Open with care.
Cuire à feu doux = Cuisez à feu doux.
Cook on a low heat.
Note: When the Infinitive is used to formulate a strong request or an
order on written notices, it is often preceded by **Prière de** (*Please. .*)
to soften its meaning:
Prière de **fermer** la porte = Fermez la porte s'il vous plaît.
Please close the door.
Prière de ne pas **fumer** = Ne fumez pas s'il vous plaît.   *Please
refrain from smoking.*
5   It can, in a limited number of cases, be used as a noun (with an
article or other determiner):
Le **pouvoir** corrompt.   *Power corrupts.*
Il fait son **devoir**.   *He is doing his duty.*

The Perfect
Formation: Present Infinitive of **avoir/être** + Past Participle of main
verb.
Usage: This form normally indicates that, at a given time, an action
is/was considered as completed.
Je crois vous **avoir dit** d'attendre.   *I think I told you (earlier) to
wait.*
Compare: Je vous remercie d'**être venu**. (Inf. Perf.)
Thank you for being with us.(lit: *having come*).
and: Je vous remercie **de venir** (Pres. Inf.)
Thank you for coming (now or later).
or: Ils croient **comprendre**.
They believe they understand (now).
and: Ils croient **avoir compris**.
They believe they have understood (already).
Specific uses: Like the present infinitive, it can:
1   replace certain subordinate clauses (s.c.):
Il pense **avoir gagné** = Il pense **qu'il a gagné**.
s.c.
He thinks he has won.
If faut **avoir vu** ce film = Il faut **que l'on ait vu ce film**.
s.c. (Subj.)

This film must be seen. (i.e. *is a 'must.'*)
2   take on the value of a noun:
    Merci de m'**avoir aidé** = Merci de votre aide.
    Thank you for your help. (lit: *for having helped me*)
3   replace parts of an interrogative sentence beginning with **pourquoi** (*why*):
    Pourquoi **être monté**? = Pourquoi êtes-vous monté?
    Why did you come up?
    Pourquoi **avoir cédé**? = Pourquoi ai-je cédé?
    Why did I give in?
Because of the absence of indication about the performer, such constructions could refer to *any* person.
4   Indicate that an action must be completed by a given deadline set in the future. In this case, it follows a verb expressing an order or a request:
    Nous devons **avoir quitté** l'hôtel à midi.   *We must be out of the hotel by twelve (noon).*
    Il faut **être revenus** ce soir.   *We must be back by tonight.*
Points to bear in mind regarding the use of infinitives:
1   When two verbs follow each other, the second one must be in the infinitive *except* when the first is one of the two auxiliaries **avoir** (*to have*) or **être** (*to be*):
    Il doit **répondre**.   *He must answer.*
    Nous aimons **voyager**.   *We like travelling.*
Note: In French, the use of a present participle (i.e. *ing* form) in this context is unacceptable.
You must say: Ils aiment **marcher**. (and not *Ils aiment marchant)
            They like walking.
2   If a verb follows the prepositions **à** (*to*), **de** (*from*), **pour** (*in order to*), **sans** (*without*), it must be in the infinitive (and *not* in the present participle as is often the case in English):
    Il commence à **pleuvoir**.   *It is beginning to rain.*
    Vous avez la chance de **gagner**. (and not *. . . de gagnant)   *You have the chance of winning.*
    Ils sont partis sans **payer**. (and not *. . . sans payant)   *They left without paying.*

The preposition **par** (*by*) is only used with a verb (in the infinitive) in two expressions: **commencer par** (*to begin by* + verb) and **finir par** (*to end up by* + verb):
    Ils ont commencé **par crier** mais ils ont fini **par accepter**
    They began by shouting but they ended up by accepting.

3   If an Infinitive follows a verb expressing desire, dislike, longing, preference, it will not be preceded by a preposition.

> Vous désirez **parler** au patron?   *Do you wish to talk to the manager?*
> Il déteste **attendre**.   *He hates waiting.*

4   If an Infinitive follows a verb expressing a claim, a statement or an assertion, it will not be preceded by a preposition:

> Il prétend **avoir été** invité.   *He claims to have been invited.*
> Elle dit **être** sa fille.   *She says she is his daughter.*

If **après** (*after*) is followed by a verb, that verb *must* be in the Infinitive Perfect (and not in the Present Infinitive or the Present Participle!)

You must say: Après **avoir parlé** il m'a regardé.
After he had spoken, he looked at me.
and not: *Après parlant (or parler), il m'a regardé.

The Participle

This Mood represents the adjectival form of the verb. The Participle can therefore have two distinct roles: that of a verb (in which case it will be invariable), and that of an adjective (in which case it will agree as required). In this Mood, the following Tenses are found.

The Present Participle

Formation: Stem + $\begin{cases} \textbf{ant} \text{ in 1st and 3rd group verbs} \\ \textbf{issant} \text{ in 2nd group verbs} \end{cases}$

NB   For an explanation of the grouping of verbs see next chapter.

Usage: As previously mentioned, this tense has two distinct roles:
1   As a verbal form it can indicate that the action it represents coincides (at any point in time) with another action. In this role, it is used to replace whole relative clauses beginning with **qui** (*who/which*), particularly after verbs of perception.

> J'ai vu le vieux **comptant** son argent = qui comptait son argent. *I saw the old man counting his money.*
> Nous les entendons **criant** à tue-tête = qui crient à tue-tête. *We hear them shouting their heads off.*

Note: In that role, the Present Participle is invariable

2   As an adjective, it indicates a distinctive quality:
   Ils lisent une histoire **intéressante**.   *They are reading an interest-
      ing story.*
   Nous ferons des choses **étonnantes**.   *We will do astonishing
      things.*
Note: In that role, the Present Participle behaves like an adjective
and agrees as appropriate.
Compare: J'entends des cris **déchirants**. (quality)
            I hear heart-breaking cries.
and: J'entends des cris **déchirant** le silence. (action)
            I hear cries breaking the silence.
In this latter case, the Present Participle indicates an action (**qui
déchirent . . .**) and is therefore invariable.

The Gerund

The Gerund is the adverbial form of the verb. It is identical in shape
with the Present Participle, but is preceded by the preposition **en**
(*by/through/whilst*). Since it has the value and role of an adverb, it is
invariable. It is used to modify the meaning of a verbal phrase. The
shades of meaning it can convey (at any point in time) are as follows:
1   It can indicate the co-occurrence of two actions:
   Elle entra **en chantant**.   *She came in singing.*
   Il sortit **en riant**.   *He went out laughing.*
2   It outlines the means by which a result is achieved (*through, by
dint of . . .*):
   C'est **en travaillant** dur que tu réussiras.   *It is by working hard
      that you will succeed.*
   On apprend beaucoup **en regardant** les gens.   *One learns a lot
      through looking at people.*
3   It can express hypothetical situations:
   En acceptant, je perds ma place.   *If I accept I lose my job.*
Be sure to distinguish between:
   J'ai vu l'homme **parlant** à un ami (qui parlait . . .).   *I saw the
      man talking to a friend.*
and: J'ai vu l'homme **en parlant** à un ami (pendant que je
   parlais . . .).   *I saw the man while I was talking to a friend.*

The Past Participle

Formation: Stem + **é/i/u** (according to the group).
Some verbs do not conform to this regular pattern (see next chapter).
Usage: The Past Participle has two distinct functions:

1 As a verb, it is used in all compound tenses and serves to emphasise *the completed aspect* of an action:

J'ai **ramassé** le sac. *I picked up the bag.*

Il se sera **endormi**. *He will have fallen asleep.*

2 As an adjective, it expresses a state:

Jette ces fleurs **fanées**! *Throw those wilted flowers out!*

Le soleil entre par la fenêtre **ouverte**. *The sun is coming in through the open window.*

Note: A small number of past participles can be used as nouns:

Donnez moi mon **dû** et je signe un **reçu**. *Give me what is owed to me and I will sign a receipt.*

Past Participle agreements

See also chapters 11 (Reflexive Pronouns) and 20 (Past Participle agreement with **avoir/être**).

As outlined earlier, the Past Participle can have several functions:

1 When used as an adjective, it will normally agree in gender and number with the noun or pronoun it relates to:

Elle regarde la robe **déchirée**. *She is looking at the torn dress.*

Laissez la fenêtre **ouverte**. *Leave the window open.*

Note: Certain Past Participles used as adjectives in set expressions *do not* agree with the noun *when placed before it,* but behave normally when placed after; the most common are: **excepté** (*except*), **passé** (*past/after*), **supposé** (*assumed*), **ci-joint/ci-inclus** (*enclosed*), **étant donné** (*given*), **non-compris** (*not included*), **y compris** (*included*).

Compare: Ouvert tous les jours, **excepté** dimanches et fêtes.

and: Ouvert tous les jours, dimanches et fêtes **exceptés**.

Open every day, Sundays and public holidays excepted.

or: Veuillez trouver **ci-joint** une photo.

and: Veuillez trouver une photo **ci-jointe**.

Please find enclosed a photograph.

2 When used as a noun, the past participle agrees as required:

Signez ces **reçus** s'il vous plaît. *Please sign these receipts.*

Debout les **morts**! *Everybody up!* (humorous)

3 When used with the auxiliary **être** in non-pronominal constructions (i.e. *without* one of the reflexive pronouns: **me, te, se, nous, vous, se**), the past participle agrees as appropriate.

Note: This includes the compound tenses of the 'famous 14': **aller, venir, descendre, monter, entrer, sortir, naître, mourir, partir, arriver, passer, retourner, rester, tomber**, as well as all passive constructions:

Ils sont **restés** à la maison. *They stayed at home.*

Elle a été **mordue** par un chien. *She has been bitten by a dog.*

(passive construction)

4 When the past participle is used pronominally (i.e. with a reflexive pronoun) two possibilities arise:

If the verb concerned admits an accusative construction (a direct object), the past participle will agree as required. A practical way of finding out whether the verb is in the accusative is to rephrase the sentence in your mind using **avoir** as the auxiliary and to ask the question **qui?** or **quoi?** after the past participle. If the answer to that question is the reflexive pronoun (representing the subject), the agreement is required. *Otherwise*, no agreement must be made.

Compare: Elle s'est **levée**. (elle a levé qui?: **s'** = elle) *She got up.*
The construction is an accusative one, hence the agreement.

and: Elle s'est **dit**: "tant pis!" (elle a dit à qui? à **s'** = à elle) *She said to herself: "too bad!".*

The construction is a dative one, hence no agreement.

Note: Beware of such sentences as:

Elle s'est **coupé** la main. (= elle a coupé la main à qui?: à **s'** = à elle — dative, no agreement) *She cut her hand.*

and: Elle s'est **coupée** à la main (elle a coupé qui?: **se** = elle — accusative, agreement)

She cut herself on the hand.

5 When the past participle is used with **avoir**, several possibilities must be envisaged:

(a) If the construction is not an accusative one (i.e. if the verb has no direct object or, practically, if the question **qui?** or **quoi?** asked after the past participle has no answer), there will be no agreement.

Ils ont **entendu** (ils ont entendu quoi? = no answer — no agreement) *They heard.*

Elle a **mangé** (elle a mangé quoi? = no answer — no agreement) *She has eaten.*

(b) If the construction is an accusative one but if the direct object is placed after the past participle, there is no agreement.

Elles ont **mangé les bonbons** (elles ont mangé quoi? = les
                Dir. obj.

bonbons *They ate the sweets.*

Elle a **vu la pièce** (elle a vu quoi? = la pièce). *She saw the*
        Dir. obj.

play.

(c) If the construction is an accusative one *and* if the direct object is placed before the past participle, the agreement will be made as applicable.

Ils nous **ont vu(e)s** (ils ont vu qui? = nous (masc. or fem. plur.) *They saw us.*

Remember, for agreement purposes, that the direct object pronouns: **me**, **te**, **le**, **la**, can represent a masculine *or* a feminine singular, and that **nous**, **vous**, **les**, refer to a masculine *or* feminine plural. In addition, **vous** could refer to one person only (polite singular). You could therefore have the following agreements.

Je vous ai { vu (to a man)
I saw you { vue (to a woman)
{ vus (to several people)
{ vues (to several women)

When a sentence contains the relative pronoun **que** (*that*), check the gender and number of its antecedent (i.e. the noun or pronoun it replaces) and, if the clause contains a past participle, make the agreement as required:

C'est la montre que j'avais **perdue** (j'avais perdu quoi?: **que** = la montre — fem. sing. agreement). *This is the watch I had lost.*

If the past participle occurs in an impersonal construction (i.e. with **il fait**, **il y a . . .**), it will remain invariable:

Vous savez la crise qu'il y a **eu** (and not *eue) *You know the crisis there was.*

If the past participle of **coûter** (*to cost*), **peser** (*to weigh*), or **valoir** (*to be worth*) is used in a 'concrete' sense, it will remain invariable; if used figuratively, it will agree as appropriate.

Compare: Je regrette les 300 Francs que cette robe a **coûté**.
I begrudge the 300F which this dress has cost.
and: Je plains les efforts que ce travail a **coûtés**.
I begrudge the efforts this job has cost.

Active and passive voice

It is often useful for the listener or reader to know whether the subject of a sentence is performing an action (*active voice*) or is merely subjected to the action (*passive voice*).

Note: the auxiliary **être** (*to be*) is used to turn an active sentence into a passive one.

Compare: Le touriste **achète** une carte postale.
The tourist is buying a postcard. (active)
and: La carte postale **est achetée** par le touriste.
The postcard is bought by the tourist. (passive)
or: Le docteur **a examiné** le malade.
The doctor examined the sick man. (active)
and: Le malade **a été examiné** par le docteur.
The sick man was examined by the doctor. (passive)

Notes:
1. *Not all* sentences can be turned into the passive voice.
   Il pleut. *It is raining.*
2. The presence of the auxiliary **être** does *not* automatically mean that a sentence is in the passive voice.
   Elle **est arrivée** ce matin. *She arrived this morning.*

Types of verbs

Verbs can also be classified according to the relationship they create between the being(s) or thing(s) performing the action and the object(s) or recipient(s) of that action. On that basis, the following categories are distinguished:

Intransitive verbs

No indication is given as to the object or recipient of the action.
   Il marche. *He is walking.*
   Elles dorment. *They are sleeping.*

Transitive verbs

They give an indication of the object or recipient of the action:
   Vous **donnez** votre passeport.
   You are giving (what?=) *your passport.*
   Il **adore** les enfants.
   He adores (who(m)?) *children.*

   Elle **parle à** sa voisine.
   She is speaking (to whom?=) *to her neighbour.*
   Nous **pensons à** vous.
   We are thinking (of whom?=) *of you.*
In the four sentences given above the first two are examples of 'transitive direct' verbs and the last two of 'transitive indirect' verbs. In the latter, the verb is followed by a preposition: **à** (*to*), **de** (*of*).

Pronominal verbs

They are preceded by one of the appropriate pronouns: **me** (*myself*), **te** (*yourself* — fam.), **se** (*himself, herself, itself, oneself, themselves*), **nous** (*ourselves*), **vous** (*yourself, yourselves*). They indicate:

a) *either* that the action of the performer(s) affects only the performer(s) (reflexive verbs):
   Nous **nous levons** tôt. *We get (ourselves) up early.*
   Ils **se sont coupés**. *They cut themselves.*

(*b*)   *or* that the performer(s) and the recipient(s) perform the same action and that *both* are affected by it (reciprocal verbs).

Nous **nous sommes battus**.   *We fought (each other)*.
Elles **se sont insultées**.   *They insulted each other*.

Although there are verbs in French which only belong to one of the above three categories, many verbs can move from one category to another depending on the pattern of the sentence they are used in. For example:

Je regarde.   *I am looking/watching*. (intransitive)
Je regarde la mer.   *I am looking at the sea*. (trans. direct)
Je regarde à la dépense.   *I am careful about expenses*. (trans. indirect)
Je me regarde.   *I am looking at myself*. (reflexive)
Nous nous regardons.   *We are looking at each other*. (reciprocal)

Impersonal verbs

There is a small group of verbs which are only used in the 3rd person singular (masculine). In that case, the pronoun **il** (*it*) does not refer to any thing or being. Those verbs are called impersonal verbs.

Il pleut et **il fait** du vent.   *It is raining and windy*.
Il faut partir.   *It is necessary to go*.

Key points

1   In order to express accurately the occurrence of an action, there are in French a selection of tenses which make it possible to situate that action in time.
2   Tenses can be made up of one word (*simple tenses*) or several words — usually two — one of which is the auxiliary and the other the main verb (*compound tenses*).
3   The verb (in simple tenses) or the auxiliary (in compound tenses) is made up of a stem and an ending which serves to indicate the performer(s) *and* the position of the action on the time axis.
4   Tenses are grouped into broader categories called Moods which are used to express definite shades of meaning: actual occurrence of an action, possibility, conjecture, command, doubt, regret, etc.
5   The Indicative Mood is used to situate the occurrence of an action on the time axis in relation to other actions or to the present.
6   The Conditional Mood expresses the fact that an action could occur in the present or the future (or could have occurred in the past) if certain conditions were (or had been) met. It is also used to soften commands into polite requests and to express indignation or guarded statements.

7   The Imperative Mood is used to express an order or a request, to give a set of instructions or directions. It has three persons only (2nd singular, 1st plural, 2nd plural) and *no* subject pronouns. It can be supplemented by the 3rd person (singular and plural) of the Subjunctive if required.

8   The Subjunctive Mood is normally used in subordinate clauses to indicate that an action is considered *not* as a reality but as a possible, hypothetical or doubtful event in the past, the present or the future. Because of the shades of meaning it conveys, it *must not* be used at random, but in very precise circumstances (after certain verbs or expressions of command, doubt, fear, longing, etc., or after certain 'prescribed' conjunctions). It can (infrequently) be found in main or independent clauses where it usually expresses such feelings as enthusiasm, indignation or disgust.

9   The Infinitive Mood is an impersonal mood. The Infinitive can have the value of a verb or a noun. As a verb, it will remain invariable; as a noun, it will agree if required. Infinitives may be used in certain circumstances to replace other grammatical elements such as subordinate clauses or nouns.

10   The Participle is also an Impersonal Mood. It can be used as a verb or as an adjective:

(*a*)   As a verb it expresses an action coinciding with that of the main verb. It may be used to replace relative clauses beginning with **qui** (*who*) and remains invariable.

(*b*)   As an adjective, it serves to indicate an 'active' quality (Present Participle) or a state (Past Participle) and, with a few restrictions, agrees like a normal adjective.

The Gerund, which is identical to the Present Participle but is preceded by **en**, is the adverbial form of the latter. It is used to modify the verb-phrase which it accompanies and may express simultaneity, 'means to an end', or hypothetical situations.

11   The Past Participle is used in conjunction with the auxiliaries **avoir** and **être** to form all compound tenses in French conjugation.

12   In compound tenses, the Past Participle follows rigid rules of agreement:

(*a*)   If the Past Participle is used with **être** in non-pronominal verb constructions, it will agree in gender and number like a normal adjective

(*b*)   If it is used pronominally (i.e. essentially with reflexive or reciprocal verbs) in *dative constructions* (when the verb accepts an Indirect Object complement), it will remain unchanged.

(*c*)   If it is used with **avoir**, it will agree as appropriate provided:

(i)   The construction is an accusative one (i.e. the verb accepts a Direct Object complement); *and*

(ii)   That Direct Object complement is placed *before* the Past Participle. The whole problem of agreement therefore hinges on the presence and position of the Direct Object Complement.

13   The actions indicated by most verbs can be expressed in the active voice (i.e. subject(s) performing the action) or in the passive voice (i.e. subject(s) undergoing the action).

13 The Verb

The verb is said to be the most important word in a sentence. It enables the speaker(s) to express actions, feelings, states of mind or body, etc. In order to situate those actions along the time axis (past-present-future) or relatively to each other, verbs are organised into Tenses. Tenses in their turn are grouped into Moods. Each Mood gives extra information (overtones) about the action: actuality, doubt, possibility, regret, wish, etc.

Introductory remarks

Although the general principles involved in the conjugation of verbs are similar in French and English, there are, between the two languages important differences which must be borne in mind:

In English, for a given tense (Present, Past Historic, etc.), the task of distinguishing between persons falls almost entirely on the Subject Pronoun (*I, you, he/she/it, we, you, they*). In French, on the other hand, that task is shared between the Subject Pronouns which are — and generally sound — different *and* the tense ending for each person. A comparative look at the behaviour of a given verb (e.g. **aller** *to go*) in the two languages will clarify that point. The tense shown is the Past Historic.

Persons		*to go*	*aller*
1st		*I went*	J'allai
2nd	sing	*You went*	Tu allas (fam. sing.)
3rd		*He/she/it went*	Il/elle alla
1st		*We went*	Nous allâmes
2nd	plural	*You went*	Vous allâtes (polite sing./normal plur.)
3rd		*They went*	Ils/elles allèrent

In English the form *went* is the same for all 6 persons; distinction in meaning is made by the pronoun alone. In French the endings **ai, as, a,** etc. change with each person which means that two clues are available (pronoun + ending) instead of one in English (pronoun), to help you recognise the person in question. It is therefore essential to match, for each tense, the correct ending with the correct person; a fairly demanding (but by no means impossible) task, which will be greatly aided by careful scrutiny of the examples given and some of the 'detective work' outlined in the introduction.

Verb groups

Broadly speaking, French verbs fall into a small number of categories organised into three groups. With some notable exceptions presented in the Irregular charts on pages 161–73, verbs in a given category tend to 'behave' in a consistent way for the purpose of stem-determination and tense-formation. Two forms are used to determine which group a given verb belongs to: its *Infinitive* and its *Present Participle*:

(i) the Infinitive is, as we know, the nominal form of the verb, the one which will appear in dictionaries. In English, the Infinitive is signalled by the presence of *to*. In French, the Infinitive is made up of a *stem + an ending*: **er**, **ir** or **re**;

(ii) the Present Participle is the adjectival form of the verb. In English the *ing* ending signals the Present Participle. In French the Present Participle is made up of a *stem + an ending*: **ant** for 1st and 3rd group verbs and **issant** for 2nd group ones.

French verb categories and groups are presented below.

Categories		*Examples*	*Meaning*
a	Infinitive ending = **er**	aim**er**	*to love*
	Pres. Part. ending = **ant**	aim**ant**	*loving*
b	Infinitive ending = **ir**	fin**ir**	*to finish*
	Pres. Part. ending = **issant**	fin**issant**	*finishing*
c	Infinitive ending = **ir**	part**ir**	*to leave*
	Pres. Part. ending = **ant**	part**ant**	*leaving*
d	Infinitive ending = **re**	ven**dre**	*to sell*
	Pres. Part. ending = **ant**	vend**ant**	*selling*
e	Infinitive ending = **oir**	rece**voir**	*to receive*
	Pres. Part. ending = **ant**	rece**vant**	*receiving*

Category a represents group I, in which there are roughly 4,000 verbs. It is the largest and the most dynamic group: most of the new verbs created in the language are **er** verbs: **bétoniser** (*to 'pollute' with concrete and buildings*), **réclamiser** (*to advertise*), **robotiser** (*to robotise*), **informatiser** (*to computerise*) are some recently-created examples.

With the notable exception of **aller**, which will be presented in the Irregular Verbs chart, this group is fairly trouble-free.

Category b represents group II which is approximately 350 strong. It has a very limited number of new additions, e.g. **alunir** (*to land on the moon*). In terms of endings and tense-formation, it is the easiest group to learn.

Categories c, d and e represent group III which is the most inconsistent, not so much in terms of endings, as in terms of changes to the *stem* (to which the endings will be added). It is approximately 100 strong and several of its members are either very rarely used today (i.e. obsolete), or not used throughout their conjugation (i.e. defective). Unfortunately, some of the most commonly used verbs in the language also belong to that group!

Tense formation

French tenses are formed in one of two ways, as outlined in Unit 12.
Simple Tenses = Stem of main verb + endings.
Compound Tenses = Auxiliary + Past Participle of main verb.
The determination of the correct endings for a given tense is *not* a difficult matter, given a few models and some reflection. The difficulty is to determine how to 'discover' the stem. Here again, some of the detective work outlined in the introduction will be invaluable. Here are some hints which may also prove useful.

(*a*)   Once you have heard or seen one person of the Future or Present Conditional of a verb, you will know the stem used for the whole of those two tenses, however irregular the verb. Let us take two examples:

Aller *to go*
Future   = **j'irai**   ⟶ stem = **ir** + ending = **ai**
                     I shall go
Pres. Cond. = **Tu irais**   ⟶ stem = **ir** + ending = **ais**
                     You would go
Prendre *to take*
Future   = **elle prendra** ⟶ stem = **prendr** + ending = **a**
                     she will take
Pres. Cond. = **nous prendrions** ⟶ stem = **prendr** + ending = **ions**
                     we would take

Having learnt the appropriate endings (which, incidentally, are *the same for all verbs*) for each of those two tenses, you will find it extremely easy to make up the rest of the tense yourself.

(*b*)   For the formation of the Future (*and* of the Present

Conditional), the stem will *normally* be either the *full* Infinitive, in the case of **er** and most **ir** verbs, or the Infinitive minus **e**, in the case of **re** verbs. For example:

chercher *to search*

Future: **Ils chercheront**—➤ stem = **chercher** + ending = **ont**
       They will search

attendre *to wait*

Pres. Cond.: **Vous attendriez**—➤ **stem =**
       attendr + ending = **iez**

(c) For all verbs, the endings of the Present Conditional are the same as the *endings* of the Imperfect Indicative. For example:
    pouvoir *to be able to*

Imperfect: **Je pouvais** ——➤ stem = **pouv** + ending **ais**
Pres. Cond.: **Je pourrais** ——➤ stem = **pourr** + ending **ais**

(d) The endings of the Present Indicative of **avoir** (minus the stem **av**), are *also* the endings of the Future Tense for all verbs.

Compare:	**J'ai**	and:	Je ser**ai**
	I have		*I shall be*
or:	Tu **as**	and:	Tu fer**as**
	You have		*You will do*
or:	Nous av**ons**	and:	Nous parler**ons**
	We have		*We shall talk*

(e) In the case of many irregular verbs, the Present Indicative exhibits two stem formations: *one* for the first three persons singular and the third person plural, *and another* for the 2nd and 3rd persons plural. For example:

boire *to drink*

Compare: Je bois, tu bois, il boit, ils boivent ——➤ stem = **boi(v)**
and: nous buvons, vous buvez ——➤ stem = **buv**

pouvoir *to be able to*

Compare: Je peux, tu peux, il peut, ils peuvent ——➤ stem = **peu**
and: nous pouvons, vous pouvez ——➤ stem = **pouv**

Note: Despite the fact that the above 'rule' has numerous exceptions, it has the advantage of showing that there is some underlying 'logic' in the language. Careful study of grammatical data will enable you to uncover further 'logical' information by yourself.

Auxiliaries

Auxiliaries are verbs which assist in the formation of Compound Tenses. The two main auxiliaries used for that purpose in French are **avoir** (*to have*) and **être** (*to be*), as previously indicated.

Être

Verbs which take **être** as an auxiliary are:

1　All those constructed pronominally (e.g. reflexive or reciprocal verbs). The pronominal construction is indicated by the presence of one of the following reflexive pronouns: **me, te, se, nous, vous, se,** (see Unit 11 on-reflexive pronouns), between the subject and the Verb. For example:

Se couper	⟶	Tu **te** coupes (reflexive)
To cut oneself		*You cut yourself*
Se battre	⟶	Nous **nous** battons (reciprocal)
To fight (one another)		*We fight (each other)*
S'enfuir	⟶	Je **m'**enfuis (pronominal)
To run away		*I run away*

2　The following 14 verbs (the 'famous 14'):

Aller　*to go*	Venir　*to come*
Arriver　*to arrive*	Partir　*to leave/go*
Descendre　*to go down*	Monter　*to go up*
Entrer　*to go in*	Sortir　*to go out*
Naître　*to be born*	Mourir　*to die*
Passer　*to go by*	Retourner　*to return/go back*
Rester　*to stay*	Tomber　*to fall*

Notes:

(i)　Most of the above verbs, when constructed with a prefix (usually **re** indicating repetition) — **re**descendre (*to go down again*), **re**partir (*to go again*), etc. — also take **être** as their auxiliary. For example:

Il est **revenu** à trois heures et il est **reparti** à sept heures.
He came back at three and went back at seven.

(ii)　Some of the 'famous 14' can also be used in transitive constructions (i.e. followed by a Direct Object Complement). In such cases, they will take the auxiliary **avoir**.

Compare:　Ils **sont** descendus.
　　　　　They went down.

and:　Ils **ont descendu** la valise.
　　　They took the case down.

or:　Ils **sont** retournés au bureau.
　　They went back to the office.

and:　Ils **ont retourné** le livre.
　　　They returned the book.

Avoir

All other verbs take **avoir** as their auxiliary, including **avoir** and être themselves. For example:

Il **a achevé** son travail.   *He finished his work.*
Elle **avait rêvé**.   *She had been dreaming.*
Ils **ont été invités**.   *They were invited.*
Nous **avons eu** des problèmes.   *We have had problems.*
In addition to the two auxiliaries examined above, other verbs may be used in a similar capacity. Two categories may be distinguished:
1 *Semi-auxiliaries*: **aller** (*to go*) and **venir** (*to come*). Both may be constructed with an Infinitive to indicate the imminent occurrence of an action (**aller**), or the recent completion of an action (**venir**) and both may be used in the Present *or* the Imperfect Indicative.
Compare: Nous **allons** fermer le magasin.
            We are going to close the shop.
and: Nous **allions** fermer le magasin.
            We were about to close the shop.
or: Il **vient de** perdre son portefeuille.
            He has just lost his wallet.
and: Il **venait de** perdre son portefeuille.
            He had just lost his wallet.
Note: In this type of construction **de** or **d'** as applicable is inserted between **venir** and the following infinitive.
2 *Modal auxiliaries*: **devoir** (*to have to*), **faire** (*to have . . . . done*), **falloir** (*to be necessary*), **pouvoir** (*to be able to*), **savoir** (*to know how to*), **vouloir** (*to want*). They may be used with an infinitive to express certain overtones (desire, moral obligation, order) reminiscent of those expressed by the various Moods (Conditional, Imperative, Subjunctive) previously examined. For example:
    Vous **devez** partir = Il faut que vous partiez.   *You must go.*
    Je **peux** gagner = Il est possible que je gagne.   *I can win.*

Model charts

The Conjugation charts of five regular verbs will now be presented in full. Please study these charts carefully, since they contain most of the clues to the secrets of correct French Conjugation. In addition, Irregular Verb charts will also be given at the end of the chapter.
Notes:
1   In order to simplify the verb charts presented below, only one form (**il** for the singular and **ils** for the plural) will be given for the 3rd person. But it is understood that **il** (*he*) also stands for **elle** (*she*) and **on** (*one*), and that **ils** (*they* masc. plur.) also stands for **elles** (*they* fem. plur.).
2   In a further attempt to simplify the model charts, the polite

singular form **vous** will not be entered separately as it was in the pronouns chapter.

Remember that, in compound tenses, the rules of agreement of the past participle will have to be adhered to whenever appropriate. Compare:

vous êtes tombé masc. sing. polite form
vous êtes tombée fem. sing. polite form
vous êtes tombés masc. plur. normal form
vous êtes tombées fem. plur. normal form

} *You have fallen*

3   Within the Past Historic, the Imperfect, the Future and the Conditional of a given verb, the *stem*, once determined, *remains constant* and the endings follow a regular pattern.

Auxiliaries: AVOIR

Simple Tenses	Compound Tenses
Indicative	
Present	*Perfect*
J'ai	J'ai eu
Tu as	Tu as eu
Il a	Il a eu
Nous avons	Nous avons eu
Vous avez	Vous avez eu
Ils ont	Ils ont eu
Past Historic	*Past Anterior*
J'eus	J'eus eu
Tu eus	Tu eus eu
Il eut	Il eut eu
Nous eûmes	Nous eûmes eu
Vous eûtes	Vous eûtes eu
Ils eurent	Ils eurent eu
Imperfect	*Pluperfect*
J' avais	J'avais eu
Tu avais	Tu avais eu
Il avait	Il avait eu
Nous avions	Nous avions eu
Vous aviez	Vous aviez eu
Ils avaient	Ils avaient eu

Avoir-*cont.*

Simple Tenses		*Compound Tenses*
Future		*Future Perfect*
J'aur**ai**		J'aurai eu
Tu aur**as**		Tu auras eu
Il aur**a**		Il aura eu
Nous aur**ons**		Nous aurons eu
Vous aur**ez**		Vous aurez eu
Ils aur**ont**		Ils auront eu
	Conditional	
Present		*Perfect*
J'aur**ais**		J'aurais eu
Tu aur**ais**		Tu aurais eu
Il aur**ait**		Il aurait eu
Nous aur**ions**		Nous aurions eu
Vous aur**iez**		Vous auriez eu
Ils aur**aient**		Ils auraient eu
	Imperative	
Present		*Perfect* (Rare)
2nd pers. sing. Aie		2nd pers. sing. Aie eu
1st pers. plur. Ayons		1st pers. plur. Ayons eu
2nd pers. plur. Ayez		2nd pers. plur. Ayez eu
	Subjunctive	
Present		*Perfect*
Que j'aie		Que j'aie eu
Que tu aies		Que tu aies eu
Qu'il ait		Qu'il ait eu
Que nous ayons		Que nous ayons eu
Que vous ayez		Que vous ayez eu
Qu'ils aient		Qu'ils aient eu
	Infinitive	
Present		*Perfect*
Avo**ir**		Avoir eu
	Participle	
Present		*Past*
Ay**ant**		(Ayant) eu

Auxiliaries: ÊTRE

Simple Tenses	*Compound Tenses*
Indicative	

Present	*Perfect*
Je suis	J'ai été
Tu es	Tu as été
Il est	Il a été
Nous sommes	Nous avons été
Vous êtes	Vous avez été
Ils sont	Ils ont été

Past Historic	*Past Anterior*
Je fus	J'eus été
Tu fus	Tu eus été
Il fut	Il eut été
Nous fûmes	Nous eûmes été
Vous fûtes	Vous eûtes été
Ils furent	Ils eurent été

Imperfect	*Pluperfect*
J'étais	J'avais été
Tu étais	Tu avais été
Il était	Il avait été
Nous étions	Nous avions été
Vous étiez	Vous aviez été
Ils étaient	Ils avaient été

Future	*Future Perfect*
Je serai	J'aurai été
Tu seras	Tu auras été
Il sera	Il aura été
Nous serons	Nous aurons été
Vous serez	Vous aurez été
Ils seront	Ils auront été

Conditional	
Present	*Perfect*
Je serais	J'aurais été
Tu serais	Tu aurais été
Il serait	Il aurait été
Nous serions	Nous aurions été
Vous seriez	Vous auriez été
Ils seraient	Ils auraient été

Être-*cont.*

	Simple Tenses		Compound Tenses
		Imperative	
	Present		*Perfect* (Rare)
	2nd pers. sing. Sois		2nd pers. sing. Aie été
	1st pers. plur. Soyons		1st pers. plur. Ayons été
	2nd pers. plur. Soyez		2nd pers. plur. Ayez été
		Subjunctive	
	Present		*Perfect*
	Que je sois		Que j'aie été
	Que tu sois		Que tu aies été
	Qu'il soit		Qu'il ait été
	Que nous soyons		Que nous ayons été
	Que vous soyez		Que vous ayez été
	Qu'ils soient		Qu'ils aient été
		Infinitive	
	Present		*Perfect*
	Être		Avoir été
		Participle	
	Present		*Past*
	Et**ant**		(Ayant) été

Points to bear in mind regarding the use of **avoir** (*to have*) and **être** (*to be*):
1 As well as being verbs in their own right, **avoir** and **être** are used as auxiliaries to form all the compound tenses in French. To do so, the Past Participle of the main verb is added to the required tense of the *appropriate* auxiliary.
Note: Because of the French system of gender and number agreement, you must *always* check, when using a Past Participle, whether its role or position in the sentence require it to agree with the Subject or the Object. The rules of Past Participle agreement are presented in Chapter 12.
2 The auxiliary **être** is used to form the Passive Voice (Subject undergoing an action). It should be noted, however, that the compound tenses of a passive construction use **avoir** as their auxiliary.
Compare: Il **est** blessé.   and   Il **a été** blessé.
            (Present)   (Perfect)
            He is wounded.   *He has been wounded.*

or:	Il **était** blessé.	and:	Il **avait été** blesse.́
	(Imperfect)		(Pluperfect)
	He was wounded.		*He had been wounded.*

Note: Some transitive verbs (i.e. admitting a Direct Object complement) can, in English, be constructed using the 'passive technique'. For example

(*a*) *He was given a watch.*
(*b*) *They were shown the door.*
(*c*) *I was told a story.*

This is *impossible* in French. Such sentences must be put in the active voice.

(*a*) On lui a donné une montre.
(*b*) On leur a montré la porte.
(*c*) On m'a raconté une histoire.

3   It is possible to create a whole new category of tenses called double-compound tenses (**temps surcomposés**) which are mainly used in spoken French and are formed as follows:

(i) *For verbs using the auxiliary* **avoir**: Suitable Compound Tense of **avoir** + Past Participle of main verb. For example:
Quand il **a eu fini** son travail, il **est parti**.   *When he had finished his work, he went.*

(ii) *For verbs using the auxiliary* **etre**: Suitable Compound Tense of **avoir** + **été** + Past Participle of main verb. For example:
Quand il **a eu été parti** je **suis rentré**.   *When he was gone I returned home.*

Such tenses are used to emphasise the *completed aspect* of a past action in constructions where traditional compound tenses may sound affected or highbrow. The double-compound Perfect is very often used as a partner for the Perfect because the Past Anterior (which was the partner of the Past Historic) sounds over-refined.

Compare:	Quand elle **eut mangé**, elle **se leva**. (Past Ant. + Past Hist.)
and:	Quand elle **a eu mangé**, elle **s'est levée**. (Pass. Surcomp. + Perfect) *When she had finished eating, she got up.*
or:	Lorsqu'il **fut sorti**, il **refusa** de parler. (Past Ant. + Past Hist.)
and:	Lorsqu'il **a eu été sorti**, il **a refusé** de parler (Pass. Surcomp. + Perf.) *Once he had gone out, he refused to talk.*

Note: All ordinary compound tenses could, if desired, be replaced using the above technique.

Important: In *all* circumstances, the Past Participle of **être** remains invariable.

1ST GROUP VERBS—aimer to love

Indicative

Simple Tenses	Compound Tenses
Present	*Perfect*
J'aime	J'ai aimé
Tu aim**es**	Tu as aimé
Il aim**e**	Il a aimé
Nous aim**ons**	Nous avons aimé
Vous aim**ez**	Vous avez aimé
Ils aim**ent**	Ils ont aimé
Past Historic	*Past Anterior*
J'aim**ai**	J'eus aimé
Tu aim**as**	Tu eus aimé
Il aim**a**	Il eut aimé
Nous aim**âmes**	Nous eûmes aimé
Vous aim**âtes**	Vous eûtes aimé
Ils aim**èrent**	Ils eurent aimé
Imperfect	*Pluperfect*
J'aim**ais**	J'avais aimé
Tu aim**ais**	Tu avais aimé
Il aim**ait**	Il avait aimé
Nous aim**ions**	Nous avions aimé
Vous aim**iez**	Vous aviez aimé
Ils aim**aient**	Ils avaient aimé
Future	*Future Perfect*
J'aim**erai**	J'aurai aimé
Tu aim**eras**	Tu auras aimé
Il aim**era**	Il aura aimé
Nous aim**erons**	Nous aurons aimé
Vous aim**erez**	Vous aurez aimé
Ils aim**eront**	Ils auront aimé

Conditional

Present	*Perfect*
J'aim**erais**	J'aurais aimé
Tu aim**erais**	Tu aurais aimé
Il aim**erait**	Il aurait aimé
Nous aim**erions**	Nous aurions aimé
Vous aim**eriez**	Vous auriez aimé
Ils aim**eraient**	Ils auraient aimé

aimer *cont.*

	Simple Tenses		Compound Tenses
		Imperative	
	Present		*Perfect* (Rare)
	2nd pers. sing. Aime		2nd pers. sing. Aie aimé
	1st pers. plur. Aim**ons**		1st pers. plur. Ayons aimé
	2nd pers. plur. Aim**ez**		2nd pers. plur. Ayez aimé
		Subjunctive	
	Present		*Perfect*
	Que j'aime		Que j'aie aimé
	Que tu aim**es**		Que tu aies aimé
	Qu'il aime		Qu'il ait aimé
	Que nous aim**ions**		Que nous ayons aimé
	Que vous aim**iez**		Que vous ayez aimé
	Qu'ils aim**ent**		Qu'ils aient aimé
		Infinitive	
	Present		*Past*
	Aim**er**		(Avoir) aim**é**
		Participle	
	Present		*Perfect*
	Aim**ant**		(Ayant) aim**é**

Note: There are two distinct stems — **aim** and **aimer** — which are used to form the simple Tenses.

Points regarding the use of 1st group (**er**) verbs:

1 **Aller** (*to go*), which is one of the most frequently used verbs in the language, does not follow the normal pattern of tense-formation. Its conjugation is presented in the Irregular Verbs Chart on page 161.

2 Some verbs in this group undergo small changes in order to preserve their phonetic (i.e. sound) pattern. The following examples will help clarify that statement:

(i) Because of the sound change of **c** from [s] to [k] when that letter is followed by **a**, **o** or **u**, **c** is replaced by **ç** = [s] whenever, in the course of conjugation, an ending beginning with one of those three vowels is expected immediately after the **c**.

Compare:	Il place	*or*	Il placera
	He is placing		*He will place*
and:	Il plaçait	*or*	Nous plaçons
	He was placing		*We are placing*

In the last two examples, if the **c** were not replaced by **ç** before the **a** or the **o**, it would be pronounced [k]. (See Appendix I.)

(ii) Because of the sound change of **g** from [ʒ] to [g] when that letter is followed by **a**, **o** or **u**, an **e** must be introduced after the **g** whenever, in the course of the conjugation, an ending beginning with **a** or **o** is expected immediately after it.

Compare: Je mange   or: Nous mangions
          I am eating   *We were eating*
and: Je mangeai   or: Nous mangeons
          I ate   *We are eating*

In the last two examples, if the **g** were not followed by **e** before **a** or **o**, it would be pronounced [g] (see Appendix I).

Note: A look at the endings for each tense will *immediately* reveal where those modifications are needed to preserve the correct sound-pattern of the verb.

3 Verbs in **ayer**, **oyer** and **uyer**: In their modern French version, those verbs change **y** to **i** whenever, in the course of the conjugation, **y** is due to be followed by a mute **e** (e without an accent = [ə]).

Compare: Nous essayons   or: Nous nettoyons
          We are trying   *We are cleaning*
and: J'essaie   or: Je nettoie
          I am trying   *I am cleaning*
But: J'ai essayé   Il a nettoyé
          I tried   *He cleaned*

Note: The endings **er** and **ez** are pronounced as **é** (= [e]); the **y** will therefore remain before them:

Essay**er**   or: Nettoy**ez**!
To try   *Clean!*

4 Verbs in **eler** and **eter**. Their pattern of behaviour is as follows:

(i) The majority double their **l** or **t** if the letter which follows is a mute **e** (e without an accent = [ə]):

Compare: Nous jetons   or: Nous appelons
          We are throwing   *We are calling*
and: Il jet**te**   or: Il appel**le**
          He is throwing   *He is calling*
But: J'ai jeté   J'ai appelé
          I threw   *I called*

Note: The 3rd person plural ending **ent** is *always* pronounced like a mute **e** [ə]. The doubling of the consonant will therefore occur:

Ils je**ttent**   or: Ils appe**llent**
They are throwing   *They are calling*

(ii)   The remainder of **eler** and **eter** verbs (see list below) *do not* double their consonant, but when the environment where they should do so occurs (see (i) above), they change the **e** preceding the consonant into **è** (= [ɛ]).

Compare:	Nous gelons	or:	Nous pelons
	We are freezing		*We are peeling*
and:	Nous gèlerons	or:	Nous pèlerons
	We shall freeze		*We shall peel*
But:	Je suis gelé		Il a pelé
	I am frozen		*He has peeled*
or:	Geler		Pelez!
	To freeze		*Peel!*

The most commonly used verbs in that category are: **acheter** (*to buy*), **démanteler** (*to dismantle*), **étiqueter** (*to label*), **geler** (*to freeze*) and its compounds: **dégeler** (*to defrost*), **congeler/surgeler** (*to deep-freeze*), **harceler** (*to badger*), **marteler** (*to hammer*), **modeler** (*to model*).

Note: The following verbs: **mener** (*to lead*), **semer** (*to sow*), **soulever** (*to lift*), change their **e** to **è** in the same phonetic environment as the above-mentioned category.

5   Verbs ending in **éder**, **éger**, **éler** or **éter** change their **é** to **è** when the syllable they are in is followed by a *final* mute **e** (pronounced [ə]).

If another syllable follows the mute **e**, the **é** remains unchanged!

Compare:	Céder	or:	Protéger
	To give in		*To protect*
and	Je cède!	or:	Ils protègent
	I give in!		*They protect*
But:	Tu céderas	or:	Elle protégerait
	You will give in		*She would protect*

Note: the previously-mentioned comments concerning **ent**, **er** and **ez** verb endings also apply here.

6   The verbs **envoyer** (*to send*) and **renvoyer** (*to send back*) do not totally conform to the normal rule of tense-formation. In the Future and Present Conditional, their stem is **enverr** and **renverr** respectively. For example:

Nous **enverr**ons	or:	Ils **renverr**aient
We shall send		*They would send back*

2ND GROUP VERBS — **finir** *to finish*

Simple Tenses	*Compound Tenses*
Indicative	

Present	*Perfect*
Je finis	J'ai fini
Tu finis	Tu as fini
Il finit	Il a fini
Nous finissons	Nous avons fini
Vous finissez	Vous avez fini
Ils finissent	Ils ont fini

Past Historic	*Past Anterior*
Je finis	J'eus fini
Tu finis	Tu eus fini
Il finit	Il eut fini
Nous finîmes	Nous eûmes fini
Vous finîtes	Vous eûtes fini
Ils finirent	Ils eurent fini

Imperfect	*Pluperfect*
Je finissais	J'avais fini
Tu finissais	Tu avais fini
Il finissait	Il avait fini
Nous finissions	Nous avions fini
Vous finissiez	Vous aviez fini
Ils finissaient	Ils avaient fini

Future	*Future Perfect*
Je finirai	J'aurai fini
Tu finiras	Tu auras fini
Il finira	Il aura fini
Nous finirons	Nous aurons fini
Vous finirez	Vous aurez fini
Ils finiront	Ils auront fini

Conditional	
Present	*Perfect*
Je finirais	J'aurais fini
Tu finirais	Tu aurais fini
Il finirait	Il aurait fini
Nous finirions	Nous aurions fini
Vous finiriez	Vous auriez fini
Ils finiraient	Ils auraient fini

Simple Tenses		*Compound Tenses*
	Imperative	
Present		*Perfect* (Rare)
2nd pers. sing. fin**is**		2nd pers. sing. Aie fini
1st pers. plur. Fin**issons**		1st pers. plur. Ayons fini
2nd pers. plur. Fin**issez**		2nd pers. plur. Ayez fini
	Subjunctive	
Present		*Perfect*
Que je finiss**e**		Que j'aie fini
Que tu finiss**es**		Que tu aies fini
Qu'il finiss**e**		Qu'il ait fini
Que nous finiss**ions**		Que nous ayons fini
Que vous finiss**iez**		Que vous ayez fini
Qu'ils finiss**ent**		Qu'ils aient fini
	Infinitive	
Present		*Perfect*
Fin**ir**		Avoir fini
	Participle	
Present		*Past*
Finiss**ant**		(Ayant) fini

Note: the three stems — **fin**, **finir** and **finiss** — and the Tenses each one occurs in.

Points regarding the use of 2nd group verbs:

NB　There are two conditions that a verb must fulfill in order to belong to this group: it must have an **ir** Infinitive, *and* a Present Participle ending in **issant**.

The formation of the simple tenses is as follows:

1　The basic stem (Infinitive minus **ir**), is used (with the appropriate endings) for the first three persons singular of the Present Indicative, for the Past Historic, and for the 2nd person singular of the Present Imperative.

2　The whole of the Present Infinitive is used as a stem to form the Future and the Present Conditional.

3　The basic stem + **iss** is used to form the last three persons of the Present Indicative, the whole of the Imperfect, the two plural persons of the Present Imperative and the whole of the Present Subjunctive:

Compare: Je réa**gis**   or: Il invest**it**
             I react   *He invests*
with: Je réa**girai**   or: Il invest**irait**
             I shall react   *He would invest*
and: Nous réa**gissions**   or: Qu'ils invest**issent**!
             We used to react   *Let them invest!*

Note: Apart from the insertion of the syllable **iss** between the stem and the endings of certain tenses, the principles of tense formation are identical with those of the 1st group verbs.

This group is the least troublesome of the three but there are, nevertheless, a few other points to note:

1 **Bénir** (*to bless*) has two possible adjectival forms for its past participle:

– **bénit** when the meaning is *blessed by a priest*. For example

    Du pain **bénit**   *Consecrated bread*

    De l'eau **bénite**   *Holy water*

– **béni** in all other cases:

    Madame, soyez **bénie** pour ces bonnes paroles. *Madam, may you be blessed for those kind words.*

2 **Fleurir** (*to blossom*) has two different stems for the Imperfect and the Present Participle:

(i) **fleur** if the action refers to trees or flowers;

(ii) **flor** if the action refers to a venture, a business, etc.

Compare: Le pommier **fleurissait**.

             The apple-tree was blossoming.

and: L'affaire **florissait**.

             The business was flourishing.

Note: No further distinction is made between the two throughout the rest of the conjugation.

3 **Haïr** (*to hate*) loses its diaeresis (¨) in the first three persons of the Present Indicative and in the second person singular of the Present Imperative.

Compare: Je **hais** les dimanches. (and not *je haïs)

             I hate Sundays.

and: Vous **haïssez** la solitude.

             You hate loneliness.

As a point of interest, it may be noted that a number of 2nd group verbs have been formed from adjectives of colour: **blanchir** (*to turn white*), **brunir** (*to turn brown*), **jaunir** (*to turn yellow*), **rosir** (*to turn pink*), **rougir** (*to turn red, to blush*), **noircir** (*to turn black*), **pâlir** (*to turn pale*), **verdir** (*to turn green*). For example:

    Elle **rougissait** de plaisir. *She was blushing with delight.*

3RD GROUP VERBS (**ir** category) — **partir** *to leave*

Simple Tenses	*Compound Tenses*
Indicative	
Present	*Perfect*
Je par**s**	Je suis parti
Tu par**s**	Tu es parti
Il par**t**	Il est parti
Nous part**ons**	Nous sommes partis
Vous part**ez**	Vous êtes partis
Ils part**ent**	Ils sont partis
Past Historic	*Past Anterior*
Je part**is**	Je fus parti
Tu part**is**	Tu fus parti
Il part**it**	Il fut parti
Nous part**îmes**	Nous fûmes partis
Vous part**îtes**	Vous fûtes partis
Ils part**irent**	Ils furent partis
Imperfect	*Pluperfect*
Je part**ais**	J'étais parti
Tu part**ais**	Tu étais parti
Il part**ait**	Il était parti
Nous part**ions**	Nous étions partis
Vous part**iez**	Vous étiez partis
Ils part**aient**	Ils étaient partis
Future	*Future Perfect*
Je partir**ai**	Je serai parti
Tu partir**as**	Tu seras parti
Il partir**a**	Il sera parti
Nous partir**ons**	Nous serons partis
Vous partir**ez**	Vous serez partis
Ils partir**ont**	Ils seront partis
Conditional	
Present	*Perfect*
Je partir**ais**	Je serais parti
Tu partir**ais**	Tu serais parti
Il partir**ait**	Il serait parti
Nous partir**ions**	Nous serions partis
Vous partir**iez**	Vous seriez partis
Ils partir**aient**	Ils seraient partis
Imperative	
Present	*Perfect* (Rare)
2nd pers. sing. Pars	2nd pers. sing. Sois parti
1st pers. plur. **Partons**	1st pers. plur. Soyons partis
2nd pers. plur. **Partez**	2nd pers. plur. Soyez partis

partir *cont.*

Simple Tenses	*Compound Tenses*
	Subjunctive
Present	*Perfect*
Que je part**e**	Que je sois parti
Que tu part**es**	Que tu sois parti
Qu'il part**e**	Qu'il soit parti
Que nous part**ions**	Que nous soyons partis
Que vous part**iez**	Que vous soyez partis
Qu'ils part**ent**	Qu'ils soient partis
	Infinitive
Present	*Perfect*
Part**ir**	Être parti
	Participle
Present	*Past*
Part**ant**	(Etant) parti

Note the different stems:
(i) Mixed: **par**/**part** for the Present Indicative and the Present Imperative;
(ii) **part** for the Past Historic, the Imperfect, the Present Subjunctive, the Past Participle;
(iii) **partir** for the Future and the Conditional.

3RD GROUP VERBS (**oir** category) – **recevoir** *to receive*

Simple Tenses	*Compound Tenses*
	Indicative
Present	*Perfect*
Je reçois	J'ai reçu
Tu reçois	Tu as reçu
Il reçoit	Il a reçu
Nous recev**ons**	Nous avons reçu
Vous recev**ez**	Vous avez reçu
Ils reçoiv**ent**	Ils ont reçu
Past Historic	*Past Anterior*
Je reç**us**	J'eus reçu
Tu reç**us**	Tu eus reçu
Il reç**ut**	Il eut reçu
Nous reç**ûmes**	Nous eûmes reçu
Vous reç**ûtes**	Vous eûtes reçu
Ils reç**urent**	Ils eurent reçu

recevoir-*cont.*

Simple Tenses	*Compound Tenses*
Imperfect	*Pluperfect*
Je recev**ais**	J'avais reçu
Tu recev**ais**	Tu avais reçu
Il recev**ait**	Il avait reçu
Nous recev**ions**	Nous avions reçu
Vous recev**iez**	Vous aviez reçu
Ils recev**aient**	Ils avaient reçu
Future	*Future Perfect*
Je recevr**ai**	J'aurai reçu
Tu recevr**as**	Tu auras reçu
Il recevr**a**	Il aura reçu
Nous recevr**ons**	Nous aurons reçu
Vous recevr**ez**	Vous aurez reçu
Ils recevr**ont**	Ils auront reçu

Conditional

Present	*Perfect*
Je recevr**ais**	J'aurais reçu
Tu recevr**ais**	Tu aurais reçu
Il recevr**ait**	Il aurait reçu
Nous recevr**ions**	Nous aurions reçu
Vous recevr**iez**	Vous auriez reçu
Ils recevr**aient**	Ils auraient reçu

Imperative

Present	*Perfect*
2nd pers. sing. reç**ois**	2nd pers. sing. Aie reçu
1st pers. plur. recev**ons**	1st pers. plur. Ayons reçu
2nd pers. plur. recev**ez**	2nd pers. plur. Ayez reçu

Subjunctive

Present	*Perfect*
Que je reç**oive**	Que j'aie reçu
Que tu reç**oives**	Que tu aies reçu
Qu'il reç**oive**	Qu'il ait reçu
Que nous recev**ions**	Que nous ayons reçu
Que vous recev**iez**	Que vous ayez reçu
Qu'ils reç**oivent**	Qu'ils aient reçu

Infinitive

Present	*Perfect*
Recev**oir**	Avoir reçu

recevoir-*cont.*

Simple Tenses		Compound Tenses
	Participle	
Present		*Past*
Rece**vant**		(Ayant) re**çu**

Note the different stems:
 (i) mixed: **reçoi**/**recev** for the Present Indicative, the Present Subjunctive and the Present Imperative;
 (ii) **reç** for Past Historic and Past Participle;
 (iii) **recev** for Imperfect and Present Participle;
 (iv) **recevr** for Future and Present Conditional.

Points regarding the use of 3rd group verbs (**ir/oir** categories):
1 Although the following verbs: **couvrir** (*to cover*), **ouvrir** (*to open*), **offrir** (*to offer*), **souffrir** (*to suffer*) belong to the 3rd group, they form their Present Indicative (and Present Imperative) in the same way as **er** verbs:
  Je couvre; tu ouvres; il souffre
  I cover; you open he suffers
2 The following verbs: **acquérir** (*to acquire*), **courir** (*to run*), **mourir** (*to die*), drop the **i** of their Infinitive (stem) in the Future and Present Conditional Tenses. For example:
  J'**acquerr**ai; tu **courr**as; il **mourr**a
  I shall acquire; you will run; he will die
3 **Mentir** (*to lie*), **partir** (*to leave*), **sentir** (*to feel*), **sortir** (*to go out*) drop the **t** of their stem in the first persons singular of the Present Indicative and in the second person singular of the Present Imperative:
  Je mens; tu sens; sors!
  I lie; you feel; get out!
4 **Tenir** (*to hold*) follows the same pattern as **venir** (*to come*) (see Irregular Verbs Charts on page 172).
5 **Fuir** (*to run away*) has two stems:

In the Present Indicative { 1st, 2nd, 3rd sing. + 3rd plur. = **fui**
{ 1st, 2nd plur. = **fuy**

In the Present Imperative { 2nd sing. = **fui**
{ 1st, 2nd plur. = **fuy**

In the Present Subjunctive { 1st, 2nd, 3rd sing. + 3rd plur. = **fui**
{ 1st, 2nd plur. = **fuy**

6 **Pouvoir** (*to be able to/can*) and **voir** (*to see*) have an irregular stem in the Future and Conditional:

Je **pourr**ai	Nous **verr**ions
I will be able to	*We would see*

3RD GROUP VERBS (**re** category) — **vendre** *to sell*

Simple Tenses	Compound Tenses
Indicative	
Present	*Perfect*
Je vend**s**	J'ai vendu
Tu vend**s**	Tu as vendu
Il vend	Il a vendu
Nous vend**ons**	Nous avons vendu
Vous vend**ez**	Vous avez vendu
Ils vend**ent**	Ils ont vendu
Past Historic	*Past Anterior*
Je vend**is**	J'eus vendu
Tu vend**is**	Tu eus vendu
Il vend**it**	Il eut vendu
Nous vend**îmes**	Nous eûmes vendu
Vous vend**îtes**	Vous eûtes vendu
Ils vend**irent**	Ils eurent vendu
Imperfect	*Pluperfect*
Je vend**ais**	J'avais vendu
Tu vend**ais**	Tu avais vendu
Il vend**ait**	Il avait vendu
Nous vend**ions**	Nous avions vendu
Vous vend**iez**	Vous aviez vendu
Ils vend**aient**	Ils avaient vendu
Future	*Future Perfect*
Je vend**rai**	J'aurai vendu
Tu vend**ras**	Tu auras vendu
Il vend**ra**	Il aura vendu
Nous vend**rons**	Nous aurons vendu
Vous vend**rez**	Vous aurez vendu
Ils vend**ront**	Ils auront vendu
Conditional	
Present	*Perfect*
Je vend**rais**	J'aurais vendu
Tu vend**rais**	Tu aurais vendu
Il vend**rait**	Il aurait vendu

vendre *cont.*

Simple Tenses		*Compound Tenses*
Nous vendr**ions**		Nous aurions vendu
Vous vendr**iez**		Vous auriez vendu
Ils vendr**aient**		Ils auraient vendu

Imperative

Present		*Perfect* (Rare)
2nd pers. sing. Vend**s**		2nd pers. sing. Aie vendu
1st pers. plur. Vend**ons**		1st pers. plur. Ayons vendu
2nd pers. plur. Vend**ez**		2nd pers. plur. Ayez vendu

Subjunctive

Present	*Perfect*
Que je vend**e**	Que j'aie vendu
Que tu vend**es**	Que tu aies vendu
Qu'il vend**e**	Qu'il ait vendu
Que nous vend**ions**	Que nous ayons vendu
Que vous vend**iez**	Que vous ayez vendu
Qu'ils vend**ent**	Qu'ils aient vendu

Infinitive

Present	*Perfect*
Vend**re**	Avoir vend**u**

Participle

Present	*Past*
Vend**ant**	(Ayant) vend**u**

Note the different stems:
(i) **vendr** for the Future and Present Conditional Tenses;
ii) **vend** for all other Tenses.

Points regarding the use of 3rd group (**re** category) verbs:
1 **Rompre** (*to break*) and its compounds: **corrompre** (*to corrupt*) and **interrompre** (*to interrupt*), take a **t** in the 3rd person singular of the Present Indicative:

Il corromp**t**	*or*: Elle interromp**t**
He corrupts	*She interrupts*

2 Verbs ending in **dre** *normally* take a **d** in the 3rd person singular of the Present Indicative:

Il pren**d** (Inf. = **Prendre**)	*or*: Elle atten**d** (Inf. = **attendre**)
He takes	*She waits*

But: Verbs ending in **indre** and **soudre** take a **t** instead of a **d** in the same context:

    Il pein**t** (Inf. = **peindre**)   *or*: Il résou**t** (Inf. = **résoudre**)
    He paints   *He solves*

3   **Dire** (*to say*) and **redire** (*to repeat*) become **dites** and **redites** (and not *disez and *redisez) in the 2nd person plural of the Present Indicative and Imperative.

But: **Contredire** (*to contradict*), **interdire** (*to forbid*), **médire** (*to slander*), **prédire** (*to foretell*) become contre**disez**, inter**disez**, mé**disez** and pré**disez** in the same context.

4   **Faire** becomes **faites** (and not *faisez) in the 2nd Person plural of the Present Indicative and Imperative.

5   Verbs ending in **aître** and **oître** (e.g. **connaître** *to know* and **croître** *to grow/increase*) preserve their circumflex accent over the **i** whenever that **i** is followed by a **t** in the conjugation.

Compare: Je connaissais   *or*: Ils croissent
              I used to know   *They are growing*
and: Il conna**î**t   *or*: Ils cro**î**tront
              He knows   *They will grow*

6   **Croître** (*to grow/increase*) takes a circumflex accent ˆ over the **u** of its Past Participle but its compounds do not.

Compare: Il a cr**û**   and: Il a décr**u**
              It has increased   *It has decreased*

Irregular Verbs

PRÉSENT de l'indicatif *Present indicative*	PASSÉ SIMPLE *Past historic*	IMPARFAIT *Imperfect*	FUTUR *Future*	CONDITIONNEL *Conditional*	Present du SUBJONCTIF *Present subjunctive*	IMPÉRATIF *Imperative*

Aller (+ **être**) *to go: Past participle:* allé *Present participle:* allant

je vais	allai	allais	irai	irais	aille	
tu vas	allas	allais	iras	irais	ailles	va
il va	alla	allait	ira	irait	aille	
nous allons	allâmes	allions	irons	irions	allions	allons
vous allez	allâtes	alliez	irez	iriez	alliez	allez
ils vont	allèrent	allaient	iront	iraient	aillent	

S'asseoir (+ **être**) *to sit:* assis — asseyant

je m'assieds	m'assis	m'asseyais	m'assiérai	m'assiérais	m'asseye	
tu t'assieds	t'assis	t'asseyais	t'assiéras	t'assiérais	t'asseyes	assieds-toi
il s'assied	s'assit	s'asseyait	s'assiéra	s'assiérait	s'asseye	
nous nous asseyons	nous assîmes	nous asseyions	nous assiérons	nous assiérions	nous asseyions	asseyons-nous
vous vous asseyez	vous assîtes	vous asseyiez	vous assiérez	vous assiériez	vous asseyiez	asseyez-vous
ils s'asseyent	s'assirent	s'asseyaient	s'assiéront	s'assiéraient	s'asseyent	

Present indicative	Past historic	Imperfect	Future	Conditional	Present subjunctive	Imperative

Boire (+ **avoir**) *to drink*: bu — buvant

Present indicative	Past historic	Imperfect	Future	Conditional	Present subjunctive	Imperative
je bois	bus	buvais	boirai	boirais	boive	
tu bois	bus	buvais	boiras	boirais	boives	bois
il boit	but	buvait	boira	boirait	boive	
nous buvons	bûmes	buvions	boirons	boirions	buvions	buvons
vous buvez	bûtes	buviez	boirez	boiriez	buviez	buvez
ils boivent	burent	buvaient	boiront	boiraient	boivent	

Conduire (+ **avoir**) *to drive*: conduit — conduisant

Present indicative	Past historic	Imperfect	Future	Conditional	Present subjunctive	Imperative
je conduis	conduisis	conduisais	conduirai	conduirais	conduise	
tu conduis	conduisis	conduisais	conduiras	conduirais	conduises	conduis
il conduit	conduisit	conduisait	conduira	conduirait	conduise	
nous conduisons	conduisîmes	conduisions	conduirons	conduirions	conduisions	conduisons
vous conduisez	conduisîtes	conduisiez	conduirez	conduiriez	conduisiez	conduisez
ils conduisent	conduisirent	conduisaient	conduiront	conduiraient	conduisent	

Connaître (+ **avoir**) *to know*: connu — connaissant

Present indicative	Past historic	Imperfect	Future	Conditional	Present subjunctive	Imperative
je connais	connus	connaissais	connaîtrai	connaîtrais	connaisse	
tu connais	connus	connaissais	connaîtras	connaîtrais	connaisses	connais
il connaît	connut	connaissait	connaîtra	connaîtrait	connaisse	
nous connaissons	connûmes	connaissions	connaîtrons	connaîtrions	connaissions	connaissons
vous connaissez	connûtes	connaissiez	connaîtrez	connaîtriez	connaissiez	connaissez
ils connaissent	connurent	connaissaient	connaîtront	connaîtraient	connaissent	

je cours	courus	courais	courrai	courrais	coure	
tu cours	courus	courais	courras	courrais	coures	cours
il court	courut	courait	courra	courrait	coure	
nous courons	courûmes	courions	courrons	courrions	courions	courons
vous courez	courûtes	couriez	courrez	courriez	couriez	courez
ils courent	coururent	couraient	courront	courraient	courent	

Craindre (+ **avoir**) *to fear*: craint — craignant

je crains	craignis	craignais	craindrai	craindrais	craigne	
tu crains	craignis	craignais	craindras	craindrais	craignes	crains
il craint	craignit	craignait	craindra	craindrait	craigne	
nous craignons	craignîmes	craignions	craindrons	craindrions	craignions	craignons
vous craignez	craignîtes	craigniez	craindrez	craindriez	craigniez	craignez
ils craignent	craignirent	craignaient	craindront	craindraient	craignent	

Croire (+ **avoir**) *to believe*: cru — croyant

je crois	crus	croyais	croirai	croirais	croie	
tu crois	crus	croyais	croiras	croirais	croies	crois
il croit	crut	croyait	croira	croirait	croie	
nous croyons	crûmes	croyions	croirons	croirions	croyions	croyons
vous croyez	crûtes	croyiez	croirez	croiriez	croyiez	croyez
ils croient	crurent	croyaient	croiront	croiraient	croient	

Present indicative	Past historic	Imperfect	Future	Conditional	Present subjunctive	Imperative

Cueillir (+ **avoir**) *to pick*: cueilli — cueillant

Present indicative	Past historic	Imperfect	Future	Conditional	Present subjunctive	Imperative
je cueille	cueillis	cueillais	cueillerai	cueillerais	cueille	
tu cueilles	cueillis	cueillais	cueilleras	cueillerais	cueilles	cueille
il cueille	cueillit	cueillait	cueillera	cueillerait	cueille	
nous cueillons	cueillîmes	cueillions	cueillerons	cueillerions	cueillions	cueillons
vous cueillez	cueillîtes	cueilliez	cueillerez	cueilleriez	cueilliez	cueillez
ils cueillent	cueillirent	cueillaient	cueilleront	cueilleraient	cueillent	

Devoir (+ **avoir**) *to have to/to owe*: dû — devant

Present indicative	Past historic	Imperfect	Future	Conditional	Present subjunctive	Imperative
je dois	dus	devais	devrai	devrais	doive	
tu dois	dus	devais	devras	devrais	doives	dois
il doit	dut	devait	devra	devrait	doive	
nous devons	dûmes	devions	devrons	devrions	devions	devons
vous devez	dûtes	deviez	devrez	devriez	deviez	devez
ils doivent	durent	devaient	devront	devraient	doivent	

Dire (+ **avoir**) *to say*: dit — disant

Present indicative	Past historic	Imperfect	Future	Conditional	Present subjunctive	Imperative
je dis	dis	disais	dirai	dirais	dise	
tu dis	dis	disais	diras	dirais	dises	dis
il dit	dit	disait	dira	dirait	dise	
nous disons	dîmes	disions	dirons	dirions	disions	disons
vous dites	dîtes	disiez	direz	diriez	disiez	dites
ils disent	disirent	disaient	disent	diraient	disent	

Dormir (+ **avoir**) *to sleep*: dormi — dormant

je dors	dormis	dormais	dormirai	dormirais	dorme	
tu dors	dormis	dormais	dormiras	dormirais	dormes	dors
il dort	dormit	dormait	dormira	dormirait	dorme	
nous dormons	dormîmes	dormions	dormirons	dormirions	dormions	dormons
vous dormez	dormîtes	dormiez	dormirez	dormiriez	dormiez	dormez
ils dorment	dormirent	dormaient	dormiront	dormiraient	dorment	

Ecrire (+ **avoir**) *to write*: écrit — écrivant

j'écris	écrivis	écrivais	écrirai	écrirais	écrive	
tu écris	écrivis	écrivais	écriras	écrirais	écrives	écris
il écrit	écrivit	écrivait	écrira	écrirait	écrive	
nous écrivons	écrivîmes	écrivions	écrirons	écririons	écrivions	écrivons
vous écrivez	écrivîtes	écriviez	écrirez	écririez	écriviez	écrivez
ils écrivent	écrivirent	écrivaient	écriront	écriraient	écrivent	

Envoyer (+ **avoir**) *to send*: envoyé — envoyant

j'envoie	envoyai	envoyais	enverrai	enverrais	envoie	
tu envoies	envoyas	envoyais	enverras	enverrais	envoies	envoie
il envoie	envoya	envoyait	enverra	enverrait	envoie	
nous envoyons	envoyâmes	envoyions	enverrons	enverrions	envoyions	envoyons
vous envoyez	envoyâtes	envoyiez	enverrez	enverriez	envoyiez	envoyez
ils envoient	envoyèrent	envoyaient	enverront	enverraient	envoient	

Present indicative	Past historic	Imperfect	Future	Conditional	Present subjunctive	Imperative

Eteindre (+ **avoir**) *to extinguish*: éteint — éteignant

j'éteins	éteignis	éteignais	éteindrai	éteindrais	éteigne	
tu éteins	éteignis	éteignais	éteindras	éteindrais	éteignes	éteins
il éteint	éteignit	éteignait	éteindra	éteindrait	éteigne	
nous éteignons	éteignîmes	éteignions	éteindrons	éteindrions	éteignions	éteignons
vous éteignez	éteignîtes	éteigniez	éteindrez	éteindriez	éteigniez	éteignez
ils éteignent	éteignirent	éteignaient	éteindront	éteindraient	éteignent	

Faire (+ **avoir**) *to do/to make*: fait — faisant

je fais	fis	faisais	ferai	ferais	fasse	
tu fais	fis	faisais	feras	ferais	fasses	fais
il fait	fit	faisait	fera	ferait	fasse	
nous faisons	fîmes	faisions	ferons	ferions	fassions	faisons
vous faites	fîtes	faisiez	ferez	feriez	fassiez	faites
ils font	firent	faisaient	feront	feraient	fassent	

Falloir (+ **avoir**) *to be necessary (impersonal only) Past participle*: fallu *No present participle*

il faut	il fallut	il fallait	il faudra	il faudrait	qu'il faille	

Lire (+ **avoir**) *to read*: lu — lisant

je lis	lus	lisais	lirai	lirais	lise	
tu lis	lus	lisais	liras	lirais	lises	lis
il lit	lut	lisait	lira	lirait	lise	
nous lisons	lûmes	lisions	lirons	lirions	lisions	lisons
vous lisez	lûtes	lisiez	lirez	liriez	lisiez	lisez
ils lisent	lurent	lisaient	liront	liraient	lisent	

Mettre (+ **avoir**) *to put*: mis — mettant

je mets	mis	mettais	mettrai	mettrais	mette	
tu mets	mis	mettais	mettras	mettrais	mettes	mets
il met	mit	mettait	mettra	mettrait	mette	
nous mettons	mîmes	mettions	mettrons	mettrions	mettions	mettons
vous mettez	mîtes	mettiez	mettrez	mettriez	mettiez	mettez
ils mettent	mirent	mettaient	mettront	mettraient	mettent	

Mourir (+ **être**) *to die*: mort — mourant

je meurs	mourus	mourais	mourrai	mourrais	meure	
tu meurs	mourus	mourais	mourras	mourrais	meures	meurs
il meurt	mourut	mourait	mourra	mourrait	meure	
nous mourons	mourûmes	mourions	mourrons	mourrions	mourions	mourons
vous mourez	mourûtes	mouriez	mourrez	mourriez	mouriez	mourez
ils meurent	moururent	mouraient	mourront	mourraient	meurent	

Present indicative	Past historic	Imperfect	Future	Conditional	Present subjunctive	Imperative

Naître (+ **être**) *to be born:* né — naissant

je nais	naquis	naissais	naîtrai	naîtrais	naisse	
tu nais	naquis	naissais	naîtras	naîtrais	naisses	nais
il naît	naquit	naissait	naîtra	naîtrait	naisse	
nous naissons	naquîmes	naissions	naîtrons	naîtrions	naissions	naissons
vous naissez	naquîtes	naissiez	naîtrez	naîtriez	naissiez	naissez
ils naissent	naquirent	naissaient	naîtront	naîtraient	naissent	

Ouvrir (+ **avoir**) *to open:* ouvert — ouvrant

j'ouvre	ouvris	ouvrais	ouvrirai	ouvrirais	ouvre	
tu ouvres	ouvris	ouvrais	ouvriras	ouvrirais	ouvres	ouvre
il ouvre	ouvrit	ouvrait	ouvrira	ouvrirait	ouvre	
nous ouvrons	ouvrîmes	ouvrions	ouvrirons	ouvririons	ouvrions	ouvrons
vous ouvrez	ouvrîtes	ouvriez	ouvrirez	ouvririez	ouvriez	ouvrez
ils ouvrent	ouvrirent	ouvraient	ouvriront	ouvriraient	ouvrent	

Partir (+ **être**)—see Model Chart on pages 154–5.

Plaire (+ **avoir**) *to please:* plu — plaisant

je plais	plus	plaisais	plairai	plairais	plaise	
tu plais	plus	plaisais	plairas	plairais	plaises	plais
il plaît	plut	plaisait	plaira	plairait	plaise	
nous plaisons	plûmes	plaisions	plairons	plairions	plaisions	plaisons

Pleuvoir (+ **avoir**) *to rain (impersonal only)*: plu — pleuvant

il pleut	il plut	il pleuvait	il pleuvra	il pleuvrait	qu'il pleuve	

Pouvoir (+ **avoir**) *to be able to (can)*: pu — pouvant

je peux	pus	pouvais	pourrai	pourrais	puisse	
tu peux	pus	pouvais	pourras	pourrais	puisses	
il peut	put	pouvait	pourra	pourrait	puisse	
nous pouvons	pûmes	pouvions	pourrons	pourrions	puissions	
vous pouvez	pûtes	pouviez	pourrez	pourriez	puissiez	
ils peuvent	purent	pouvaient	pourront	pourraient	puissent	

Prendre (+ **avoir**) *to take*: pris — prenant

je prends	pris	prenais	prendrai	prendrais	prenne	
tu prends	pris	prenais	prendras	prendrais	prennes	prends
il prend	prit	prenait	prendra	prendrait	prenne	
nous prenons	prîmes	prenions	prendrons	prendrions	prenions	prenons
vous prenez	prîtes	preniez	prendrez	prendriez	preniez	prenez
ils prennent	prirent	prenaient	prendront	prendraient	prennent	

Present indicative	Past historic	Imperfect	Future	Conditional	Present subjunctive	Imperative

Recevoir (+ **avoir**) — see Model Chart on pages 155–7.

Rire (+ **avoir**) *to laugh*: ri — riant

Present indicative	Past historic	Imperfect	Future	Conditional	Present subjunctive	Imperative
je ris	ris	riais	rirai	rirais	rie	
tu ris	ris	riais	riras	rirais	ries	ris
il rit	rit	riait	rira	rirait	rie	
nous rions	rîmes	riions	rirons	ririons	riions	rions
vous riez	rîtes	riiez	rirez	ririez	riiez	riez
ils rient	rirent	riaient	riront	riraient	rient	

Savoir (+ **avoir**) *to know*: su — sachant

Present indicative	Past historic	Imperfect	Future	Conditional	Present subjunctive	Imperative
je sais	sus	savais	saurai	saurais	sache	
tu sais	sus	savais	sauras	saurais	saches	sache
il sait	sut	savait	saura	saurait	sache	
nous savons	sûmes	savions	saurons	saurions	sachions	sachons
vous savez	sûtes	saviez	saurez	sauriez	sachiez	sachez
ils savent	surent	savaient	sauront	sauraient	sachent	

Sentir (+ **avoir**) *to feel/smell*: senti — sentant

Present indicative	Past historic	Imperfect	Future	Conditional	Present subjunctive	Imperative
je sens	sentis	sentais	sentirai	sentirais	sente	
tu sens	sentis	sentais	sentiras	sentirais	sentes	sens
il sent	sentit	sentait	sentira	sentirait	sente	
nous sentons	sentîmes	sentions	sentirons	sentirions	sentions	sentons
vous sentez	sentîtes	sentiez	sentirez	sentiriez	sentiez	sentez

Servir (+ **Avoir**) *to serve*: servi — servant

	Present	Passé simple	Imperfect	Future	Conditional	Subjunctive	Imperative
je	sers	servis	servais	servirai	servirais	serve	
tu	sers	servis	servais	serviras	servirais	serves	sers
il	sert	servit	servait	servira	servirait	serve	
nous	servons	servîmes	servions	servirons	servirions	servions	servons
vous	servez	servîtes	serviez	servirez	serviriez	serviez	servez
ils	servent	servirent	servaient	serviront	serviraient	servent	

Sortir (+ **être**) *to go out*: sorti — sortant

	Present	Passé simple	Imperfect	Future	Conditional	Subjunctive	Imperative
je	sors	sortis	sortais	sortirai	sortirais	sorte	
tu	sors	sortis	sortais	sortiras	sortirais	sortes	sors
il	sort	sortit	sortait	sortira	sortirait	sorte	
nous	sortons	sortîmes	sortions	sortirons	sortirions	sortions	sortons
vous	sortez	sortîtes	sortiez	sortirez	sortiriez	sortiez	sortez
ils	sortent	sortirent	sortaient	sortiront	sortiraient	sortent	

Suivre (+ **Avoir**) *to follow*: suivi — suivant

	Present	Passé simple	Imperfect	Future	Conditional	Subjunctive	Imperative
je	suis	suivis	suivais	suivrai	suivrais	suive	
tu	suis	suivis	suivais	suivras	suivrais	suives	suis
il	suit	suivit	suivait	suivra	suivrait	suive	
nous	suivons	suivîmes	suivions	suivrons	suivrions	suivions	suivons
vous	suivez	suivîtes	suiviez	suivrez	suivriez	suiviez	suivez
ils	suivent	suivirent	suivaient	suivront	suivraient	suivent	

Present indicative	Past historic	Imperfect	Future	Conditional	Present subjunctive	Imperative

Valoir (+ **avoir**) *to be worth*: valu — valant

Present indicative	Past historic	Imperfect	Future	Conditional	Present subjunctive	Imperative
je vaux	valus	valais	vaudrai	vaudrais	vaille	
tu vaux	valus	valais	vaudras	vaudrais	vailles	*(not used)*
il vaut	valut	valait	vaudra	vaudrait	vaille	
nous valons	valûmes	valions	vaudrons	vaudrions	valions	
vous valez	valûtes	valiez	vaudrez	vaudriez	valiez	
ils valent	valurent	valaient	vaudront	vaudraient	vaillent	

Venir (+ **être**) *to come*: venu — venant

Present indicative	Past historic	Imperfect	Future	Conditional	Present subjunctive	Imperative
je viens	vins	venais	viendrai	viendrai	vienne	
tu viens	vins	venais	viendrais	viendras	viennes	viens
il/elle vient	vint	venait	viendrait	viendra	vienne	
nous venons	vînmes	venions	viendrions	viendrons	venions	venons
vous venez	vîntes	veniez	viendriez	viendrez	veniez	venez
ils/elles viennent	vinrent	venaient	viendraient	viendront	viennent	

Vivre (+ **avoir**) *to live*: vécu — vivant

Present indicative	Past historic	Imperfect	Future	Conditional	Present subjunctive	Imperative
je vis	vécus	vivais	vivrai	vivrais	vive	
tu vis	vécus	vivais	vivras	vivrais	vives	vis
il vit	vécut	vivait	vivra	vivrait	vive	
nous vivons	vécûmes	vivions	vivrons	vivrions	vivions	vivons

Voir (+ **avoir**) *to see:* vu — voyant

	Present	Imperfect	Past historic	Future	Conditional	Subjunctive	Imperative
je vois	vis	voyais	vis	verrai	verrais	voie	
tu vois	vis	voyais	vis	verras	verrais	voies	vois
il voit	vit	voyait	vit	verra	verrait	voie	
nous voyons	vîmes	voyions	vîmes	verrons	verrions	voyions	voyons
vous voyez	vîtes	voyiez	vîtes	verrez	verriez	voyiez	voyez
ils voient	virent	voyaient	virent	verront	verraient	voient	

Vouloir (+ **avoir**) *to want:* voulu — voulant

	Present	Imperfect	Past historic	Future	Conditional	Subjunctive	Imperative
je veux	voulus	voulais	voulus	voudrai	voudrais	veuille	
tu veux	voulus	voulais	voulus	voudras	voudrais	veuilles	veuille
il veut	voulut	voulait	voulut	voudra	voudrait	veuille	
nous voulons	voulûmes	voulions	voulûmes	voudrons	voudrions	voulions	veuillons
vous voulez	voulûtes	vouliez	voulûtes	voudrez	voudriez	vouliez	veuillez
ils veulent	voulurent	voulaient	voulurent	voudront	voudraient	veuillent	

Key points

1　The verb is considered the most important word in a sentence: it enables us *to express* actions, states of mind or body, feelings; *to situate* them along the time axis through its various Tenses and, through the various Moods, *to add* particular overtones (doubt, possibility, etc.).

2　There are significant differences in the conjugation systems of the two languages. In French, verb endings are far more significant than in English to determine the *Tense* (Present, Imperfect, etc.) and the *Person* of the verb (1st, 2nd, 3rd, singular or plural).

3　Verbs fall into several categories according to the endings of their infinitives *and* of their present participle. Those categories are themselves organised into the three following groups:

- 1st group: Infinitive = er — Present Participle = **ant**
- 2nd group: Infinitive = ir — Present Participle = **issant**
- 3rd group: Infinitive = ir/oir/re — Present participle = **ant**

4　With very few exceptions, notably **aller** (*to go*), the verbs of the 1st and 2nd groups are regular, i.e. they follow a fixed pattern as regards tense formation. Close examination of the Model Charts for those 2 groups will reveal the way the stem is selected *and* the endings used within each Tense.

5　Some of the 'exceptions' encountered in the first group are *phonetic* and not grammatical: the stem of the verb only changes to preserve the same sound-pattern throughout the conjugation. Such is the case for verbs ending in **cer** and **ger**.

- *the first* change **c** to **ç** before **a** or **o**;
- *the second* insert an **e** between the **g** and any subsequent ending beginning with **a** or **o**.

6　*Normally*, verbs use two stems in their conjugation

(*a*)　the Infinitive *minus* the ending (**er/ir/re**) for the present, Past Historic, Imperfect Indicative; the Present Imperative and the Present Subjunctive

(*b*)　the *full* Infinitive (ending included) — except for the **e** of **re** verbs — for the Future Indicative and the Present Conditional.

7　There are, however, some *notable exceptions* to this rule, particularly in the 3rd group, which is the smallest but also the most troublesome. A Model Chart of three of its verbs (**partir, recevoir, vendre**) has been given so as to present the most likely variations in *stem and endings* for that group.

8　The most frequently used irregular verbs have been presented in the Irregular Charts.

9　In order to form compound tenses, auxiliaries are needed. The main auxiliaries are **avoir** (*to have*) and **être** (*to be*); the Past Participle of the main verb is then added to the selected tense of the appropriate auxiliary.

Remember:　Verbs conjugated with **être** are: pronominal verbs (e.g. reflexives) and the 'famous 14' (**aller, venir**, etc.). All other verbs form their compound tenses with **avoir**.

10　It is possible to create a whole new category of *double compound tenses* which may be used in *spoken French* to replace some of the more 'highbrow' or 'old fashioned' tenses (Past Historic or Past Anterior). They are called **temps surcomposés** and are constructed as follows:

(*a*) For verbs using **avoir** as an auxiliary:
  – appropriate compound tense of **avoir** + Past Participle of main verb.

(*b*) For tenses using **être** as an auxiliary:
  – appropriate compound tense of **avoir** + Past Part. of **être** (= **été**) + Past Part. of main verb

11 For the conjugation of verbs (i.e. formation of tenses with stems and endings), some of the 'detective work' outlined in the introduction will prove invaluable.

14 Adverbs

Adverbs are words — or expressions — which in French as in English modify (i.e. refine) the meaning of verbs, adjectives, other adverbs or their equivalents. For example:

Je *chante* **mal**. *I sing badly*. (Here the adverb modifies a verb.)

Cette photo est **très** *jolie*. *This photo is very pretty*. (Here the adverb modifies an adjective.)

Vous dansez **extrêmement** *bien*. *You dance extremely well*. (Here the adverb modifies another adverb.)

In the above examples, the adverb is indicated in bold type, and the word the adverb modifies in italic bold.

In a way, adverbs are to the words they modify, the equivalent of what adjectives are to nouns. The similarity is further highlighted by the following facts:

1 Some adjectives can be used as adverbs (this point is also mentioned on page 53 in the chapter dealing with adjectives).

Je vais le dire **haut** et **clair**. *I am going to say it loud(ly) and clear(ly)*.

Elle chante **faux**. *She sings off-key*.

Ils tiennent **ferme**. *They are holding on firmly/fast*.

2 A great many French adjectives can be turned into adverbs by addition of the ending **ment**. The adverbs thus obtained are often labelled 'adverbs of manner'. In fact, some of them can also be adverbs of time, quantity, etc. (see categories below).

Unlike adjectives, however, adverbs do not vary in gender or number.

Compare: Il marche **droit**. *He walks straight = in a straight line*.

and: Elle marche **droit**. *She walks straight = in a straight line*.

Rules governing the formation of adverbs in *ment*

The rules of formation of such adverbs are as follows:

1 *Normally*, the adverb is obtained by adding **ment** to the feminine-singular form of the adjective. Examples are shown in the table below.

masc. sing.	fem. sing.	adverb	meaning
fort	forte	fortement	*strongly*
normal	normale	normalement	*normally*
partiel	partielle	partiellement	*partially*
sage	sage	sagement	*wisely/quietly*
vif	vive	vivement	*quickly/swiftly*

2   In certain cases, however, there are some modifications to this 'normal' formation rule:

(*a*)   If the masculine singular form of the adjective ends in **i**, **e** or **u**, the adverb will be formed directly from it, and the **e** of the feminine omitted, as shown in the table below:

masc. sing.	fem. sing.	adverb	meaning
absolu	absolue	absolument	*absolutely*
*cru	crue	crûment	*crudely*
*gai	gaie	gaîment	*gaily*
joli	jolie	joliment	*prettily*
vrai	vraie	vraiment	*truly*

Notes:

(i)   In the case of **beau** (*beautiful*), **nouveau** (*new*), **fou** (*mad*) and **mou** (*limp*), the adverbs will be formed in the normal way: **bellement** (*beautifully*), **nouvellement** (*newly*), **follement** (*madly*) and **mollement** (*limply*).

(ii)   In two of the above examples (marked *), the absence of the **e** of the feminine is signified by a circumflex accent˄. The circumflex accent often indicates in this way the disappearance of a letter which used to be present in old French.

(*b*)   If the masculine singular form of the adjective ends in **ant**, the adverb will be formed by deleting that ending and replacing it with **amment**. Adjectives ending in **ent** in the masculine singular will lose that ending and replace it with **emment**:

Vous vous battez **vaillamment**.   *You fight valiantly.* (from adj. **vaillant**)

Elles se disputaient **constamment**.   *They used to argue constantly.* (from adj. **constant**)

Elle le frappa **violemment** au visage.   *She hit him violently in the face.* (from adj. **violent**)

Avançons **prudemment**.   *Let's proceed cautiously.* (from adj. **prudent**)

Note: **lent** (*slow*), **présent** (*present*) and **véhément** (*vehement*) follow the normal pattern of formation (i.e. fem. sing. adj. + **ment**). For example:

> La voiture avançait **lentement**. *The car was moving slowly forward.*
>
> *Ils refusèrent* **véhémentement** de partir. *They vehemently refused to leave.*

(*c*) A small number of adjectives, whilst following the normal pattern of formation, take an acute accent (´) on the **e** before adding the ending **ment**:

masc. sing.	fem. sing.	adverb	meaning
aveugle	aveugle	aveuglément	*blindly*
commode	commode	commodément	*conveniently*
commun	commune	communément	*commonly*
confus	confuse	confusément	*vaguely*
énorme	énorme	énormément	*enormously*
immense	immense	immensément	*immensely*

(*d*) A limited number of adjectives undergo a change in spelling before adding the ending **ment**:

masc. sing.	fem. sing.	adverb	meaning
bref	brève	*or* brièvement / brèvement	*briefly*
grave	grave	*or* grièvement / gravement	*gravely (ill)*
traître	traîtresse	traîtreusement	*treacherously*

Position of adverbs

The position of French adverbs is not always absolutely fixed and can, at times, be quite different from that of English adverbs. (In the following examples the adverb is shown in bold with the word it modifies in italic bold:

Compare:	He **often** *comes* to see us.
and:	Il *vient* **souvent** nous voir.
or	We shall **never** *forget* you.
and:	Nous ne vous *oublierons* **jamais**.

It is, however, possible to formulate general rules concerning the position of French adverbs. They are as follows:

1 Adverbs modifying simple tense verbs (i.e. without an auxiliary) are normally placed after those verbs:

Ils reviendront **souvent** nous voir. *They will often come back to see us.*

Nous parlons **rarement** du passé. *We rarely talk about the past.*

2 Adverbs modifying compound tense verbs (i.e. with an auxiliary) are normally placed between the auxiliary and the past participle:

J'ai **souvent** parlé à cet homme. *I have often talked to that man.*

Vous êtes **quelquefois** arrivés en retard au bureau. *You sometimes arrived late at the office.*

3 Adverbs modifying adjectives, past participles, other adverbs or expressions of similar value, are generally placed before those words or expressions:

Votre chien est **très** fidèle mais **peu** obéissant. *Your dog is very faithful but not very obedient.*

Les deux hommes parlaient **trop** fort. *The two men were speaking too loudly.*

Notes:

(a) The position of the adverb can sometimes be changed to create a special effect. In the two examples which follow, the brackets indicate the place the adverb should normally occupy.

Soudain, il se tourna ( ) vers moi.

Suddenly he turned towards me. (dramatic effect)

Tu as ( ) été trompé, **incontestablement**.

You have been swindled, no doubt about it. (emphasis)

(b) Adverbs of place and many adverbs of time (see categories below) modifying a compound tense verb are placed after the past participle and not immediately after the auxiliary:

Ils ont dîné **ici** hier soir. *They dined here last night.*

Nous étions arrivés **là** par hasard. *We had arrived there by chance.*

Je l'ai revue **souvent**. *I have often seen her again.*

(c) If the adverb, because of its meaning, links two sentences together, it will be placed between them:

Il a refusé de nous voir. **Néanmoins**, il a accepté de lire notre lettre. *He refused to see us. Nevertheless, he accepted to read our letter.*

L'argent a disparu. **Pourtant** il était là il y a deux minutes! *The money has disappeared. Yet it was here two minutes ago!*

Types of adverbs

Adverbs are generally grouped by meaning into seven broad categories. It is, of course, possible for the same adverb to occur in more than one category with a different meaning:

Compare: Il travaille **bien**.
            He works well. (adverb of manner)
and: Il est **bien** malade.
            He is very ill. (adverb of quantity)

The seven categories are given below.

1   **Adverbs of manner:**

ainsi *thus*, **à tort** *wrongly*, **bien** *well*, **comme** *as/how*, **exprès** *on purpose*, **mal** *badly*, **mieux** *better*, **pis** *worse*, **plutôt** *rather*, **vite** *quickly*, **volontiers** *willingly*, etc. (To these must be added a great many adverbs ending in **ment** which are derived from adjectives.) For example:

> Je suis sûr que vous le faites **exprès** dit-il **méchamment**.   *I am sure you do it on purpose, he said viciously.*
>
> Les choses vont **de mal en pis**. (set expression)   *Things are going from bad to worse.*
>
> Il est accusé **à tort**.   *He is wrongfully accused.*

2   **Adverbs of quantity:**

à peine *hardly*, **assez** *enough*, **aussi** *as much*, **beaucoup/bien** *a great deal/much*, **comme** *how much*, **davantage** *more*, **guère** *little*, **moins** *less*, **pas mal** *a good deal* (familiar), **peu** *little*, **plus** *more*, **quelque** *approximately*, **si** *so*, **tant/tellement** *so much*, **tout** *totally*, **très** *very*, **trop** *too much*, etc. For example:

> Nous avons **beaucoup** marché et nous sommes **très** fatigués.   *We have walked a great deal and we are very tired.*
>
> Ils ont **tant** souffert!   *They have suffered so much!*
>
> J'ai **assez** mangé, merci **bien**.   *I have eaten enough, thank you very much.*

Notes:

(*a*)   Do not confuse the adverb **quelque** (*approximately*) and the indefinite adjective **quelques** (*some/a few*). The adverb is invariable, whereas the adjective can vary in number (see chapter on indefinite adjectives)

Compare: Le train est resté **quelque** dix minutes en gare.   *The train stayed approximately ten minutes in the station.* (adverb = no agreement)

and: Le train est resté **quelques** minutes en gare.   *The train stayed a few minutes in the station.* (indefinite adjective = agreement) (*b*) As mentioned previously, adverbs are invariable. **Tout**, however, violates the rule in the following cases: *if* **tout** modifies a feminine adjective, *and if* that adjective begins with a consonant or with an aspirated 'h' (on this point see appendix I), **tout** will agree in gender and number with that adjective.

Compare: Elle était **tout** émue.

She was quite moved. (followed by vowel = no agreement)

and: Elle était **toute** contente.

She was quite pleased. (followed by consonant = agreement)

or: Elles sont **toutes** honteuses.

They are quite ashamed. (followed by aspirated 'h' = agreement)

and: Elles sont **tout** étonnées.

They are quite astonished. (followed by vowel = no agreement)

3 **Adverbs of time:**
d'abord *firstly*, **alors** *then*, **après** *afterwards*, **aujourd'hui** *today*, **auparavant** *previously*, **aussitôt** *immediately/at once*, **autrefois** *previously/formerly*, **avant** *before*, **bientôt** *soon*, **déjà** *already*, **demain** *tomorrow*, **depuis** *since*, **désormais** *from now on/henceforth*, **de suite** *straight afterwards*, **encore** *again/still*, **enfin** *finally*, **ensuite** *afterwards*, **hier** *yesterday*, **jadis** *a long time ago*, **jamais** *ever/never*, **longtemps** *for a long time*, **immédiatement** *at once*, **maintenant** *now*, **parfois/quelquefois** *sometimes*, **soudain/tout à coup** *suddenly*, **toujours** *always/still*, **tout de suite** *at once*.

For example:

Téléphonez **d'abord**; vous partirez **ensuite**. *Telephone first, you will go afterwards.*

La neige ne reste **jamais** bien **longtemps**. *The snow never stays (for) very long.*

Ils ont **quelquefois** reçu des nouvelles de leur fils. *They sometimes heard from their son.*

Notes:
(*a*) Some of the above adverbs have two distinct meanings or nearly identical forms which may lead to confusion. Extra care will be needed when dealing with those:

Compare: Il finira ce travail et il viendra **de suite**.

He will finish this job and will come afterwards.

and: Il vient **tout de suite**!

He is coming at once!

or: Elle est insupportable; elle est **toujours** en colère.
           She is unbearable; she is always cross.
and: Elle n'était pas contente; elle est **toujours** en colère.
           She wasn't pleased; she is still angry.
or: Vous n'avez **jamais** répondu.
           You have never replied.
and: Avez-vous **jamais** répondu?
           Have you ever replied?

(*b*) **tout à coup** (*suddenly*) has a near-equivalent in the 'adverbs of manner' category. Care should be taken not to confuse the two.

Compare: Il ouvrit **tout à coup** la porte.
           He suddenly opened the door.
and: Il ouvrit **tout d'un coup** la porte.
           He opened the door all in one go. (adverb of manner)

4 Adverbs of place/position:

Ailleurs *elsewhere*, **alentour/autour** *around*, **ça et là** *here and there*, **-ci** *here*, **contre** *against*, **dedans** *inside*, **dehors** *outside*, **derrière** *behind*, **dessous** *below/underneath*, **ici** *here*, **-là** *there*, **loin** *far*, **nulle part** *nowhere*, **où** *where*, **partout** *everywhere*, **près** *near*, **quelque part** *somewhere*. For example:

Les rescapés couraient **ça et là**. *The survivors were running here and there.*
Attendez **dehors**! *Wait outside!*
Ils voient des espions **partout**! *They see spies everywhere!*

In the last example, note the unusual position of the adverb (for emphasis)

Note: **ici** (*here*) can also be an adverb of time meaning up to now
so: Jusqu'**ici** la route a été bonne. could mean:
either: *Up to now* (adv. of time) *the road has been good.*
or: *Up to this point* (adv. of place) *the road has been good.*

5 Adverbs of affirmation:

Assurément *assuredly*, **aussi** *also/too*, **bien/fort bien** *very well*, **certainement** *certainly*, **certes** *indeed*, **oui** *yes*, **précisément** *precisely*, **sans aucun doute** *without any doubt*, **sans doute** *probably/certainly*, **si** *yes*, **soit** *alright/granted*, **vraiment** *indeed/definitely*. For example:

Je crois **vraiment** qu'ils ont raison. *I definitely believe they are right.*
Pensez-vous que vous réussirez? **Certes!** *Do you think you will succeed? Indeed (I do)!*
Sortirez-vous seul? **Sans aucun doute!** *Will you go out alone? Without a doubt!*

> **Aussi**, placed at the beginning of a sentence/clause, is a 'sentence connector' meaning *consequently/therefore*. In that case it is normally followed by an inversion.
>
> Compare: Vous avez donné votre parole. **Aussi** irons-nous les voir. *You have given your word. Consequently we shall go and see them.*
>
> and: Vous avez donné votre parole. Nous irons **aussi** les voir. *You have given your word. We will go and see them too.*

Note: Although they *both* mean *yes*, **oui** and **si** must be clearly distinguished:
— **Oui** is used to reply to a straight-forward question:
  Il est malade? **Oui**. *Is he ill? Yes (he is).*
  Est-ce que le film est fini? **Oui**. *Is the film over? Yes (it is).*
— **Si** is used as a reply to a question *formulated in the negative*:
  Tu n'as pas froid? **Si!** *Aren't you cold? Yes (I am).*
  Les agents ne vous ont jamais arrêté? **Si**, une fois! *Have the police ever stopped you? Yes once!*

6 Adverbs of negation:
The main adverbs of negation are **non** (*no*) and **ne** (*not* . . .). A clear distinction should be made between them.
— *Non* can be used on its own to express the negation, whether the sentence is affirmative or interrogative:
  Descends! **Non!** *Come down! No (I shan't)!*
  Prendrez-vous l'avion? **Non!** *Will you take the plane? No (I won't)!*
  Vous n'avez pas froid? **Non!** *Aren't you cold? No (I'm not)!*
— **Non** can also be used with some other adverbial expression like **pas, point, point du tout, pas le moins du monde** to emphasise the negative meaning (=*not in the least/not in the slightest*):
  Avez vous soif? **Non, pas le moins du monde.** *Are you thirsty? (No) not in the least.*
Note: In modern French, the English expression *why not*? is translated by **Pourquoi pas**? rather than **pourquoi non**?
  Irons-nous en Espagne cet été? Pourquoi **pas**? *Shall we go to Spain this summer? Why not?*
— **Ne** is *normally* unable to express the negative idea on its own and is therefore used in connection with other suitable words or expressions. The most common are listed below.
NB Words in brackets can be used with the word they appear next to. If so, they must appear in the position shown.

1 *followed by*		*2* *accompanying phrase*	*3* *meaning*
ne	+ verb/aux	+ aucun/aucune	*not a single one* (masc/fem.)
		+ aucunement	*not in the least*
		+ (plus) guère	*hardly (any more)*
		+ jamais	*not . . . ever*
		+ jamais plus	*not . . . ever again*
		+ jamais (plus) personne	*not anyone (ever) again*
		+ jamais (plus) rien	*not anything (ever) again*
		+ ni . . . ni	*neither . . . nor*
		+ non plus	*not . . . either*
		+ nul	*not . . . anyone/anything*
		+ nullement	*not . . . in the slightest*
		+ pas	*not . . . any*
		+ pas du tout	*not . . . at all*
		+ personne	*not . . . anybody*
		+ plus	*not . . . any longer*
		+ plus personne	*not . . . anyone any more*
		+ plus que	*not any more/no more than . .*
		+ que	*. . . only*
		+ (plus) quiconque	*not . . . anyone (any longer)*
		+ (plus) rien	*not . . . anything (any more)*

For example:

Vous **ne** payez **plus** votre loyer.   *You no longer pay your rent.*

Laissez-moi tranquille! Je **n'**ai **rien** fait!   *Leave me alone! I have done nothing!*

Que se passe-t-il? Il **n'**y a **plus personne** sur la plage.   *What is happening? There is no longer anybody on the beach.*

Nous **ne** resterons **que** cinq minutes.   *We shall only stay five minutes.*

Pourquoi **ne** dites-vous **plus rien?**   *Why are you not saying anything any more?*

Note: Except for those appearing *on the same line*, the expressions in column 2 are mutually exclusive:

Do not say or write:

*Nous **ne** dormons **pas jamais** avec les fenêtres fermées.

Say or write instead:

Nous **ne** dormons **jamais** avec les fenêtres fermées.   *We never sleep with the windows closed.*

Do not say or write:

*Vous **ne** mangez **pas plus**.

Say or write instead:

Vous **ne** mangez **plus**.   *You no longer eat.*

> However, if the sense of **plus** is comparative (= *more*) rather than
> negative (= *no longer*) the association **pas plus** is possible:
> Compare: Il **ne** paie **plus**! *He no longer pays!*
> and: Il **ne** paie **pas plus** (que moi).
> *He does not pay any more (than I do).*

Note:
(a) In colloquial French **ne** is very often omitted:
Tu travailles **pas**. (for: tu **ne** travailles **pas**)
You do not work.
Elle arrête **jamais**. (for: elle **n'**arrête **jamais**)
She never stops.
As a learner you should use such constructions with great care to
avoid possible ambiguities:
Compare: Je fume **plus**. (for: je **ne** fume **plus**)
I no longer smoke. (in this case the **s** of **plus** is *never*
sounded)
and: Je fume **plus**!
I smoke more! (in this case the **s** of **plus** is *usually*
sounded)
(b) Conversely, **ne** can sometimes be used on its own in re-
fined/literary French for **ne pas** or **ne point**, i.e. to express a
negative idea:
Je **ne** sais si vous comprenez. (for: je **ne** sais **pas** . . .)
I do not know if you understand.
Partez donc! Je **ne** peux! (for: je **ne** peux **pas**)
Do go! I cannot!

> A small number of verbs or expressions are, in good French,
> used with a **ne** called 'expletive ne' which is *not* a negative. The
> most common of those verbs/expressions are: **avoir peur que** *to
> be afraid that*, **craindre que** *to fear that*, **à moins que** *unless* . . . ,
> **avant que** *before*, **de crainte que/de peur que** *for fear that* . . . For
> example:
> Finis ton chocolat **avant que** ton frère **n'**arrive. *Finish
> your chocolate before your brother arrives.*
> J'**ai peur** qu'il **ne** refuse. *I fear he may refuse.*
> Compare: Nous craignons qu'il **n'**accepte.
> *We fear that he may accept.*
> and: Nous craignons qu'il **n'**accepte **pas**.
> *We fear he may not accept*

(c)   The following negative adverbial expressions can be placed at the beginning of a sentence/clause, provided the order of the two words is reversed: **ne . . . aucun** *none/no one*, **ne . . . jamais** *never*, **ne . . . nul** *no one*, **ne . . . personne** *nobody*, **ne . . . rien** *nothing*. In such cases the negative **ne** will be placed before the verb.

Jamais les gens **ne** signeront ce document.   *People will never sign this document.*

Rien n'avait **plus** d'importance.   *Nothing mattered any longer.*

Personne ne souhaite vous offenser.   *Nobody wishes to offend you.*

(d)   When modifying an infinitive, the following expressions are placed before it in one block instead of being, as is normal, separated by the verb: **ne pas** *not to*, **ne jamais** *not ever*, **ne plus** *not any longer*, **ne rien** *not anything*. For example:

Le vieux monsieur décida de **ne plus** sortir.   *The old man decided not to go out any more.*

Prière de **ne pas** marcher sur la pelouse.   *You are requested not to walk on the grass.*

Je t'ai dit de **ne jamais** m'écrire.   *I told you never to write to me.*

But: La vieille dame décida de **ne** voir **personne**.   *The old lady decided not to see anyone.*

7   **Adverbs of doubt:**

Apparemment *apparently*, **peut-être** *perhaps*, **probablement/sans doute** *probably*, **vraisemblablement** *in all probability*. For example:

Il faudrait **peut-être** faire quelque chose.   *Perhaps we should do something.*

Apparemment, les étrangers ont besoin d'un visa.   *Apparently, foreigners need a visa.*

Note: If **peut-être**, **probablement** and **sans doute** are placed at the beginning of the sentence and are *not* followed by **que**, a change in the word-order (i.e. inversion) is necessary.

Compare: Le docteur a **peut-être** tort.

and: **Peut-être** le docteur a-t-il tort.
           The doctor may be wrong.

or: Les prix vont **sans doute** baisser.

and: **Sans doute** les prix vont-ils baisser.
        Prices are probably about to go down.

> If the subject of such sentences is a noun, it must appear immediately after the adverb; the corresponding subject pronoun will then be used to form the inversion (in other words the subject will appear twice).
>
> Compare: **Peut-être** vont-ils réussir. (pronoun only)
> *They may succeed.*
> and: **Peut-être** les journalistes vont-ils réussir.
> *The journalists may succeed.*(noun + pronoun)
> *Note*: * **Peut-être vont les journalistes réussir** (noun only) is unacceptable.

Key points

1 Adverbs are words or expressions which can modify verbs, adjectives, past participles, other adverbs, or phrases of similar value.

2 Adverbs are invariable: they do not alter in gender or number.

3 A great many adverbs are formed by adding the ending **ment** to the feminine (and in some cases to the masculine) form of the required adjective.

4 Although the position of adverbs is not absolutely fixed and can sometimes be changed for stylistic reasons, there are some general rules concerning their placement which can be of help to the learner.

5 Adverbs modifying *simple tense* verbs (i.e. without an auxiliary) follow the verb; adverbs modifying *compound tense* verbs (i.e. with an auxiliary) are normally placed between the auxiliary and the past participle; adverbs modifying adjectives and other adverbs generally precede them.

6 There are 7 main categories of adverbs; they express the following notions: manner; quantity; time; place/position; affirmation; negation; doubt.

7 Some adverbs, when placed at the beginning of a sentence or clause, undergo a change in meaning and/or require a change in word order.

8 A small number of adverbs may appear in more than one of the 7 categories. In such cases, their meaning will obviously be different in each of the categories in which they appear.

9 A very small number of pairs of adverbial expressions look almost identical but have different meanings. They should be carefully distinguished and remembered.

SECTION III
Building the Complete Picture

15 Prepositions

Note: Making proper use of prepositions is probably the most difficult stage in the acquisition of a foreign language, but it is by no means impossible. In this case, as in any other, be attentive to the examples given and to any new material you will come across, and refine your knowledge accordingly.

Prepositions are words, or groups of words, which are used to express a relationship (usually of time, space, purpose, etc.) between two phrases. The first phrase may have the shape or the value of a noun, an adjective, a verb or an adverb, and the second that of a noun, a pronoun or a verb:

Les clients attendent **devant** le magasin. *The customers are waiting in front of the shop.*

C'est à cause **de** lui qu'elle a décidé de partir. *It is because of him that she decided to leave.*

Notes:

(a) Prepositions may be made of one word only (simple prepositions) or several (compound prepositions or prepositional phrases). In the second case, the last words will very often be **à** (*at, to, in*, etc. or **de** (*of, from*, etc.), which are the two most common prepositions in the language.

(b) **à** (*at, to, in*, etc.) and **de** (*of, from*, etc.) combine with the definite articles **le** and **les** (*the*) in the following way:

à + le ⟶ au
à + les ⟶ aux
de + le ⟶ du
de + les ⟶ des

For example:

Les employés allaient **au** travail. *The employees were going to work.*

Les spectateurs sortent **du** cinéma. *The spectators are coming out of the cinema.*

(c) In an attempt to facilitate learning, the prepositions introduced in the chapter have been grouped into broad categories: position; movement; constraint-restriction-exclusion; inclusion or participation; manner or purpose. But it should be noted that such a classification, although useful, can be somewhat arbitrary.

(*d*)   The same preposition may be found in more than one of the above-mentioned categories, each time with a different shade of meaning. For example:

Il est **à** Paris.   *He is in Paris.* (position in space)
Il va **à** Paris.   *He is going to Paris.* (movement)
C'est une machine **à** coudre.   *It is a sewing machine.* (lit: *a machine for sewing* — purpose)
Le car arrivera **à** six heures.   *The coach will arrive at 6 o'clock.* (position in time)

The main prepositions are given below in their categories.

Position or location

1   *In space*: **à** *at, in,* **à côté de** *beside,* **à l'arrière de** *at the back of,* **à l'avant de** *at the front of,* **à l'intérieur de** *inside,* **à l'exterieur de** *outside,* **à l'extrémité de** *at the far end of,* **au bout de** *at the end of,* **au-dessous de** *below,* **au-dessus de** *above,* **au milieu de** *in the middle of,* **auprès de** *close to,* **autour de** *around,* **aux environs de** *in the vicinity of,* **avant** *before,* **chez** *at someone's,* **contre** *against,* **derrière** *behind,* **devant** *in front of,* **en** *in,* **en arrière de** *further back from,* **en avant de** *ahead of,* **en travers de** *across,* **entre** *between,* **hors de** *outside,* **le long de** *along,* **parmi** *among,* **sur** *on,* **sous** *under,* etc. For example:

Ton fils est **au** lit.   *Your son is in bed.*
Il est tombé **au milieu de** la rue.   *He fell in the middle of the street.*
Il y a un arbre **en travers de** la route.   *There is a tree lying across the road.*

2   *In time*: **à** *at,* **après,** *after,* **au milieu de** *in the middle of,* **au moment de** *at the time of,* **aux environs de** *around,* **avant** *before,* **dès** *from/as early as,* **en début de** *at the beginning of,* **en dehors de** *outside,* **en fin de** *at the end of,* **entre** *between,* **pendant** *during,* **vers** *towards,* etc. For example:

Ils ont sonné **au milieu de** la nuit.   *They rang (the bell) in the middle of the night.*
Je vous écrirai **dès** demain.   *I shall write to you no later than tomorrow.*
Est-ce que vous fermez **avant** ou **après** huit heures?   *Do you close before or after 8 o'clock?*

Movement

1 *In space*: **à** *to*, **après** *after*, **au-dehors de** *outside*, **au-delà de** *beyond*, **au-devant de** *before/towards*, **au travers de** *through*, **en** *in/to*, **le long de** *along*, **passé** *after/past*, **par** *through*, **pour** *to/towards*, **vers** *towards*, **via** *via*, etc. For example:

N'allez pas **au-delà de** la rivière! *Do not go beyond the river!*

Il est toujours **par** monts et **par** vaux. (saying) *He is always gallivanting about.* (lit: *through mountains and valleys*)

Elle se tourna **vers** lui. *She turned towards him.*

2 *In time*: **à** *to*, **à partir de** *from*, **après** *after* **au-delà de** *beyond*, **avant** *before*, **de** *from*, **durant** *during*, **en** *within*, **jusqu'à** *up to/until*, **passé** *after*, **pour** *for*, **vers** *towards*, etc. For example:

A partir d'aujourd' hui, je prends les décisions. *As from today, I make the decisions.*

Ne m'appelez pas **avant** dix heures ce soir. *Do not call me before ten o'clock tonight.*

Restez **jusqu'à** dimanche! *Stay until Sunday!*

Constraint-restriction-exclusion

A cause de *because of*, **à force de** *by dint of*, **à défaut de** *for want of*, **à l'exception de** *except for*, **à l'exclusion de** *excluding*, **à l'insu de** *unbeknown to*, **à moins de** *unless*, **au péril de** *at the risk of*, **aux dépens de** *at the expense of*, **au lieu de** *instead of*, **de peur de** *for fear of*, **contre** *against*, **en dépit de** *in spite of*, **en raison de** *by reason of*, **étant donné** *given*, **excepté** *except*, **faute de** *through lack of*, **hormis** *except*, **malgré** *in spite of*, **quant à** *as for*: idea of opposition, **sans** *without*, **sauf** *except*, **selon** *according to*, **vu** *in view of*, etc. For example:

Ne restez pas trop longtemps **de peur de** le fatiguer. *Do not stay too long for fear of tiring him.*

En dépit de nos efforts, il a échoué. *In spite of our efforts, he has failed.*

Vous pouvez partir; **quant à** moi, je reste. *You may go; (as for me) I am staying.*

Participation — inclusion

A l'aide de *with the help of — something*, **avec** *with*, **avec l'aide de** *with the help of — someone*, **dans** *in*, **en** *in*, **en compagnie de** *in the company of*, **en plus de** *besides*, **grâce à** *thanks to*, **parmi** *among*, **outre** *besides*, **y compris** *including*, etc. For example:

Reste **avec** moi!   *Stay with me!*
Il est **dans** la marine.   *He is in the Navy.*
Tout a disparu, **y compris** l'argent.   *Everything has gone, including the money.*

Manner — purpose

A *to/for*, **avec** *with*, **afin de** *in order to*, **à la mode de** *in the manner of*, **au moyen de** *by means of*, **contre** *against*, **dans le but de** *with a view to*, **de façon à/de manière à** *so as to*, **en vue de** *with a view to*, **par** *by/through*, **pour** *in order to*, **sans** *without*, **suivant** *according to*, etc. For example:

C'est une machine **à** laver.   *It is a washing machine.* (lit: *a machine for washing*)
Je vous dis cela **afin de** vous aider.   *I tell you that in order to help you.*
Il est sorti **sans** chapeau.   *He went out without a hat.*

Use of prepositions

1   A limited number of prepositions can be followed by a verb. In each case, the verb must be in the infinitive (present or past). Those prepositions are:
à *to/for*, **de** *to/of/from*, **pour** *for/to*, **sans** *without*, **après** *after*, **par** *by*. For the last two, see notes below.
For example:

Préparez-vous **à** partir.   *Get ready to go.*
Ça ne coûte rien **de** dire merci.   *It does not cost anything to say thank you.*
Il se baissa **pour** ramasser la pièce.   *He bent down to pick up the coin.*
Vous partirez **sans** le voir.   *You will leave without seeing him.*

Notes:
(*a*)   When a verb occurs after **après**, it must be in the past infinitive (infinitive of the auxiliary + past participle) *except* if it can take the value of a noun:

Après manger, il est sorti. (**manger** = **le repas**)   *After the meal he went out.*
Il est amusant **après** boire. (**boire** = **la boisson**)   *He is amusing after he has had a few drinks.*
But: **Après avoir fini** le travail, il sort.
and not: *Après finir le travail, il sort.
   After finishing work he goes out.
or: **Après être descendue**, elle ferma la porte.

and not: *Après descendre elle ferma la porte.

After going down, she closed the door.

Avoir fini and **être descendue** are the past infinitives of **finir** (*to finish*) and **descendre** (*to go down*) respectively.

b) **Par** (*by*) can be followed by an infinitive in *two set phrases only*: **commencer par** (*to begin by*) and **finir par** (*to end up by*).

Nous commencerons **par** prendre un apéritif.   *We shall begin by taking an aperitif.*

Je vais finir **par** perdre patience.   *I am going to end up by losing my patience.*

2   Elimination of certain prepositions:

Since prepositions are supposed to link two words or phrases within a sense-group, it is not generally acceptable to leave them out in French. Otherwise, the link may not be obvious and an ambiguity may be created. In the following examples the words in bold are linked, and the sign // indicates the end of a sense group.

Compare: Je parle **à mon voisin** et **à sa femme**// . . .

I speak to my neighbour and (to) his wife . . .

and: Je parle **à mon voisin** // et sa femme . . .

In the second example, the reader or listener expects a verb to follow **femme** explaining what that lady is doing while I'm speaking to her husband!

Remember: In English it is acceptable to avoid repeating the preposition. In French it is generally unwise to do so.

Exceptions:

a)   With set expressions made up of several elements, but considered as one word, the preposition is not repeated:

Il habite en **Seine-et-Marne**. *He lives in Seine-et-Marne.* (region near Paris)

Je passe mon temps **à aller et venir**. *I spend my time going to and fro.*

b)   If the word **ou** (*or*) is used to indicate an alternative, the preposition is not normally repeated:

Un voyage **de** deux **ou** trois jours. (*and not* *de deux ou de trois jours*) *A two or three-day journey.*

La maison est **à** trois **ou** quatre cents mètres (*and not* *à trois ou à quatre cents mètres*). *The house is three or four hundred metres away.*

c)   **Pour** (*for*) is often not repeated:

Voici la note **pour** la chambre et le repas. (*and not* *pour la chambre et pour le repas*). *Here is the bill for the bedroom and the meal.*

(*d*)   **Entre** (*between*) is never repeated:
Entre vous et moi, il n'est pas très doué.(*and not* *entre vous e
entre moi . . .*)   *Between you and me, he is not very gifted.*

3   Prepositions indicating 'position in' or 'movement to or from' ;
country:

(*a*)   Position and movement to a feminine singular country: **en**:
Nous allons **en** France. (movement)   *We are going to France*
Il habite **en** Espagne. (position)   *He lives in Spain.*

(*b*)   Position and movement to a masculine country: **au** (sing.), **au**:
(plur.):
Il va **au** Canada? Non, **aux** Etats-Unis. (movement)   *Is h*
going to Canada? No, to the United States.
Elle vit **au** Japon. (position)   *She lives in Japan.*

(*c*)   Movement from a feminine country: **de** (sing.), **des** (plur.):
Cette vague de froid arrive **d**'Allemagne.   *This cold wave i*
coming from Germany.
Voici une lettre **des** Seychelles.   *Here is a letter from th*
Seychelles.

(*d*)   Movement from a masculine country: **du** (sing.), **des** (plur.):
J'aime le café **du** Brésil.   *I like coffee from Brazil.*
J'ai reçu un coup de téléphone **des** USA.   *I have received* (
phone call from the States.

Notes:

(i)   The general rules stated for countries also apply for regions
'départements' and counties, with the following modifications
– In the case of 'movement to' or 'position in' a 'masculine
area, region, county or 'département', **au** (sing.) will b(
replaced by **dans le**, and **aux** (plur.) by **dans les**:
Il a une villa **dans le** Midi de la France.   *He has a villa in th*
South of France.
Je fais du ski **dans les** Alpes.   *I go skiing in the Alps.*

(ii)   English counties are masculine in French:
Nous avons passé cinq jours **dans le** Kent.   *We spent five days ir*
Kent.

4   Prepositions indicating 'position in', 'movement to', or 'move
ment from' a town:

(*a*)   Position or movement to = **à** (or **au**, if the name of the town
includes the article **le**):
Ils resteront deux jours **à** Marseille. (position)   *They will sta*
two days in Marseilles.
Nous irons **à** Paris. (movement)   *We shall go to Paris.*

Le bateau arrive **au** Havre à midi. (movement) *The boat arrives in Le Havre at 12 noon.*

(b) Movement from = **de** (or **du**, if the name of the town includes the article **le**):

Je viens **de** Londres. *I am coming from London.*

C'est le train **du** Touquet. *It is the train from Le Touquet.*

5 Prepositions used to introduce the name of the material(s) or substance(s) constituting an object. **De** and **en** are used for this purpose.

Note: In modern French, **en** has become relatively more frequent than **de**. Although there is little difference in meaning between the two, it is generally agreed that **en** emphasises the material/substance slightly more than **de**:

Compare: Une table **de** chêne = *an oak table*

and: Une table **en** chêne = *a table made of oak*

or: Un vase **de** cristal = *a crystal vase*

and: Un vase **en** cristal = *a vase made of crystal*

6 The prepositions **entre** (*between*) and **parmi** (*among*) are not interchangeable.

– **entre** suggests a position or movement *between* two things or beings;

– **parmi** suggests a position or movement *among* a larger number of things or beings.

Compare: Je vois la maison **entre** la rivière et la route.

I see the house between the river and the road.

and: Je vois la maison **parmi** les arbres.

I see the house among the trees.

When the preposition **de** precedes, **parmi** is replaced by **entre**:

Plusieurs **d'entre** eux ont visité le château. *Several of them* (i.e. *among them*) *visited the castle.*

---

7 The preposition **pour** may be used to indicate:

(a) *destination*:

Nous partons **pour** Londres ce soir. *We leave for London tonight.*

(b) *anticipated duration*:

Nous partons **pour** une semaine. *We are going for a week.*

Note: In this latter sense, **pour** must be distinguished from **pendant**, which insists on the actual duration or time span (and which can often be omitted).

Compare: J'y vais **pour** trois semaines.
            I am going there for three weeks.
and: J'y resterai (pendant) trois semaines.
            I shall stay there (for) three weeks.

(*c*)   *purpose*:
        Je voudrais des cachets **pour** calmer la douleur.   *I would like*
        pain-killing tablets. (lit: *to calm pain*)

8   The preposition **depuis** (*since/for*) may be used to indicate a time
span (duration):
Compare: Il habite ici **depuis** 1945. (precise date).
            He has been living here since 1945.
            Il habite ici **depuis** la fin de la guerre. (precise event)
            He has been living here since the end of the war.
            Il habite ici **depuis** 40 ans. (duration)
            He has been living here for 40 years.

Note: If **depuis** is followed by an expression denoting duration, as in
the last of the above examples, it will normally be used with a tense
also emphasising duration (i.e. Present or Imperfect Indicative).
Do not say: *Il travailla ici depuis 10 ans.
say instead: Il **travaillait** ici **depuis** 10 ans.
               He had been working here for 10 years.

9   The preposition **de** is often used with the meaning of **avec** (*with*) or
par (*by*):
        Je l'ai vu **de** mes propres yeux. (**de** = **avec**)   *I saw it with my own*
        eyes.
        Elle est aimée **de** tous. (**de** = **par**)   *She is loved by all.*

10   The preposition **de** is also used in French to express possession:
     Où est le stylo **de** Jean?   *Where is John's pen?*
     Le frère **de** Robert est malade.   *Robert's brother is ill.*

11   The preposition **chez** may have the following meanings:
(*a*)   *to* or *at* someone's house, apartment, shop, etc.
        Va **chez** le boucher!   *Go to the butchers!*
(*b*)   *among* when referring to the attitudes, habits, etc. of a group of
        people:
        La délinquance **chez** les jeunes.   *Delinquency among young*
        people.

Note: If a firm, shop, etc. bears the name of the founder(s) **chez** will
be used:
        Il travaillait **chez** Citroën.   *He was working for the Citroen*
        Company.

Elle s'habille **chez** Christian Dior.   *She buys her clothes at Christian Dior's.*

12   When used with an expression of the type **l'un l'autre** (*one another*) the preposition will be placed between the two elements:

Ils se battent les uns **contre** les autres.   *They are fighting against each other.*

Key points

1   Prepositions are words or expressions used to link together certain words or phrases, to indicate the relationship (time, space, manner, purpose, etc.) which exists between them.

2   Prepositions are invariable: they do not agree in gender or number with the words they link together.

3   It is possible for a given preposition to have a variety of meanings and therefore express different relationships.

4   In general, it is essential to repeat prepositions as required, since failure to do so may cause confusion in the mind of the reader or listener. There are, however, cases when the preposition *must not* be repeated: set expressions, presence of **ou** (*or*) or **entre** (*between*).

5   Certain prepositions are subject to *elision* (removal of the final vowel) whenever there is the danger of a vowel-vowel clash, or *fusion* (combination with the definite articles **le** or **les**).

6   The preposition **de** can be used in certain circumstances to express possession.

7   The prepositions **entre** (*between*) and **parmi** (*among*) are not normally interchangeable; the former expresses a position or movement *between* two things or beings, the latter a position or movement *among* a greater number of things or beings. There are, however, some cases when **entre** is used with the meaning of *among*.

8   The preposition **chez** is used to indicate 'movement to' *or* 'position in' the abode or shop of a person. In this case, *either* the name *or* the profession of the person concerned may be used. **Chez** is also used to express the attitudes, habits, etc. of a given group of people.

16 Conjunctions

Conjunctions are invariable expressions composed of one or more words which are used to link:
1 Words or phrases of equal grammatical status:
  Il est entré **et** Il a commandé une bière.

      (1)   (2)
  He went in and ordered a beer.
  J'ai refusé **mais** ma femme a accepté.

      (1)   (2)
  I refused but my wife accepted.
The elements 1 and 2 are linked by **et** (*and*) and **mais** (*but*) but they could both stand as sentences in their own right.
2 Phrases or clauses (i.e. sense groups with subject, verb, etc.) of unequal status, but closely related; one being the *main clause* (m.c.) and the other, the *subordinate clause* (s.c.), serving to 'complete the picture', as it were, by underlining the relationship (time-opposition-restriction) which exists between the two clauses and by giving extra information:
  Il vient me voir **bien que** je sois malade.   (opposition)

      m.c.   s.c.
  He comes to see me although I am ill.
  Elle doit prendre ce sirop **jusqu'à ce qu'**elle ne tousse plus

      m.c.   s.c.
She must take this mixture until she stops coughing.
The conjunctions of type 1 are called *coordinating conjunctions* and those of type 2 are known as *subordinating conjunctions*. The two types will now be examined in turn. In order to facilitate learning, broad categories have been created to outline the relationships the conjunctions create between the elements they join together.

Coordinating conjunctions

Time: **comme** *as*, **ensuite** *afterwards*, **et** *then*, **lorsque** *when*, **puis** *then* = *afterwards*, **quand** *when*. For example:

Finissez cette lettre; **ensuite**, venez dans mon bureau. *Finish this letter; then come into my office.*

Vous ferez la vaisselle **quand** vous aurez fini de manger. *You will wash up when you have finished eating.*

Comme je me levais, on frappa à la porte. *As I was getting up, someone knocked on the door.*

Cause/consequence: **ainsi** *so = thus*, **aussi** *so = therefore*, **car** *for = because*, **donc** *therefore*, **en effet** *indeed = that is so*, **partant** *consequently*. For example:

Ainsi il est d'accord! Vous m'étonnez. *So he agrees! You astonish me.*

Je vais au restaurant **car** j'ai une faim de loup. *I'm going to the restaurant because I am starving.* (lit: *I have a wolf's hunger*)

Je pense, **donc** je suis. *I think, therefore I am.*

Il perdra sa réputation et, **partant**, son emploi. *He will lose his reputation and consequently his job.*

Constraint/restriction/exclusion: **au contraire** *on the contrary*, **cependant** *yet*, **et** *but*, **néanmoins** *nevertheless*, **ni . . . ni** *neither . . . nor*, **or** *yet*, **ou/ou bien** *or*, **pourtant** *however*, **quoique** *although*, **si** *if*, **sinon** *except/if not*, **soit . . . soit** *either . . . or*. For example:

Vous le détestez et **cependant** vous restez? Bizarre! *You detest him and yet you stay? Strange!*

Tu te reposes **et** je fais tout le travail. *You are resting and* (i.e. *whilst*) *I do all the work.*

Quoique riche il vivait simplement. *Although rich, he lived simply.*

Emphasis: **à savoir** *namely*, **bien** *jolly well*, **donc** *so, therefore*, **en effet** *indeed*. For example:

Pourquoi n'y allez-vous pas? J'y suis **bien** allé, moi! *Why don't you go? I jolly well went (didn't I)!*

Vous voilà **donc**! *So there you are!*

Je crois que vous êtes au courant. **En effet**! *I think you know Indeed I do!*

Points to bear in mind regarding the use of co-ordinating conjunctions:

1 **Et**, which is normally used to indicate association (*and = with*), may also be used to express:

(a) *Opposition*:

Je sais tout **et** je ne dis rien. *I know everything and (= but) I say nothing.*

(b)   *Simultaneity*:
   Papa fume **et** maman lit.   *Father is smoking and (= whilst) Mother is reading.*
(c)   *Posteriority*:
   Fermez le magasin **et** venez prendre un verre.   *Close the shop and (= then) come for a drink.* (lit: *to take a glass*)

2   **Si**, which is normally used to express a condition (= *if*), may also express:
(a)   *Doubt*:
   Je ne sais pas **si** elle répondra.   *I do not know whether she will reply.*
(b)   *Hope or wish*:
   Ah **si** j'étais jeune!   *Ah, if only I were young (again)!*
(c)   *Supposition*:
   Et **s'**ils avaient eu un accident?   *And what if they'd had an accident?*
(d)   *Repetition*:
   Si elle allait au bal, tout le monde l'admirait.   *Whenever she went dancing, everyone admired her.*

3   Whenever **quand** (*when*) is used to refer to a future action, it will be followed by the Future (simple or Perfect) and not the Present as in English.
Compare: **Quand** vous aurez fini, vous fermerez.
and: *When you have finished, you will lock up.*
or: **Quand** ils arriveront laissez-les entrer.
and: *When they arrive let them come in.*

4   The English word *then* has two distinct meanings: *afterwards* and *in that case*. You must take care to distinguish clearly between them:

(a)   *then = afterwards* will be translated by:
   (i)   **puis** if there is no significant time-lapse between the two actions referred to:
   J'ai fait la vaisselle, **puis** j'ai essuyé la poussière.   *I washed up, then I dusted.*
   (ii)   **ensuite** if there is a significant time-lapse between the two actions referred to:
   J'ai fait la vaisselle, **ensuite** j'ai essuyé la poussière.   *I washed up, afterwards I dusted.*
(b)   *then = in that case* is an adverb and must be translated by **alors, dans ce cas** or **dans ces conditions**:
   Tu ne dis rien? **Alors** je m'en vais.   *Aren't you saying anything? In that case I am going.*

5 Ni ... Ni (*neither ... nor*) is normally accompanied by the negative particle **ne** (*not*) *but not* by **pas**. You must say or write:

Il n'est **ni** riche **ni** célèbre.   *He is neither rich nor famous.*

and not: * Il n'est pas ni riche ni célèbre.

However, when used in a negative sentence **ni ... ni** will be reduced to **ni**.

Tu n'es pas bête, **ni** paresseux.   *You are not stupid, nor (are you) lazy.*

6 Comme (*as*), **lorsque quand** (*when*), **puisque** (*since*), **si** (*if*), etc. are not normally repeated in the same sentence; if necessary, they can be replaced by **que**.

It should be noted that if **que** replaces **quand**, **comme**, **lorsque** or **puisque** it will *not* be followed by a verb in the subjunctive:

Quand vous serez riche et **que** je serai vieux ...   *When you are rich and (when) I am old ...*

However, if **que** replaces **si**, the verb which follows will be in the subjunctive:

Si vous tombez malade et **que** vous ayez besoin de moi, appelez-moi. (**ayez** = 2nd pers. plur. subjunctive of **avoir**).   *If you fall ill and you need me, call me.*

Subordinating conjunctions

They, too, have been grouped into broad categories according to the relationship they create between the clauses they link together.

Note: Certain subordinating conjunctions *always* require the verb which follows to be in the subjunctive mood; in such cases, the conjunction will be accompanied by the mark $+S$. Some other conjunctions may *sometimes* be followed by a subjunctive; this will be expressed by the mark $(+S)$ placed immediately after the conjunction.

Time = **alors que** *as/while*, **à mesure que** *as*, **après que** *after*, **aussitôt que** *as soon as*, **avant que** $+ S$ *before*, **cependant que** *while*, **depuis que** *since*, **dès que** *as soon as*, **en attendant que** $+ S$ *until*, **jusqu'à ce que** $+ S$ *until*, **maintenant que** *now that*, **pendant que** *while*, **sitôt que** *as soon as*, **tandis que** *while*, **tant que** *so long as*, etc.

For example:

Ils l'ont arrêté **alors qu**'il ouvrait le coffre.   *They arrested him as he was opening the safe.*

Je veux vous dire deux mots **avant qu**'ils n'arrivent.   *I want to say a few words to you before they arrive.*

Dès que midi sonne, il s'en va! *As soon as it is twelve o'clock, he is off!*

Restez assis **jusqu'à ce que** l'avion s'arrête. *Remain seated until the aircraft stops.*

Constraint-restriction-exclusion = **afin** **que** + *S* *so that*, **alors que** *whereas*, **à moins que** + *S* *unless*, **attendu que** *bearing in mind that*, **au lieu que** + *S* *whereas*, **bien que** + *S* *although*, **de crainte que** + *S* *for fear that*, **de façon que** + *S* *in such a way that*, **de manière que** + *S* *so that*, **de peur que** + *S* *for fear that*, **de sorte que** (+ *S*) *in such a way that*, **encore que** + *S* *although*, **étant donné que** *given that*, **parce que** *because*, **plutôt que** + *S* *rather than*, **pour que** + *S* *so that*, **pour . . . que** + *S* *however*, **puisque** *since*, **quoique** + *S* *although*, **quoi** **que** + *S* *whatever*, **sans que** + *S* *without*, **sauf que** *except that*, **selon que** *depending*, **si ce n'est que** *except for the fact that*, **soit que** (+ *S*) *whereas*, **suivant que** *depending whether*, **supposé que** + *S* *assuming that*, **tandis que** *whereas*, **vu que** *in view of the fact that*, etc. For example:

Venez plus près, **afin que** je vous voie. *Come closer so that I may see you.*

Bien qu'il soit vieux, il n'est pas gâteux. *Although he is old, he is not senile.*

Travaille bien **de sorte qu'**ils soient contents. *Work well so that they will be pleased.*

Il ne l'épousera pas, **parce qu'**il ne l'aime pas. *He will not marry her, because he does not love her.*

Vu que vous êtes directeur, vous pouvez prendre cette décision. *In view of the fact that you are a director you can take this decision.*

Comparison: **ainsi que** *as*, **autant que** + *S* *so far as*, **comme si** *as though*, **d'autant plus que** *all the more so that*, **de même que** *in the same way as*, **moins que** *less than*, **non moins que** *no less than*, **plus que** *more than*. For example:

Le plan a réussi, **ainsi que** nous l'avions prévu. *The plan succeeded, as we had forecast.*

Faisons **comme si** tout allait bien. *Let us act as if everything was going well.*

Ils ont dépensé **moins que** nous. *They spent less than we did.*

Points to bear in mind regarding the use of subordinating conjunctions:

1 In the lists given above, there are many words which also appear in the chapters dealing with adverbs or prepositions. This is because there is a close relationship between those grammatical categories:

alors (*then* = adv.) ←→ alors que (*while* = conjunction)
après (*after* = prep.) ←→ après que (*after* = conjunction)
avant (*before* = prep.) ←→ avant que (*before* = conjunction)
In most cases, those words are followed by **que** (*that*) which is the most commonly encountered subordinating conjunction.

2   As well as being a conjunction in its own right, **que** is also used in the following ways:

(*a*)   As an elliptic (shorter) version of other conjunctions: **afin que** *so that*, **avant que** *before*, **de telle façon que/de telle sorte que** *so that*, **pour que** *in order that*, etc. For example:
Viens ici **que** je te voie. (= **afin que**)   *Come here so that I can see you.*
Faites du bon travail, **qu'**il soit content. (= **de sorte que**)   *Do a good job so that he'll be pleased.*

(*b*)   Almost systematically as an 'alternative' to avoid the repetition of an already-used subordinating conjunction. For example:
Je l'ai fait **afin que** tu comprennes et **que** tu acceptes.   *I did it so that you understand and accept.*
Tu resteras ici **jusqu'à ce que** le brouillard se lève et **que** la pluie cesse.   *You will stay here until the fog lifts and the rain stops.*

3   Care must be taken not to confuse the following two conjunctions (both followed by a subjunctive):
(i)   **quoique** = *although*:
Quoiqu'il soit souffrant il est allé au bureau.   *Although he was unwell, he went to the office.*
(ii)   **quoi que** = *whatever/no matter what*:
Quoi que vous disiez, je refuse de vous croire.   *Whatever you say, I refuse to believe you.*

4   The conjunctions **à moins que** *unless*, **avant que** *before*, **de crainte que/de peur que** *for fear that which* are all followed by the subjunctive, are normally constructed with the expletive particle **ne**. In such cases, the particle **ne** has no negative value whatever.

Compare: Attendez ici de peur qu'il **ne** vous voie. (expletive).
              Wait here for fear he may see you.
and: Attendez ici de peur qu'il **ne** vous voie **pas** (negation).
              Wait here for fear he may not see you.

5   As previously stated, many subordinating conjunctions must be followed by a verb in the subjunctive. However, since that tense is felt to be stylistically 'heavy', French people will try to avoid, it if at all possible. To that end, *and so long as the subject (performer) is the same in the main clause (m.c.) and the subordinate clause (s.c.);* a preposition equivalent in meaning to the conjunction and often

containing **de** will be used. This will allow the replacement of the subjunctive by an infinitive:

Compare: <u>Nous avons attendu</u> afin que nous puissions vous parler.

    (same subject)

        m.c.   s.c.

and: Nous avons attendu **afin de** pouvoir vous parler.
We have waited in order to speak to you (i.e. *so that we may speak to you*).

or: Vous mangerez un sandwich avant que vous partiez.

    (same subject)

        m.c.   s.c.

and: Vous mangerez un sandwich **avant de** partir.
You will eat a sandwich before going (i.e. *before you go*).

or: Je n'ai rien ajouté de peur que je dise une bêtise.

    (same subject)

        m.c.   s.c.

and: Je n'ai rien ajouté **de peur de** dire une bêtise.
I did not add anything for fear of saying something stupid (i.e. *for fear I may say something stupid*).

> If the subject is not the same in the two clauses, the subjunctive must be used if the conjunction requires it.

Note: If the subject of the main clause is the impersonal pronoun **il** (*it*), it will be possible for the subordinate clause to be constructed with an infinitive.

Compare: Il faut que vous partiez.

        m.c.   s.c.

and: Il vous faut **partir.**
You must go.

or: Il est important que nous acceptions

        m.c.   s.c.

and: Il est important pour nous d'**accepter**.
It is important for us to accept

Any ambiguity about the subject (performer) can be removed by using an additional pronoun: **moi, toi**, etc. (*me, you*, etc.)

6 The conjunctions **pendant que** and **tandis que** (*while*) have two possible meanings.

(a) They can indicate the straightforward occurrence of two actions *at the same time*. For example

Elle lit le journal $\begin{cases} \text{tandis que} \\ \text{pendant que} \end{cases}$ j'écoute la radio.

She is reading the paper while I am listening to the radio.

(b) They can introduce an idea of opposition (*while = whereas*).

Il se repose $\begin{cases} \text{tandis que} \\ \text{pendant que} \end{cases}$ je me tue au travail.

He is resting while I am working my fingers to the bone.
(lit: . . . *while I am killing myself working*)

7 After certain verbs (constructed with the preposition **à**) **que** must be preceded by the expression **à ce** (lit: *to that*). The most common of those verbs are: **s'attendre à** *to expect*, **consentir à** *to agree to*, **se décider à** *to make up one's mind to*, **s'habituer à** *to get used to*, **s'opposer à** *to be opposed to*, **se refuser à** *to refuse to* and **renoncer à** *to give up*. For example:

Je m'attends **à ce qu**'il refuse. (and not *je m'attends qu'il refuse) *I expect he will refuse.*

Nous nous opposons **à ce qu**'ils entrent. (and not * nous nous opposons qu'ils entrent) *We are opposed to them coming in.*

8 As well as introducing subordinate clauses, **que** can also be found:
(a) At the beginning of a main clause:

$\underbrace{\textbf{Qu}\text{'il parle,}}_{\text{m.c.}} \underbrace{\text{s'il en a le courage.}}_{\text{s.c.}}$

Let him talk if he has the courage to do so.
(b) At the beginning of an independent clause (i.e. not followed by a subordinate one):

Que dieu vous garde! *May God be with you.* (lit: *let God keep you*)

9 Although the presence of **que** often indicates that the verb of the subordinate clause it introduces will be in the Subjunctive, it is by no means always the case. This is very important and should always be borne in mind.

Compare: Nous pensons **que** vous **refuserez**. (Future Indicative)
   We think you will refuse.
and: Nous ne pensons pas **que** vous **refusiez**. (Present Subjunctive)
   We do not think you will refuse.

or: Je crois que vous **avez** raison. (Present Indicative)
         I think you are right.
and: Je ne crois pas que vous **ayez** raison. (Perfect Subjunctive).
         I do not think you are right.

Key points

1   Conjunctions are invariable words or expressions which are used to link:

(*a*)   Words or expressions of equal grammatical status (nouns, adjectives, verbs, adverbs). Such conjunctions are called *coordinating conjunctions*.

(*b*)   Phrases or clauses of unequal status, one being a *main clause* and the other(s) giving useful additional information about the first and called *subordinate clause(s)*. Such conjunctions are called *subordinating conjunctions*.

2   Conjunctions serve to indicate the relationship which exists between the elements they link together (time; cause/consequence; constraint/restriction/exclusion; opposition; emphasis; etc.)

3   It is possible for a given conjunction to have several distinct meanings according to context.

4   There is a close relationship between conjunctions, prepositions and even adverbs: similar expressions can sometimes be found in more than one of those categories.

5   Certain subordinating conjunctions introduce clauses in which the verb must be in the subjunctive mood; others do not.

6   Because of its 'ponderous' quality, the subjunctive can sometimes be avoided in subordinate clauses. In such cases, the conjunction is replaced by the corresponding preposition which is then followed by an infinitive or by a noun.

7   Normally, the repetition of a given subordinating conjunction in one sentence is not acceptable. This can easily be avoided by using **que** as a substitute, as many times as required.

8   Although the conjunction **que** often indicates the presence of a subjunctive in the subordinate clause it introduces, this is by no means systematic. Careful note should be made of which conjunctions require which mood.

17 Interjections

Interjections are invariable words or expressions which can be slipped into the speech chain, either to convey certain commands, emotions or moods, or to represent, as faithfully as practicable, noises made by things or beings (onomatopoeias). Interjections may be nouns, adjectives, adverbs, verbs, etc. They can also be modifications of blasphemous expressions referring to God, the Virgin Mary or even Satan. For example:

Parbleu! (*You bet!*) comes from **Par Dieu** (*by God*)
Diantre! (*By Jove!*) comes from **Par le Diable** (*by the devil*)
Dame! (Of course!) comes from **Par Notre-Dame** (*by Our Lady*)

Note: Very often, the interjection is an elliptical (shortened) sentence:

Patience! = Prenez patience!
Patience! Have patience!
Attention! = Faites attention!
Careful! Be careful!

The interjections presented in this chapter have, for the sake of convenience, been divided into three groups: interjections proper, oaths and onomatopoeias.

Interjections proper

1 *Appreciation*: **A la bonne heure!** *None too soon!*, **bon!** *good!*, **bien!** *well done!*, **bravo!** *hurrah!*, **chic!** *great!*, **enfin!** *at last*, **fichtre!** *by God!*, **hip hip hip hourra!** *hip hip hooray!*, **ô!** *oh!*

2 *Disappointment*: **Bah!** *too bad!*, **bof!** *what the heck!*, **flûte!** *blast!*, **fichtre!** *blast!*, **hélas** *alas*, **mince!** *drat!*, **zut!** *blast!*

3 *Encouragement*: **Allez!** *Go on!*, **allons!** *come on!*, **chiche!** *I dare you!*, **courage!** *take heart!*, **hardi!** *go on!*, **hue!** *gee-up!*, **patience!** *patience!*

4 *Greeting*: **Adieu!** *Goodbye!*, **allô!** *hallo!*, **bonjour** *hallo!*, **bonsoir** *good evening!*, **hé!** *hey!*, **salut!** *Hi!*, etc.

5 *Relief*: **Ah!** *Well done!*, **enfin!** *at last!*, **ouf!** *phew!*

6 *Sadness or pain*: **Ah!** *Oh!*, **aïe** *ouch!*, **hélas!** *alas!*, **oh là là!** *oh dear!*, **ouille!** *ouch!*

7 *Surprise*: **Ah!** *Oh!*, **bonté divine!** *good gracious!*, **grand dieu!** *good God!*, **juste ciel!** *good heavens!*, **sapristi!** *gosh!*, **tiens!** *I say!*
8 *Warning*: **Attention!/gare!** *Watch out!*, **au secours!** *help!*, **chut!** *hush!*, **halte!** *halt/stop!*, **hé bien!** *watch out!*, **ho!** *hey!*, **holà!** *watch out!*, **silence!** *silence!*, **tout doux!** *take it easy!*

For example:
> Voilà le garçon! **A la bonne heure!** *Here is the waiter! And about time too!*
> **Flûte!** J'ai oublié de téléphoner. *Blast! I forgot to telephone.*
> **Allez!** Avancez! *Go on! Move!*
> **Allô!** Je voudrais parler au gérant. *Hallo! I'd like to speak to the manager.*
> **Attention!** Vous allez tomber! *Watch out! You are going to fall!*

Oaths

Dame! *Of course!*, **diable/diantre!** *by Jove!*, **nom de dieu!** *by God!*, **parbleu!** *of course*, **sacrebleu!/ventrebleu!** *by God!*
Note: Most of the oaths containing **bleu** (a deformation of **dieu** = *God*) are now old-fashioned and humorous; modern versions have been created to replace them. For example:
> Nom d'une pipe! (lit: *in the name of a pipe!*) = *Good God!*
> Nom d'un chien! (lit: *in the name of a dog!*) = *Damn!*
> Nom d'un petit bonhomme! (lit: *in the name of a small man!*) = *Blast!*

Onomatopoeias

Some of the most commonly used onomatopoeias are given below along with the context in which they normally occur, or the thing or being associated with them:
Badaboum *noisy and spectacular fall*, **clic-clac** *key locking a door*, **clac** *sharp noise or slap*, **cocorico** *cock crowing*, **crac** *wood snapping*, **cui-cui** *small bird chirping*, **ding-dong** *big bell*, **drelin-drelin** *small bell*, **flic-floc** *noise in mud or water*, **hi-han** *donkey*, **hi-hi** *laugh*, **meuh** *cow*, **miaou** *cat*, **ouah-ouah** *dog*, **paf** *hard slap or thud*, **pan** *shot-like noise*, **patatras** *fall*, **pif** *sharp slap-like noise*, **plouf** *object falling in water*, **teuf-teuf** *an old engine*, **tic-tac** *clock or watch*, **toc-toc** *knocking on a door*, **vlan** *slamming noise*:
> Ses chaussures faisaient **flic-floc** dans la boue! *His shoes were making squelching noises in the mud!*
> Elle le gifla violemment, **paf!** *She slapped him very hard!*

J'ai glissé dans l'herbe mouillée et **plouf!**   *I slipped on the damp grass and fell into the water!*

Note: Some of the above may also be used figuratively.

Compare: La porte se referme. Vlan!
           The door closes, bang!

and: Je le lui ai dit tout net! Vlan!
           I told him! Straight between the eyes!

As with slang words, it is extremely important to be aware of the context (social and linguistic) in which interjections are used. So, whenever you hear them, pay particular attention to who is saying them and the circumstances in which they are used.

Key points

1   Interjections are invariable words or phrases used in speech to convey a command, a feeling, a mood or to imitate the sounds made by a thing or being.

2   Some interjections are disguised oaths. They should be used with care. In modern French, oaths ending in **bleu** (a deformation of **dieu** = *God*) are generally seen as old-fashioned and humorous.

3   If used properly (and sparingly), interjections can liven up a conversation, but it is essential to be sensitive to the social and linguistic context in which they occur.

4   Although interjections can be found in written form, they were (and are) essentially a means of expressing feelings in the spoken language.

18 Comparatives and Superlatives

In certain circumstances, we need to express a comparison between two or more things, beings or actions, to state which of them possess(es) a given characteristic, to a lesser degree (inferiority), to the same degree (equality), to a higher degree (superiority) or even to the highest degree possible (superlative).

In general, comparisons involve adjectives or adverbs, but they can also involve nouns and verbs:

> Il y avait **plus** de monde **que** d'habitude. (noun) *There were more people than usual.*
>
> Tu travailles **moins que** moi. (verb) *You work less than I do.*

In English, those various degrees are expressed in the following way:

Inferiority = lesser degree:	*less . . . than (not so . . . as)*
Equality = same degree:	*as . . . as (no more . . . than)*
Superiority = higher degree:	*more . . . than (. . . er than . . .)*
Superlative highest degree:	*the most . . . (the . . . est)*
very high degree:	*extremely . . . , infinitely . . . , very . . .*

Note: A small number of adjectives and adverbs do not follow the regular pattern of formation. This is also the case in French. They will be studied separately.

The French comparative and superlative structures are presented below. For each example, the part of speech affected by the comparison is given in brackets.

Inferiority

Moins . . . que *(less . . . than)*. For example:

> Nous sommes **moins** riches **qu'** eux. (adjective) *We are less rich than they are.*
>
> Il y a **moins** de travail **qu'**hier. (noun) *There is less work than yesterday.*
>
> Sa voiture va **moins** vite **que** la nôtre. (adverb) *His car goes less fast than ours.*

Il a **moins** bu **que** d'habitude. (verb)   *He drank less than usual.*

Notes:

1   It is possible to convey the same meaning (inferiority) by using the negative structure **ne . . . pas (aus) si . . . que**   (*not as . . . as*)

Compare: Il est **moins** intelligent **que** toi. (adjective)

and: Il **n'**est **pas (aus)si** intelligent **que** toi.

   He is less intelligent than you.

If this comparison is constructed with a noun or a verb instead of an adjective, **ne pas (aus)si** will become **ne pas (au)t ant**:

   Le vieux monsieur **n'**avait **pas autant** de courage qu'autrefois.   *The old man did not have as much courage as in the old days.*

2   To express an idea of continuous reduction, the phrase **de moins en moins** (*less and less*) can be used:

   J'ai **de moins en moins de** courage. (noun)   *I have less and less courage.*

   C'est **de moins en moins** facile. (adjective)   *It's getting less and less easy.*

Equality

Aussi . . . que (*as . . . as*). For example:

   Elle est **aussi** charmante **que** sa mère. (adjective)   *She is as charming as her mother.*

   Nous crierons **aussi** fort **que** vous. (adverb)   *We shall shout as loud(ly) as you.*

Notes:

1   If this degree of comparison is used with a noun or a verb, **aussi** *must* be replaced by **autant**:

   Il y a **autant** de bruit **que** ce matin. (noun)   *There is as much noise as this morning.*

   Ils ont **autant** travaillé **que** moi. (verb)   *They have worked as much as I have.*

2   It is possible to convey the idea of equality by using the negation **ne pas** (*not*) with a construction expressing superiority or inferiority:

   Elle **n'**est **pas plus** riche **que** toi. (adjective)   *She is no richer than you (= as rich as).*

   Je **ne** suis **pas moins** prudent **que** lui. (adjective)   *I am no less careful than he is (= as careful as).*

3   The idea of equality can also be conveyed by using the adverb **comme** (*as*):

   Il est têtu **comme** une mule.   *He is (as) stubborn as a mule.*

   Des cheveux blancs **comme** neige.   *Hair (as) white as snow.*

Superiority

Plus . . . que (*more . . . than/ . . . er than*). For example:

>Son voisin est **plus** raisonnable **que** lui. (adjective)   *His neighbour is more reasonable than he is.*
>
>Il parle **plus** vite **que** moi. (adverb)   *He speaks faster than I do.*
>
>Elle a **plus** de soucis **que** vous. (noun)   *She has more cares than you have.*
>
>Tu manges **plus que** nous deux. (verb)   *You eat more than both of us.*

Notes:

1   In cases when a noun or a verb are used in this type of comparison, **plus** is normally replaced by **davantage**:

>Ils ont **davantage** d'idées **que** leur patron. (noun)   *They have more ideas than their boss.*

2   When the point of reference for the comparison is a noun, **de** or **d'** (as applicable) is inserted immediately after **plus** or **davantage:**

>Ils ont **plus d'**argent **que** nous.   *They have more money than we have.*

3   To express an idea of continual increase, the expression **de plus en plus** (*more and more*) can be used.

>Nous recevons **de plus en plus** de lettres. (noun)   *We are receiving more and more letters.*
>
>Il est **de plus en plus** déçu. (adj.)   *He is getting more and more disappointed.*

A similar meaning can be obtained by using **toujours plus** (or **toujours davantage** when required) or **chaque jour plus** (or **chaque jour davantage** when required):

>Les trains vont **chaque jour plus** vite. (adverb)   *Trains are getting faster every day.*
>
>La tension augmente **toujours davantage**. (verb)   *Tension is ever increasing.*

Superlative degree

Highest degree

le plus . . . (*the . . . est* or *the most . . .*). For example:

>C'est **le plus** beau jour de ma vie. (adjective)   *It is the best day of my life.*
>
>C'est ce remède qui agit **le plus** vite. (adverb)   *It is this remedy which works the fastest.*

Note: When this structure is used with an adjective, the article which is part of the superlative expression must vary in gender *and* number with the noun which the adjective qualifies. In addition, the required agreement must be made at the end of the adjective.

Compare: Elle avait **la plus** jolie robe et **le plus** beau collier.
                She had the prettiest dress and the most beautiful necklace.

and: Elle avait **les plus** jolies robes et **les plus** beaux colliers.
                She had the prettiest dresses and the most beautiful necklaces.

In all other cases (i.e. with nouns, adverbs, verbs), the superlative expression will be invariable:

    Elle a **le plus** de travail. (noun)   *She has the most work.*

    Ce sont eux qui ont **le plus** mangé. (verb)   *It is they who ate the most.*

Very high degree

For the expression of *a very high degree*, the adjective or adverb will be preceded by an adverb such as: **bien** or **fort** (*very*), **extraordinairement** (*extraordinarily*), **extrêmement** (*extremely*), **infiniment** (*infinitely*), etc. For example:

    Nous avons **extrêmement** peur. (noun)   *We are extremely frightened.*

    Je suis **infiniment** touché. (adjective)   *I am extremely touched.*

Notes:

1   This second category of superlatives can sometimes be expressed by a prefix: **extra**, **super**, **hyper**, **ultra** or by a suffix: **issime** usually welded to the appropriate adjective:

    Elle est **hypersensible**. (adjective)   *She is hypersensitive.*

    Ce vin est **extra sec**. (adjective)   *This wine is extra dry.*

    Cet homme est **richissime** (adjective)   *This man is incredibly rich.*

2   This superlative meaning can also be expressed by the repetition of the adjective or adverb concerned:

    C'est **dur-dur**. (adjective)   *Things are very hard.*

    Il faut partir **vite-vite**. (adverb)   *We must leave very quickly.*

3   The same effect can also be achieved by using **des plus** (*most*):

    La décision est **des plus** importante.   *The decision is most important.*

(Note the absence of agreement!)

4   In many cases, the construction of a French comparative or superlative sentence will involve a word order which is different from the one used in English.

Compare: *A more important discovery has been made.*

and: Une découverte **plus** importante a été faite.
or: *Here is the strongest man in the world.*
and: Voici l'homme **le plus fort** du monde.
or: *The most stringent experiments are carried out.*
and: Les expériences **les plus** rigoureuses sont effectuées.

NB   In such sentences, the noun-phrase is placed *before* the comparative or superlative and *not after* it as in English.

Exceptional forms

A small number of adjectives and adverbs do not follow the regular rules of formation for comparatives and superlatives. Their list is given below.

Category	Positive form	Meaning	Comparative	Superlative
adjective	bon	*good*	meilleur	le meilleur
	mauvais	*bad*	pire	le pire
	petit	*slight*/small	moindre	le moindre
adverb	beaucoup	*much*	plus	le plus
	bien	*well*	mieux	le mieux
	mal	*badly*	pis	le pis
	peu	*little*	moins	le moins

For example:
Ici le climat est **meilleur** que là-bas. (adjective)   *Here the climate is better than over there.*
C'est **mieux** que la dernière fois. (adverb)   *It's better than last time.*
Tout va de **mal** en **pis**. (adverbs)*Everything is getting from bad to worse.*

Notes:
1   In the case of the adjectives, it must be remembered that the appropriate agreements must be made according to the gender and number of the noun concerned:
Prenez **la meilleure** chambre et **le meilleur** lit.   *Take the best room and the best bed.*
2   **Mauvais** (*bad*), **petit** (*slight*/*small*) and **mal** (*badly*), can also be constructed in the normal way. The two forms are used in different circumstances:

(i) the regular form is used particularly when a concrete characteristic is expressed. It is the most frequent;

(ii) the irregular form is used in abstract cases.

Compare: De deux maux il faut choisir **le moindre**. (abstract)
We must choose the lesser of two evils.

and: De ces deux hôtels je préfère **le plus petit**. (concrete)
Of those two hotels I prefer the smaller.

or: La situation est **pire qu'**hier. (abstract)
The situation is worse than yesterday.

and: La soupe est **plus mauvaise qu'**hier. (concrete)
The soup is worse than it was yesterday.

Idiomatic uses of comparative structures

1 $\begin{cases} \textbf{plus} \dots \textbf{plus} \ (the\ more \dots the\ more) \\ \textbf{moins} \dots \textbf{moins} \ (the\ less \dots the\ less): \end{cases}$

Plus je joue, **plus** je gagne. *The more I play, the more I win.*

Plus on est (de fous) **plus** on rit. (saying) *The more, the merrier.*

Moins je le vois, **plus** je suis heureux. *The less I see him, the happier I am.*

2 $\begin{cases} \textbf{de plus en plus} \ (more\ and\ more) \\ \textbf{de moins en moins} \ (less\ and\ less): \end{cases}$

Elle devient **de plus en plus** forte. *She is becoming stronger and stronger.*

Votre travail est **de moins en moins** acceptable. *Your work is getting less and less acceptable.*

3 $\begin{cases} \textbf{Plus de} \ (more\ than) \\ \textbf{moins de} \ (less\ than): \end{cases}$

Those two expressions are used in sentences where the idea of a limit is formulated (distance, time, age, weight, etc.), to indicate that the limit has been exceeded (**plus de**), or has not been reached (**moins de**):

Ils sont restés **plus de** trois jours. *They stayed more than three days.*

Elle a **moins de** 18 ans. *She is under 18.*

Certain adjectives cannot normally be used in comparative or superlative constructions because their meaning *already* implies a comparative or superlative value. Such is the case for:

aîné *elder*, **cadet** *younger*, **dernier** *last*, **excessif** *excessive*, **majeur** *major*, **mineur** *minor*, **ultime** *ultimate*, **unique** *unique*, etc.

Key points

1   There are in French, as in English, phrases which enable us:
(*a*)   to express various degrees of comparison between things, beings or actions; or
(*b*)   to state that certain things, beings, etc., possess a certain characteristic to the highest degree or to 'a very high degree'.
The first are known as comparatives, the second as superlatives.

2   There are 3 degrees of comparison: (i) *inferiority*, (ii) *equality* and (iii) *superiority*. They are rendered in French by (i) **moins . . . que** (*less than*) (ii) **aussi . . . que** (*as . . . as*) (iii) **plus . . . que** (*more than*).
3   There are alternatives to express two of the degrees mentioned:
(*a*)   *inferiority* can also be expressed as 'negative equality' with **ne . . . pas aussi que** (*not so . . . as*), or **ne . . . pas comme** (*not . . . like . . .*)
(*b*)   *equality* can also be expressed as 'negative superiority': **ne . . . pas plus . . . que** (*not any more than*) or 'negative inferiority': **ne . . . pas . . . moins . . . que** (*not any less than . . .*). Equality can also be expressed by using **comme** (*as, like*).
4   If a comparison involves an adjective, the necessary agreements (gender and number) must be made as required.
5   If a comparison involves a nominal or verbal phrase instead of an adjective or adverb, the expressions used will have to be modified in the following way:
aussi . . . que (equality) must be replaced by **autant . . . que:**
plus . . . que (superiority) should be replaced by **davantage . . . que**.
6   There are two main types of superlatives:
a superlative conveying the idea of 'the highest degree';
a superlative conveying the idea of 'a very high degree'.
–   The first one is expressed in French by: **le plus . . .** (*the . . . est/the most . . .*).
–   The second by placing before the appropriate element (adjective/adverb) an adverb such as: **excessivement** (*excessively*), **extrêmement** (*extremely*), **infiniment** (*infinitely*), **merveilleusement** (*wonderfully*), **très** (*very*), etc.
7   It is important to remember that in many sentences where a comparative (or superlative) is present, the word-order may be different in French and English. In particular, nouns which are placed after the comparative or superlative in English will be placed before it in French.
8   Although most adjectives and adverbs follow the normal rules for the formation of comparatives and superlatives, a small number of them are irregular; they are: *adjectives* = **bon** (*good*), **mauvais** (*bad*) and **petit** (*small/slight*). *adverbs* = **beaucoup** (*much*), **bien** (*well*), **mal** (*badly*) and **peu** (*little*).
9   The irregular comparatives and superlatives of adjectives *must agree* in gender and number as required by the grammatical context.

10   The regular method of formation for comparatives and superlatives can also be used with **mauvais** (*bad*), **petit** (*small/slight*), and **mal** (*badly*). The two forms (regular and irregular) have a slightly different use:
– the regular form is used in a concrete context;
– the irregular form is used in an abstract context.

11   Certain adjectives cannot normally be used in comparative or superlative constructions, because they already express a comparative or superlative idea on their own.

19 The Agreement of Tenses in Main and Subordinate Clauses

When speaking and writing in French, it is important to have the opportunity to situate a series of actions in relation to one another. In other words, it is useful to indicate whether:

1 One action occurred *before* the other(s) (= *anteriority*);
2 All actions occurred *at the same time* (= *simultaneity*);
3 One action occurred *after* the other(s) (= *posteriority*).

This can be done through careful use of tenses. The problem of tense agreement becomes particularly acute in the case of a sentence composed of a main clause (m.c.) and one (or more) subordinate clause(s) (s.c.) which, as previously stated, help(s) to give a fuller picture of the situation through added information.

Compare:

	perfect	perfect
C'est l'homme	que j'ai rencontré à la gare	qui m'a donné la lettre
m.c.	s.c. 1	s.c. 2

It is the man (whom) I met at the station who gave me the letter.

and:

	perfect	future
C'est l'homme	que j'ai rencontré à la gare	qui me donnera la lettre
m.c.	s.c. 1	s.c. 2

It is the man (whom) I met at the station who will give me the letter.

There are three types of possibilities

1 The main clause is in the Indicative mood and the subordinate clause does *not* require a verb in the subjunctive. In this case the verb of the subordinate clause may be in the Indicative, the Conditional, or even the Infinitive. An example is shown on pages 222–3 overleaf.

2 The main clause is in the Indicative, but the subordinate clause requires a subjunctive, because it expresses a possibility, a hypothesis, a doubt, etc. or because it is introduced by a conjunction requiring the subjunctive (see chapter on conjunctions).

There are two cases to envisage:
(i) the action expressed in the subordinate clause *may already have occurred*;
(ii) the action expressed in the subordinate clause *may yet occur* (now or later).

Main clause	Subordinate clause in the subjunctive	
(Indicative)	(i) *The action may have occurred*	(ii) *The action may yet occur*
Present je doute *I doubt* **Future** je douterai *I shall doubt* **Perfect** j'ai douté *I doubted* **Past Historic** je doutai *I doubted* **Imperfect** je doutais *I was doubting*	Perfect subjunctive qu'il soit venu *that he has/had come*	Present subjunctive qu'il vienne *that he is coming* *that he will come* *that he would come*

Note: There are other subjunctive tenses (Imperfect and Pluperfect) which could be used. But because of their increasing rarity in everyday French, it was deemed unnecessary to include them here.

3 The subordinate clause is introduced by **si** (*if*) *expressing a condition*. At this level, you are advised to consider that the three possibilities given below are *the only acceptable ones* for a sentence *in which a condition is expressed*. In each case the arrow indicate the only possible combination.
Note: Very often, the subordinate clause beginning with **si** is *placed first* and followed by the main clause.

Main Clause	*Subordinate Clause (Indicative or Conditional)*		
	1 *Anteriority*	*2* *Simultaneity*	*3* *Posteriority*
(Indicative mood)			
Present Je pense *I think* →	**Perfect Indicative** qu'il est venu *he has come*	**Present Indicative** qu'il vient *he is coming*	**Future Indicative** qu'il viendra *he will come*
Future je penserai *I shall think* →	**Perfect Indicative** (as above)	**Present Indicative** (as above)	**Future Indicative** (as above)
Perfect j'ai pensé *I thought* →	**Pluperfect Indicative** qu'il était venu *he had come*	**Imperfect Indicative** qu'il venait *he was coming*	**Present conditional** qu'il viendrait *he would come*
Past Historic → je pensai	**Pluperfect Indicative** (as above)	**Imperfect Indicative** (as above)	**Present Conditional** (as above)
Imperfect → je pensais	**Pluperfect Indicative** (as above)	**Imperfect Indicative** (as above)	**Present Conditional** (as above)

	Perfect Infinitive	Present Infinitive	Present Infinitive
Present je pense *I think* →	**Perfect Infinitive** être venu *I have come*	**Present Infinitive** venir *I am coming*	**Present Infinitive** venir *I shall come*
Future je penserai →	**Perfect Infinitive** (as above)	**Present Infinitive** (as above)	**Present Infinitive** (as above)
Perfect j'ai pensé *I thought* →	**Perfect Infinitive** être venu *I had come*	**Present Infinitive** venir *I was coming*	**Present Infinitive** venir *I would come*
Past Historic je pensai →	**Perfect Infinitive** (as above)	**Present Infinitive** (as above)	**Present Infinitive** (as above)
Imperfect je pensais →	**Perfect Infinitive** (as above)	**Present Infinitive** (as above)	**Present Infinitive** (as above)

Notes:

1 The use of an infinitive in a subordinate clause implies that the subject of the two clauses is the same. For example:

Je pense **être** venu = Je pense que je suis venu.
I think I came.

Tu espères venir = Tu espères que tu viendras.
You hope that you will come.

2 If an infinitive clause is used, there is no way of distinguishing simultaneity or posteriority with the help of the infinitive alone: **J'espère venir** could mean either *I hope I am coming* or *I hope I will be coming*. The context should however make matters clear in most cases.

	Subordinate Clause	Main Clause
	(Indicative)	(Indicative or Conditional)
	Present Indicative ⟶	**Present Indicative/Future**
1	Si tu refuses	je pars/je partirai
	If you refuse	*I am leaving shall leave*
	Imperfect Indicative ⟶	**Present Conditional**
2	Si tu refusais	je partirais
	If you refused	*I would go*
	Pluperfect Indicative ⟶	**Perfect Conditional**
3	Si tu avais refusé	je serais parti
	If you had refused	*I would have gone*

In addition to the above possibilities, there are other instances when tenses need to be modified to comply with the 'agreement of tenses' rules. Two such instances are given below.

Direct and indirect speech

As already mentioned, *direct speech* is someone's speech presented as if the listener or reader were face to face with the person uttering the words in question. The quotation marks are used as well as exclamation or question marks. Indirect speech is someone's speech *reported* as though by a witness. No speech marks and no question or exclamation marks are used. In the table below the arrows indicate which way the changes should be made.

Direct speech		Indirect speech	
introducing clause	*quotation*	*introducing clause*	*reported speech*
Present	+ **Present**	↔ **Present**	+ **Present**
Il dit:	"je sors"	Il dit	qu'il sort
He says:	*"I am going out"*	*He says*	*he is going out*
Present	+ **Perfect**	↔ **Present**	+ **Perfect**
Il dit:	"je suis sorti"	Il dit	qu'il est sorti
He says:	*"I have gone out"*	*He says*	*he has gone out*
Future	+ **Present**	↔ **Future**	+ **Present**
Il dira:	"je sors"	Il dira	qu'il sort
He will say:	*"I am going out"*	*He will say*	*he is going out*
Perfect	+ **Present**	↔ **Perfect**	+ **Imperfect**
Il a dit:	"je sors"	Il a dit	qu'il sortait
He said:	*"I am going out"*	*He said*	*he was going out*

Direct speech (cont.)		*Indirect speech* (cont.)	
introducing clause	*quotation*	*introducing clause*	*reported speech*
Perfect	+ **Perfect** ↔	**Perfect**	+ **Pluperfect**
Il a dit:	"je suis sorti"	Il a dit	qu'il était sorti
He said:	*"I have gone out"*	*He said*	*he had gone out*
Perfect	+ **Future** ↔	**Perfect**	+ **†Present conditional**
Il a dit:	"je sortirai"	Il a dit	qu'il sortirait
He said:	*"I shall go out"*	*He said*	*he would go out*
Imperfect	+ **Present** ↔	**Imperfect**	+ **Imperfect**
Il disait:	"je sors"	Il disait	qu'il sortait
He was saying:	*"I am going out"*	*He was saying*	*he was going out*
Imperfect	+ **Perfect** ↔	**Imperfect**	+ **Pluperfect**
Il disait:	"je suis sorti"	Il disait	qu'il était sorti
He was saying:	*"I have gone out"*	*He was saying*	*he had gone out*

† This tense is not, properly speaking, a Present Conditional but a *Future of the Past* which is the indirect speech equivalent of a *direct speech Future* uttered in the past.

Compare: Il **a dit** (Perfect): "Je **sortirai**" (Future)
He said *"I will go out"*
and: Il **a dit** (Perfect) qu'il **sortirait** (Future of the Past)
He said *he would go out*

For the sake of convenience, and because both tenses are identical, only the appellation Present Conditional has so far been given.

Modal attraction (the 'chameleon effect')

In sentences where the main clause is followed by several other clauses introduced by a relative pronoun: **qui** (*who*), **que** (*that*), **dont** (*whose*), **où** (*where*), etc. (see relative pronouns on pages 94–5), the first subordinate clause (s.c. 1), may require a subjunctive because of its meaning (doubt, hypothesis, etc.). In such cases the second relative clause (s.c. 2), may also take the subjunctive (by a sort of 'chameleon effect') even though the sense may not require it; this phenomenon is called *Modal attraction*. For example:

Je veux un ouvrier   qui **fasse** bien son travail,

m.c.   s.c. 1   (Present Subjunctive)
I want a worker who will do his work well,

et { qui **sera** ponctuel. (Future Indicative)
{ qui **soit** ponctuel. (Present Subjunctive)

s.c. 2
and who will be punctual.

Donnez–moi un remède qui **soit** efficace, (Present subjunctive)

m.c.   s.c. 1
Give me a remedy, which will be efficient,

et $\left\{ \begin{array}{l} \text{que je } \textbf{pourrai} \text{ prendre facilement. (Future Indicative)} \\ \text{que je } \textbf{puisse} \text{ prendre facilement. (Present subjunctive)} \end{array} \right.$

s.c. 2

and which I can take easily.

Key points

1   Tense agreement enables the speaker or writer to express the timing of a given action in relation to other actions.

2   If a subordinate clause does not require a verb in the Subjunctive, the range of tenses which can be used is very large and may include the indicative as well as the Conditional Mood.

3   If a subordinate clause requires the Subjunctive, two tenses can be used depending on sense:
 − the Perfect Subjunctive to express actions that may have occurred
 − the Present Subjunctive to express actions that may yet occur.

4   In the case of a sentence composed of a subordinate clause (s.c.) beginning with **si** (*if*) expressing a condition, and a main clause (m.c.), 3 combinations only are possible.

 s.c. = Present/Perfect   ⟶   m.c. = Present/Future
 s.c. = Imperfect   ⟶   m.c. = Present Conditional
 s.c. = Pluperfect   ⟶   m.c. = Perfect Conditional

5   The rules governing changes of tense from direct to indirect speech (or vice versa) are fairly rigid and should be learned with care.

6   In certain sentences where the main clause is followed by several relative clauses (introduced by **qui**, **que**, etc.), the first of which requires the subjunctive, the other(s) may also take the subjunctive by virtue of modal attraction ('chameleon effect').

20 Problems and Solutions

When studying a language, one always comes across problems which are hard to solve, or mistakes which are difficult to eliminate. This chapter has been written with this point in mind.

Some of the most commonly encountered problems are examined. The entries are made in alphabetical order. For a fuller treatment of the grammatical categories involved, you should refer to the relevant chapter when appropriate.

Adjectives

With very few exceptions, adjectives agree in gender and number with the noun they qualify. The following, however, are exceptions and remain invariable.

1 Adjectives of colour derived from nouns: **aurore** *dawn*, **cerise** *cherry*, **chocolat** *chocolate*, **orange** *orange*, **marron** *chestnut*, **mastic** *putty*, **noisette** *hazel*:

Elle a les yeux **noisette**. *She has hazel eyes.*

2 Compound adjectives of colour:

J'aime les chemises **bleu-clair**. *I like light-blue shirts.*

3 **Nu** (*bare*) and **demi** (*half*), when placed before the noun (note the hyphen!):

Il est **nu-tête** et **nu-pieds**. *He is bare-headed and barefoot.*

4 **Grand** (*great/main*), when used in a feminine (singular or plural) compound:

Voilà la **grand-route**! *Here is the main road.*

5 Adjectives placed after a verb and used as adverbs: **bas** *low*, **bon** *good*, **cher** *dear*, **dur** *hard*, **fort** *very/loud*, etc.

Ces fleurs sentent **bon**. *These flowers smell good.*

Adverbs

Adverbs are invariable. They are *normally* placed as follows.

1 After the verb in a simple tense:

Il travaille **bien**. *He is working well.*

2 Between the auxiliary and the past participle in compound tenses:

Il a **bien** travaillé. *He has worked well.*

3   Before an adjective or an adverb:
  Elle est **très** jeune.   *She is very young.*
  Tu vas **trop** vite.   *You are going too fast.*

After (*Après*)

Après (preposition) can be followed by:
1   A noun or a pronoun:
  Il est arrivé **après** le repas.   *He arrived after the meal.*
  Après vous!   *After you!*
2   A Perfect Infinitive (Infinitive of **être** (*to be*) or **avoir** (*to have*) + Past
Participle) and *not* a Present Participle as in English:
  Il est parti **après avoir payé** sa note. (and not* . . . après payant
  sa note)   *He left after paying his bill.*

Age

In French, the verb **avoir** (*to have*) is used to express age. It must be
followed by the cardinal number *and* the word **an(s)** (*year(s)*):
  Il **a** vingt-cinq **ans**. (lit: *he has twenty-five years*)   *He is twenty-
  five.*

Attributive verbs

The following verbs: **demeurer** (*to remain*), **devenir** (*to become*), **être**
(*to be*), **paraître** (*to seem*), **rester** (*to remain*) and **sembler** (*to seem*) are
called 'attributive verbs'. They cannot, unlike other verbs, be
modified by an adverb but they can be qualified by an adjective which
will *vary in gender and number* as required:
  Ils **semblent** tristes et fatigués. (masc. plur. agreement)   *They
  seem sad and tired.*
  La porte **reste** ouverte. (fem. sing. agreement)   *The door remains
  open.*
Compare: Ils **sont** rapides. (and not *ils sont vite) *They are quick.*
  (adjective)
and: Ils vont vite. *They go quickly.* (adverb)
Notes:
1   In sentences of the type Il est **très** rapide (*He is very fast*), the
adverb **très** modifies the adjective and not the verb.
2   Expressions like **C'est bien** (*it is good = it is well done*) and **C'est
mal** (*it is bad = it is badly done*) are not exceptions but are merely
elliptical (shortened) sentences where the Past Participle **fait** (*done*) is
missed out.

Auxiliaries

Être (*to be*) and **avoir** (*to have*) are the verbs which are used in the formation of *compound tenses* (Perfect, Pluperfect, etc.); the rule is as follows:

1 **être** is used to form the compound tenses of:

(*a*) the 'famous 14': **aller** *to go*, **venir** *to come*, **arriver** *to arrive*, **partir** *to leave*, **descendre** *to go down*, **monter** *to go up*, **entrer** *to go in*, **sortir** *to go out*, **mourir** *to die*, **naître** *to be born*, **passer** *to go by*, **retourner** *to return*, **rester** *to stay*, **tomber** *to fall*:

Ils **sont partis** mais je **suis resté**. *They went but I stayed.*

(*b*) pronominal verbs (reflexive and reciprocal):

Je **me suis coupé**. *I cut myself.* (reflexive)

Nous **nous sommes battus**. *We fought each other.* (reciprocal)

2 **Avoir** is used in all other cases (including the compound tenses of passive verbs):

Ils **ont été insultés** par vous. *They have been insulted by you.*

For the agreement of past participles with **avoir** and **être**, see *Past Participle agreement* on page 240.

Because

It can be translated in two ways:

1 **à cause de**, if it is followed by a noun or a pronoun:

L'accident est arrivé **à cause de** cet idiot. *The accident happened because of this fool.*

2 **parce que**, if it introduces a subordinate clause (s.c.) with subject, verb, etc.:

Je vous téléphone parce que je ne suis pas satisfait.
s.c.

I am ringing you because I am not satisfied.

By

It can be translated by:

1 **en** + Present Participle of a verb if, in English, it was followed by an *ing* form:

C'est **en travaillant** qu'il réussira. *It's by working that he will succeed.*

2 **par**, when a noun follows:

Prenez-moi **par** la main. *Take me by the hand.*

Note: If the meaning of *by* is *at the side of* or *near*, it should be translated by **près de**:

Je me promène **près de** la rivière. *I am walking by the river.*

3   **en**, when the idea of transport is present:
  Ils sont allés aux Etats-Unis **en** avion.   *They went to the United*
  States by plane.

Collective nouns

Nouns such as: **l'armée** (*the army*), **l'église** (*the Church*), **la famille**
(*the family*), **le gouvernement** (*the government*), **la police** (*the police*),
le public (*the public*), etc. *must* be used in the singular, despite the fact
that they represent a large collection of beings, and the verb they are
associated with *must* be in the 3rd person singular. For example:
  Le gouvernement est tombé. (and not *sont tombés)   *The*
  government has fallen.
  Le public est content. (and not *sont contents)   *The public is*
  pleased.
  La famille est arrivée. (and not *sont arrivés)   *The family has*
  arrived.

Dates and days

Dates, with the exception of the first day of the month, require the
cardinal number in French.
Compare: Le **premier** mai
      May 1st
and: Le **deux** mai (and not *le deuxième mai)
      May 2nd
      Du **premier** janvier au **trente et un** décembre. (and not * . . . au
      trente et unième . . .)   *All the year round.* (lit: *from January*
      1st to December 31st)
Note: Neither the name of the day nor that of the month begin with a
capital letter (unless they are at the start of a sentence).

Definite articles

The definite article, which varies according to the gender and number
of the noun it relates to, serves as an *advance warning system*. It is
therefore used more systematically than in English, not only to
indicate very precise and clearly defined categories of things or
beings, but also to refer to broad categories or concepts.
Compare: **Les** loups sont féroces.
      Wolves (as a species) *are ferocious.*
and: **Les** loups du zoo sont superbes.
      The wolves at the zoo (very precise group) *are superb.*

The fact that, with very few exceptions, the plural form of French nouns sounds exactly the same as their singular form, *makes it imperative* to use the definite article (or another determiner) to signal the difference:

Compare: Il adore **le** cadeau.
He loves the present.

The only sound difference between those two French sentences is

and: Il adore **les** cadeaux.
He loves presents.

le [lə] v. **les** [le]
(see appendix I)

Note: The definite article must also be used with the name of a country, or the rank or title of a person (whether or not followed by the name of that person):

Compare: *General de Gaulle did a lot for France.*
and: **Le** Général de Gaulle a beaucoup fait pour **la** France.

Direct (accusative) and indirect (dative) object pronouns

1 If a verb is constructed in the *accusative*, i.e. admits an answer to the question **qui?** (*who(m)?*) or **quoi?** (*what?*), one of the object pronouns — **me** (*me*), **te** (*you* fam.), **le/la** (*him/her/it*), **nous** (*us*) **vous** (*you* sing. or plur.), **les** (*them*) — must be used. For example:

Nous **le** regardons. (nous regardons qui? = **le**)
We are watching him/it.
Je **les** vois. (je vois qui? = **les**)
I see them.

Note: **me** (*me*) changes to **moi** in the 2nd person (sing./plur.) of the Present Imperative (*positive*) tense.

Compare: Regarde-**moi**! (positive)
Watch me!
and: Ne **me** regarde pas! (negative)
Do not watch me!

2 If a verb is constructed in the *dative*, i.e. is followed by à and admits an answer to the question **à qui?** (*to whom?*) or **a quoi?** (*to what?*), one of the object pronouns -**me** (*to me*), **te** (*to you* fam.), **lui** (*to him/her*), **nous** (*to us*), **vous** (*to you* sing. or plur.), **leur** (*to them*) -must be used:

Nous **lui** téléphonons. (nous téléphonons à qui? = à **lui**)
We are telephoning (to) him/her.
Je **leur** parle. (je parle à qui? = à eux = **leur**)
I am talking to them.

Note: **me** (*to me*) changes to **moi** in the 2nd person (sing./plur.) of the Present Imperative (*positive*) tense:

Compare: Ecrivez-**moi**! (positive)
          Write to me!
and: Ne **m**'écrivez pas! (negative)
          Do not write to me!

The two sets of pronouns (direct and indirect object) presented above, are almost identical *except for the 3rd persons* (singular and plural). Be particularly careful about constructions involving those 3rd persons.

Disjunctive pronouns

Those pronouns are: **moi** (*me*), **toi** (*you* fam.), **lui** (*him/it*), **elle** (*she/it*), **nous** (*us*), **vous** (*you* sing. or plur.), **eux** (*them* masc. plur.), **elles** (*them* fem. plur.). They are used:

1 After a preposition: **à** (*at/to*), **de** (*of/from*), **pour** (*for*), **sans** (*without*), **vers** (*towards*), etc. For example:

Elle se tourna vers **eux**. *She turned towards them.*

2 As emphatic reinforcement of the corresponding subject pronoun:

Moi, je pense que vous avez tort. *I (for one) think you are wrong.*

3 To replace the corresponding subject pronoun in constructions involving a coordinating conjunction: **et** (*and*), **mais** (*but*), **ni** (*neither/nor*), **ou** (*or*):

Nous travaillons dur **lui** et **moi**. *He and I work hard.*

Ni **eux** ni **moi** n'avons rien vu. *Neither they nor I saw anything.*

4 In reply to a question where, in English, an auxiliary would follow the subject pronoun:

Qui a parlé? **Moi**! *Who spoke? I did!*

Qui est coupable? **Eux**! *Who is guilty? They are!*

Faire

Apart from its straightforward meanings (*to do/to make*), **faire** also occurs in a number of useful idiomatic constructions. The most common are presented below.

1 To translate the expressions *to have something done* or *to cause something to be done*. In this case, **faire** is followed by another Infinitive:

Nous **faisons construire** une maison. *We are having a house built.*

Il **a fait fermer** le magasin. *He had the shop closed* (i.e. *he caused the shop to be closed*).

Notes:
a) It is possible to have a construction where **faire** is used twice: once as the auxiliary and once in its own right:

Elle a **fait faire** sa robe a Paris. *She had her dress made in Paris.*

b) In certain expressions, particularly in cooking recipes, **faire** is often used as an auxiliary where in English only the main verb would be present.

Faire cuire à feu doux. *Cook on a low heat.*
Faites monter la crème. *Whisk up the cream.*

c) **Faire** is also used in orders or requests to indicate that a person other than the one you are addressing should perform the action requested:

Faites ouvrir la porte. *Have someone open the door.*
Fais appeler le docteur. *Have somebody call the doctor.*

To translate impersonal expression relating to the weather:

	beau	*fine*
	du brouillard	*foggy*
	chaud	*hot*
Il fait	frais	*cool*
The weather is	froid	*cold*
It is	humide	*damp*
	orage	*stormy*
	sec	*dry*
	soleil	*sunny*
	du vent	*windy*

To translate the expression of assent **do!** in reply to a request (this use is informal):

Je peux fumer? **Faites,** je vous en prie! *May I smoke? Please do!*
Vous permettez? **Faites** donc! *Do you mind . . . ? By all means!*

In a pronominal construction to translate the English *to get*:

Il **se fait** tard. *It is getting late.*
Ta voix **se fait** dure. *Your voice is getting harsh.*

To translate the following English expressions:

to hurt somebody = faire mal à quelqu'un
to frighten somebody = faire peur à quelqu'un
to shame somebody = faire honte à quelqu'un
to please somebody = faire plaisir à quelqu'un
to mollify somebody = faire pitié à quelqu'un

Note: The above verbs can also be used pronominally:

Je **me fais** peur. *I frighten myself.* (reflexive)
Ils **se** sont **fait** mal. *They hurt themselves.* (reflexive)
They hurt each other. (reciprocal)

6 In certain constructions with 'passive' overtones:
 Il s'est **fait** tuer. *He was killed* (i.e. *someone killed him*).
 Je me suis **fait** voler. *I was robbed* (i.e. *someone robbed me*).
 Ils se sont **fait** prendre. *They have been caught* (i.e. *someone caught them*).
In all the above constructions, **fait** bears no gender or number agreement.
7 To translate expressions like *to play* . . . , *to act* . . . For example:
 Vous **faites** l'idiot! *You are playing the fool!*
 Arrêtez de **faire** le singe! *Stop acting the goat!* (lit. *the monkey*)

For (duration)

This word can be translated in different ways, according to its precise meaning.
1 If it indicates a period (in the past, present or future) seen from the point of view of its *actual* duration, it may be translated as **pendant** (*for = during*), or totally omitted. You may say:
either: Il a vécu **pendant** vingt ans à Londres.
or: Il a vécu vingt ans à Londres.
 He lived in London for twenty years.
either: Je resterai ici **pendant** trois jours.
or: *Je resterai ici trois jours.*
 I shall stay here for three days.
2 If it indicates an *anticipated duration*, particularly with a verb of movement -**aller**/**se rendre** (*to go*), **arriver** (*to arrive*), **partir** (*to leave*), **venir** (*to come*), etc.-it will be translated as **pour**:
 Nous partons **pour** un mois. *We are leaving for a month.*
Note: *for* expressing a duration in the past can be translated by the expression **il y a . . . que** with one of the appropriate tenses emphasising duration (i.e. present, imperfect, etc. *but not* past historic):
 Il y a deux heures **que** j'attends. (present) *I have been waiting for two hours.*
 Il y avait deux ans **qu**'il était parti. (imperfect) *He had been gone for two years.*

For example

This is translated by **par exemple** (and not * pour exemple).
Note: In an exclamative sentence **par exemple** is used in familiar French to express incredulity or great surprise:
 Vous ici? Ça **par exemple**! *You are here? Well I never!*

Generally/in general

This is translated in French by:

1 **En général** (often used in informal situations):
   En général, il est assez compréhensif. *Generally, he is fairly understanding.*

2 **Généralement** (often used is slightly more elevated style):
   Je le vois **généralement** le mercredi. *Generally, I see him on Wednesdays.*

Note: *Generally speaking* can be translated by **Généralement parlant**:
   Généralement parlant, ça marche bien. *Generally speaking, things are going well.*

Imperfect v. Perfect (or Past Historic)

This is one of the most common sources of errors.

1   The Perfect or the Past Historic indicate that an action occurred as an isolated event in the past *regardless of its duration*. It permits the faithful recording of a sequence of *separate* events (A, B, C) along the time axis, as shown below:

```
                            Present
Past ——————×———×———×———————————— Future
            A    B    C
```

Il s'est assis, a appelé le garçon et a commandé son déjeuner.
        A   B   C
He sat down, called the waiter and ordered his lunch.
Il fréquenta l'Université pendant trois ans.
He attended University for 3 years.

Note: Here, the duration is irrelevant to the tense; the action is seen as a finite, isolated event.

2   The imperfect emphasises:

(a)   The habitual recurrence of an action in the past, seen from the point of view of its *duration* or *repetition*:
   Tous les lundis il **allait** au cinéma. *Every Monday he used to go to the pictures.*

(b)   The fact that an action was in progress when another *isolated* action occurred:
   Je finissais mon travail quand elle est arrivée.
     Imperf.   Perf.
   I was finishing my work when she arrived.

(c)   The fact that an action used to occur *every time* another did:

Chaque fois qu'il sortait il prenait, un taxi.

<u>Imperf.</u>   <u>Imperf.</u>

Every time he went out, he used to take a taxi.

(*d*) The fact that an action used to be the 'hallmark' of a period in which another used to occur:

Quand j'étais jeune, je vivais à la campagne.

Imperf   Imperf.

When I was young, I used to live in the country.

Infinitives

The Infinitive is the 'nominal' form of a verb. In French, it is recognisable by its ending: **er**, **ir** or **re**. The following important points should always be borne in mind:

1 Some infinitives can be used as nouns: **l'avoir** (*'nest egg'* or *credit note*), **l'être** (*the being*), **le devoir** (*duty*), **le manger** (*food*), **le pouvoir** (*power to act*), **le savoir** (*knowledge*), etc.

2 After the prepositions **à** (*at/to*), **de** (*of/from*), **pour** (*to*) and **sans** (without) the verb *must be in the infinitive*:

Il vient de **partir** sans **dire** merci. *He has just left without saying thank you.*

3 If two verbs follow each other the second one *must be in the infinitive* unless the first is an auxiliary (**avoir** or **être**):

J'aime **marcher**. (and not* j'aime marchant) *I like walking.*

Elle déteste **sortir**. (and not * elle déteste sortant) *She hates going out.*

Note: The English Present Participle found in such constructions must only be translated *either* by an infinitive (as above) *or* by a noun equivalent in meaning. For example:

J'aime marcher.

= J'aime **la marche**.

Elle déteste sortir.

= Elle déteste **les sorties**.

4 The infinitive can be used with the value of an imperative in written instructions:

Assembler avec soin. *Assemble with care.*

Ouvrir ici. *Open here.*

It is

This expression can be translated in a variety of ways according to the context in which it occurs. The main possibilities are given below.

If *it* is impersonal (i.e. does not refer to any thing or being) and is onstructed as follows:

$$\text{it is} + \text{adjective} + \begin{cases} \text{subordinate clause beginning} \\ \text{with } \textit{that} \\ \qquad\qquad\qquad \textit{or} \\ \text{infinitive clause introduced by } \textit{to} \end{cases}$$

'or example:

$$\textit{It is important} \begin{cases} \textit{that you work.} \\ \textit{or} \\ \textit{(for you) to work.} \end{cases}$$

'he French structure will be:

$$\textbf{Il est} + \text{adjective} + \begin{cases} \text{subordinate clause (usually subjunctive)} \\ \text{beginning with } \textbf{que} \\ \textit{or} \text{ infinitive clause beginning with 'de'} \end{cases}$$

'or example:

$$\text{Il est important} \begin{cases} \text{que tu travailles.} \\ \textit{or} \\ \text{(pour toi) de travailler.} \end{cases}$$

Jote: The real subject of such sentences is not **il** but the subordinate r infinitive clauses themselves. You could therefore say:

:ither: (Le fait de) travailler est important.
          Working is important.
r: (Le fait) que tu travailles est important.
          (The fact) that you should work is important.

If *it* refers to a precise masculine or feminine noun already ientioned in the same or a previous sentence, the translation will be **il** r **elle** as required by the noun's gender:

Lisez cette lettre qui vient d'arriver. **Elle** est urgente. *Read this letter which has just arrived. It* (i.e. this letter) *is urgent.*

J'ai examiné votre dossier. **Il** est impressionnant. *I have examined your dossier. It* (i.e. your dossier) *is impressive.*

If *it* refers to something which cannot directly be assimilated to a iasculine or feminine noun quoted before, but has nevertheless been inted at 'in substance', the translation will be: **c'**, **ceci**, **cela**, **ça** *his/that*) and the adjective will be in the masculine singular:

Lisez cette lettre. C'est urgent. *Read this letter. It* (i.e. the fact that you should read this letter) *is urgent.*

J'ai examiné votre dossier. C'est impressionnant! *I have examined your dossier. It* (i.e. what you have achieved or what is in it . . .) *is impressive!*

'ompare: Ce cheval ne gagne jamais. **Il** est ridicule.
            This horse never wins. It (i.e. this horse) *is ridiculous.*

and: Ce cheval ne gagne jamais. C'est ridicule.
             This horse never wins. It (i.e. the fact that it never wins) *is*
             ridiculous.
4 If *it is* is followed by a noun or a pronoun, the translation will be
c'est (or **ce sont** if the verb which follows is in the 3rd person
plural):
             C'est la plage que je préfère. *It is the beach I prefer.*
             Ce sont les invités qui arrivent. *It is the guests who are arriving*

It is cannot be used on its own in reply to a question, as in
English. The adverbs **oui** or **si** (as appropriate) will have to be
used and, if required, accompanied by a repetition of the
relevant adjective, noun or pronoun.
Compare: *Is it your car? (Yes) it is!*
and: C'est votre voiture? Oui! (c'est la mienne).
and *not just*: *oui c'est!

More and less

Those words are used in a variety of constructions:
1 *More than/less than* (or equivalent) = comparative; this is translated as: **plus . . . que/moins . . . que**:
             Il court **plus** vite **que** moi. *He runs faster than I.*
2 *The more . . . the more/the less . . . the less* (or equivalent) =
augmentative; this is translated as: **plus . . . plus . . .
moins . . . moins . . .** (and not* le plus . . . le plus or le moins . . . le
moins):
             Plus nous avançons, **plus** il fait sombre. *The more we advance,*
             the darker it gets.
3 *More than/less than* + a limit expressed by a figure (i.e. over/
under): this is translated by **plus de . . . /moins de . . .** (and not*
plus que . . . /moins que . . .).
             Il nous reste **moins de** trois jours. *We have less than three days*
             left.
             Une absence de **plus de** six mois. *An absence of over six months*
4 *More and more/less and less* (or equivalent) = idea of progression
or deterioration. This is translated in French by **de plus en
plus . . . /de moins en moins . . .** (and not *plus et plus/moins et
moins):
             Ils ont **de plus en plus** de temps libre. *They have more and more*
             free time.

5 *More or less*. This is translated by **plus ou moins**:
  Je crois qu'il a **plus ou moins** compris. *I think he has more or less understood.*

Notes:
(*a*) *More* expressing a request/order for a greater amount is translated by **encore**!
(*b*) *More* followed by a noun can be translated by **davantage de** as well as **plus de**:
  Nous avons **plus de** temps.
  = Nous avons **davantage de** temps.
  We have more time.

In certain sentences **plus que** . . . followed by a noun or equivalent may have the meaning of *only . . . left!*:
  Plus que deux heures à attendre! *Only two more hours to wait.*
  Il ne reste **plus que** lui. *He is the only one left* (lit: *There is only him left*).

Neuter

Although it is accepted that there are only two genders in French, there are a number of expressions which do not refer specifically to any masculine or feminine thing or being, e.g. **ce** or **c'** (*this/that*), **ça** (*that*), **ceci** (*this*), **cela** (*that*), **quelque chose** (*something*), **quelqu'un** (*someone*), etc. They are considered neutral in value, but any agreement will be made in the *masculine singular*.

Such neutral expressions are used when the speaker or writer does not know (or want to tell) what the gender of the thing or being referred to is, or when the subject of the sentence is too vague to be clearly labelled masculine or feminine. For example:
  Il est encore ici. **C'est** étrange. *He is still here. That's strange.*
  (i.e. the fact that he is still here is strange)
  J'ai entendu **quelque chose** d'intéressant. *I have heard something interesting.*
  Quelqu'un frappe à la porte. *Someone is knocking at the door.*
  (it could be a man or a woman)

Note: If **quelque chose** and **quelqu'un** are followed by an adjective, the preposition **de** must be used:
  Mangez **quelque chose de** bon. *Eat something good.*
  Je cherche **quelqu'un de** consciencieux. *I am looking for somebody conscientious.*

Past participle agreement with *avoir* and *être*

1   With **être** there are two main cases:

(a) *If the verb concerned is not a 'reflexive' verb* (or more precisely a pronominal verb) the past participle will agree in gender and number with the subject, like an adjective:
Ils **sont** partis mais elle **est** restée.   *They* (masc. plur.) *went but she stayed.*

(b) *If the verb concerned is a pronominal verb,* the past participle will agree *if* the construction is an accusative one (i.e. if the performer of the action is also the answer to the questions **qui?** or **quoi?** posed after the past participle reconstructed with **avoir**).
Compare: **Elle** s'est coupée. (elle a coupé qui? = elle)
She cut herself. (accusative = agreement)
and: **Elle** s'est **dit**. (elle a dit à qui? = à elle)
She said to herself. (dative = no agreement)

2   With **avoir** the principle of agreement is as follows:

(a) If the construction is not an accusative one (i.e. no answer to the question **qui?** or **quoi?**) there is no agreement:
Elle a fermé. (Elle a fermé quoi?-no answer available = no agreement) *She locked up.*
Ils lui ont parlé (Ils ont parlé à qui? dative = no agreement) *They talked to him/her.*

(b) If the construction is accusative but if the answer to the question **qui?** or **quoi?** comes too late (i.e. after the past participle), there is no agreement:
Ils ont **vu** la mer. (Ils ont vu quoi? = la mer)   *They saw the sea.*

(c) If the construction is accusative *and* if the answer to the question **qui?** or **quoi?** precedes the past participle, then the latter agrees *in gender and number* with the direct object.
La mer est là; ils l'ont **vue**.
(ils ont vu quoi? = l' = la mer = agreement)
The sea is there; they saw it.

People/persons

There are two possible translations of those words:
1   **Gens** (masc. plur.) This word *cannot* be used to refer to one person only.
You can say: Il y a **des gens** sur la place. *There are people in the square.*

but not: *Il y a un gens sur la place.
This word *cannot* be used with an exact number.
You can say: Une centaine de **gens**. *Approximately a hundred people.*
but not: *Cent trente gens. One hundred and thirty people.
2 *Personnes* (fem. plur.) This word *can* be used to refer to one person only.
   Il y a une **personne** qui attend. *There is a person (who is) waiting.*
It *can* be used with a precise *or* approximate number of people:
   Cent **personnes** attendaient. *A hundred people were waiting.*
   Quelques **personnes** sont descendues. *Some people went down.*
Note: After **quelques** (*a few*) and **plusieurs** (*several*), it is **personnes** *and not* **gens** which is used:
   Il a parlé à **plusieurs** personnes. (and not *. . . à plusieurs gens)

Adjectives used immediately before **gens** are put in the *feminine*, although subsequent agreements remain masculine plural.
   Les **vieilles gens** sont isolés. (and not *isolées) *Old people are isolated.*
   Certaines gens sont furie**ux**. (and not *furieuses) *Certain people are furious.*

Present participles

The Present Participle is the adjectival form of a verb. In English, it is recognisable by its *ing* ending. It can appear in four types of constructions in French.
1 *As an adjective.* In this case, it will agree in gender and number with the noun it qualifies:
   Une étoile **filante**. *A shooting star.*
2 *As an invariable word*, often replacing a relative clause beginning with **qui** (*who*):
   Elle aperçoit la voiture **roulant** à toute vitesse. (roulant = qui roule) *She sees the car going at full speed.*
3 *To indicate the simultaneity of two actions.* In this case the French Present Participle will be preceded by **en**:
   Ils montent **en sifflant**. *They come up whistling.*
   Il est parti **en pleurant**. *He went away crying.*
4 *To express manner* (= by/through) The French equivalent is also constructed with **en**:
   Vous réussirez **en travaillant** bien. *You will succeed by working well.*

English Present Participles immediately following a verb and relating to the same subject *must*, in French, be translated by *an Infinitive*:

Compare: J'aime **manger** des pommes.

and: *I like eating apples.*

or: Ils détestent **se lever** tôt.

and: *They hate getting up early.*

Requests and orders

In French, as in English, there are many different ways of formulating a request or an order. The expression chosen may depend on the force of the request, the degree of urgency, the status of the person formulating the request, the social context, etc. Some examples are given below. Non standard usage will be mentioned where appropriate.

It should be noted, however, that in most cases a strong request may be 'toned down' by adding such expressions as **s'il te/vous plaît**, **je te/vous prie** (*please*), **si tu veux/vous voulez bien, si cela ne te/vous dérange pas** (*if you do not mind*), etc. The following categories may be considered:

1 *Strong requests or commands*

(*a*) The Present Imperative can be used at all levels of language to convey such a meaning:

Fermez la porte (s'il vous plaît)! *Close the door (please)!*

Ouvre la bouche (je te prie)! *Open your mouth (please)!*

Note: In the case of a construction involving the second person plural of the Imperative, the corresponding form of **vouloir** (*to want*) may be used as a softener.

Compare: Attendez un moment, je vous prie.

Wait a moment, please.

and: Veuillez attendre un moment, je vous prie.

Would you mind waiting a moment please.

In certain situations, the verb may be omitted altogether; the tone of the command is then quite abrupt and can verge on rudeness:

Un moment, s'il vous plaît! *Just a moment, if you please!*

Deuxième porte à droite! *Second door on the right!*

(*b*) The Present Indicative of verbs of request — **demander** (*to ask*), **désirer** (*to wish*), **exiger** (*to demand*), **ordonner** (*to order*)- followed, as appropriate, by an Infinitive or subjunctive clause can also be used for the purpose:

J'exige que vous partiez immédiatement. *I demand that you go immediately.*

Il **désire** parler au directeur. *He wishes to talk to the director.*

Nous vous **demandons** de bien vouloir attendre. *We ask you to be good enough to wait.*

Note: In certain administrative circles, a distinction is sometimes drawn between the softeners **bien vouloir** and **vouloir bien** (*to be kind enough to. . .*): the former is used by a subordinate when making a request to a superior and the latter by a superior politely instructing a subordinate to do something.

Compare: Je vous demande de **bien vouloir** lire ce dossier. (subordinate to superior) *I would be pleased if you could read this dossier.*

and: Je vous demande de **vouloir bien** lire ce dossier. (superior to subordinate) *Would you be good enough to read this dossier?*

Both constructions are quite formal. In normal French, the distinction is often no longer made.

(*c*) Certain impersonal expressions such as **il faut/il est nécessaire de/que** (*it is necessary to/that*) can also be used to indicate an order or a strong request:

Il faut que j'aille à la banque. *I must go to the bank.*

Il est nécessaire d'obéir aux ordres. *It is necessary to obey orders.*

(*d*) Certain words or expressions may be used on their own to convey an order or strong request:

Halte! *Halt!*

Attention! *Beware!*

En avant, marche! *Forward, march!*

2 *Softened requests or toned-down orders*

(*a*) The Future Indicative of such verbs as **demander** (*to ask*), **devoir** (*to have to*), **falloir** (*to be necessary*), etc. can be used to tone down a request.

Compare: **Il faut** que je vous parle.
            I must talk to you.

and: **Il faudra** que je vous parle.
            I shall have to talk to you.

or: Je vous **demande** de ne rien dire.
            I ask you not to say anything.

and: Je vous **demanderai** de ne rien dire.
            I would ask you not to say anything.

(*b*) The Present Conditional of some verbs may be used to soften a request even further:

Compare: Vous **devez** accepter.
You must accept.
and: Vous **devriez** accepter.
You should accept.
or: Nous **voulons** sortir.
We want to go out.
and: Nous **voudrions** sortir.
We would like to go out.

Note: The expression **je vous serais reconnaissant de ...** (*I would be grateful if you would ...*) belongs to the same category, but sounds more formal and could be interpreted as condescending.

(*c*) Requests expressed in the form of a question are often used in French. Their level of stylistic acceptability will depend on the way the question is phrased.

Compare: Pouvez-vous venir, s'il vous plaît (formal)
and: Est-ce que vous pouvez venir, s'il vous plaît (standard)
and: Vous pouvez venir, s'il vous plaît? (familiar)
Could you come please?
or: Venez-vous prendre l'apéritif? (formal)
and: Est-ce que vous venez prendre''apéritif? (standard)
and: Vous venez prendre l'apéritif? (familiar)
Will you come for an aperitif?

(*d*) A reduced sentence beginning with **si** (*if*) can be used to convey a fomal request:

Si vous voulez bien me suivre ... *Would you care to follow me?*

Si Monsieur veut bien s'asseoir ... *Would you care to sit down, Sir?*

The following phrases, also expressing a command, are very colloquial and should be used with great care:

La ferme! *Shut up!*
Ta gueule! *Shut your trap*!

Since

This word can have two distinct meanings:

1 *As a preposition*, it can express a duration with a clear starting point (date or event). In this case, it is translated by **depuis**:

Ils habitent ici **depuis** la guerre. *They have been living here since the war.*

Ils habitent ici **depuis** 1945.   *They have been living here since 1945.*

2   *As a conjunction*, it can introduce a cause-consequence relation (i.e. *given the fact that* . . .). It is translated by **puisque**:

Puisque vous refusez, j'irai ailleurs.   *Since you refuse, I shall go elsewhere.*

Note: *Since*, as a preposition expressing duration, should only be used with tenses also emphasising duration (e.g. Present, Imperfect), and *not* with tenses stressing the mere occurrence of an event (e.g. Perfect or Past Historic).

You should say: Il **est** ici **depuis** trois mois.
He has been here for three months.
or: Il **était** ici **depuis** trois mois.
He had been here for three months
and not: * Il **a été** ici **depuis** trois mois.
or: * Il **fut** ici **depuis** trois mois

Some

It is translated by **quelque**, but it can have three distinct meanings as indicated below.

1   *some . . . or other* + singular:
Quelque voisin l'aura averti.   *One or other of his neighbours must have warned him.* (lit:. . *will have warned him*)

2   *a few/some* + plural:
Nous passerons **quelques** jours chez vous.   *We shall spend a few days at your house.*

3   *approximately* (adverb = invariable):
Il a gagné **quelque** vingt courses.   *He has won some* (i.e. *approximately*) *twenty races.*

There is/there are

Both expressions are translated by a single French form: **il y a**. Care must be taken *not to change anything to* the expression, *except* the tense of the verb **avoir** (as required):

Il y avait une vieille dame dans cette maison.   *There used to be an old lady in this house.*

Il y aura beaucoup d'invités ce soir.   *There will be many guests this evening.*

Soudain **il y eut** une terrible explosion.   *Suddenly there was a terrible explosion.*

Notes:
(*a*)   For the opening sentence of a fairy tale the expression **il était une fois** is used instead of **il y avait une fois**.
(*b*)   **Il y a** is sometimes replaced by such expressions as **il existe** (*there exist(s)*), **il se trouve** (*there is/are to be found*):
   Il existe des gens qui n'ont pas de scrupules.   *There exist (i.e. are) people who have no scruples.*

This/these — that/those

Those words can have two grammatical roles, either demonstrative adjectives (followed by a noun) or demonstrative pronouns (followed by a verb):
1   *As demonstrative adjectives*, they agree in gender and number with the noun which follows; they are: **ce** (masc. sing.), **cette** (fem. sing.), **ces** (masc./fem. plur.); in addition there exists the form **cet** (masc. sing.), used when the next word begins with a vowel or a mute 'h'. For example:
   Regardez **cet** énorme embouteillage.   *Look at this (that) enormous traffic jam.*
Note: The above-mentioned words can have the meaning of *this* or *that*. If a distinction is needed, the words **-ci** (here) or **-là** (*there*) can be added to the noun concerned:
   Je n'aime pas **ce** livre-**ci**.   *I do not like this book.*
   Il adore **cette** plage-**là**.   *He loves that beach.*
2   *As demonstrative pronouns*, with the exception of **c', ça, ceci, cela** (which have a neutral value but are still considered to be masculine singular), they vary according to the gender and number of the noun they represent. They are:
   celui + **-ci/-là** (masc. sing.); **celle** + **-ci/-là** (fem. sing.)
   ceux + **-ci/-là** (masc. plur.); **celles** + **-ci/-là** (fem. plur.)
For example:
   Vous qui aimez les chats, regardez **celui-ci**.   *You who love cats, look at this one.*

Towards

The word has two meanings and requires two different translations as indicated below.
1   If *towards* indicates a *movement* (in space or time) *towards a goal*, it will be translated by **vers**:
   Ils vont **vers** la ville.   *They are going towards the town.*
   Je vous appellerai **vers** six heures.   *I shall call you towards (i.e. around) six o'clock.*

2 If *towards* indicates *feelings* it will be translated by **envers**:
  Quels sont tes sentiments **envers** lui? *What are your feelings towards him?*
Note: In this latter sense, its is the equivalent of the expression **vis à vis de**:
  Quels sont tes sentiments **vis à vis de** lui? *What are your feelings towards him?*

Until

Two constructions are possible depending whether:
1 *Until* is followed by a noun *or* by **hier** (*yesterday*), **aujourd'hui** (*today*) or **demain** (*tomorrow*). In this case, its French equivalent is **jusqu'à**:
  Restez **jusqu'à** demain. *Stay until tomorrow.*
2 *Until* introduces a subordinate clause (subject, verb, etc.). In this case it *must* be translated by **jusqu'à ce que** and the verb of the subordinate *must* be in the Subjunctive:
  Tenez bon **jusqu'à ce que** nous arrivions. *Hold on tight until we arrive.*
  s.c.

Verbs without prepositions

The following verbs do not require a preposition when followed by another verb (which *must be* in the infinitive): **compter** (*to bank on*), **croire** (*to believe*), **désirer** (*to wish*), **devoir** (*to have to*), **espérer** (*to hope*), **faire** (*to cause/to do*), **falloir** (impersonal = *must*), **oser** (*to dare*), **penser** (*to hope*), **pouvoir** (*to be able to*), **sembler** (*to seem*), **vouloir** (*to want*). For example:
  Nous **comptons** réussir. *We bank on succeeding.*
  Il **faut** faire quelque chose. (lit: *It is necessary to do something*) *Something must be done.*
  Vous **osez** me demander de l'argent? *You dare to ask me for money?*
Note: The reason why some English learners tend to over-use prepositions in that context is because they have difficulty in accepting that *to* when placed before a verb in English is often merely a 'signal' for the infinitive and has, in that case, no value in French (which signals its infinitives by a special ending: **er**, **ir** or **re**). It must therefore be considered that a preposition is attached *to the verb that precedes* rather than to the verb that follows. In the following examples the verb and preposition appear in bold type:
  Je **commence à** comprendre. *I am beginning to understand.*
  Ils **refusent de** manger. *They refuse to eat.*
  Elle **s'est décidée à** sortir. *She has made up her mind to go out.*

NB   Any good dictionary will give the list of acceptable prepositions (if any) which may be used with a given verb.

When

This word is generally translated by **quand** or **lorsque** and is used to introduce a clause clarifying a certain time-sequence. Several shades of meaning may be distinguished depending on the tenses used in the two clauses.

1   **Quand/lorsque** = *after* when the tense of the subordinate clause indicates that the action it describes has been fully completed *before* the start of the action expressed by the main clause.

Quand tu auras fini, tu partiras.

      s.c.   m.c.
When you have finished, you will go.
Lorsqu'il eut fini, il partit.

      s.c.   m.c.
When he had finished, he went.

2   **Quand/lorsque** = *as soon as* when the tenses in the subordinate and the main clause are the same, thereby indicating the absence of any time-lag between the two actions:

Quand je crie, tu lâches la corde.

      s.c.   m.c.
When (i.e. as soon as) I shout, you let go of the rope.
Lorsque je l'ai appelé il s'est enfui.

      s.c.   m.c.
When (i.e. as soon as) I called him, he ran away.

Notes:

(*a*)   If a tense expressing duration (Imperfect, Present) is used in both clauses **quand** indicates a repetition and can be translated by *whenever*:

Quand il me voyait, il tournait la tête.

      s.c.   m.c.
Whenever he saw me, he looked away.
Lorsque je vais au marché, j'achète des fleurs

        s.c.   m.c.
When I go to the market I (always) buy flowers

(*b*)   If the sense of *whenever* needs to be emphasised, the expression **chaque fois que** (*every time*) may be used instead of **quand** or **lorsque**:

Chaque fois qu'il me voyait, il souriait
             s.c.   m.c.

Every time he saw me he smiled.

It is not possible, as it is in English, to use a Present or Perfect Indicative in the subordinate clause, if the verb of the main clause is in the Future Indicative; you *must* say or write:

Quand je le verrai, je lui parlerai
         s.c.   m.c.

When I see him I shall talk to him.

and not* : Quand je le vois, je lui parlerai.

Remember: Expressions such as *the day when, the time when,* etc. are translated into French as **le jour où, le moment où** (and not ***le jour/le moment quand**):

Compare: *I long for the day when we'll all be free.*

and: J'attends impatiemment **le jour où** nous serons tous libres.

If the sense of *when* is *as soon as*, it may be translated by **aussitôt que** or **dès que** with the tense-sequences outlined above.

Year

There are two ways of translating the word *year*:

1 If it refers to a precise or 'objective' number of years it will be translated by **an(s)**:

    Nous avons passé **deux ans** au Pérou.   *We spent two years in Peru.*

2 If it refers to an imprecise number of years, or if there is an overtone of nostalgia, fondness, hate, etc. it will be translated by **année(s)**:

    Il a habité quelques **années** en Italie. (and not * quelques ans . . .)   *He has lived a few years in Italy.*

    Nous avons passé deux **années** au Maroc.   *We spent two* ('long' or 'happy') *years in Morocco.*

In this latter example (where one would expect **an**) **année** gives the idea of a subjective overtone (happiness, boredom, etc.).

Note:

(*a*) *last year* and *next year* may be translated respectively by:

    l'an dernier *or* **l'année dernière**

    l'an prochain *or* **l'année prochaine**

without any particular overtone.

(*b*) *this year*, however, must *always* be translated by **cette année** (* cet an is *not* acceptable).

Appendix 1
The Sounds of French

It may seem strange that, in a grammar book, there should be a section on pronunciation. Yet there are very good reasons why this should be so and that is why most modern grammars now include a chapter on phonetics. The first reason is that, when learning to speak French, many people find that a good potential performance is marred by bad pronunciation. The second is that, in modern reference books like dictionaries, useful information is available to those who are familiar with the International Phonetic Alphabet (IPA) symbols: each word is transcribed using those symbols, which are the ones introduced in this chapter. Thirdly, and most importantly, many so-called grammatical rules are, in fact, dictated by phonetic considerations. This point will be clearly and abundantly illustrated in this section. You should not try to take in every detail of it at once, but return to it as often as you wish or need to.

Although the letters used to write French words are the same as for English, the sounds that the French associate with these letters are sometimes quite different. You must therefore try not to carry the rules of English pronunciation into French.

The following example may make things clearer: take the English word *party* and the French one **parti** both meaning a political group. They look reasonably alike and you may well be tempted to pronounce the French word in the same way as the English one. By doing so you would break a whole series of 'rules' governing the French language. These are as follows:

Rule 1
In French, the sounds **p**, **t** and **k** are *not* followed by an escape of breath before the next sound. A simple trick will enable you to become aware of the fact. Take a piece of paper approximately 15 cm by 10 cm. Hold it down in front of your face so that the bottom part of the paper rests lightly on your lips. When you pronounce the *p* of the English word *party* the paper should move away from your lips. Learn to pronounce the French word in such a way that the paper hardly moves at all.

Rule 2
There are 2 **a** sounds in French. The one you need here is not the one you would expect, but an **a** closer to the one found in standard English *cat* and *bat* or the Northern pronunciation of such words as *bath* or *path*.

Rule 3
Whereas in most English accents the *r* is present in spelling but not normally sounded, the **r** is always pronounced in standard French. This is a very difficult sound for an English person to master, but another simple trick may help you: insert into your mouth the end of a pencil (preferably not the sharp one!) just far enough — one inch or so — to hold the tip of your tongue down. With your tongue tip in that position, try to make a friction noise by lifting the back of your tongue as if you were gargling. You should succeed in producing a French **r** or something fairly close to it.

Rule 4
The **i** sound in French is similar in quality to the *ee* sound in *beef* but shorter; in other words quite different from the sound of the *y* in *party*.

Rule 5
In English the emphasis is on the first section of the word: PArty, whereas in French it is on the last: parTI.

Do not be discouraged! The aim of the above example is to show you that French and English have each got their own identity. Be critical in your listening and then try to reproduce the sounds faithfully.

As we have seen, letters are sometimes misleading. So, in order to simplify matters, it is often very useful to have a special way of writing up words, a code which will be immediately recognisable and pronounceable by anyone who is familiar with it. This code is used in all good dictionaries and is now more or less standardised; it is called the International Phonetic Alphabet (IPA). We shall list the elements of it in two broad categories, *consonants* and *vowels*. Those units of sound, arranged in certain ways, make up the words we use. Whenever a phonetic transcription is given, it will appear in square brackets: [ ].

Important remarks

Unless otherwise stated, 'English pronunciation' should be taken as meaning 'standard English pronunciation' and 'French pronunciation' as meaning 'Educated Parisian French'.

Consonants

			sea note
[p]	la **p**orte	*door*	
[t]	la **t**our	*tower see Rule* 1 above	
[k]	la **c**our	*courtyard*	
[b]	le **b**ain	*bath*	
[d]	le **d**oute	*doubt*	
[g]	le **g**arde	*guard*	
[m]	la **m**ère	*mother*	
[n]	**n**ous	*we*	
[ɲ]	l'a**gn**eau	*lamb*	1
[l]	le **l**ivre	*book*	2
[f]	le **f**our	*oven*	
[s]	le **s**ac	*bag*	
[ʃ]	le **ch**ou	*cabbage*	3
[v]	le **v**erre	*glass*	
[z]	le **z**èbre	*zebra*	
[ʒ]	le **j**our	*day*	4
[R]	le **r**oi	*king* (see Rule 3 above)	5
[w]	**ou**i	*yes*	
[ɥ]	**t**u**er**	*to kill*	6
[J]	le **y**oga	*yoga*	

Notes: The following notes correspond to the numbers appearing in the right-hand column above.

1   It is very rare to pronounce the two letters **gn** as [g+n] (as in *to ignore*). Normally, **gn** sounds like the first section of *n*ew and is transcribed [ɲ].

2   [l]   In English this *l* has two values (which you may not even be aware of), according to its position. If you say the word *lull* and think about how you pronounce it, you will notice that the qualities of the first *l* and of the last two (pronounced as one) are quite different. If you tried to reverse their position the word *lull* would sound 'foreign'. In French, whatever its position in the word, the **l** sounds like the first sound in *l*ull, *l*ate, *l*ine, etc. There is no 'dark' quality to it.

3   [ʃ]   In French, except in rare cases, the combination **c+h** is pronounced [ʃ]. This sound is similar to that of the first element of the words *sh*ape, *sh*eep and *sh*oe: la **ch**asse (*hunting*), le **ch**at (*cat*), le **ch**ien (*dog*).

4   [ʒ] This sound does occur in English in le**is**ure, ple**as**ure and in borrowed words like rou**g**e and gara**g**e. Essentially, it is very much like the sound of *j* in *Jack*, but without the [d] before it:

	English	*French*
	[dʒ]	[ʒ]
	Jack	**Jacques**
	[dʒak]	[ʒak]

5 [R] We have already mentioned the difference in quality of the **r** in French. You may find that, in addition to the standard [R] value, you will come across others. Do not be put off, stick to the standard one!

6 The [w] sound is the same as the one in *w*et and *w*ith. The [J] sound is the same as the one in *y*ear and *y*olk. The [ɥ] has no equivalent in English, but if while saying [i] you push your lips forward and round them, you may produce a sound close to it.

Vowels

[i]	le **lit**	*bed*	7
[y]	la **rue**	*street*	8
[e]	le **pré**	*meadow*	9
[ø]	**peu**	*little*	10
[ɛ]	la **mer**	*sea*	11
[ɛ̃]	la **main**	*hand*	12
[œ]	la **peur**	*fear*	13
[œ̃]	br**un**	*brown*	14
[a]	la **patte**	*paw*	15
[ɑ]	la **pâte**	*paste*	16
[ɑ̃]	gr**and**	*tall*	17
[ɔ]	le **corps**	*body*	18
[ɔ̃]	le coch**on**	*pig*	19
[o]	l'**eau**	*water*	20
[u]	la r**ou**e	*wheel*	21
[ə]	la premi**è**re	*the first*	22

Notes

7 [i] As mentioned in Rule 4 above, this [i] is close in value to the *ee* in *beef* or *meet*, but it is *shorter*.

8 [y] The tongue position is the same as for [i] but the lips are pushed outwards and rounded. This feature of lip-rounding plays a very important part in French. The purpose of it is to increase the volume of air contained in the mouth. This, as a result, changes the sound quite dramatically. It is important to master the lip-rounding technique because there are many pairs of words which are distinguished solely by that feature:

Compare: la vie [la vi] *life* (= spread)
and: la vue [la vy] *sight* (= rounded)
or: la biche [la biʃ(ə)] *doe* (= spread)
and: la bûche [la byʃ(ə)] *log* (= rounded)

It is very important that the *tongue position* should *not* be changed (see note 21 below).

9   [e] This sound is similar to that of the last section in words like health*y*, nutt*y*, part*y*, etc., as pronounced in standard English.

   le nez [lə ne] *nose*
   le bébé [lə bebe] *baby*

10   [ø] The tongue position is the same as for [e] but the lips are rounded—here again take great care to distinguish from [e]

Compare: le nez [lə ne] *nose*
and: le noeud [lə nø] *knot*
or: le dé [lə de] *die/thimble*
and: le deux [lə dø] *Second day of the month*

11   [ɛ] This sound is identical to the vowel sound in n*e*t, b*e*t, p*e*t:

   le fait [lə fɛ] *fact*
   le lait [lə lɛ] *milk*

12   [ɛ̃] The tongue position is the same as for 11, but this time some air escapes through the nose as well as through the mouth — this is known as nasalisation and is phonetically represented by [˜] placed above the sound concerned. Again, it is very important for you to master this nuance because, as in the case of lip-rounding, many word-pairs are distinguished by nasalisation alone.

Compare: le lait [lə lɛ] *milk*
and: le lin [lə lɛ̃] *linen*
or: fait [fɛ] *done*
and: fin [fɛ̃] *fine/thin*

13   [œ] This sound is similar to the vowel sound in f*i*r (*tree*) or in p*u*rr:

   le coeur [lə kœR] *heart*
   la soeur [la sœR] *sister*

14   [œ̃] The tongue and lip positions are similar to those used for 13 but, here again, there is an escape of air through the nose as well as through the mouth:

   brun [bRœ̃] *dark-haired/*brown
   un [œ̃] *a/one*

15   [a] As mentioned at the beginning of this chapter (Rule 3), this sound is roughly similar to that of the vowel in the Standard English words c*a*t, m*a*t, b*a*t, or in the Northern pronunciation b*a*th. Keep it distinct from the sound of 11: [ɛ]

   la dame [la dam(ə)] *lady*
   la flamme [la flam(ə)] *flame*

16   [ɑ] This sound is similar to the vowel sound in the English words c*a*r, d*a*rk and p*a*rk:

   la pâte [la pɑt] *paste/dough*
   le mât [lə mɑ] *mast*

17   [ɑ̃] The lip and tongue positions are similar to those required for 16 but, in addition, air escapes through the nose as in 12 and 14:

   en [ɑ̃] *in*
   lent [lɑ̃] *slow*

8 [ɔ] Very close to the vowel sound in the English words d*o*t, n*o*t and, sh*o*t:
la b**o**tte [la bɔt(ə)] *boot*
la n**o**te [la nɔt(ə)] *note/bill*

9 [ɔ̃] Similar tongue position to that in [ɔ]; lips slightly more closed and, here again, some air escaping through the nose as for 12, 14 and 17:
b**on** [bɔ̃] *good*
le p**on**t [lə pɔ̃] *bridge*

10 [o] This sound is 'half way' between [ɔ] and [u]–see 21:
l'**eau** [lo] *water*
b**eau** [bo] *beautiful*

11 [u] This sound is not very different from the vowel sound in English words b*oo*m, c*oo*l, l*oo*p, but the lips are pushed out and rounded:
le l**ou**p [lə lu] *wolf*
le c**ou** [lə ku] *neck*

12 [ə] This is a vowel with 'reduced value'. It never apppears in a stressed syllable (see below). The sound is not very different from that of vowel 13 [œ], and of the vowel sound in English *fi*rm, t*u*rn but the jaws are closer together. This sound is sometimes omitted from the pronunciation of certain words and some dictionaries will give it in brackets to indicate that fact:
la port**e** [la pɔRt(ə)] *door*
la bouch**e** [la buʃ(ə)] *mouth*

Warning: All French vowel sounds are *tense*. In other words, when you are saying them, your articulators—jaws, lips and tongue—should not change position at all.
Be aware of the sound difference between:

English	and	**French**
(a) note		**(une) note**
[nout]		[nɔt (ə)]

The vowels and consonants which we have seen in the first section of this chapter combine to form syllables, words, phrases and sentences, which make up the speech-chain. We shall now look at the most basic of those units: the syllable.

The syllable

Every word is made up of sections called syllables. Although there is a great deal of disagreement among specialists as to the definition of the syllable, it is generally agreed that it is a group of sounds composed of a central element-the vowel-and either no consonant at all or a limited number of consonants on each side of that vowel. The vowel is

essential but the consonant(s) may be absent in some syllables:
 il a (*he has*) has 2 syllables [il/a] = VC/V
                            1 2

NB: Please be sure to distinguish between *letters* (written alphabe
and *sounds* (phonetic alphabet). The following examples in Frenc
will make the difference clear:

1   **exact** (*exact*) has 5 letters, 4 sounds [εgza] and 2 syllables[εg/z;
                                                  1 2

2   **comptons** (*let's count*) has 8 letters, 4 sounds [kɔ̃tɔ̃] and 2 sy
    lables [kɔ̃/tɔ̃].   1234
          1 2

3   **joli** (*pretty*) has 4 letters, 4 sounds [ʒɔli] and 2 syllables [ʒɔ/li
                                    1234   1

The vowel-vowel clash

The French language has a natural tendency to regularity and th
pattern of syllables CV/CV/CV, etc. is preferred not only within on
word but *between words* and an arrangement like CV/VC/etc.
avoided whenever possible. This point is very important because
explains many so called 'grammatical oddities' which are sometime
puzzling to the learner. For instance:

1   It explains why the difinite article **le** or **la** (*the*) loses its **e** or **a** if th
next word begins with a vowel or a mute'h' (see 7 below fo
distinction between mute and aspirated 'h'). For example *le am
(*friend*) is *not* acceptable because the pattern is CV/V CV. So
becomes: **l'ami**. *la/auto* (*car*) is, for the same reason, not ac
ceptable either (CV/V CV), so it becomes:**l'auto**.

2   It also explains why some words add on a letter in certain case
       *ce enfant (*this child*) ⟶ cet enfant
       CV V   CV   CVC VCV

3   It also explains why some masculine adjectives like **beau** (*beautifu
and **nouveau** (*new*) change before nouns starting with a vowel or mut
'h' (see 7 below)
       *le nouveau/ami (*the new friend*) ⟶ le nouvel/ami
           CV/VCV   CVC/VCV
       *le beau/hôtel (*the beautiful hotel*) ⟶ le bel/hôtel
           CV / VC   CVC/ VC

4   It clarifies the reason why, when the 3 feminine possessives **ma, t;**

a (*my, your, his/her*) are followed by a word beginning with a vowel or a mute 'h' they are replaced by the 3 corresponding masculines: **mon, ton** and **son**:

    *ma/auto (*my car*) ——➤ mon/auto
    CV/V CV   CVC/V CV

    *ta/amie (*your friend*) ——➤ ton/amie
    CV/VCV   CVC/VCV

It explains why sometimes an 'intrusive' sound is put in between 2 words:

    *a-il? (*has he?*) ——➤ a-t-il?
    V/VC   V/C/VC

    *va-elle? (*does she go*) ——➤va-t-elle . . ?
    CV/VCV   CV/C/VCN

It also sheds some light on the phenomenon of 'liaison' (= linking 2 words with a sound which, in normal circumstances, is not pronounced; this phenomenon is more frequent in careful speech). Compare: Il est content. *He is pleased.* [il ɛ kɔ̃tɑ̃]
and: Est-il content? *Is he pleased?* [ɛ t il kɔ̃tɑ̃]Here the **t** of **est** is sounded.
or: Vous travaillez. *You work.* [vu tRavaje]
and: Vous allez. *You go.* [vuz ale] Here the **s** of **vous** is sounded as [z].

It helps solve the mystery of the mute and aspirated 'h'. There are, in French, a number of words beginning with 'h'. Before some of these words, the article **le** or **la** (*the*), or other small words, lose their, final vowel. (This only happens to 'lesser' words. You do not cut vowels off nouns or verbs or adjectives!) But this is not the case with the words in the list given below. These words start with an aspirated 'h'.

[In fact there is, in modern French, no sign of that 'h' in pronunciation (but in old French, it used to be sounded, as it is in English).Nevertheless, it is as if a 'ghost consonant' were still present, thus preventing the vowel-vowel clash. So we say:

    l'hôtel (*hotel*) or ce**t** horrible enfant (*this horrid child*) but:
    le hasard (*chance*) or **ce** héros (*this hero*)

The following is a list of the words beginning with an aspirated 'h' which you are most likely to encounter. There are others, but they are less frequently used. In any case, a good dictionary will indicate which words begin with an aspirated 'h' *either* by preceding the word with an asterisk (*), *or* by beginning the phonetic transcription with an apostrophe (').

la hache *axe*	le héros *hero*
la haie *hedge*	le hêtre *beech*
le hall *hall*	le hibou *owl*
la halle *market hall*	la hiérarchie *hierarchy*
la halte *pause*	la Hollande *Holland*
le hameau *hamlet*	le homard *lobster*
la hanche *hip*	la Hongrie *Hungary*
le handicap *handicap*	la honte *shame*
le hangar *hangar*	le hoquet *hiccup*
le hareng *herring*	la horde *horde*
le haricot *bean*	la houille *coal*
le hasard *chance*	le houx *holly*
la hâte *haste*	le huit *eight*
la hausse *increase*	le hurlement *scream*
le haut *top/summit*	la hutte *hut*
le havre *haven*	

Stress (accentuation)

A section on phonetics would not be complete without a mention of stress (or accentuation). Stress is sometimes explained as the relatively greater force with which we pronounce some syllables. In English, there is stress on certain parts of important words (stressed syllables are underlined):

Paul went to the *door* and (he) *o*pened it. Total = 4 stresses

In French, the system is totally different. For the purpose of stressing, the speech-chain is divided into sense-groups, i.e. phrases having a meaning in themselves, and it is the last syllable of the sense-group *only* which will be stressed. (If the last syllable ends with an [ə] it does not count!)

Words on their own are treated as sense-groups. Compare:

1 | *Paul!*   *Paul!*

| Sense group | 1 stress

2 | Paul est allé à la **por**te.   *Paul went to the door.*

| *Sense group* | 1 stress

3 | Paul est allé à la **por**te   et (il)l'a ou**ver**te

| Sense group | Sense group   2 stresses

   Paul went to the door   and (he) opened it.

The temptation is great, particularly when words look the same in the 2 languages, to use the English system of stress and say:

*Il continue la démonstration. *He carries on with the demonstration.*

instead of:

| *Il continue la démonstration.* |

<------------------------------->

| sense group |

r

*Il a cessé ces activités. *He gave up these activities.*

instead of:

| Il a cessé ces activités. |

<------------------------->

| sense group |

he above is the general rule. Sometimes, for the sake of emphasis, xtra stresses are put in (particularly in radio and television reports).

ey points

French sounds are sometimes quite different from English ones.

There are 2 types of sounds: vowels [i, e, ɛ etc.] and consonants [p, t, m, c.]

In the 'speech chain', the French avoid, as much as possible, a clash etween two vowels by a variety of tricks.

French is not stressed in the same way as English. Only the last word of e sense-group carries the stress, so the rhythm of the two languages is quite ifferent.

Appendix II
Accents and Other Signs; Punctuation Marks

When writing French, it is necessary to make use of certain signs marks. Those signs are important and must be used properly. The are introduced and explained below.

Accents

Accents are marks used in writing over certain letters. In French the are only found on **a**, **e**, **i**, **o** and **u**.
Note: These accents have a definite role to play and *cannot* be use at random.

There are 3 types of accents:

1 *The acute accent*: ´. It can only be found on an **e**, and it changes the sound of that letter from [ə] to [e]. (See vowel list in Appendix I
Compare: Porte! [pɔRt(ə)]   *Carry!*
and: porté [pɔRte]   *carried*
or: Cherche! [ʃɛRʃ(ə)]   *Look (for)!*
and: cherché [ʃɛRʃe]   *looked (for)*
2 *The grave accent*: (`). It is found on **e**, and, much more rarely, on and **u**.
(*a*) When over the **e**, it changes the sound of that letter to [ɛ]. (S vowel list in Appendix I.)
       Compare: protégé [pRɔteʒe]   *protected*
       and: Protège! [pRɔtɛʒ(ə)]   *Protect!*
       or: acheté [aʃ(ə)te]   *bought*
       and: Achète! [aʃɛt(ə)]   *Buy!*
(*b*) When over an **a** or **u**, it does not change the sound of the lette but it helps to distinguish between words which would otherwi look alike:
       La voiture est **là**.   *The car is there.*

Il **a** rendez-vous **à** cinq heures.   *He has an appointment at five o'clock.*

Jean **ou** Paul vont **où** ils veulent.   *John or Paul go where they like.*

The circumflex accent: (ˆ). It can be found on all five vowels: **a, e, i, , and u**.

ᵇ)   When over the **e** it changes the sound of that letter to [ɛ]. (See vowel list of Appendix I.)

Bête [bɛt(ə)]   *silly*

Être [ɛtR(ə)]   *to be*

ᵇ)   On the other four vowels, it used to have the effect of lengthening the sound, but in modern French this is generally no longer the case. This accent also acts as an indicator that, in old French, the vowel used to be followed by an **s** which has now disappeared. (Often, however, this **s** is still present in the corresponding English words.) For example:

Un abîme   *an abysm*

La bête   *beast*

La côte   *coast*

La hâte   *haste*

Un hôte   *a host/guest*

Le mât   *mast*

La pâte   *paste/dough*

So, the letter most affected by accents is **e**; but there are certain circumstances where the sound of **e** changes to [e] or [ɛ] without the help of an accent. This is the case before geminated (i.e. double) consonants: **cc, dd, ff, ll, nn, ss, tt**, etc. For example:

Belle [bɛl(ə)]   *beautiful* (fem.)

Effacer [efase]   *to rub out*

Jette! [ʒɛt(ə)]   *throw!*

This is also the case when **e** is followed by two different consonants, provided the second one is *not* an **r** or an **l**:

Restons [Rɛstɔ̃]   *let's stay*

Le lecteur [lə lɛktœR]   *reader*

but: Réfléchir [RefleʃiR]   *to reflect*

La pègre [la pɛgR(ə)]   *the underworld*

Exception: If **e** is followed by the group of consonants **rl**, it does not take an accent:

La perle [la pɛRlə]   *pearl*

Le merle [lə mɛRlə]   *blackbird*

Apostrophe, cedilla, diaeresis and hyphen

1 *The apostrophe* (') is used to indicate that a letter, usually **e**, **a** or **i**, has been removed to avoid the vowel-vowel clash (see Appendix I). This is the written representation of the phenomenon called *elision*:

*Le arbre	⟶ l'arbre	*tree*
*La amie	⟶ l'amie	*girlfriend*
*Ce est	⟶ c'est	*this/that is*
*Quelque un	⟶ quelqu'un	*someone*

2 *The cedilla* (¸). It is placed under a **c** before **a**, **o** or **u**, to indicate that the **c** is to be pronounced [s]; if the cedilla were not there, the sound of **c** would be [k].

Compare: Recevoir [RəsəvwaR] *to receive*

Reçu [Rəsy] *received*

Reculer [R ə kyle] *to go backwards*

Celui-ci [səlцisi] *this one*

Ça [sa] *that thing*

Remember:
c = [s] before
e or **i**
c = [k] before
a, **o**, **u**

3 *The diaeresis* (¨). This mark is used in writing to indicate to the reader that two consecutive vowels *must* be pronounced separately, because they usually belong to two different syllables.

Compare: Oui [wi] *yes*

and: Ouï [u/i] *heard*

    1 2

or: (La) haie [ɛ] *hedge*

and: Haïe [a/i] *hated*. (fem.)

    1 2

4 *The hyphen* (-). Unlike the previous signs, it does not alter the sound of a word. It is simply used to link together words which are meant to form a whole:

Celui-ci *this one* (masc.)

Quatre-vingt-dix *ninety*

Le porte-parole *spokesman*

Punctuation

Broadly speaking, punctuation is the written representation of oral pauses and a marker for changes in voice pitch for the benefit of the reader:

1 The *full stop* indicates to the reader that he/she has come to the end of a sentence and that the voice must go down.

2 The *comma* signals the end of a sense-group but the voice must not go down.

3 The *semi-colon* indicates that a self-contained part of a sentence has ended, but that some more related information is to follow. The pitch should go down as for a full stop.

4 The *colon* indicates that direct speech is about to be reported or an explanation given. The voice should not go down, but the pitch at the beginning of the utterance which follows should be higher or lower than what preceded.

5 *Dots* (. . .) indicate that some things have remained unsaid. The voice should not go down.

6 The *exclamation mark* signals the end of a forceful statement. There should be an increase in volume and a change of pitch.

7 The *question mark* indicates a question has been asked. Generally, the voice will *either* go down if the question starts with words like **qui** (*who*), **où** (*where*), **quand** (*when*), **pourquoi** (*why*), etc. *or* go up with the other types of questions.

8 *Speech marks* (" ") are used to signal the beginning and end of sections of speech as uttered by the speaker (direct speech). The pitch of the voice at the start of the quotation should be markedly different (higher or lower) from that of the preceding section.

Key points

1 Accents have specific roles in French and they cannot be used indiscriminately. They are particularly important on **e**, because they change the sound of that letter.

2 The cedilla changes the sound of **c** from [k] to [s] before **a**, **o** and **u**.

3 The diaeresis warns that two consecutive vowels usually belong to two distinct syllables and should be pronounced separately.

4 Punctuation tells the reader that the pitch of the voice should go up, stay the same or go down, depending on the sign used, and that pauses should be inserted as appropriate.

French–English Vocabulary

The vocabulary list includes most of the words which have been used in the examples. It does not, however, include words which appear in lists or charts since in such cases the translation of each word has already been given. The meanings are those applicable in the context of the examples. The feminine of adjectives, when irregular, appears alongside the masculine.

Abbreviations
f = feminine	s = Singular
m = masculine	sthg = something
pl = plural	sbdy = somebody

à *at, to*
abandonner *to abandon*
d'abord *at first*
absence (f) *absence*
acceptable *acceptable*
accepter *to accept*
accident (m) *accident*
accord (m) *agreement;*
　d'—*OK*
accueillant *welcoming*
accuser *to accuse*
acheter *to buy, purchase*
achever *to finish*
acteur (m) *actor*
admirer *to admire*
adorer *to adore*
advenir *to occur*
affiche (f) *poster*
afin de/que *in order to*
Afrique (f) *Africa*
agent (m) *policeman*
agir *to act*
agréable *pleasant*
ah! *oh!*
aider *to help*
aigu, -ë *sharp, acute*
ailleurs *elsewhere*
aimé *loved*

aimer *to love*
ainsi *thus*
air (m) *air*
ajouter *to add*
aller *to go*
allô *hallo*
allumette (f) *match*
allusion (f) *allusion; faire — à*
　to allude to
alors *then; - que whilst*
Alpes (f. pl.) *Alps*
amasser *to gather*
ambitieux, euse *ambitious*
américain *American*
ami (m) *friend*
amusant *amusing*
an (m) *year*
ancien,-ne *former, old*
anglais *English*
Angleterre (f) *England*
animal (m) *animal*
année (f) *year*
annoncer *to announce*
août (m) *August*
apercevoir *to catch sight of*
s'apercevoir de/que *to notice*
　that
apéritif (m) *aperitif*

apparemment *apparently*
appeler *to call*
s'appeler *to be called*
applaudir *to clap, applaud*
apporter *to bring*
apprécier *to appreciate*
apprendre *to learn*
apprenti (m) *apprentice*
approcher *to bring near*
s'approcher *to approach*
après *after*
arbre (m) *tree*
argent(m) *silver, money*
arme (f) *weapon*
arrêt (m) *stop*; sans— *non-stop*
arrêter *to stop (sthg or sbdy)*
s'arrêter *to stop, to come to a standstill*
arrhes (f. pl) *deposit*
arriver *to arrive*
aspirateur (m) *vacuum cleaner*
(s')assembler *to gather, assemble*
(s')asseoir *to sit*
assez *enough*
assis *seated*
assurance (f) *assurance, insurance*
atteindre *to reach*
attendre *to wait*
attente (f) *wait*
attention (f) *attention*
attitude (f) *attitude*
au, à la *at the, to the*
aucun *none, no-one*
d'aucuns (m.pl) *some people*
au delà de *beyond*
aujourd'hui *today*
aussi *also, therefore*
autant *as much*
auto (f) *car*
automne (m) *autumn*
autre *other*
autrefois *in the past*
autrui (m. sing.) *other people*
aux *at the, to the*
avancer *to advance*
avant *before*
avec *with*

avenir (m) *future*
avertir *to warn*
avion (m) *plane*
avoir *to have*

bagages (m. pl) *luggage*
bague (f) *ring*
(se) baisser *to lower (oneself)*
bal (m) *dance, ball*
banque (f) *bank*
barbu *bearded*
bas, basse *low*
bateau (m) *boat*
bâtiment (m) *building*
battre *to beat*
se battre *to fight*
beau, belle *beautiful*
beaucoup *much, a great deal*
beaujolais (m) *Beaujolais wine*
béni *blessed*
bénin, bénigne *slight (illness)*
bénir *to bless*
besoin (m) *need;* avoir — *to need*
bête *silly, stupid*
bêtise (f) *silly mistake*
bien *well*
bien que *although*
bière (f) *beer*
bijou, -x (m) *jewel*
bizarre *peculiar, odd*
boire *to drink*
bois (m) *wood*
bon, bonne *good*
bonbon (m) *sweet*
bonhomme (m) *chap*
bonjour *Good day, hello*
boucher (m) *butcher*
boue (f) *mud*
bouger *to move*
bougie (f) *candle*
boulanger (m) *baker*
bourgogne (m) *Burgundy wine*
brave *kind, brave*
Brésil (m) *Brazil*
Bretagne (f) *Brittany*
brioche (f) *bun*

(se) brosser *to brush (oneself)*
brouillard (m) *fog*
bruit (m) *noise*
brun *brown*
bureau (m) *office, desk*

ça *that*
ça et là *here and there*
cacher *to hide*
cachet (m) *tablet*
cadeau (m) *gift*
café (m) *coffee, cafe*
calme *calm, quiet*
calmer *to calm down*
campagne (f) *countryside*
capitaine (m) *captain*
capitale (f) *capital city*
car *for*
car (m) *coach*
carte (f) *card; map;* — postale
   postcard
cassé *broken*
casser *to break*
cathédrale (f) *cathedral*
catholique (f) *catholic*
cause (f) *cause*
ce, cet, cette *this, that*
ceci *this*
céder *to give in*
cela *that*
célèbre *famous*
celui-ci, celle-ci *this one*
celui-là, celle-là *that one*
cendrier (m) *ashtray*
cent *hundred*
centaine (f) *a hundred or so*
centime (m) *centime*
cependant *meanwhile, nevertheless*
certain *certain*
certains (m. pl) *some people*
certes *indeed*
ces *these, those*
cesser *to cease, to stop*
c'est *it is*
ceux-ci, celles-ci *these*
ceux-là, celles-là *those*
chacun *each*

chaise (f) *chair*
chambre (f) *bedroom*
chance (f) *luck*
changement (m) *change*
changer *to change*
chanter *to sing*
chapeau (m) *hat*
charbon (m) *coal*
charmant *charming*
chasse (f) *chase, hunt*
chat (m) *cat*
château (m) *castle*
chauffeur (m) *driver*
chaussure (f) *shoe*
chauve *bald*
chemise (f) *shirt*
chêne (m) *oak*
chèque (m) *cheque*
cher *dear*
chercher *to look for*
cheval, chevaux (m) *horse(s)*
cheveux (m. pl) *hair*
chez *at the house of*
chien (m) *dog*
chimie (f) *chemistry*
choisir *to choose*
chose (f) *thing*
ciel (m) *sky, heaven*
cigare (m) *cigar*
ci-joint *herewith*
ciment (m) *cement*
cinéma (m) *cinema*
cinq *five*
cinquantaine (f) *about fifty*
cinquante *fifty*
clac! *slam!, bang!*
clair *clear*
classe (f) *class*
clef (f) *key*
client (m) *customer*
climat (m) *climate*
cloche (f) *bell*
cœur (m) *heart*
coffre-fort (m) *safe*
coin (m) *corner*
colère (f) *anger*
colis (m) *parcel*

collier (m) *necklace*
colline (f) *hill*
combien *how much*
commander *to order*
comme *as, like*
commencer *to begin*
comment *how*
complet *complete, full*
compréhensif, -ive *understanding*
comprendre *to understand*
compris *understood*
confiture (f) *jam*
connaître *to know*
consciencieux, -euse *conscientious*
conseil (m) *advice*
constamment *constantly*
construire *to build*
content *pleased*
continuer *to carry on*
contre *against*
corde (f) *rope*
cordial *cordial*
corrompre *to corrupt*
corrupteur, -trice *corrupting*
costume (m) *suit*
coudre *to sew*
coup (m) *blow*
(se) couper *to cut (oneself)*
courage (m) *courage*
courageux, -euse *courageous*
courir *to run*
course (f) *race*
court *short*
coûter *to cost*
craindre *to fear*
crâne (m) *skull*
cri (m) *scream, shout*
crier *to scream, to shout*
crime (m) *crime*
crise (f) *crisis*
cristal (m) *crystal*
croire *to believe*
cruel, -elle *cruel*
cuire *to cook*
curieux, -euse *curious, strange*

dame (f) *lady*

dans *in*
danser *to dance*
davantage *more*
débarquement (m) *landing*
débarquer *to land*
debout *standing*
décembre *December*
déchirant *heart-rending*
déchirer *to tear*
décider *to decide*
décision (f) *decision*
découvert *discovered, uncovered*
déçu *disappointed*
défaut (m) *fault*
déficit (m) *deficit*
dehors *outside*
déjeuner (m) *lunch*
déjeuner *to have lunch*
délinquance (f) *delinquency*
demain *tomorrow*
(se) demander *to ask (oneself)*
demi *half*
démonstration (f) *demonstration*
dent (f) *tooth*
départ (m) *departure*
dépense (f) *expenditure*
dépenser *to spend*
dépit (m) *spite;* en —
    de *in spite of*
depuis *since*
député (m) *member of parliament*
dernier, -ière *last*
derrière *behind*
des *some*
dès (que) *as soon as*
désastre (m) *disaster*
descendre *to go down*
désir (m) *desire, wish*
désirer *to desire, to wish*
destin (m) *fate*
détester *to hate*
deux *two*
devant *in front (of)*
devenir *to become*
devoir (m) *duty*
devoir *to have to*
diamant (m) *diamond*

dieu (m) *God*
difficile *difficult*
dimanche (m) *Sunday*
dîner *to dine*
(se) dire *to tell (oneself)*
directeur (m) *director*
discret *discreet*
discuter *to discuss*
disparaître *to disappear*
disparu *disappeared, missing*
se disputer *to quarrel*
disque (m) *record*
dix *ten*
dizaine (f) *ten or so*
docteur (m) *doctor*
donc *therefore*
donner *to give*
dont *whose, of which*
dormir *to sleep*
dossier (m) *dossier*
doué *gifted*
douleur (f) *pain*
doute (m) *doubt;* sans — *doubtless*
douter *to doubt*
doux, douce *soft*
douzaine (f) *dozen*
douze *twelve*
droit *right;* tout — *straight on*
dû, due *owed, due*
duquel, de laquelle *of which, of whom*
dur *hard*

eau (f) *water*
échapper *to escape*
écharpe (f) *scarf*
échouer *to fail*
éclatant *dazzling*
écouter *to listen*
écrire *to write*
édenté *toothless*
effectuer *to perform*
effet (m) *effect;* en — *indeed*
efficace *effective, efficient*
effort (m) *effort*
égal *equal*
égalité (f) *equality*

église (f) *church*
éléphant (m) *elephant*
élisabéthain *Elizabethan*
elle *she, her*
embouteillage (m) *traffic jam*
s'emparer de *to seize*
emploi (m) *employment*
ému *touched, moved*
en *in*
encore *again, still*
endormir *to put to sleep*
s'endormir *to fall asleep*
endroit (m) *place, spot*
enfant (m, f) *child*
s'enfuir *to flee*
énorme *enormous*
ensuite *then*
entendre *to hear*
entre *between*
entrée (f) *entrance, entry*
entrer *to enter*
entretien (m) *conversation*
envers *towards*
envoyer *to send*
épais, épaisse *thick*
épinards (m. pl) *spinach*
époque (f) *era*
épouser *to marry*
Espagne (f) *Spain*
espagnol *Spanish*
espérer *to hope*
espion (m) *spy*
essayer *to try*
et *and*
Etats-Unis (m. pl) *United States*
été (m) *summer*
été *been*
étoile (f) *star;*-filante *shooting star*
étonnant *astonishing*
étonner *to astonish*
étrange *strange*
étranger,-ère (m, f) *foreigner*
étranger (m) à l'— *abroad*
étude (f) *study*
eux, elles (m, f) *them*
s'évanouir *to faint*
événement (m) *event*

examiner *to examine*
excellent *excellent*
excepté *except*
excuser *to excuse*
exemple (m) *example;* par - *for instance*
exiger *to demand*
exister *to exist*
expérience (f) *experience*
exploiter *to exploit*
explosion (f) *explosion*
exprès *on purpose*
extra *extra*
extrêmement *extremely*

facile *easy*
facilement *easily*
faim (f) *hunger;* avoir - *to be hungry*
faire *to do, make*
falloir *to be necessary;* il faut que *it is necessary that*
famille (f) *family*
fané *wilted*
fatal *fatal*
fatigué *tired*
fatiguer *to tire*
faute (f) *mistake*
fauteuil (m) *armchair*
faux, fausse *false*
femelle (f) *female*
femme (f) *woman, wife*
fenêtre (f) *window*
ferme (f) *farm*
fermé *closed*
fermer *to close*
féroce *ferocious*
fête (f) *festival*
feu (m) *fire;* - rouge *traffic light*
fidèle *faithful*
fier, fière *proud*
figure (f) *face*
fille (f) *girl, daughter*
fillette (f) *little girl*
film (m) *film*
fils (m) *son*
fin (f) *end*

fini *finished*
finir *to finish, to end*
fixe *fixed*
flamme (f) *flame*
fleur (f) *flower*
fleurir *to bloom, to blossom*
flûte! *blast!*
fois (f) *time;* une — *once*
foncé *dark* (colour)
football (m) *football*
fort *strong, hard*
fou, folle *mad*
foule (f) *crowd*
fracture (f) *fracture*
frais, fraîche *cool, fresh*
frais (m. pl) *costs*
franc, franche *frank*
français *French*
France (f) *France*
frapper *to knock, to strike*
fraternité (f) *fraternity*
frère (m) *brother*
froid *cold;* avoir — *to be cold*
fromage (m) *cheese*
fruit (m) *fruit*
fumée (f) *smoke*
fumer *to smoke*
furieux, –ieuse *furious*

gaffe (f) *gaffe, blunder*
gagner *to earn, to win*
gant (m) *glove*
garçon (m) *boy, waiter*
garder *to keep, to guard*
gare (f) *station*
gâteux, -euse *senile*
gauche *left;* à – *on the left*
geler *to freeze*
général (m) *general*
généralement *generally*
genou (m) *knee*
gens (m. pl) *people*
gérant (m) *manager*
gifler *to slap (face)*
glisser *to slide, to slip*
gourmandise (f) *greed*
gouvernement (m) *government*

grand *tall, large, great*
grand-mère (f) *grandmother*
grand-route (f) *main road*
grand-tante (f) *great-aunt*
gris *grey*
gros, grosse *big, bulky*
guerre (f) *war*
guider *to guide*

(s')habiller *to dress (oneself)*
habiter *to dwell*
habitude (f) *habit;* d' — *usually*
haïr *to hate*
hasard (m) *chance;* par — *by chance*
haut *high*
herbe (f) *grass*
heure (f) *hour;* à l' — *on time*
heureux, -euse *happy*
hier *yesterday;* — soir *last night*
hiver (m) *winter*
Hollande (f) *Holland*
homme (m) *man*
honnête *honest*
honnêteté (f) *honesty*
honteux, -euse *ashamed*
hôtel (m) *hotel*
hôtesse (f) *hostess*
huit *eight*
hypersensible *hypersensitive*

ici *here*
idéal *ideal*
idée (f) *idea*
idiot *silly, stupid*
il *he*
ils *they*
imbécile (m, f) *fool, idiot*
impatient *impatient*
impatiemment *impatiently*
important *important*
importer *to be important, to import*
impressionnant *impressive*
incident (m) *incident*
incontestablement *unquestionably*
individualiste *individualistic*
information (f) *information*
ingénieur (m) *engineer*

inquiet, -iète *anxious*
inquiéter *to worry*
insulter *to insult*
insupportable *unbearable*
intéressant *interesting*
intervention (f) *intervention*
invité *invited*
invité (m) *guest*
inviter *to invite*
irritant *irritating*
isolé *isolated*

jamais *never*
jambe (f) *leg*
janvier *January*
Japon (m) *Japan*
jardin *garden*
jardinier (m) *gardener*
je *I*
jeter *to throw*
jeune *young*
joli *pretty*
jour (m) *day*
journal (m) *newspaper*
journaliste (m, f) *journalist*
juillet *July*
juin *June*
jusqu'à *until*

kaki *khaki*
kilomètre (m) *kilometre*

la (f) *the*
là *there;* — bas *over there*
lâcher *to release, to let go*
laisser *to leave, to let*
langue (f) *language, tongue*
(se) laver *to wash (oneself)*
le (m) *the*
lecture (f) *reading*
légume (m) *vegetable*
lentement *slowly*
le plus *the most*
lequel, laquelle (m, f s) *who, whom which*
les (m, f pl) *the*

lesquels, lesquelles (m, f pl) *who, whom, which*
les uns les autres *each other*
lettre (f) *letter*
leur (f) *their, to them*
lever *to raise*
se lever *to arise*
libérer *to free*
liberté (f) *freedom*
libre *free*
lire *to read*
lit (m) *bed*
livre (m) *book*
livre (f) *pound*
logique *logical*
Londres *London*
long, longue *long*
longtemps *a long time*
lorsque *when*
loup (m) *wolf*
loyer (m) *rent*
lu *read*
lui *(to) him, (to) her*
lundi (m) *Monday*
lutter *to fight*
lycée (m) *high school*

ma *my*
machine (f) *machine*
madame (f) *Madam, Mrs*
magasin (m) *shop*
magazine (m) *magazine*
magnifique *magnificent, splendid*
mai *May*
main (f) *hand*
mais *but*
maison (f) *house*
mal *badly, bad*
mal (m), maux (pl) *evil*
malade *ill*
malade (m, f) *sick person*
maladie (f) *illness*
mâle (m) *male*
malheureux, -euse *unhappy*
malin, maligne *shrewd*
maman (f) *Mum*
manger *to eat*

manifestation (f) *demonstration*
marche (f) *walk*
marché (m) *market*
marcher *to work, to function*
mari (m) *husband*
marine (f) *Navy*
mastic (m) *putty*
matin (m) *morning*
mauvais *bad*
me *(to) me*
méchant *unkind, nasty*
méchamment *nastily*
médecin (m) *doctor*
meilleur *better*
ménage (m) *housework, household*
menu (m) *menu*
mer (f) *sea*
merci *thank you*
mercredi (m) *Wednesday*
mère (f) *mother*
mètre (m) *metre*
mettre *to put*
midi *midday*
Midi (m) *South of France*
mieux *better*
milieu (m) *middle*
mille *thousand*
milliard (m) *thousand million*
minérale *mineral*; eau –*mineral water*
ministre (m) *minister*
minute (f) *minute*
moi *me;* –même *myself*
moindre *least*
moins *less*
mois (m) *month*
mon, ma, mes *my*
monde (m) *world*
monsieur (m) *Mr, Sir*
monter *to climb*
montre (f) *watch*
montrer *to show*
monts (m. pl) *mountains*; par —
   et par vaux *always on the move*
monument (m) *monument*
morceau (m) *piece*
mordre *to bite*

mort *dead*
mort (m) *dead man*
mortel, -elle *deadly*
mot (m) *word*
mouchoir (m) *handkerchief*
mouillé *wet*
mourir *to die*
mousse (f) *foam*
mule (f) *mule*
mur (m) *wall*

naître *to be born*
néanmoins *nevertheless*
neige (f) *snow*
neiger *to snow*
ne . . . pas *not*
ne . . . plus *no longer*
ne . . . que *only*
net *neat, nett*
nettoyer *to clean*
neuf, neuve *new*
nez (m) *nose*
ni . . . ni *neither . . . nor*
Noël *Christmas*
noir *black*
noir (m) *darkness*
noisette (f) *hazel nut*
nom (m) *name*
nombre (m) *number*
note (f) *bill, note*
nous *we, us*
nouveau, nouvelle *new*
nouvelle (f) *piece of news*
nu *bare;* – tête *bareheaded*
nuit (f) *night*
numéro (m) *number*

obéissant *obedient*
œil, yeux (m) *eye, eyes*
œuf (m) *egg*
on *one, we*
s'opposer à *to oppose (sthg or sbdy)*
or (m) *gold*
orange (f) *orange*
ordre (m) *order*
oreille (f) *ear*

oser *to dare*
ou *or*
où *where*
oublier *to forget*
ouf! *phew!*
oui *yes*
ouvert *open*
ouvrier (m) *worker*
ouvrir *to open*

page (f) *page*
pain (m) *bread*
paire (f) *pair*
pâlot *wan, pale*
pantalon (m) *trousers*
papa (m) *Dad*
papier (m) *paper*
par *by*
paraître *to appear*
parce que *because*
pardon (m) *pardon*
parent (m) *parent*
paresse (f) *laziness*
paresseux, -euse *lazy*
parler *to talk*
parmi *among*
parole (f) *word*
part (f) *part;* de ma – *on my behalf*
parti *gone*
partir *to go*
partout *everywhere*
pas (m) *footstep*
(ne . . .) pas *not*
passeport (m) *passport*
passer *to pass*
se passer de *to do without (sthg or sbdy)*
patience (f) *patience*
patrie (f) *home country*
patron (m) *owner, manager*
pauvre *poor*
pauvreté (f) *poverty*
payer *to pay*
péché (m) *sin*
peindre *to paint*
peler *to peel*
pelouse (f) *lawn*

penser *to think*
(se) perdre *to lose (oneself)*
perdu *lost*
père (m) *father*
période (f) *period*
périr *to perish*
permettre *to allow*
Pérou (m) *Peru*
Perse (f) *Persia*
personne (f) *person*
personne *nobody*
petit *small*
petit-déjeuner (m) *breakfast*
pétrole (m) *petroleum*
peu *little*
peur (f) *fear;* de – que *for fear that*
peut-être *perhaps*
photo (f) *photograph*
pièce (f) *coin, room, piece, play*
pied (m) *foot;* à – *on foot*
pierre (f) *stone*
pincée (f) *pinch*
pipe (f) *pipe*
pis *worse, worst;* tant — *too bad*
place (f) *place, square*
placer *to place*
plage (f) *beach*
plaindre *to begrudge, to pity*
se plaindre *to complain*
plainte (f) *complaint*
plaisir (m) *pleasure*
plan (m) *plan*
plante (f) *plant*
planter *to plant*
plat *flat*
pleurer *to cry*
pleuvoir *to rain*
pluie (f) *rain*
plus *more*
plus . . . plus *the more . . . the more*
plusieurs *several*
plus tard *later*
poche (f) *pocket*
poignée (f) *handle;* — de main *handshake*
(ne . . .) point *not*

police (f) *police*
politicien (m) *politician*
pomme (f) *apple*
pommier (m) *apple tree*
ponctuel, -elle *punctual*
porte (f) *door*
portefeuille (m) *wallet*
porter *to carry, to wear*
Portugal (m) *Portugal*
poterie (f) *pottery*
poudre (f) *powder*
pour *for*
pour que *so that*
pourquoi *why;* — pas? *why not?*
pourtant *however*
pouvoir *to be able to*
prairie (f) *meadow*
pré (m) *meadow*
préférer *to prefer*
premier, -ière *first*
prendre *to catch, to take*
(se) préparer *to prepare (oneself)*
près *near*
présenter *to present*
président (m) *president*
prêt *ready*
prétendre *to pretend*
prêter *to lend*
prévoir *to forecast*
prière (f) *prayer;* — de . . . *please* . . .
prix (m) *price*
problème (m) *problem*
prochain *next*
professeur (m) *professor, teacher*
promenade (f) *walk, outing*
se promener *to go for a walk*
prometteur, -euse *promising*
propre *own, clean*
protéger *to protect*
prudent *cautious*
prudemment *cautiously*
public, -ique *public*
public (m) *public*
puis *then*
puissance (f) *power*
Pyrénées (f. pl) *Pyrenees*

quai (m) *quay, platform*
qualité *quality*
quand *when*
quant à *as regards*
quatre *four*
que *whom, which, that*
quel, quelle, quels, quelles *what, which*
quelque *some*
quelque chose *something*
quelquefois *sometimes*
quelques *several*
quelqu'un *someone*
qui *who*
quiconque *whoever*
quitter *to leave*
quoi? *what?*
quoi que *whatever*
quoique *although*

réagir *to react*
recevoir *to receive*
refaire *to do (sthg) again*
(se) refermer *to close again*
refuser *to refuse*
regard (m) *look, glance*
regarder *to look at*
regretter *to regret*
reine (f) *queen*
remarque (f) *remark*
remède (m) *remedy*
remercier *to thank*
rencontre (f) *meeting*
rencontrer *to meet*
rendez-vous (m) *meeting*
rendre *to give back*
rentrer *to return home, to go back in*
renvoyer *to send back*
réparation (f) *repair*
repas (m) *meal*
répondre *to answer, to reply*
réponse (f) *answer, reply*
reposant *restful*
se reposer *to rest*
république (f) *republic*

réputation (f) *reputation*
rescapé (m) *survivor*
restaurant (m) *restaurant*
rester *to stay*
retard (m) *delay;* en — *late*
retour (m) *return*
retourner *to return*
se retourner *to turn round*
réunion (f) *meeting*
réussir *to succeed*
rêve (m) *dream*
réveiller *to wake (sbdy) up*
se réveiller *to wake up*
revenir *to come back*
rêver *to dream*
revoir *to see again;* au — *goodbye*
rhume (m) *cold*
riche *rich*
richissime *extremely rich*
ridicule *ridiculous*
rien *nothing*
rigoureux, -euse *harsh, rigorous*
rire *to laugh*
rivière (f) *river*
robe (f) *dress*
rocher (m) *rock*
roman (m) *novel*
rouge *red*
rougir *to turn red, blush*
rouler *to drive along, to roll*
route (f) *road*
rue (f) *street;* grand- — *main street*

sa *his, her, its*
sable (m) *sand*
sac (m) *bag*
samedi (m) *Saturday*
sandwich (m) *sandwich*
satisfait *satisfied*
savoir *to know*
scandale (m) *scandal*
scandaleux, -euse *scandalous*
scrupules (m. pl) *scruples*
sec, sèche *dry*
sel (m) *salt*
selon *according to*

semaine (f) *week*
sembler *to seem*
sentiment (m) *feeling*
sentir *to feel, to smell*
sept *seven*
servir *to serve*
seul *alone*
sévère *strict, severe*
si *if, yes*
siffler *to whistle*
signer *to sign*
silence (m) *silence*
simple *simple*
simplement *simply*
situation (f) *situation*
six *six*
sœur (f) *sister*
soi *oneself*
soif (f) *thirst*
soin (m) *care*
soir (m) *evening*
soirée (f) *evening*
soldat (m) *soldier*
soleil (m) *sun*
solitude (f) *solitude*
solution (f) *solution*
sombre *dark, gloomy*
son, sa, ses *his, her, its*
sonner *to ring*
sorte (f) *sort*
sortir *to go out*
sot, sotte *silly, stupid*
souci (m) *care, worry*
soudain *suddenly*
souffrant *suffering, ill*
souffrir *to suffer*
souhaitable *desirable*
souhaiter *to wish*
soupe (f) *soup*
sourire *to smile*
souris (f) *mouse*
souvent *often*
spectateur, -trice (m, f) *spectator*
stock (m) *stock*
stylo (m) *pen*
suite (f) *follow-up;* tout de — *at once*

suivant *following, next;* au — ! *next!*
suivre *to follow*
superbe *superb*
sur *on*
sûr *sure*
surprise (f) *surprise*

ta *your*
table (f) *table*
tableau (m) *picture*
Tamise (f) *Thames*
tant *so much;* — pis! *too bad!*
tapis (m) *carpet*
tard *late;* trop —! *too late!*
taureau (m) *bull*
taxi (m) *taxi;* chauffeur de — *taxi driver*
te *(to) you*
téléphoner *to telephone*
temps (m) *time, weather*
tendre *tender, soft*
tenir *to hold*
se tenir *to behave*
tension (f) *tension*
terminer *to finish, to end (sthg)*
terrible *terrible*
tête (f) *head*
têtu *stubborn*
toi *you*
toit (m) *roof*
tomber *to fall*
ton, ta, tes *your*
tort *wrong;* avoir — *to be wrong*
tôt *early*
toucher *to touch*
toujours *always, still*
tour (m) *turn*
tour (f) *tower*
touriste (m, f) *tourist*
tourner *to turn (sthg)*
se tourner (vers) *to turn (towards)*
tous *(pl) all*
tousser *to cough*
tout *everything, quite*
tout à coup *suddenly*
train (m) *train*

tranquille *calm, quiet*
travail (m) *work*
travailler *to work*
travers: en travers *across*
trentaine (f) *thirty or so*
trente *thirty*
très *very*
triste *sad*
tromper *to deceive*
se tromper *to make a mistake*
trop *too, too much*
trouver *to find*
tu *you*
tuer *to kill*

un, une *a, one*
uniforme (m) *uniform*
union (f) *union*
université (f) *university*
urgent *urgent*
usine (f) *factory*
utiliser *to use*

vacances (f. pl) *holiday*
vache (f) *cow*
vague (f) *wave*
vaillamment *bravely*
vaisselle (f) *washing up, crockery*
valise (f) *suitcase*
vase (m) *vase*
véhémentement *vehemently*
vendeur (m) *salesman*
vendre *to sell*
venir *to come*
vent (m) *wind*
vérifier *to check*
vers *towards*
vert *green*
veste (f) *jacket*
viande (f) *meat*
vice (m) *vice*
victime (f) *victim*
vieille (f) *old woman*
vieux, vieille *old*
vieux (m) *old man*

villa (f) *villa*
village (m) *village*
ville (f) *town*
vin (m) *wine*
vingt *twenty*
vingtaine (f) *twenty or so*
violemment *violently*
visa (m) *visa*
visite (f) *visit*
visiter *to visit*
visiteur, -euse (m, f) *visitor*
vite *fast*
vitesse (f) *speed*
vitrail, -aux (m) *stained glass
    window*
vive . . . ! *long live . . . !*
vivre *to live*
voici *here is, here are*
voilà *there is, there are*
voir *to see*
voisin (m) *neighbour*
voiture (f) *car*
voler *to fly, to steal*
volet (m) *shutter*
votre, vos *your*
vôtre (m, f) *yours;* à la — ! *your
    health!*
vouloir *to want, to require*
voulu *wanted, required*
voyage (m) *travel*
voyager *to travel*
voyageur, -euse (m, f) *traveller*
vrai *true*
vraiment *truly*
vu *seen*
vu que . . . *considering that . . .*
vue (f) *sight, view*

y *there*
y compris *included*
yeux (m, pl) *eyes*

zéro *nought, zero*
zoo (m) *zoo*
zut! *blast!*